MW00667541

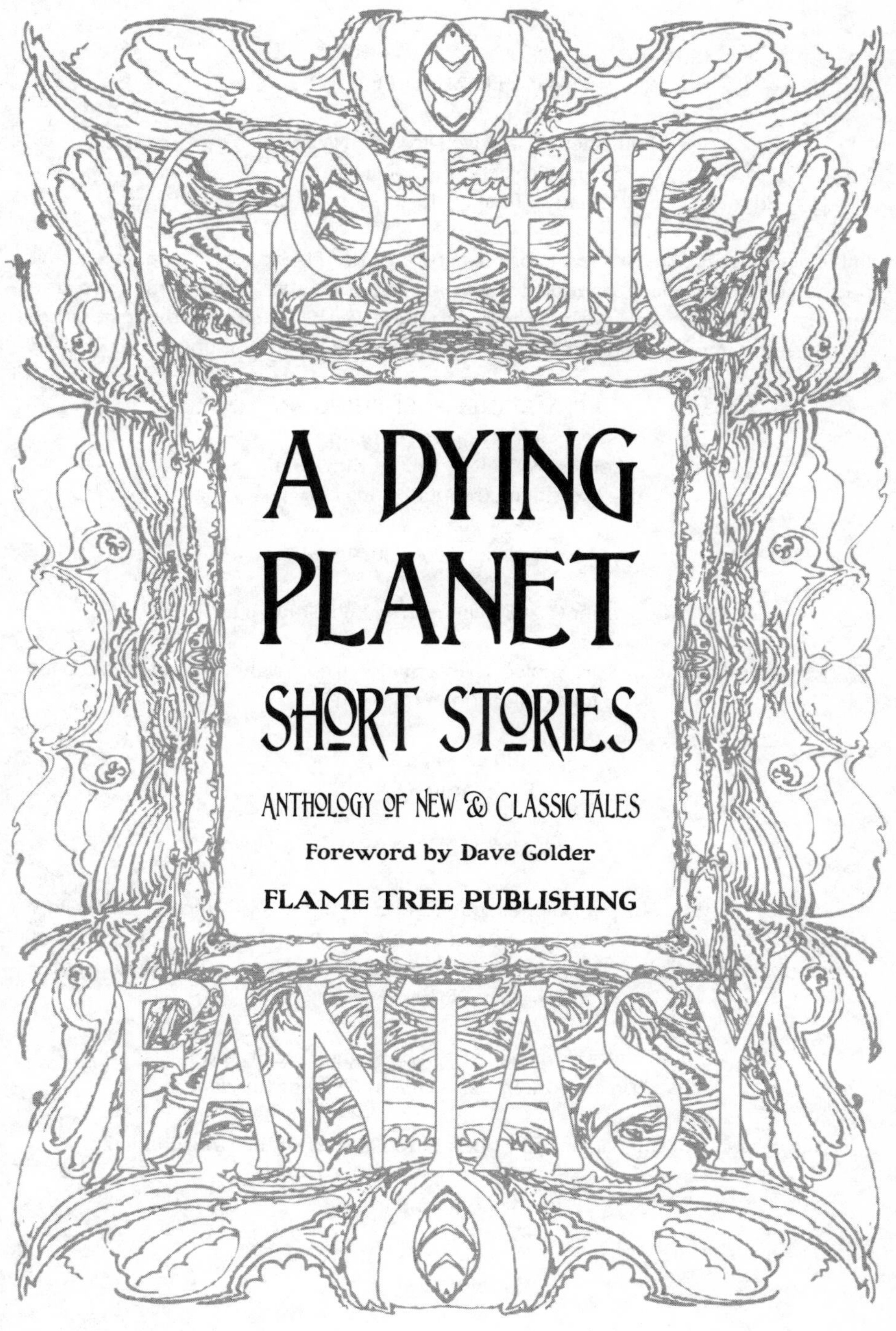

A DYING PLANET SHORT STORIES

ANTHOLOGY OF NEW & CLASSIC TALES

Foreword by Dave Golder

FLAME TREE PUBLISHING

This is a FLAME TREE Book

Publisher & Creative Director: Nick Wells
Senior Project Editor: Josie Karani

Publisher's Note: Due to the historical nature of the classic text, we're aware that there may be some language used which has the potential to cause offence to the modern reader. However, wishing overall to preserve the integrity of the text, rather than imposing contemporary sensibilities, we have left it unaltered.

FLAME TREE PUBLISHING
6 Melbray Mews, Fulham,
London SW6 3NS, United Kingdom
www.flametreepublishing.com

First published 2020

20 22 24 23 21
1 3 5 7 9 10 8 6 4 2

ISBN: 978-1-78755-781-9

The cover image is created by Flame Tree Studio
based on artwork by Slava Gerj and Gabor Ruszkai.

A copy of the CIP data for this book is available from the British Library.

Printed and bound in China

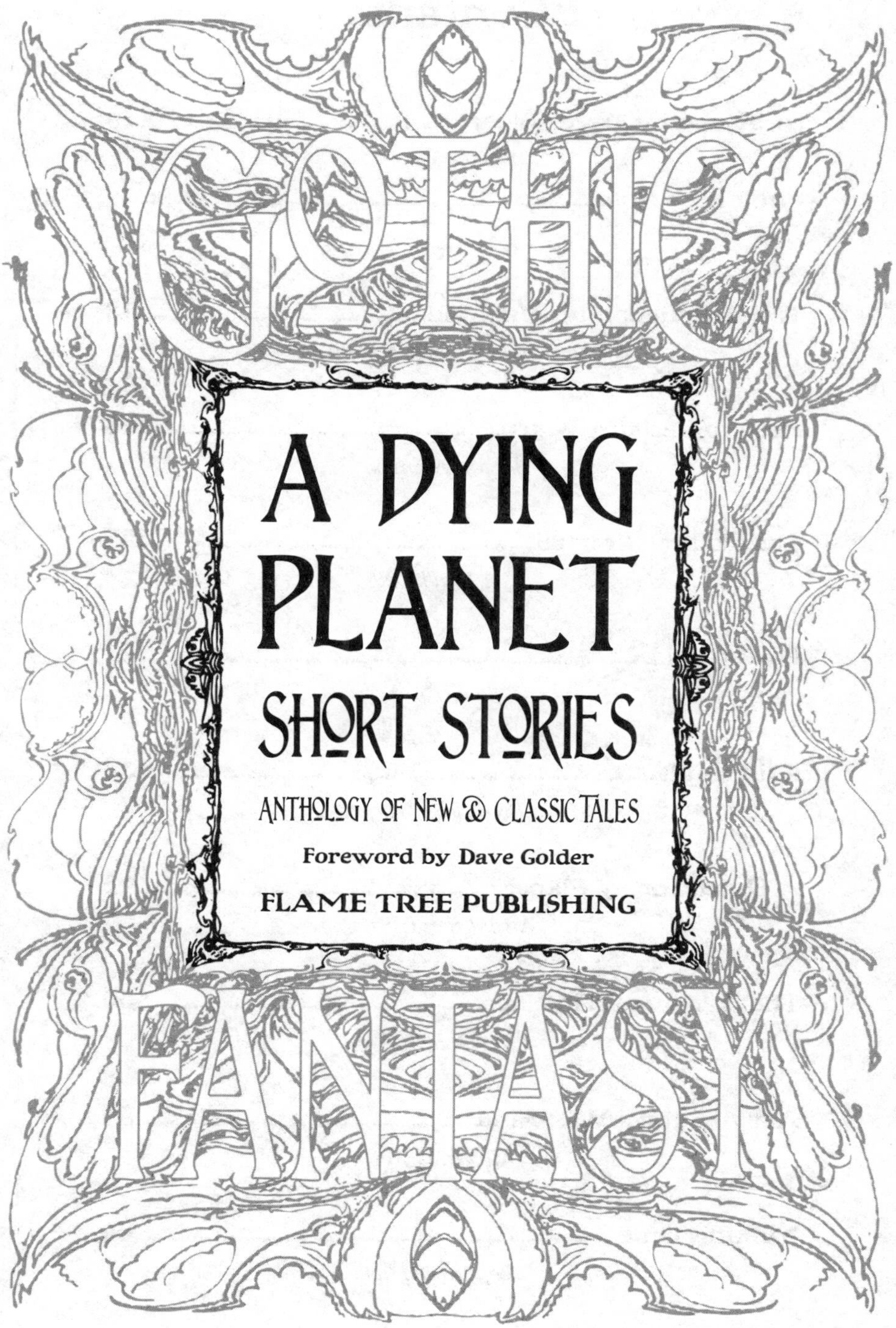

GOTHIC FANTASY

A DYING PLANET

SHORT STORIES

ANTHOLOGY OF NEW & CLASSIC TALES

Foreword by Dave Golder

FLAME TREE PUBLISHING

Contents

Foreword: A Dying Planet Short Stories

WHILE THERE'S little evidence that T.S. Eliot – of 'The Waste Land' fame – spent much time pondering the subject of science fiction during his life, he did inadvertently pen the perfect mission statement for one of science fiction's most enduring sub-categories:

'This is the way the world ends
Not with a bang but a whimper.'

These are the endlessly quoted final lines of 'The Hollow Men' (1925). The poem is about many things (post-war Europe, religion, the death of hope) but not, literally, the end of the world. However, there's an intrinsic melancholy to those lines that's at the heart of Dying Earth fiction – or Dying Worlds fiction as it has evolved into as SF authors have increasingly broadened their scale of reference (for example, Edgar Rice Burroughs' Mars-based pulp series are often considered part of the genre).

Because Dying Worlds fiction is distinct from that other great end-of-the-world sub-genre, apocalyptic fiction. Instead of humanity pluckily trying to survive one great disaster that's caused (or threatening to cause) the collapse of civilisation as we know it, Dying World is about humanity facing up to the fact that our planet's on its last legs, usually, though not always, because the Sun's about to give up the ghost. Civilisation hasn't collapsed; rather it's slowly unravelling as entropy takes an ever stronger hold. The world is doomed, but it's in no hurry getting there, so let's make the most of the time left, yeah?

The term Dying Earth was coined in the title of Jack Vance's 1950 short story collection, but that was far from the origins of the genre. It's always fun to try to find the earliest example of any SF sub-genre in the Bible but in this case the Gospels are clearly on team apocalypse. Norse mythology, with its wonderfully evocative 'Twilight of the Gods' and Zoroastrianism, which foretells of a future in which 'the sun is more unseen and more spotted…and the Earth is more barren' feel more like they contain the seeds of the genre.

It wan't until the 19th century that SF writers truly began to consider the end of time, partly as a response to science beginning to grapple with the fact that the Sun, and indeed the universe, may have an expiration date (the term 'entropy' was coined in 1865).

H.G. Wells' *The Time Machine* (1895) is often cited as an early example, with the latter chapters of the book taking the unnamed time traveller to a far future in which the Earth's spin in slowing and the Sun is dimming. But other SF writers were also experimenting the as-yet-unnamed genre, and the stories collected here provide some fascinating SF archeology for contemporary readers as you can see the Dying Earth tropes begin to form.

Camille Flammarion's *Omega: The Last Days of the World* (1894) – the first section of which is reprinted here – starts like a Victorian prequel to Armageddon before spinning off into a cerebral and philosophical exploration of the various long lingering deaths that may face the planet. The two Clark Ashton Smith tales in this anthology are set in his imagined, dying world of Zothique and feel as much fantasy as they do SF, another common theme of the genre (the idea being that we're so far in the future, the boundaries between science and magic have blurred).

Also included in this anthology is William Hope Hodgson's mind-bending *The House on the Borderland* (1908), which influenced writers as diverse as H.P. Lovecraft and Terry Pratchett.

Some might say it's better to burn out than fade away, but with the best Dying Worlds stories, you just want them to keep lingering on.

Dave Golder
@DaveGolder
SFX Magazine

Publisher's Note

Whether it is due to nuclear war, a climate disaster, societal reasons or something otherworldly the end days of a planet can tell us so much about humanity. A subgenre of science fiction and fantasy, the Dying Worlds genre has provided us with some of the most thought-provoking stories – they make us analyze our own struggles and put minor complaints into perspective. This collection brings together classic stories from well-known and lesser-known writers, including Camille Flammarion, Jack London and Stanley G. Weinbaum. We hope there are a few gems in this collection that you may not have come across before.

We received an incredible number of new submissions for this anthology, and have loved reading so many powerful and gripping stories. The standard of the writing submitted to us has always been impressive and the final selection is always an incredibly hard decision, but ultimately we chose a collection of stories we hope sit alongside each other and with the classic tales, to provide a brilliant *A Dying Planet* book for all to enjoy.

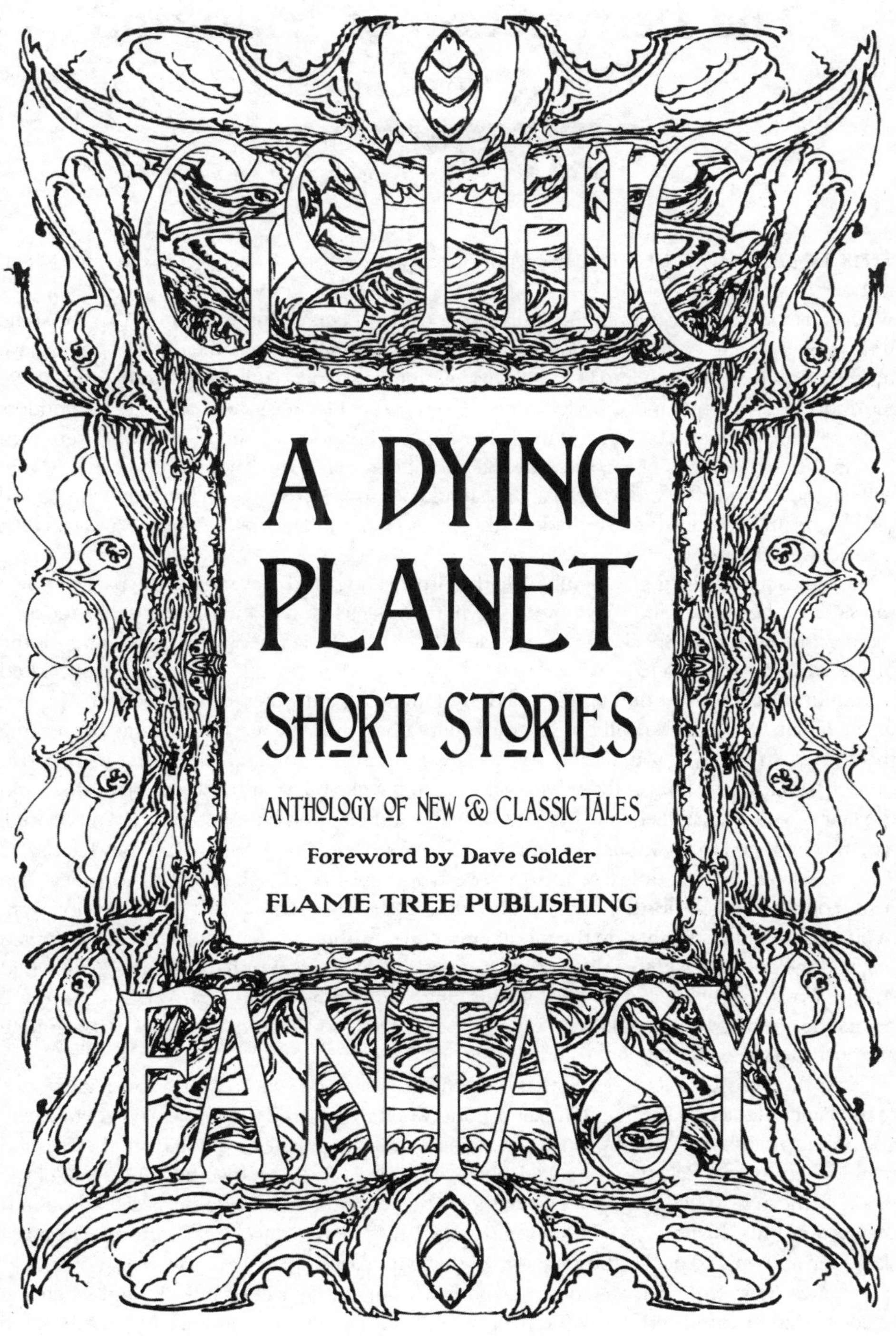
GOTHIC
A DYING PLANET
SHORT STORIES
ANTHOLOGY OF NEW & CLASSIC TALES
Foreword by Dave Golder
FLAME TREE PUBLISHING
FANTASY

The Destruction of Mankind

Ancient Egyptian Myth

THIS LEGEND WAS CUT in hieroglyphs on the walls of a small chamber in the tomb of Seti I, about 1350 bc.

When Ra, the self-begotten and self-formed god, had been ruling gods and men for some time, men began to complain about him, saying, 'His Majesty has become old. His bones have turned into silver, his flesh into gold, and his hair into real lapis-lazuli.' His Majesty heard these murmurings and commanded his followers to summon to his presence his Eye (i.e. the goddess Hathor), Shu, Tefnut, Keb, Nut, and the father and mother gods and goddesses who were with him in the watery abyss of Nu, and also the god of this water, Nu. They were to come to him with all their followers secretly, so that men should not suspect the reason for their coming, and take flight, and they were to assemble in the Great House in Heliopolis, where Ra would take counsel with them.

In due course all the gods assembled in the Great House, and they ranged themselves down the sides of the House, and they bowed down in homage before Ra until their heads touched the ground, and said, 'Speak, for we are listening.' Then Ra, addressing Nu, the father of the first-born gods, told him to give heed to what men were doing, for they whom he had created were murmuring against him. And he said, 'Tell me what you would do. Consider the matter, invent a plan for me, and I will not slay them until I have heard what you shall say concerning this thing.' Nu replied, 'You, Oh my son Ra, are greater than the god who made you (i.e. Nu himself), you are the king of those who were created with you, your throne is established, and the fear of you is great. Let your Eye (Hathor) attack those who blaspheme you.' And Ra said, 'Lo, they have fled to the mountains, for their hearts are afraid because of what they have said.' The gods replied, 'Let your Eye go forth and destroy those who blasphemed you, for no eye can resist you when it goes forth in the form of Hathor.' Thereupon the Eye of Ra, or Hathor, went in pursuit of the blasphemers in the mountains, and slew them all. On her return Ra welcomed her, and the goddess said that the work of vanquishing men was dear to her heart. Ra then said that he would be the master of men as their king, and that he would destroy them. For three nights the goddess Hathor-Sekhmet waded about in the blood of men, the slaughter beginning at Hensu (Herakleopolis Magna).

Then the Majesty of Ra ordered that messengers should be sent to Abu, a town at the foot of the First Cataract, to fetch mandrakes (?), and when they were brought he gave them to the god Sekti to crush. When the women slaves were bruising grain for making beer, the crushed mandrakes (?) were placed in the vessels that were to hold the beer, together with some of the blood of those who had been slain by Hathor. The beer was then made, and seven thousand vessels were filled with it. When Ra saw the beer he ordered it to be taken to the scene of slaughter, and poured out on the meadows of the four quarters of heaven. The object of putting mandrakes (?) in the beer was to make those who drank fall asleep quickly, and when the goddess Hathor came and drank the beer mixed with blood and mandrakes (?) she became very merry, and, the sleepy stage of drunkenness coming on her, she forgot all about men, and slew no more. At every festival of Hathor ever after 'sleepy beer' was made, and it was drunk by those who celebrated the feast.

Now, although the blasphemers of Ra had been put to death, the heart of the god was not satisfied, and he complained to the gods that he was smitten with the 'pain of the fire of sickness'. He said, 'My heart is weary because I have to live with men; I have slain some of them, but worthless men still live, and I did not slay as many as I ought to have done considering my power.' To this the gods replied, 'Trouble not about your lack of action, for your power is in proportion to your will.' Here the text becomes fragmentary, but it seems that the goddess Nut took the form of a cow, and that the other gods lifted Ra on to her back. When men saw that Ra was leaving the earth, they repented of their murmurings, and the next morning they went out with bows and arrows to fight the enemies of the Sun-god. As a reward for this Ra forgave those men their former blasphemies, but persisted in his intention of retiring from the earth. He ascended into the heights of heaven, being still on the back of the Cow-goddess Nut, and he created there Sekhet-hetep and Sekhet-Aaru as abodes for the blessed, and the flowers that blossomed therein he turned into stars. He also created the millions of beings who lived there in order that they might praise him. The height to which Ra had ascended was now so great that the legs of the Cow-goddess on which he was enthroned trembled, and to give her strength he ordained that Nut should be held up in her position by the godhead and upraised arms of the god Shu. This is why we see pictures of the body of Nut being supported by Shu. The legs of the Cow-goddess were supported by the various gods, and thus the seat of the throne of Ra became stable.

When this was done Ra caused the Earth-god Keb to be summoned to his presence, and when he came he spoke to him about the venomous reptiles that lived in the earth and were hostile to him. Then turning to Thoth, he bade him to prepare a series of spells and words of power, which would enable those who knew them to overcome snakes and serpents and deadly reptiles of all kinds. Thoth did so, and the spells which he wrote under the direction of Ra served as a protection of the servants of Ra ever after, and secured for them the help of Keb, who became sole lord of all the beings that lived and moved on and in his body, the earth. Before finally relinquishing his active rule on earth, Ra summoned Thoth and told him of his desire to create a Light-soul in the Tuat and in the Land of the Caves. Over this region he appointed Thoth to rule, and he ordered him to keep a register of those who were there, and to mete out just punishments to them. In fact, Thoth was to be ever after the representative of Ra in the Other World.

How to Reclaim Water

Barton Aikman

Dear M,

Cry. I've found that's the easiest way to reclaim water. I'm always on the brink of it. There's more to cry about than to not cry about, don't you think? Maybe it's funny to think about me crying, but I do it all the time. In my camo and boots and this heavy olive jacket, I cry. I just wait till everyone else in camp has fallen asleep.

Thank you for the crackers you left with your last letter. Don't worry, they weren't too stale, not as stale as you thought they would be. I played with the plastic wrapper the crackers came in after I was done eating. I held it up to my ear and made crinkling sounds. I closed my eyes and, depending on how I played the plastic with my fingers, could picture different things. A shallow creek passing over a rock bed. Rain. Rapid gunfire off in the distance. There isn't much to do here at the hideout until we have everything ready for the reclaiming, and it was a nice way to pass the time.

I think that's another reason I enjoy it, the crying. It takes time. Feeling the tears pool in my eyes and spill over, rolling down my cheeks, and waiting for the streams to make it to my mouth. I've come to like the salty taste. I imagine the water they're holding hostage at the facility isn't as salty, but that's okay. I know I'll enjoy the difference, the crisp cleanness I'm sure the captive water has. I can't wait for the chance to taste it. And I'll always have more tears anyway.

I hope this letter isn't too creased for you. I folded it a lot to get it to fit completely into the plastic cracker wrapper, and I hope the wrapper keeps the letter from getting as dirty as you've said the last few have gotten. I look forward to the day where we don't have to pass messages through an old foxhole to talk. That day will come soon. I promise.

Attached with string, please find a gift, as requested. If you asked for a gift does it still count as a gift? For some reason I feel like it doesn't count. It's more like a request. Regardless, I was happy to get it for you, specifically for you.

Be safe. I can't imagine what it's like to live inside one of the militarized zones. I can't imagine how it actually feels. I only have your words, and so few of them sound good. Here I go again, wanting to cry. See what I mean?

At least I'll make more water.

Flow freely,

R

* * *

Dear R,

Thank you for the pocketknife. I just want it as a precaution, but I appreciate it. In addition to taking away all of the metal cutlery in our homes, they've now stopped using metal utensils in the dining tents. I guess too many steak knives went missing. I hate the feeling of eating with plastic utensils. It cheapens the food, tarnishes it somehow, not that it's that great to begin with, but still. Besides, I'm sure if someone tried hard enough, they could hurt someone plenty with a plastic knife.

I'm sorry to hear about your crying but I'm glad you're looking at it in a positive way. Maybe if enough of us had stored our tears we wouldn't have needed militarized zones to begin with. A device comes to mind. A type of helmet or headgear that keeps tiny vials resting against your cheeks while you weep and fill them up. It would be like giving blood.

Anyway, don't cry for me, R. I'm okay. It's true that living behind the blockades and fences is hard. Knowing those types of objects are how I mark the edges of my life weighs on me sometimes. I'm still waiting to get used to the constant presence of soldiers, but it hasn't happened yet. They keep the resources guarded in shifts. From a distance they appear unified and sleepless, especially with them all having the same haircut, shaved down to the scalp except for a thin sliver of buzzcut on top. I don't think I like the style. But there's food here, and yes, water. It's all handled by the soldiers, but I'm given enough rations to get by for now.

More importantly, there's the foxhole and our letters. As always, I make sure to keep the hole well covered and disguised on this side of the barrier. I know you're doing the same on the other side. Remember not to pat down the dirt too much to cover the hole. They'll be able to tell someone was there. I've been happy with a combination of bluegrass and tumbleweed and loose soil. I don't fill the hole so much as cover it. I've been watching the soldiers very carefully and I still don't see any signs that they suspect anything. They don't seem interested in watching me do the work they've assigned me, which makes sense. Who would want to watch someone dig graves? Lucky me, I guess. If they liked watching me dig, they probably would have seen when I first discovered the hole.

But they didn't. They didn't see me find the foxhole, and the message your group had hidden inside. I don't know why I looked inside, but I still remember reading that first note.

If you need help, please write, it said.

Now look at us.

This last letter of yours was much cleaner than the ones before it. Thank you for taking the time to fold it into the plastic. The creases didn't bother me at all. I know you know that I destroy these after reading them, but I value the reading of them so much, the ability to communicate with someone outside of the zone, and sometimes the dirt and rips make me sad. There's something satisfying, even comforting, about reading something on clean paper.

To answer a question you asked in a previous letter, I do not have a sense of how much ammunition the soldiers have. Seldom do they fire their rifles or handguns. When they do, it's usually a single shot that rings out, and our zone is a large enough territory that I imagine there are shots I don't always hear. All I know is that, often enough, there are new holes to dig.

Attached, a surprise. Something to celebrate another month of letter writing.

Flow freely,

M

* * *

Dear M,

Photo paper?! I can't remember the last time I've felt photo paper. It's so smooth and slick. You probably saw this coming, but it reminds me of water. I shared it with some of the others and I had a hard time getting it back from them. I watched some of them rub it against their faces and necks. They all closed their eyes to imagine things.

The paper also reminded me of running errands with my mother when I was a kid. She was very adamant that I hold her hand in crowded places, so I didn't get lost. She loved lotions and oils, I think that's why the photo paper made me think of her, of her and her hands. It's funny now to think about someone actually spending time liking something as superfluous as lotion or oil.

Can you imagine if you had a camera to use the photo paper with? Don't get me wrong, even just looking at the exposed paper is nice, the density of the black. What do you think you'd take a picture of in the militarized zone? Or what do you wish you had a picture of to look at it while you're living there? You don't have to answer, but I'd love to know.

Thank you for the information about the ammunition. I've shared it with the others. Every bit of intel helps us prepare for the reclaiming. Do you ever notice if soldiers are falling asleep during night shifts? Do you ever see them check their magazines or clean their guns? Do you think it's possible most of them don't have bullets, that what few bullets they have are saved for executions?

Let me know.

Our resources are scarce, or I would have attached an anniversary gift as well. I hope it's okay if we count the knife as my gift toward that. Something else I can offer is that once we've taken the militarized zone, you'll never have to worry about destroying letters. You can nail them to the front of your house for all we care. Yes, you'll have a house again too. No more tent. I promise.

We'll avenge all of the bodies you've had to bury.

Thank you for helping us.

Flow freely,

R

* * *

Dear R,

At first, I thought I'd want a photo of my extended family, but no, I think I'd miss them too much if I kept seeing their faces but not their actual selves. I try very hard not to worry about how they're doing right now, with communication being what it is.

Instead, I would want a photo of a railroad. I'd prefer it to not have a train in it. Rather I would want it to be taken looking straight down the tracks, focused on the horizon, with nothing else but the surrounding landscape and the track itself. I love anything that implies what exists outside of the thing itself, the futility of capturing something, thinking about how humble having eyes is, how so much escapes our perception. I also enjoy thinking about vacated forms of transportation, and in particular, trains. I don't think my tent and its flappable walls would be well suited for hanging a picture, but I would keep the photo of the train hidden in my pillowcase and look at it inside of my sleeping bag at night.

No, I haven't seen any soldiers fall asleep. I don't see them clean or fiddle with their guns, I just know they have them. These are both hard things for me to see, given the curfew and the logistics of their executions. One might imagine they'd make the rest of us watch, but no, they're actually very private about it. I never see the bodies, despite the final resting place I make for them. I dig a hole, tell a soldier when I'm done, and then a group of them come and place a black shimmering body bag into the hole. When I go to fill the hole back up, I can hardly make out an impression of a silhouette.

The soldiers always pray together before calling me back over to cover the grave.

Weird, huh?

Sometimes, when the soldiers have all returned to their posts, I'll put one of your letters into a grave and bury it with someone.

I'm sorry I can't be of more help with your questions.

They've started searching our tents at random to find the missing steak knives. A few arguments broke out amongst us in my section of the zone about coming forward if you had taken one. I didn't say anything for or against. I don't like getting directly involved in those kinds of things. As to be expected, they started with the chefs' tents, and two chefs in particular had dozens of knives taped to the bottom of their cots, which probably wasn't the best spot to hide them to begin with. That wasn't all of the knives, however. Maybe some of them were sent to your group? I'm not sure how many contacts you have inside of my zone. I imagine that's not something you'd tell me. Maybe you don't even know.

Their search for the rest of the knives continues, but I don't think they'll find the pocketknife you gave me. I hope they'll let me keep my paper and pens if they search my tent. I'm worried about what they might do to punish us depending on how long it takes to retrieve all of the cutlery. I've come to quite like writing, R. It passes time in a way few other things do. It's such a quiet and little thing to do.

I'm afraid I don't have much to offer you in this letter. I haven't answered your questions and I haven't attached any gifts. I hope you are well, along with the rest of your group, wherever it is you all are hiding nearby.

I'm certain I dug graves for those two chefs the other day. It's impossible to know for sure. Where I am, we all look the same in death, under those slick black bags. It feels weird to say, but when I see the blackness of the bags, I think of the exposed photo paper. I'm glad I gave it to you. I'm sure that unwanted association will go away with enough time.

Flow freely,

M

* * *

Dear M,

If you see anything change in the behavior of the soldiers, let me know right away, even if it means doubling up your letters inside of the foxhole. Even small things, like how they behave with each other. It's all very good for me to know.

I hope the missing steak knives don't give you too much trouble. I would hate for you to lose your paper and pen.

I think you know what I would want a picture of if I had a choice.

There's more to do here now. Sorry for such a short letter. Again, let me know if you notice anything.

Flow freely,

R

* * *

Dear R,

The soldiers searched the row of tents I live on. They searched my tent and some of them stayed by my side while others went through my things. One of the soldiers beside me had a clipboard with text I tried to peer over and read, but ultimately couldn't see. The soldier called out to the others searching my things that I was a digger. Not a grave digger, just a digger. After the soldier beside me said that, the searching ones disassembled my tent. They left my possessions inside the deflated tent and, holding opposite corners, a small group of them moved all of my jumbled things a few feet away from its original spot.

It was a strange feeling seeing how easily all of my things could be picked up and moved. It was a mixture of a good and a bad feeling. Comforting, but also sad.

I didn't disguise the hole I'd dug under my tent as well as the foxhole. I honestly didn't think they'd ever check underneath the tent. Even at the distance they kept me, I could see the freshness of the dirt I had patted down, how it contrasted with the rest of the ground. I had made a shallow hole and within moments they dug up the shoe box I had buried there.

One of the soldiers opened the box, still hunched over, and looked inside. They stayed like that for a long time, hunched over, looking inside. At least it felt like a long time for me, just having to stand there next to a bunch of shaved heads and camouflage. I watched as they didn't bother to take your pocket knife out of the shoebox. Instead, they put the lid back on and reburied the box. Then they put my tent back over the shallow hole and pitched it back up.

They didn't say anything else to me, just kept making their way down the rows of tents on my block. I stayed inside the green shell of my tent the rest of the day, doing nothing, too afraid to write. Too afraid to see if they had in fact not touched the pocketknife. The soldier beside me with the clipboard didn't even make a note of what they had found, at least from what I saw. I almost wish they had done something. Taken me away, taken my things, at least taken the knife. Doing something, I've continued to realize, is almost always better than doing nothing. There's assuredness there.

They still haven't said anything to me.

They've just assigned me new holes to dig. Not more than usual or anything, so I wonder if they are having any luck tracking down the rest of the steak knives. They still don't keep an eye on me while I work. I think about you a lot, R, and running to you. I've lost weight steadily for a while, even before the rationing, even before the establishment of the militarized zone. It's been two days since the search, and I've thought and thought about squeezing myself through the foxhole. I think about how cool the dirt inside the hole would be. I think of the moments of darkness I would experience inside, brief but intense, and finding the light on the other side, of emerging from the hole and coming out on the other side of the barrier.

But I don't know where you are, R. For all I know you watch me dig graves hidden behind nearby rocks, but I doubt that. Maybe you hike down one of the mountains to get my letters, to leave yours. I find that easier to believe.

I think right now I should wait before writing you another letter. I probably shouldn't even be writing this one.

What if one of the graves I dig becomes my own?

I wish I had something better to say.

Flow freely,

M

* * *

Dear M,

I think you should get rid of the pocketknife. Throw it away in the trash during dinner, bury it in one of the graves you dig, something. I worry about why they didn't reprimand you for having it. They might be preparing lots of careful questions for you and are considering where it might have come from. It concerns me that you weren't interrogated already.

Of course, I'm glad you weren't.

I know you wanted the knife just in case, to feel a little safer around the soldiers, but it doesn't seem to have helped. I don't think it was advisable to bury it under your tent. Most emergencies unfold in an instant. Do you think you would have had the time to get it out when you needed it? I wish you had asked me about where you should hide it. I might have recommended somewhere like a neighbor's tent, even if it was in an obvious place. It'd still be easier to get to than digging it up, and if the soldiers found it, it'd be your neighbor that took the blame.

It's likely too late for that now. On second thought, maybe it's too late to even get rid of it. It might irritate them even more. No matter what, this complicates things. I, like you, am spending time worrying about this. My time should be spent preparing for the reclaiming of the water, liberating it to serve all of us, not just some. I wanted for us to help each other, M, not distract.

I have consulted with the group about whether or not I should continue to write to you. For now, they have voted to allow it. They want to be sure that I thank you for destroying my letters after you read them. It has alleviated some tension about the situation. We are confident in our abilities, in our plan, and believe your correspondence is still of value. We are willing to risk this for intel about the inside.

They want me to be sure I mention that they hope you are alright. It sounds like the soldiers did not harm you in any way, and for that, they are glad.

I'm glad you're okay too, M.

The group has now agreed that it is probably best for you to hold onto the pocketknife. Once again, ignore my initial suggestion. I'd scratch it out, or tear off that part of the letter, but that just feels like a waste of paper and ink.

Right now, I shouldn't waste anymore.

Flow freely,

R

* * *

Dear R,

A few soldiers approached me at dinner. They brought over an extra cup of tea and chatted about small things. The weather. The comfort of keeping a good sleeping schedule. They sat and ate with plastic utensils beside me. It felt okay, being there.

We all walked out together, and they asked me to stop by their tent. The way they asked actually felt very natural. I had never seen the inside of the soldiers' tents and was curious. I thought, at the very least, I'd just take a peek inside. From the outside, the tents are big. Not as big as the dining tents, but definitely larger than my personal tent.

Turns out the inside of their tents are no more luxurious than mine. We still couldn't completely stand up, and we found it most comfortable to sit on the floor together. Most of them, maybe all of them, confessed their jealousy for personal tents like mine. They said it was nice getting to know each other, but after a while anyone, no matter who they are, craves a little personal space. I agreed, and thought of my time writing, but of course I didn't mention it, let alone writing to you.

They asked if was okay with my work. Not happy, but okay, like they knew it would be stupid to ask if I was happy digging graves, which it would be.

I said that it was what it was.

They nodded and listened.

They had reservations about their own work. All of them agreed that, at least once, they felt the urge to stop guarding the food and water, to let everyone come in and take whatever they wanted, to be able to keep extra supplies in their tents. They wanted to let us move back into the houses, but they understood why not. In case things got worse, there was a possibility the houses would need to be torn down, to repurpose their wood, plastics, and metals. Their superiors felt it would be better to have everyone, including them, to be used to living in tents, to have the houses become meaningless backdrops, should they need to be destroyed.

That made sense to me.

Then one of them introduced themselves. By name.

Her name was Whitney. It still is, I just saw her walking around this morning, before writing you this letter, R. R, that's all I know you by. I don't know your name, even after all the time we've spent writing to each other. Although, to be fair, you don't know mine either. I still understand why it has to be that way.

Whitney offered to cut my hair, in the same style of her and the other soldiers.

I said yes. Sitting on the ground in the tent with them I wanted to say yes, and I did.

So, Whitney shaved my head. She left a thin strip of buzzcut on top, from front to back. It looks like a mohawk but without having to spike it up.

I checked my reflection again today using the surface of my water ration, the extra one Whitney snuck for me, and I like how I look. I actually like it a lot. The style reminds me of spontaneous things I used to do.

I'm worried that you'll be worried reading this letter from me. Don't worry, I haven't said anything. Not about the knife or about writing. I didn't even complain about my job because I was worried they might move me to something else, and it'd be harder to find a way to get to the foxhole so often.

I'm still keeping an eye on them. In fact, now I'm able to keep an even closer eye on some of them.

Kinsley is the name of another one of the soldiers.

Nobu is another.

All of the soldiers rotate the resources they guard. They all have, and will again, guard the water. They all seem to like each other, and I get the sense that has remained the same for a while now. I know that's not much, but I wanted to give you something.

Flow freely,

M

* * *

Dear R,

I know I'm leaving you a second letter, even though you haven't come to take the last one I left, but I was too excited to not write to you.

Can you see the lights from where you are? We have electricity. It's limited, and sporadic, but some of the solar panels have been repaired and output energy in short bursts. One of the first things the soldiers did during one of these electric periods was set up a comm link with another militarized zone. The soldiers had a radio tent set up and ready to go for whenever they got the power to come back on, so they wasted no time once the panels started to function again. Smart, huh?

Whitney told me once the power becomes steady, we'll be able to talk to our families living in the other militarized zones. Can you imagine? I'll be able to talk to my family again. I hope they're okay. I've wanted so badly to make sure that they're okay for a long time now. I know you of all people can understand that.

I hope you can see the lights. It's so nice to have a powerful source of illumination in the dark. They work so much better than candles, and we have to be careful how often we use the candles to begin with.

Today I saw someone else get the same haircut as me. Someone who also isn't a soldier.

I'm trying to keep this letter short to save paper. I've also thought of a new sign off for myself, but I still like the one you started very much.

Use wisely,

M

* * *

Dear M,

Why didn't you pay close attention to the soldiers' guns while you were in the tent? Because you were too busy getting your hair cut. At the very least, I wish you had pressed them about their superior officers, about their orders, about the resources they guard. You had a lot of opportunities in there that you failed to capitalize on.

It is very good to know there is no one regularly occupying the houses.

And thank you for telling me their names.

You seem happier in your last two letters, M, and I don't know how to feel about that. I'm sorry to say that I don't know how to feel about your happiness, but I really don't. I urge you not to trust Whitney and the others.

Yes, I have seen the lights. I believe they are fleeting. Those solar panels broke for a reason. They will never be restored to their original optimization. I wouldn't be surprised to learn that they had kept a few dormant, half-functional panels stashed away for some time, and are using the stored energy to keep you and the others complicit.

I think what Whitney told you about speaking to your family is a false promise.

I'm sorry if this reads like I'm being short with you, M. Writing this, I feel like I'm being terse. I agree it is important to conserve, to reduce our usage. You're right that paper, like all resources, is precious. But what's even more important is that that conservation doesn't happen via the hands of an authority, of a few maintaining control over many. If that requires using a few more things, some more paper, then so be it.

The group is skeptical about me writing more letters to you. I just want to be honest about that. I almost didn't send this one out.

Flow freely,

R

* * *

Dear R,

We want the same thing. To survive, to make it through this hard time and build something better. I need to hold onto something to get through this. If there's a chance I can reconnect with people I love, people who could be dead for all I know, I'll hold onto that. I don't appreciate your cynicism. I've helped you a lot.

How do you even plan to ration the food and water after the reclaiming?

I've started to worry about those kinds of logistics. You've kept me in the dark for so long. I have to walk around with secrets and have no realistic comfort in return.

Use wisely,

M

* * *

Dear M,

What matters is that a free people make those decisions together. I thought you understood that. I didn't think it needed to be reiterated. Yes, we both want to survive, but I will not do so as a lesser human to others. I will not allow decisions to be made about my well-being without my input. I would not expect others to let me do the same to them. I hope the same can still be said for you.

Telling you any more than that would be unacceptable, and the group doesn't approve for me to tell you anything more.

Has it also not occurred to you that if the militarized zones didn't exist to begin with, you wouldn't have to worry about your family? You could just go to them.

Take comfort in knowing that someday soon those fences and barricades will be torn down. They'll fall from both the inside and the outside.

I promise.

Flow freely,

R

* * *

Dear R,

What if I went to my family, travelled all of that way, and there weren't enough resources to sustain my presence? What if I became a burden to them? I likely wouldn't even be able to survive the trip back if I had to turn around.

See, this is what I mean.

I'm sorry, but your supposed comforts are still abstract concepts to me. Wishful thinking. What if people here don't agree with you and your group? How much dissent or disagreement before a gridlock is created, or worse?

Let's also not forget that it's I that have been able to spare food for you. You have mentioned time and time again that resources are sparse where you are, hiding where you are. There are resources here. We just have to be smart about how we use them.

I'm worried you haven't thought all of this through.

I want you to know, that still, despite the direction these letters have taken, despite my doubts, I have not mentioned you to anyone. That being said, those are the same reasons I haven't given you anymore information. About Whitney, Kinsley, Nobu, or any of the other soldiers I've met. About anything at all.

And, for the record, the power has lasted more and more every day.

Use wisely,

M

* * *

Dear M,

Give up, M. That is how you have reclaimed water.

Has it not occurred to you that you have no concept as to how many resources you actually have? That information is kept from you, as is how much energy your panels are producing and if they're being stored with maximum efficiency. Those details are kept from you for a reason. To keep you placid, to create a system with a false sense of security. You expect your rations of food and water like you expect the sun to rise and set each day. These are all things expected out of habit. None of them are actually guaranteed to occur.

Do not forget that it is soldiers like Whitney, Kinsley, and Nobu that tasked you with digging graves, that have given you bodies to fill those graves with.

The group has agreed, and I with them, that this will be my last letter to you.

When the reclaiming happens, I'm sure I will find you within the militarized zone, M. We have not used our names in these letters. We have not described ourselves very much, although I know now you have the same haircut as the soldiers. Regardless, I have a feeling we'll be able to tell who the other is. We know each other well enough. Our eyes will know.

I hope when that moment comes, we will be able to reconcile.

Either way, I would like my knife back.

See you soon.

Flow freely,

R

* * *

Dear R,

I spoke with my family today. Whitney helped me get one of the first spots in line for the radio. She pulled a few strings. Most of them are still alive, R. It sounds worse in that militarized zone, the choices they've had to make to make the rations work. I don't want to go into more detail about it.

I hesitated to write this letter at all, given your last one. I'm holding onto the hope that you'll stop by the foxhole at least one more time before your group attempts to reclaim the water. There are a few things I want to tell you, or at the very least, I think writing them down will be good for me. Writing has been much more helpful for me personally than I ever thought it would be, despite it wasting a precious resource.

Here are a few things I've wanted to say.

I told Whitney about you. Just her, although I know she's told others. I didn't tell her right away, but I did. I have a feeling you know, you already seemed to suspect it. I didn't tell her much, just that you were out there with your group, a group of I don't know how many people. You did a good job keeping me in the dark. She was sure you were watching us, and she made sure none of the other soldiers spent more time over by the foxhole. She didn't want you to become suspicious.

Telling Whitney about you was how I was able to talk to my family. I'm sorry, R, but I don't regret that. I don't regret hearing their voices or having closure and knowing which voices I won't hear again.

You might be happy to hear that she looked scared when I told her about you. I get the sense that the other soldiers are too. I think you were right. I think they're almost out of bullets, and they never found the other steak knives. I'm sure your group has them.

There's something else, the most important thing.

When I came out of the radio tent, I saw Whitney coming back from the water facility. She was crying. She tried to hide it, but that's a hard thing to hide, even when the tears have stopped. She wouldn't talk to me about it, and I didn't want to talk much either. But I knew what her tears meant.

We're running out of water, R.

We're fighting over nothing now, nothing but a carcass.

There is nothing to reclaim.

Maybe you'll find this letter before your group moves in. Maybe you'll hold them back, forgo the plan altogether. Either way, at this point, I don't think I'd blame you either way. Maybe it will feel good to have the victory of taking this place before having to figure out what to do next, if there can even be a next. I might try to make it to my family's militarized zone, but I don't know, I just don't. It might not be feasible. Maybe I'll just stay here, wait this out for a while.

If I'm here when you arrive, when you finally emerge from the perimeters of paper, I think you'll be right. I think we'll recognize each other right way.

One way or another, we'll find a way to stop fighting over the knife.

The Hollow Journal

V.K. Blackwell

MY NAME IS Kieran Hollow and I want my children to know what we did.

I woke my family early. We planned the whole day – a pancake breakfast, a trip to the zoo, and supper at the diner down the street. Just a mundane spring vacation, one of life's simple pleasures. Nothing but a few precious moments with my wife, Marianne, and our two children.

My little boy, Morgan, was almost three. My baby girl, Nora, was eighteen months. They'll never know what life was like before the end.

I had just finished the first batch of blueberry pancakes when Marianne rushed down the stairs. Only half her hair was curled, and she wore no makeup. Nora balanced on her hip. She demanded to know if I checked my phone. Of course not, I told her, why would I check my phone? She squeezed behind me to reach the small television we kept in the kitchen, switching it to the local news.

Inbound nuclear threat. Evacuate to the nearest public shelter.

I tossed every valuable into luggage while Marianne kept the children out of the way, huddled by the television to await more news. The whole threat could be called off any moment, she told me, even as she dialed family with shaking hands. Her parents first, then mine. Siblings, then neighbors and friends. Her parents refused to leave for an underground bunker. We've lived through thirty hurricanes, they declared, and two national bomb threats. This would be another nothing, just one more second in the long hours of their lives. My parents were out in the countryside, stocked up for the season. They, too, refused to leave their home. I heard Marianne reassuring them everything would be fine, but we were leaving regardless. We would not gamble with our children's safety.

Two hours later we inched through bumper-to-bumper traffic, creeping ever closer to the edge of the city. Constant updates flooded through the radio, calm but urging immediate evacuation. I found my gaze directed to the sky. Cloudless, brilliant blue – perfect weather for the family outing we would never have. I never saw any sign of the impending nuclear doom. But every car around us was packed to bursting with luggage and furniture and pets. I started to wonder if there really was a threat at all.

When we arrived, processed through a police line with our belongings, the bunker appeared nearly empty. Those in charge assigned us a small room – two beds, a dresser, and a shelf. Good enough for a few weeks in the emergency.

The updates filtered in slowly through the radio. Natural gas explosions destroyed Asian and African countries. Fighting broke out in the east on suspicion of terrorism. Entire oil fields burned, engulfing cities in smog. Anarchy spread like wildfire in a dry forest, grinding Europe to a halt, infecting South America, sparking in North American urban capitals. Infrastructure began to collapse across the globe – no internet, no natural gas pipelines, no power stations. Out came the nuclear warheads, to restore order. Two cities on the west coast were hit, a thousand miles away. Every source predicted more to come, with unknown landing zones.

Whispers filled the shelter, of blackened skies and seas on fire. Would we ever leave? What would we find outside these concrete walls?

Now, nearly a week since we arrived, the bunker reached full capacity. The police sealed every door. No one enters; no one leaves. We have enough supplies for a lifetime, they're telling us. The means to grow food. A way to purify the water. Enough stockpiled coal for centuries of power. One day, they promise, it will be safe to return to the world above.

Marianne is running through the list of those who were meant to meet us here. Her brother and cousins. My sister and her in-laws. Our neighbors, who had a boy Morgan's age. We've yet to find any of them.

I want to say that the world ended all at once on a perfect Saturday, but we all knew the end was coming for a long time. It came with our fracking and our drilling and our strip mining. It came with our atom splitting and our in-fighting. Even now, as I etch this family record onto paper – another product ripped from our Earth – the seas swallow another inch of the coast and the deserts eat another inch of the forest.

One day, they keep promising, one day. The police and the politicians down here with us – one day. But I can see it in their eyes, in how they cast their gaze upward, as if God could possibly bear to be watching us now, after what we've done. We all knew the end was coming. We just thought we had more time.

We killed the Earth for convenience.

I'm sorry.

* * *

My name is Morgan Hollow and I was raised in the bunker.

My father said that the bunker could provide for us all indefinitely. We had the means for healthy food, clean water, and fresh air. Until the growing lights burnt out, one by one. Until the filters clogged, overloaded with radioactive soot from the world above.

They forgot about the medicine, when they stocked the bunker. Millions of analgesics, but not enough anti-depressants, and every day someone new desperately needs them. Thousands of syringes, but too few filled with vaccines. Our food supply dwindles with our population. Most of the deceased now are from plague or suicide.

We lost Nora to the former. We lost Mother to the latter, not long after. Their deaths are some of my first memories.

Father also said that before the outside world collapsed for good, we were told the United States had enough energy for the next century. That every bunker would be able to ride out the storm. And that we had plenty of renewable energy options for when the doors finally opened again. This was the last lie they told us, and the most devastating.

My bunker will collapse under its own weight if we cannot generate electricity in the next six months.

As mayor, my father chose me to be part of the first group to leave the bunker. My boots were first to touch outside soil in three decades. I led a team of ten brave people, my friends and my family. Each of us wore multiple layers over every inch of skin, the clothing lined in tin foil, and full-face gas masks to protect against the toxic air. We all carried a firearm, but none of us were soldiers. Teachers, nurses, farmers, engineers.

Now we are all scavengers.

Our goal was to return to the nearby city and scout what remained. If people lived outside the shelter, if they began to set the world to right, we needed to know. Our radio was decades dead; what if there was place for us to join society above? We set a timer for one week outside the shelter to investigate. We had no advance knowledge, no expectations, and all the hope that something – *anything* – would be left for us to bring home.

My first step on the surface all but crushed those hopes. Smog stained the sky in gray and brown, choking the barren ground in a perpetual twilight. A sun shined behind that suffocating blanket, but I could not see it. The elders of the shelter kept pictures and paintings of the world above, before the doors closed. Greenery and vibrant flowers, birds and squirrels and trees. If any of that exists on the planet now, I have yet to find it.

We hiked the crumbling highways, littered with rusted cars and piles of detritus. Our duty compelled us to check every vehicle, even though we found each to be empty. Winds whistled across the wasteland, clearing the smog just enough for us to see the outline of the old city in the distance, a slumbering behemoth clothed in a poisonous burial shroud. Even with the incessant gusts, I sweat through my layers, clouding the interior of my face mask. I dared not remove it to clear the stinging drops in my eyes.

It took us a day to reach the edge of the city. Wind could not pierce the shelter of the towers. Without the sharp breeze, the smog hangs low, obscuring everything beyond ten paces. I lead my people over concrete ground, treading lightly around shapes in the dust.

When we stopped to evaluate our location, checking broken street signs against an outdated map, I sensed eyes on my back. I turned, looking through the window of a building that was once a pharmacy. In the moment between one heartbeat and the next, a face peered back. To call it human would have been a lie. Skin like ash, paper-thin over a sharp skeleton. Eyes, too large for a gaunt head, were red and bloodshot. Thin, cracked lips hardly disguise a jagged, ravenous maw. Before I could even gasp, the figure darted from sight into the dark recesses of the empty building.

My team inquired if I was fine. I nodded numbly, still staring past the smudged glass. If I tilted my flashlight just right through the window, I could see the flash of the hungry gaze, refracting the beam in a color like firelight. Only twin disks glared out of the darkness, face invisible to the shadows.

We carried on through streets that no longer felt abandoned. Hands shaking, I turn my light into the occasional window. Behind every pane I saw pairs of burning orbs, like pits into Hell, only growing in frequency as we traveled deeper into the city. I wondered if our newness kept them at bay or our numbers. Could any sentience remain beyond those unblinking eyes, to warn them our weapons meant danger? Many times, I considered turning back, leaving the city to the ghouls. The thought of watching my people starve drove me onward.

Halfway through the week, while marking places of interest, we found an old news station. Carlos, our shelter historian, urged us to search the inside for any old computers. The parts could be gutted, he argued, and maybe something remained to tell us what happened to those left aboveground. I already knew what happened to those that refused to leave the surface, but I held my tongue and agreed to his request regardless.

That was how we found the launchpad.

From the top of the radio tower, looking out past the edge of the city, the clouds cleared just enough to see the shape of scaffolds in the distance. Perfect for experimental passenger rockets, the kind the private sector was beginning to use for Mars colonies before the end, my father told me. The maps declared the city never had an aerospace industry, but the evidence sat before our very eyes. Even squinting through binoculars, I could tell the empty launchpad served no purpose now. The scorched scaffolds appeared at least a decade out of use, if not longer.

How much *fuel* had they burned to reach the stars – how much did they waste? How long did they wait, after the radios failed, to declare the people in the bunkers a lost cause?

In my anger, I turned my back on the evidence of betrayal. My team stood around me on the roof, shoulders heavy with the burden we all shared. Those rockets could only carry so many. Even if we had known, if our shelter had been opened, how many of us would have truly been permitted a chance to venture off this world?

I looked out over the horizon, infested buildings like broken teeth, crumbled into a darkening sky. More expeditions would be planned after this one, but I doubted anything of value remained in this obliterated husk, and I had no desire to make a return trip. I guided my team back to the shelter. We arrived home only hours ago; just in time to bathe ourselves of radioactive dust before a safe night's sleep behind a sealed vault door. We discuss our findings and next steps in the morning. I cannot imagine what we will do next.

I will tell no one of the urban phantoms, the last of humanity on the surface of the Earth.

* * *

My name is Bailey Hollow and I built the village of Penance.

For much time my people wandered across North America in search of a home. The underground shelter struggled onward, a prolonged death, and my ancestors stayed until the last moment. We eked out years, then decades, pilfering from the nearby city to resuscitate the bunker. The dream finally died with my mother. Thousands of lives were her burden to bear on the surface of a new planet. And then mine, when she passed. We were nomads of a hostile world, once custodians of this Earth and now nothing.

I fought for a place to call home. Seeking, waiting, but never finding a haven for more than a few years. Every new location had problems, seemingly insurmountable.

At the first attempt, the gardeners among us warned the soil was too sandy. With the desert in every direction, our half-way oasis would be swallowed in decades. For the second attempt, the carpenters found every building material too brittle. With torrential acid rain dissolving the rooftops every other week, I could not risk the people under my care. Our third attempt was a wooded caldera, but the rising sun made the natural crater a brutal oven, even with the shade of the trees. The plants had adapted to the heat, but even the strongest among us felt light-headed within hours.

It took many tries, but I finally found Penance. Cradled by a mountainside, surrounded by lush forest, a freshwater river less than a mile away. The abundance of natural stone made for good houses and the air was not too thin to support life. We arrived just in time to spread seeds and the forest provided plenty to scavenge in the meantime.

Best of all, it is far from a city. Our doctor, an aging woman named Moira, gravely informed us that life in the bunker and exposure to the elements damaged us. The radiation of the surface – our own doing, added to the oppressive sun – shortened our lives. Contaminants in the air abraded our lungs. Heavy metals and synthetic toxins in the water and food shred our intestines. Here, leagues away from a city, beyond the reach of our ancestors, we can make our own future. We rely only on ourselves and the yet untouched Earth.

I await first harvest, to see if we are blessed or cursed.

* * *

My name is Lorin Hollow and I transcribed every family journal entry, every mislaid and poorly preserved scrap, into this book.

My eldest, Leanora, lies abed recovering from her fourth miscarriage in as many years. Every woman in Penance suffers such, even secluded away from the noxious ancestral metropolises. The nearest is hundreds of miles away, a smog-filled jungle of hard angles and sharp edges, where specters haunt the crumbling streets with burning eyes. Even so, the poison seeps into our mountainside homes. We all succumb to it in the end, with aching lungs and aching hearts, feeding back to the Earth that gives and takes from us in turn.

My Earth-given gift, little Lacey, is the only child in our village. Leanora had just the one, but it seems no more. Today I took Lacey up the barren slope to an overlook we call Godsreach, so we do not watch her mother suffer. The journey grows more burdensome with every passing year; my old bones yearn for rest.

The thick clouds parted for us on a crystalline canopy, revealing the great stellar masterpiece. I pointed out the ones I knew to my grandchild and named each insignificant speck in turn. Whispered to her which humanity hoped to make their new home, back when everyone decided to leave. Had they made it up there, beyond the grasp of a choked world? Not a soul on the ground could contact them now, if they ever left. Debris fell from the heavens every other day, sparkling across the bruised brown sky like embers in ash, and I wondered if those pieces were all that remained of the Skybound.

I taught my people to track the dying arcs through the atmosphere, to figure out where they land. When I had their youth, the fallen objects set the clouds alight. Just the flammable wisps in lower atmosphere, but we used to gape in wonder and call them Dragonfires. Now, though, with the combustibles kindled away, any falling wyrms only leave temporary burns on the clouds.

Once, before I married, a group of men left to investigate an impact site, put reality into the Dragonfire myth. When no one returned, we forbade all future scavenging of the plummeting debris. If you see scorched Earth, we whisper to the children, turn and *run*. It might be a dragon, we warn them, but it might be a demon, too. My mother told me the demons were from beyond this world, crashed from the stars to see if it was time for us to be forgiven for the ancestral crimes.

I do not know if we deserve to be forgiven.

I once thought her stories all nonsense. That was before she passed a bundle of paper to me when I came of age. Read these, Lorin, and save them all. Those torn and yellowed scraps were all that remained of the Hollow generations, centuries of calculations and drawings and musings. Tales of a world so foreign it could have circled a distant star. Legends of cities with millions, of underground caves housing thousands. I scarcely believe them, even with written proof. Never have I met someone outside my village, and we number only a hundred. All I had were the stories.

The Hollow Journal recorded the population of every place we called home for every year we lived. My census date soon approaches and the number I write will be less than last autumn. On these pages I have circled those numbers, if only to show myself how sand flows so quickly through the hourglass of our creation.

Humanity reaches its final seconds.

If the countdown isn't enough, I can feel it in the forest. The skies may begin to clear, but after every winter fewer fresh sprigs poke through ashen ground. Every harvest brings us less bounty. Though I expressly forbid the youth from venturing outside the boundary of the fields, I know they explore beyond the forest. I hear them whisper about sandy soil, about withered underbrush.

Atop Godsreach with Lacey, I tried to find the line where sky met ground. Once, towering conifers brushed the sky, the fingers of the world caressing the heavens as far as the eye could see. That lover's embrace retreated over the sunsets of my life. Now the horizon blends into a haze, the suffocating clouds blanketing the consuming desert. By the time my granddaughter reads this book, I fear the forest will be eaten entirely.

All the stories I know, none of them tell of life in the desert. I squeeze gently the small hand in mine. Bright stars glitter above, silent and indifferent in a swirl of eternity. I wonder how many barren planets orbit those distant suns. How many lifeless rocks spin through space with a cargo of corpses?

The Earth is quiet.

* * *

My name is Yas DeBurro and I found this journal in a buried time capsule.

I have not read every page yet. It has been a long time since I've read anything at all. My family has a few novels, a couple textbooks, all on the verge of crumbling – and yet here I am, holding an entirely new text in my hands, hundreds of pages of words.

For years, we lived in the gulf lowlands. Both my mother and father were raised there, and their parents before them, going back since the beginning of the end. We avoided the cities at all costs, welcomed in the stray traveler every few years, and created a community from nothing. By luck or the grace of God, the place we called home sheltered us from the worst of the heat, of the drought, of the storms. The land was arable and suited to farm animals.

Every few years, as summer turned to autumn, hurricanes swept through our little Elysium. At first, we only needed to protect crops from the rain. But each storm caused more damage than the last, dragging the shoreline inland. Last year the hurricane brought with it black tides, flooding fields with oil and garbage. When the abrasive winds finally died down enough to venture outside, the sun created rainbows on the rows of spoiled crops.

Lina DeBurro founded life in that valley, and now we move our home elsewhere.

The mountains, we thought. Even with the thinner atmosphere, the natural caverns of the land could protect us. No petroleum hurricanes, no sweltering drought, no spontaneous grass fires. A fresh start, taking with us everything we could carry.

We found this village in the shadow of a short mountain, surrounded by fertile soil. All that remained are stones ground into dust, the outline of cabins. There were no bodies, very little to scavenge. In the center of the crumbled ruins was one large fir tree – withered, warped like it has been struck by lightning, but grappling with the Earth for life. It was eldest in the young forest surrounding the village. In the shade of the evergreen, buried among the roots, was a ceramic and metal capsule. And in that capsule, this journal. My parents moved on, to inspect the suitability of the ground and see if it can support all twenty-three of us, but I already know this will be our new home. I stayed to investigate this village further.

I found a wooden sign, overgrown with moss, reading "Penance" in black letters. That sign was the first thing we burned to feed our dinner fire. As it went up in smoke, I carved a new one.

Kieran Hollow, I welcome you to Amnesty.

Power Grid

Steve Carr

MA'S TOMATO PLANTS are wilting in the sun-scorched earth. Tied by old shoe laces to wood stakes to hold them up, the plants look as if they're being held in the garden against their will and being subjected to torture by the heat. The vines are limp; many of their leaves droop, with their tips and edges curled. They had been stripped that morning of the few tomatoes they had produced. Ma put the tomatoes in a birch basket on top of some scrawny carrots and undersized cucumbers.

Before carrying the basket into the house, she wiped sweat from her forehead with the back of her gloved hand, looked up at the hazy white sky, and said, "God save us."

From the edge of the garden that is surrounded by mesh wire to keep out raccoon, rabbits and deer, the flat earth beyond our property is carpeted in dying brown grass that stretches out to the horizon. Electric power lines stretch from one metal transmission tower to the next that stand a good distance apart on a broad path that bisects the prairie. There's something comforting in the almost inaudible humming coming from the wires.

* * *

The fan above the dining room table swirls slowly, making little difference in the stillness of the hot air. With each completed turn of the fan's blades it makes a loud clicking noise, something Pa has said he would fix for as long as I can recall.

He's sitting at one end of the table and rubbing an ice cube across his stubbled cheeks. There are large sweat stains under his arms. His plate of food sits in front of him, untouched. Visible waves of heat rise up from the mound of mashed potatoes. Butter flows over them like bright yellow lava.

Before sunrise Pa and I saddled up our last two horses, Jupiter and Sassy, and rode out to the back ten acres of our ranch to see how the cattle were faring. The last bales of hay we had placed in the fields four days ago was gone and the cows and their calves stood about listlessly. They weren't starving, not this morning at least, but it would only be a matter of time. When we returned the horses to the barn, Pa took his rifle from his saddle, and with tears streaming down his face, shot Jupiter and then Sassy.

"Better they die this way," he said. We didn't tell Ma about it.

"Eat, Henry," Ma says. "Your food is going to get cold."

She stifles a gasp, and repeats quietly the word 'cold' as if uncertain of its meaning.

Pa dips his fingers into his ice tea and takes out another ice cube. He runs it across his lips and then puts it in his mouth. While making sucking sounds he says, "The water in the stream that flows under Pony Bridge was warm, really warm, this afternoon. There was dead catfish and bass floating on the top."

I push cooked carrots around on my plate, wishing I had grown to like them long before this.

Suddenly the fan stops rotating. The house has become silent, free of the subtle, persistent drone of electricity. Every appliance has stopped.

I grip the edge of the table. My knuckles are white.

Ma and Pa look at each other, searching for something indefinable in one another's eyes.

Then the blades of the fan begin to move.

I lean my head back and feel the hot air circulated by the fan on my cheeks. I long for a cool breeze, even one generated by electricity, as if it has been years since I felt one, but it wasn't that long ago.

* * *

The chain holding the swinging chair to the roof of the porch squeaks loudly with every swing backward. Night hasn't brought cooler weather and it feels like I'm breathing with a plastic bag over my head. It's too hot to sit with my arm around Jennifer's shoulders. She sits at the other end of the seat, her legs drawn up to her chest with her arms wrapped around them. Strands of her long brunette hair is glued by perspiration to her face.

"The grocery store was sold out of almost everything," she says. "But there was a whole bunch of folks just standing in the aisles because of the air conditioning."

She swats at a horsefly that was buzzing around her head.

A coyote's bark reverberates from the darkness of the prairie. A shooting star slices across the sky, disappearing as abruptly as it appeared.

"Are you sure you want to put off the wedding until October?" I say.

She combs back her hair with her fingers and runs her tongue across her lower lip. "No one wants to travel in this heat to a wedding, even if they could."

"It could just be our immediate families. The ones nearby," I say.

As if propelled off the swing, she unfurls her legs and leaps off of the seat. In the glare of the light cast by the uncovered bulb in the socket above the door, the features of her face look flattened, as if her face had been ironed.

"Not now. Not in this heat," she says breathlessly, as if gulping for air. She slumps against the porch railing and softly cries.

The bulb flickers, then goes out.

I stare at the dark bulb, bite into my index finger, and wait.

When the bulb comes back on a few minutes later I realize I've peed in my pants.

Jennifer has left the porch and is going to her car. The gasoline she used coming to see me and to get back home was the last available at the gas station in town.

* * *

In my bedroom the lamp on the stand by my bed is on. The hot breeze blowing in through the open window carries with it grit and flying insects. A hawk's screech comes from very near the house. Lying naked on the sheet, rivulets of sweat runs down my chest and between my legs. My body feels restrained, weighed down on the bed, held in place by imaginary boulders sitting on my chest. I try to not think about how difficult it is to take each breath.

Ringo is curled up on the end of the mattress. His heavy panting causes the bed to vibrate. Twice he's emptied his water bowl in the past few hours.

I hear my parents in the hallway outside my door.

"I don't want you going hunting tomorrow," Ma says.

"A single deer would put enough venison in the freezer for a month if the electricity holds out that long," Pa says.

"It's not hunting season," Ma says. "You could get arrested, or in this heat, something worse…"

"I know enough to have water with me in this weather," Pa says.

There is a moment of silence, and then Ma says, "It got up to 120 degrees in Washington, DC today. People are dying on the streets."

"I know," Pa says.

When I hear the door to their bedroom open and close I turn off the lamp. The four nightlights plugged into the outlets along the floorboards glow like lighthouse beacons.

I close my eyes, listening for the sounds of electricity.

* * *

Jess is tightly gripping the steering wheel of his old Ford pickup truck. A muscle in his cheek pulsates as he chews on the end of a blade of dead prairie grass. The wheels of his speeding truck spit up clouds of dirt that are quickly blown away by the constant wind. He suddenly slams on the brakes, causing my seat belt to dig into my chest and abdomen.

"Damn, Jess, what are you doing?" I say.

He quickly unbuckles his seat belt and throws open his door. "You have to see this," he says as he leaps out of the truck.

I undo my seat belt and get out of the truck.

We're at the beginning of a usually dry, narrow river bed that leads to a swimming pool sized pond that we've swam in since we were young boys. He runs along the edge, his boots knocking off large chunks of dirt that fall into the river bed.

"C'mon slowpoke," he yells, his voice almost bordering on hysteria.

Even running a few yards, my lungs are taxed from breathing in the scorching heat. He has been standing near the bank of the pond for a few minutes when I come up beside him.

The water is gone. A large, oval-shaped, shallow bowl of dried, cracked mud, remains. An old, rusted bicycle, a car tire and the skeleton of a cow stick out of the dirt.

"Where did it go?" I say.

"I came out here yesterday and this is how I found it." He takes off his Stetson and runs his hand through his sweat-soaked hair. "Did you notice how quiet it is?" he says. "Where have the birds gone to?"

I scan the prairie, and then the sky. There isn't a bird, or cloud, in sight. Far off I see the power lines and imagine I can hear their hum.

* * *

Ringo is lying on the floor in the corner of the living room. He doesn't move as I enter the room, and looks at me indifferently. I bend down and hold a dog biscuit in front of his nose. He turns his head away. I lay the dog biscuit on the floor in front of him. He rests his head listlessly on his front paw.

"He's stopped eating and he's gotten lethargic," I say as I stand.

"It's this weather," Ma says. She's sitting in Pa's Barcalounger. The box fan is on the floor and aimed at her, bathing her in hot air. She's sewing a button on one of Pa's shirts. Her sewing basket is on the stand next to the chair.

"It's almost dark. I thought Pa would be home from hunting by now," I say.

She bites into her lower lip and pulls the thread through a button hole. "Me too."

The television is on, but the sound is off. News coverage of massive wildfires in California and Oregon is playing.

"I should have gone with him," I say.

"He wanted you here in case," she says.

"In case of what?"

Ma inserts the needle into a button hole and pulls the thread through.

I go to the front screen door and watch as small dust devils dance across the driveway. The twilight sky is streaked with rays of dark purple and blood red. Pa's pickup is coming down the road toward our house.

"Pa's home," I say.

Ma throws aside Pa's shirt and accidentally knocks the sewing basket from the stand as she jumps up. Spools of thread, needles, a pin cushion, thimbles and pieces of ribbon scatter across the floor. She pushes past me and rushes out the door. She reaches the truck just as Pa pulls to a stop. He opens his door and Ma throws her arms around him as he gets out of the truck.

Pa's face is sunburned.

Both Ma and Pa are crying as they cling to each other.

"Everything out there is dying," he says.

* * *

"It's only until all this is over," Jennifer says.

"The same thing is going on in Canada. And Mexico. And France. And India. Everywhere," I answer, knowing it's meaningless.

She is silent for a moment. "I have to go north with my family," she says.

I switch my phone to my other ear. "At least here we still have electricity," I say. "As long as we have that, then we'll be okay."

"I love you," she says, and then hangs up.

The night is quiet. Too quiet. On my bed I stare at the light cast on the ceiling by the lamp.

Ringo stayed in the living room, curled up in a corner, whining.

The bulb in the lamp and the nightlights flicker, and then go out.

Rainclouds

Brandon Crilly

"MAYBE YOU want to put that weapon down, son."

I never figured out how Moore could sound so calm with the barrel of a gun pointed at him. The two strangers standing on the edge of our lands were haggard, thin and twitchy – the worst kind of travelers on Nuaga. Moore looked like royalty compared to them, just in comparison to their threadbare clothes. But the way he squared his shoulders, the way his low baritone issued smoothly through the dry air – that was the real source of his authority, which set him apart from the wanderers and from me.

The stranger holding the gun flicked his eyes between us. I was pressed against the old, long-dead harvester on the edge of our land, with my gloves wrapped around an old rifle that was leveled at the man's head. I wasn't a very confident shot, but I tried to pretend by borrowing some of Moore's calm.

"We just need some water," the gunman said. His companion nodded in rapid agreement. "Please."

"And like I said, we don't have any to spare." Moore shook his head. "I wish the condensers were working better this season, but they aren't. If I had anything to spare for you, I would."

"How do I know you're not just feeding me lies?" the gunman hissed.

"You've visited a few homesteads, I imagine?" The gunman nodded. "Is anyone faring well these days? Is anyone sitting on some miracle cache of water that no one else knows about? Has someone figured out how to tame the clouds?"

I felt the usual anxiety at the back of my neck – a bizarre mix of hopefulness and fear of that hope being broken again. Moore asked the same question of everyone that passed by their homestead: has someone tamed the clouds? Had someone else solved the puzzle and saved the world?

But the gunman just hissed again. "No one controls the clouds, old man. They drop water whenever they please."

Moore sighed and spread his hands. "Then we're at an impasse here, son. The clouds don't favor me anymore than they favor you. More time spent demanding something I don't have just means you'll be thirstier when you find someone who can help you. And if you decide to shoot, odds are that you and your friend won't walk away alive."

I caught the gunman's eye again and decided to wink.

"Let's just go," the gunman's companion said. He grabbed his friend's scrawny shoulder. "Let's just go."

The gunman blinked a few times and turned away. The two of them started down the rocky slope, and I saw Moore's shoulders relax. Conveying that kind of authority took energy, he had once told me. I blew out a cautious breath.

I didn't see the gunman turn until it was too late.

His face tightened into a mad, desperate snarl as he raised the gun. It clicked twice in the time it took me to level the rifle again and fire. Despite not being much of a shot, I hit the gunman square in the forehead. His companion cried out and started running.

I didn't even think. It took two shots to bring him down, and then the rifle was out of my hands and I was running to Moore.

One of the gunman's wild shots had missed. The other had struck Moore almost in the center of his chest. Blood was pumping furiously from the wound; it swirled around my hands as I pressed them to his shirt. I had no way of knowing what damage might have been done, and in my panic I had no idea how to save him. Applying pressure seemed natural, but other than that I was at a loss.

I heard shouts from the homestead and saw two shapes running toward me: Warren and Lecea. They had been watching from a distance – just in case, Warren always said.

One of Moore's hands gripped my shoulder. Even then, his eyes were still surprisingly calm.

"The work…" he whispered weakly.

Then his hand dropped to the stony ground, and he closed his eyes.

* * *

We buried Moore on a hill behind the homestead, where the cracked ground was a little softer. The two strangers went in a deep crevice off our property, and weren't spared another glance. There were people elsewhere on Nuaga, supposedly, who extracted all the fluids from the dead before they were buried, not wanting to waste an ounce of liquid. None of us believed in that.

Warren was silent through the entire process. He and Moore had been married for almost forty years, back on Earth. Where Moore was calm and approachable, Warren was firm and tight-lipped; they had seemed to complement each other perfectly, though I didn't have any couples to compare them to. He barely breathed as he stared at the grave.

Lecea stood apart from us, chewing on a fingernail. Part of me wanted to take that hand and hold it, but I got the feeling she wouldn't want that. We were close in ways that were mostly physical, but that kind of comfort didn't seem like one of them.

There were a few clouds in the sky as the sun started to set. None of them passed directly overhead, and none of the Tamrynites within chose to drop any rain.

We walked back to the homestead in silence. Lecea said something about checking the condensers and drifted away. Warren said nothing as he opened the door to the old habitation pod. He and Moore had lived there alone for six years after the Landing, before taking Lecea in, and me the year after. I watched him pause at the threshold and rub the back of his broad, brawny shoulders before he disappeared inside.

I ended up at Moore's makeshift workshop without really thinking about it. I shut the door to the converted supply container, turned on the one working light and sat down on the stool beside Moore's desk. The metal chair he had made for himself sat empty a few meters away.

The workshop was a mess of cobbled machinery, bundles of wire, and scattered notes written on old multi-use sheets. A lot of the settlement equipment that had proven useless on Nuaga had ended up in there: fertilizing pods, drones for monitoring crops, hydroelectric converters. There was little tangible evidence of Moore's various attempts to attract the Tamrynites; there weren't a ton of materials on hand, so we had to keep recycling components over and over. Some of his original notes were stuck to the walls, as well as transcripts and screenshots from before the communications network went down. I remembered from my first homestead how people had shared ideas freely after the Landing, having realized that Nuaga wasn't the temperate gem the people of Earth had thought. It didn't take long after the network died for people to turn into savages.

One of the screenshots was a photo of Professor Tamryn: the man who had figured out how Nuaga could have so many clouds and such arid terrain. The man who had discovered the Tamrynites and shared sensor data showing the tiny aliens living in the clouds, feeding on hydrogen and oxygen molecules. Moore had explained Tamryn's theories to me a couple times, and while some of it had gone over my head, I understood that the rain we depended on for survival was just waste to the Tamrynites, full of nitrates and other substances that they either couldn't ingest or just didn't enjoy. They stored this waste water for a while, dumped it on whoever was lucky enough to be beneath them at the time, and drifted higher into the atmosphere to collect fresher H_2O.

Moore had idolized Tamryn, always saying that he wished he had half of the professor's genius. I thought the two were a match. It was Moore who had built the collectors and spread them out to catch the water the Tamrynites discarded, Moore who had adapted the habitation pod's water purification system into condensers to draw moisture from the air. Moore was the smartest man I had ever known.

I must have sat there for a while, just staring at the notes and the hodgepodge of equipment, before Lecea came inside. The open doorway didn't cast any light into the room.

"You should get some sleep. Warren wants to run a full diagnostic on the condensers tomorrow."

"Okay."

I thought she had left, but she eventually said, "It wasn't your fault, by the way."

"I've read that line in a lot of stories in the Library," I said without turning. "Doesn't make much of a difference."

She closed the door without saying anything else.

I decided to sleep on the floor of the workshop.

* * *

The condenser diagnostics were pushed aside when a packer wandered onto our land. Every meager life form on Nuaga had adapted some way to survive the Tamrynites' unpredictable water cycles; for the four-legged packers, that equaled two fleshy sacks hanging from their torsos, which stored water for their body to slowly siphon from. A lot of them were hunted and killed when people's water stores started to disappear, but there were a few in our area that didn't fear us.

I was halfway through drawing water from the sedated packer – not enough to harm it, but a sizable quantity for us – when I heard a crash from Warren's lab. I left Lecea to finish up and ran over there as quickly as I could, imagining some stupid accident taking my last remaining father figure the day after I lost Moore.

The door to the lab – another converted storage container, like the workshop – was hanging open when I got there. Inside, I saw our meager root vegetables untouched to the left, along with Warren's meticulous workstation. Further down, Warren was leaning over a jumble of equipment, disconnecting wires from circuit boards and organizing the parts.

"What are you doing?"

"None of this has gotten any results," Warren said as he finished with another board.

"I thought you were making progress," I said. "Reverse-engineering the crops could—"

"Could what?" Warren snapped. He grabbed a container of plants – part of an experiment he had started a year earlier – and dumped them into the organic reducer, to be mulched.

"It could save us."

Warren grimaced as he started cleaning out one of the jars he used as a beaker.

"Nothing is going to save us." I had never heard the burly old man speak in such a harsh whisper. "Moore was the only one who was close enough to that, and look what happened to him. This has all been a waste of my time."

"Look, maybe if you just—"

The jar shattered against the far wall. "It was a waste! Do you understand? My greatest mistake was thinking that I could actually accomplish something here. That any of us could. The only thing that matters is staying alive in this God-forsaken place, not…not screwing around with toys, thinking we can change the world."

Before I realized it, I was inches from Warren's face. "How dare you? Moore dedicated his life to this kind work. He believed that—"

"Oh, he believed, all right." Some of the anger seemed to leave Warren. He leaned over the edge of one of his little gardens, staring down at the tiny vegetables inside as they tried to grow with their limited water. "And he was wrong. Every experiment…they were just forestalling the inevitable. Foolish ideas aren't going to keep us alive. I've wasted enough time and energy as it is. I'm done with it."

Warren went back to dismantling his equipment. I wanted to berate him some more, maybe convince him that he was wrong. But I couldn't think of what to say. Both of us seemed to be out of words. I left and stalked across the homestead to Moore's workshop, ignoring Lecea's questioning glance from afar.

I couldn't give up on what Moore was doing. He had spent years trying to figure out a way to communicate with the Tamrynites – tame the clouds, like he always said. I looked around at the half-finished machinery and the fresh notes Moore left behind.

I knew then that surviving wasn't enough for me. Just like it wasn't enough for Moore.

* * *

Moore had tried a few different ideas to coax rain out of the Tamrynites, based on what he could cobble together from the equipment inside the pod, but nothing had panned out.

His latest project had involved sound. He figured the Tamrynites had to have a way to coordinate expelling their waste water – even that they might be semi-sentient – and that doing so via a particular noise or vibration would be the most efficient way for creatures their size. He had scavenged the speakers from the pod's communications system and connected them to one of the portable Libraries, intending to use its vast store of music to try to replicate the Tamrynites' signals. The only thing left was to boost the speakers' range and fiddle with the acoustics, since there was no way of knowing what particular frequency might work.

I spent the rest of that first day tinkering, and then into the next. Technical work and programming had always been my knack, Moore had said. Warren stepped into the workshop partway through the second day, saw what I was doing, and wandered back out with a low grumble. I kept working, and when the door opened again, I thought Warren had finally decided to force me to be more useful.

Lecea appeared beside me. "You're making some progress."

"Yeah."

She leaned on the back of Moore's chair; I had switched its position with the stool. "Warren says we're going to fall behind out there, just me and him. Our stores are already really low."

I put down the soldering iron I had been using. "Did he send you in here to make me stop?"

"No." I glanced over, but she didn't meet my eyes. I admired her long hair instead. "I wanted you to know I'll pick up the slack for you, until you're done."

"Oh. Thanks."

She caught me off guard by reaching out to touch my hand. We usually only held hands after we'd finished making love in the back of the pod. This was different, and not in a bad way.

"Let me know if you need any help," she said, and left before I could say anything else.

* * *

When I was done, I had four speakers hooked up to a heavy amplifier; the portable Library doubled as my control board, for modulating frequencies and so on. I fabricated a wheeled cart for the board, since I was afraid of dropping it. Lecea helped me haul everything out to the tallest hill on our land, after dark when the rest of the day's work was done.

A group of small clouds passed over our northern collectors about an hour later.

I turned on the machine and picked a particular frequency from a list Moore had jotted down. Lecea and I stood back as sound blasted at the cloud. Nothing happened, so I dialed up the volume until we had to cover our ears. When the cloud still didn't seem affected, I switched to a second frequency, and then a third as I worked down the list. The Tamrynites continued on their slow path; their cloud didn't even shift in form.

"It's not working!" Lecea shouted over the noise.

I refused to admit that until we had tried the last frequency, and the cloud drifted away.

* * *

A week later, after more failed attempts, I started rummaging through the discarded equipment in the workshop, mulling things over. It was hard to admit that Moore might have been wrong, and I didn't trust myself to brainstorm another theory. I was worried about Warren's reaction if I admitted defeat.

I picked up one of the crop-monitoring drones and rotated the disc-like machine in my hands. I wondered what Warren would say if I got them working again and used them to watch for approaching strangers; that would be a useful contribution. I started thinking about how to do it, and how high I could get the drones to go – maybe even get one among the Tamrynites, to learn a little more about them.

Something else occurred to me, and I froze. Then I raced back to Moore's desk and started writing.

Lecea came to the workshop that night, and I explained my idea.

"The needs of the many," I said, and she just blinked at me. "I think Moore was right about using sound, but we're sending our signal from the wrong place. Moore said that the Tamrynites have to communicate with each other – but how do they decide as a group *when* to release their water? If one Tamrynite starts signaling, but the others aren't ready or don't sense the need, the cloud does nothing. But if multiple Tamrynites signal, then the rest of the cloud would naturally follow suit, right?"

"Okay…but how does that help us?"

I held up one of the drones. My grin was only partly forced; I was still getting past the desire to share my bright idea with Moore.

"I can attach the speakers to the drones and reprogram them. They'll go up into the cloud, spread out, and start broadcasting the same frequency. Once the Tamrynites respond, the control board will lock in that frequency in all the speakers. That'll trick the Tamrynites into releasing their waste water."

"But you would still have to figure out the right frequency," Lecea said. I nodded, and she added, "Assuming they even use sound waves to talk to each other."

I frowned. "You don't think this is going to work, do you?"

Lecea studied the equipment, and I noticed her brilliant, blue eyes were sparkling. "I don't know. Moore thought it would. I'll keep an open mind."

* * *

We brought the equipment back to the hill the next day, as the sun was setting. There was a massive cloud up in the distance, heading directly toward us. Warren was nowhere to be seen; he had started ignoring me completely during the day, and disappearing into the habitation pod before the sun went down.

Lecea helped me set up the equipment. The control board went in the same place as before, and we spaced out the drones so they wouldn't hit each other when they lifted off. There were four drones, each with a speaker attached to their underside, remotely linked to my control board. I spent a long while hunched over the board. The program I had come up with was entirely automated – the drones would find the Tamrynites, spread out in the cloud, and test different frequencies until they registered a response – but for some reason that made me even more anxious about technical failure.

Something crunched in front of me.

I looked up and saw three people standing in front of the drones. They were hard and disheveled, like the ones from before. The lead man was older, with gray in his receding hairline and a scruffy beard. Something more than the gun at his hip reminded me of the one that had shot Moore. I wasn't entirely sure why, until he started speaking.

"Name's Hoston." His voice was low and raw, like so many people who survived on too little water. He glanced at the drones. "Looking for my brother. Last I heard he came out this way."

I stepped around the control board, thinking of the drones. Hoston slowly drew his gun and I froze. Again I couldn't find my words.

"We don't get many visitors here," Lecea said.

"I know. Figure my brother would stick out in your minds."

"And if we told you we haven't seen anyone in months?"

"Then I'd call you both liars," Hoston said grimly, "since I'm the one that sent him here to steal from you."

Just like that, there was a sick feeling in my gut, a sort of fearful certainty that we were both going to die. My old rifle was back at the homestead. It hadn't crossed my mind to bring it, even after what happened to Moore. Hoston's eyes flicked between us, as though he was deciding who to kill first.

"Hold it."

I glanced back as Warren stepped onto the hill, clutching our only other weapon: a battered shotgun he and Moore had traded for before they took me in. He stepped up beside one of the drones, and Hoston was smart enough not to even twitch.

"Your brother killed a member of our family." Warren's voice sounded oddly flat to me. "I'd like to assume that wasn't part of your plan. But I'd be happy to blow your head off, just in case."

Hoston studied the shotgun. "That the weapon that killed my brother?"

"Time for you and your friends to leave."

The bizarre déjà vu of the scenario struck me. I had already lost one father figure like this. I couldn't lose another.

"It's going to pass us," Lecea whispered behind me.

My eyes flicked to the cloud. It was almost directly overhead, but I knew there was nothing I could do.

Lecea didn't feel the same way. I felt her move behind me, and saw Hoston's eyes widen as he lifted his gun. I threw myself to the side, reached for Lecea and missed, and saw the control board light up in the darkness. The gun went off behind me.

The drones whirred to life, kicking up dust and tiny pebbles, and surged into the sky. I flailed and fell onto my back. The shotgun roared and Hoston stumbled toward me, clutching his shoulder.

I was close enough to Hoston to kick his legs out from under him. He fell to the ground, his cry of surprise and the sound of him hitting the rocks drowned out by a loud chirp from the control board. Warren's next shot sprayed into the air overhead. I kicked Hoston in the side for good measure. His two friends were scrambling away, hands held high in the air.

The control board chirped again as I got to my feet – that meant the drones were in position, and testing the first frequency. Hoston started to rise, but I leapt onto his chest and punched him hard in the face. His gun was already gone, but I raised my fist to punch him again.

Warren caught my wrist and pulled me to my feet. "Lecea," he barked, and pushed me away.

She was sitting with her back against the control board's makeshift cart, arms slack at her sides. I landed on my knees beside her and stared at the bloody wound in her chest. It was almost in the same place as Moore's, and once again I felt helpless.

The control board chirped again – a different tone, but I didn't register it.

I started fumbling with my shirt, thinking that I should press it to Lecea's wound, but she caught one of my hands. Her beautiful, brilliantly blue eyes were on the sky. "Look."

At first, I thought she'd be watching the cloud, but she was trying to look behind her at the control board. I looked up, and saw green lights shining bright from the controls. There were no more chirps. There didn't need to be.

Rain started to patter around us.

"It worked," Lecea said. Her lips curled upward in amazement. "You did it."

The cloud kept drifting with a strangely ponderous graze, and my cheeks were wet before the raindrops fell against them. I glanced behind me and saw Warren still standing over Hoston, but neither of them were paying attention to the other. Their stunned looks were fixed upward as the rain started to fall more heavily than I had ever seen before.

"Moore did it," I said to Lecea. "He's the one who saved us."

But she was already gone, the tiny smile of amazement permanently etched across her face.

Oblivious to us, the Tamrynites eventually moved on.

A Quiet, Lonely Planet

AnaMaria Curtis

WALKING UP the muddy hill felt like home to Arendt, even though the grass here was blue, and the mud was siltier and grainier than that on Earth.

The shed was built of violet Corladian wood, soft with age. The wood smelled sweet and sour and sharp, like a combination of fruit just past ripe and the barn she'd grown up in. She sat on the soft dirt floor, leaning against the wall with a careful eye for nearby tools. She lay a possessive arm across the crate next to her. In it, wrapped carefully, were seeds she had saved from every Earth vegetable she had managed to get her hands on since coming to Corlad.

Her communications chip flashed. Her mother's voice streamed through almost before she hit accept.

"Honey—"

"Yeah, Mom, I know. It was in the news here too." She swallowed. She'd only skimmed the article when she woke up, unable to look for detail without the words blurring in front of her. "How are you and Brandon?"

"Everyone in the neighborhood here is planning a funeral for a week from now," her mother said. "You should come."

Arendt laughed, and the hollow sound chased her around the tiny shed. "You're having a funeral for a planet?"

"It was our planet."

"Yeah." Arendt rested her head against the wall. Dust settled on her clothing, and she thought of the barn at home again. It had been red and sturdy and a little gross, everything a barn ought to be. "I've been putting off a business trip into the city," she said. "I can be there."

Her mother chuckled. "My daughter, putting off a trip?"

Arendt twisted her lip in an insult that her mother couldn't see and considered all the places she'd run away from, the fact that she had been here for the longest of any of them: seven Earth years, four Corladian years. Long enough to do more than work for hire. Long enough to start a business and try not to fuck her roommates because she'd probably still be living with them in another quarter of a year.

"Point is," she said, "I'll be there."

"Okay," her mother said, "great! There's a new restaurant I want to take you to and people for you to meet."

"Unless they're interested in farming, I don't want to meet anybody in your business."

"*My business* paid for your starter loan."

Arendt sighed. Only because nobody in Leima province wanted to loan to a human. "Bye, Mom," she said. "I'll see you soon." She hung up without waiting for a response.

She couldn't remember what she'd needed from the shed. She looked at the tools hopefully. They were Corladian tools, only somewhat recognizable to Arendt as hoe, rake, tiller blades, trowels, shovels, and irrigation tubes. But she couldn't remember which one she needed.

She'd go to the shop; work would focus her.

Arendt tiptoed around the house as she gathered her jacket, tablet, keys, and socks. Enry and Mero, her roommates, were kind, but she didn't want to see them. Mero was a native Corladian, neutral in every way, and Enry's home planet, Frisb, was on the other side of the galaxy from Earth. They wouldn't understand.

She was putting her boots on in the kitchen when Mero poked two long blue arms and a cautious face around the corner.

"Oh, Arendt," they said, "I was afraid you'd gone."

"Just heading out."

Mero's full body entered the room, four arms fluttering nervously in search of something to do or say. But they were using Arendt's spoken language, a courtesy, though their voice was soft from less practice and a weaker throat. "Can I make you something before you go? Tea?"

Arendt's stomach flipped at the thought. Humans as homesick as Arendt would have cleared every warehouse of Earth tea by now. It would be on the black market for a few months, but not at prices she could afford. She had three tea bags left in the box in the pantry, had meant to order more last week.

"No, thanks," she said. Mero gave her a long, sad look with three unblinking eyes.

"I'm sorry," they said. "About Earth."

"I gotta go," Arendt said.

* * *

Arendt spent the next few days sorting and packing seeds into boxes, marveling as always at the color and size of them. Corladian seeds, like the plants they came from, were bigger than any equivalents from Earth. These were the size of her knuckles, perfectly round and incredibly dense. They had to be strong and hard to fight through the dense soil, to bloom into shelled potato-like synamests and bright, stringy telo beans.

She wondered sometimes if she couldn't take the cucumber and blueberry and broccoli seeds that she'd saved in a box in the shed and paint bright shells onto them until they were as strong and as colorful as these. But she couldn't risk them, not yet. There might be better soil for them somewhere else, if she chose to leave. And that was looking more likely by the minute.

At home, she cleaned her room and packed her essentials into her suitcases, playing her music out loud even though she knew it hurt Mero's more sensitive ears. She had two suitcases, and for five years they had carried her whole life. One was as blue as the grass, its plastic edges worn and round; the other, a bright yellow with a hard shell, was plastered with stickers, their images cracked and faded. They smelled like the imitation-cedar packets she'd stuffed in when she'd arrived, sure she'd leave in another six months.

Of course, she wasn't taking those suitcases with her on a brief trip to the city to take care of some business and see her mother. If she needed them, it would be easy enough to have them shipped. Besides, if she really wanted to leave, she would need an open visa. Something to discuss with her mother.

Arendt spent time with Enry and Mero, watching the dramas Mero liked so much and letting Enry do her makeup, even though she looked ridiculous with purple brows and grey lipstick. None of them talked about Earth, but for all that they would offer her food, they never went near the odds and ends of Earth food she had.

Arendt spent lots of time in the garden too. She finally fixed the wheelbarrow wheel in the shed, mulched the mirtleberries, and thinned the two rows of the corladcorn that Mero liked so much. It was a good garden, but the soil was dense, and she always worried that her plants wouldn't anchor properly to the soil. Sometimes she would sit on the dirt patch that she'd left in the center of her orderly rows of plants and look at them, run her fingers through the dirt that still felt a little wrong against her fingers, a little too hard, too gritty. Some of these times Mero and Enry came into the garden themselves, watching her sadly.

She wondered if she could teach them a little bit, just enough that they could get some of the hardier plants through a season. Just enough that if she left the garden wouldn't turn to weeds. It wasn't hard, but they'd have to learn to watch for things, to care about the color of the undersides of leaves. She wasn't sure if they noticed those kinds of things.

They all ate breakfast together before Mero drove Arendt to the train station. As a treat for herself, Arendt had some of the strawberry jam from the fridge on her toast, though the bread wasn't made with wheat.

At the train station she bought a one-way ticket.

* * *

She had dinner with her mother and sibling at a restaurant that served old-school human-style food made from Corladian ingredients. Arendt missed the restaurant from their first neighborhood. That restaurant sometimes had shipments of vegetables from Earth, cooked and measured out carefully. Whenever they'd had a shipment of carrots, she'd asked her mother to visit the restaurant every day. Arendt put a spoon to her mouth and thought that they'd probably go out of business, now.

"Someone finally bought our first apartment," her mother was saying. "Charities are buying up property in the neighborhood to house anyone who might have escaped." Her voice was very firm, but Arendt saw the corners of her mouth tremble.

Arendt had been thirteen in that apartment, not understanding why they'd had to leave Earth or home, missing pine trees and Japanese turnips and her friends. She had made her first Corladian friend there, had dug her bare fingers into Corladian soil for the first time. In fact, she had planted carrot seeds there and hoped and hoped and cried salty tears into the ground when nothing came up. Arendt knew better now. She was glad someone else would have the apartment. It belonged, Arendt knew, to a thirteen-year-old who came on the last ship from Earth and didn't know how or where to belong.

"That's great," she said.

Her sibling stirred the soup in front of them. "Arendt, how's business?"

"Not bad. I could do with a bigger customer base, but people are starting to see the advantages of sourcing things locally."

"They still won't let you own land up there?" That was her mother now, eyes narrowed.

Arendt shook her head. "They're not as used to us."

Her mother put her spoon into her soup bowl, where it sank. "I don't understand what the point of a planet with two intelligent species is if they haven't learned to accept others."

"Says the woman profiting from the war between species." Arendt had really tried not to say it, but there it was.

Brandon shifted uncomfortably. "Can't we just have dinner before we fight?"

Arendt's mother rescued her spoon by the tip of the handle. "I'm just trying to set you up well. We came to this planet with almost nothing. And now we have nothing to return to."

Arendt couldn't argue with that.

* * *

They watched the funeral parade from the balcony of her mother's apartment. Dozens of people, mostly her mother's friends, came over to watch with them, filling the apartment. They wore dresses and suits and saris and qipaos, all of the highest quality. Arendt tried calculating how many of them could get her an open visa if she asked the right way. She wondered what the right way was.

In the parade, people walked under the flag of their countries, under pictures of their cities, to the sound of dented and out-of-tune instruments that they had learned to play in schools once. Some of the instruments had been brought from Earth, but some of them had been made on Corlad, the planet of silence, and these were obvious by the shine on their bells and buttons, for the way they were never quite in tune. The people in the parade tried to play old, familiar songs, but they sounded just off enough that nothing was quite recognizable, like the melody they were supposed to be carrying was smoke, trailing through their instruments and moving on. Arendt wondered if this was the result of the slightly different chemical makeup of the air on Corlad, but she hadn't taken enough science to know. She sent Mero and Enry a little video of it, warning Mero about the noise.

The parade went and went, banner by banner and haunting song by haunting song, and Arendt watched this and thought that she should feel something. People next to her were weeping, reciting names of people and cities left behind. Arendt felt a little numb. She thought she might faint. Vendors on the sides of the street sold human food made with a mix of human and Corladian ingredients, and when Brandon said they were going to go buy something she convinced them to get her a nut butter and jelly sandwich.

Maybe it didn't feel like a funeral to her because she wasn't saying goodbye to her home, not really. Beijing and New New York had never meant anything to her, and nobody else in the crowd of hundreds of thousands was mourning her barn and her hills and the farmhouse with uneven floors and the weedy garden, except maybe Brandon. But Brandon had been so young when they left, and her mother had never cared for the farmhouse. She had always wanted an apartment in a city. Now she had several. And Arendt had three bags of tea left and flavors that lingered in her memory. Arendt let her eyes go unfocused over the crowd. Nobody would ever figure out how to grow mulberry trees or tea in hydroponics. Some things were just gone forever.

The sandwich Brandon brought her didn't taste like the ones she'd grown up with, with peanut butter from a brightly-branded jar and jam they'd made from the berries in the woods behind the farmhouse, but the nut butter was only a little too thick, and they'd put plenty of sugar in the berries. The bread smelled like real bread. Arendt ate it slowly, letting the nut butter accumulate at the top of her mouth and using it as an excuse not to talk to anybody. She was crying too, she realized when her eyelids felt sticky. All of this, all the humans here, trying too hard to recreate something that couldn't be brought back to life, it was too much. She needed something utterly unlike Earth. She needed something totally new. She scrubbed at her eyes. Newness would cleanse her.

After the end of the parade passed, the other people gathered in the apartment and along the balcony went to follow it to the main square, where many old human religions had temples. Arendt had no religion – no beliefs, either – so she stayed and finished her sandwich.

Her mother, even less of a believer, was the only one left in the apartment by the time Arendt finished the last bite.

They didn't talk. Her mother put on quiet music, jazz. Arendt sat on a wooden chair – Earth wood – and watched her mother turn water on and pull a crate of tea out from under the sink. Loose-leaf tea, a crate three quarters full. Her mother filled a mug with it and another with wine old enough to have been made from grapes harvested before there was such a thing as an intergalactic war. She placed the tea in front of Arendt and kept the wine.

"We should talk about this," she said. Her lips were cracked; Arendt could tell by the way her lipstick was beginning to flake off. And Arendt had just witnessed a planet's funeral.

"Let's not," she said, but she said it gently.

Her mother looked at her with the level eyes that she had always had when she explained why she was going to punish Arendt for something. But they were softer now, and tears were gathering at the corners.

"You'll feel better if we talk about it," she said.

"Mother, I guarantee you I won't."

"Well, I might."

Arendt put down her cup of tea, and it clinked unevenly on the table. Her hand was shaking a little. "You don't feel bad about things," she said.

Her mother tried to smile. "We can think of it as a new experience for both of us."

Arendt stood up. "That's not really the kind of new experience I'm looking for."

She was nearly to the door when her mother spoke. "Are you really going to leave your old mother alone here?"

"You're barely fifty." Arendt reached for the doorknob.

"But I'm still your mother."

Arendt turned. "Fine. But I'm not going to talk about anything, and I need a favor."

Her mother took another sip of wine. "What do you need?"

"An open visa. Leima is getting stifling. I might want to leave soon, go to Lispa or Ferlan or back to Fandar. Only Lispie planets, of course."

Her mother blinked. "And here I thought you were settling down."

Arendt tipped her chair back a touch too far, reveling in the momentary weightlessness in her chest. "The Rafers have a weapon," she said, "that can destroy any planet they wish. Maybe this is my last chance to visit these places."

Her mother tilted her head. "Do you *want* to get blown up on one of these planets? Is that what you want? Do you think that will make you feel better?"

Arendt took a sip of her tea, and the taste shot straight to her throat, drawing tears she didn't want to shed. It was strong and bitter and *good*. Her suitcases were already packed, her wares already stored. She stared back down at the cup.

"It can't make me feel worse."

* * *

Arendt skipped her business meeting the next day, sleeping in and reading instead. Her mother's apartment was nice. It had everything.

She was just getting to the most interesting part of her book when her comm chip dinged, and a voice message from Brandon started to play. "Arendt," they said, "Mom told me you might want to leave. A friend of mine is going to Fandar – you went there a couple years ago, right? – to see if there's anything they can do for their agriculture. Apparently, a few of their major grains are failing, and it could be bad there. Any chance you want to go pitch in for a bit? Would only be for a couple of months, but they're leaving tomorrow. Mom says she can get your visa tonight if you go down and sign something this afternoon."

Arendt put her book down. This was sudden. She wouldn't have time to go back for anything. She'd have to explain to Enry and Mero over the comms.

Arendt didn't reply to Brandon, giving herself at least an hour to think, but when Enry sent her a picture of burnt nurlach slices and noodles arranged to say, "We miss you," she didn't reply to that either.

* * *

Arendt went to get her visa in an office that smelled like canned pine and played human music at just the volume to make the lyrics indistinguishable but the melody ever-present. Arendt hummed along to it as she went over the forms, which were simpler than she'd expected. Arendt had heard that maybe the ambassadors from Earth on other planets had decided to make Corlad their official governmental base; perhaps this bureaucratic ease was a step in that direction. Then again, maybe it was just a sign of her mother's influence.

After she'd turned in the forms, it was only another half hour before a suited man brought her in for a quick interview, which went quickly as she stated the circumstances of her birth, her arrival in Corlad, and her attempt to start a small business.

He retrieved the document for her immediately after the interview, handing the small waterproof book to her mere moments after he had ushered her back into the waiting room. An electronic version would be sent within six weeks as they verified all her forms. He wrapped the visa in thick brown paper.

Arendt thanked him as she headed out the door, stuffing the package in her pocket. She couldn't stop holding it, though. Her fingers rubbed curiously at the smooth paper, at the edge where he'd taped it. This would let her run anywhere she wished.

* * *

She headed to the train station early the next day to meet Brandon's friend, Kento. He was a doctoral student in agriculture, a Corladian of the kind Mero was not, with six arms instead of four, three eyes in a diamond-shaped head, and skin a darker blue. They met by the entrance of a stationery shop and walked toward the train that would take them to the ship station.

"What's your interest in agriculture?" Kento asked her. His hands moved very quickly.

"I like being outside," Arendt said, only narrowly avoiding a Corladian going very fast in a mobility scooter as she looked back ahead of her while she signed. "And working with my hands is nice. I started gardening as a kid, and it helped me get work while I traveled, so I just kept going."

"That's interesting," he said. "I hate the actual work, personally, but I find agricultural patterns biologically very interesting. We seem to be opposites."

They bought their tickets, but they had just missed one train, and the next one didn't leave for another thirty minutes. Where they stood to wait was crowded, smelling of sweat and the metal of train batteries. People flowed around her, trying to converse even in the rush. They wore coats and skirts and the wraps favored on Corlad in muted colors, but the lack of brightness didn't make Arendt's head spin any less watching them. It was very quiet for a train station. Only the sounds of trains arriving and infrequent auditory announcements punctured the silence.

"Let's look around," she said. "Maybe there?" She pointed to a small shop selling wood products. Kento nodded his agreement.

The shop was small, but Arendt found amusement looking at the statues and picture frames done in different colored wood. There were even a few statues made of Earth wood, but those were inside glass cases. Arendt drifted further back in the shop. Kento followed a few steps behind.

There were several shelves of seeds in the back corner, mostly for decorative bushes that Arendt had no interest in, but she picked up a packet anyway. "For thin soils," read one. She put it back and picked up another. "For dense soils," it said.

Earth plants were the same way, of course. Arendt took a deep breath to calm her heart, which was beating faster than she could make sense of, and when she did so her nose caught a scent, sweet and sour and sharp. She glanced down – where was it coming from? – and saw the violet wood of the shelves. It smelled sour and sweet, and she could almost see dust coming off it, settling on her shirt. She thought of her shed and her garden, which she still needed to irrigate, and the crate of Earth seeds in the corner of the shed. She thought of the tea in her bag and wondered for the first time what kind of soil a tea plant needed.

"Kento," she said, barely hearing herself, "biologically, how different is Corlad's soil from that of Earth? I know it's denser, but chemically, what's the difference?"

He clasped his hands together in three pairs. "I never had the chance to visit your planet in person myself, of course, and there are lots of observations that nobody ever took the trouble of making."

"Why not?"

"My understanding is that you didn't have the instruments for it, or the inclination."

Arendt let that slide. "What does that mean? For the soil, I mean."

"We just don't know. Scientists have grown a few plants from Earth, broccoli and lettuce, for example, on Corlad, but nothing more has been attempted."

Arendt put a hand on the violet shelf to steady herself. "Those are plants that need clay soil," she said. Lists were running through her head: blueberries, brussels sprouts, even rice. Dense soil. Clay soil. Not carrots.

"Yes," Kento said.

"Why haven't they tried any other vegetables?" she said.

He shrugged. "It's not that interesting. Scientifically, I mean. Funding is limited, and most food can be made well enough with Corladian vegetables."

She gripped the shelf so hard she thought she might be creating finger-shaped indents. "That's despicable."

He looked at her, surprised.

"Other planets are going to get destroyed too," she said. "Shouldn't someone be making sure that their people have something that reminds them of home?"

Kento sighed. "That's not the responsibility of scientists."

Arendt thought of Enry's parents. They had come to Corlad before Enry was born. She had never had the chance to eat the vegetables and fruits her parents told her about. Arendt put the packet of seeds back on the shelf.

"I'm very sorry," she said to the scientist, "but I have to go home." She went back to the ticket booth and bought a ticket for the next train to Leima.

She couldn't have gardens on spaceships, no matter how far they took her. Especially not if she was going to experiment with new kinds of seeds. For a garden she needed time.

* * *

When she got off the train, the sky was growing dark. No one else got off at her stop. Arendt watched the train rush away and studied the curve of the planet – this strange, small planet – under the rails.

Enry and Mero were waiting for her in the truck. She wanted to pause and look at them for another minute, with the strange red sun setting on them, making the truck and their faces and limbs bright, but they ushered her in.

Enry drove with the one long arm and hugged her with the other, latching on a little tighter than usual. Arendt thought she might have bruises on her shoulder the next day, but she didn't really mind.

When they got back, Mero put the water on for tea and shushed Arendt's protests, gesturing to the table. There, collected in an awkward mound, were five boxes of tea, full to varying degrees.

"We got it from the neighbors," Enry explained. "They wanted to help, and most of them don't like human tea anyway, just tried it as a novelty."

Arendt just clutched her, then Mero, then the two together.

After she'd wiped her eyes and gotten her cup of tea, Arendt wandered out to look at the garden. In the moonlight – stronger than that of Earth, a convenient strangeness of this planet – she saw neat rows, untroubled by weeds.

She grabbed the watering can and headed for the pump.

"What are you doing?" Enry asked, sticking her head out the door.

"Gotta water the corladcorn."

Enry shook her head. "Mero watered it this morning. They looked up how often it needed water to make sure it was good." She rolled her eyes. "You know how much they love that stuff."

Enry was from a planet like Earth, small and insignificant in the grand scheme of things. She would have been sorry if Arendt was blown up somewhere. Arendt was suddenly, violently glad to be home.

She looked up toward the purple shed on the hill and the crate of seeds in it. She would go through them tomorrow.

"Can you ask your parents what grows in dense soil on your planet?" she asked Enry. It would be good, she thought, to try for a mixed garden. It was time to let her roots grow.

The Arrow of Time

Kate Dollarhyde

WE ABIDE in the small, thin hours of dawn, my mother and I. Her hand is slack and paper-thin in mine, her lips just parted. The ghost of breath slides between her gritted teeth, insistent still but ebbing, the slow draining away of an overfull life.

She has cancer. There's no point in saying what kind because it's everywhere. Its tiny grasping hands are ten hundred million strong and sunk deep in every turned-out pocket of her sagging flesh. She's dying, and in this moment I'm so furious with her that I can't speak. So, I hold her hand.

My mother is a scientist – an astrophysicist and an engineer. She is a clever, brilliant woman. And she has long thought, must still surely think under all those comatic layers of drug-induced sleep, that if she could gaze far enough back into time, she could figure out just where we'd gone so wrong. That's why she built the time machine.

* * *

I was born at the start of summer, of *the* summer – the first summer the North Pole turned to slurry. California shriveled under skies washed red with wildfire haze. Shasta Lake, the state's largest reservoir, surrendered her last drops of water. Communities too long disempowered and disenfranchised were made to reckon with a reality that scientists like my mother had warned them of for decades: this hot, dry world was their new home, and there would be no going back. Millions of people lost their jobs, their homes, their lives. Many of those remaining fled to the cities, and the cities buckled under the weight of their untold griefs, their justified furies.

My mother was born in a century that still held close to its chest the naive belief that anything could be fixed if you could just divine the correct number of resolutions to sign, could just levy the proper sanctions on the country of time. From what I've read of her journals, it was a beautiful place. Stuffed among her calculations, her frustrations and her many miseries, are memories of it sketched in a spidery hand:

> *Yesterday I drove down to the ocean. Green hills rolled right to the beach where they became dunes, sand, sea. I stood at the top of one of them and for a moment felt as if I were tilting down, as if the green of the bobbing grass and the white of the waves were all rushing up to greet me in a great tsunami tide. The swirl of color made me dizzy, and I fell hard to my knees. The grass was soft and caught me.*
>
> *I took off my sandals and buried my toes in the grass. It felt obscene, unreal, almost grotesquely taboo. It felt so good – the rain-fed grasses between my toes, that heady smell of bright and blinding life.*
>
> *I wanted to embrace it, the coast, and let it come into me. I believed, even if briefly, that I could carry its seeds and give birth to something new, better – a child*

of seafoam skin and driftwood bones who would demand water from the desert with thunderous lungs.

Every long entry read so, like stories she told herself, stories that gathered up the unraveling strands of the world she knew and knit them back together into a comforting whole.

I am sick with anger when I imagine her in green hills, standing on an impermeable coastline. Sick not because it's what I've never had – even if I haven't – but because she always longed to go back there, back to that time. Or maybe it's the guilt that turns my stomach; she tried to save the world, and I wanted her to read to me bedtime stories. Noble goals mean nothing to a child, but as adult I think I understand – she did it for love. If I could have stood beside her in green hills, to her, it would be worth any sacrifice.

* * *

There's light on the horizon now. A nurse shuffles through the door, a coffee-scented cloud in the shape of a human being. She pulls the curtain aside and checks my mother's vitals. She spares a moment to check on me, too, sympathy thick in the lines of her forehead. She tells me to get some rest, that it could be hours yet, but I don't want to. My fury keeps me awake, burning like slag down through my gut. My mother traded her life for an impossible dream, and now we will never have another chance to make things right between us.

I stare into my mother's face hoping I might see through her skin to the knot of longing that must live lodged behind her brow. I want to understand. I pinch the insides of her wrists, and she doesn't even blink. *Wake up, wake up, wake up. One last time – you owe me that much.*

* * *

When I was fourteen, she me took out West, out as far as we could go, out to where her dream for me was grown. It was her first visit to the coast since that day she dug her toes into the seaside grass, a day almost fifteen years dead.

We drove through the desert. We drove through coastal mountains barren or burned. The heat was unbearable, radiating from the ground in dancing silver sheets. She wouldn't let me turn on the air conditioner, and I could feel my heart racing, a headache coming on, nausea rising in my chest. "Energy is so expensive now," she said. "Not like when I was your age." Our two carboys of stale, cloudy water clinked in the back of the car, crashing together with every pothole bounce. "Shit," she'd laughed, "that was a big one."

We rode in silence past long-fallow fields of wizened almond trees, their black limbs stretched like clawed hands in supplication to a sky that had long ago stopped answering prayers for rain. The twisting highway led us past towns now a graveyard of tumbledown buildings all huddled together.

She stared ahead, eyes narrowed and always scanning for something only she could see. I tried to imagine her past overlaid on the brown hills, a flickering superimposition of beryl and chartreuse, malachite and verdigris. I saw flickers of all that had once been reflected in her eyes. Her knuckles whitened on the steering wheel. She patted me on the knee. "You'll see," she said, and grinned. "You'll see."

She parked the car. We stood together on the porous border between earth and sea. We were miles still from the old coast. There was no dense coastal forest, no grassy, sloping hill, nor even any dunes, no scrubby shrubs, no sand at all, just seething, wild seas screaming into an implacable wind.

She stared unblinking until her eyes watered and tears tracked down her cheeks. "There's nothing left. *Cupressus abramsiana*, *Sequoia sempervirens* – they're all gone." She tried to take my hand, but I pulled away.

I couldn't understand her tears because I felt only joy. I had never known the cities that this once pacific sea had swallowed up on its slow crawl inland, so I never knew to miss them. This was the only coast I had ever known, and as far I could confirm with my own eyes, the only coast that had ever been. It was a feral land, this new California. It was fierce and angry. It was there I discovered the wonder humans hold for uncontrollable places. I wouldn't have given that wonder up for anything, not even green hills, not even my mother's arms around my shoulders. My wild California, my only home.

She changed after that. She filled journal after journal. They fell from her shelves like water and puddled on the floor, lakes of calculations woven through with memories, stitched with a thread longing I couldn't cut. She drowned herself in old nature magazines and museums brimming with dioramas of lush ecosystems that no longer exist. She became more textbook than mother. She grew frighteningly thin, like the past was eating her alive. Her thoughts turned from observing the past to visiting it, and she spent the next twenty years figuring out how.

* * *

She built her machine in the basement of our falling-down house in our huge, hot city. The machine was her solution to the arrow of time, a physical expression of her refutation of entropy. She would copy herself into the past – a fork in the road, a divergence, a rebuilding, identical in the now and then, both conscious, both her, but separated by thirty-four years. *Time moves both ways* – she'd underlined it in her final notebook several times; her hand was so insistent the pen tore deep grooves into the pages beneath it.

She built it from the bones of scrapped airliners, from the guts of abandoned hospital machinery. She built it to run on intention and believed her clarity of purpose was more than power enough.

At thirty-four I watched her, then fifty-seven, step into that machine. It closed around her like a flower unfurling in reverse. She was hidden for moments, only the space of a few breaths. The machine's door slid open and she stumbled out, then collapsed. Her smile was bright and her breath short. She pushed sweat-damp hair away from her face, and I saw that her hands shook. Tears shone in the corners of her eyes.

I helped her up from the floor. She wobbled as she stood.

"What happened? Did it work?" I asked.

She pulled me into a rib-crushing hug. "*Yes.*" And smiled only wider. Then, she fainted.

* * *

It's midday. The hospital that hours ago was so quiet now grows loud. Patients cough and shift in their beds. Nurses' shoes squeak as they rush down the halls, always in a hurry. Beside me, my mother's skin grows slowly blue. Her breath comes fast and slow in cycles, as if still deciding whether to stay or go. Her eyes no longer draw sliding loops beneath her lids. Too soon, she's still. The afternoon light through the blinds is golden. Bars of buttery yellow divide the room into long slivers of dark and light. My shadow lays across my mother as if in mourning. It does the work of the living that I can't yet bring myself to do.

She's dead, and the fury that had kept me together during her brief illness leaches from me like water from the earth. Without it to sustain me, I am dry, desiccated. Now I am loose topsoil, and I fear at any moment I might be carried off by a light breeze. A part of me wants to believe her last thought was for me, but another hopes it was for her green hills, for her long-gone country. The two hopes twist in my chest, slippery eels in a bag, as I sign the hospital's interminable paperwork.

She is cremated, and I am filled with a longing for her touch so acute I can hardly breathe for its sharp talons in my ribs. I wanted her to ask me if I'd miss her.

Months before she finished the machine, she begged me to go with her; she wanted me to see it once with her, her century. A copy of me and a copy of her that could stand hand-in-hand and taste the old world's living wind.

But I was afraid, and she went alone.

* * *

I stand before it now, my mother's machine. My toes, bare and cold, edge toward the threshold. I hold her ashes in a simple urn in the crook of my arm. They're surprisingly heavy, but then, she was an unusually tall woman.

I have only the vaguest notion of how it works – world lines, light cones, the second law of thermodynamics, and other, more impenetrable things scribbled in her characteristically cramped hand – but I know how to push buttons. One of them says OPEN; I press it and the door slides away.

The machine is a metal womb. My feet are silent on the thick steel as I climb inside. There are buttons here, too: OPEN, CLOSE, and one unlabeled. I press CLOSE and the door slides back into place. The womb is dark and silent. "Think of it as a camera," she said, "a camera that records the unseen parts of you and sends you like a telegraph across an impossible distance." The half of me that holds a fierce allegiance to 'now' wrestles with the reluctant half that wants to know my mother's 'then', to finally know all of her.

I am still afraid, because I know what the machine does to you if not exactly what it *does*. She hadn't known, and had pressed the buttons anyway. Nothing had happened that we could see, and in three months she was dying of cancer. She never said so, but I think she knew it would kill her – she was too clever not to consider the possibility. Perhaps she did that careful calculus and decided it was worth it. I wish she would have told me, but then, I also didn't think to ask.

I want to know what she was expecting. A coin flip of consciousness? Press the button, hope that consciousness prime took the leftmost path and fell into the past? She knew that if it had worked it wouldn't work that way, that she would press the button and nothing would happen, that she'd climb out of the womb and still be in the world she loathed. She knew also that she would press the button and fall a few feet onto a cold cement floor and be in the world of then. Both branches of the fork would be her-prime, equal and identical. That's what she believed, anyway. That much I understand from her journals.

I sit curled in the cool metal womb. I can't decide if I will press the button. I want a version of me to go back and see what so moved her, but I want a version of me to live on, too. I could die in a hospital bed in three months' time because I was drawn in by my mother's dream of those green rolling hills. I could die like she did while letting one of me live in distant light. I could let one of me watch the earth turn brown, the oceans rise, the coast dissolve like sugar-glass in water. I could sacrifice my 'now' self for a glimpse of what is gone.

I think of my dusty city, my thirsty, sprawling city clinging to the face of a swiftly changing earth. Solar stills that I built bob in its bay like a flock of sea birds, stills that bring fresh water to our dry land. They water our small garden plots, they wash the dust from our eyes, from our skin, from our hair. They wet our sticky tongues. They keep us alive. But their design is not perfect, and we need so many more to do better than just *survive*.

Mine is the world I want my mother to see. Mine is a world that does not need saving. The unlabeled button is warm beneath my fingertip. I remember: the machine runs on intention. I am no longer afraid.

I hold my mother's ashes hard against my chest. I hear her calling to me from twenty years away. I smell the wild sea breeze. The burned-brown hills hold us up to the hazy sky. When I touch the button, I am holding her hand. Together we can love this world. I only have to go back and show her how.

I press the button.

Acrylics for a Wasteland

Megan Dorei

THE SIGN is overgrown, though not with anything that could be considered living. Aster doesn't need to read it to know what it says, but she brushes the oozing vines back with her hatchet anyway.

Sol's Grove, 7 miles

Her hollow stomach twists. She reminds herself that this isn't her destination, simply an unfortunate gatekeeper at the end of the line. As weak as she's grown, struggling to live off crumbs and the memory of meals and the thinning, humid air, going around is no longer an option. She will cut straight through, in exactly the same way this town splits her heart.

She belts the hatchet, keeping her left hand and the shard of mirror in it held aloft. It reflects back the brooding tangle over her shoulder, what was once insistent wilderness. The music blasting through her headphones masks her thoughts, but it makes it impossible to hear what might be moving behind her.

The gnarled, leaning trees glisten dully under bleached clouds, but nothing stirs among them. Not the ambling, massive frame of a mutation, nor the Others in their gleaming black suits. Not yet.

Thunder rumbles. She turns her glare on the sky.

Migraine weather, she thinks balefully, and indeed the tell-tale throb radiates ears to temples.

Maybe there'll be some peppermint oil in town.

She adds it to the list of things to scavenge for, which mostly consists of food, batteries, an oxygen tank if she's lucky. Though that last she fears might be more necessary than previously assumed.

Beneath these thoughts and her headphones shoveling sound over them, Emilita's faint, familiar voice reminds her of the first, most paramount rule.

Keep going.

She does.

* * *

When the rain starts, she pauses to pull a half-eaten granola bar from her backpack and then takes out Harold.

At three inches, he's nearly outgrown his toy egg, the only terrarium she could provide. His leaves press at the plastic dome, begging for space.

"Soon, little buddy." Her lips barely move; it's not even a whisper. The mutations hunt primarily through telepathic sonar, but that doesn't mean their other senses are less keen.

She's still not entirely sure what Harold is, or why, like herself, he remained untouched when the rest of the world mutated. She found him peeking out from under a knot of monstrous, stygian thistle on the day she decided to throw herself off the Bank Tower. It was only his simple, impossible existence, and a few promises whispered to a grave, that convinced her otherwise.

We're almost there, she thinks at him. 'Almost there' meaning the center of the country, where it was rumored there remained pockets of land unscorched by the Pulse. She can't decide if it's luck or cruelty that the closest pocket lies right outside of her old hometown. She can't decide if it's wise to go back.

But...she promised. Emilita and Harold, she promised them both. And what could possibly come after that? What the hell is there if she stops?

* * *

The Last Day began like many before it. Sunny. Frenzied. Coffee brewing, spilled sugar, Aster rubbing her burning eyes as Emilita scarfed a bowl of cereal. A month prior, Aster took a third shift maintenance position at a factory. Their new, opposing schedules were temporary but it was a struggle adjusting all the same.

Nothing stood out among the standard chaos. Aster adjusted Emilita's collar in the doorway and suggested she steal a few extra minutes of sleep during her morning meeting. Emilita wiped a smudge of paint off Aster's nose, nagged her not to stay up too late and kissed her goodbye. That was it.

For some people, she knew, the morning was something more extraordinary. TELETHER's launch was all anyone could talk about.

Imagine the entirety of the internet, readily available in your mind. Think of it and you know it, the commercials claimed.

The first telepathic connection to the internet as well as other people via a tiny chip implanted in the brain. It was meant to pick up signals from router towers across the country. Japan and Australia were preparing their own for introduction; the U.S. rushed to catch up.

In the year leading up to the official debut, those that could afford it were shortlisted for the procedure – less invasive than other keyhole surgeries. Still, many more were barred by the price tag, Aster and Emilita included.

Aster couldn't care less. She was tired and happy and breathing freely.

That last morning, she returned to her paints and canvas, despite her drooping eyes. The portrait was going to be a gift for Emilita's birthday. She wet her brush and began.

She felt the soundless screech move through her seconds before she heard the crash.

The brush slipped from her fingers. Her breath hung in the air while reality pinballed.

The can tipped as she scrambled from the room, gorging the carpet with red. Ears ringing, she flung through the front door.

From every direction, people screamed. Like the world had gone mad all at once. Car alarms. Sirens. The world was suddenly so *loud.*

Emilita staggered in the middle of the street, her car crumpled against a streetlamp. She clutched her head in both hands and shrieked.

Aster's legs moved in a dream. Eternity churned between her and Emilita, and she feared she would be caught there forever. Running with no end.

The weight of Emilita's limp frame when that distance finally closed turned her knees to water.

"'Lita. Sweetheart. Look at me."

Yards away, a man collapsed in the street and writhed like a wounded snake. Emilita's screams drowned his moans.

"*Make it stop! Make it stop!*"

Blood trickled from her nose and ears. Aster's throat closed around her next words.

And then Emilita's eyes rolled back, and she went silent but the world continued to scream, and Aster shuddered as her heart cracked down the middle. The man in the street kinked like a hose, spine popping. His skin split, exposing a nest of muscular, uncoiling tentacles, and Aster couldn't move.

"'Lita." Her lips formed the name but made no sound.

The man rose. Upside down. Creaking on all fours. Strange, complicated flesh spilled from his torso.

"'Lita."

His blood-gorged eyes snapped to her. A snarl as dark as the void of space left his throat.

In that moment, she longed to be swallowed by it.

* * *

She doesn't remember the violence after. Only coming back from a blank space to find herself crouched above the mutation's mangled frame, clutching a bloodied hubcap. The streets were full at that point, mutations, corpses. Every mutation in the area targeted her like prowling tigers. She barely survived carrying Emilita's body into the backyard to bury her.

Of the weeks that followed, only fragments remain in her memory. Clouds claiming the sky, hunger, rain, dark-skinned reflections in broken windows that she only barely recognized as herself. She was one of few humans left unchanged, but she felt irreversibly altered all the same.

She remembers lying under a starless sky, fingers pushing into grave soil. Emilita's voice in waking dreams. Asking her to keep going, keep breathing, and promising that she would.

She remembers the corpses sprouting tentacles a few days into decomposition. Creeping monstrosities spidering out into the landscape, choking away the last memories of normalcy.

Survivors, too, names and faces she can't put together. Survivors converting the neighborhood into a provisional community. Though her time with them was brief, she clings to these memories the most. They shared food and resources, but most importantly, they shared what they knew. This information always demanded a price; Aster gave what she had freely. Everything that mattered had already been taken from her.

Before news stations stopped broadcasting altogether, they disclosed that the effects of the Pulse were not self-contained. "No less than global disintegration," they said. Tens of thousands who had gotten the chip mutated and appeared to target prey through telepathic sonar. Except for a margin of anomalies, all others perished, including a frightening percentage of flora and fauna.

Where the knowledge ended, speculation began. Speculation about the reason for their survival. Speculation about clusters of unaffected land. And speculation about the cause of it all.

That TELETHER was the catalyst seemed almost unavoidably true. But why? What went wrong?

Or had something gone right? Some sinister plot for widespread extinction?

Aster rolled her eyes at that one. Reality was dying from some global fuck-up. Nothing behind it but a few miscalculations.

She thought that right up to the day the Others raided the neighborhood.

A cacophony woke her. Screams, gunshots, shattering glass. The Others wandered the neighborhood in black hazmat suits, armed, casually arrogant.

Aster and the other survivors fought back, but the hazmat suits doubled as riot gear and were not easily penetrated. Loud, clipped voices ordered them to stand down. It was those voices that put the doubt in her mind. They were official. Trained. Police, military, *someone.* Someone who demanded compliance without explanation.

The resistance burned out like a match flare. Everyone was beaten, handcuffed and shoved into a black van. Everyone but Aster, who only escaped by a breath.

Adrenaline carried her into the city. Terror drove her further. By the time she collapsed to a halt, she was alone.

She doesn't allow herself near survivors anymore, if there are even any left.

They all get taken in the end.

* * *

Sol's Grove beckons her darkly.

The rain stopped but the clouds remain, casting the streets in hazy twilight gray. Mutant growth webs the old brick buildings, a cinder-black latticework steaming in the evening cool.

She knows these streets. She could walk them blindfolded. Childhood rushes to engulf her and her skin breaks out in goosebumps.

Dubstep screeches in her headphones, disharmonizing with her eldritch surroundings. She focuses on that.

She's not that kid anymore, not even close.

There's no way to avoid passing her parents' house. It's on the way to the hospital. Exhaustion digs at her bones and going around requires an energy she feels permanently incapable of.

Of course, so does revisiting this town, but here she is...

When it looms into view, her muscles lock down, fighting a flinch. The two-story is almost entirely overgrown with mutation, with the exception of her bedroom. It leers out from the forbidding snarl like a great beast's eye, mad and dull and deceptively empty.

She climbed out that window the night she ran off to California, too numb to taste the tears in her throat. Driving till her tank tiptoed on empty. Watching the sun rise from the hood of her car and waiting for her parents to call.

When they never did, she dialed her aunt to plead for a place to stay, all the while picturing that damn window, the way her mother's face became a wall shuttering her off, the way her father wouldn't even look at her.

She wasn't their daughter. They hadn't raised her up to kiss other girls. She was going to stop that shit, no arguments.

How do you stop who you are? she wanted to ask them. *How do you just...stop?*

But the words stayed coiled in her throat, a burn like swallowing venom, and she waited until they closed the door behind them before packing her things.

As she skulks past the front yard, a horrifying, insistent urge sinks a talon into her chest.

She could go inside.

Thirty steps or so, and she would be in that foyer. Lemon and cinnamon would lurk beneath the stench of corrosion. Her mother was likely gone, but her reflection would remain in the oven door. Her father was likely gone, but his shadow would remain in the garden. She could climb the stairs, she could touch the murals she painted on her bedroom walls—

Don't think about it.

Emilita's whisper hails her like a distant bell, or a song just on the edge of identifying.

Keep going.

"Okay," Aster whispers. "Okay."

She trails limply down the road, watching the house grow smaller in her makeshift rear-view mirror. It takes everything to ignore the pull of that place, like the sticky dragging of cobwebs. She spent years stitching the hole her parents left. It won't do to reopen it here, at the end of the world.

She is almost to the end of the block when a lumbering mass emerges from her parents' backyard.

Her lungs shrivel. The drum and bass shrouding her thoughts won't matter if she stays where she is.

But fatigue weighs her down. She lifts a weary foot to duck behind a tree laden with tentacles. The beast swivels its fleshy head and spots her.

"*Fuck.*"

She drops her backpack, draws her hatchet and raises it only seconds before the mutant descends on her.

Heat and muscle suffocate her. Pavement scrapes her raw. Every vein in her body thrums with terror. She buries the axe head in the creature's collarbone. It roars in fury but continues snapping at her face, spattering her with saliva.

Only an echo of its face is human, the rest a gruesome patchwork of sinew and spurs of what can only be bone.

But…its eyes. They're blue.

Not her father. Not her mother.

Her heart squeezes undefinably.

There is not enough strength left in her to resist as the beast crushes her. Rows upon rows of broken, obsidian teeth click toward her throat.

One final jolt of desperation drives her left hand up, impaling both her palm and the mutant's eye with the shard of glass.

The beast reels back, howling its own thunder at the sky. Aster leans up to twist the hatchet a few inches to the left.

Pitchy blood sprays as its artery severs. She scrambles to the side before the beast collapses on top of her.

The silence after stings. Gasping, sprawled like a ragdoll, she realizes her headphones must've broken in the melee.

"…Fuck."

* * *

Vines eat their way through most of the hospital. Her flashlight illuminates their greasy imprint as she slouches down the hall, breathing deeply, quickly.

Her lungs feel paper-thin, like the confrontation with her parents' house and the mutant immediately after stripped away layers of their structure.

Music thumps in her ears once again, though vague instinct keeps the volume low.

She lucked out at the convenience store near the hospital. New earphones as well as two back-ups; cookies, jerky, and a few other non-perishables she isn't entirely sick of eating; a few dozen batteries; peppermint gum in lieu of oil; and a small acrylic paint set.

The paints are frivolous. She knows she'll probably have to drop them at some point, but for now she clings to them. She is too raw to do anything else.

The first two floors prove fruitless. Everything is buried beneath broods of thick mutation; it's a struggle simply climbing through them. The third floor is less infested, though the appendages of strange almost-flesh rib the walls like tree roots shaping a cave.

She checks each room methodically, but her hope plummets with each one. There are thankfully no bodies, likely eaten by some mutation or other, but no oxygen tanks, either. Empty hospital beds lay tipped on their sides, monuments to the ghost of what this place used to be. Her nerves prickle; she rubs her wrist over the back of her neck as if to soothe them.

Finally, a closet at the end of the hall rewards her efforts. Gas tanks of varying sizes stand like stone sentinels, regulators and other paraphernalia she doesn't recognize scattered among them. Nitrogen, CO_2…and oxygen. The tension in her chest eases. She coughs out a weak laugh, fingers trembling. She takes what she can carry and heads back the way she came. One tank alone won't be enough, but maybe she can figure out a way to transport the rest later…

Near the corner of an intersecting hallway, voices, loud enough to be heard over her music, jar her to a halt. The walls ahead flicker with flashlight beams.

"…doesn't matter, there will be oxygen on this floor, there has to be. The O.R.—"

Three figures round the corner before Aster can hide, and halt at the sight of her. Their black, beetle-like suits are instantly recognizable.

The Others.

Her heart sputters. The air turns to ash in her throat. Her fingers twitch toward her hatchet, a mindless reflex; whatever their suits are made of, an axe won't save her.

They raise their guns and her heart stops altogether. They step forward.

"Halt—"

She spins and flees. It's a simple miracle she keeps her balance stumbling through the gloom. Her quaking knees threaten to catapult her to the floor at any moment.

They gain ground on her quickly, obviously stronger. Her blood thunders.

Keep going. Keep going.

Fingers brush her shoulder blade. She launches herself into the closet and slams the door shut.

It shudders as she presses her back against it. It won't take them long to break in, but she can't imagine fighting them. There's no way she can hold them off long enough to escape, no exits nearby, no weapons that will do enough damage.

Her stomach lurches in frantic somersaults. Air whistles up and down her tight throat…

Air.

Air.

Mind racing, she catalogs her options before snatching three tanks. *Nitrogen* is printed at the top of each. The type isn't terribly large, but if the Others notice…

"Paint," she mouths. She digs the acrylics from her pack and spills them on the floor, mixing colors furiously. Once she approximates the color of the tanks, she veils the writing with thin, quick strokes that will likely dry quickly. The pounding continues the entire time.

"Stop," she rasps, clears her throat, tries again. "*Stop.*"

The pounding stops.

"Come out hands up and this will be easier on all of us."

Sweat trickles to her chin. Her body shakes but her voice is surprisingly steady.

"I won't be doing that. I'm not letting you take me wherever you've been taking people."

A pause.

"You don't have a choice."

Ice seizes her bones. Patting the paint dry, she says, "Please, I—I have oxygen. There are tanks in here, that's why I was scoping this place. If I let you have them, will you let me go?"

Another pause.

"Fine. Roll the tanks out – slow, followed by any weapons."

"I don't have anything except a hatchet."

"Surrender it."

She takes a measured breath. Opens the door. No one attacks her, but she doesn't lower her guard.

One by one, she slides the tanks through the gap. Then the hatchet. Then herself.

The Others are already unzipping the rectangular humps on the back of each other's suits and slipping the tanks inside.

One of them points a gun at her.

"Stay back."

She stays.

"Hands behind your back."

"But— I— You agreed!"

"It was the only way to get you out peaceably. We can't let you leave."

Aster doesn't move. The tanks are in place, the suits zipped up. She waits.

"I said, *hands behind your back.*"

Something strains beneath the voice. Like there isn't enough air to fill each word. The Others stumble, clutching at their hoods.

Aster narrows her eyes, abandoning her timid guise.

"I told you I wouldn't let you take me."

"Get your...hands..."

But the voice drifts to nothing. All three figures collapse like stringless puppets.

Shock holds her captive for a moment. Poised to act if they regain consciousness.

They never do.

She...killed them. She suffocated them, she took their air.

"I had to," she says, louder than she should. Her teeth snap shut.

A whisper, soft as approaching spring: *Keep going.*

She does.

* * *

The hill is steep. Even with the oxygen she is out of breath. But she's so *close.* Just beyond the ridge of this hill is her destination, the first spot of only a few where the land remained green, fertile, *alive.*

We're almost there, she thinks at Harold. She can almost feel his eagerness mirroring her own, to live outside of his cage, to breathe.

She climbs the last few yards on all fours, clawing at the wasted grass and rotten soil. She hasn't slept since leaving the hospital. The bulky hazmat suit – a last minute theft – only makes her limbs clumsier. But she has to keep going. She has to reach the top, she has to see...

She crests the hill. Familiar wasteland sprawls below.

Mildew. Decay. Death.

Gravity compresses her bones. She stares, not blinking, not breathing.

Where was the green? Where was the lush memory of what came before, where was *life?*

Something creeps slowly up her spine, insidious and sharp. She staggers down the slope without conscious decision to do so, ethereal wave music buzzing her skin like static cling.

She stops at the bottom. Cracks honeycomb the emaciated ground, and from them scorched vines emerge, an insectoid blight.

She presses her heel down on one of the tendrils, hard enough to make her leg shake.

"Fuck you."

Her vision blurs. She digs in, scrapes the tendril back and forth.

"*Fuck* you."

Beads of ink burst through its flesh, muddying the soil. Heat surges from her gut to her skull, threatening to split her like an overripe fruit.

"*Fuck you!*"

Her hoarse scream seems louder within the confines of her hood. She buckles from the force of the heat beating within her, tugging and slashing at the tentacles, billowing dust into the half-dead air.

Nothing here. Nothing here nothing here nothing here.

This land is as dead as the rest, and how was she stupid enough to believe there was anything else?

Tears burn a path down her cheeks. She wails her despair at the sky.

* * *

Awareness comes back to her in increments. Dust. Glaring white clouds. Sticky black speckling her arms. Silence. Her nails throb. Numbness perches on her chest like a vulture.

I am alive.

Why am I alive?

She sits up, slow so as not to slosh the blood in her brain. Tattered mutation enwreathes her, inking the earth with its blood. Her earphones and hazmat suit are slumped a few feet away.

Why is she alive? The faded wasteland stretches so far in every direction, horizon to horizon, and she knows now, she knows…

There is nothing. Nothing more than this. Death wears the crown and she is alive anyway and why, *why?*

Mid-scan of her surroundings, her eyes fall on the backpack.

Harold.

You promised him…

Yes, she promised him soil to sink his roots in and fresh air, she promised him *life.*

He's alive already. Just like you.

Why—

And you promised me. You promised.

Aster swallows hard, feeling rough, feeling naked.

"I promised," she whispered.

She eyes the horizon a moment longer, and then she stands.

So this is it. But it isn't the end. Maybe there is nothing out there, maybe she and Harold are the only ones left, maybe there is no reason for that.

They're alive.

She thinks of that house, her parents, all the words she never said.

How do you just…stop?

How could she? What else came after that?

Lethargy drags her body. She manages to stand. Brittle and breathing, she gathers up her suit and supplies. Puts in her earphones and faces that unattainable, unchanging horizon.

Keep going.

She does.

Milking Time

Stephanie Ellis

A CLOCK CHIMED. Milking time. Andrew got up to fetch the herd, the dog he'd been given, just in case any tried to make a run for it, at his heels. They trailed in slowly, each heading for their own particular booth. They had been trained well.

Andrew looked at the women either side of Ellen. Their faces reflecting the grief all still felt. They had all lost their children, although that implied they had simply misplaced them as if no more than a sock or set of keys. 'Lost' though was the preferred euphemism for the reality of the shallow grave, the empty womb. And still they were forced to go through this 'privilege'. Part of man's last stand against an approaching extinction.

The nurses came round. Wiped their breasts with anti-bacterial lotion. Did the blood test. As if that would have changed in the last four hours. Viruses and bacteria mutated rapidly however these days and resistance to the few remaining drugs available meant they could not take the risk if the next generation were to survive.

Andrew moved along the ward, the women at least screened for the purposes of modesty. The tests were all satisfactory. Farming practices applied to humans. Cows could only produce milk if they'd calved. The calves slaughtered as collateral damage. Women who'd lost a child would still produce milk, vital in this world of scarcity.

Ten women could be milked, ten babies, not their own, fed. He paused at Ellen's bed. He wanted to drag her out of there, away from the place, but he couldn't. It was only her contribution which kept the family alive. *They were lucky.*

"Ellen," he whispered. "Ellen, are you okay?"

"Go away, Andy," she said. "Not here." She sounded tired.

"We need to talk about this."

"Later."

The nurses were moving towards him, workers had been known to steal milk intended for paying customers.

"Andrew? Is something wrong?" asked Sister Mary.

"No," he said. "I just…it's just I was thinking about our own baby." He didn't want to appear ungrateful. Mary was an old friend, had got him the job at the clinic.

"You poor thing," she said, her eyes full of sympathy, her hand resting lightly on his arm. "So many are suffering these days…"

"Except those with money," he said, unable to keep the bitterness from his voice.

She gave him a reproving look, flicked her eyes to the camera monitoring the ward. He understood. Time to leave.

In the small kitchen, she made them both a coffee, or at least the synthetic version of the bean.

"What's on your mind?" he asked, as she looked about to say something and then appeared to think better of it.

"The yield of some of the women is dropping," she said. "Not just here but in other clinics supporting the approved children."

Approved children. He hated that term, the law which had been passed to declare 'approved' children were to take priority over all others. The children of the common man? They had no value. Instead everything was being given to a minority, every precious resource, in order to ensure the survival of humanity.

"I've heard the Board are discussing new measures."

"New measures? What can they do? We have no dairy herds anymore, the land is either a dust bowl or under several feet of water. Millions have already died. Everything is getting scarcer."

"But if *some* survive," said Mary, "doesn't that mean our planet has hope, a future? That's why we do all this." She waved her arm around to include the clinic.

"The next generation," muttered Andrew. "Why their children though?" It was an old argument, a scab they continued to pick at.

"Money talks doesn't it," said Mary. "Even when the planet is dying, it still comes down to money."

He looked at her closely. "What *are* the new measures?"

"Some have proposed the…detention…of all pregnant women, especially those near to term."

"When milk production kicks in," said Andrew, understanding immediately. "And the women's babies?"

"Will be delivered and unfortunately…complications, you know the drill. And of course, that'll relieve pressures on food supplies."

Christ, yes, he knew the drill. Operation Herod they'd called it, that original roundup. He'd been promised it had been a one-off, a necessity. The royal baby. The figurehead of the nation. A wet-nurse could not be allowed, not in this time of creeping infection. Yet the mother had no milk and the child could not be allowed to die.

And his own? *Oh, I'm so sorry, Andrew, but out of the darkness can come some good. Would your wife consider?*

God help them, they had. Their dead baby had given them and their young son the chance of extra rations.

"When will they start?" he asked.

"They already have. The delivery rooms were brought back online today."

"I suppose we should be thankful people still want to procreate," said Andy.

"They don't have much choice," said Mary. "Contraception is no longer available. Sterilisation operations are too risky. Old methods are unreliable. And a lot of men won't accept celibacy. There's always going to be children."

Man's selfish gene, the desire to reproduce had betrayed the very women they professed to love.

"So now we live in a world where the authorities murder children *for the sake* of the children," said Andrew.

"Well, they've killed everyone else," said Mary, matter of fact as always.

She had never been this cold. Everyone had their own coping mechanisms, however. It was not for him to judge, still, he couldn't bear it, pushed his cup away, left without another word.

Ellen was home before him. She'd fulfilled her quota for the day, was allowed home on condition she took the mobile expressing machine; one of the privileged few. They even had the luxury of a small fridge to store the milk. Something that would be taken as soon as she dried up.

He told her Mary's news.

"It's got to stop," she whispered, a glass of water shaking in her hands. "If this goes ahead, then what sort of race do we become?"

He hadn't told her about his part in the original Operation Herod. His shame had been too much for that.

"Will they announce it or just round them up?"

He shrugged. She would find out that part soon enough and he didn't want to say anything. The usual government messengers had gone out onto the streets of the few remaining functioning cities and announced the good news:

> ***Attention.*** *A brighter future beckons. Recent advancements have allowed us to bring facilities online so that all members of the public can deliver their babies in safety. This is your chance to help build our future. The times are changing. Change with us!*
> *If you, or anyone you know needs our support, please attend the maternity clinic at the address below.*

The flyers had also been stuck up on the government news boards dotted around the city. Andrew wasn't sure how many people continued to live within its limits, the country's population had been decimated and nobody really paid attention to anything anymore. The need to survive overwhelmed everything else, everyone retreating into their own little bubbles. It was always the way.

The one thing he was sure of was that the women who would come forward would be the last. There couldn't be that many scrabbling around these derelict streets. He was right.

After walking Ellen to the milking parlour as they termed it, Andrew was told his services would be required elsewhere that morning.

"What will you do?" she asked as they kissed goodbye.

"I don't know yet. Not without seeing how many, who…"

One man on his own. He couldn't do much. Would the husbands be there, the fathers?

Andrew was joined by two other 'herders' from the clinic. The women would be under the sole care of the nurses today.

The three walked along the empty streets, the closed-down signs and homeless sleeping in doorways mere wallpaper now, familiarity breeding contempt, or the mind filtering out as much unpleasantness as possible. Homeless though? The thought suddenly struck him. They no longer needed to be homeless with so many flats and houses empty. He paid closer attention now and noticed for the first time, bright eyes peering at him over the edge of a sleeping bag or out from under wild hair. There was none of the drink or drug induced stupefaction of previous times. They were being watched.

"We're being followed."

Mark's comment caused Andrew to look back and he noticed some of the vagrants he had observed were indeed following them. The hairs on his neck started to prickle.

"We're armed," said Colin, his other companion.

That knowledge did not make him feel better.

"They've never followed us before," he said.

"We've never been this way before," said Mark.

Andrew glanced at him. He didn't know. Mark and Colin had not taken part in that original round up, kept to the 'safe' part of the city. Had those who'd followed been around then? Did they recognise him as one of those who'd taken the women on that horrific day?

He looked back again. There were six now.

"We'll be at the collection centre soon," said Colin. "Security will be tight there."

But they would have to walk the women back through these streets.

Around the corner and Andrew saw them. So few! His heart sank. He should have been overjoyed that so few had responded to the summons, perhaps guessing there was something more going on. The other part though acknowledged his true fear. The human race was dying. How long before true extinction? And still they were finding new ways to kill each other.

Ten women lined up. They looked pale and nervous. Worn-out by their condition and by their circumstances. Behind Andrew stood ten men.

"Hey," called one of the guards. "Disperse. Nothing to see here. These women will be well looked after."

The men remained stationary. The guard simply shrugged his shoulder, satisfied the power lay with them.

"When can we come and see them?" shouted one of the ten. He was ignored.

So, they *were* the women's partners. Desperate for their children but still rightly suspicious.

He remembered when Ellen had gone through that awful labour to produce only a stillbirth. The little boy had been perfectly formed and it had torn them apart at the time, still continued to rip and tear at their emotions, their relationship.

Stillbirths were sadly increasingly common, the doctor had said at Mary's clinic, now his workplace.

But Ellen's pregnancy had seemed healthy, despite their near starvation rations. The supplements they had been given had seen to that. A thought filtered across his mind. *The tablets.*

"You will be our escort?" he asked the guards.

"Not all, we can only spare a few," said their spokesman. "That's why you had to come out today. Plus, we figured if anything happens on the way, you know what to do."

Oh, they knew what to do alright. They knew how to deliver a baby, what had to be done next. But that part he had *never* done. It had always been left to the senior nurse or the doctor. He had been spared *that*.

"Why can't you come?" asked Mark. "Something going on?"

"Relocation of the children," said the guard.

He meant the ones being fed by the milk of his wife and the rest of the *herd*. Breast milk was insisted upon for these children until at least three years of age. Far longer than anything society had normally accepted but needed now to continue to boost immunity, fill in the gaps for bodily development left by the lack of fresh food.

"Where to?" asked Colin.

"That, my friend, is classified but it means that you soon you will no longer be needed."

"The women?"

"Have provided a considerable stockpile."

"But there's only ten of them." How could Ellen and the others have satisfied this need?

"You think your clinic is the only one? We've had them pumping out the goods for ages now. The boss has been impressed with our productivity levels. Guaranteed us a place with them when they go."

Their productivity levels? He looked for any sign of emotion in the guard, anything that would indicate a human being still resided within. There was nothing. He was doing what they all did. Justifying his actions to ensure his own survival.

"Yet you're rounding up *these* women," said Mark, puzzled now. He had never really commented on their situation before. He looked to Andrew like a man finally waking up.

"A final collection, a safety buffer."

Stock. Cargo. Collection. So many terms were now applied to these women. Except one which seemed to have been lost in the process. Human.

"We'd better get moving," said the guard, indicating the conversation was at an end. "This lot look as though they might pop at any minute."

It took Andrew a while to realise he was talking about the women and not the men from the street, they'd moved closer despite the earlier warning.

Back the way they came. The guards ahead and behind with their rifles. Andrew, Mark and Colin alongside the group. Five men against the ten who followed, but they had their guns.

The women didn't speak, shot occasional anxious looks around them, hands resting protectively on their swollen stomachs. Only when they neared the clinic and saw two nurses outside waiting for them, did they allow small smiles of relief to brighten their faces. The sight of other women always reassured those who entered the clinic, after all, what harm would one woman do another?

Once inside, the guards departed. They too were smiling. For some a brighter future appeared to beckon. The men who had followed settled down on the pavement opposite. Kept their eyes fixed firmly on the clinic.

"Take them down to the delivery rooms," said Doctor Angelicus, after each had been examined.

"Why?" asked one of the women. "It's too soon. I mean, I haven't had any contractions yet."

"You appreciate the need to put the safety of your child first," said the doctor, smoothly. "You are all near enough to your time for the babies to be able to be delivered now."

"No," said the woman, moving away from the group, back towards the door. "No." She'd grabbed hold of the door handle now, opened it. Across the street, Andrew could see one of the men stand.

Mark slammed the door shut.

"Don't worry, Mrs...er Mrs Griffiths. You're in safe hands. Think of the baby. A child is the symbol of hope for us all. Wouldn't you do *anything* for that child?"

Mrs Griffiths nodded her head, not realising the doctor was actually thinking about a totally different child.

"Come along," said one of the nurses. "Let's get you down to delivery and prepped. It'll be over before you know it and you'll be sat up in bed with a nice cup of tea and some toast. We've even got a little strawberry jam."

Jam today, literally, but not tomorrow.

"Better go back to the wards," said Mark, as the women were finally led away.

"That won't be necessary," said Sister Mary.

Andrew jumped. He hadn't seen her appear.

"Their yield is down and the quality has fallen below allowable parameters. They are free to return to their own lives."

Ellen stood just behind her. They both knew what that meant. Their extra food rations would be stopped. At least *he* had his job. Then he thought about the men outside. Watching and waiting. That was all the men did these days, watch and wait, occasionally offer up a wife, a partner...*their child*. They were complicit. He was complicit. The tablets. He needed to know. He was done with the place.

"Mary," he asked. "Was there something in those supplements you gave Ellen?"

His wife stared at him for a minute, then understanding dawned and she turned her horrified gaze on Mary. The nurse had been her *friend*, had promised to help.

"I said I'd help," hissed Mary. "And I did. It was the only way."

"You helped murder my baby," said Ellen. "I..."

"I helped keep your family alive," said Mary. "I don't regret it."

All it had done though was postpone the inevitable.

Ellen had moved over to the door, opened it. Mark and Colin were no longer there. Just the women, now surplus to requirements, Mary and Ellen.

A breeze stirred up and sent in desiccated leaves and yellowed papers, the smell of decay and neglect. The scent of unwashed bodies. The ten men had crossed the street and stood just beyond the door. Ellen opened the door wider. Mary went to try and close it, but Andrew grabbed her arm.

A decision had been made.

"Get in here," he shouted. "You'll need to move quick."

The men glanced at him suspiciously but still entered.

"Down here," said Ellen, leading the way. How she could go back down there after what she'd gone through, he didn't know. If she could though, so could he.

Andrew pulled out his gun, gestured Ellen to move ahead of him. Dim lights flickered on and off as they passed. Old consultation rooms no longer used, a pharmacy practically empty. The delivery ward.

Nine women stood in the waiting area, nurses scribbling notes, none of which would be read.

"Get them and get out," said Andrew, as they were finally noticed. One of the nurses went to press the alarm. "I wouldn't do that. Sit down, all of you." He gestured the four nurses to the seats. Gave his gun to Ellen.

One man remained. "My wife, Stella," he said. "What are they doing to her?"

"Oh, she's perfectly safe," said Ellen. "It's your baby you need to save."

"I don't understand. We were promised safe delivery."

"But still you followed. Shows you still had some suspicions," said Andrew.

The man nodded. "Yeah, but what choice did we have? No medical care, precious little food, nothing."

It was time for the truth. Bring the whole sordid business out into the open. "They take our wives, our partners. They rip out the child or trigger a late miscarriage, a...stillbirth," he swallowed and then continued, "they force the mothers to express milk for their non-existent babies so the children of the privileged can be 'properly nourished' as they described it. They harvest the stem cells from the umbilical cord, they take the placenta..."

The man looked shocked. "They do that? To the women? How can they, *you*, put up with that?"

Andrew smiled sadly. "To repeat your own words. What choice did we have? We didn't know then our babies had been murdered. We got extra rations for the milk our wives could produce. Wouldn't you have done the same?"

"But you know now, and still go through with this?"

"I have a son, three years old."

"And so we have become monsters of men," said the man, quietly.

Andrew didn't answer. Led him down the corridor towards the one door from which a light glowed. A woman screamed. He sped up, the husband close behind. Crashing through the door, they discovered the woman cowering in the corner, a nurse trying to pull her back to the delivery table, a doctor with a syringe in his hand. It was empty.

"You bastard," cried the husband and punched the doctor squarely in the face. He crumpled easily beneath the blow, hitting his head on a cupboard on the way down, blood pooling swiftly beneath him.

"Get her out and get her out quickly," said Andrew, noticing the camera in the corner of the room blinking red.

He said nothing to the nurse, left her kneeling over the doctor, trying to staunch the wound. Ellen rose from her seat as he reappeared. Screams from the nurse left behind began to sweep down the corridor. Mary swiftly headed towards the sound, her staff following her.

He took Ellen's hand and they headed out of the building, catching up with the couple who hadn't made it very far.

"You need to get off the streets as soon as possible," he said.

"Can't you help us?" asked the man.

"There's nothing more we can do," said Ellen. "I'm sorry, but we've got a son. They'll come looking for us."

"Please," begged the woman, crying out as another contraction took hold.

"I'm sorry," said Ellen, distraught now. "Our son."

"Come on, love," said the man, supporting his wife. "It's not far. We'll get home, we'll make it."

They struggled away down the street leaving Andrew and Ellen looking after them.

"We can't do anything for them," he said. "You know that. We have to think of ourselves. We have to be selfish."

"And that makes us no better than the one who murdered our child," said Ellen. "It's just a degree of scale. No wonder the planet's turned against us."

He stared at their house. Paint peeled, the garden was mere bare soil and gravel, the windows were filthy. The neighbouring houses were empty. The residents had either died or fled to greener pastures, wherever those were. There was so little life left around them.

"We can leave," said Ellen. "Do you think our caravan is still standing?"

"Perhaps." He was looking back towards the clinic. No guards had followed. No one was chasing them. It meant the city had been abandoned. They were safe.

"We could go there," she said.

"We could," he agreed. "A better place."

They spent the evening curled up together with Nicholas between them, describing the countryside around the van, the green meadows, the soft blue sky, the birdsong. Then there was the short walk to a golden beach and the clearest sea. Nicholas listened as Andrew described how the sand felt between your toes, how the waves tickled, smiling at the description of the starfish, laughing at the nip of the crab. His eyelids drooped as he finished the last of the drink Ellen had given him took effect.

"It was a beautiful day," she said, of the memory.

He watched her finish her own cup, her own lids closing swiftly, breathing steadying, slowing.

Andrew held them both a bit longer before he emptied his own cup.

"Tomorrow," he whispered, "the sun will rise and we'll meet your little brother. You'll like that, won't you Nicky." His family lay smiling in his arms. Then he too, closed his eyes.

The Air Trust
Chapters I–XV
George Allan England

Chapter I
The Birth of an Idea

SUNK FAR BACK in the huge leather cushions of his morris chair, old Isaac Flint was thinking, thinking hard. Between narrowed lids, his hard, gray eyes were blinking at the morning sunlight that poured into his private office, high up in the great building he had reared on Wall Street. From his thin lips now and then issued a coil of smoke from the costly cigar he was consuming. His bony legs were crossed, and one foot twitched impatiently. Now and again he tugged at his white mustache. A frown creased his hard brow; and, as he pondered, something of the glitter of a snake seemed reflected in his pupils.

"Not enough," he muttered, harshly. "It's not enough – there must be more, more, more! Some way must be found. Must be, and shall be!"

The sunlight of early spring, glad and warm over Manhattan, brought no message of cheer to the Billionaire. It bore no news of peace and joy to him. Its very brightness, as it flooded the metropolis and mellowed his luxurious inner office, seemed to offend the master of the world. And presently he arose, walked to the window and made as though to lower the shade. But for a moment he delayed this action. Standing there at the window, he peered out. Far below him, the restless, swarming life of the huge city crept and grovelled. Insects that were men and women crowded the clefts that were streets. Long lines of cars, toy-like, crept along the "L" structures. As far as the eye could reach, tufted plumes of smoke and steam wafted away on the April breeze. The East River glistened in the sunlight, its bosom vexed by myriad craft, by ocean liners, by tugs and barges, by grim warships, by sailing-vessels, whose canvas gleamed, by snow-white fruitboats from the tropics, by hulls from every port. Over the bridges, long slow lines of traffic crawled. And, far beyond to the dim horizon, stretched out the hives of men, till the blue depths of distance swallowed all in haze.

And as Flint gazed on this marvel, all created and maintained by human toil, by sweat and skill and tireless patience of the workers, a hard smile curved his lips.

"All mine, more or less," said he to himself, puffing deep on his cigar. "All yielding tribute to me, even as the mines and mills and factories I cannot see yield tribute! Even as the oil-wells, the pipe-lines, the railroads and the subways yield – even as the whole world yields it. All this labor, all this busy strife, I have a hand in. The millions eat and drink and buy and sell; and I take toll of it – yet it is not enough. I hold them in my hand, yet the hand cannot close, completely. And until it does, it is not enough! No, not enough for me!"

He pondered a moment, standing there musing at the window, surveying "all the wonders of the earth" that in its fulness, in that year of grace, 1921, bore tribute to him who toiled not, neither spun; and though he smiled, the smile was bitter.

"Not enough, yet," he reflected. "And how – how shall I close my grip? How shall I master all this, absolutely and completely, till it be mine in truth? Through light? The mob can do with less, if I squeeze too hard! Through food? They can economize! Transportation? No, the traffic will bear only a certain load! How, then? What is it they all must have, or die, that I can control? What universal need, vital to rich and poor alike? To great and small? What absolute necessity which shall make my rivals in the Game as much my vassals as the meanest slave in my steel mills? What can it be? For power I must have! Like Caesar, who preferred to be first in the smallest village, rather than be second at Rome, I can and will have no competitor. I must rule *all*, or the game is worthless! But how?"

Almost as in answer to his mental question, a sudden gust of air swayed the curtain and brushed it against his face. And, on the moment, inspiration struck him.

"What?" he exclaimed suddenly, his brows wrinkling, a strange and eager light burning in his hard eyes. "Eh, what? Can it – could it be possible? My God! If so – if it might be – the world would be my toy, to play with as I like!

"If *that* could happen, kings and emperors would have to cringe and crawl to me, like my hordes of serfs all over this broad land. Statesmen and diplomats, president and judges, lawmakers and captains of industry, all would fall into bondage; and for the first time in history one man would rule the earth, completely and absolutely – *and that man would be Isaac Flint!*"

Staggered by the very immensity of the bold thought, so vast that for a moment he could not realize it in its entirety, the Billionaire fell to pacing the floor of his office.

His cigar now hung dead and unnoticed between his thinly cruel lips. His hands were gripped behind his bent back, as he paced the priceless Shiraz rug, itself having cost the wage of a hundred workmen for a year's hard, grinding toil. And as he trod, up and down, up and down the rich apartments, a slow, grim smile curved his mouth.

"What editor could withstand me, then?" he was thinking. "What clergyman could raise his voice against my rule? Ah! Their 'high principles' they prate of so eloquently, their crack-brained economics, their rebellions and their strikes – the dogs! – would soon bow down before *that* power! Men have starved for stiff-necked opposition's sake, and still may do so – but with my hand at the throat of the world, with the world's very life-breath in my grip, what then? Submission, or – ha! well, we shall see, we shall see!"

A subtle change came over his face, which had been growing paler for some minutes. Impatiently he flung away his cigar, and, turning to his desk, opened a drawer, took out a little vial and uncorked it. He shook out two small white tablets, on the big sheet of plate-glass that covered the desk, swallowed them eagerly, and replaced the vial in the desk again. For be it known that, master of the world though Flint was, he too had a master – morphine. Long years he had bowed beneath its whip, the veriest slave of the insidious drug. No three hours could pass, without that dosage. His immense native will power still managed to control the dose and not increase it; but years ago he had abandoned hope of ever diminishing or ceasing it. And now he thought no more of it than of – well, of breathing.

Breathing! As he stood up again and drew a deep breath, under the reviving influence of the drug, his inspiration once more recurred to him.

"Breath!" said he. "Breath is life. Without food and drink and shelter, men can live a while. Even without water, for some days. But without *air* – they die inevitably and at once. And if I make the air my own, then I am master of all life!"

And suddenly he burst into a harsh, jangling laugh.

"Air!" he cried exultantly, "An Air Trust! By God in Heaven, it can be! It shall be! – it must!"

His mind, somewhat sluggish before he had taken the morphine, now was working clearly and accurately again, with that fateful and undeviating precision which had made him master of billions of dollars and uncounted millions of human lives; which had woven his network of possession all over the United States, Europe and Asia and even Africa; which had drawn, as into a spider's web, the world's railroads and steamship lines, its coal and copper and steel, its oil and grain and beef, its every need – save air!

And now, keen on the track of this last great inspiration, the Billionaire strode to his revolving book-case, whirled it round and from its shelves jerked a thick volume, a smaller book and some pamphlets.

"Let's have some facts!" said he, flinging them upon his desk, and seating himself before it in a costly chair of teak. "Once I get an outline of the facts and what I want to do, then my subordinates can carry out my plans. Before all, I must have facts!"

For half an hour he thumbed his references, noting all the salient points mentally, without taking a single note; for, so long as the drug still acted, his brain was an instrument of unsurpassed keenness and accuracy.

A sinister figure he made, as he sat there poring intently over the technical books before him, contrasting strangely with the beauty and the luxury of the office. On the mantel, over the fireplace of Carrara marble, ticked a Louis XIV clock, the price of which might have saved the lives of a thousand workingmen's children during the last summer's torment. Gold-woven tapestries from Rouen covered the walls, whereon hung etchings and rare prints. Old Flint's office, indeed, had more the air of an art gallery than a place where grim plots and deals innumerable had been put through, lawmakers corrupted past counting, and the destinies of nations bent beneath his corded, lean and nervous hand. And now, as the Billionaire sat there thinking, smiling a smile that boded no good to the world, the soft spring air that had inspired his great plan still swayed the silken curtains.

Of a sudden, he slammed the big book shut, that he was studying, and rose to his feet with a hard laugh – the laugh that had presaged more than one calamity to mankind. Beneath the sweep of his mustache one caught the glint of a gold tooth, sharp and unpleasant.

A moment he stood there, keen, eager, dominant, his hands gripping the edge of the desk till the big knuckles whitened. He seemed the embodiment of harsh and unrelenting Power – power over men and things, over their laws and institutions; power which, like Alexander's, sought only new worlds to conquer; power which found all metes and bounds too narrow.

"Power!" he whispered, as though to voice the inner inclining of the picture. "Life, air, breath – the very breath of the world in my hands – power absolutely, at last!"

Chapter II
The Partners

THEN, AS WAS HIS HABIT, translating ideas into immediate action, he strode to a door at the far end of the office, flung it open and said:

"See here a minute, Wally!"

"Busy!" came an answering voice, from behind a huge roll-top desk.

"Of course! But drop it, drop it. I've got news for you."

"Urgent?" asked the voice, coldly.

"Very. Come in here, a minute. I've got to unload!"

From behind the big desk rose the figure of a man about five and forty, sandy-haired, long-faced and sallow, with a pair of the coldest, fishiest eyes – eyes set too close together – that ever looked out of a flat and ugly face. A man precisely dressed, something of a fop, with just a note of the "sport" in his get-up; a man to fear, a man cool, wary and dangerous – Maxim Waldron, in fact, the Billionaire's right-hand man and confidant. Waldron, for some time affianced to his eldest daughter. Waldron the arch-corruptionist; Waldron, who never yet had been "caught with the goods," but who had financed scores of industrial and political campaigns, with Flint's money and his own; Waldron, the smooth, the suave, the perilous.

"What now?" asked he, fixing his pale blue eyes on the Billionaire's face.

"Come in here, and I'll tell you."

"Right!" And Waldron, brushing an invisible speck of dust from the sleeve of his checked coat, strolled rather casually into the Billionaire's office.

Flint closed the door.

"Well?" asked Waldron, with something of a drawl. "What's the excitement?"

"See here," began the great financier, stimulated by the drug. "We've been wasting our time, all these years, with our petty monopolies of beef and coal and transportation and all such trifles!"

"So?" And Waldron drew from his pocket a gold cigar-case, monogrammed with diamonds. "Trifles, eh?" He carefully chose a perfecto. "Perhaps; but we've managed to rub along, eh? Well, if these are trifles, what's on?"

"Air!"

"Air?" Waldron's match poised a moment, as with a slight widening of the pale blue eyes he surveyed his partner. "Why – er – what do you mean, Flint?"

"The Air Trust!"

"Eh?" And Waldron lighted his cigar.

"A monopoly of breathing privileges!"

"Ha! Ha!" Waldron's laugh was as mirthful as a grave-yard raven's croak. "Nothing to it, old man. Forget it, and stick to—"

"Of course! I might have expected as much from you!" retorted the Billionaire tartly. "You've got neither imagination nor—"

"Nor any fancy for wild-goose chases," said Waldron, easily, as he sat down in the big leather chair. "Air? Hot air, Flint! No, no, it won't do! Nothing to it nothing at all."

For a moment the Billionaire regarded him with a look of intense irritation. His thin lips moved, as though to emit some caustic answer; but he managed to keep silence. The two men looked at each other, a long minute; then Flint began again:

"Listen, now, and keep still! The idea came to me not an hour ago, this morning, looking over the city, here. We've got a finger on everything but the atmosphere, the most important thing of all. If we could control *that*—"

"Of course, I understand," interrupted the other, blowing a ring of smoke. "Unlimited power and so on. Looks very nice, and all. Only, it can't be done. Air's too big, too fluid, too universal. Human powers can't control it, any more than the ocean. Talk about monopolizing the Atlantic, if you will, Flint. But for heaven's sake, drop—"

"Can't be done, eh?" exclaimed Flint, warmly, sitting down on the desk-top and levelling a big-jointed forefinger at his partner. "That's what every new idea has had to meet. It's no argument! People scoffed at the idea of gas lighting when it was new. Called it 'burning smoke,' and made merry over it. That was as recently as 1832. But ten years later, gas-illumination was in full sway.

"Electric lighting met the same objection. And remember the objection to the telephone? When Congress, in 1843, granted Morse an appropriation of $30,000 to run the first telegraph line from Baltimore to Washington, one would-be humorist in that supremely intelligent body tried to introduce an amendment that part of the sum should be spent in surveying a railroad to the moon! And—"

"Granted," put in Waldron, "that my objection is futile, just what's your idea?"

"This!" And Flint stabbed at him with his forefinger, while the other financier regarded him with a fishily amused eye. "Every human being in this world – and there are 1,900,000,000 of them now! – is breathing, on the average, 16 cubic feet of air every hour, or about 400 a day. The total amount of oxygen actually absorbed in the 24 hours by each person, is about 17 cubic feet, or *over 30 billions of cubic feet of oxygen*, each day, in the entire world. Get that?"

"Well?" drawled the other.

"Don't you see?" snapped Flint, irritably. "Imagine that we extract oxygen from the air. Then—"

"You might as well try to dip up the ocean with a spoon," said Waldron, "as try to vitiate the atmosphere of the whole world, by any means whatsoever! But even if you could, what then?"

"Look here!" exclaimed the Billionaire. "It only needs a reduction of 10 per cent. in the atmospheric oxygen to make the air so bad that nobody can breathe it without discomfort and pain. Take out any more and people will die! We don't have to monopolize *all* the oxygen, but only a very small fraction, and the world will come gasping to us, like so many fish out of water, falling over each other to buy!"

"Possibly. But the details?"

"I haven't worked them out yet, naturally. I needn't. Herzog will take care of those. He and his staff. That's what they're for. Shall we put it up to him? What? My God, man! Think of the millions in it – the billions! The power! The—"

"Of course, of course!" interposed Waldron, calmly, eyeing his smoke. "Don't get excited, Flint. Rome wasn't built in a day. There may be something in this; possibly there may be the germ of an idea. I don't say it's impossible. It looks visionary to me; but then, as you well say, so has every new idea always looked. Let me think, now; let me think."

"Go ahead and think!" growled the Billionaire. "Think and be hanged to you! *I'm* going to act!"

Waldron vouchsafed no reply, but merely eyed his partner with cold interest, as though he were some biological specimen under a lens, and smoked the while.

Flint, however, turned to his telephone and pulled it toward him, over the big sheet of plate glass. Impatiently he took off the receiver and held it up to his ear.

"Hello, hello! 2438 John!" he exclaimed, in answer to the query of "Number, please?"

Silence, a moment, while Waldron slowly drew at his cigar and while the Billionaire tugged with impatience at his gray mustache.

"Hello! That you, Herzog?"

"All right. I want to see you at once. Immediately, understand?"

"Very well. And say, Herzog!"

"Bring whatever literature you have on liquid air, nitrogen extraction from the atmosphere, and so on. Understand? And come at once!"

"That's all! Good-bye!"

Smiling dourly, with satisfaction, he hung up and shoved the telephone away again, then turned to his still reflecting partner, who had now hoisted his patent leather boots to the window sill and seemed absorbed in regarding their gloss through a blue veil of nicotine.

"Herzog," announced the Billionaire, "will be here in ten minutes, and we'll get down to business."

"So?" languidly commented the immaculate Waldron. "Well, much as I'd like to flatter your astuteness, Flint, I'm bound to say you're barking up a false trail, this time! Beef, yes. Steel, yes. Railroads, steamships, coal, iron, wheat, yes. All tangible, all concrete, all susceptible of being weighed, measured, put in figures, fenced and bounded, legislated about and so on and so forth. But *air*—!"

He snapped his manicured fingers, to show his well-considered contempt for the Billionaire's scheme, and, throwing away his smoked-out cigar, chose a fresh one.

Flint made no reply, but with an angry grunt flung a look of scorn at the calm and placid one. Then, furtively opening his desk drawer, he once more sought the little vial and took two more pellets – an action which Waldron, without moving his head, complacently observed in a heavily-bevelled mirror that hung between the windows.

"Air," murmured Waldron, suavely. "Hot air, Flint?"

No answer, save another grunt and the slamming of the desk-drawer.

And thus, in silence, the two men, masters of the world, awaited the coming of the practical scientist, the proletarian, on whom they both, at last analysis, had to rely for most of their results.

Chapter III
The Baiting of Herzog

HERZOG WAS NOT LONG in arriving. To be summoned in haste by Isaac Flint, and to delay, was unthinkable. For eighteen years the chemist had lickspittled to the Billionaire. Keen though his mind was, his character and stamina were those of a jellyfish; and when the Master took snuff, as the saying is, Herzog never failed to sneeze.

He therefore appeared, now, in some ten minutes – a fat, rubicund, spectacled man, with a cast in his left eye and two fingers missing, to remind him of early days in experimental work on explosives. Under his arm he carried several tomes and pamphlets; and so, bowing first to one financier, then to the other, he stood there on the threshold, awaiting his masters' pleasure.

"Come in, Herzog," directed Flint. "Got some material there on liquid air, and nitrogen, and so on?"

"Yes, sir. Just what is it you want, sir?"

"Sit down, and I'll tell you," – for the chemist, hat in hand, ventured not to seat himself unbidden in presence of these plutocrats.

Herzog, murmuring thanks for Flint's gracious permission, deposited his derby on top of the revolving book-case, sat down tentatively on the edge of a chair and clutched his books as though they had been so many shields against the redoubted power of his masters.

"See here, Herzog," Flint fired at him, without any preliminaries or beating around the bush, "what do you know about the practical side of extracting nitrogen from atmospheric air? Or extracting oxygen, in liquid form? Can it be done – that is, on a commercial basis?"

"Why, no, sir – yes, that is – perhaps. I mean—"

"What the devil *do* you mean?" snapped Flint, while Waldron smiled maliciously as he smoked. "Yes, or no? I don't pay you to muddle things. I pay you to *know*, and to tell me! Get that? Now, how about it?"

"Well, sir – hm! – the fact is," and the unfortunate chemist blinked through his glasses with extreme uneasiness, "the fact of the matter is that the processes involved haven't been really perfected, as yet. Beginnings have been made, but no large-scale work has been done, so far. Still, the principle—"

"Is sound?"

"Yes, sir. I imagine—"

"Cut that! You aren't paid for imagining!" interrupted the Billionaire, stabbing at him with that characteristic gesture. "Just what do you know about it? No technicalities, mind! Essentials, that's all, and in a few words!"

"Well, sir," answered Herzog, plucking up a little courage under this pointed goading, "so far as the fixation of atmospheric nitrogen goes, more progress has been made in England and Scandinavia, than here. They're working on it, over there, to obtain cheap and plentiful fertilizer from the air. Nitrogen *can* be obtained from the air, even now, and made into fertilizers even cheaper than the Chili saltpeter. Oxygen is liberated as a by-product, and—"

"Oh, it is, eh? And could it be saved? In liquid form for instance?"

"I think so, sir. The Siemens & Halske interests, in Germany, are doing it already, on a limited scale. In Norway and Austria, nitrogen has been manufactured from air, for some years."

"On a paying, commercial basis?" demanded Flint, while Waldron, now a trifle less scornful, seemed to listen with more interest as his eyes rested on the rotund form of the scientist.

"Yes, sir, quite so," answered Herzog. "It's commercially feasible, though not a very profitable business at best. The gas is utilized in chemical combination with a substantial base, and—"

"No matter about that, just yet," interrupted Flint. "We can have details later. Do you know of any such business as yet, in the United States?"

"Well, sir, there's a plant building at Great Falls, South Carolina, for the purpose. It is to run by waterpower and will develop 5000 H.P."

"Hear that, Waldron?" demanded the Billionaire. "It's already beginning even here! But not one of these plants is working for what I see as the prime possibility. No imagination, no grasp on the subject! No wonder most inventors and scientists die poor! They incubate ideas and then lack the warmth to hatch them into general application. It takes men like us, Wally – practical men – to turn the trick!" He spoke a bit rapidly, almost feverishly, under the influence of the subtle drug. "Now if *we* take hold of this game, why, we can shake the world as it has never yet been shaken! Eh, Waldron? What do you think now?"

Waldron only grunted, non-committally. Flint with a hard glance at his unresponsive partner, once more turned to Herzog.

"See here, now," directed he. "What's the best process now in use?"

"For what, sir?" ventured the timid chemist.

"For the simultaneous production of nitrogen and oxygen, from the atmosphere!"

"Well, sir," he answered, deprecatingly, as though taking a great liberty even in informing his master on a point the master had expressly asked about, "there are three processes. But all operate only on a small scale."

"Who ever told you I wanted to work on a large scale?" demanded Flint, savagely.

"I – er – inferred – beg pardon, sir – I—" And Herzog quite lost himself and floundered hopelessly, while his mismated eyes wandered about the room as though seeking the assurance he so sadly lacked.

"Confine yourself to answering what I ask you," directed Flint, crisply. "You're not paid to infer. You're paid to answer questions on chemistry, and to get results. Remember *that!*"

"Yes, sir," meekly answered the chemist, while Waldron smiled with cynical amusement. He enjoyed nothing so delightedly as any grilling of an employee, whether miner, railroad man, clerk, ship's captain or what-not. This baiting, by Flint, was a rare treat to him.

"Go on," commanded the Billionaire, in a badgering tone. "What are the processes?" He eyed Herzog as though the man had been an ox, a dog or even some inanimate object, coldly and with narrow-lidded condescension. To him, in truth, men were no more than Shelley's "plow or sword or spade" for his own purpose – things to serve him and to be ruled – or broken – as best served his ends. "Go on! Tell me what you know; and no more!"

"Yes, sir," ventured Herzog. "There are three processes to extract nitrogen and oxygen from air. One is by means of what the German scientists call *Kalkstickstoff*, between calcium carbide and nitrogen, and the reaction-symbols are—"

"No matter," Flint waived him, promptly. "I don't care for formulas or details. What I want is results and general principles. Any other way to extract these substances, in commercial quantities, from the air we breathe?"

"Two others. But one of these operates at a prohibitive cost. The other—"

"Yes, yes. What is it?" Flint slid off the edge of the table and walked over to Herzog; stood there in front of him, and bored down at him with eager eyes, the pupils contracted by morphine, but very bright. "What's the best way?"

"With the electric arc, sir," answered the chemist, mopping his brow. This grilling method reminded him of what he had heard of "Third Degree" torments. "That's the best method, sir."

"Now in use, anywhere?"

"In Notodden, Norway. They have firebrick furnaces, you understand, sir, with an alternating current of 5000 volts between water-cooled copper electrodes. The resulting arc is spread by powerful electro-magnets, so." And he illustrated with his eight acid-stained fingers. "Spread out like a disk or sphere of flame, of electric fire, you see."

"Yes, and what then?" demanded Flint, while his partner, forgetting now to smile, sat there by the window scrutinizing him. One saw, now, the terribly keen and prehensile intellect at work under the mask of assumed foppishness and jesting indifference – the quality, for the most part masked, which had earned Waldron the nickname of "Tiger" in Wall Street.

"What then?" repeated Flint, once more levelling that potent forefinger at the sweating Herzog.

"Well, sir, that gives a large reactive surface, through which the air is driven by powerful rotary fans. At the high temperature of the electric arc in air, the molecules of nitrogen and oxygen dissociate into their atoms. The air comes out of the arc, charged with about one per cent. of nitric oxide, and after that—"

"Jump the details, idiot! Can't you move faster than a paralytic snail? What's the final result?"

"The result is, sir," answered Herzog, meek and cowed under this harrying, "that calcium nitrate is produced, a very excellent fertilizer. It's a form of nitrogen, you see, directly obtained from air."

"At what cost?"

"One ton of fixed nitrogen in that form costs about $150 or $160."

"Indeed?" commented Flint. "The same amount, combined in Chile saltpeter, comes to—?"

"A little over $300, sir."

"Hear that, Wally?" exclaimed the Billionaire, turning to his now interested associate. "Even if this idea never goes a step farther, there's a gold mine in just the production of fertilizer from air! But, after all, that will only be a by-product. It's the oxygen we're after, and must have!"

He faced Herzog again.

"Is any oxygen liberated, during the process?" he demanded.

"At one stage, yes, sir. But in the present process, it is absorbed, also."

Flint's eyebrows contracted nervously. For a moment he stood thinking, while Herzog eyed him with trepidation, and Waldron, almost forgetting to smoke, waited developments with interest. The Billionaire, however, wasted but scant time in consideration. It was not money now, he lusted for, but power. Money was, to him, no longer any great desideratum. At most, it could now mean no more to him than a figure on a check-book or a page of statistics in his private memoranda. But power, unlimited, indisputable power over the whole earth and the fulness thereof, power which none might dispute, power before which all humanity must bow – God! the lust of it now gripped and shook his soul.

Paling a little, but with eyes ablaze, he faced the anxious scientist.

"Herzog! See here!"

"Yes, sir?"

"I've got a job for you, understand?"

"Yes, sir. What is it?"

"A big job, and one on which your entire future depends. Put it through, and I'll do well by you. Fail, and by the Eternal, I'll break you! I can, and will, mark that! Do you get me?"

"I – yes, sir – that is, I'll do my best, and—"

"Listen! You go to work at once, immediately, understand? Work out for me some process, some practicable method by which the nitrogen and oxygen can both be collected in large quantities from the air. Everything in my laboratories at Oakwood Heights is at your disposal. Money's no object. Nothing counts, now, but *results!*

"I want the process all mapped out and ready for me, in its essential outlines, two weeks from today. If it isn't—" His gesture was a menace. "If it is – well, you'll be suitably rewarded. And no leaks, now. Not a word of this to any one, understand? If it gets out, you know what I can do to you, and will! Remember Roswell; remember Parker Hayes. *They* let news get to the Dillingham-Saunders people, about the new Tezzoni radio-electric system – and one's dead, now, a suicide; the other's in Sing-Sing for eighteen years. Remember that – and keep your mouth shut!"

"Yes, sir. I understand."

"All right, then. A fortnight from today, report to me here. And mind you, have something to report, or—!"

"Yes, sir."

"Very well! Now, go!"

Thus dismissed, Herzog gathered together his books and papers, blinked a moment with those peculiar wall-eyes of his, arose and, bowing first to Flint and then to the keenly-watching Waldron, backed out of the office.

When the door had closed behind him, Flint turned to his partner with a nervous laugh.

"That's the way to get results, eh?" he exclaimed. "No dilly-dallying and no soft soap; but just lay the lash right on, hard – they jump then, the vermin! Results! That fellow will work his head off, the next two weeks; and there'll be something doing when he comes again. You'll see!"

Waldron laughed nonchalantly. Once more the mask of indifference had fallen over him, veiling the keen, incisive interest he had shown during the interview.

"Something doing, yes," he drawled, puffing his cigar to a glow. "Only I advise you to choose your men. Some day you'll try that on a real man – one of the rough-necks you know, and—"

Flint snapped his fingers contemptuously, gazed at Waldron a moment with unwinking eyes and tugged at his mustache.

"When I need advice on handling men, I'll ask for it," he rapped out. Then, glancing at the Louis XIV clock: "Past the time for that C.P.S. board-meeting, Wally. No more of this, now. We'll talk it over at the Country Club, tonight; but for the present, let's dismiss it from our minds."

"Right!" answered the other, and arose, yawning, as though the whole subject were of but indifferent interest to him. "It's all moonshine, Flint. All a pipe-dream. Defoe's philosophers, who spent their lives trying to extract sunshine from cucumbers, never entertained any more fantastic notion than this of yours. However, it's your funeral, not mine. You're paying for it. I decline to put in any funds for any such purpose. Amuse yourself; you've got to settle the bill."

Flint smiled sourly, his gold tooth glinting, but made no answer.

"Come along," said his partner, moving toward the door. "They're waiting for us, already, at the board meeting. And there's big business coming up, today – that strike situation, you remember. Slade's going to be on deck. We've got to decide, at once, whether or not we're going to turn him loose on the miners, to smash that gang of union thugs and Socialist fanatics, and do it right. *That's* a game worth playing, Flint; but this Air Trust vagary of yours – stuff and nonsense!"

Flint, for all reply, merely cast a strange look at his partner, with those strongly-contracted pupils of his; and so the two vultures of prey betook themselves to the board room where already, round the long rosewood table, Walter Slade of the Cosmos Detective Company was laying out his strike-breaking plans to the attentive captains of industry.

Chapter IV
An Interloper

ON THE ELEVENTH DAY after this interview between the two men who, between them, practically held the whole world in their grasp, Herzog telephoned up from Oakwood Heights and took the liberty of informing Flint that his experiments had reached a point of such success that he prayed Flint would condescend to visit the laboratories in person.

Flint, after some reflection, decided he would so condescend; and forthwith ordered his limousine from his private garage on William Street. Thereafter he called Waldron on the 'phone, at his Fifth Avenue address.

"Mr. Waldron is not up, yet, sir," a carefully-modulated voice answered over the wire. "Any message I can give him, sir?"

"Oh, hello! That you, Edwards?" Flint demanded, recognizing the suave tones of his partner's valet.

"Yes, sir."

"All right. Tell Waldron I'll call for him in half an hour with the limousine. And mind, now, I want him to be up and dressed! We're going down to Staten Island. Got that?"

"Yes, sir. Any other message, sir?"

"No. But be sure you get him up, for me! Good-bye!"

Thirty minutes later, Flint's chauffeur opened the door of the big limousine, in front of the huge Renaissance pile that Waldron's millions had raised on land which had cost him more than as though he had covered it with double eagles; and Flint himself ascended the steps of Pentelican marble. The limousine, its varnish and silver-plate flashing in the bright spring sun, stood by the curb, purring softly to itself with all six cylinders, a thing of matchless beauty and rare cost. The chauffeur, on the driver's seat, did not even bother to shut off the gas, but let the engine run, regardless. To have stopped it would have meant some trifling exertion, in starting again; and since Flint never considered such details as a few gallons of gasoline, why should *he* care? Lighting a Turkish cigarette, this aristocrat of labor lolled on the padded leather and indifferently – with more of contempt than of interest – regarded a swarm of iron-workers, masons and laborers at work on a new building across the avenue.

Flint, meanwhile, had entered the great mansion, its bronze doors – ravished from the Palazzo Guelfo at Venice – having swung inward to admit him, with noiseless majesty. Ignoring the doorman, he addressed himself to Edwards, who stood in the spacious, mahogany-panelled hall, washing both hands with imaginary soap.

"Waldron up, yet, Edwards?"

"No, sir. He – er – I have been unable—"

"The devil! Where is he?"

"In his apartments, sir."

"Take me up!"

"He said, sir," ventured Edwards, in his smoothest voice. "He said—"

"I don't give a damn what he said! Take me up, at once!"

"Yes, sir. Immediately, sir!" And he gestured suavely toward the elevator.

Flint strode down the hall, indifferent to the Kirmanshah rugs, the rare mosaic floor and stained-glass windows, the Parian fountain and the Azeglio tapestries that hung suspended up along the stairway – all old stories to him and as commonplace as rickety odds and ends of furniture might be to any toiler "cribbed, cabin'd and confined" in fetid East Side tenement or squalid room on Hester Street.

The elevator boy bowed before his presence. Edwards hesitated to enter the private elevator, with this world-master; but Flint beckoned him to come along. And so, borne aloft by the smooth force of the electric motor, they presently reached the upper floor where "Tiger" Waldron laired in stately splendor, like the nabob that he was.

Without ceremony, Flint pushed forward into the bed-chamber of the mighty one – a chamber richly finished in panels of the rare sea-grape tree, brought from Pacific isles at great cost of money and some expenditure of human lives; but this latter item was, of course, beneath consideration.

By the softened light which entered through rich curtains, one saw the famous frieze of De Lussac, that banded the apartment, over the panelling – the frieze of Bacchantes, naked and unashamed, revelling with Satyrs in an abandon that bespoke the age when the world was young. Their voluptuous forms entwined with clustering grapes and leaves, they poured tipsy libations of red wine from golden chalices; while old Silenus, god of drink, astride a donkey, applauded with maudlin joy.

Flint, however, had no eyes for this scene which would have gladdened a voluptuary's heart – and which, for that reason was dear to Waldron – but walked toward the huge, four-posted bed where Wally himself, now rather paler than usual, with bloodshot eyes, was lying. This bed, despite the fact that it had been transported all the way from Tours, France, and that it once had belonged to an archbishop, had only too often witnessed its owner's insomnia.

"Hm! You're a devil of a man to keep an appointment, aren't you?" Flint sneered at the master of the house. "Eleven o'clock, and not up, yet!"

"Pardon me for remarking, my dear Flint," replied Waldron, stretching himself between the silken sheets and reaching for a cigarette, "that the appointment was not of my making. Also that I was up, last night – this morning, rather – till three-thirty. And in the next place, that scoundrel Hazeltine, trimmed me out of eighty-six thousand in four hours—"

"Roulette again, you idiot?" demanded Flint.

"And in conclusion," said Wally, "that the bigness of my head and the brown taste in my mouth are such as no 'soda and sermons, the morning after' can possibly alleviate. So you understand my dalliance.

"Damn those workmen!" he exclaimed, with sudden irritation, as a louder chattering of pneumatic riveters from the new building all at once clattered in at the window. "A free country, eh? And men are permitted to make *that* kind of a racket when a fellow wants to sleep! By God, if I—"

"Drop that, Wally, and get up!" commanded Flint. "There's no time for this kind of thing today. Herzog has just informed me his experiments have brought results. We're going down to Oakwood Heights to sea a few things for ourselves. And the quicker you get dressed and in your right mind, the better. Come along, I tell you!"

"Still chasing sunbeams from cucumbers, eh?" drawled the magnate, inhaling cigarette smoke and blowing a thin cloud toward the wanton Bacchantes. He affected indifference, but his dull eyes brightened a trifle in his wan face, deep-lined by the savage dissipations of the previous night. "And you insist on dragging me out on the same fatuous errand?"

"Don't be an ass!" snapped the Billionaire. "Get up and come along. The sooner we have this thing under way, the better."

"All right, anything to oblige," conceded Waldron, inwardly stirred by an interest he took good care not to divulge in word or look. "Give me just time for a cold plunge, a few minutes with my masseur and my barber, a bite to eat and—"

Flint laid hold on his partner and shook him roughly.

"Move, you sluggard!" he commanded. And Tiger Waldron obeyed.

Forty-five minutes later, the two financiers were speeding down the asphalt of the avenue at a good round clip. Flint's gleaming car formed one unit of the never-ending procession of motors which, day and night, year in and year out, spin unceasingly along the great, hard, splendid, cruel thoroughfare.

"I tell you," Flint was asserting as they swung into Broadway, at Twenty-third Street, and headed for South Ferry, "I tell you, Wally, the thing is growing vaster and more potent every moment. The longer I look at it, the huger its possibilities loom up! With air under our control, as a source of manufacturing alone, we can pull down perfectly inconceivable fortunes. We shan't have to send anywhere for our raw material. It will come to us; it's everywhere. No cost for transportation, to begin with.

"With oxygen, nitrogen and liquid air as products, think of the possibilities, will you? Not an ice-plant in the country could compete with us, in the refrigerating line. With liquid air, we could sweep that market clean. By installing it on our fruit cars and boats, and our beef cars, the saving effected in many ways would run to millions. The sale of nitrogen, for fertilizer, would net us billions. And, above all, the control of the world's air supply, for breathing, would make us the absolute, undisputed masters of mankind!

"We'd have the world by the windpipe. Its very life-breath would be at our disposal. Ha! What about revolution, then? What about popular discontent, and stiff-necked legislators, and cranky editors? What about commercial and financial rivals? What about these damned Socialists, with their brass-lunged bazoo, howling about monopoly and capitalism and all the rest of it? Eh, what? Just one squeeze," here Flint closed his corded, veinous fingers, "just one tightening of the fist, and – all over! We win, hands down!"

"Like shutting the wind off from a runaway horse, eh?" suggested Waldron, squinting at his cigar as though to hide the involuntary gleam of light that sparkled in his narrow-set eyes.

"Precisely!" assented Flint, smiling his gold-toothed smile. "The wildest bolter has got to stop, or fall dead, once you close his nostrils. That's what we'll do to the world, Wally. We'll get it by the throat – and there you are!"

"Yes, there we are," repeated Waldron, "but—"

"But what, now?"

Waldron did not answer, for a moment, but squinted up at the tall buildings, temples of Mammon and of Greed, filled from pave to cornice with toiling, sweated hordes of men and women, all laboring for Capitalism; many of them, directly or indirectly, for him. Then, as the limousine slowed at Spring Street, to let a cross-town car pass – a car whose earnings he and Flint both shared, just as they shared those of every surface and subway and "L" car in the vast metropolis – he said:

"Have you weighed the consequences carefully, Flint? Quite carefully? This thing of cornering all the oxygen is a pretty big proposition. Do you think you really ought to undertake it?"

"Why not?"

"Have you considered the frightful suffering and loss of life it might entail? Almost certainly would entail? Are you quite sure you *want* to take the world by the throat and – and choke it? For money?"

"No, not for money, Waldron. We're both staggering under money, as it is. But power! Ah, that's different!"

"I know," admitted Waldron. "But ought we – you – to attempt this, even for the sake of universal power? Your plan contemplates a monopoly such that everybody who refused or was unable to buy your product would, at best, have to get along with vitiated air, and at worst would have to stifle. Do you really think we ought to undertake this?"

Keenly he eyed Flint, as he thus sounded the elder man's inhuman determination. Flint, fathoming nothing of his purpose, retorted with some heat:

"Ha! Getting punctilious, all at once, are you? Talk ethics, eh? Where were your scruples, a year ago, when people were paying 25 cents a loaf for bread, because of that big wheat pool you put through? How about the oil you've just lately helped me boost by a 20 per cent. increase? And when the papers – though mostly those infernal Socialist or Anarchist papers, or whatever they were – shouted that old men and women were freezing in attics, last winter, what then? Did you vote to arbitrate the D.K. coal strike? Not by a jugful! You stood shoulder to shoulder with me, then, Wally, while *now*—!"

"It's a bit different, now," interposed "Tiger," with an evil smile, still leading his partner along. "Since then I've had the – ah – the extreme happiness to become engaged to your daughter, Catherine. New thoughts have entered my mind. I've experienced a – a—"

"You quitter!" burst out Flint. "No, by God! you aren't going to put this thing over on me. I'll have no quitter for *my* son-in-law! Wally, I'm astonished at you. Astonished and disappointed. You're not yourself, this morning. That eighty-six thousand you dropped last night, has shaken your heart. Come, come, pull together! Where's your nerve, man? Where's your nerve?"

Waldron answered nothing. In silence the partners watched the press of traffic, each busy with his own thoughts, Waldron waiting for Flint to reopen fire on him, and the Billionaire decided to say no more till his associate should make some move. Thus the limousine reached the Staten Island ferry, that glorious monument of municipal ownership wrecked by Tammany grafting. In silence they smoked while the car rolled down the incline and out onto the huge ferry boat. Then, as the crowded craft got under way, a minute later, both men left the car and strolled to the rail to watch the glittering sparkle of the sunlight on the harbor; the teeming commerce of the port; the creeping liners and busy tugs; the towering figure of Liberty, her flameless torch held far aloft in mockery.

Suddenly Waldron spoke.

"You can't do it, I tell you!" said he, waving an eloquent hand toward the sky. "It's too big, the air is, as I said before. Too damned big! Own coal and copper, if you will, and steel and ships, here; own those buildings back there," with a gesture at the frowning line of skyscrapers buttressing

Manhattan, "but don't buck the impossible! And incidentally, Flint, don't misunderstand me, either. When I asked you if we *ought* to try it, I merely meant, would it be *safe?* The world, Flint, is a dangerous toy to play with, too hard. The people are perilous baubles, if you step on their corns a bit too often or too heavily. Every Caesar has a Brutus waiting for him somewhere, with a club.

"Once let the unwashed get an idea into their low brows, and you can't tell where it may lead them. Even a rat fights, in its last corner. These human rats of ours have been getting a bit nasty of late. True, they swallowed the Limited Franchise Bill, three years ago, with only a little futile protest, so that now we've got them politically hamstrung. True, there's the Dick Military Bill, recently enlarged and perfected, so they can't move a hand without falling into treason and court-martial. True again, they've stood for the Censorship and the National Mounted Police – the Grays – all in the last year. But how much more will they stand, eh? You close your hand on their windpipes, and by God! something may happen even yet, after all!"

Flint snapped his fingers with contempt.

"Machine guns!" was all he said.

"Yes, of course," answered Waldron. "But there may be life in the old beast yet. They may yet kick the apple cart over – and us with it. You never can tell. And those infernal Socialists, always at it, night and day, never letting up, flinging firebrands into the powder magazine! *Sometime* there's going to be one hell of a bang, Flint! And when it comes, *suave qui peut!* So go slow, old man – go damned slow, that's all I've got to say!"

"On the contrary," said Flint, blinking in the golden spring sunshine as he peered out over the swashing brine at a raucous knot of gulls, "on the contrary, Wally, I'm going to push it as fast as the Lord will let me. You can come in, or not, as you see fit – but remember this, no quitter ever gets a daughter of mine! And another thing; we're in the year 1921, now, not 1910 or 1915. Developments, political and otherwise, have moved swiftly, these few years past. Then, there might have been trouble. Today, there can't be. We've got things cinched too tight for that!

"Ten years ago, they might have had our blood, the people might, or given us a hemp-tea party in Wall Street. today, all's safe. Come, be a man and grip your courage! We can put the initial stages through in absolute secrecy – and then, once we get our clutch on the world's breath, what have we to fear?"

"Go slow, Flint!"

"Nonsense! Oxygen is life itself. There's no substitute. Vitiate the air by removing even 10 per cent. of it, and the world will lick our boots for a chance to breathe! Everybody's got to have oxygen, all the way from kings and emperors down to the toiling cattle, the Henry Dubbs, as I believe they're commonly called in vulgar speech. Shut off the air, and 'the captains and the kings' will run to heel like the rabble itself. Run to heel, and pay for the privilege of doing it! We've got the universities, press, churches, laws, judges, army and navy and everything already in our hands. We'll be secure enough, no fear!"

"Shhhhh!" And Waldron nudged the Billionaire with his elbow.

In his excitement, Flint had permitted his voice to rise, a little. Not far from him, leaning on the rail, a stockily built young fellow in overalls, a cap pulled down firmly over his well-shaped head, was apparently watching the gulls and the passing boats, with eyes no less blue than the bay itself; eyes no less glinting than the sunlight on the waves. He seemed to be paying no heed to anything but what lay before him. But "Tiger" Waldron, possessed of something of the instinct of the beast whose name he bore, subconsciously sensed a peril in his nearness. The man's ear – if unusually quick – might, just *might* possibly have caught a word or two meant for no interloper. And at that thought, Waldron once more nudged his partner.

"Shhh!" he repeated, "Enough. We can finish this, in the limousine."

Flint looked at him a moment, in silence, then nodded.

"Right you are," said he. And both men climbed back into the closed car.

"You never can tell what ears are primed for news," said Waldron. "Better take no chances."

"Before long, we can throw away all subterfuge," the Billionaire replied as he shut the door. "But for now, well, you're correct. Once our grasp tightens on the windpipe of the world, we're safe. From our office in Wall Street you and I can play the keys of the world-machine as an organist would finger his instrument. But there must be no leak; no publicity; no suspicion aroused. We'll play our music *pianissimo*, Wally, with rare accompaniments to the tune of 'great public utility, benefit to the public health,' and all that – the same old game, only on a vastly larger scale.

"Every modern composer in the field of Big Business knows that score and has played it many times. *We* will play it on a monstrous pipe organ, with the world's lungs for bellows and the world's breath to vibrate our reeds – and all paying tribute, night and day, year after year, all over the world, Wally, all over the world!

"God! What power shall be ours! What infinite power, such as, since time began, never yet lay in mortal hands! We shall be as gods, Waldron, you and I – and between us, we shall bring the human race wallowing to our feet in helpless bondage, in supreme abandon!"

The ferry boat, nearing the Staten Island landing, slowed its ponderous screws. The chauffeur flung away his cigarette, drew on his gauntlets and accelerated his engine. Forward the human drove began to press, under the long slave-driven habit of haste, of eagerness to do the masters' bidding.

The young mechanic by the rail – he of the overalls and keen blue eyes – turned toward the bows, picked up a canvas bag of tools and stood there waiting with the rest.

For a moment his glance rested on the limousine and the two half-seen figures within. As it did so, a wanton breeze from off the Island flapped back the lapel of his jumper. In that brief instant one might have seen a button pinned upon his blue flannel shirt – clasped hands, surrounded by the legend: "Workers of the World, Unite!"

But neither of the plutocrats observed this; nor, had they seen, would they have understood.

And whether the sturdy toiler had overheard aught of their infernal conspiring – or, having heard it, grasped its dire and criminal significance – who, who in all this weary and toil-burdened world, could say?

Chapter V
In the Laboratory

HALF AN HOUR'S run down Staten Island, along smooth roads lined with sleepy little towns and through sparse woods beyond which sparkled the shining waters of the harbor, brought the two plutocrats to the quiet settlement of Oakwood Heights.

Now the blasé chauffeur swung the car sharply to the left, past the aviation field, and so came to the wide-scattered settlement – almost a colony – which, hidden behind high, barb-wire-topped fences, carried on the many and complex activities of the partners' experiment station. Here were the several laboratories where new products were evolved and old ones refined, for Flint's and Waldron's greater profit. Here stood a complete electric power plant, for lighting and heating the works, as well as for current to use in the retorts and many powerful machines of the testing works.

Here, again, were broad proving grounds, for fuel and explosives; and, at one side, stood a low, skylighted group of brick buildings, known as the electro-chemical station.

Dormitories and boarding-houses for the small army of employees occupied the eastern end of the enclosure, nearest the sea. Over all, high chimney stacks and the aerials of a mighty wireless plant dominated the entire works. A private railroad spur pierced the western side of the enclosure, for food and coal supplies, as well as for the handling of the numerous imports and exports of this wonderfully complete feudal domain. As the colony lay there basking in the sunshine of early spring, under its drifting streamers of smoke, it seemed an ideal picture of peaceful activities. Here a locomotive puffed, shunting cars; there, a steam-jet flung its plumes of snowy vapor into air; yonder, a steam hammer thundered on a massive anvil. And forges rang, and through open windows hummed sounds of industry.

And yet, not one of all those sounds but echoed more bitter slavery for men. Not one of all those many activities but boded ill to humanity. For the whole plan and purpose of the place was the devising of still wider forms of human exploitation and enslavement. Its every motive was to serve the greed of Flint and Waldron. Outwardly honest and industrious, it inwardly loomed sinister and terrible, a type and symbol of its masters' swiftly growing power. Such, in its essence, was the great experiment station of these two men who lusted for dominion over the whole world.

As the long, glittering car drew up at the main gate of the enclosure, a sharp-eyed watchman peered through a sliding wicket therein. Satisfied by his inspection, he withdrew; and at once the big gate rolled back, smoothly actuated by electricity. The car purred onward, into the enclosure. When the gate had closed noiselessly behind it, the chauffeur ran it down a splendidly paved roadway, swung to the right, past the machine shops, and drew it to a stand in front of the administration building.

Flint and his partner alighted, and stood for a moment surveying the scene with satisfaction. Then Flint turned to the chauffeur.

"Put the car in the garage," he directed. "We may not want it till afternoon."

The blasé one touched his cap and nodded, in obedience. Then, as the car withdrew, the partners ascended the broad steps.

"Good chap, that Herrick," commented Waldron, casting a glance at the retreating chauffeur. "Quick-witted, and mum. Give me a man who knows how to mind *and* keep still about it, every time!"

"Right," assented Flint. "Obedience is the first of all virtues, and the second is silence. Well, it looks to me as though we had the whole world coming our way, now, along that very same path of virtue. Once we get this air proposition really to working, the world will obey. It will have to! And as for silence, we can manage that, too. The mere turn of a valve, and—!"

Waldron smiled grimly, as though in derision of what he seemed to think his partner's chimerical hopes, but made no answer. Together they entered the administration building. Five minutes later, Herzog, their servile experimenter, stood bowing and cringing before them.

"Got it, Herzog?" demanded Flint, while Waldron lighted still another of those costly cigars – each one worth a good mechanic's daily wage.

"Yes, sir, I believe so, sir," the scientist replied, depreciatingly. "That is, at least, on a small scale. Two weeks was the time you allowed me, sir, but—"

"I know. You've done it in eleven days," interrupted, the Billionaire. "Very well. I knew you could. You'll lose nothing by it. So no more of that. Show us what you've done. Everything all ready?"

"Quite ready, sir," the other answered. "If you'll be so good as to step into the electro-chemical building?"

Flint very graciously signified his willingness thus to condescend; and without delay, accompanied by the still incredulous Waldron, and followed by Herzog, he passed out of the administration building, through a covered passage and into the electro-chemical works.

A variety of strange odors and stranger sounds filled this large brick structure, windowless on every side and lighted only by broad skylights of milky wire-glass – this arrangement being due to the extreme secrecy of many processes here going forward. The partners had no intention that any spying eyes should ever so much as glimpse the work in this department; work involving foods, fuels, power, lighting, almost the entire range of the vast network of exploiting media they had already flung over a tired world.

"This way, gentlemen," ventured Herzog, pointing toward a metal door at the left of the main room. He unlocked this, which was guarded by a combination lock, like that of a bank vault, and waited for them to enter; then closed it after them, and made quite sure the metal door was fast.

A peculiar, pungent smell greeted the partners' nostrils as they glanced about the inner laboratory. At one side an electric furnace was glowing with graphite crucibles subjected to terrific heat. On the other a dynamo was humming. Before them a broad, tiled bench held a strange assortment of test tubes, retorts and complex apparatus of glass and gleaming metal. The whole was lighted by a strong white light from above, through the milk-hued glass – one of Herzog's own inventions, by the way; a wonderful, light-intensifying glass, which would bend but not break; an invention which, had he himself profited by it, would have brought him millions, but which the partners had exploited without ever having given him a single penny above his very moderate salary.

"Is that it?" demanded Flint, a glitter lighting up his morphia-contracted pupils. He jerked his thumb at a complicated nexus of tubes, brass cylinders, coiled wires and glistening retorts which stood at one end of the broad work-bench.

"That is it, sir," answered Herzog, apologetically, while "Tiger" Waldron's hard face hardened even more. "Only an experimental model, you understand, sir, but—"

"It gets results?" queried Flint sharply. "It produces oxygen and nitrogen on a scale that indicates success, with adequate apparatus?"

"Yes, sir. I believe so, sir. No doubt about it; none whatever."

"Good!" exclaimed the Billionaire. "Now show us!"

"With pleasure, sir. But first, let me explain, a little."

"Well, what?" demanded Flint. His partner, meanwhile, had drawn near the apparatus, and was studying it with a most intense concentration. Plain to see, beneath this man's foppish exterior and affected cynicism, dwelt powerful purposes and keen intelligence.

"Explain what?" repeated the Billionaire. "As far as details go, I'm not interested. All I want is results. Go ahead, Herzog; start your machine and let me see what it can do."

"I will, sir," acceded the scientist. "But first, with your permission, I'll point out a few of its main features, and—"

"Damn the main features!" cried Flint. "Get busy with the demonstration!"

"Hold on, hold on," now interrupted Waldron. "Let him discourse, if he wants to. Ever know a scientist who wasn't primed to the muzzle with expositions? Here, Herzog," he added, turning to the inventor, "I'll listen, if nobody else will."

Undecided, Herzog smiled nervously. Even Flint had to laugh at his indecision.

"All right, go on," said the Billionaire. "Only for God's sake, make it brief!"

Herzog, thus adjured, cleared his throat and blinked uneasily.

"Oxygen," he said. "Yes, I can produce it quickly, easily and in large quantities. As a gas, or as a liquid, which can be shipped to any desired point and there transformed into gaseous form. Liquid air can also be produced by this same machine, for refrigerating purposes. You understand, of course, that when liquid air evaporates, it is only the nitrogen that goes back into the atmosphere at 313 degrees below zero. The residue is pure liquid oxygen. In other words, this apparatus will make money as a liquid air plant, and furnish you oxygen as a by-product.

"It will also turn out nitrogen, for fertilizing purposes. The income from a full-sized machine, on this pattern, from all three sources, should be very large indeed."

"Good," put in Waldron. "And liquid air, for example, would cost how much to produce?"

"With power-cost at half a cent per H.P. hour, about $2.50 a ton. The oxygen by-product alone will more than pay for that, in purifying and cooling buildings, or used to promote combustion in locomotives and other steam engines. The liquid air itself can be used as a motive power for a certain type of expansion engine, or—"

"There, there, that's enough!" interposed Flint, brusquely. "We don't need any of your advice or suggestions, Herzog. As far as the disposal of the product is concerned, we can take care of that. All we want from you is the assurance that that product can be obtained, easily and cheaply, and in unlimited quantities. Is that the case?"

"It is, sir."

"All right. And can liquid oxygen be easily transported any considerable distance?"

"Yes, sir. In what is known as Place's Vacuum-jacketed Insulated Container, it can be kept for weeks at a time without any appreciable loss."

Flint pondered a moment, then asked, again:

"Could large tanks, holding say, a million gallons, be built on that principle, for wholesale storage? And could vacuum-jacketed pipes be laid, for conveying liquid oxygen or its gas?"

"No reason why not, sir. Yes, I may say all that is quite feasible."

"Very well, then," snapped Flint. "That's enough for the present. Now, show us your machine at work! Start it Herzog. Let's see what you can do!"

The Billionaire's eyes glittered as Herzog laid a hand on a gleaming switch. Even Waldron forgot to smoke.

"Gentlemen, observe," said Herzog, as he threw the lever.

Chapter VI
Oxygen, King of Intoxicators

A SOFT HUMMING note began to vibrate through the inner laboratory – a note which rose in pitch, steadily, as Herzog shoved the lever from one copper post to another, round the half-circle.

"I am now heating the little firebrick furnace," said the scientist. "In Norway, they use an alternating current of only 5,000 volts, between water-cooled copper electrodes, as I have already told you. I am using 30,000 volts, and my electrodes, my own invention, are—"

"Never mind," growled Flint. "Just let's see some of the product – some liquid oxygen, that's all. The why and wherefore is your job, not ours!"

Herzog, with a pained smile, bent and peered through a red glass bull's-eye that now had begun to glow in the side of his apparatus.

"The arc is good," he muttered, as to himself. "Now I will throw in the electro-magnets and spread it; then switch in my intensifying condenser, and finally set the turbine fans to work, to throw air through the field. Then we shall see, we shall see!"

Suiting the action to the words, he deftly touched here a button, there a lever; and all at once a shrill buzzing rose above the lower drone of the induction coils.

"Gentlemen," said Herzog, straightening up and facing his employers, "the process is now already at work. In five minutes – yes, in three – I shall have results to show you!"

"Good!" grunted Waldron. "That's all we're after, results. That's the only way you hold your job, Herzog, just getting results!"

He relighted his cigar, which had gone out during Herzog's explanation – for "Tiger" Waldron, though he could drop thousands at roulette without turning a hair, never yet had been known to throw away a cigar less than half smoked. Flint, meanwhile, took out a little morocco-covered note book and made a few notes. In this book he had kept an outline of his plan from the very first; and now with pleasure he added some memoranda, based on what Herzog had just told him, as well as observations on the machine itself.

Thus two minutes passed, then three.

"Time's up, Herzog!" exclaimed Waldron, glancing at the electric clock on the wall. "Where's the juice?"

"One second, sir," answered the scientist. Again he peeked through the glowing bull's-eye. Then, his face slightly pale, his bulging eyes blinking nervously, he took two small flint glass bottles, set them under a couple of pipettes, and deftly made connections.

"Oxygen cocktail for mine," laughed Waldron, to cover a certain emotion he could not help feeling at sight of the actual operation of a process which might, after all, open out ways and means for the utter subjugation of the world.

Neither Flint nor the inventor vouchsafed even a smile. The Billionaire drew near, adjusted a pair of pince-nez on his hawk-like nose, and peered curiously at the apparatus. Herzog, with a quick gesture, turned a small silver faucet.

"Oxygen! Unlimited oxygen!" he exclaimed. "I have found the process, gentlemen, commercially practicable. Oxygen!"

Even as he spoke, a lambent, sparkling liquid began to flow through the pipette, into the flask. At sight of it, the Billionaire's eyes lighted up with triumph. Waldron, despite his assumed nonchalance, felt the hunting thrill of Wall street, the quick stab of exultation when victory seemed well in hand.

"These bottles," said Herzog, "are double, constructed on the principle of the Thermos bottle. They will keep the liquid gases I shall show you, for days. Huge tanks could be built on the same principle. In a short time, gentlemen, you can handle tons of these gases, if you like – thousands of tons, unlimited tons.

"The Siemens and Halske people, and the Great Falls, S.C., plant, will be mere puttering experimenters beside you. For neither they nor any other manufacturers have any knowledge of the vital process – my secret, polarizing transformer, which does the work in one-tenth the time and at one-hundredth the cost of any other known process. For example, see here?"

He turned the faucet, disconnected the flask and handed it to Flint.

"There, sir," he remarked, "is a half-pint of pure liquid oxygen, drawn from the air in less than eight minutes, at a cost of perhaps two-tenths of a cent. On a large scale the cost can be vastly reduced. Are you satisfied, sir?"

Flint nodded, curtly.

"You'll do, Herzog," he replied – his very strongest form of commendation. "You're not half bad, after all. So this is liquid oxygen, eh? Very cheap, and very cold?"

His eyes gleamed with joy at sight of the translucent potent stuff – the very stuff of life, its essence and prime principle, without which neither plant nor animal nor man can live – oxygen, mother of all life, sustainer of the world.

"Very cheap, yes, sir," answered the scientist. "And cold, enormously cold. The specimen you hold in your hand, in that vacuum-protected flask, is more than three hundred degrees below zero. One drop of it on your palm would burn it to the bone. Incidentally, let me tell you another fact—"

"And that is?"

"This specimen is the allotropic or condensed form of oxygen, much more powerful than the usual liquified gas."

"Ozone, you mean?"

"Precisely. Would you like to sense its effect as a ventilating agent?"

"No danger?"

"None, sir. Here, allow me."

Herzog took the flask, pressed a little spring and liberated the top. At once a whitish vapor began to coil from the neck of the bottle.

"Hm!" grunted Waldron, smiling. "Mountain winds and sea breezes have nothing on that!" He sniffed with appreciation. "Some gas, all right!"

"You're right, Wally," answered the Billionaire. "If this works out on a large scale, in all its details – well – I needn't impress its importance on you!"

Yielding to the influence of the wonderful, life-giving gas, the rather close air of the laboratory, contaminated by a variety of chemical odors, and vitiated by its recent loss of oxygen, had begun to freshen and purify itself in an astonishing manner. One would have thought that through an open window, close at hand, the purest ocean breeze was blowing. A faint tinge of color began to liven the somewhat pasty cheek of the Billionaire. Waldron's big chest expanded and his eye brightened. Even the meek Herzog stood straighter and looked more the man, under the stimulus of the life-giving ozone.

"Fine!" exclaimed Flint, with unwonted enthusiasm, and nearly yielded to a laugh. Waldron went so far as to slap Herzog on the shoulder.

"You're some wizard, old man!" he exclaimed, with a warmth hitherto never known by him – for already the subtle gas was beginning to intoxicate his senses. "And you can handle nitrogen with the same ease and precision?"

"Exactly," answered Herzog. "This other vial contains pure nitrogen. With enlarged apparatus, I can supply it by the trainload. The world's fertilizer problem is solved!"

"Great work!" ejaculated Waldron, even more excited than before, but Flint, his natural sourness asserting itself, merely growled some ungracious remark.

"Nitrogen can go hang," said he. "It's oxygen we're after, primarily. Once we get our grip on that, the world will be—"

Waldron checked him just in time.

"Enough of this," he interrupted sharply. "I admit, I'm not myself, in this rich atmosphere. I know *you're* feeling it, already, Flint. Come along out of this, where we can regain our aplomb. We've seen enough, for once."

He turned to Herzog.

"For God's sake, man," cried he, "cork that magic bottle of yours, before all the oxygen-genii escape, or you'll have us both under the table! And, see here," he added, pulling out his check-book, while Flint stared in amazed disgust. "Here, take a blank check." He took his fountain pen and scrawled his name on one. "The amount? That's up to you. Now, let us out," he bade, as Herzog stood there regarding the check with entire uncomprehension. "Out, I say, before I get extravagant!"

Herzog, perfectly comprehending the magnates' unusual conduct as due to oxygen-intoxication in its initial stage, made no comment, but walked to the door, spun the combination and flung it open.

"Glad to have had the pleasure of demonstrating the process to you, gentlemen," said he. "If you're convinced it's practicable, I'm at your orders for any larger extension of the work. Have you any other question or suggestion?"

Neither magnate answered. Flint was trying hard to hold his self-control. Waldron, red-faced now and highly stimulated, looked as though he had been drinking even more than usual.

Both passed out of the laboratory with rather unsteady steps. Together they retraced their way to the administration building; and there, safe at last in the private inner office, with the door locked, they sat down and stared at each other with expressions of amazement.

Chapter VII
A Freak of Fate

WALDRON was the first to speak. With a sudden laugh, boisterous and wild, he cried:

"Flint, you old scoundrel, you're drunk!"

"Drunk yourself!" retorted the Billionaire, half starting from his chair, his fist clenched in sudden passion. "How dare you—?"

"Dare? I dare anything!" exclaimed Waldron. "Yes, I admit it – I *am* half seas over. That ozone – God! what a stimulant! Must be some wonderfully powerful form. If we – could market it—"

Flint sank back in his chair, waving an extravagant hand.

"Market it?" he answered. "Of course we can market it, and will! Drunk or sober, Wally, I know what I'm talking about. The power now in our grasp has never yet been equalled on earth. On the one side, we can half-stifle every non-subscriber to our service, or wholly stifle every rebel against us. On the other, we can simply saturate every subscriber with health and energy, or even – if they want it – waft them to paradise on the wings of ozone. The old Roman idea of 'bread and circus' to rule the mob, was child's play compared to this! Science has delivered the whole world into our hands. Power, man, power! Absolute, infinite power over every living, breathing thing!"

He fell silent, pondering the vast future; and Waldron, gazing at him with sparkling eyes, nodded with keen satisfaction. Thus for a few moments they sat, looking at each other and letting imagination ran riot; and as they sat, the sudden, stimulating effect of the condensed oxygen died in their blood, and calmer feelings ensued.

Presently Waldron spoke again.

"Let's get down to brass tacks," said he, drawing his chair up to the table. "I'm almost myself again. The subtle stuff has got out of my brain, at last. Generalities and day-dreams are all very well, Flint, but we've got to lay out some definite line of campaign. And the sooner we get to it the better."

"Hm!" sneered Flint. "If it's not more practical than your action in giving Herzog that blank check, it won't be worth much. As an extravagant action, Wally, I've never seen it equalled. I'm astonished, indeed I am!"

Waldron laughed easily.

"Don't worry," he answered his partner. "That temporary aberration of judgment, due to oxygen-stimulus, will have no results. Herzog won't dare fill out the check, anyhow, because he knows he'd get into trouble if he did; and even though he should, he can collect nothing. I'll have payment stopped, at once, on that number. No danger, Flint!"

"I don't know," mused the Billionaire. "It may be that this man has us just a little under his thumb. He, and he alone, understands the process. We've got to treat him with due consideration, or he may leave us and carry his secret to others – to Masterson, for instance, or the Amalgamated people, or—"

"Nothing doing on that, old man!" interrupted "Tiger." "Have no fear. The first move he makes, off to Sing Sing he goes, the way we jobbed Parker Hayes. Slade and the Cosmos Agency can take care of *him*, all right, if he asserts himself!"

"Very likely," answered Flint, who had now at last entirely recovered his sang-froid. "But in that event, our work would be at a standstill. No, Waldron, we mustn't oppose this fellow. Better let the check go through, if he has nerve enough to fill it out and cash it. He won't dare gouge very deep; and no matter what he takes, it won't be a drop in the ocean, compared to the golden flood now almost within our grasp!"

Waldron pondered a moment, then nodded assent.

"All right. Correct," he finally answered. "So then, we can dismiss that trifle from our minds. Now, to work! We've got the process we were after. What next?"

"First of all," answered the Billionaire, "we'll let this Herzog understand that he's to have a share in the results; that in this, as in everything so far, he's merely a tool – and that when tools lose their cutting edge we break 'em. He's a meek devil. We can hold *him* easily enough."

"Right. And then?" asked Waldron.

"Then? First of all, a good, big, wide-sweeping publicity campaign. That must begin today, to prepare opinion for the forthcoming development of the new idea."

"Henderson can handle that, all right," said Wally, leaning forward in his chair. "Give him the idea, and turn him loose, and he'll get results. A clever dog, that. He and his press bureau, working through all the big dailies and many of the magazines, can turn this country upside down in six months. Let him get on this job, and before you know it the public will be demanding, be fighting for a chance to subscribe to the new ventilating-service. That part of it is easy!"

"Yes, you're right," replied Flint. "We'll see Henderson no later than this afternoon. He and his writers can lay out a series of popular articles and advertisements, to be run as pure reading matter, with no distinguishing mark that they *are* ads, which will get the country – the whole world, in fact – coming our way."

"Good," the other assented. "Meantime, we can begin installing oxygen machines on a big scale, a huge scale, to supply the demand that's bound to arise. Where do you think we'd best manufacture? Herzog says water power is the correct thing. We might use Niagara – use some of the surplus power we already own there."

"Niagara would do, very well," answered Flint. He had once more taken out his little morocco-covered note book, and was now jotting down some further memoranda. "It's a good location. Pipe-lines could easily be extended, from it, to cover practically a quarter to a third of the United States. Eventually we'll put in another plant in Chicago, one in Denver and one on the Pacific Coast. Then, in time, there must be distributing centers in Europe, Africa, Asia and Australia. But for the present, we'll begin with the Niagara plant. After we get that under full operation, the others will develop in due course of time."

"Our charter covers this new line of work. There will be no need of any legal technicalities," said Waldron, with a smile. "Some charter, if I do say it, who shouldn't. I drew it, you remember. Nothing much in the way of possible business-extension got past *me!*"

Flint nodded.

"You're right," he answered. "Nothing stands in our way, now. Positively nothing. We have land, power and capital without limit. We have the process. We control press, law, courts, judges, military and every other form of government. All we need look out for is to secure public confidence and keep the bandage on the eyes of the world till our system is actually in operation – then there will be no redress, no come back, no possible rebellion. As I've already said, Wally, we'll have the whole world by the windpipe; and let the mob howl *then*, if they dare!"

"Yes, let 'em howl!" chimed in "Tiger," with a snarl that proved his nickname no misnomer. "Inside of a year we'll have them all where we want them. You were right, Flint, when you called oil, coal, iron and all the rest of it mere petty activities. Air – ah! that's the talk! Once we get the *air* under our control, we're emperors of all life!"

His words rang frank and bold, but something in his look, as he blinked at his partner, might have given Flint cause for uneasiness, had the Billionaire noticed that oblique and dangerous glance. One might have read therein some shifty and devious plan of Waldron's to dominate even Flint himself, to rule the master or to wreck him, and to seize in his own hands the reins of universal power. But Flint, bending over his note-book and making careful memoranda, saw nothing of all this.

Waldron, an inveterate smoker, lighted a fresh cigar, leaned back, surveyed his partner and indulged in a short inner laugh, which hardly curved his cruel lips, but which hardened still more those pale-blue, steely eyes of his.

"All right," said he, at last. "Enough of this, Flint. Let's get back to town, now, and have a conference with Henderson. That's the first step. By tonight, the whole campaign of publicity must be mapped out. Come, come; you can finish your memoranda later. I'm impatient to be back in Wall Street. Come along!"

Five minutes later, having left orders that Herzog was to attend upon them in their private offices, next morning, they had ordered the limousine and were making way along the hard road toward the gate of the enclosure.

The gate opened to let them pass, then swung and locked again, behind them. At a good clip, the powerful car picked up speed on the homeward way. The two magnates, exultant and flushed with the consciousness of coming victory, lolled in the deeply-cushioned seat and spoke of power.

As they swung past the aviation field and neared the Oakwood Heights station, a train pulled out. Down the road came tramping a workingman in overalls and jumper, with a canvas bag of tools swinging from his brawny right hand. As he walked, striding along with splendid energy, he whistled to himself – no cheap ragtime air, but Handel's Largo, with an appreciation which bespoke musical feeling of no common sort.

The Billionaire caught sight of him, just as the car slowed to take the sharp turn by the station. Instant recognition followed. Flint's eyes narrowed sharply.

"Hm! The same fellow," he grunted to himself. "The same rascal who stood beside us on the ferry boat, as we were talking over our plans. Now, what the devil?"

Shadowed by a kind of instinctive uneasiness, not yet definite or clear but more in the nature of a premonition of trouble, Flint gazed fixedly at the mechanic as the car swung round the bend in the road. The glance was returned.

Yielding to some kind of imperative curiosity, the Billionaire leaned over the side of the car – leaned out, with his coat flapping in the stiff wind – and for a moment peered back at the disquieting workman.

Then the car swept him out of sight, and Flint resumed his seat again.

He did not know – for he had not seen it happen – that in that moment the slippery, leather-covered note-book had slid from his lolling coat pocket and had fallen with a sharp slap on the white macadam, skidded along and come to rest in the ditch.

The workingman, however, who had paused and turned to look after the speeding car, *he* had seen all this.

A moment he stood there, peering. Then, retracing his steps with resolution he picked up the little book and slid it into the pocket of his jeans.

Deserted was the road. Not a soul was to be seen, save the crossing flagman, musing in his chair beside his little hut, quite oblivious to everything but a rank cob pipe. The workman's act had not been noticed.

Nobody had observed him. Nobody knew. Not a living creature had witnessed the slight deed on which, by a strange freak of fate, the history of the world was yet to turn.

Chapter VIII
One Unbidden, Shares Great Secrets

IMMEDIATELY ON DISCOVERING his loss – which was soon after having reached his office – Flint, in something like a fright, telephoned down to the Oakwood Heights laboratory and instructed Herzog, in person, to make a careful search for it and to report results inside an hour. Even though some of the essentials of his plan were written in a code of his own devising, Flint paled before the possible results should the book fall into the hands of anybody intelligent enough to fathom its meaning.

"Damn the luck!" he ejaculated, pacing the office floor, his fists knotted. "If it had been a pocket book with a few thousand inside, that would have been a trifle. But to lose my plan of campaign – God grant no harm may come of it!"

Waldron, slyly observing him, could not suppress a smile.

"Calling on God, eh?" sneered he. "You *must* be agitated. I haven't heard that kind of entreaty on your lips, Flint, since the year of the big coal strike, when you prayed God the gun-men might 'get' the strikers before they could organize. Come, come, man, brace up! Your book will turn up all right; and even if it doesn't there's no cause for alarm. It would take a man of extraordinary acumen to read *your* hieroglyphics! Cheer up, Flint. There's really nothing to excite you."

The Billionaire thus adjured, sat down and tried to calm his agitation.

"Rotten luck, eh?" he queried. "But after all, Herzog is likely to find the book. And even if he doesn't, I guess we're safe enough. The very boldness of the plan – supposing even that the finder could grasp it – would put it outside the seeming range of the possible. It's hardly a hundred to one shot any harm may come of it."

"All right, then, let it go at that," said Waldron. "And now, to business. Suppose, for example, you've got a perfectly unlimited supply of oxygen-gas and liquid. How are you going to market it? Just what details have you worked out?"

Flint pondered a moment, before replying. At last he said:

"Of course you understand, Wally, I can't give you every point. The whole thing will be an evolution, and new ideas and processes, new uses and demands will develop as time passes. But in the main, my idea is this: The big producing stations will steadily extract oxygen from the atmosphere, thus leaving the air increasingly poorer and less adapted to sustaining human life.

"I shall store the oxygen in vast tanks, like the ordinary gas-tanks to be found in every city, only much bigger. These tanks will be fed by pipe-lines from the central stations, thus."

Flint drew toward him a sheet of his heavily embossed letter-paper, and, picking up a pencil, began to sketch a rough diagram. Waldron, making no comment, followed every stroke with keen interest.

"From these tanks," the Billionaire continued, "smaller pipes will convey the gaseous oxygen to every house taking our service."

"Just like ordinary gas?"

"Precisely. Each room will be fitted with an oxygen jet apparatus, something like a gas burner, with a safety device to prevent over supply and avoid the dangers of combustion."

"Combustion?"

"Yes. In pure oxygen, a glowing bit of wire will burst into flame. Your cigar, there, would catch fire, from the merest spark in its inmost folds. Too much oxygen in a room not only intoxicates the occupants – we've already seen *that* effect – but also develops a great fire risk. So we shall have to make some provision for that, Wally. It will be absolutely essential."

"All right. Allowing it's been made, what then?" asked "Tiger," with extraordinary interest.

"Can't you see? We'll have every household under our absolute thumb?" And Flint pressed his thumb on the table to illustrate. "My God, man, think of it! Every city honeycombed by our pipes – yes, and every village and hamlet too, and even every farm house that can afford it! At first, the cost will be very low, till people have become accustomed to ozone as they are to water. The whole ventilation problem will be solved, at once and for all time. Where we can't pipe in the ozone, we can use portable vaporizers, to be supplied once a month, and of sufficient capacity to keep the air of an average-sized house perfectly pure for thirty days.

"Pure? More than pure! Exhilarating, life-giving, delicious! Under this system, Wally, the middle and upper classes will thrive as never before. They'll grow in size and weight, in health and intelligence, under the steady influence of ozone, day and night. Every vital process will be stimulated. Our invention will mark a new era in the welfare of the world!"

"Bunk!" sneered Wally. "That's all very well for your prospectuses and newspaper articles, old man, but the fact is we don't give a damn whether it helps the world or wrecks it. We're out for money and power. My motto is, Get 'em and do good, if you can – but *get* 'em anyhow! So you had better can the philanthropic part of it. Just show me the cash, and you can have all the credit!"

Flint shot a grim look at his partner, then continued:

"Don't be flippant, Wally. This is a serious business and must be treated as such. In addition to the respiratory service, we can put in water-cooling and refrigerating services, at low cost, also cold-pipes for cooling houses in summer. In fine, we can immeasurably add to the health and comfort of the better classes; and can at last have everybody using our gas, which, registering through our own sealed meters, will flood us with wealth so vast as to make that of these Standard Oil pifflers look like the proverbial thirty cents!"

"Fine!" exclaimed Waldron, nodding approval. "Also, any time any rebellion develops we can merely shut off the supply in that quarter, and quickly reduce it. Or, again, we can increase the potency of the gas, and fairly intoxicate the people, till they stand for anything. Just fancy, now, our pipes connected with the sacred Halls of Congress and with the White House! Even if any difficulty could possibly be expected from these sources, just imagine how quickly we could nip it in the bud!"

"Quickly isn't the word, Wally," answered the Billionaire. "I tell you, old man, the world lies in our hands, today. And we have only to close our fingers, in order to possess it!"

He glanced at his own fingers, as though he visibly perceived the great world lying there for him to squeeze. Waldron's eyes, following the Billionaire's, saw that Flint's hand was trembling, and understood the reason. More than three hours had passed – nay, almost four – since Flint had had any opportunity to take his necessary dose of morphia. Waldron arose, paced to the window and stood there looking out over the vast panorama of city, river and harbor, apparently absorbed in contemplation, but really keen to hear what Flint might do.

His expectations were not disappointed. Hardly had he turned his back, when he heard the desk-drawer open, furtively, and knew the Billionaire was taking out the little vial of white tablets, dearer to him than ever the caress of woman to a Don Juan. A moment later, the drawer closed again.

"He'll do now, for a while," thought Waldron, with satisfaction. "Let him go the limit, if he likes – the fool! The more he takes, the quicker I win. It'll kill him yet, the dope will. And *that* means, my mastery of the world will be complete. Let him go it! The harder, the better!"

He turned back toward Flint, again, veiling in that impenetrable face of his the slightest hint or expression which might have told Flint that he understood the Billionaire's vice. If Flint were Vulture, Waldron was Tiger, indeed. And so, for a brief moment, these two soulless men of gold and power stood eyeing each other, in silence.

Suddenly Waldron spoke.

"There's one thing you've forgotten to speak of, Flint," he said.

"And that is?" demanded the other, already calmed by the quick action of the subtle, enslaving drug.

"The effect on the world's poor – on the toiling millions! The results of this innovation, in slum, and slave-quarter, and in the haunts of poverty. Your talk has all been of the middle and upper classes, and of the benefits accruing to them, from increased oxygen-consumption. But how about the others? Every ounce of oxygen you take out of the air, leaves it just so much poorer. Store thousands of tons of the life-giving gas, in monster tanks, and you vitiate the entire atmosphere. How about that? How can even the well-to-do breathe, then, out-doors, to say nothing of the poverty-stricken millions?"

Flint grimaced, showing a glint of his gold tooth – his substitute for a smile.

"That's all reckoned for," he answered. "I thought I made it quite clear, in our previous talk. To begin with, we will withdraw the oxygen from the atmosphere so slowly that at first there won't be any noticeable effect on the out-door air. For a while, the only thing that will be noticed by the world will be that our gas service, to private residences and institutions, will result in greatly increased comfort and health to the better classes. And the cost will be so low – at first, mind you, only at first – that every family of any means at all can take it. In fact, Wally, we can afford practically to give away the service, for the first year, until we get our grip firmly fixed on the throat of the world. Do you get the idea?"

Waldron nodded, as he drew leisurely on his cigar.

"Practical to a degree," he answered. "That is, until the poor begin to gasp for breath. But what then?"

"By the time the outer atmosphere really begins to show the effect of withdrawing a considerable percentage of the oxygen," Flint answered, "we will have our pocket respirators on the market. Well-to-do people will as soon think of going out without their shoes, as they will with their respirators. No, there won't be any visible tubes or attachments, Wally. Nothing of that kind. Only, each person will carry a properly insulated cake of solidified oxygen that will evaporate through the special apparatus and surround him with a normally rich atmosphere. And—"

"Yes, but the poor? The workers? What of them?"

"Devil take *them*, if it comes to that!" retorted Flint, with some heat. "Who ever gives them any serious attention, as it is? Who bothers about their health? They eat and drink and breathe the leavings, anyhow – eat the cheapest and most adulterated food, drink the vilest slop and breathe the most vitiated slum air. Nobody cares, except perhaps those crazy Socialists that once in a while get up on the street-corner and howl about the rights of man and all that rubbish! Working-class? What do *I* care about the cattle? Let them die, if they want to! D'you suppose, for one minute, I'm going to limit or delay this big innovation, because there's a working-class that may suffer?"

"They'll do more than suffer, Flint, if you seriously depreciate the atmosphere. They'll die!"

"Well, let them, and be damned to them!" retorted Flint, already showing symptoms of drug-stimulation. Waldron, smoking meanwhile, eyed him with a dangerous smile lurking in his cold eyes. "Let them, I say! They die off, now, twice or thrice as fast as the better classes, but what difference does it make? Great breeders, those people are. The more they die, the faster they multiply. Let them go their way and do as they like, so long as they don't interfere with *us!* The only really important factor to reckon on is this, that with an impoverished air to breathe, their rebellious spirit will die out – the dogs! – and we'll have no more talk of social revolution. We'll draw their teeth, all right enough; or rather, twist the bowstring round their damned necks so tight that all their energy, outside of work, will be consumed in just keeping alive. Revolution, then? Forget it, Waldron! We'll kill *that* viper once and for all!"

"Good idea, Flint," the other replied, with approbation. "Only a master-mind like yours could have conceived it. I'm with you, all right enough. Only, tell me – do you really believe we can put this whole program through, without a hitch? Without a leak, anywhere? Without barricades in the streets, wild-eyed agitators howling, machine-guns chattering, and Hell to pay?"

Flint smiled grimly.

"Wait and see!" he growled.

"Maybe you're right," his partner answered. "But slow and easy is the only way."

"Slow and easy," Flint assented. "Of course we can't go too fast. In 1850, for example, do you suppose the public would have tolerated the sudden imposition of monopolies? Hardly! But now they lie down under them, and even vote and fight to keep them! So, too, with this Air Trust. Time will show you I'm right."

Waldron glanced at his watch.

"Long past lunch-time, Flint," said he. "Enough of this, for now. And this afternoon, I've got that D. K. & E. directors' meeting on hand. When shall we go on with our plans, and get down to specific details?"

"This evening, say?"

"Very well. At my house?"

"No. Too noisy. Run out to Englewood, to mine. We'll be quiet there. And come early, Waldron. We've no end of things to discuss. The quicker we get the actual work under way, now, the better. You can see Catherine, too. Isn't that an inducement?"

Thus ended the conference. It resumed, that night, in Flint's luxurious study at "Idle Hour," his superb estate on the Palisades. Waldron paid only a perfunctory court to Catherine, who manifested her pleasure by studied indifference. Both magnates felt relieved when she withdrew. They had other and larger matters under way than any dealing with the amenities of life.

Until past midnight the session in the study lasted, under the soft glow of the Billionaire's reading-light. And many choice cigars were smoked, many sheets of paper covered with diagrams and calculations, many vast schemes of conquest expanded, ere the two masters said good-night and separated.

At the very hour of Waldron's leave-taking, another man was pondering deeply, studying the problem from quite another angle, and – no less earnestly, than the two magnates – laying careful plans.

This man, sturdy, well-built and keen, smoked an old briar as he worked. A flannel shirt, open at the throat, showed a well-sinewed neck and powerful chest. Under the inverted cone of a shaded incandescent in his room, at the electricians' quarters of the Oakwood Heights enclosure, one could see the deep lines of thought and careful study crease his high and prominent brow.

From time to time he gazed out through the open window, off toward the whispering lines of surf on the eastern shores of Staten Island – the surf forever talking, forever striving to give its mystic message to the unheeding ear of man. And as he gazed, his blue eyes narrowed with the intensity of his thought. Once, as though some sudden understanding had come to him, he smote the pine table with a corded fist, and swore below his breath.

It was past two in the morning when he finally rose, stretched, yawned and made ready for sleep on his hard iron bunk.

"Can it be?" he muttered, as he undressed. "Can it be possible, or am I dreaming? No – this is no dream! This is reality; and thank God, I understand."

Then, before he extinguished his light, he took from the table the material he had been studying over, and put it beneath his pillow, where he could guard it safe till morning.

The thing he thus protected was none other than a small note-book, filled with diagrams, jottings and calculations, and bound in red morocco covers.

That night, at Englewood – in the Billionaire's home and in the workman's simple room at Oakwood Heights – history was being made.

The outcome, tragic and terrible, who could have foreseen?

Chapter IX
Discharged

ALMOST ALL the following morning, working at his bench in the electro-chemical laboratories of the great Oakwood Heights plant, Gabriel Armstrong pondered deeply on the problems and responsibilities now opening out before him.

The finding of that little red-leather note-book, he fully understood, had at one stroke put him in possession of facts more vital to the labor-movement and the world at large than any which had ever developed since the very beginning of Capitalism. A Socialist to the backbone, thoroughly class-conscious and dowered with an incisive intellect, Gabriel thrilled at thought that he, by chance, had been chosen as the instrument through which he felt the final revolution now must work. And though he remained outwardly calm, as he bent above his toil, inwardly he was aflame. His heart throbbed with an excitement he could scarce control. His brain seemed on fire; his soul pulsed with savage joy and magnificent inspiration. For he was only four-and-twenty, and the bitter grind of years and toil had not yet worn his spirit down nor quelled the ardor of his splendid strength and optimism.

Working at his routine labor, his mind was not upon it. No, rather it dwelt upon the vast discovery he had made – or seemed to have made – the night before. Clearly limned before his vision, he still saw the notes, the plans, the calculations he had been able to decipher in the Billionaire's lost note-book – the note-book which now, deep in the pocket of his jumper that hung behind him on a hook against the wall, drew his every thought, as steel draws the compass-needle.

"Incredible, yet true!" he pondered, as he filed a brass casting for a new-type dynamo. "These men are plotting to strangle the world to death – to strangle, if they cannot own and rule it! And, what's more, I see nothing to prevent their doing it. The plan is sound. They have the means. At this very moment, the whole human race is standing in the shadow of a peril so great, a slavery so imminent, that the most savage war of conquest ever waged would be a mere skirmish, by comparison!"

Mechanically he labored on and on, turning the tremendous problem in his brain, striving in vain for some solution, some grasp at effective opposition. And, as he thought, a kind of dumb hopelessness settled down about him, tangible almost as a curtain black and heavy.

"What shall I do?" he muttered to himself. "What can I do, to strike these devils from their villainous plan of mastery?"

As yet, he saw nothing clearly. No way seemed open to him. Alone, he knew he could do nothing; yet whither should he turn for help? To rival capitalist groups? They would not even listen to him; or, if they listened and believed, they would only combine with the plotters, or else, on their own hook, try to emulate them. To the labor movement? It would mock him as a chimerical dreamer, despite all his proofs. At best, he might start a few ineffectual strikes, petty and futile, indeed, against this vast, on-moving power. To the Socialists? They, through their press and speakers – in case they should believe him and co-operate with him – could, indeed, give the matter vast publicity and excite popular opposition; but, after all, could they abort the plan? He feared they could not. The time, he knew, was not yet ripe when Labor, on the political field, could meet and overthrow forces such as these.

And so, for all his fevered thinking, he got no radical, no practical solution of the terrible problem. More and more definitely, as he weighed the pros and cons, the belief was borne in upon him that in this case he must appeal to nobody but himself, count on nobody, trust in nobody save Gabriel Armstrong.

"I must play a lone hand game, for a while at least," he concluded, as he finished his casting and took another. "Later, perhaps, I can enlist my comrades. But for now, I must watch, wait, work, all alone. Perhaps, armed with this knowledge – invaluable knowledge shared by no one – I can meet their moves, checkmate their plans and defeat their ends. Perhaps! It will be a battle between one man, obscure and without means, and two men who hold billions of dollars and unlimited resources in their grasp. A battle unequal in every sense; a battle to the death. But I may win, after all. Every probability is that I shall lose, lose everything, even my life. Yet still, there is a chance. By God, I'll take it!"

The last words, uttered aloud, seemed to spring from his lips as though uttered by the very power of invincible determination. A sneer, behind him, brought him round with a start. His gaze widened, at sight of Herzog standing there, cold and dangerous looking, with a venomous expression in those ill-mated eyes of his.

"Take it, will you?" jibed the scientist. "You thief!"

Gabriel sprang up so suddenly that his stool clattered over backward on the red-tiled floor. His big fist clenched and lifted. But Herzog never flinched.

"Thief!" he repeated, with an ugly thrust of the jaw. Servile and crawling to his masters, the man was ever arrogant and harsh with those beneath his authority. "I repeat the word. Drop that fist, Armstrong, if you know what's good for you. I warn you. Any disturbance, here, and – well, you know what we can do!"

The electrician paled, slightly. But it was not through cowardice. Rage, passion unspeakable, a sudden and animal hate of this lick-spittle and supine toady shook him to the heart's core. Yet he managed to control himself, not through any personal apprehension, but because of the great work he knew still lay before him. At all hazards, come what might, he must stay on, there, at the Oakwood Heights plant. Nothing, now, must come between him and that one supreme labor.

Thus he controlled himself, with an effort so tremendous that it wrenched his very soul. This trouble, whatever it might be, must not be noised about. Already, up and down the shop, workers were peering curiously at him. He must be calm; must pass the insult, smooth the situation and remain employed there.

"I – I beg pardon," he managed to articulate, with pale lips that trembled. He wiped the beaded sweat from his broad forehead. "Excuse me, Mr. Herzog. I – you startled me. What's the trouble? Any complaint to make? If so, I'm here to listen."

Herzog's teeth showed in a rat-like grin of malice.

"Yes, you'll listen, all right enough," he sneered. "I've named you, and that goes! You're a thief, Armstrong, and this proves it! Look!"

From behind his back, where he had been holding it, he produced the little morocco-covered book. Right in Armstrong's face he shook it, with an oath.

"Steal, will you?" he jibed. "For it's the same thing – no difference whether you picked it out of Mr. Flint's pocket or found it on the floor here, and tried to keep it! Steal, eh? Hold it for some possible reward? You skunk! Lucky you haven't brains enough to make out what's in it! Thought you'd keep it, did you? But you weren't smart enough, Armstrong – no, not quite smart enough for me! After looking the whole place over, I thought I'd have a go at a few pockets – and, you see? Oh, you'll have to get up early to beat *me* at the game you – you thief!"

With the last word, he raised the book and struck the young man a blistering welt across the face with it.

Armstrong fell back, against the bench, perfectly livid, with the wale of the blow standing out red and distinct across his cheek. Then he went pale as death, and staggered as though about to faint.

"God – God in heaven!" he gasped. "Give me – strength – not to kill this animal!"

A startled look came into Herzog's face. He recognized, at last, the nature of the rage he had awakened. In those twitching fists and that white, writhen face he recognized the signs of passion that might, on a second's notice, leap to murder. And, shot through with panic, he now retreated, like the coward he was, though with the sneer still on his thin and cruel lips.

"Get your time!" he commanded, with crude brutality. "Go, get it at once. You're lucky to get off so easily. If Flint knew this, you'd land behind bars. But we want no scenes here. Get your money from Sanderson, and clear out. Your job ended the minute my hand touched that book in your pocket!"

Still Armstrong made no reply. Still he remained there, dazed and stricken, pallid as milk, a wild and terrible light in his blue eyes.

An ugly murmur rose. Two or three of his fellow-workmen had come drifting down the shop, toward the scene of altercation. Another joined them, and another. Not one of them but hated Herzog with a bitter animosity. And now perhaps, the time was come to pay a score or two.

But Armstrong, suddenly lifting his head, faced them all, his comrades. His mind, quick-acting, had realized that, now his possession of the book had been discovered, his chances of discovering anything more, at the works, had utterly vanished. Even though he should remain, he could do nothing there. If he were to act, it must be from the outside, now, following the trend of events, dogging each development, striving in hidden, devious ways – violent ways, perhaps – to pull down this horrible edifice of enslavement ere it should whelm and crush the world.

So, acting as quickly as he had thought, and now ignoring the man Herzog as though he had never existed, Armstrong faced his fellows.

"It's all right, boys," said he, quite slowly, his voice seeming to come from a distance, his tones forced and unnatural. "It's all right, every way. I'm caught with the goods. Don't any of you butt in. Don't mix with my trouble. For once I'm glad this is a scab shop, otherwise there might be a strike, here, and worse Hell to pay than there will be otherwise. I'm done. I'll get my time, and quit. But – remember one thing, you'll understand some day what this is all about.

"I'm glad to have worked with you fellows, the past few months. You're all right, every one of you. Good-bye, and remember—"

"Here, you men, get back to work!" cried Herzog, suddenly. "No hand-shaking here, and no speech-making. This man's a sneak-thief and he's fired, that's all there is to it. Now, get onto your job! The first man that puts up a complaint about it, can get through, too!"

For a moment they glowered at him, there in the white-lighted glare of the big shop. A fight, even then, was perilously near, but Armstrong averted it by turning away.

"I'm done." he repeated. He gathered up a few tools that belonged to him, personally, gave one look at his comrades, waved a hand at them, and then, followed by Herzog, strode off down the long aisle, toward the door.

"Herzog," said he, calmly and with cold emphasis, "listen to this."

"Get out! Get your time, I tell you, and go!" repeated the bully. "To Hell with you! Clear out of here!"

"I'm going," the young man answered. "But before I do, remember this; you grazed death, just now. Well for you, Herzog, almighty well for you, my temper didn't best me. For remember, you struck me and called me 'thief' – and that sort of thing can't be forgotten, ever, even though we live a thousand years.

"Remember, Herzog – not now, but sometime. Remember that one word – sometime! That's all!"

With no further speech, and while Herzog still stood there by the shop door, sneering at him, Armstrong turned and passed out. A few minutes later he had been paid off, had packed his knapsack with his few belongings, and was outside the big palisade, striding along the hard and glaring road toward the station.

"I did it," his one overmastering thought was. "Thank heaven, I did it! I held my temper and my tongue, didn't kill that spawn of Hell, and saved the whole situation. I'm out of a job, true enough, and out of the plant; but after all, I'm free – and I know what's in the wind!

"There's yet hope. There'll be a way, a way to do this work! What a man *must* do, he *can* do!"

Up came Armstrong's chin, as he walked. His shoulders squared, with strength and purpose, and his stride swung into the easy machine gait that had already carried him so many thousand miles along the hard and bitter highways of the world.

As he strode away, on the long road toward he knew not what, words seemed to form and shape in his strengthened and refortified mind – words for long years forgotten – words that he once had heard at his mother's knee:

"He that ruleth his spirit is better than he that taketh a city!"

Chapter X
A Glimpse at the Parasites

The Longmeadow Country Club, on the Saturday afternoon following Armstrong's abrupt dismissal, was a scene of gaiety and beauty without compare. Set in broad acres of wood and lawn, the club-house proudly dominated far-flung golf-links and nearer tennis-courts. Shining motors stood parked on the plaza before the club garage, each valued at several years' wages of a workingman. Men and women – exploiters all, or parasites – elegantly and coolly clad in white, smote the swift sphere upon the tennis-court, with jest and laughter. Others, attended by caddies – mere proletarian scum, bent beneath the weight of cleeks and brassies – moved across the smooth-cropped links, kept in condition by grazing sheep and by steam-rollers. On putting-green and around bunkers these idlers struggled with artificial difficulties, while in shops and mines and factories, on railways and in the blazing Hells of stoke-holes, men of another class, a slave-class, labored and agonized, toiled and died that *these* might wear fine linen and spend the long June afternoon in play.

From the huge, cobble-stone chimney of the Country Club, upwafting smoke told of the viands now preparing for the idlers' dinner, after sport – rich meats and dainties of the rarest. In the rathskeller some of the elder and more indolent men were absorbing alcohol while music played and painted nymphs of abundant charms looked down from the wall-frescoes. Out on the broad piazzas, well sheltered by awnings from the rather ardent sun, men and women sat at spotless tables, dallying with drinks of rare hues and exalted prices. Cigarette-smoke wafted away on the pure breeze from over the Catskills, far to northwest, defiling the sweet breath of Nature, herself, with fumes of nicotine and dope. A Hungarian orchestra was playing the latest Manhattan ragtime, at the far end of the piazza. It was, all in all, a scene of rare refinement, characteristic to a degree of the efflorescence of American capitalism.

At one of the tables, obviously bored, sat Catherine Flint, only daughter of the Billionaire. A rare girl, she, to look upon – deep-bosomed and erect, dressed simply in a middy-blouse with a blue tie, a khaki skirt and low, rubber-soled shoes revealing a silk-stockinged ankle that would have attracted the enthusiastic attention of gentlemen in any city of the world. No hat disfigured the coiled and braided masses of coppery hair that circled her shapely head. A healthy tan on face and arms and open throat bespoke her keen devotion to all outdoor life. Her fingers, lithe and strong, were graced by but two rings – a monogram, of gold, and the betrothal ring that Maxim Waldron had put there, only three weeks before.

Impatience dominated her. One could see that, in the nervous tapping of her fingers on the cloth; the slight swing of her right foot as she sat there, one knee crossed over the other; the glance of her keen, gray eyes down the broad drive-way that led from the huge stone gates up to the club-house.

Beside her sat a nonentity in impeccable dress, dangling a monocle and trying to make small-talk, the while he dallied with a Bronx cocktail, costing more than a day's wage for a childish flower-making slave of the tenements, and inhaled a Rotten Row cigarette, the "last word" from London in the tobacco line. To the sallies of this elegant, the girl replied by only monosyllables. Her glass was empty, nor would she have it filled, despite the exquisite's entreaties. From time to time she glanced impatiently at the long bag of golf-sticks leaning against the porch rail; and, now and then, her eyes sought the little Cervine watch set in a leather wristlet on her arm.

"Inconsiderate of him, I'm sure – ah – to keep so magnificent a Diana waiting," drawled her companion, blowing a lungful of thin blue smoke athwart the breeze. "Especially when you're so deuced keen on doing the course before dinner. Now if *I* were the favored swain, wild horses wouldn't keep me away."

She made no answer, but turned a look of indifference on the shrimp beside her. Had he possessed the soul of a real man, he would have shriveled; but, being oblivious to all things save the pride of wealth and monstrous self-conceit, he merely snickered and reached for his cocktail – which, by the way, he was absorbing through a straw.

"I say, Miss Flint?" he presently began again, stirring the ice in the cocktail.

"Well?" she answered, curtly.

"If you – er – are really very, *very* impatient to have a go at the links, why wait for Wally? I – I should be only too glad to volunteer my services as your knight-errant, and all that sort of thing."

"Thanks, awfully," she answered, "but Mr. Waldron promised to go round the course with me, this afternoon, and I'll wait."

The impeccable one grinned fatuously, invited her again to have a drink – which she declined – and ordered another for himself, with profuse apologies for drinking alone; apologies which she hardly seemed to notice.

"Deuced bad form of Wally, I must say," the gilded youth resumed, trying to make capital for himself, "to leave you in the lurch, this way!"

Silence from Catherine. The would-be interloper, feeling that he was on the wrong track, took counsel with himself and remained for a moment immersed in what he imagined to be thought. At last, however, with an oblique glance at his indifferent companion, he remarked.

"Devilish hard time women have in this world, you know! Don't you sometimes wish you were a man?"

Her answer flashed back like a rapier:

"No! Do you wish *you* were?"

Stunned by this "facer," Reginald Van Slyke gasped and stared. That he, a scion of the Philadelphia Van Slykes, in his own right worth two hundred million dollars – dollars ground out of the Kensington carpet-mill slaves by his grandfather – should be thus flouted and put upon by the daughter of Flint, that parvenu, absolutely floored him. For a moment he sat there speechless, unable even to reach for his drink; but presently some coherence returned. He was about to utter what he conceived to be a strong rejoinder, when the girl suddenly standing up, turned her back upon him and ignored him as completely as she might have ignored any of the menials of the club.

His irritated glance followed hers. There, far down the drive, just rounding the long turn by the artificial lake, a big blue motor car was speeding up the grade at a good clip. Van Slyke recognized it, and swore below his breath.

"Wally, at last, damn him!" he muttered. "Just when I was beginning to make headway with Kate!"

Vexed beyond endurance, he drummed on the cloth with angry fingers; but Catherine was oblivious. Unmindful of the merry-makers at the other tables, the girl waved her handkerchief at the swiftly-approaching motor. Waldron, from the back seat, raised an answering hand – though without enthusiasm. Above all things he hated demonstration, and the girl's frank manner, free, unconventional and not yet broken to the harness of Mrs. Grundy, never failed to irritate him.

"Very incorrect for people in our set," he often thought. "But for the present I can do nothing. Once she is my wife, ah, then I shall find means to curb her. For the present, however, I must let her have her head."

Such was now his frame of mind as the long car slid under the porte-cochère and came to a stand. He would have infinitely preferred that the girl should wait his coming to her, on the piazza; but already she had slung her bag of sticks over her strong shoulder, and was down the steps to meet him. Her leave-taking of the incensed Van Slyke had been the merest nod.

"You're late, Wally," said she, smiling with her usual good humor, which had already quite dissipated her impatience. "Late, but I'll forgive you, this time. I'm afraid we won't have time to do all eighteen holes round. What kept you?"

"Business, business!" he answered, frowning. "Always the same old grind, Kate. You women don't understand. I tell you, this slaving in Wall Street isn't what it's cracked up to be. I couldn't get away till 11:30. Then, just had a quick bite of lunch, and broke every speed law in New York getting here. Do you forgive me?"

He had descended from the car, in speaking. They shook hands, while the chauffeur stood at attention and all the gossips on the piazza, scenting the possibility of a disagreement, craned discreetly eager necks and listened intently.

"Forgive you? Of course – this time, but never again," the girl laughed. "Now, run along and get into your flannels. I'll meet you on the driving green, in ten minutes. Not another second, mind, or—"

"I'll be on the dot," he answered. "Here, boy," beckoning a caddy, "take Miss Flint's sticks. And have mine carried to the green. Look sharp, now!"

Then, with a nod at the girl, he ran up the steps and vanished in the club-house, bound for the locker-room.

Fifteen minutes the girl waited on the green, watching others drive off from the little tees and inwardly chafing to be in action. Fifteen, and then twenty, before Waldron finally appeared, immaculate in white, bare-armed and with a loose, checked cap shading his close-set eyes. The fact was, in addition to having changed his clothes, he had felt obliged to linger in the bar for a little Scotch; and one drink had meant another; and thus precious moments had sped.

But his smile was confident as he approached the green. Women, after all, he reflected, were meant to be kept waiting. They never appreciated a man who kept appointments exactly. Not less fatuous at heart, in truth, was he, than the unfortunate Van Slyke. But his manner was perfection as he saluted her and bade the caddy build their tees.

The girl, however, was now plainly vexed. Her mouth had drawn a trifle tight and the tilt of her chin was determined. Her eyes were far from soft, as she surveyed this delinquent fiancé.

"I don't like you a bit, today, Wally," said she, as he deliberated over the club-bag, choosing a driver. "This makes twice you've kept me waiting. I warn you don't let it happen again!"

Under the seeming banter of her tone lurked real resentment. But he, with a smile – partly due to a finger too much Scotch – only answered, in a low tone:

"You're adorable, today, Kate! The combination of fresh air and annoyance has painted the most wonderful roses on your cheeks!"

She shrugged her shoulders with a little motion she had inherited from French ancestry, stooped, set her golf ball on the little mound of sand, exactly to suit her, and raised her driver on high.

"Nine holes," said she, "and I'm going to beat you, today!"

He frowned a little at the spirit of the threat, for any self-assertion in a woman crossed his grain; but soon forgot his pique in admiration of the drive.

Swishing, her club flashed down in a quick circle. *Crack!* It struck the gutta-percha squarely. The little white sphere zipped away like a rocket, rose in a far trajectory, up, up, toward the water-hazard at the foot of the grassy slope, then down in a long curve.

Even while the girl's cry of "Fore!" was echoing across the green, the ball struck earth, ricochetted and sped on, away, across the turf, till it came to rest not twenty yards from the putting green of the first hole.

"Wheeoo!" whistled Waldron. "Some drive. I guess you're going to make good your threat, today, Kate of my heart!"

The smile she flashed at him showed that her resentment had, for the moment, been forgotten.

"Come on, Wally, now let's see what *you* can do," said she, starting off down the slope, while her meek caddy tagged at a respectful distance.

Waldron, thus adjured, teed up and swung at the ball. But the Scotch had by no means steadied his aim. He foozled badly and broke his pet driver, into the bargain. The steel head of it flew farther even than the ball, which moved hardly ten yards.

"Damn!" he muttered, under his breath, choosing another stick and glancing with real irritation at Catherine's lithe, splendidly poised figure already some distance down the slope.

His second stroke was more successful, nearly equalling hers. But her advantage, thus early won, was not destined to be lost again. And as the game proceeded, Waldron's temper grew steadily worse and worse.

Thus began, for these two people, an hour destined to be fraught with such pregnant developments – an hour which, in its own way, vitally bore on the great loom now weaving warp and woof of world events.

Chapter XI
The End of Two Games

TRIVIAL EVENTS SOMETIMES precipitate catastrophies. It has been said that had James MacDonald not left the farm gate open, at Hugomont, Waterloo might have ended otherwise. So now, the rupture between Catherine Flint and Maxim Waldron was precipitated by a single unguarded oath.

It was at the ninth hole, down back of the Terrace Woods bunker. Waldron, heated by exercise and the whiskey he had drunk, had already dismissed the caddies and had undertaken to carry the clubs, himself, hoping – man-fashion – to steal a kiss or two from Catherine, along the edge of the close-growing oaks and maples. But all his plans went agley, for Catherine really made good and beat him, there, by half a dozen strokes; and as her little sphere, deftly driven by the putting-iron gripped in her brown, firm hands, rolled precisely over the cropped turf and fell into the tinned hole, the man ejaculated a perfectly audible "*Hell!*"

She stood erect and faced him, with a singular expression in those level gray eyes – eyes the look of which could allure or wither, could entice or command.

"Wally," said she, "did you swear?"

"I – er – why, yes," he stammered, taken aback and realizing, despite his chagrin, how very poor and unsportsmanlike a figure he was cutting.

"I don't like it," she returned. "Not a little bit, Wally. It isn't game, and it isn't manly. You must respect me, now and always. I can't have profanity, and I won't."

He essayed lame apologies, but a sudden, hot anger seemed to have possessed him, in presence of this free, independent, exacting woman – this woman who, worst of all, had just beaten him at the game of all games he prided himself on playing well. And despite his every effort, she saw through the veil of sheer, perfunctory courtesy; and seeing, flushed with indignation.

"Wally," she said in a low, quiet tone, fixing a singular gaze upon him, "Wally, I don't know what to make of you lately. The other night at Idle Hour, you hardly looked at me. You and father spent the whole evening discussing some business or other—"

"Most important business, my dear girl, I do assure you," protested Waldron, trying to steady his voice. "Most vitally—"

"No matter about that," she interposed. "It could have been abridged, a trifle. I barely got six words out of you, that evening; and let me tell you, Wally, a woman never forgets neglect. She may forgive it; but forget it, never!"

"Oh, well, if you put it that way—" he began, but checked himself in time to suppress the cutting rejoinder he had at his tongue's end.

"I do, and it's vital, Wally," she answered. "It's all part and parcel of some singular kind of change that's been coming over you, lately, like a blight. You haven't been yourself, at all, these few days past. Something or other, I don't know what, has been coming between us. You've got something else on your mind, beside me – something bigger and more important to you than I am – and – and—"

He pulled out his gold cigar-case, chose and lighted a cigar to steady his nerve, and faced her with a smile – the worst tactic he could possibly have chosen in dealing with this woman. Supremely successful in handling men, he lacked finesse and insight with the other sex; and now that lack, in his moment of need, was bringing him moment by moment nearer the edge of catastrophe.

"I don't like it at all, Waldron," she resumed, again. "You were late, the other night, in taking me to the Flower Show. You were late, today, for our appointment here; and the ten minutes I gave you to get ready in, stretched out to twenty before you—"

He interrupted her with a gesture of uncontrollable vexation.

"Really, my dear Kate," he exclaimed, "if you – er – insist on holding me to account for every moment—"

"You've been drinking, too, a little," she kept on. "And you know I detest it! And just now, when I beat you in a square game, you so far forgot yourself as to swear. Now, Waldron—"

"Oh, puritanical, eh?" he sneered, ignoring the danger signals in her eyes. Even yet there might have been some chance of avoiding shipwreck, had he heeded those twin beacons, humbled himself, made amends by due apology and promised reformation. For though Catherine never had truly loved this man, some years older than herself and of radically different character, still she liked and respected him, and found him – by his very force and dominance – far more to her taste than the insipid hangers-on, sons of fortune or fortune-hunters, who, like the sap-brained Van Slyke, made up so great a part of her "set."

So, all might yet have been amended; but this was not to be. Never yet had "Tiger" Waldron bowed the neck to living man or woman. Dominance was his whole scheme of life. Though he might purr, politely enough, so long as his fur was smoothed the right way, a single backward stroke set his fangs gleaming and unsheathed every sabre-like claw. And now this woman, his fiancée though she was, her beauty dear to him and her charm most fascinating, her fortune much desired and most of all, an alliance with her father – now this woman, despite all these considerations, had with a few incisive words ruffled his temper beyond endurance.

So great was his agitation that, despite his strongest instinct of saving, he flung away the scarcely-tasted cigar.

"Kate," he exclaimed, his very tongue thick with the rage he could not quell, "Kate, I can't stand this! You're going too far. What do you know of men's work and men's affairs? Who are you, to judge of their times of coming and going, their obligations, their habits and man of life? What do *you* understand—?"

"It's obvious," she replied with glacial coldness, "that I don't understand *you*, and never have. I have been living in a dream, Wally; seeing you through the glass of illusion; not reality. After all, you're like all men – just the same, no different. Idealism, self-sacrifice, con true nobility of character, where are these, in you? What is there but the same old selfishness, the same innate masculine conceit and—"

"No more of this, Kate!" cried the financier, paling a little. "No more! I can't have it! I won't – it's impossible! You – you don't understand, I tell you. In your narrow, untrained, woman's way, you try to set up standards for me; try to judge me, and dictate to me. Some old puritanical streak in you is cropping out, some blue-law atavism, some I know not what, that rebels against my taking a drink – like every other man. That cries out against my letting slip a harmless oath – again, like every other man that lives and breathes. Every man, that is, who *is* a man, a real man, not a dummy! If you've been mistaken in me, how much more have I, in you! And so—"

"And so," she took the very words from his pale lips, "we've both been mistaken, that's all. No, no," she forbade him with raised hand, as he would have interrupted with protests. "No, you needn't try to convince me otherwise, now. A thousand volumes of speeches, after this, couldn't do it. An hour's insight into the true depths of a man's character – yes, even a moment's – perfectly suffices to show the truth. You've just drawn the veil aside, Wally, for me, and let me look at the true picture. All that I've known and thought of you, so far, has been sham and illusion. Now, I *know* you!"

"You – you don't, Catherine!" he exclaimed, half in anger, half contrition, terrified at last by the imminent break between them, by the thought of losing this rich flower from the garden of womanhood, this splendid financial and social prize. "I – I've done wrong, Kate. I admit it. But, truly—"

"No more," said she, and in her voice sounded a command he knew, at last, was quite inexorable. "I'm not like other women of our set, perhaps. I can't be bought and sold, Wally, with money and position. I can't marry a man, and have to live with him, if he shows himself petty, or small, or narrow in any way. I must be free, free as air, as long as I live. Even in marriage, I must be free. Freedom can only come with the union of two souls that understand and help and inspire each other. Anything else is slavery – and worse!"

She shuddered, and for a moment turned half away from him, as, now contrite enough for the minute, he stood there looking at her with dazed eyes. For a second the idea came to him that he must take her in his arms, there in the edge of the woods, burn kisses on her ripe mouth, win her back to him by force, as he had won all life's battles. He would not, could not, let this prize escape him now. A wave of desire surged through his being. He took a step toward her, his trembling arms open to seize her lithe, seductive body. But she, retreating, held him away with repellant palms.

"No, no, no!" she cried. "Not now – never that, any more! I must be free, Wally – free as air!"

She raised her face toward the vast reaches of the sky, breathed deep and for a moment closed her eyes, as though bathing her very soul in the sweet freedom of the out-of-doors.

"Free as air!" she whispered. "Let me go!"

He started violently. Her simile had struck him like a lash.

"Free – as what?" he exclaimed hoarsely. "As *air?* But – but there's no such freedom, I tell you! Air isn't free any more – or won't be, soon! It will be everything, anything but free, before another year is gone! Free as air? You – you don't understand! Your father and I – we shall soon own the air. Free as air? Yes, if you like! For that – that means you, too, must belong to me!"

Again he sought to take her, to hold her and overmaster her. But she, now wide-eyed with a kind of sudden terror at this latest outbreak, this seeming madness on his part, which she could nowise fathom or comprehend, retreated ever more and more, away from him.

Then suddenly with a quick effort, she stripped off the splendid, blazing diamond from her finger, and held it out to him.

"Wally," said she, calm now and quite herself again, "Wally, let's be friends. Just that and nothing more. Dear, good, companionable friends, as we used to be, long years ago, before this madness seized us – this chimera of – of love!"

As a bull charging, is struck to the heart by the sword of the matador, and stops in his tracks, motionless and dazed before he falls, so "Tiger" Waldron stopped, wholly stunned by this abrupt and crushing denouement.

For a moment, man and woman faced each other. Not a word was spoken. Catherine had no word to say; and Waldron, though his lips worked, could bring none to utterance. Then their eyes met; and his lowered.

"Good-bye," said she quietly. "Good-bye forever, as my betrothed. When we meet again, Wally, it will be as friends, and nothing more. And now, let me go. Don't come with me. I prefer to be alone. I'd rather walk, a bit, and think – and then go back quietly to the club-house, and so home, in my car. Don't follow me. Here – take this, and – good-bye."

Mechanically he accepted the gleaming jewel. Mechanically, like a man without sense or reason, he watched her walk away from him, upright and strong and lithe, voluptuous and desirable in every motion of that splendid body, now lost to him forever. Then all at once, entering a woodland path that led by a short cut back to the club-house, she vanished from his sight.

Vanished, without having even so much as turned to look at him again, or wave that firm brown hand.

Then, seeming to waken from his daze, "Tiger" laughed, a terrible and cruel laugh; and then he flung a frightful blasphemy upon the still June air; and then he dashed the wondrous diamond to earth, and stamped and dug it with a perfect frenzy of rage into the soft mold.

And, last of all, with lowered head and lips that moved in fearful curses, he crashed away into the woods, away from the path where the girl was, away from the club-house, away, away, thirsting for solitude and time to quell his passion, salve his wounded pride and ponder measures of terrible revenge.

The diamond ring, crushed into the earth, and the golf clubs, lying where they had fallen from the disputants' hands, now remained there as melancholy reminders of the double game – love and golf – which had so suddenly ended in disaster.

Chapter XII
On the Great Highway

AS VIOLENTLY rent from his job as Maxim Waldron had been torn from his alliance with Catherine, Gabriel Armstrong met the sudden change in his affairs with far more equanimity than the financier could muster. Once the young electrician's first anger had subsided – and he had pretty well mastered it before he had reached the Oakwood Heights station – he began philosophically to turn the situation in his mind, and to rough out his plans for the future.

"Things might be worse, all round," he reflected, as he strode along at a smart pace. "During the seven months I've been working for these pirates, I've managed to pay off the debt I got into at the time of the big E. W. strike, and I've got eighteen dollars or a little more in my pocket. My clothes will do a while longer. Even though Flint blacklists me all over the country, as he probably will, I can duck into some job or other, somewhere. And most important of all, I know what's due to happen in America – I've seen that note-book! Let them do what they will, they can't take *that* knowledge away from me!"

The outlook, on the whole, was cheering. Gabriel broke into a whistle, as he swung along the highway, and slashed cheerfully with his heavy stick at the dusty bushes by the roadside. A vigorous, pleasing figure of a man he made, striding onward in his blue flannel shirt and corduroys, stout boots making light of distance, somewhat rebellious black hair clustering under his cap, blue eyes clear and steady as the sunlight itself. There must have been a drop of Irish blood somewhere or other in his veins, to have given him that ruddy cheek, those eyes, that hair, that quick enthusiasm and that swiftness to anger – then, by reaction, that quick buoyancy which so soon banished everything but courageous optimism from his hot heart.

Thus the man walked, all his few worldly belongings – most precious among them his union card and his red Socialist card – packed in the knapsack strapped to his broad shoulders. And as he walked, he formulated his plans.

"Niagara for mine," he decided. "It's there these hellions mean to start their devilish work of enslaving the whole world. It's there I want to be, and must be, to follow the infernal job from the beginning and to nail it, when the right time comes. I'll put in a day or two with my old friend, Sam Underwood, up in the Bronx, and maybe tell him what's doing and frame out the line of action with him. But after that, I strike for Niagara – yes, and on foot!"

This decision came to him as strongly desirable. Not for some time, he knew, could the actual work of building the Air Trust plant be started at Niagara. Meanwhile, he wanted to keep out of sight, as much as possible. He wanted, also to save every cent. Again, his usual mode of travel had always been either to ride the rods or "hike" it on shanks' mare. Bitterly opposed to swelling the railways' revenues by even a penny, Armstrong in the past few years of his life had done some thousands of miles, afoot, all over the country. His best means of Socialist propaganda, he had found, was in just such meanderings along the highways and hedges of existence – a casual job, here or there, for a day, a week, a month – then, quick friendships; a little talk; a few leaflets handed to the intelligent, if he could find any. He had laced the continent with such peregrinations, always sowing the seed of revolution wherever he had passed; getting in touch with the Movement all over the republic; keeping his finger on the pulse of ever-growing, always-strengthening Socialism.

Such had his habits long been. And now, once more adrift and jobless, but with the most tremendous secret of the ages in his possession, he naturally turned to the comfort and the calming influence of the broad highway, in his long journey towards the place where he was to meet, in desperate opposition, the machinations of the Air Trust magnates.

"It's the only way for me," he decided, as he turned into the road leading toward Saint George and the Manhattan Ferry. "Flint and Herzog will be sure to put Slade and the Cosmos people after me. Blacklisting will be the least of what they'll try to do. They'll use slugging tactics, sure, if they get a chance, or railroad me to some Pen or other, if possible. My one best bet is to keep out of their way; and I figure I'm ten times safer on the open road, with a few dollars to stave off a vagrancy charge, and with two good fists and this stick to keep 'em at a distance, than I would be on the railroads or in cheap dumps along the way.

"The last place they'll ever think of looking for me will be the big outdoors. *Their* idea of hunting for a workman is to dragnet the back rooms of saloons – especially if they're after a Socialist. That's the limit of their intelligence, to connect Socialism and beer. I'll beat 'em; I'll hike – and it's a hundred to one I land in Niagara with more cash than when I started, with better health, more knowledge, and the freedom that, alone, can save the world now from the most damnable slavery that ever threatened its existence!"

Thus reasoning, with perfect clarity and a long-headedness that proved him a strategist at four-and-twenty, Gabriel Armstrong whistled a louder note as he tramped away to northward, away from the hateful presence of Herzog, away from the wage-slavery of the Oakwood Heights plant, away – with that precious secret in his brain – toward the far scene of destined warfare, where stranger things were to ensue than even he could possibly conceive.

Saturday morning found him, his visit with Underwood at an end, already twenty miles or more from the Bronx River, marching along through Haverstraw, up the magnificent road that fringes the Hudson – now hidden from the mighty river behind a forest-screen, now curving on bold abutments right above the sun-kissed expanses of Haverstraw Bay, here more than two miles from wooded shore to shore.

At eleven, he halted at a farm house, some miles north of the town, got a job on the woodpile, and astonished the farmer by the amount of birch he could saw in an hour. He took his pay in the shape of a bountiful dinner, and – after half an hour's smoke and talk with the farmer, to whom he gave a few pamphlets from the store in his knapsack – said good-bye to all hands and once more set his face northward for the long hike through much wilder country, to West Point, where he hoped to pass the night.

Thus we must leave him, for a while. For now the thread of our narration, like the silken cord in the Labyrinth of Crete, leads us back to the Country Club at Longmeadow, the scene, that very afternoon, of the sudden and violent rupture between the financier and Catherine Flint.

Catherine, her first indignation somewhat abated, and now vastly relieved at the realization that she indeed was free from her loveless and long-since irksome alliance with Waldron, calmly enough returned to the club-house. Head well up, and eyes defiant, she walked up the broad steps and into the office. Little cared she whether the piazza gossips – The Hammer and Anvil Club, in local slang – divined the quarrel or not. The girl felt herself immeasurably indifferent to such pettinesses as prying small talk and innuendo. Let people know, or not, as might be, she cared not a whit. Her business was her own. No wagging of tongues could one hair's breadth disturb that splendid calm of hers.

The clerk, behind the desk, smiled and nodded at her approach.

"Please have my car brought round to the porte-cochère, at once?" she asked. "And tell Herrick to be sure there's plenty of gas for a long run. I'm going through to New York."

"So soon?" queried the clerk. "I'm sure your father will be disappointed, Miss Flint. He's just wired that he's coming out tomorrow, to spend Sunday here. He particularly asks to have you remain. See here?"

He handed her a telegram. She glanced it over, then crumpled it and tossed it into the office fire-place.

"I'm sorry," she answered. "But I can't stay. I must get back, to-night. I'll telegraph father not to come. A blank, please?"

The clerk handed her one. She pondered a second, then wrote:

> *Dear Father: A change of plans makes me return home at once. Please wait and see me there. I've something important to talk over with you.*
> *Affectionately,*
> *Kate.*

Ordinarily people try to squeeze their message to ten words, and count and prune and count again; but not so, Catherine. For her, a telegram had never contained any space limit. It meant less to her than a post-card to you or me. Not that the girl was consciously extravagant. No, had you asked her, she would have claimed rigid economy – she rarely, for instance, paid more than a hundred dollars for a morning gown, or more than a thousand for a ball-dress. It was simply that the idea of counting words had never yet occurred to her. And so now, she complacently handed this verbose message to the clerk, who – thoroughly well-trained – understood it was to be charged on her father's perfectly staggering monthly bill.

"Very well, Miss Flint," said he. "I'll send this at once. And your car will be ready for you in ten minutes – or five, if you like?"

"Ten will do, thank you," she answered. Then she crossed to the elevator and went up to her own suite of rooms on the second floor, for her motor-coat and veils.

"Free, thank heaven!" she breathed, with infinite relief, as she stood before the tall mirror, adjusting these for the long trip. "Free from that man forever. What a narrow escape! If things hadn't happened just as they did, and if I hadn't had that precious insight into Wally's character – good Lord! – catastrophe! Oh, I haven't been so happy since I – since – why, I've *never* been so happy in all my life!

"Wally, dear boy," she added, turning toward the window as though apostrophizing him in reality, "now we can be good friends. Now all the sham and pretense are at an end, forever. As a friend, you may be splendid. As a husband – oh, impossible!"

Lighter of heart than she had been for years, was she, with the added zest of the long spin through the beauty of the June country before her – down among the hills and cliffs, among the forests and broad valleys – down to New York again, back to the father and the home she loved better than all else in the world.

In this happy frame of mind she presently entered the low-hung, swift-motored car, settled herself on the luxurious cushions and said "Home, at once!" to Herrick.

He nodded, but did not speak. He felt, in truth, somewhat incapable of quite incoherent speech. Not having expected any service till next day, he had foregathered with others of his ilk in the servants' bar, below-stairs, and had with wassail and good cheer very effectively put himself out of commission.

But, somewhat sobered by this quick summons, he had managed to pull together. Now, drunk though he was, he sat there at the wheel, steady enough – so long as he held on to it – and only by the redness of his face and a certain glassy look in his eye, betrayed the fact of his intoxication. The girl, busy with her farewells as the car drew up for her, had not observed him. At the last moment Van Slyke waved a foppish hand at her, and smirked adieux. She acknowledged his good-bye with a smile, so happy was she at the outcome of her golf-game; then cast a quick glance up at the club windows, fearing to see the harsh face of Wally peeping down at her in anger.

But he was nowhere to be seen; and now, with a sudden acceleration of the powerful six-cylinder engine, the big gray car moved smoothly forward. Growling in its might, it swung in a wide circle round the sweep of the drive, gathered speed and shot away down the grade toward the stone gates of the entrance, a quarter mile distant.

Presently it swerved through these, to southward. Club-house, waving handkerchiefs and all vanished from Kate's view.

"Faster, Herrick," she commanded, leaning forward, "I must be home by half past five."

Again he nodded, and notched spark and throttle down. The car, leaping like a wild creature, began to hum at a swift clip along the smooth, white road toward Newburgh on the Hudson.

Thirty miles an hour the speedometer showed, then thirty-five and forty. Again the drunken chauffeur, still master of his machine despite the poison pulsing in his dazed brain, snicked the little levers further down. Forty-five, fifty, fifty-five, the figures on the dial showed.

Now the exhaust ripped in a crackling staccato, like a machine gun, as the chauffeur threw out the muffler. Behind, a long trail of dust rose, whirling in the air. Catherine, a sportswoman born, leaned back and smiled with keen pleasure, while her yellow veil, whipping sharply on the wind, let stray locks of that wonderful red-gold hair stream about her flushed face.

Thus she sped homeward, driven at a mad race by a man whose every sense was numbed and stultified by alcohol – homeward, along a road up which, far, far away, another man, keen, sober and alert, was trudging with a knapsack on his broad back, swinging a stick and whistling cheerily as he went.

Fate, that strange moulder of human destinies, what had it in store for these two, this woman and this man? This daughter of a billionaire, and this young proletarian?

Who could foresee, or, foreseeing, could believe what even now stood written on the Book of Destiny?

Chapter XIII
Catastrophe!

FOR A TIME no danger seemed to threaten. Kate was not only fearless as a passenger, but equally intrepid at the wheel. Many a time and oft she had driven her father's highest-powered car at dizzying speeds along worse roads than the one her machine was now following. Velocity was to her a kind of stimulant, wonderfully pleasurable; and now, realizing nothing of the truth that Herrick was badly the worse for liquor, she leaned back in the tonneau, breathed the keen slashing air with delight, and let her eyes wander over the swiftly-changing panorama of forest, valley, lake and hill that, in ever new and more radiant beauty, sped away, away, as the huge car leaped down the smooth and rushing road.

Dust and pebbles flew in the wake of the machine, as it gathered velocity. Beneath it, the highway sped like an endless white ribbon, whirling back and away with smooth rapidity. No common road, this, but one which the State authorities had very obligingly built especially for the use of millionaires' motor cars, all through the region of country-clubs, parks, bungalows and summer-resorts dotting the west shore region of the Hudson. Let the farmer truck his produce through mud and ruts, if he would. Let the country folk drive their ramshackle buggies over rocks and stumps, if they so chose. Nothing of that sort for millionaires! No, *they* must have macadam and smooth, long curves, easy grades and – where the road swung high above the gleaming river – retaining walls to guard them from plunging into the palisaded abyss below.

At just such a place it was, where the road made a sharper turn than any the drunken chauffeur had reckoned on, that catastrophe leaped out to shatter the rushing car.

Only a minute before, Kate – a little uneasy now, at the truly reckless speeding of the driver, and at the daredevil way in which he was taking curves without either sounding his siren or reducing speed – had touched him on the shoulder, with a command: "Not *quite* so fast, Herrick! Be careful!"

His only answer had been a drunken laugh.

"Careful nothing!" he slobbered, to himself. "You wanted speed – an' now – hc! – b'Jesus, you *get* – hc! – speed! *I* ain't 'fraid – are – hc! – *you?*"

She had not heard the words, but had divined their meaning.

"Herrick!" she commanded sharply, leaning forward. "What's the matter with you? Obey me, do you hear? Not so fast!"

A whiff of alcoholic breath suddenly told her the truth. For a second she sat there, as though petrified, with fear now for the first time clutching at her heart.

"Stop at once!" she cried, gripping the man by the collar of his livery. "You – you're drunk, Herrick! I – I'll have you discharged, at once, when we get home. Stop, do you hear me? You're not fit to drive. I'll take the wheel myself!"

But Herrick, hopelessly under the influence of the poison, which had now produced its full effect, paid no heed.

"Y' – can't dri' *thish* car!" he muttered, in maudlin accents. "Too big – too heavy for – hc! – woman! I – *I* dri' it all right, drunk or sober! Good chauffeur – good car – I know thish car! You won't fire me – hc! – for takin' drink or two, huh? I drive you all ri' – drive you to New York or to – hc! – Hell! Same thing, no difference, ha! ha! – I—"

A sudden blaze of rage crimsoned the girl's face. In all her life she never had been thus spoken to. For a second she clenched her fist, as though to strike down this sodden brute there in the seat before her – a feat she would have been quite capable of. But second thought convinced her of the peril of such an act. Ahead of them a long down-grade stretched away, away, to a turn half-hidden under the arching greenery. As the car struck this slope, it leaped into ever greater speed; and now, under the erratic guidance of the lolling wretch at the wheel, it began to sway in long, unsteady curves, first toward one ditch, then the other.

Another woman would have screamed; might even have tried to jump out. But Kate was not of the hysteric sort. More practical, she.

"I've got to climb over into the front seat," she realized in a flash, "and shut off the current – cut the power off – stop the car!"

On the instant, she acted. But as she arose in the tonneau, Herrick, sensing her purpose, turned toward her in the sudden rage of complete intoxication.

"Naw – naw y' don't!" he shouted, his face perfectly purple with fury and drink. "No woman – he! – runs this old boat while I'm aboard, see? Go on, fire me! *I* don't give – damn! But you don't run – car! Sit down! *I* run car – New York or Hell – no matter which! *I*—"

Hurtling down the slope like a runaway comet, now wholly out of control, the powerful gray car leaped madly at the turn.

Catherine, her heart sick at last with terror, caught a second's glimpse of forest, on one hand; of a stone wall with tree-tops on some steep abyss below, just grazing it, on the other. Through these trees she saw a momentary flash of water, far beneath.

Then the leaping front wheels struck a cluster of loose pebbles, at the bend.

Wrenched from the drunkard's grip, the steering wheel jerked sharply round.

A skidding – a crash – a cry!

Over the roadway, vacant now, floated a tenuous cloud of dust and gasoline-vapor, commingled.

In the retaining-wall at the left, a jagged gap appeared. Suddenly, far below, toward the river, a crashing detonation shattered harsh echoes from shore to shore.

Came a quick flash of light; then thick, black, greasy smoke arose, and, wafting through the treetops, drifted away on the warm wind of that late June afternoon.

A man, some quarter of a mile to southward, on the great highway, paused suddenly at sound of this explosion.

For a moment he stood there listening acutely, a knotted stick in hand, his flannel shirt, open at the throat, showing a brown and corded neck. The heavy knapsack on his shoulders seemed no burden to that rugged strength, as he stood, poised and eager, every sense centered in keen attention.

"Trouble ahead, there, by the Eternal!" he suddenly exclaimed. His eye had just caught sight of the first trailing wreaths of smoke, from up the cliff. "An auto's gone to smash, down there, or I'm a plute!"

He needed no second thought to hurl him forward to the rescue. At a smart pace he ran, halloo'ing loudly, to tell the victims – should they still live – that help was at hand. At his right, extended the wall. At his left, a grove of sugar-maples, sparsely set, climbed a long slope, over the ridge of which the descending sun glowed warmly. Somewhat back from the road, a rough shack which served as a sugar-house for the spring sap-boiling, stood with gaping door, open to all the winds that blew. These things he noted subconsciously, as he ran.

Then, all at once, as he rounded a sharp turn, he drew up with a cry.

"Down the cliff!" he exclaimed. "Knocked the wall clean out, and plunged! Holy Mackinaw, what a smash!"

In a moment he had reached the scene of the catastrophe. His quick eye took in, almost at a glance, the skidding mark of the wheels, the ragged rent in the wall, the broken limbs of trees below.

"Some wreck!" he ejaculated, dropping his stick and throwing off his knapsack. "*Hello, Hello, down there!*" he loudly hailed, scrambling through the gap.

From below, no answer.

A silence, as of death, broken only by the echo of his own voice, was all that greeted his wild cry.

Chapter XIV
The Rescue

GABRIEL ARMSTRONG leaped, rather than clambered, through the gap in the wall, and, following the track of devastation through the trees, scrambled down the steep slope that led toward the Hudson.

The forest looked as though a car of Juggernaut had passed that way. Limbs and saplings lay in confusion, larger trees showed long wounds upon their bark, and here and there pieces of metal – a gray mud-guard, a car door, a wind-shield frame, with shattered plate glass still clinging to it – lay scattered on the precipitous declivity. Beside these, hanging to a branch, Gabriel saw a gaily-striped auto robe; and, further down, a heavy, fringed shawl.

Again he shouted, holding to a tree-trunk at the very edge of a cliff of limestone, and peering far down into the abyss where the car had taken its final plunge. Still no answer. But, from below, the heavy smoke still rose. And now, peering more keenly, Armstrong caught sight of the wreck itself.

"There it is, and burning like the pit of Hell!" he exclaimed. "And – what's that, under it? A man?"

He could not distinctly make out, so thick the foliage was. But it seemed to him that, from under the jumbled wreckage of the blazing machine, something protruded, something that suggested a human form, horribly mangled.

"Here's where I go down this cliff, whatever happens!" decided Gabriel. And, acting on the instant, he began swinging himself down from tree to bush, from shrub to tuft of grass, clinging wherever handhold or foothold offered, digging his stout boots into every cleft and cranny of the precipice.

The height could not have been less than a hundred and fifty feet. By dint of wonderful strength and agility, and at the momentary risk of falling, himself, to almost certain death, Gabriel descended in less than ten minutes. The last quarter of the distance he practically fell, sliding at a tremendous rate, with boulders and loose earth cascading all about him in a shower.

He landed close by the flaming ruin.

"Lucky this isn't in the autumn, in the dry season!" thought he, as he approached. "If it were, this whole cliff-side, and the woods beyond, would be a roaring furnace. Some forest-fire, all right, if the woods weren't wet and full of sap!"

Parting the brush, he made his way as close to the car as the intense heat would let him. The gasoline-tank, he understood, had burst with the shock, and, taking fire, had wrapped the car in an Inferno of unquenchable flame. Now, the woodwork was entirely gone; and of the wheels, as the long machine lay there on its back, only a few blazing spokes were left. The steel chassis and the engine were red-hot, twisted and broken as though a giant hammer had smitten them on some Vulcanic anvil.

"There's a few thousand dollars gone to the devil!" thought he. But his mind did not dwell on this phase of the disaster. Still he was hoping, against hope, that human life had not been dashed and roasted out, in the wreck. And again he shouted, as he worked his way to the other side of the machine – to the side which, seen from the cliff above, had seemed to show him that inert and mangled body.

All at once he stopped short, shielding his face with his hands, against the blaze.

"Good God!" he exclaimed; and involuntarily took off his cap, there in the presence of death.

That the man *was* dead, admitted of no question. Pinned under the heavy, glowing mass of metal, his body must already have been roasted to a char. The head could not be seen; but part of one shoulder and one arm protruded, with the coat burned off and the flesh horribly crackled; while, nearer Gabriel, a leg showed, with a regulation chauffeur's legging, also burned to a crisp.

"Nothing for me to do, here," said Gabriel aloud. "He's past all human help, poor chap. I don't imagine there can be anybody else in this wreck. I haven't seen anybody, and nobody has answered my shouts. What's to be done next?"

He pondered a moment, then, looking at the license plate of the machine – its enamel now half cracked off, but the numbers still legible – drew out his note-book and pencil and made a memo of the figures.

"Four-six-two-two, N.Y.," he read, again verifying his numbers. "That will identify things. And now – the quicker I get back on the road again, and reach a telephone at West Point, the better."

Accordingly, after a brief search through the bushes near at hand, for any other victim – a search which brought no results – he set to work once more to climb the cliff above him.

The fire, though still raging, was obviously dying down. In half an hour, he knew, it would be dead. There was no use in trying to extinguish it, for gasoline defies water, and no sand was to be had along that rocky river shore.

"Let her burn herself out," judged Gabriel. "She can't do any harm, now. The road for mine!"

He found the upward path infinitely more difficult than the downward, and was forced to make a long detour and do some hard climbing that left him spent and sweating, before he again approached the gap in the wall. Pausing here to breathe, a minute or two, he once more peered down at the still-smoking ruin far below. And, as he stood there all at once he thought he heard a sound not very far away to his right.

A sound – a groan, a half-inchoate murmur – a cry!

Instantly his every sense grew keen. Holding his breath he listened intently. Was it a cry? Or had the breeze but swayed one tree limb against another; or did some boatman's hail, from far across the river, but drift upward to him on the cliff?

"Hello! *Hello!*" he shouted again. "Anybody there?"

Once more he listened; and now, once more, he heard the sound – this time he knew it was a cry for help!

"Where are you?" shouted he, plunging forward along the steep side of the cliff. "Where?"

No answer, save a groan.

"Coming! Coming!" he hailed loudly. Then, guided as it seemed by instinct, almost as much as by the vague direction of the moaning call, he ploughed his way through brush and briar, on rescue bent.

All at once he stopped short in his tracks, wild-eyed, a stammering exclamation on his lips.

"A woman!" he cried.

True. There, lying as though violently flung, a woman was half-crouched, half-prone behind the roots of a huge maple that leaned out far above a sheer declivity.

He saw torn clothing, through the foliage; a white hand, out-stretched and bleeding; a mass of golden-coppery hair that lay dishevelled on the bed of moss and last autumn's leaves.

"A woman! Dying?" he thought, with a sudden stab of pity in his heart.

Then, forcing his way along, he reached her, and fell upon his knees at her side.

"Not dead! Not dying! Thank God!" he exclaimed. One glance showed him she would live. Though an ugly gash upon her forehead had bathed her face in blood, and though he knew not but bones were broken, he recognized the fact that she was now returning, fast, to consciousness.

Already she had opened her eyes – wild eyes, understanding nothing – and was staring up at him in dazed, blank terror. Then one hand came up to her face; and, even as he lifted her in both his powerful arms, she began to sob hysterically.

He knew the value of that weeping, and made no attempt to stop it. The overwrought nerves, he understood, must find some outlet. Asking no question, speaking no word – for Gabriel was a man of action, not speech – he gathered her up as though she had been a child. A tall woman, she; almost as tall as he himself, and proportioned like a Venus. Yet to him her weight was nothing.

Sure-footed, now, and bursting through the brambles with fine energy, he carried her to the gap in the wall, up through it, and so to the roadway itself.

"Where – where am I?" the woman cried incoherently. "O – what – where—?"

"You're all right!" he exclaimed. "Just a little accident, that's all. Don't worry! I'll take care of you. Just keep quiet, now, and don't think of anything. You'll be all right, in no time!"

But she still wept and cried out to know where she might be and what had happened. Obviously, Gabriel saw, her reason had not yet fully returned. His first aim must be to bathe her wound, find out what damage had been done, and keeping her quiet, try to get help.

Swiftly he thought. Here he and the woman were, miles from any settlement or house, nearly in the middle of a long stretch of road that skirted the river through dense woods. At any time a motor might come along; and then again, one might not arrive for hours. No dependence could be put on this. There was no telephone for a long distance back; and even had one been near he would not have ventured to leave the girl.

Could he carry her back to Fort Clinton, the last settlement he had passed through? Impossible! No man's strength could stand such a tremendous task. And even had it been within Gabriel's means, he would have chosen otherwise. For most of all the girl needed rest and quiet and immediate care. To bear her all that distance in his arms might produce serious, even fatal results.

"No!" he decided. "I must do what I can for her, here and now, and trust to luck to send help in an auto, down this road!"

His next thought was that bandages and wraps would be needed for her cut and to make her a bed. Instantly he remembered the shawl and the big auto-robe that he had seen caught among the trees.

"I must have those at once!" he realized. "When the machine went over the edge, they were thrown out, just as the girl was. A miracle she wasn't carried down, with the car, and crushed or burned to death down there by the river, with that poor devil of a chauffeur!"

Laying her down in the soft grass along the wall, he ran back to where the wraps were, and, detaching them from the branches, quickly regained the road once more.

"Now for the old sugar-house in the maple-grove," said he. "Poor shelter, but the best to be had. Thank heaven it's fair weather, and warm!"

The task was awkward, to carry both the girl and the bulky robes, but Gabriel was equal to it She had by now regained some measure of rationality; and though very pale and shaken, manifested her nerve and courage by no longer weeping or asking questions.

Instead, she lay in his arms, eyes closed, with the blood stiffening on her face; and let him bear her whither he would. She seemed to sense his strength and mastery, his tender care and complete command of the situation. And, like a hurt and tired child, outworn and suffering, she yielded herself, unquestioningly, to his ministrations.

Thus Gabriel, the discharged, blacklisted, outcast rebel and proletarian, bore in his arms of mercy and compassion the only daughter of old Isaac Flint, his enemy, Flint the would-be master of the world.

Thus he bore the woman who had been betrothed to "Tiger" Waldron, unscrupulous and cruel partner in that scheme of dominance and enslavement.

Such was the meeting of this woman and this man. Thus, in his arms, he carried her to the old sugar-house.

And far below, the mighty river gleamed, unheeding the tragedy that had been enacted on its shores, unmindful of the threads of destiny even now being spun by the swift shuttles of Fate.

In the branches, above Gabriel and Catherine, birdsong and golden sunlight seemed to prophesy. But what this message might be, neither the woman nor the man had any thought or dream.

Chapter XV
An Hour and a Parting

ARRIVING AT the sugar-house, tired yet strong, Gabriel put the wounded girl down, quickly raked together a few armfuls of dead leaves, in the most sheltered corner of the ramshackle structure, and laid the heavy auto-robe upon this improvised bed. Then he helped his patient to lie down, there, and bade her wait till he got water to wash and dress her cut.

"Don't worry about anything," he reassured her. "You're alive, and that's the main thing, now. I'll see you through with this, whatever happens. Just keep calm, and don't let anything distress you!"

She looked at him with big, anxious eyes – eyes where still the full light of understanding had not yet returned.

"It – it all happened so suddenly!" she managed to articulate. "He was drunk – the chauffeur. The car ran away. Where is it? Where is Herrick – the man?"

"I don't know," Gabriel lied promptly and with force. Not for worlds would he have excited her with the truth. "Never you mind about that. Just lie still, now, till I come back!"

Already, among the rusty utensils that had served for the "sugaring-off," the previous spring, he had routed out a tin pail. He kicked a quantity of leaves in under the sheet-iron open stove, flung some sticks atop of them, and started a little blaze. Warm water, he reflected, would serve better than cold in removing that clotting blood and dressing the hurt.

Then, saying no further word, but filled with admiration for the girl's pluck, he seized the pail and started for water.

"Nerve?" he said to himself, as he ran down the road toward a little brook he remembered having crossed, a few hundred yards to southward. "Nerve, indeed! Not one complaint about her own injuries! Not a word of lamentation! If this isn't a thoroughbred, whoever or whatever she is, I never saw one!"

He returned, presently, with the pail nearly full of cold and sparkling water. Ignoring rust, he made her drink as deeply as she would, and then set a dipperful of water on the now hot sheet-iron.

Then, tearing a strip off the shawl, he made ready for his work as an amateur physician.

"Tell me," said he, kneeling there beside her in the hut which was already beginning to grow dusk, "except for this cut on your forehead, do you feel any injury? Think you've got any broken bones? See if you can move your legs and arms, all right."

She obeyed.

"Nothing broken, I guess," she answered. "What a miracle! Please leave me, now. I can wash my own hurt. Go – go find Herrick! He needs you worse than I do!"

"No he doesn't!" blurted Gabriel with such conviction that she understood.

"You mean?" she queried, as he brought the dipper of now tepid water to her side. "He – he's dead?"

He hesitated to answer.

"Dead! Yes, I understand!" she interpreted his silence. "You needn't tell me. I know!"

He nodded.

"Yes," said he. "Your chauffeur has paid the penalty of trying to drive a six-cylinder car with alcohol. Now, think no more of him! Here, let me see how badly you're cut."

"Let me sit up, first," she begged. "I – I'm not hurt enough to be lying here like – like an invalid!"

She tried to rise, but with a strong hand on her shoulder he forced her back. She shuddered, with the horror of the chauffeur's death strong upon her.

"Please lie still," he begged. "You've had a terrific shock, and have lived through it by a miracle, indeed. You're wounded and still bleeding. You *must* be quiet!"

The tone in his voice admitted no argument. Submissive now to his greater strength, this daughter of wealth and power lay back, closed her tired eyes and let the revolutionist, the proletarian, minister to her.

Dipping the piece of shawl into the warm water, he deftly moistened the dried blood on her brow and cheek, and washed it all away. He cleansed her sullied hair, as well, and laid it back from the wound.

"Tell me if I hurt you, now," he bade, gently as a woman. "I've got to wash the cut itself."

She answered nothing, but lay quite still. And so, hardly wincing, she let him lave the jagged wound that stretched from her right temple up into the first tendrils of the glorious red-gold hair.

"H'm!" thought Gabriel, as he now observed the cut with close attention. "I'm afraid there'll have to be some stitches taken here!" But of this he said nothing. All he told her was: "Nothing to worry over. You'll be as good as new in a few days. As a miracle, it's *some* miracle!"

Having completed the cleansing of the cut, he fetched his knapsack and produced a clean handkerchief, which he folded and laid over the wound. This pad he secured in place by a long bandage cut from the edge of the shawl and tied securely round her shapely head.

"There," said he, surveying his improvisation with considerable satisfaction. "Now you'll do, till we can undertake the next thing. Sorry I haven't any brandy to give you, or anything of that sort. The fact is, I don't use it, and have none with me. How do you feel, now?"

She opened her eyes and looked up at him with the ghost of a smile on her pale lips.

"Oh, much, much better, thank you!" she answered. "I don't need any brandy. I'm – awfully strong, really. In a little while I'll be all right. Just give me a little more water, and – and tell me – who are you?"

"Who am I?" he queried, holding up her head while she drank from the tin cup he had now taken from his knapsack. "I? Oh, just an out-of-work. Nobody of any interest to you!"

A certain tinge of bitterness crept into his voice. In health, he knew, a woman of this class would not suffer him even to touch her hand.

"*Don't* ask me who I am, please. And I – I won't ask *your* name. We're of different worlds, I guess. But for the moment, Fate has levelled the barriers. Just let it go at that. And now, if you can stay here, all right; perhaps I can hike back to the next house, below here, and telephone, and summon help."

"How far is it?" she asked, looking at him with wonder in her lovely eyes – wonder, and new thoughts, and a strange kind of longing to know more of this extraordinary man, so strong, so gentle, so unwilling to divulge himself or ask her name.

"How far?" he repeated. "Oh, four or five miles. I can make it in no time. And with luck, I can have an auto and a doctor here before dark. Well, does that suit you?"

"Don't go, please," she answered. "I – I may be still a little weak and foolish, but – somehow, I don't want to be left alone. I want to be kept from remembering, from thinking of those last, awful moments when the car was running away; when it struck the wall, at the turn; when I was thrown out, and – and knew no more. Don't go just yet," the girl entreated, covering her eyes with both hands, as though to shut out the horrible vision of the catastrophe.

"All right," Gabriel answered. "Just as you please. Only, if I stay, you must promise to stop thinking about the accident, and try to pull together."

"I promise," she agreed, looking at him with strange eyes. "Oh dear," she added, with feminine inconsequentiality, "my hair's all down, and Lord knows where the pins are!"

He smiled to himself as she managed, with the aid of such few hairpins as remained, to coil the coppery meshes once more round her head and even somewhat over the bandage, and secure them in place.

At sight of his face as he watched her, she too smiled wanly – the first time he had seen a real smile on her mouth.

"I'm only a woman, after all," she apologized. "You don't understand. You can't. But no matter. Tell me – why need you go, at all?"

"Why? For help, of course."

"There's sure to be a motor, or something, along this road, before very long," she answered. "Put up some signal or other, to stop it. That will save you a long, long walk, and save me from – remembering! I need you here with me," she added earnestly. "Don't go – please!"

"All right, as you will," the man made reply. "I'll rig a danger-signal on the road; and then all we can do will be to wait."

This plan he immediately put into effect, setting his knapsack in the middle of the road and piling up brush and limbs of trees about it.

"There," he said to himself, as he surveyed the result, "no car will get by *that*, without noticing it!"

Then he returned to the sugar-house, some hundred yards back from the highway in the grove, now already beginning to grow dim with the shadows of approaching nightfall. The glowing coals of the fire gleamed redly, through the rough place. The girl, still lying on her bed of leaves and auto-robes, with the mutilated shawl drawn over her, looked up at him with an expression of trust and gratitude. For a second, only one, something quick and vital gripped at the wanderer's heart – some vague, intangible longing for a home and a woman, a longing old as our race, deep-planted in the inmost citadel of every man's soul. But, half-impatiently, he drove the thought away, dismissed it, and, smiling down at her with cheerful eyes and white, even teeth, said reassuringly:

"Everything's all right now. The first machine that passes, will take you to civilization."

"And you?" she asked. "What of you, then?"

"Me? Oh, I'll hike," he answered. "I'll plug along just as I was doing when I found you."

"Where to?"

"Oh, north."

"What for?"

"Work. Please don't question me. I'd rather you wouldn't."

She pondered a moment.

"Are you – what they call a – workingman?" she presently resumed.

"Yes," said he. "Why?"

"And are you happy?"

"Yes. In a way. Or shall be, when I've done what I mean to do."

"But – forgive me – you're very poor?"

"Not at all! I have, at this present moment, more than eighteen dollars in my pocket, and I have *these!*"

He showed her his two hands, big and sinewed, capable and strong.

"Eighteen dollars," she mused, half to herself. "Why, I have spent that, and more, for a single ounce of a new perfume – something very rare, you know, from Japan."

"Indeed? Well, don't tell *me*," he replied. "I'm not interested in how you spend money, but how you get it."

"Get it? Oh, father gives me my allowance, that's all."

"And he squeezes it out of the common people?"

She glanced at him quickly.

"You – you aren't a Socialist, into the bargain, are you?" she inquired.

"At your service," he bowed.

"This is strange, strange indeed," she said. "Tell me your name."

"No," he refused. "I'd still rather not. Nor shall I ask yours. Please don't volunteer it."

Came a moment's silence, there in the darkening hut, with the fire-glow red upon their faces.

"Happy," said the girl. "You say you're happy. While I—"

"Are not unhappy, surely?" asked Gabriel, leaning forward as he sat there beside her, and gazing keenly into her face.

"How should I know?" she answered. "Unhappy? No, perhaps not. But vacant – empty – futile!"

"Yes, I believe you," Gabriel judged. "You tell me no news. And as you are, you will ever be. You will live so and die so. No, I won't preach. I won't proselytize. I won't even explain. It would be useless. You are one pole, I the other. And the world – the whole wide world – lies between!"

Suddenly she spoke.

"You're a Socialist," said she. "What does it mean to be a Socialist?"

He shook his head.

"You couldn't understand, if I told you," he answered.

"Why not?"

"Oh, because your ideas and environments and interests and everything have been so different from mine – because you're what you are – because you can never be anything else."

"You mean Socialism is something beyond my understanding?" she demanded, piqued. "Of course, that's nonsense. I'm a human being. I've got brains, haven't I? I can understand a scheme of dividing up, or levelling down, or whatever it is, even if I can't believe in it!"

He smiled oddly.

"You've just proved, by what you've said," he answered slowly, "that your whole concepts are mistaken. Socialism isn't anything like what you think it is, and if I should try to explain it, you'd raise ten thousand futile objections, and beg the question, and defeat my object of explanation by your very inability to get the point of view. So you see—"

"I see that I want to know more!" she exclaimed, with determination. "If there's any branch of human knowledge that lies outside my reasoning powers, it's time I found that fact out. I thought Socialists were wild, crazy, erratic cranks; but if you're one, then I seem to have been wrong. You look rational enough, and you talk in an eminently sane manner."

"Thank you," he replied, ironically.

"Don't be sarcastic!" she retorted. "I only meant—"

"It's all right, anyhow," said he. "You've simply got the old, stupid, wornout ideas of your class. You can't grasp this new ideal, rising through the ruck and waste and sin and misery of the present system. I don't blame you. You're a product of your environment. You can't help it. With that environment, how can you sense the newer and more vital ideas of the day?"

For a moment she fixed eager eyes on him, in silence. Then asked she:

"Ideals? You mean that Socialism has ideals, and that it's not all a matter of tearing down and dividing up, and destroying everything good and noble and right – all the accumulated wisdom and resources of the world?"

He laughed heartily.

"Who handed you that bunk?" he demanded.

"Father told me Socialism was all that, and more,"

"What's your father's business?"

"Why, investments, stocks, bonds, industrial development and all that sort of thing."

"Hm!" he grunted. "I thought as much!"

"You mean that father misinformed me?"

"Rather!"

"Well, if he did, what is Socialism?"

"Socialism," answered the young man slowly, while he fixed his eyes on the smouldering fire, "Socialism is a political movement, a concept of life, a philosophy, an interpretation, a prophecy, an ideal. It embraces history, economics, science, art, religion, literature and every phase of human activity. It explains life, points the way to better things, gives us hope, strengthens the weary and heavy-laden, bids us look upward and onward, and constitutes the most sublime ideal ever conceived by the soul of man!"

"Can this be true?" the girl demanded, astonished.

"Not only can, but is! Socialism would free the world from slavery and slaves, from war, poverty, prostitution, vice and crime; would cleanse the sores of our rotting capitalism, would loose the gyves from the fettered hands of mankind, would bid the imprisoned soul of man awake to nobler and to purer things! How? The answer to that would take me weeks. You would have to read and study many books, to learn the entire truth. But I am telling you the substance of the ideal – a realizable ideal, and no chimera – when I say that Socialism sums up all that is good, and banishes all that is evil! And do you wonder that I love and serve it, all my life?"

She peered at him in wonder.

"You serve it? How?" she demanded.

"By spreading it abroad; by speaking for it, working for it, fighting for it! By the spoken and the printed word! By every act and through every means whereby I can bring it nearer and nearer realization!"

"You're a dreamer, a visionary, a fanatic!" she exclaimed.

"You think so? No, I can't agree. Time will judge that matter. Meanwhile, I travel up and down the earth, spreading Socialism."

"And what do you get out of it, personally?"

"I? What do you mean? I never thought of that question."

"I mean, money. What do you make out of it?"

He laughed heartily.

"I get a few jail-sentences, once in a while; now and then a crack over the head with a policeman's billy, or maybe a peek down the muzzle of a rifle. I get—"

"You mean that you're a martyr?"

"By no means! I've never even thought of being called such. This is a privilege, this propaganda of ours. It's the greatest privilege in the world – bringing the word of life and hope and joy to a crushed, bleeding and despairing world!"

She thought a moment, in silence.

"You're a poet, I believe!" said she.

"No, not that. Only a worker in the ranks."

"But do you write poetry?"

"I write verses. You'd hardly call them poetry!"

"Verses? About Socialism?"

"Sometimes."

"Will you give me some?"

"What do you mean?"

"Tell me some of them."

"Of course not! I can't recite my verses! They aren't worth bothering you with!"

"That's for me to judge. Let me hear something of that kind. If you only knew how terribly much you interest me!"

"You mean that?"

"Of course I do! Please let me hear something you've written!"

He pondered a moment, then in his well-modulated, deep-toned voice began:

HESPERIDES.

I.

My feet, used to pine-needles, moss and turf, And the gray boulders at the lip o' the sea, Where the cold brine jets up its creamy surf, Now tread once more these city ways, unloved by me, Hateful and hot, gross with iniquity. And so I grieve, Grieve when I wake, or at high blinding noon Or when the moon Mocks this sad Ninevah where the throngs weave Their jostling ways by day, their paths by night;

Where darkness is not – where the streets burn bright With hectic fevers, eloquent of death! I gasp for breath.... Visions have I, visions! So sweet they seem That from this welter of men and things I turn, to dream Of the dim Wood-world, calling out to me. Where forest-virgins I half glimpse, half see With cool mysterious fingers beckoning! Where vine-wreathed woodland altars sunlit burn, Or Dryads dance their mystic rounds and sing, Sing high, sing low, with magic cadences That once the wild oaks of Dodona heard; And every wood-note bids me burst asunder The bonds that hold me from the leaf-hid bird. I quaff thee, O Nepenthe! Ah, the wonder Grows, that there be who buy their wealth, their ease By damning serfs to cities, hot and blurred, Far from thy golden quest, Hesperides!...

II.

I see this August sun again Sheer up high heaven wheel his angry way; And hordes of men Bleared with unrestful sleep rise up another day, Their bodies racked with aftermaths of toil. Over the city, in each gasping street, Shudders a haze of heat, Reverberant from pillar, span and plinth. Once more, cribbed in this monstrous labyrinth Sacrificed to the Minotaur of Greed Men bear the turmoil, glare, sweat, brute inharmonies; Denial of each simplest human need, Loss of life's meaning as day lags on day; And my rebellious spirit rises, flies In dreams to the green quiet wood away, Away! Away!

III.

And now, and now...I feel the forest-moss... Come! On these moss-beds let me lie with Pan, Twined with the ivy-vine in tendrill'd curls, And I will hold all gold, that hampers man, Only the ashes of base, barren dross! On with the love-dance of the pagan girls! The pagan girls with lips all rosy-red, With breasts upgirt and foreheads garlanded, With fair white foreheads nobly garlanded! With sandalled feet that weave the magic ring! Now...let them sing, And I will pipe a tune that all may hear, To bid them mind the time of my wild rhyme; To warn profaning feet lest they draw near. Away! Away! Beware these mystic trees! Who dares to quest you now, Hesperides?

IV.

Great men of song, what sing ye? Woodland meadows? Rocks, trees and rills where sunlight glints to gold? Sing ye the hills, adown whose sides blue shadows Creep when the westering day is growing old? Sing ye the brooks where in the purling shallows The small fish dart and gleam? Sing ye the pale green tresses of the willows That stoop to kiss the stream? Or sing ye burning streets, foul with the breath Of sweatshop, tenement, where endlessly Spawned swarms of folk serve tyrant masters twain— Profit, and his twin-brother, grinning Death? Where millions toil, hedged off from aught save pain? Far from thee ever, O mine Arcady?...

His voice ceased and silence fell between the man and woman in the old sugar-house. Gabriel sat there by the dying fire, which cast its ruddy light over his strongly virile face, and gazed into the coals. The girl, lying on the rude bed, her face eager, her slim strong hands tightly clasped, had almost forgotten to breathe.

At last she spoke.

"That – that is wonderful!" she cried, a tremor of enthusiasm in her voice.

He shook his head.

"No compliments, please," said he.

"I'm not complimenting you! I think it *is* wonderful. You're a true poet!"

"I wish I were – so I might use it all for Socialism!"

"You could make a fortune, if you'd work for some paper or magazine – some regular one, I mean, not Socialist."

He shook his head.

"Dead sea fruit," he answered. "Fairy gold, fading in the clutch, worthless through and through. No, if my work has any merit, it's all for Socialism, now and ever!"

Silence again. Neither now found a word to say, but their eyes met and read each other; and a kind of solemn hush seemed to lie over their hearts.

Then, as they sat there, looking each at each – for now the girl had raised herself on the crude bed and was supporting herself with one hand – a sudden sound of a motor, on the road, awakened them from their musing.

Came the raucous wail of a siren. Then the engine-exhaust ceased; and a voice, raised in some annoyance, hailed loudly through the maple-grove:

"Hello! Hello? What's wrong here?"

Gabriel stepped to the sugar-house door:

"Here! Come here!" he shouted in a ringing voice that echoed wildly from between his hollowed palms.

As the motorist still sat there, uncomprehending, Gabriel made his way toward the road.

"Accident here," said he. "Girl in here, injured. Can you take her to the nearest town, at once? She needs a doctor."

Instantly the man was out of his car, and hastening toward Gabriel.

"Eh? What?" he asked. "Anything serious?"

In a few words, Gabriel told him the outlines of the tale.

"The quicker you get the girl to a town, and let her have a doctor and communication with her family, the better," he concluded.

"Right! I'll do all in my power," said the other, a rather stout, well-to-do, vulgar-looking man.

"Good! This way, then!"

The man followed Gabriel to the sugar-house. They found the girl already on her feet, standing there a bit unsteadily, but with determination to be game, in every feature.

Five minutes later she was in the new-comer's car, which had been turned around and now was headed back toward Haverstraw. The shawl and robe serving her as wraps, she was made comfortable in the tonneau.

"Think you can stand it, all right?" asked Gabriel, as he took in his the hand she extended. "In half an hour, you'll be under a doctor's care, and your father will be on his way toward you."

She nodded, and for a second tightened the grasp of her hand.

"I – I'm not even going to know who you are?" she asked, a strange tone in her voice.

"No," he answered. "And now, good luck, and good-bye!"

"Good-bye," she echoed, her voice almost inaudible. "I – I won't forget you."

He made no answer, but only smiled in a peculiar way.

Then, as the car rolled slowly forward, their hands separated.

Gabriel, bareheaded and with level gaze, stood there in the middle of the great highway, looking after her. A minute, under the darkening arches of the forest road, he saw her, still. Then the car swung round a bend, and vanished.

Had she waved her hand at him? He could not tell. Motionless he stood, a while, then cleared away the barrier of branches that obstructed the road, took up his knapsack, and with slow steps returned to the sugar-house.

Almost on the threshold, a white something caught his eye. He picked it up. Her handkerchief! A moment he held the dainty, filmy thing in his rough hand. A vague perfume reached his nostrils, disquieting and seductive.

"More than eighteen dollars an ounce, perhaps!" he exclaimed, with sudden bitterness; but still he did not throw the handkerchief away. Instead, he looked at it more keenly. In one corner, the fading light just showed him some initials. He studied them, a moment.

"C. J. F." he read. Then, yielding to a sudden impulse, he folded the kerchief and put it in his pocket.

He entered the sugar-house, to make sure, before departing, that he had left no danger of fire behind him.

Another impulse bade him sit down on a rough box, there, before the dying embers. He gazed at the bed of leaves, a while, immersed in thought, then filled his pipe and lighted it with a glowing brand, and sat there – while the night came – smoking and musing, in a reverie.

The overpowering lure of the woman who had lain in his arms, as he had borne her thither; her breath upon his face; the perfume of her, even her blood that he had washed away – all these were working on his senses, still. But most of all he seemed to see her eyes, there in the ember-lit gloom, and hear her voice, and feel her lithe young body and her breast against his breast.

For a long time he sat there, thinking, dreaming, smoking, till the last shred of tobacco was burned out in the heel of his briar; till the last ember had winked and died under the old sheet-iron stove.

At last, with a peculiar laugh, he rose, slung the knapsack once more on his shoulders, settled his cap upon his head, and made ready to depart.

But still, one moment, he lingered in the doorway. Lingered and looked back, as though in his mind's eye he would have borne the place away with him forever.

Suddenly he stooped, picked up a leaf from the bed where she had lain, and put that, too, in his pocket where the kerchief was.

Then, looking no more behind him, he strode off across the maple-grove, through which, now, the first pale stars were glimmering. He reached the road again, swung to the north, and, striking into his long marching stride, pushed onward northward, away and away into the soft June twilight.

The complete and unabridged text is available online, from *flametreepublishing.com/extras*

The Last Day on Earth

Gini Koch writing as Anita Ensal

"DO YOU want anything?" she asked him, while straightening a picture on the wall.

"No, I'm good. Dinner was wonderful, as always." He put the food bowls down for their dogs, scratched one cat gently behind her ear, and wandered into their living room. He turned on the television and sat down on the sofa.

She joined him in the living room, but she didn't sit down or look at the picture on the screen. Instead she moved some of their few knickknacks and mementos around into their proper places. "Do you think they're really going to make it?"

"Yes. Whether they'll find someplace liveable is the question. But, we won't have to worry about it."

"Not after today." She plumped the pillows on the loveseat.

The news announcer's voice attracted their attention. "…and scientific authorities of all the major continental governments state that the eruption *will* begin within eight hours, which they have confirmed will trigger explosions within the Earth's core immediately after. Total world implosion is expected within twenty-four hours. Here in the Americas, the Citizens' Action Group is still protesting in Washington, D.C., over what they consider a worldwide conspiracy to hide the truth about the Grand Canyon's volcanic underbelly from the common people—"

He clicked the remote and changed the channel. They looked at scenes of people in other countries climbing to the highest points they could find. Mount Fuji was thick with people, even at the top, despite the snow.

She sighed. "Might be safer in a submarine."

He chuckled and changed the channel again. This time he found what he was truly searching for.

She sat down next to him on the sofa and they watched the shuttles launch, one after another. He put his arm around her and she snuggled closer. "They'll be fine up to the Moon Station, I would think." He could hear the worry in her voice, though.

"Oh yes. It's old hat."

The televised launch coverage finished with Japan and moved over to China.

"I can't imagine what it must have been like, only being given one slot for every three families."

"They're so restricted, most Chinese couples don't even have one child," he reminded her. "And they had the fewest shuttles, anyway."

"True."

They felt a tremor, very slight. The dogs seemed to ignore it, though the cats both got up and paced a bit.

The image on the television switched to the Americas launches. They both tried to see if they could tell which shuttle their child was in, though neither one said so aloud.

"Will they keep them together, do you think?" she asked, as the announcer commented on he superior quality of the Americas shuttles, their range and passenger capacity, their safety and stability. They could ignore this – they'd been hearing it for months now.

"Yes. They're listed as a family group now, and the governments don't want to separate family groups."

She sighed. "They're so young."

"Not all that young anymore, since they're all teenagers. And that means they'll be given berth on one of the Alpha Centauri ships for sure. They'll just be young adults when they get there – plenty of time to build new lives."

"I'm glad we only had one daughter." The fifty-third ship from The Americas went up.

"So're the neighbors." He hugged her gently.

"They're glad they only had *three* children." She gave a soft laugh. "I remember when they found out she needed a hysterectomy. Can you imagine what they'd be going through if they'd really had six?"

"It's also a good thing each Americas family was given two shuttle slots so we could share our spare slot with them. Guess we paid our taxes for something."

She giggled. "True. You know, in a way I'm glad they decided not to come over and spend tonight with us."

"Me, too. And I didn't want to go to that End of the World Explosion Party they got tickets to, either."

"I know. I'd rather be home, here, just us."

They continued to watch the shuttle departures. The last shuttle from The Americas went up, and the television coverage switched to Europe. "Europe was the worst," he commented. "That lottery was not what I'd have wanted to go through."

"I like the Auzealand attitude."

He grinned. "True. Send your top students in your two shuttles, everyone else stays home and parties until the world ends." He knew they'd both lost interest in watching the launches, so he turned the channel again, to a local station. Streams of people were heading for higher ground.

"Should we do that?"

He knew she was just asking. "No," he said, as he always did. "I've studied the reports. There's no way anyone on this continent can be safe. Even if they survive the lava eruption, the fumes will be poisonous, and the land's going to cave in on itself. And when that happens, the domino effect will cause the same to happen everywhere else, to all the exterior and underground volcanic chains, just like they've been telling us for months now."

"They won't be safe anywhere else, either." Her voice trembled a bit.

"Nope, not even in your submarine. The oceans aren't going to be calm, or safe. Tsunamis, earthquakes, and the water heated to the boiling point will ensure it. The world's going to be over. But at least it'll go out with a bang."

The cats wandered over and sat with them. One went right to sleep while the other groomed himself. The dogs finished eating and joined them as well, one on each side of their feet.

They sat like this for a while, in silence, watching the images on the screen, occasionally stroking one of the pets.

She broke the silence. "I'm scared."

"I know." He shifted her onto his lap, and she curled up, her face in his neck. "It'll be over quickly, for us."

"What if it hurts? I don't want to be burned alive."

"I won't let that happen. You know our plan."

"Yes. But…what if something goes wrong?"

"You have your gun with you?"

"In my apron pocket."

"And I've got mine in my shoulder holster. You know the backup plan. We have enough bullets for us and the pets." He considered something. "Will you be able to do it, if you have to?"

"Yes. I don't want to be burned alive and I don't want any of you burned alive either. A bullet to the brain is much faster." She moved and looked at him. "And, I am an excellent shot, you know."

He grinned. "You had a wonderful teacher."

"Modest to a fault as always," she said with a genuine laugh.

"Yep." He kissed her, a long, lingering kiss.

She leaned her head back onto his shoulder. "I'm glad we're still together."

He stroked her hair and shoulder. "I told you I'd love you and stay with you until my last day on earth."

"I'm glad you meant it." She gave another sigh. "So, do you want to watch a movie?"

"Sure. A comedy would be nice."

"Yes. I'm not in the mood for a disaster picture." He laughed as she got up and picked out one of their favorites. "Popcorn?"

"Sure. And a beer, while you're up."

"We'll probably have time for another movie, maybe two," she said, as she went into the kitchen. "Before we have to worry about anything."

"The pets will let us know when it's time to get ready." He listened to the kernels pop and looked around the room. It wasn't overly decorated – just comfortable furniture, pictures they both liked, some souvenirs from the years together, books, and family photos. They could have had more – a bigger house, more possessions, more friends – but had never felt the need. They'd been a happy, self-contained unit from the first day they'd met, and nothing had changed that, not even the impending cataclysm.

He liked their home, and he was glad they were staying in tonight. Their last night together. The last hours of the life they'd built and loved, spent as they had always spent them – together, with the world kept away as much as possible.

She came back with the popcorn, a beer for him, and a soda for herself. She set them down, went back into the kitchen, and returned with a box of dog biscuits and two bags of cat treats. She shrugged at his questioning look. "It's not like we need to save them. They might as well have a feast before dying."

"True." He gave a biscuit to each dog, and then, as they settled down, munching happily, divided the box between them. She gave the cats a bag of treats each and sat back down on the sofa next to him.

Then, they settled in to watch their movies and wait for the end of the world.

Omega: The Last Days of the World

Part I

Camille Flammarion

Chapter I

THE MAGNIFICENT marble bridge which unites the Rue de Rennes with the Rue de Louvre, and which, lined with the statues of celebrated scientists and philosophers, emphasizes the monumental avenue leading to the new portico of the Institute, was absolutely black with people. A heaving crowd surged, rather than walked, along the quays, flowing out from every street and pressing forward toward the portico, long before invaded by a tumultuous throng. Never, in that barbarous age preceding the constitution of the United States of Europe, when might was greater than right, when military despotism ruled the world and foolish humanity quivered in the relentless grasp of war – never before in the stormy period of a great revolution, or in those feverish days which accompanied a declaration of war, had the approaches of the house of the people's representatives, or the Place de la Concorde presented such a spectacle. It was no longer the case of a band of fanatics rallied about a flag, marching to some conquest of the sword, and followed by a throng of the curious and the idle, eager to see what would happen; but of the entire population, anxious, agitated, terrified, composed of every class of society without distinction, hanging upon the decision of an oracle, waiting feverishly the result of the calculations which a celebrated astronomer was to announce that very Monday, at three o'clock, in the session of the Academy of Sciences. Amid the flux of politics and society the Institute survived, maintaining still in Europe its supremacy in science, literature and art. The center of civilization, however, had moved westward, and the focus of progress shone on the shores of Lake Michigan, in North America.

This new palace of the Institute, with its lofty domes and terraces, had been erected upon the ruins remaining after the great social revolution of the international anarchists who, in 1950, had blown up the greater portion of the metropolis as from the vent of a crater.

On the Sunday evening before, one might have seen from the car of a balloon all Paris abroad upon the boulevards and public squares, circulating slowly and as if in despair, without interest in anything. The gay aerial ships no longer cleaved the air; aeroplanes and aviators had all ceased to circulate. The aerial stations upon the summits of the towers and buildings were empty and deserted. The course of human life seemed arrested, and anxiety was depicted upon every face. Strangers addressed each other without hesitation; and but one question fell from pale and trembling lips: "Is it then true?" The most deadly pestilence would have carried far less terror to the heart than the astronomical prediction on every tongue; it would have made fewer victims, for already, from some unknown cause, the death-rate was increasing. At every instant one felt the electric shock of a terrible fear.

A few, less dismayed, wished to appear more confident, and sounded now and then a note of doubt, even of hope, as: "It may prove a mistake;" or, "It will pass on one side;" or, again: "It will amount to nothing; we shall get off with a fright," and other like assurances.

But expectation and uncertainty are often more terrible than the catastrophe itself. A brutal blow knocks us down once for all, prostrating us more or less completely. We come to our senses, we make the best of it, we recover, and take up life again. But this was the unknown, the expectation of something inevitable but mysterious, terrible, coming from without the range of experience. One was to die, without doubt, but how? By the sudden shock of collision, crushed to death? By fire, the conflagration of a world? By suffocation, the poisoning of the atmosphere? What torture awaited humanity? Apprehension was perhaps more frightful than the reality itself. The mind cannot suffer beyond a certain limit. To suffer by inches, to ask every evening what the morning may bring, is to suffer a thousand deaths. Terror, that terror which congeals the blood in the veins, which annihilates the courage, haunted the shuddering soul like an invisible spectre.

For more than a month the business of the world had been suspended; a fortnight before the committee of administrators (formerly the chamber and senate) had adjourned, every other question having sunk into insignificance. For a week the exchanges of Paris, London, New York and Pekin, had closed their doors. What was the use of occupying oneself with business affairs, with questions of internal or foreign policy, of revenue or of reform, if the end of the world was at hand? Politics, indeed! Did one even remember to have ever taken any interest in them? The courts themselves had no cases; one does not murder when one expects the end of the world. Humanity no longer attached importance to anything; its heart beat furiously, as if about to stop forever. Every face was emaciated, every countenance discomposed, and haggard with sleeplessness. Feminine coquetry alone held out, but in a superficial, hesitating, furtive manner, without thought of the morrow.

The situation was indeed serious, almost desperate, even in the eyes of the most stoical. Never, in the whole course of history had the race of Adam found itself face to face with such a peril. The portents of the sky confronted it unceasingly with a question of life and death.

But, let us go back to the beginning.

Three months before the day of which we speak, the director of the observatory of Mount Gaurisankar had sent the following telephonic message to the principal observatories of the globe, and especially to that of Paris:

> *For about 300 years the observatory of Paris had ceased to be an observing station, and had been perpetuated only as the central administrative bureau of French astronomy. Astronomical observations were made under far more satisfactory conditions upon mountain summits in a pure atmosphere, free from disturbing influences. Observers were in direct and constant communication by telephone with the central office, whose instruments were used only to verify certain discoveries or to satisfy the curiosity of savants detained in Paris by their sedentary occupation.*

"A telescopic comet discovered tonight, in 290°, 15′ right ascension, and 21°, 54′ south declination. Slight diurnal motion. Is of greenish hue."

Not a month passed without the discovery of telescopic comets, and their announcement to the various observatories, especially since the installation of intrepid astronomers in Asia on the lofty peaks of Gaurisankar, Dapsang and Kanchinjinga; in South America, on Aconcagua

Illampon and Chimborazo, as also in Africa on Kilimanjaro, and in Europe on Elburz and Mont Blanc. This announcement, therefore, had not excited more comment among astronomers than any other of a like nature which they were constantly receiving. A large number of observers had sought the comet in the position indicated, and had carefully followed its motion. Their observations had been published in the Neuastronomischenachrichten, and a German mathematician had calculated a provisional orbit and ephemeris.

Scarcely had this orbit and ephemeris been published, when a Japanese scientist made a very remarkable suggestion. According to these calculations, the comet was approaching the sun from infinite space in a plane but slightly inclined to that of the ecliptic, an extremely rare occurrence, and, moreover, would traverse the orbit of Saturn. "It would be exceedingly interesting," he remarked, "to multiply observations and revise the calculation of the orbit, with a view to determining whether the comet will come in collision with the rings of Saturn; for this planet will be exactly at that point of its path intersected by the orbit of the comet, on the day of the latter's arrival."

A young laureate of the Institute, a candidate for the directorship for the observatory, acting at once on this suggestion, had installed herself at the telephone office in order to capture on the wing every message. In less than ten days she had intercepted more than one hundred despatches, and, without losing an instant, had devoted three nights and days to a revision of the orbit as based on this entire series of observations. The result proved that the German computor had committed an error in determining the perihelion distance and that the inference drawn by the Japanese astronomer was inexact in so far as the date of the comet's passage through the plane of the ecliptic was concerned, this date being five or six days earlier than that first announced; but the interest in the problem increased, for the minimum distance of the comet from the earth seemed now less than the Japanese calculator had thought possible. Setting aside for the moment, the question of a collision, it was hoped that the enormous perturbation which would result from the attraction of the earth and moon would afford a new method of determining with exhaustive precision the mass of both these bodies, and perhaps even throw important light upon the density of the earth's interior. It was, indeed, established that the celestial visitor was moving in a plane nearly coincident with that of the ecliptic, and would pass near the system of Saturn, whose attraction would probably modify to a sensible degree the primitive parabolic orbit, bringing it nearer to the belated planet. But the comet, after traversing the orbits of Jupiter and of Mars, was then to enter exactly that described annually by the earth about the sun. The interest of astronomers was not on this account any the less keen, and the young computor insisted more forcibly than ever upon the importance of numerous and exact observations.

It was at the observatory of Gaurisankar especially that the study of the comet's elements was prosecuted. On this highest elevation of the globe, at an altitude of 8000 meters, among eternal snows which, by newly discovered processes of electro-chemistry, were kept at a distance of several kilometers from the station, towering almost always many hundred meters above the highest clouds, in a pure and rarified atmosphere, the visual power of both the eye and the telescope was increased a hundred fold. The craters of the moon, the satellites of Jupiter, and the phases of Venus could be readily distinguished by the naked eye. For nine or ten generations several families of astronomers had lived upon this Asiatic summit, and had gradually become accustomed to its rare atmosphere. The first comers had succumbed; but science and industry had succeeded in modifying the rigors of the temperature by the storage of solar heat, and acclimatization slowly took place; as in former times, at Quito and Bogota, where, in the eighteenth and nineteenth centuries, a contented population lived in plenty, and young women might be seen dancing all night long without fatigue; whereas on Mont Blanc in Europe, at the same elevation, a few steps only were attended with painful respiration. By degrees a small colony was installed upon the slopes of the Himalayas, and, through their researches and discoveries, the observatory had acquired the reputation of being the first in the world. Its principal instrument was the celebrated equatorial of one hundred meters focal length, by whose aid the hieroglyphic signals, addressed in vain for several thousand years by the inhabitants of the planet Mars to the earth, had finally been deciphered.

While the astronomers of Europe were discussing the orbit of the new comet and establishing the precision of the computations which foretold its convergence upon the earth and the collision of the two bodies in space, a new phonographic message was sent out from the Himalayan observatory:

"The comet will soon become visible to the naked eye. Still of greenish hue. Its course is earthward."

The complete agreement between the astronomical data, whether from European, American, or Asiatic sources, could leave no further doubt of their exactness. The daily papers sowed broadcast this alarming news, embellished with sinister comments and numberless interviews in which the most astonishing statements were attributed to scientists. Their only concern was to outdo the ascertained facts, and to exaggerate their bearing by more or less fanciful additions. As for that matter, the journals of the world had long since become purely business enterprises. The sole preoccupation of each was to sell every day the greatest possible number of copies. They invented false news, travestied the truth, dishonored men and women, spread scandal, lied without shame, explained the devices of thieves and murderers, published the formulæ of recently invented explosives, imperilled their own readers and betrayed every class of society, for the sole purpose of exciting to the highest pitch the curiosity of the public and of "selling copies."

Everything had become a pure matter of business. For science, art, literature, philosophy, study and research, the press cared nothing. An acrobat, a runner or a jockey, an air-ship or water-velocipede, attained more celebrity in a day than the most eminent scientist, or the most ingenious inventor – for these two classes made no return to the stockholders. Everything was adroitly decked out with the rhetoric of patriotism, a sentiment which still exercised some empire over the minds of men. In short, from every point of view, the pecuniary interests of the publication dominated all considerations of public interest and general progress. Of all this the public had been for a long time the dupe; but, at the time of which we are now speaking, it had surrendered to the situation, so that there was no longer any newspaper, properly speaking, but only sheets of notices and advertisements of a commercial nature. Neither the first announcement of the press, that a comet was approaching with a high velocity and would collide with the earth at a date already determined; nor the second, that the wandering star might bring about a general catastrophe by rendering the atmosphere irrespirable, had produced the slightest impression; this two-fold prophecy, if noticed at all by the heedless reader, had been received with profound incredulity, attracting no more attention than the simultaneous announcement of the discovery of the fountain of perpetual youth in the cellars of the Palais des Fées on Montmartre (erected on the ruins of the cathedral of the Sacré-Cœur).

Moreover, astronomers themselves had not, at first, evinced any anxiety about the collision so far as it affected the fate of humanity, and the astronomical journals (which alone retained any semblance of authority) had as yet referred to the subject simply as a computation to be verified. Scientists had treated the problem as one of pure mathematics, regarding it only as an interesting case of celestial mechanics. In the interviews to which they had been subjected they had contented themselves with saying that a collision was possible, even probable, but of no interest to the public.

Meanwhile, a new message was received by telephone, this time from Mount Hamilton in California, which produced a sensation among the chemists and physiologists:

"Spectroscopic observation establishes the fact that the comet is a body of considerable density, composed of several gases the chief of which is carbonic-oxide."

Matters were becoming serious. That a collision with the earth would occur was certain. If astronomers were not especially preoccupied by this fact, accustomed as they were for centuries to consider these celestial conjunctions as harmless: if the most celebrated even of their number had, at last, coldly shown the door to the many beardless reporters constantly importuning them, declaring that this prediction was of no interest to the people at large and was a strictly astronomical question which did not concern them, physicians, on the other hand, had begun to agitate the subject and to discuss gravely, among each other, the possibilities of asphyxia, or poisoning. Less indifferent to public opinion, so far from turning a cold shoulder to the journalists, they had welcomed them, and in a few days the subject suddenly entered upon a new phase. From the domain of astronomy it had passed into that of philosophy, and the name of every well-known or famous physician appeared in large letters on the title-pages of the daily papers; their portraits were reproduced in the illustrated journals, and the formula, "Interviews on the Comet," was to be seen on every hand. Already, even, the variety and diversity of conflicting opinions had created hostile camps, which hurled at each other the most grotesque abuse, and asserted that all physicians were "charlatans eager for notoriety."

In the mean time the director of the Paris observatory having at heart the interests of science, was profoundly disturbed by an uproar which had more than once, on former occasions, singularly misrepresented astronomical facts. He was a venerable old man who had grown gray in the study of the great problems of the constitution of the universe. His utterances were respected by all, and he had decided to make a statement to the press in which he declared that all conjectures, made prior to the technical discussion authorized by the Institute, were premature.

It has been remarked, we believe, that the Paris observatory, always in the van of every scientific movement, by virtue of the labors of its members, and more especially, of improved methods of observation, had become, on the one hand, the sanctuary of theoretical research, and on the other the central telephone bureau for stations established at a distance from the great cities on elevations favored by a perfectly transparent atmosphere.

It was an asylum of peace, where perfect concord reigned, where astronomers disinterestedly consecrated their whole lives to the advancement of science, and mutually encouraged each other, without experiencing any of the pangs of envy, each forgetting his own merit to proclaim that of his colleagues. The director set the example, and when he spoke it was in the name of all.

He published a technical discussion, and he was listened to – for a moment. For the question appeared to be no longer one of astronomy. No one denied or disputed the meeting of the comet with the earth. That was a fact which mathematics had rendered certain. The absorbing question now was the chemical constitution of the comet. If the earth, in its passage through it, was to lose the oxygen of its atmosphere, death by asphyxia was inevitable; if, on the other hand, the nitrogen was to combine with the cometary gases, death was still certain; but death preceded by an ungovernable exhilaration, a sort of universal intoxication, a wild delirium of the senses being the necessary result of the extraction of nitrogen from the respirable air and the proportionate increase of oxygen.

The spectroscope indicated especially the presence of carbonic-oxide in the chemical constitution of the comet. The chief point under discussion in the scientific reviews was whether the mixture of this noxious gas with the atmosphere would poison the entire population of the globe, human and animal, as the president of the academy of medicine affirmed would be the case.

Carbonic-oxide! Nothing else was talked of. The spectroscope could not be in error. Its methods were too sure, its processes too precise. Everybody knew that the smallest admixture of this gas with the air we breathe meant a speedy death. Now, a later despatch from the observatory of Gaurisankar had more than confirmed that received from Mount Hamilton This despatch read:

"The earth will be completely submerged in the nucleus of the comet, whose diameter is already thirty times that of the globe and is daily increasing."

Thirty times the diameter of the earth! Even then, though the comet should pass between the earth and the moon, it would touch them both, since a bridge of thirty earths would span the distance between our world and the moon.

Then, too, during the three months whose history we have recapitulated, the comet had emerged from regions accessible only to the telescope and had become visible to the naked eye. In full view of the earth it hovered now like a threat from heaven among the army of stars Terror itself, advancing slowly but inexorably, was suspended like a mighty sword above every head. A last effort was made, not indeed to turn the comet from its path – an idea conceived by that class of visionaries who recoil before nothing, and who had even imagined that an electric storm of vast magnitude might be produced by batteries suitably distributed over that face of the globe which was to receive the shock – but to examine once more the great problem under every aspect, and perhaps to reassure the public mind and rekindle hope by the discovery of some error in the conclusions which had been drawn, some forgotten fact in the observations or computations. This collision might not after all prove so fatal as the pessimists had foretold. A general presentation of the case from every point of view was announced for this very Monday at the Institute, just four days before the prophesied moment of collision, which would take place on Friday, July 13th. The most celebrated astronomer of France, at that time director of the Paris observatory; the president of the academy of medicine, an eminent physiologist and chemist; the president of the astronomical society, a skillful mathematician, and other orators also, among them a woman distinguished for her discoveries in the physical sciences, were among the speakers announced. The last word had not yet been spoken. Let us enter the venerable dome and listen to the discussion.

But before doing so, let us ourselves consider this famous comet which for the time being absorbed every thought.

Chapter II

THE STRANGER had emerged slowly from the depths of space. Instead of appearing suddenly, as more than once the great comets have been observed to do, – either because coming into view immediately after their perihelion passage, or after a long series of storms or moonlight nights has prevented the search of the sky by the comet-seekers – this floating star-mist had at first remained in regions visible only to the telescope, and had been watched only by astronomers. For several days after its discovery, none but the most powerful equatorials of the observatories could detect its presence. But the well-informed were not slow to examine it for themselves. Every modern house was crowded with a terrace, partly for the purpose of facilitating aerial embarkations. Many of them were provided with revolving domes. Few well-to-do families were without a telescope, and no home was complete without a library, well furnished with scientific books.

The comet had been observed by everybody, so to speak, from the instant it became visible to instruments of moderate power. As for the laboring classes, whose leisure moments were always provided for, the telescopes set up in the public squares had been surrounded by impatient crowds from the first moment of visibility, and every evening the receipts of these astronomers of the open air had been incredible and without precedent. Many workmen, too, had their own instruments, especially in the provinces, and justice, as well as truth, compels us to acknowledge that the first discoverer of the comet (outside of the professional observers) had not been a man of the world, a person of importance, or an academician, but a plain workman of the town of Soissons, who passed the greater portion of his nights under the stars, and who had succeeded in purchasing out of his laboriously accumulated savings an excellent little telescope with which he was in the habit of studying the wonders of the sky. And it is a notable fact that prior to the twenty-fourth century, nearly all the inhabitants of the earth had lived without knowing where they were, without even feeling the curiosity to ask, like blind men, with no other preoccupation than the satisfaction of their appetites; but within a hundred years the human race had begun to observe and reason upon the universe about them.

To understand the path of the comet through space, it will be sufficient to examine carefully the accompanying chart. It represents the comet coming from infinite space obliquely towards the earth, and afterwards falling into the sun which does not arrest it in its passage toward perihelion. No account has been taken of the perturbation caused by the earth's attraction, whose effect would be to bring the comet nearer to the earth's orbit. All the comets which gravitate about the sun – and they are numerous – describe similar elongated orbits, – ellipses, one of whose foci is occupied by the solar star. On studying the intersections of the cometary and planetary orbits, and the orbit of the earth about the sun, we perceive that a collision is neither an impossible nor an abnormal event.

The comet was now visible to the naked eye. On the night of the new moon, the atmosphere being perfectly clear, it had been detected by a few keen eyes without the aid of a glass, not far from the zenith near the edge of the milky way to the south of the star Omicron in the constellation of Andromeda, as a pale nebulæ, like a puff of very light smoke, quite small, almost round, slightly elongated in a direction opposed to that of the sun – a gaseous elongation, outlining a rudimentary tail. This, indeed, had been its appearance since its first discovery by the telescope. From its inoffensive aspect no one could have suspected the tragic role which this new star was to play in the history of humanity. Analysis alone indicated its march toward the earth.

But the mysterious star approached rapidly. The very next day the half of those who searched for it had detected it, and the following day only the near-sighted, with eyeglasses of insufficient power, had failed to make it out. In less than a week every one had seen it. In all the public squares, in every city, in every village, groups were to be seen watching it, or showing it to others.

Day by day it increased in size. The telescope began to distinguish distinctly a luminous nucleus. The excitement increased at the same time, invading every mind. When, after the first quarter and during the full moon, it appeared to remain stationary and even to lose something of its brilliancy, as it had been expected to grow rapidly larger, it was hoped that some error had crept into the computations, and a period of tranquillity and relief followed. After the full moon the barometer fell rapidly. A violent storm-center, coming from the Atlantic, passed north of the British Isles. For twelve days the sky was entirely obscured over nearly the whole of Europe.

Once more the sun shone in purified atmosphere, the clouds dissolved and the blue sky reappeared pure and unobscured; it was not without emotion that men waited for the setting of the sun – especially as several aerial expeditions had succeeded in rising above the cloud-belts, and aeronauts had asserted that the comet was visibly larger. Telephone messages sent out from the mountains of Asia and America announced also its rapid approach. But great was the surprise when at nightfall every eye was turned heavenward to seek the flaming star. It was no longer a comet, a classic comet such as one had seen before, but an aurora borealis of a new kind, a gigantic celestial fan, with seven branches, shooting into space seven greenish streamers, which appeared to issue from a point hidden below the horizon.

No one had the slightest doubt but that this fantastical aurora borealis was the comet itself, a view confirmed by the fact that the former comet could not be found anywhere among the starry host. The apparition differed, it is true, from all popularly known cometary forms, and the radiating beams of the mysterious visitor were, of all forms, the least expected. But these gaseous bodies are so remarkable, so capricious, so various, that everything is possible. Moreover, it was not the first time that a comet had presented such an aspect. Astronomy contained among its records that of an immense comet observed in 1744, which at that time had been the subject of much discussion, and whose picturesque delineation, made de visu by the astronomer Chèzeaux, at Lausanne, had given it a wide celebrity. But even if nothing of this nature had been seen before, the evidence of one's eyes was indubitable.

Meanwhile, discussions multiplied, and a veritable astronomical tournament was commenced in the scientific reviews of the entire world – the only journals which inspired any confidence amid the epidemic of buying and selling which had for so long a time possessed humanity. The main question, now that there was no longer any doubt that the star was moving straight toward the earth, was its position from day to day, a question depending upon its velocity. The young computor of the Paris observatory, chief of the section of comets, sent every day a note to the official journal of the United States of Europe.

A very simple mathematical relation exists between the velocity of every comet and its distance from the sun. Knowing the former one can at once find the latter. In fact the velocity of the comet is simply the velocity of a planet multiplied by the square root of two. Now the velocity of a planet, whatever its distance, is determined by Kepler's third law, according to which the squares of the times of revolution are to each other as the cubes of the distances. Nothing evidently, can be more simple. Thus, for example, the magnificent planet, Jupiter, moves about the sun with a velocity of 13,000 meters per second. A comet at this distance moves, therefore, with the above-mentioned velocity, multiplied by the square root of two, that is to say by the number 1.4142. This velocity is consequently 18,380 meters per second.

The planet Mars revolves about the sun at the rate of 24,000 meters per second. At this distance the comet's velocity is 34,000 meters per second.

The mean velocity of the earth in its orbit is 29,460 meters per second, a little less in June, a little more in December. In the neighborhood of the earth, therefore, the velocity of the comet is 41,660 meters, independently of the acceleration which the earth might occasion.

These facts the laureate of the Institute called to the attention of the public which, moreover, already possessed some general notions upon the theory of celestial mechanics.

When the threatening star arrived at a distance from the sun equal to that of Mars, the popular fear was no longer a vague apprehension; it took definite form, based, as it was, upon the exact knowledge of the comet's rate of approach. Thirty-four thousand meters per second meant 2040 kilometers per minute, or 122,400 kilometers per hour!

As the distance of the orbit of Mars from that of the earth is only 76,000,000 of kilometers, at the rate of 122,400 kilometers an hour, this distance would be covered in 621 hours, or about twenty-six days. But, as the comet approached the sun, its velocity would increase, since at the distance of the earth its velocity would be 41,660 meters per second. In virtue of this increase of speed, the distance between the two orbits would be traversed by a comet in 558 hours, or in twenty-three days, six hours.

But the earth at the moment of meeting with the comet, would not be exactly at that point of its orbit intersected by a line from the comet to the sun, because the former was not advancing directly toward the latter; the collision, therefore, would not take place for nearly a week later, namely: at about midnight on Friday, the 13th of July. It is unnecessary to add that under such circumstances the usual arrangements for the celebration of the national fête of July 14th had been forgotten. National fête! No one thought of it. Was not that date far more likely to mark the universal doom of men and things? As to that, the celebration by the French of the anniversary of that famous day had lasted – with some exceptions, it is true – for more than five centuries: even among the Romans anniversaries had never been observed for so long a period, and it was generally agreed that the 14th of July had outlived its usefulness.

It was now Monday, the 8th of July. For five days the sky had been perfectly clear, and every night the fan-like comet hovered in the sky depths, its head, or nucleus, distinctly visible and dotted with luminous points which might well be solid bodies several kilometers in diameter, and which, according to the calculations, would be the first to strike the earth, the tail being in a direction away from the sun and in the present instance behind and obliquely situated with reference to the direction of motion. The new star blazed in the constellation of Pisces. According to observations taken on the preceding evening, July 8th, its exact position was: right ascension, 23h., 10m., 32s.; declination north, 7°, 36′, 4″. The tail lay entirely across the constellation of Pegasus. The comet rose at 9h., 49m. and was visible all night long.

During the lull of which we have spoken, a change in public opinion had occurred. From a series of retrospective calculations an astronomer had proved that the earth had already on several occasions encountered comets, and that each time the only result had been a harmless shower of shooting stars. But one of his colleagues had replied that the present comet could not in any sense be compared to a swarm of meteors, that it was gaseous, with a nucleus composed of solid bodies and he had in this connection recalled the observations made upon a comet famous in history, that of 1811.

This comet of 1811 justified, in a certain respect, a real apprehension. Its dimensions were recalled to mind: its length of 180,000,000 kilometers, that is to say, a distance greater than that of the earth from the sun; and the width of its tail at its extreme point, 24,000,000 kilometers. The diameter of its nucleus measured 1,800,000 kilometers, forty thousand times that of the earth, and its nebulous and remarkably regular elliptical head was a spot brilliant as a star, having itself a diameter of no less than 200,000 kilometers. The spot appeared to be of great density. It was observed for sixteen months and twenty-two days. But the most remarkable feature of this comet was the immense development to which it attained without approaching very close to the sun; for it did not reach a point nearer than 150,000,000 kilometers, and thus remained more than 170,000,000 kilometers from the earth. As the size of comets increases as they near the sun, if this one had experienced to a greater degree the solar action, its appearance would certainly have been still more wonderful, and, doubtless, terrifying to the observer. And as its mass was far from insignificant, if it had fallen directly into the sun, its velocity, accelerated to the rate of five or six hundred thousand meters per second at the moment of collision, might, by the transformation of mechanical energy into thermal energy, have suddenly increased the solar radiations to such a degree as to have utterly destroyed in a few days every trace of vegetable and animal life upon the earth.

A physicist, indeed, had made this curious remark, that a comet of the same size as that of 1811, or greater, might thus bring about the end of the world without actual contact, by a sort of expulsion of solar light and heat, analogous to that observed in the case of temporary stars. The impact would, indeed, give rise to a quantity of heat six times as great as that which would be produced by the combustion of a mass of coal equal to the mass of the comet.

It had been shown that if such a comet in its flight, instead of falling into the sun, should collide with our planet, the end of the world would be by fire. If it collided with Jupiter it would raise the temperature of that globe to such a point as to restore to it its lost light, and to make it for a time a sun again, so that the earth would be lighted by two suns, Jupiter becoming a sort of minor night-sun, far brighter than the moon, and shining by its own light – of a ruby-red or garnet color, revolving about the earth in twelve years. A nocturnal sun! That is to say, no more real night for the earth.

The most classical astronomical treatises had been consulted; chapters on comets written by Newton, Halley, Maupertuis, Lalande, Laplace, Arago, Faye, Newcomb, Holden, Denning, Robert Ball, and their successors, had been re-read. The opinion of Laplace had made the deepest impression and his language had been textually cited: "The earth's axis and rotary motion changed; the oceans abandoning their old-time beds, to rush toward the new equator; the majority of men and animals overwhelmed by this universal deluge, or destroyed by the violent shock; entire species annihilated; every monument of human industry overthrown; such are the disasters which might result from collision with a comet."

Thus discussion, researches into the past, calculations, conjectures succeeded each other. But that which made the deepest impression on every mind was first that, as proved by observation, the present comet had a nucleus of considerable density, and second, that carbonic-oxide gas was unquestionably the chief chemical constituent. Fear and terror resumed their sway. Nothing else was thought of, or talked about, but the comet. Already inventive minds sought some way, more or less practicable, of evading the danger. Chemists pretended to be able to preserve a part of the oxygen of the atmosphere. Methods were devised for the isolation of this gas from the nitrogen and its storage in immense vessels of glass hermetically sealed. A clever pharmacist asserted that he had condensed it in pastilles, and in a fortnight expended eight millions in advertising. Thus commerce made capital out of everything, even universal death. All hope was not, however, abandoned. People disputed, trembled, grew anxious, shuddered, died even – but hoped on.

The latest news was to the effect that the comet, developing, as it approached the thermal and electric influences of the sun, would have at the moment of impact a diameter sixty-five times that of the earth, or 828,000 kilometers.

It was in the midst of this state of general anxiety that the session of the Institute, whose utterance was awaited as the last word of an oracle, was opened.

The director of the observatory of Paris was naturally to be the first speaker; but what seemed to excite the greatest interest in the public was the opinion of the president of the academy of medicine on the probable effects of carbonic-oxide. The president of the geological society of France was also to make an address, and the general object of the session was to pass in review all the possible ways in which our earth might come to an end. Evidently, however, the discussion of its collision with the comet would hold the first place.

As we have just seen, the threatening star hung above every head; everybody could see it; it was growing larger day by day; it was approaching with an increasing velocity; it was known to be at a distance of only 17,992,000 kilometers, and that this distance would be passed over in five days. Every hour brought this menacing hand, ready to strike, 149,000 kilometers nearer. In six days anxious humanity would breathe freely – or not at all.

Chapter III

NEVER, WITHIN THE HISTORY of man, had the immense hemicycle, constructed at the end of the twentieth century, been invaded by so compact a crowd. It would have been mechanically impossible for another person to force an entrance. The amphitheater, the boxes, the tribunes, the galleries, the aisles, the stairs, the corridors, the doorways, all, to the very steps of the platform, were filled with people, sitting or standing. Among the audience were the president of the United States of Europe, the director of the French republic, the directors of the Italian and Iberian republics, the chief ambassador of India, the ambassadors of the British, German, Hungarian and Muscovite republics, the king of the Congo, the president of the committee of administrators, all the ministers, the prefect of the international exchange, the cardinal-archbishop of Paris, the director-general of telephones, the president of the council of aerial navigation and electric roads, the director of the international bureau of time, the principal astronomers, chemists, physiologists and physicians of France, a large number of state officials (formerly called deputies or senators), many celebrated writers and artists, in a word, a rarely assembled galaxy of the representatives of science, politics, commerce, industry, literature and every sphere of human activity. The platform was occupied by the president, vice-presidents, permanent secretaries and orators of the day, but they did not wear, as formerly, the green coat and chapeau or the old-fashioned sword, they were dressed simply in civil costume, and for two centuries and a half every European decoration had been suppressed; those of central Africa, on the contrary, were of the most brilliant description.

Domesticated monkeys, which for more than half a century had filled every place of service – impossible otherwise to provide for – stood at the doors, in conformity to the regulations, rather than to verify the cards of admission; for long before the hour fixed upon every place had been occupied.

The president opened the session as follows (it is needless to remind the reader that the language of the XXXVth century is here translated into that of the XIXth):

"Ladies and gentlemen: You all know the object for which we are assembled. Never, certainly, has humanity passed through such a crisis as this. Never, indeed, has this historic room of the twentieth century contained such an audience. The great problem of the end of the world has been for a fortnight the single object of discussion and study among savants. The results of their discussions and researches are now to be announced. Without further preamble I give place to the director of the observatory."

The astronomer immediately arose, holding a few notes in his hand. He had an easy address, an agreeable voice, and a pleasant countenance. His gestures were few and his expression pleasing. He had a broad forehead and a magnificent head of curling, white hair framed his face. He was a man of learning and of culture, as well as of science, and his whole personality inspired both sympathy and respect. His temperament was evidently optimistic, even under circumstances of great peril. Scarcely had he begun to speak when the mournful and anxious faces before him became suddenly calm and reassured.

"Ladies," he began, "I address myself first to you, begging you not to tremble in this way before a danger which may well be less terrible than it seems. I hope presently to convince you, by the arguments which I shall have the honor to lay before you, that the comet, whose approach is expected by the entire race, will not involve the total ruin of the earth. Doubtless, we may, and should, expect some catastrophe, but as for the end of the world, really, everything would lead us to believe that it will not take place in this manner. Worlds die of old age, not by accident, and, ladies, you know better than I that the world is far from being old.

"Gentlemen, I see before me representatives of every social sphere, from the highest to the most humble. Before a danger so apparent, threatening the destruction of all life, it is not surprising that every business operation should be absolutely suspended. Nevertheless, as for myself, I confess that if the bourse was not closed, and if I had never had the misfortune to be interested in speculation, I should not hesitate today to purchase securities which have fallen so low."

This sentence was finished before a noted American Israelite – a prince of finance – director of the journal The Twenty-fifth Century, occupying a seat on one of the upper steps of the amphitheater, forced his way, one hardly knows how, through the rows of benches, and rolled like a ball to the corridor leading to an exit, through which he disappeared.

After the momentary interruption caused by this unexpected sequel to a purely scientific remark, the orator resumed:

"Our subject," he said, "may be considered under three heads: 1. Is the collision of the comet with the earth certain? If this question is answered in the affirmative, we shall have to examine: 2. The nature of the comet, and, 3. The possible effects of a collision. I have no need to remind so intelligent an audience as this that the prophetic words 'End of the world,' so often heard today, signify solely 'End of the earth,' which moment indeed, of all others, has the most interest for us.

"If we are able to answer the first question in the negative, it will be quite superfluous to consider the other two, which would become of secondary interest.

"Unfortunately, I must admit that the calculations of the astronomers are in this case, as usual, entirely correct. Yes, the comet will strike the earth, and, doubtless, with maximum force, since the impact will be direct. The velocity of the earth is 29,400 meters per second; that of the comet is 41,660 meters, plus the acceleration due to the attraction of our planet. The initial velocity of contact, therefore, will be 72,000 meters per second. The collision, is inevitable, with all its consequences, if the impact of the comet is direct; but it will be slightly oblique. But do not for this reason, take matters so to heart. In itself the collision proves nothing. If it were announced, for example, that a railway train was to encounter a swarm of flies, this prediction would not greatly trouble the traveller. It may well be that the collision of our earth with this nebulous star will be of the same nature.

"Permit me now to examine, calmly, the two remaining questions.

"First, what is the nature of the comet? That everyone knows already; it is a gas whose principal constituent is carbonic-oxide. Invisible under ordinary conditions, at the temperature of stellar space (273 degrees below zero), this gas is in a state of vapor, even of solid particles. The comet is saturated with them. I shall not in this matter dispute in the least the discoveries of science."

This confession deepened anew the painful expression on the faces of most of the audience, and here a long sigh was drawn.

"But, gentlemen," resumed the astronomer, "until one of our eminent colleagues of the section of physiology, or of the academy of medicine, deigns to prove for us that the density of the comet is sufficient to admit of its penetration into our atmosphere, I do not believe that its presence is likely to exert a fatal influence upon human life. I say is likely, for it is not possible to affirm this with certainty, although the probability is very great. One might perhaps wager a million to one. In any case, only those affected with weak lungs will be victims. It will be a simple influenza, which may increase three or fivefold the daily death rate.

"If, however, as the telescope and camera agree in indicating, the nucleus contains large mineral masses, probably of a metallic nature, uranolites, measuring several kilometers in diameter, and weighing some millions of tons, one cannot but admit that the localities where these masses will fall, with the velocity referred to a moment ago, would be utterly destroyed. Let us observe, however, that three-fourths of the globe is covered with water. Here again is a contingency, not so important doubtless as the first, but, nevertheless, in our favor; these masses may perhaps fall into the sea, forming possibly new islands of foreign origin, bringing in any case elements new to science, and, it may be, germs of unknown life; Geodesy would in this case be interested, and the form and rotary movement of the earth might be modified. Let us note also that not a few deserts mark the earth's surface. Danger exists, assuredly, but it is not overwhelming.

"Besides these masses and these gases, perhaps also the bolides of which we were speaking, coming in clouds, will kindle conflagrations at various places on the continents; dynamite, nitroglycerine, panclastite and royalite would be playthings in comparison with what may overtake us, but this does not imply a universal cataclysm; a few cities in ashes cannot arrest the history of humanity.

"You see, gentlemen, from this methodical examination of the three points before us, it follows that the danger, while it exists, and is even imminent, is not so great, so overwhelming, so certain, as is asserted. I will even say more: this curious astronomical event, which sets so many hearts beating and fills with anxiety so many minds, in the eyes of the philosopher scarcely changes the usual aspect of things. Each one of us must some day die, and this certainty does not prevent us from living tranquilly. Why should the apprehension of a somewhat more speedy death disturb the serenity of so many of us? Is the thought of our dying together so disagreeable? This should prove rather a consolation to our egotism. No, it is the thought that a stupendous catastrophe is to shorten our lives by a few days or years. Life is short, and each clings to the smallest fraction of it; it would even seem, from what one hears, that each would prefer to see the whole world perish, provided he himself survived, rather than die alone and know the world was saved. This is pure egoism. But, gentlemen, I am firm in the belief that this will be only a partial disaster, of the highest scientific importance, but leaving behind it historians to tell its story. There will be a collision, shock, and local ruin. It will be the history of an earthquake, of a volcanic eruption, of a cyclone."

Thus spoke the illustrious astronomer. The audience appeared satisfied, calmed, tranquillized – in part, at least. It was no longer the question of the absolute end of all things, but of a catastrophe, from which, after all, one would probably escape. Whispered murmurs of conversation were to be heard; people confided to each other their impressions; merchants and politicians even seemed to have perfectly understood the arguments advanced, when, at the invitation of the presiding officer, the president of the academy of medicine was seen advancing slowly toward the tribune.

He was a tall man, spare, slender, erect, with a sallow face and ascetic appearance, and melancholy countenance – bald-headed, and wearing closely-trimmed, gray side-whiskers. His voice had something cadaverous about it, and his whole personality called to mind the undertaker rather than the physician fired with the hope of curing his patients. His estimate of affairs was very different from that of the astronomer, as was apparent from the very first word he uttered.

"Gentlemen," said he, "I shall be as brief as the eminent savant to whom we have just listened, although I have passed many a night in analyzing, to the minutest detail, the properties of carbonic-oxide. It is about this gas that I shall speak to you, since science has demonstrated that it is the chief constituent of the comet, and that a collision with the earth is inevitable.

"These properties are terrible; why not confess it? For the most infinitesimal quantity of this gas in the air we breathe is sufficient to arrest in three minutes the normal action of the lungs and to destroy life.

"Everybody knows that carbonic-oxide (known in chemistry as CO) is a permanent gas without odor, color or taste, and nearly insoluble in water. Its density in comparison with the air is 0.96. It burns in the air with a blue flame of slight illuminating power, like a funereal fire, the product of this combustion being carbonic anhydride.

"Its most notable property is its tendency to absorb oxygen. (The orator dwelt upon these two words with great emphasis.) In the great iron furnaces, for example, carbon, in the presence of an insufficient quantity of air, becomes transformed into carbonic-oxide, and it is subsequently this oxide which reduces the iron to a metallic state, by depriving it of the oxygen with which it was combined.

"In the sunlight carbonic-oxide combines with chlorine and gives rise to an oxychlorine ($COCL^2$) – a gas with a disagreeable, suffocating odor.

"The fact which deserves our more serious attention, is that this gas is of the most poisonous character – far more so than carbonic anhydride. Its effect upon the hemoglobin is to diminish the respiratory capacity of the blood, and even in very small doses, by its cumulative effect, hinders, to a degree altogether out of proportion to the apparent cause, the oxygenizing properties of the blood. For example: blood which absorbs from twenty-three to twenty-four cubic centimeters of oxygen per hundred volumes, absorbs only one-half as much in an atmosphere which contains less than one-thousandth part of carbonic-oxide. The one-ten-thousandth part even has a deleterious effect, sensibly diminishing the respiratory action of the blood. The result is not simple asphyxia, but an almost instantaneous blood-poisoning. Carbonic-oxide acts directly upon the blood corpuscles, combining with them and rendering them unfit to sustain life: hematosis, that is, the conversion of venous into arterial blood, is arrested. Three minutes are sufficient to produce death. The circulation of the blood ceases. The black venous blood fills the arteries as well as the veins. The latter, especially those of the brain, become surcharged, the substance of the brain becomes punctured, the base of the tongue, the larynx, the wind-pipe, the bronchial tubes become red with blood, and soon the entire body presents the characteristic purple appearance which results from the suspension of hematosis.

"But, gentlemen, the injurious properties of carbonic-oxide are not the only ones to be feared; the mere tendency of this gas to absorb oxygen would bring about fatal results. To suppress, nay, even only to diminish oxygen, would suffice for the extinction of the human species. Everyone here present is familiar with that incident which, with so many others, marks the epoch of barbarism, when men assassinated each other legally in the name of glory and of patriotism; it is a simple episode of one of the English wars in India. Permit me to recall it to your memory:

"One hundred and forty-six prisoners had been confined in a room whose only outlets were two small windows opening upon a corridor; the first effect experienced by these unfortunate captives was a free and persistent perspiration, followed by insupportable thirst, and soon by great difficulty in breathing. They sought in various ways to get more room and air; they divested themselves of their clothes; they beat the air with their hats, and finally resorted to kneeling and rising together at intervals of a few seconds; but each time some of those whose strength failed them fell and were trampled under the feet of their comrades. Before midnight, that is, during the fourth hour of their confinement, all who were still living, and who had not succeeded in obtaining purer air at the windows, had fallen into a lethargic stupor, or a frightful delirium. When, a few hours later, the prison door was opened, only twenty-three men came out alive; they were in the most pitiable state imaginable; every face wearing the impress of the death from which they had barely escaped.

"I might add a thousand other examples, but it would be useless, for doubt upon this point is impossible. I therefore affirm, gentlemen, that, on the one hand, the absorption by the carbonic-oxide of a portion of the atmospheric oxygen, or, on the other, the powerfully toxic properties of this gas upon the vital elements of the blood, alike seem to me to give to the meeting of our globe with the immense mass of the comet – in the heart of which we shall be plunged for several hours – I affirm, I repeat, that this meeting involves consequences absolutely fatal. For my part, I see no chance of escape.

"I have not spoken of the transformation of mechanical motion into heat, or of the mechanical and chemical consequences of the collision. I leave this aspect of the question to the permanent secretary of the academy of sciences and to the learned president of the astronomical society of France, who have made it the subject of important investigations. As for me, I repeat, terrestrial life is in danger, and I see not one only, but two, three and four mortal perils confronting it. Escape will be a miracle, and for centuries no one has believed in miracles."

This speech, uttered with the tone of conviction, in a clear, calm and solemn voice, again plunged the entire audience into a state of mind from which the preceding address had, happily, released them. The certainty of the approaching disaster was painted upon every face; some had become yellow, almost green; others suddenly became scarlet and seemed on the verge of apoplexy. Some few among the audience appeared to have retained their self-possession, through scepticism or a philosophic effort to make the best of it. A vast murmur filled the room; everyone whispered his opinions to his neighbor, opinions generally more optimistic than sincere, for no one likes to appear afraid.

The president of the astronomical society of France rose in his turn and advanced toward the tribune. Instantly every murmur was hushed. Below we give the main points of his speech, including the opening remarks and the peroration:

"Ladies and gentlemen: After the statements which we have just heard, no doubt can remain in any mind as to the certainty of the collision of the comet with the earth, and the dangers attending this event. We must, therefore, expect on Saturday—"

"On Friday," interrupted a voice from the desk of the Institute.

"On Saturday, I repeat," continued the orator, without noticing the interruption, "an extraordinary event, one absolutely unique in the history of the world.

"I say Saturday, although the papers announce that the collision will take place on Friday, because it cannot occur before July 14th. I passed the entire night with my learned colleague in comparing the observations received, and we discovered an error in their transmission."

This statement produced a sensation of relief among the audience; it was like a slender ray of light in the middle of a somber night. A single day of respite is of enormous importance to one condemned to death. Already chimerical projects formed in every mind; the catastrophe was put off; it was a kind of reprieve. It was not remembered that this diversion was of a purely cosmographic nature, relating to the date and not to the fact of the collision. But the least things play an important role in public opinion. So it was not to be on Friday!

"Here," he said, going to the black-board, "are the elements as finally computed from all the observations." The speaker traced upon the black-board the following figures:

Perihelion passage August 11, at 0h., 42m., 44s.
Longitude of perihelion, 52°, 43′, 25″.
Perihelion distance, 0.7607.
Inclination, 103°, 18′, 35″.
Longitude of ascending node, 112°, 54′, 40″.

"The comet," he resumed, "will cross the ecliptic in the direction of the descending node 28 minutes, 23 seconds after midnight of July 14th just as the earth reaches the point of crossing. The attraction of the earth will advance the moment of contact by only thirty seconds.

"The event, doubtless, will be altogether exceptional, but I do not believe either, that it will be of so tragical a nature as has been depicted, or that it can really bring about blood poison or universal asphyxia. It will rather present the appearance of a brilliant display of celestial fireworks, for the arrival in the atmosphere of these solid and gaseous bodies cannot occur without the conversion into heat of the mechanical motion thus destroyed; a magnificent illumination of the sky will doubtless be the first phenomenon.

"The heat evolved must necessarily be very great. Every shooting star, however small, entering the upper limits of our atmosphere with a cometary velocity, immediately becomes so hot that it takes fire and is consumed. You know, gentlemen, that the earth's atmosphere extends far into space about our planet; not without limit, as certain hypotheses declare, since the earth turns on its axis and moves about the sun: the mathematical limit is that height at which the centrifugal force engendered by the diurnal rotary motion becomes equal to the weight; this height is 6.64 times the equatorial radius of the earth, the latter being 6,378,310 meters. The maximum height of the atmosphere, therefore, is 35,973 kilometers.

"I do not here wish to enter into a mathematical discussion. But the audience before me is too well informed not to know the mechanical equivalent of heat. Every body whose motion is arrested produces a quantity of heat expressed in caloric units by mv^2 divided by 8338, in which m is the mass of the body in kilograms and v its velocity in meters per second. For example, a body weighing 8338 kilograms, moving with a velocity of one meter per second, would produce, if suddenly stopped, exactly one heat unit; that is to say, the quantity of heat necessary to raise one kilogram of water one degree in temperature.

"If the velocity of the body be 500 meters per second, it would produce 250,000 times as much heat, or enough to raise a quantity of water of equal mass from 0° to 30°.

"If the velocity were 5000 meters per second, the heat developed would be 5,000,000 times as great.

"Now, you know, gentlemen, that the velocity with which a comet may reach the earth is 72,000 meters per second. At this figure the temperature becomes five milliards of degrees.

"This, indeed, is the maximum and, I should add, a number altogether inconceivable; but, gentlemen, let us take the minimum, if it be your pleasure, and let us admit that the impact is not direct, but more or less oblique, and that the mean velocity is not greater than 30,000 meters per second. Every kilogram of a bolide would develop in this case 107,946 heat units before its velocity would be destroyed by the resistance of the air; in other words, it would generate sufficient heat to raise the temperature of 1079 kilograms of water from 0° to 100° – that is, from the freezing to the boiling point. A uranolite weighing 2000 kilograms would thus, before reaching the earth, develop enough heat to raise the temperature of a column of air, whose cross-section is thirty square meters and whose height is equal to that of our atmosphere, 3000°, or, to raise from 0° to 30° a column whose cross-section is 3000 square meters.

"These calculations, for the introduction of which I crave your pardon, are necessary to show that the immediate consequence of the collision will be the production of an enormous quantity of heat, and, therefore, a considerable rise in the temperature of the air. This is exactly what takes place on a small scale in the case of a single meteorite, which becomes melted and covered superficially by a thin layer of vitrified matter, resembling varnish. But its fall is so rapid that there is not sufficient time for it to become heated to the center; if broken, its interior is found to be absolutely cold. It is the surrounding air which has been heated.

"One of the most curious results of the analysis which I have just had the honor to lay before you, is that the solid masses which, it is believed, have been seen by the telescope in the nucleus of the comet, will meet with such resistance in traversing our atmosphere that, except in rare instances, they will not reach the earth entire, but in small fragments. There will be a compression of the air in front of the bolide, a vacuum behind it, a superficial heating and incandescence of the moving body, a roar produced by the air rushing into the vacuum, the roll of thunder, explosions, the fall of the denser metallic portions and the evaporation of the remainder. A bolide of sulphur, of phosphorus, of tin or of zinc, would be consumed and dissipated long before reaching the lower strata of our atmosphere. As for the shooting stars, if, as seems probable, there is a veritable cloud of them, they will only produce the effect of a vast inverted display of fire-works.

"If, therefore, there is any reason for alarm, it is not, in my opinion, because we are to apprehend the penetration of the gaseous mass of carbonic-oxide into our atmosphere, but a rise in temperature, which cannot fail to result from the transformation of mechanical motion into heat. If this be so, safety may be perhaps attained by taking refuge on the side of the globe opposed to that which is to experience the direct shock of the comet, for the air is a very bad conductor of heat."

The permanent secretary of the academy rose in his turn. A worthy successor to the Fontenelles and Aragos of the past, he was not only a man of profound knowledge, but also an elegant writer and a persuasive orator, rising sometimes even to the highest flights of eloquence.

"To the theory which we have just heard," he said, "I have nothing to add; I can only apply it to the case of some comet already known. Let us suppose, for example, that a comet of the dimensions of that of 1811 should collide squarely with the earth in its path about the sun. The terrestrial ball would penetrate the nebula of the comet without experiencing any very sensible resistance. Admitting that this resistance is very slight, and that the density of the comet's nucleus may be neglected, the passage of the earth through the head of a comet of 1,800,000 kilometers in diameter, would require at least 25,000 seconds – that is, 417 minutes, or six hours, fifty-seven minutes – in round numbers, seven hours – the velocity being 120 times greater than that of a cannon-ball; and the earth continuing to rotate upon its axis, the collision would commence about six o'clock in the morning.

"Such a plunge into the cometary ocean, however rarified it might be, could not take place without producing as a first and immediate consequence, by reason of the thermodynamic principles which have been just called to your attention, a rise in temperature such that probably our entire atmosphere would take fire! It seems to me that in this particular case the danger would be very serious.

"But it would be a fine spectacle for the inhabitants of Mars, and a finer one still for those of Venus. Yes, that would indeed be a magnificent spectacle, analogous to those we have ourselves seen in the heavens, but far more splendid to our near neighbors.

"The oxygen of the air would prove insufficient to maintain the combustion, but there is another gas which physicists do not often think of, for the simple reason that they have never found it in their analyses – hydrogen. What has become of all the hydrogen freed from the soil these millions of years which have elapsed since prehistoric times? The density of this gas being one-sixteenth that of the air, it must have ascended, forming a highly rarified hydrogen envelope above our atmosphere. In virtue of the law of diffusion of gases, a large part of this hydrogen would become mixed with the atmosphere, but the upper air layers must contain a considerable portion of it. There, doubtless, at an elevation of more than one hundred kilometers, the shooting stars take fire, and the aurora borealis is lighted. Notice here that the oxygen of the air would furnish the carbon of the comet ample material during collision to feed the celestial fire.

"Thus the destruction of the world will result from the combustion of the atmosphere. For about seven hours – probably a little longer, as the resistance to the comet cannot be neglected – there will be a continuous transformation of motion into a heat. The hydrogen and the oxygen, combining with the carbon of the comet, will take fire. The temperature of the air will be raised several hundred degrees; woods, gardens, plants, forests, habitations, edifices, cities, villages, will all be rapidly consumed; the sea, the lakes and the rivers will begin to boil; men and animals, enveloped in the hot breath of the comet, will die asphyxiated before they are burned, their gasping lungs inhaling only flame. Every corpse will be almost immediately carbonized, reduced to ashes, and in this vast celestial furnace only the heart-rending voice of the trumpet of the indestructible angel of the Apocalypse will be heard, proclaiming from the sky, like a funeral knell, the antique death-song: 'Solvet sæculum in favilla.' This is what may happen if a comet like that of 1811 collides with the earth."

At these words the cardinal-archbishop rose from his seat and begged to be heard. The astronomer, perceiving him, bowed with a courtly grace and seemed to await the reply of his eminence.

"I do not desire," said the latter, "to interrupt the honorable speaker, but if science announces that the drama of the end of the world is to be ushered in by the destruction of the heavens by fire, I cannot refrain from saying that this has always been the universal belief of the church. 'The heavens,' says St. Peter, 'shall pass away with a great noise, and the elements shall meet with fervent heat, the earth also and the works that are therein shall be burned up.' St. Paul affirms also its renovation by fire, and we repeat daily at mass his words: 'Eum qui venturus est judicare vivos et mortuos et sæculum per ignem.'"

"Science," replied the astronomer, "has more than once been in accord with the prophecies of our ancestors. Fire will first devour that portion of the globe struck by the huge mass of the comet, consuming it before the inhabitants of the other hemisphere realize the extent of the catastrophe; but the air is a bad conductor of heat, and the latter will not be immediately propagated to the opposite hemisphere.

"If our latitude were to receive the first shock of the comet, reaching us, we will suppose, in summer, the tropic of Cancer, Morocco, Algeria, Tunis, Greece and Egypt would be found in the front of the celestial onset, while Australia, New Caledonia and Oceanica would be the most favored. But the rush of air into this European furnace would be such that a storm more violent than the most frightful hurricane and more formidable even than the air-current which moves continuously on the equator of Jupiter, with a velocity of 400,000 kilometers per hour, would rage from the Antipodes towards Europe, destroying everything in its path. The earth, turning upon its axis, would bring successively into the line of collision, the regions lying to the west of the meridian first blasted. An hour after Austria and Germany it would be the turn of France, then of the Atlantic ocean, then of North America, which would enter somewhat obliquely the dangerous area about five or six hours after France – that is, towards the end of the collision.

"Notwithstanding the unheard-of velocities of the comet and the earth, the pressure cannot be enormous, in view of the extremely rarified state of the matter traversed by the earth; but this matter, containing so much carbon, is combustible, and at perihelion these bodies are not infrequently seen to shine by their own as well as by reflected light: they become incandescent. What, then, must be the result of a collision with the earth? The combustion of meteorites and bolides, the superficial fusion of the uranolites which reach the earth's surface on fire, all lead us to believe that the moment of greatest heat will be that of contact, which evidently will not prevent the massive elements forming the nucleus of the comet from crushing the localities where they fall, and perhaps even breaking up an entire continent.

"The terrestrial globe being thus entirely surrounded by the cometary mass for nearly seven hours, and revolving in this incandescent gas, the air rushing violently toward the center of disturbance, the sea boiling and filling the atmosphere with new vapors, hot showers falling from the sky-cataracts, the storm raging everywhere with electric deflagrations and lightnings, the rolling of thunder heard above the scream of the tempest, the blessed light of former days having been succeeded by the mournful and sickly gleamings of the glowing atmosphere, the whole earth will speedily resound with the funeral knell of universal doom, although the fate of the dwellers in the Antipodes will probably differ from that of the rest of mankind. Instead of being immediately consumed, they will be stifled by the vapors, by the excess of nitrogen – the oxygen having been rapidly abstracted – or poisoned by carbonic-oxide; the fire will afterwards reduce their corpses to ashes, while the inhabitants of Europe and Africa will have been burned alive.

"The well-known tendency of carbonic-oxide to absorb oxygen will doubtless prove a sentence of instant death for those farthest from the initial point of the catastrophe.

"I have taken as an example the comet of 1811; but I hasten to add that the present one appears to be far less dense."

"Is it absolutely sure?" cried a well-known voice (that of an illustrious member of the chemical society) from one of the boxes. "Is it absolutely sure the comet is composed chiefly of carbonic-oxide? Have not the nitrogen lines also been detected in its spectrum? If it should prove to be protoxide of nitrogen, the consequence of its mixture with our atmosphere might be anæsthesia. Every one would be put to sleep – perhaps forever, if the suspension of the vital functions were to last but a little longer than is the case in our surgical operations. It would be the same if the comet was composed of chloroform or ether. That would be an end calm indeed.

"It would be less so if the comet should absorb the nitrogen instead of the oxygen, for this partial or total absorption of nitrogen would bring about, in a few hours, for all the inhabitants of the earth – for men and women, for the young and the aged – a change of temperament, involving at first nothing disagreeable – a charming sobriety, then gayety, followed by universal joy, a feverish exultation, finally delirium and madness, terminating, in all probability, by the sudden death of every human being in the apotheosis of a wild saturnalia, an unheard-of frenzy of the senses. Would that death be a sad one?"

"The discussion remains open," replied the secretary. "What I have said of the possible consequences of a collision applies to the direct impact of a comet like that of 1811; the one that threatens us is less colossal, and its impact will not be direct, but oblique. In common with the astronomers who have preceded me on this floor, I am inclined to believe, in this instance, in a mighty display of fire-works."

While the orator was still speaking, a young girl belonging to the central bureau of telephones, entered by a small door, conducted by a domesticated monkey, and, darting like a flash to the seat occupied by the president, put into his hands a large, square, international envelope. It was immediately opened, and proved to be a despatch from the observatory of Gaurisankar. It contained only the following words:

"The inhabitants of Mars are sending a photophonic message. Will be deciphered in a few hours."

"Gentlemen," said the president, "I see several in the audience consulting their watches, and I agree with them in thinking that it will be physically impossible for us to finish in a single session this important discussion, in which eminent representatives of geology, natural history and geonomy are yet to take part. Moreover, the despatch just read will doubtless introduce new problems. It is nearly six o'clock. I propose that we adjourn to nine o'clock this evening. It is probable that we shall have received, by that time, from Asia the translation of the message from Mars. I will also beg the director of the observatory to maintain constant communication, by telephone, with Gaurisankar. In case the message is not deciphered by nine o'clock, the president of the geological society of France will open the meeting with a statement of the investigations which he has just finished, on the natural end of the world. Everybody, at this moment, is absorbingly interested in whatever relates to the question of the end of our world, whether this is dependent upon the mysterious portent now suspended above us, or upon other causes, of whatsoever nature, subject to investigation."

Chapter IV

THE MULTITUDE stationed without the doors of the Institute had made way for those coming out, every one being eager to learn the particulars of the session. Already the general result had in some way become known, for immediately after the speech of the director of the Paris observatory the rumor got abroad that the collision with the comet would not entail consequences so serious as had been anticipated. Indeed, large posters had just been placarded throughout Paris, announcing the reopening of the Chicago stock exchange. This was an encouraging and unlooked for indication of the resumption of business and the revival of hope.

This is what had taken place. The financial magnate, whose abrupt exit will be remembered by the reader of these pages, after rolling like a ball from the top to the bottom row of the hemicycle, had rushed in an aero-cab to his office on the boulevard St. Cloud, where he had telegraphed to his partner in Chicago that new computations had just been given out by the Institute of France, that the gravity of the situation had been exaggerated, and that the resumption of business was imminent; he urged, therefore, the opening of the central American exchange at any cost, and the purchase of every security offered, whatever its nature. When it is five o'clock at Paris it is eleven in the morning at Chicago. The financier received the despatch from his cousin while at breakfast. He found no difficulty in arranging for the reopening of the exchange and invested several millions in securities. The news of the resumption of business in Chicago had been at once made public, and although it was too late to repeat the same game in Paris, it was possible to prepare new plans for the morrow. The public had innocently believed in a spontaneous and genuine revival of business in America, and this fact, together with the satisfactory impression made by the session of the Institute, was sufficient to rekindle the fires of hope.

No less interest, however, was manifested in the evening session than in that of the afternoon, and but for the exertions of an extra detachment of the French guard it would have been impossible for those enjoying special privileges to gain admission. Night had come, and with it the flaming comet, larger, more brilliant, and more threatening than ever; and if, perhaps, one-half the assembled multitude appeared somewhat tranquillized, the remaining half was still anxious and fearful.

The audience was substantially the same, every one being eager to know at first hand the issue of this general public discussion of the fate of the planet, conducted by accredited and eminent scientists, whether its destruction was to be the result of an extraordinary accident such as now threatened it, or of the natural process of decay. But it was noticed that the cardinal archbishop of Paris was absent, for he had been summoned suddenly to Rome by the Pope to attend an œcumenical council, and had left that very evening by the Paris-Rome-Palermo-Tunis tube.

"Gentlemen," said the president, "the translation of the despatch received at the observatory of Gaurisankar from Mars has not arrived yet, but we shall open the session at once, in order to hear the important communication previously announced, which the president of the geological society, and the permanent secretary of the academy of meteorology, have to make to us."

The former of these gentlemen was already at the desk. His remarks, stenographically reproduced by a young geologist of the new school, were as follows:

"The immense crowd gathered within these walls, the emotion I see depicted upon every face, the impatience with which you await the discussions yet to take place, all, gentlemen, would lead me to refrain from laying before you the opinion which I have formed from my own study of the problem which now excites the interest of the entire world, and to yield the platform to those gifted with an imagination or an audacity greater than mine. For, in my judgment, the end of the world is not at hand, and humanity will have to wait for it several million years – yes, gentlemen, I said *millions*, not thousands.

"You see that I am at this moment perfectly calm, and that, too, without laying any claim to the sang froid of Archimedes, who was slain by a Roman soldier at the siege of Syracuse while calmly tracing geometric figures upon the sand. Archimedes knew the danger and forgot it; I do not believe in any danger whatever.

"You will not then be surprised if I quietly submit to you the theory of a natural end of the world, by the gradual levelling of the continents and their slow submergence beneath the invading waters; but I shall perhaps do better to postpone for a week this explanation, as I do not for an instant doubt that we may all, or nearly all, reassemble here to confer together upon the great epochs of the natural history of the world."

The orator paused for a moment. The president had risen: "My dear and honorable colleague," he said, "we are all here to listen to you. Happily, the panic of the last few days is partially allayed, and it is to be hoped that the night of July 13–14 will pass like its predecessors. Nevertheless, we are more than ever interested in all which has any bearing upon this great problem and we shall listen to no one with greater pleasure than to the illustrious author of the classic Treatise on Geology."

"In that case, gentlemen," resumed the president of the geological society of France, "I shall explain to you what, in my judgment, will be the natural end of the world, if, as is probable, nothing disturbs the present course of events; for accidents are rare in the cosmical order.

"Nature does not proceed by sudden leaps, and geologists do not believe in such revolutions or cataclysms; for they have learned that in the natural world everything is subject to a slow process of evolution. The geological agents now at work are permanent ones.

"The destruction of the globe by some great catastrophe is a dramatic conception; far more so, certainly, than that of the action of the forces now in operation, though they threaten our planet with a destruction equally certain. Does not the stability of our continent seem permanent? Except through the intervention of some new agency, how is it possible to doubt the durability of this earth which has supported so many generations before our own, and whose monuments, of the greatest antiquity, prove that if they have come down to us in a state of ruin, it is not because the soil has refused to support them, but because they have suffered from the ravages of time and especially from the hand of man? The oldest historical traditions show us rivers flowing in the same beds as today, mountains rising to the same height; and as for the few river-mouths which have become obstructed, the few land-slides which have occurred here and there, their importance is so slight relatively to the enormous extent of the continents, that it seems gratuitous indeed to seek here the omens of a final catastrophe.

"Such might be the reasoning of one who casts a superficial and indifferent glance upon the external world. But the conclusions of one accustomed to scrutinize closely the apparently insignificant changes taking place about him would be quite different. At every step, however little skilled in observation, he will discover the traces of a perpetual conflict between the external powers of nature and all which rises above the inflexible level of the ocean, in whose depths reign silence and repose. Here, the sea beats furiously against the shore, which recedes slowly from century to century. Elsewhere, mountain masses have fallen, engulfing in a few moments entire villages and desolating smiling valleys. Or, the tropical rains, assailing the volcanic cones, have furrowed them with deep ravines and undermined their walls, so that at last nothing but ruins of these giants remain.

"More silent, but not less efficacious, has been the action of the great rivers, as the Ganges and the Mississippi, whose waters are so heavily laden with solid particles in suspension. Each of these small particles, which trouble the limpidity of their liquid carrier, is a fragment torn from the shores washed by these rivers. Slowly but surely their currents bear to the great reservoir of the sea every atom lost to the soil, and the bars which form their deltas are as nothing compared with what the sea receives and hides away in its abysses. How can any reflecting person, observing this action, and knowing that it has been going on for many centuries, escape the conclusion that the rivers, like the ocean, are indeed preparing the final ruin of the habitable world?

"Geology confirms this conclusion in every particular. It shows us that the surface of the soil is being constantly altered over entire continents by variations of temperature, by alterations of drought and humidity, of freezing and thawing, as also by the incessant action of worms and of plants. Hence, a continuous process of dissolution, leading even to the disintegration of the most compact rocks, reducing them to fragments small enough to yield at last to the attraction of gravity, especially when this is aided by running water. Thus they travel, first down the slopes and along the torrent beds, where their angles are worn away and they become little by little transformed into gravel, sand and ooze; then in the rivers which are still able, especially at flood-times, to carry away this broken up material, and to bear it nearer and nearer to their outlets.

"It is easy to predict what must necessarily be the final result of this action. Gravity, always acting, will not be satisfied until every particle subject to its law has attained the most stable position conceivable. Now, such will be the case only when matter is in the lowest position possible. Every surface, must therefore disappear, except the surface of the ocean, which is the goal of every agency of motion; and the material borne away from the crumbling continents must in the end be spread over the bottom of the sea. In brief, the final outcome will be the complete levelling of the land, or, more exactly, the disappearance of every prominence from the surface of the earth.

"In the first place, we readily see that near the river mouths *the final form of the dry land will be that of nearly horizontal plains.* The effect of the erosion produced by running water will be the formation on the water-sheds of a series of sharp ridges, succeeded by almost absolutely horizontal plains, between which no final difference in height greater than fifty meters can exist.

"But in no case can these sharp ridges, which, on this hypothesis, will separate the basins, continue long; for gravity and the action of the wind, filtration and change of temperature, will soon obliterate them. It is thus legitimate to conclude that the end of this erosion of the continents will be *their reduction to an absolute level*, a level differing but little from that at the river outlets."

The coadjutor of the archbishop of Paris, who occupied a seat in the tribune reserved for distinguished functionaries, rose, and, as the orator ceased speaking, added: "Thus will be fulfilled, to the letter, the words of holy writ: 'For the mountains shall depart and the hills be removed.'"

"If, then," resumed the geologist, "nothing occurs to modify the reciprocal action of land and water, we cannot escape the conclusion that every continental elevation is inevitably destined to disappear.

"How much time will this require?

"The dry land, if spread out in a layer of uniform thickness, would constitute a plateau of about 700 meters altitude above the sea-level. Admitting that its total area is 145,000,000 square kilometers, it follows that its volume is about 101,500,000, or, in round numbers, 100,000,000 cubic kilometers. Such is the large, yet definite mass, with which the external agencies of destruction must contend.

"Taken together, the rivers of the world may be considered as emptying, every year, into the sea 23,000 cubic kilometers of water (in other words, 23,000 milliards of cubic meters). This would give a volume of solid matter carried yearly to the sea, equal to 10.43 cubic kilometers, if we accept the established ratio of thirty-eight parts of suspended material in 100,000 parts of water. The ratio of this amount to the total volume of the dry land is one to 9,730,000. If the dry land were a level plateau of 700 meters altitude, it would lose, by fluid erosion alone, a slice of about *seven one-hundredths of a millimeter in thickness yearly*, or one millimeter every fourteen years – say *seven millimeters per century*.

"Here we have a definite figure, expressing the actual yearly continental erosion, showing that, if only this erosion were to operate, the entire mass of unsubmerged land would disappear in *less than 10,000,000 years*.

"But rain and rivers are not the only agencies; there are other factors which contribute to the gradual destruction of the dry land:

"First, there is the erosion of the sea. It is impossible to select a better example of this than the Britannic isles; for they are exposed, by their situation, to the onslaught of the Atlantic, whose billows, driven by the prevailing southwest wind, meet with no obstacle to their progress. Now, the average recession of the English coast is certainly less than three meters per century. Let us apply this rate to the sea-coasts of the world, and see what will happen.

"We may proceed in two ways: First, we may estimate the loss in volume for the entire coast-line of the world, on the basis of three centimeters per year. To do this, we should have to know the length of the shore-line and the mean height of the coast. The former is about

200,000 kilometers. As to the present average height of the coasts above the sea, 100 meters would certainly be a liberal estimate. Hence, a recession of three centimeters corresponds to an annual loss of three cubic meters per running meter, or, for the 200,000 kilometers of coast-line, 600,000,000 cubic meters, which is only six-tenths of a cubic kilometer. In other words, the erosion due to the sea would only amount to one-seventeenth that of the rivers.

"It may perhaps be objected, that, as the altitude actually increases from the coast-line toward the interior, the same rate of recession would, in time, involve a greater loss in volume. Is this objection well founded? No; for the tendency of the rain and water-courses being, as we have said, to lower the surface-level, this action would keep pace with that of the sea.

"Again, the area of the dry land being 145,000,000 square kilometers, a circle of equal area would have a radius of 6800 kilometers. But the circumference of this circle would be only 40,000 kilometers; that is to say, the sea could exercise upon the circle but one-fifth the erosive action which it actually does upon the indented outline of our shores. We may, therefore, admit that the erosive action of the sea upon the dry land is *five times greater* than it would be upon an equivalent circular area. Certainly this estimate is a maximum; for it is logical to suppose that, when the narrow peninsulas have been eaten away by the sea, the ratio of the perimeter to the surface will decrease more and more – that is, the action of the sea will be less effective. In any event, since, at the rate of three centimeters per year, a radius of 6800 kilometers would disappear in 226,600,000 years, one-fifth of this interval, or about 45,000,000 years, would represent the minimum time necessary for the destruction of the land by the sea; this would correspond to an intensity of action scarcely more than *one-fifth* that of the rivers and rain.

"Taken together, these mechanical causes would, therefore, involve every year a loss in volume of twelve cubic kilometers, which, for a total of 100,000,000, would bring about the complete submergence of the dry land in a little more than *8,000,000 years*.

"But we are far from having exhausted our analysis of the phenomena in question. Water is not only a mechanical agent; it is also a powerful dissolvent, far more powerful than we might suppose, because of the large amount of carbonic acid which it absorbs either from the atmosphere or from the decomposed organic matter of the soil. All subterranean waters become charged with substances which it has thus chemically abstracted from the minerals of the rocks through which it percolates.

"River water contains, per cubic kilometer, about 182 tons of matter in solution. The rivers of the world bring yearly to the sea, nearly *five cubic kilometers* of such matter. The annual loss to the dry land, therefore, from these various causes, is *seventeen* instead of twelve cubic kilometers; so that the total of 100,000,000 would disappear, not in eight, but in *a little less than six million years*.

"This figure must be still further modified. For we must not forget that the sediment thus brought to the sea and displacing a certain amount of water, will cause a rise of the sea-level, accelerating by just so much the levelling process due to the wearing away of the continents.

"It is easy to estimate the effect of this new factor. Indeed, for a given thickness lost by the plateau heretofore assumed, the sea-level must rise by an amount corresponding to the volume of the submarine deposit, which must exactly equal that of the sediment brought down. Calculation shows that, in round numbers, the loss in volume will be *twenty-four cubic kilometers*.

"Having accounted for an annual loss of twenty-four cubic kilometers, are we now in a position to conclude what time will be necessary for the complete disappearance of the dry land, always supposing the indefinite continuance of present conditions?

"Certainly, gentlemen; for, after examining the objection which might be made apropos of volcanic eruptions, we find that the latter aid rather than retard the disintegrating process.

"We believe, therefore, that we may fearlessly accept the above estimate of twenty-four cubic kilometers, as a basis of calculation; and as this figure is contained 4,166,666 times in 100,000,000, which represents the volume of the continents, we are authorized to infer that under the *sole action of forces now in operation*, provided no other movements of the soil occur, *the dry land will totally disappear within a period of about 4,000,000 years.*

"But this disappearance, while interesting to a geologist or a thinker, is not an event which need cause the present generation any anxiety. Neither our children nor our grandchildren will be in a position to detect in any sensible degree its progress.

"If I may be permitted, therefore, to close these remarks with a somewhat fanciful suggestion, I will add that it would be assuredly the acme of foresight to build today a new ark, in which to escape the consequences of this coming universal deluge."

Such was the learnedly developed thesis of the president of the geological society of France. His calm and moderate statement of the secular action of natural forces, opening up a future of 4,000,000 years of life, had allayed the apprehension excited by the comet. The audience had become wonderfully tranquillized. No sooner had the orator left the platform and received the congratulations of his colleagues than an animated conversation began on every side. A sort of peace took possession of every mind. People talked of the end of the world as they would of the fall of a ministry, or the coming of the swallows – dispassionately and disinterestedly. A fatality put off 40,000 centuries does not really affect us at all.

But the permanent secretary of the academy of meteorology had just ascended the tribune, and every one gave him at once the strictest attention:

"Ladies and gentlemen: I am about to lay before you a theory diametrically opposed to that of my eminent colleague of the Institute, yet based upon facts no less definite and a process of reasoning no less rigorous.

"Yes, gentlemen, diametrically opposed—"

The orator, gifted with an excellent voice, had perceived the disappointment settling upon every face.

"Oh," he said, "opposed, not as regards the time which nature allots to the existence of humanity, but as to the manner in which the world will come to an end; for I also believe in a future of several million years.

"Only, instead of seeing the subsidence and complete submergence of the land beneath the invading waters, I foresee, on the contrary, death by drouth, and the gradual diminution of the present water supply of the earth. Some day there will be no more ocean, no more clouds, no more rain, no more springs, no more moisture, and vegetable as well as animal life will perish, not by drowning, *but through lack of water.*

"On the earth's surface, indeed, the water of the sea, of the rivers, of the clouds, and of the springs, is decreasing. Without going far in search of examples, I would remind you, gentlemen, that in former times, at the beginning of the quaternary period, the site now occupied by Paris, with its 9,000,000 of inhabitants, from Mount Saint-Germain to Villeneuve-Saint-Georges, was almost entirely occupied by water; only the hill of Passy at Montmartre and Pere-Lachaise, and the plateau of Montrouge at the Panthéon and Villejuif emerged above this immense liquid sheet. The altitudes of these plateaus have not increased, there have been no upheavals; it is the water which has diminished in volume.

"It is so in every country of the world, and the cause is easy to assign. A certain quantity of water, very small, it is true, in proportion to the whole, but not negligible, percolates through the soil, either below the sea bottoms by crevices, fissures and openings due to submarine eruptions, or on the dry land; for not all the rain water falls upon impermeable soil. In general, that which is not evaporated, returns to the sea by springs, rivulets, streams and rivers; but for this there must be a bed of clay, over which it may follow the slopes. Wherever this impermeable soil is lacking, it continues its descent by infiltration and saturates the rocks below. This is the water encountered in quarries.

"This water is lost to general circulation. It enters into chemical combination and constitutes the hydrates. If it penetrates far enough, it attains a temperature sufficient for its transformation into steam, and such is generally the origin of volcanoes and earthquakes. But, within the soil, as in the open air, a sensible proportion of the water in circulation becomes changed into hydrates, and even into oxides; there is nothing like humidity for the rapid formation of rust. Thus recombined, the elements of water, hydrogen and oxygen, disappear as water. Thermal waters also constitute another interior system of circulation; they are derived from the surface, but they do not return there, nor to the sea. The surface water of the earth, either by entering into new combinations, or by penetrating the lower rock-strata, is diminishing, and it will diminish more and more as the earth's heat is dissipated. The heat-wells which have been dug within a hundred years, in the neighborhood of the principal cities of the world, and which afford the heat necessary for domestic purposes, will become exhausted as the internal temperature diminishes. The day will come when the earth will be cold to its center, and that day will be coincident with an almost total disappearance of water.

"For that matter, gentlemen, this is likely to be the fate of several bodies in our solar system. Our neighbor the moon, whose volume and mass are far inferior to those of the earth, has grown cold more rapidly, and has traversed more quickly the phases of its astral life; its ancient ocean-beds, on which we, today, recognize the indubitable traces of water action, are entirely dry; there is no evidence of any kind of evaporation; no cloud has been discovered, and the spectroscope reveals no indication of the presence of the vapor of water. On the other hand, the planet Mars, also smaller than the earth, has beyond a doubt reached a more advanced phase of development, and is known not to possess a single body of water worthy of the name of ocean, but only inland seas of medium extent and slight depth, united with each other by canals. That there is less water on Mars than on the earth is a fact proved by observation; clouds are far less numerous, the atmosphere is much dryer, evaporation and condensation take place with greater rapidity, and the polar snows show variations, depending upon the season, much more extensive than those which take place upon the earth. Again, the planet Venus, younger than the earth, is surrounded by an immense atmosphere, constantly filled with clouds. As for the large planet Jupiter, we can only make out, as it were, an immense accumulation of vapors. Thus, the four worlds of which we know the most, confirm, each in its own way, the theory of a secular decrease in the amount of the earth's water.

"I am very happy to say in this connection that the theory of a general levelling process, maintained by my learned colleague, is confirmed by the present condition of the planet Mars. That eminent geologist told us a few moments ago, that, owing to the continuous action of rivers, plains almost horizontal would constitute the final form of the earth's surface. That is what has already happened in the case of Mars. The beaches near the sea are so flat that they are easily and frequently inundated, as every one knows. From season to season hundreds of thousands of square kilometers are alternately exposed or covered by a thin layer of water. This is notably the case on the western shores of the Kaiser sea. On the moon this levelling process has not taken place. There was not time enough for it; before its consummation, the air, the wind and the water had vanished.

"It is then certain that, while the earth is destined to undergo a process of levelling, as my eminent colleague has so clearly explained, it will at the same time gradually lose the water which it now possesses. To all appearances, the latter process is now going on more rapidly than the former. As the earth loses its internal heat and becomes cold, crevasses will undoubtedly form, as in the case of the moon. The complete extinction of terrestrial heat will result in contractions, in the formation of hollow spaces below the surface, and the contents of the ocean will flow into these hollows, without being changed into vapor, and will be either absorbed or combined with the metallic rocks, in the form of ferric hydrates. The amount of water will thus go on diminishing indefinitely, and finally totally disappear. Plants, deprived of their essential constituent, will become transformed, but must at last perish.

"The animal species will also become modified, but there will always be herbivora and carnivora, and the extinction of the former will involve, inevitably, that of the latter; and at last, the human race itself, notwithstanding its power of adaption, will die of hunger and of thirst, on the bosom of a dried-up world.

"I conclude, therefore, gentlemen, that the end of the world will not be brought about by a new deluge, but by the loss of its water. Without water terrestrial life is impossible; water constitutes the chief constituent of every living thing. It is present in the human body in the enormous proportion of seventy per cent. Without it, neither plants nor animals can exist. Either as a liquid, or in a state of vapor, it is the condition of life. Its suppression would be the death-warrant of humanity, and this death-warrant nature will serve upon us a dozen million years hence. I will add that this will take place before the completion of the erosion explained by the president of the geological society of France; for he, himself, was careful to note that the period of 4,000,000 years was dependent upon the hypothesis that the causes now in operation continued to act as they do today; and, furthermore, he, himself, admits that the manifestations of internal energy cannot immediately cease. Upheavals, at various points, will occur for a long period, and the growth of the land area from such causes as the formation of deltas, and volcanic and coral islands, will still go on for some time. The period which he indicated, therefore, represents only the minimum."

Such was the address of the permanent secretary of the academy of meteorology. The audience had listened with the deepest attention to both speakers, and it was evident, from its bearing, that it was fully reassured concerning the fate of the world; it seemed even to have altogether forgotten the existence of the comet.

"The president of the physical society of France has the floor."

At this invitation, a young woman, elegantly dressed in the most perfect taste, ascended the tribune.

"My two learned colleagues," she began, without further preamble, "are both right; for, on the one hand, it is impossible to deny that meteorological agents, with the assistance of gravity, are working insensibly to level the world, whose crust is ever thickening and solidifying; and, on the other hand, the amount of water on the surface of our planet is decreasing from century to century. These two facts may be considered as scientifically established. But, gentlemen, it does not seem to me that the end of the world will be due to either the submergence of the continents, or to an insufficient supply of water for plant and animal life."

This new declaration, this announcement of a third hypothesis, produced in the audience an astonishment bordering upon stupor.

"Nor do I believe," the graceful orator hastened to add, "that the final catastrophe can be set down to the comet, for I agree with my two eminent predecessors, that worlds do not die by accident, but of old age.

"Yes, doubtless, gentlemen," she continued, "the water will grow less, and, perhaps, in the end totally disappear; yet, it is not this lack of water which in itself will bring about the end of things, but its climatic consequences. The decrease in the amount of aqueous vapor in the atmosphere will lead to a general lowering of the temperature, and humanity will perish *with cold*.

"I need inform no one here that the atmosphere we breathe is composed of seventy-nine per cent. of nitrogen and twenty per cent. of oxygen, and that of the remaining one per cent. about one-half is aqueous vapor and three ten-thousandths is carbonic acid, the remainder being ozone, or electrified oxygen, ammonia, hydrogen and a few other gases, in exceedingly small quantities. Nitrogen and oxygen, then, form ninety-nine per cent. of the atmosphere, and the vapor of water one-half the remainder.

"But, gentlemen, from the point of view of vegetable and animal life, this half of one per cent. of aqueous vapor is of supreme importance, and so far as temperature and climate are concerned, I do not hesitate to assert that it is more essential than all the rest of the atmosphere.

"The heat waves, coming from the sun to the earth, which warm the soil and are thence returned and scattered through the atmosphere into space, in their passage through the air meet with the oxygen and nitrogen atoms and with the molecules of aqueous vapor. These molecules are so thinly scattered (for they occupy but the hundredth part of the space occupied by the others), that one might infer that the retention of any heat whatever is due rather to the nitrogen and oxygen than to the aqueous vapor. Indeed, if we consider the atoms alone, we find two hundred oxygen and nitrogen atoms for one of aqueous vapor. Well, this one atom has eighty times more energy, more effective power to retain radiant heat, than the two hundred others; consequently, a molecule of the vapor of water is 16,000 times more effective than a molecule of dry air, in absorbing and in radiating heat – for these two properties are reciprocally proportional.

"To diminish by any great amount the number of these invisible molecules of the vapor of water, is to immediately render the earth uninhabitable, notwithstanding its oxygen; even the equatorial and tropical regions will suddenly lose their heat and will be condemned to the cold of mountain summits covered with perpetual snow and frost: in place of luxurious plants, of flowers and fruits, of birds and nests, of the life which swarms in the sea and upon the land; instead of murmuring brooks and limpid rivers, of lakes and seas, we shall be surrounded only by ice in the midst of a vast desert – and when I say *we*, gentlemen, you understand we shall not linger long as witnesses, for the very blood would freeze in our veins and arteries, and every human heart would soon cease to beat. Such would be the consequences of the suppression of this half hundredth part of aqueous vapor which, disseminated through the atmosphere, beneficently protects and preserves all terrestrial life as in a hot-house.

"The principles of thermodynamics prove that the temperature of space is 273° below zero. And this, gentlemen, is the more than glacial cold in which our planet will sleep when it shall have lost this airy garment in whose sheltering warmth it is today enwrapped. Such is the fate with which the gradual loss of the earth's water threatens the world, and this death by cold will be inevitably ours, if our earthly sojourn is long enough.

"This end is all the more certain, because not only the aqueous vapor is diminishing, but also the oxygen and nitrogen, in brief, the entire atmosphere. Little by little the oxygen becomes fixed in the various oxides which are constantly forming on the earth's surface; this is the case also with the nitrogen, which disappears in the soil and vegetation, never wholly regaining a gaseous state; and the atmosphere penetrates by its weight into the land and sea, descending into subterranean depths. Little by little, from century to century, it grows less. Once, as for example in the early primary period, it was of vast extent; the earth was almost wholly covered by water, only the first granite upheaval broke the surface of the universal ocean, and the atmosphere was saturated with a quantity of aqueous vapor immeasurably greater than that it now holds. This is the explanation of the high temperature of those bygone days, when the tropical plants of our time, the tree ferns, such as the calamites, the equisetaceæ, the sigillaria and the lepidodendrons flourished as luxuriously at the poles as at the equator. Today, both the atmosphere and aqueous vapor have considerably diminished in amount. In the future they are destined to disappear. Jupiter, which is still in its primary period, possesses an immense atmosphere full of vapors. The moon does not appear to have any at all, so that the temperature is always below the freezing point, even in the sunlight, and the atmosphere of Mars is sensibly rarer than ours.

"As to the time which must elapse before this reign of cold caused by the diminution of the aqueous atmosphere which surrounds the globe, I also would adopt the period of 10,000,000 years, as estimated by the speaker who preceded me. Such, ladies, are the stages of world-life which nature seems to have marked out, at least for the planetary system to which we belong. I conclude, therefore, that the fate of the earth will be the same as that of the moon, and that when it loses the airy garment which now guarantees it against the loss of the heat received from the sun, it will perish with cold."

At this point the chancellor of the Columbian academy, who had come that very day from Bogota by an electric air-ship to participate in the discussion, requested permission to speak. It was known that he had founded on the very equator itself, at an enormous altitude, an observatory overlooking the entire planet, from which one might see both the celestial poles at the same time, and which he had named in honor of a French astronomer who had devoted his whole life to making known his favorite science and to establishing its great philosophical importance. He was received with marked sympathy and attention.

"Gentlemen," he said, on reaching the desk, "in these two sessions we have had an admirable resumé of the curious theories which modern science is in a position to offer us, upon the various ways in which our world may come to an end. The burning of the atmosphere, or suffocation caused by the shock of the rapidly approaching comet; the submergence of the continents in the far future beneath the sea; the drying up of the earth as a result of the gradual loss of its water; and finally, the freezing of our unhappy planet, grown old as the decaying and frozen moon. Here, if I mistake not, are five distinct possible ends.

"The director of the observatory has announced that he does not believe in the first two, and that in his opinion a collision with the comet will have only insignificant results. I agree with him in every respect, and I now wish to add, after listening attentively to the learned addresses of my distinguished colleagues, that I do not believe in the other three either.

"Ladies," continued the Columbian astronomer, "you know as well as we do that nothing is eternal. In the bosom of nature all is change. The buds of the spring burst into flowers, the flowers in their turn become fruit, the generations succeed each other, and life accomplishes its mission. So the world which we inhabit will have its end as it has had its beginning, but neither the comet, nor water, nor the lack of water are to cause its death agony. To my mind the whole question hangs upon a single word in the closing sentence of the very remarkable address which has just been made by our gracious colleague, the president of the physical society.

"The sun! Yes, here is the key to the whole problem.

"Terrestrial life depends upon its rays. I say depends upon them – life is a form of solar energy. It is the sun which maintains water in a liquid state, and the atmosphere in a gaseous one; without it all would be solid and lifeless; it is the sun which draws water from the sea, the lakes, the rivers, the moist soil; which forms the clouds and sets the air in motion; which produces rain and controls the fruitful circulation of the water; thanks to the solar light and heat, the plants assimilate the carbon contained in the carbonic acid of the atmosphere, and in separating the oxygen from the carbon and appropriating the latter the plant performs a great work; to this conversion of solar into vital energy, as well as to the shade of the thick-leaved trees, is due the freshness of the forests; the wood which blazes on our hearthstones does but render up to us its store of solar heat, and when we consume gas or coal today, we are only setting free the rays imprisoned millions of years ago in the forests of the primary age. Electricity itself is but a form of energy whose original source is the sun. It is, then, the sun which murmurs in the brook, which whispers in the wind, which moans in the tempest, which blossoms in the rose, which trills in the throat of the nightingale, which gleams in the lightning, which thunders in the storm, which sings or wails in the vast symphony of nature.

"Thus the solar heat is changed into air or water currents, into the expansive force of gases and vapors, into electricity, into woods, flowers, fruits and muscular energy. So long as this brilliant star supplies us with sufficient heat the continuance of the world and of life is assured.

"The probable cause of the heat of the sun is the condensation of the nebula in which this central body of our system had its origin. This conversion of mechanical energy must have produced 28,000,000 degrees centigrade. You know gentlemen, that a kilogram of coal, falling from an infinite distance to the sun, would produce, by its impact, six thousand times more heat than by its combustion. At the present rate of radiation, this supply of heat accounts for the emission of thermal energy for a period of 22,000,000 years, and it is probable that the sun has been burning far longer, for there is nothing to prove that the elements of the nebula were absolutely cold; on the contrary they themselves were originally a source of heat. The temperature of this great day-star does not seem to have fallen any; for its condensation is still going on, and it may make good the loss by radiation. Nevertheless, everything has an end. If at some future stage of condensation the sun's density should equal that of the earth, this condensation would yield a fresh amount of heat sufficient to maintain for 17,000,000 years the same temperature which now sustains terrestrial life, and this period may be prolonged if we admit a diminution in the rate of radiation, a fall of meteorites, or a further condensation resulting in a density greater than that of the earth. But, however far we put off the end, it must come at last. The suns which are extinguished in the heavens, offer so many examples of the fate reserved for our own luminary; and in certain years such tokens of death are numerous.

"But in that long period of seventeen or twenty million years, or more, who can say what the marvellous power of adaptation, which physiology and paleontology have revealed in every variety of animal and vegetable life, may not do for humanity, leading it, step by step, to a state of physical and intellectual perfection as far above ours, as ours is above that of the iguanodon, the stegosaurus and the compsognathus? Who can say that our fossil remains will not appear to our successors as monstrous as those of the dinosaurus? Perhaps the stability of temperature of that future time may make it seem doubtful whether any really intelligent race could have existed in an epoch subjected, as ours is, to such erratic variations of temperature, to the capricious changes of weather which characterize our seasons. And, who knows if before that time some immense cataclysm, some general change may not bury the past in new geological strata and inaugurate new periods, quinquennial, sexennial, differing totally from the preceding ones?

"One thing is certain, that the sun will finally lose its heat; it is condensing and contracting, and its fluidity is decreasing. The time will come when the circulation, which now supplies the photosphere, and makes the central mass a reservoir of radiant energy, will be obstructed and will slacken. The radiation of heat and light will then diminish, and vegetable and animal life will be more and more restricted to the earth's equatorial regions. When this circulation shall have ceased, the brilliant photosphere will be replaced by a dark opaque crust which will prevent all luminous radiation. The sun will become a dark red ball, then a black one, and night will be perpetual. The moon, which shines only by reflection, will no longer illumine the lonely nights. Our planet will receive no light but that of the stars. The solar heat having vanished, the atmosphere will remain undisturbed, and an absolute calm, unbroken by any breath of air, will reign.

"If the oceans still exist they will be frozen ones, no evaporation will form clouds, no rain will fall, no stream will flow. Perhaps, as has been observed in the case of stars on the eve of extinction, some last flare of the expiring torch, some accidental development of heat, due to the falling in of the sun's crust, will give us back for a while the old-time sun, but this will only be the precursor of the end; and the earth, a dark ball, a frozen tomb, will continue to revolve about the black sun, travelling through an endless night and hurrying away with all the solar system into the abyss of space. *It is to the extinction of the sun that the earth will owe its death, twenty, perhaps forty million years hence.*"

The speaker ceased, and was about to leave the platform, when the director of the academy of fine arts begged to be heard:

"Gentlemen," he said, from his chair, "if I have understood rightly, the end of the world will in any case result from cold, and only several million years hence. If, then, a painter should endeavor to represent the last day, he ought to shroud the earth in ice, and cover it with skeletons."

"Not exactly," replied the Columbian chancellor. "It is not cold which produces glaciers, – it is *heat.*

"If the sun did not evaporate the sea water there would be no clouds, and but for the sun there would be no wind. For the formation of glaciers a sun is necessary, to vaporize the water and to transport it in clouds and then to condense it. Every kilogram of vapor formed represents a quantity of solar heat sufficient to raise five kilograms of cast-iron to its fusing point (110°). By lessening the intensity of the sun's action we exhaust the glacier supply.

"So that it is not the snow, nor the glaciers which will cover the earth, but the frozen remnant of the sea. For a long time previously streams and rivers will have ceased to exist and every atmospheric current will have disappeared, unless indeed, before giving up the ghost, the sun shall have passed through one of those spasms to which we referred a moment ago, shall have released the ice from sleep and have produced new clouds and aerial currents, reawakened the springs, the brooks and the rivers, and after this momentary but deceitful awakening, shall have fallen back again into lethargy. That day will have no morrow."

Another voice, that of a celebrated electrician, was heard from the center of the hemicycle.

"All these theories of death by cold," he observed, "are plausible. But the end of the world by fire? This has been referred to only in connection with the comet. It may happen otherwise.

"Setting aside a possible sinking of the continents into the central fire, brought about by an earthquake on a large scale, or some widespread dislocation of the earth's crust, it seems to me that, without any collision, a superior will might arrest our planet midway in its course and transform its motion into heat."

"A will?" interrupted another voice. "But positive science does not admit the possibility of miracles in nature."

"Nor I, either," replied the electrician. "When I say 'will,' I mean an ideal, invisible force. Let me explain.

"The earth is flying through space with a velocity of 106,000 kilometers per hour, or 29,460 meters per second. If some star, active or extinct, should emerge from space, so as to form with the sun a sort of electro-dynamic couple with our planet on its axis, acting upon it like a brake – if, in a word, for any reason, the earth should be suddenly arrested in its orbit, its mechanical energy would be changed into molecular motion, and its temperature would be suddenly raised to such a degree as to reduce it entirely to a gaseous state."

"Gentlemen," said the director of the Mont Blanc observatory, from his chair, "the earth might perish by fire in still another manner. We have lately seen in the sky a temporary star which, in a few weeks, passed from the sixteenth to the fourth magnitude. This distant sun had suddenly become 50,000 times hotter and more luminous. If such a fate should overtake our sun, nothing living would be left upon our planet. It is probable, from the study of the spectrum of the light emitted by this burning star, that the cause of this sudden conflagration was the entrance of this sun and its system into some kind of nebula. Our own sun is travelling with a frightful velocity in the direction of the constellation of Hercules, and may very well some day encounter an obstacle of this nature."

"To resume," continued the director of the Paris observatory, "after all we have just now heard, we see that our planet will be at a loss to choose among so many modes of death. I have as little fear now as before of any danger from the present comet. But it must be confessed that, solely from the point of view of the astronomer, this poor, wandering earth is exposed to more than one peril. The child born into this world, and destined to reach the age of maturity, may be compared to a person stationed at the entrance to a narrow street, one of those picturesque streets of the sixteenth century, lined with houses at whose every window is a marksman armed with a good weapon of the latest model. This person must traverse the entire length of the street, without being stricken down by the weapons levelled upon him at close range. Every disease which lies in wait and threatens us, is on hand: dentition, convulsion, croup, meningitis, measles, smallpox, typhoid fever, pneumonia, enteritis, brain fever, heart disease, consumption, diabetes, apoplexy, cholera, influenza, etc., etc., for we omit many, and our hearers will have no difficulty in supplementing this off-hand enumeration. Will our unhappy traveller reach the end of the street safe and sound? If he does, it will only be to die, just the same.

"Thus our planet pursues its way along its heavenly path, with a speed of more than 100,000 kilometers per hour, and, at the same time, the sun hurries it on, with all the planets, toward the constellation of Hercules. Recapitulating what has just been said, and allowing for what may have been omitted: it may meet a comet ten or twenty times larger than itself, composed of deleterious gases which would render the atmosphere irrespirable; it may encounter a swarm of uranolites, which would have upon it the effect of a charge of shot upon a meadow lark; it may meet in its path an invisible sun, much larger than itself, whose shock would reduce it to vapor; it may encounter a sun which would consume it in the twinkling of an eye, as a furnace would consume an apple thrown into it; it may be caught in a system of electric forces, which would act like a brake upon its eleven motions, and which would either melt it, or set it afire, like a platinum wire in a strong current; it may lose the oxygen which supports life; it may be blown up like the crust over a crater; it may collapse in some great earthquake; its dry land may disappear, in a second deluge, more universal than the first; it may, on the contrary, lose all its water, an element essential to its organic life; under the attraction of some passing body, it may be detached from the sun and carried away into the cold of stellar space; it may part, not only with the last vestige of its internal heat, which long since has ceased to have any influence upon its surface, but also with the protecting envelope which maintains the temperature necessary to life; one of these days, when the sun has grown dark and cold, it may be neither lighted, nor warmed, nor fertilized; on the other hand, it may be suddenly scorched by an outburst of heat, analogous to what has been observed in temporary stars; not to speak of many other sources of accidents and mortal peril, whose easy enumeration we leave to the geologists, paleontologists, meteorologists, physicists, chemists, biologists, physicians, botanists, and even to the veterinary surgeons, inasmuch as the arrival of an army of invisible microbes, if they be but deadly enough, or a well-established epidemic, would suffice to destroy the human race and the principal animal and vegetable species, without working the least harm to the planet itself, from a strictly astronomical point of view."

Just as the speaker was uttering these last words, a voice, which seemed to come from a distance, fell, as it were, from the ceiling overhead. But a few words of explanation may here perhaps be desirable.

As we have said, the observatories established on the higher mountains of the globe were connected by telephone, with the observatory of Paris, and the sender of the message could be heard at a distance from the receiver, without being obliged to apply any apparatus directly to the ear. The reader doubtless recollects that, at the close of the preceding session, a phonogram from Mt. Gaurisankar stated that a photophonic message, which would be at once deciphered, had been received from the inhabitants of Mars. As the translation of this cipher had not arrived at the opening of the evening session, the bureau of communications had connected the Institute with the observatory by suspending a telephonoscope from the dome of the amphitheater.

The voice from above said:

"The astronomers of the equatorial city of Mars warn the inhabitants of the earth that the comet is moving directly toward the earth with a velocity nearly double that of the orbital velocity of Mars. Mechanical motion to be transformed into heat, and heat into electrical energy. Terrible magnetic storms. Move away from Italy."

The voice ceased amid general silence and consternation. There were, however, a few sceptics left, one of whom, editor of La Libre Critique, raising his monocle to his right eye, had risen from the reporters desk and had exclaimed in a penetrating voice:

"I am afraid that the venerable doctors of the Institute are the victims of a huge joke. No one can ever persuade me that the inhabitants of Mars – admitting that there are any and they have really sent us a warning – know Italy by name. I doubt very much if one of them ever heard of the Commentaries of Cæsar or the History of the Popes, especially as—"

The orator, who was launching into an interesting dithyrambus, was at this point suddenly squelched by the turning off of the electric lights. With the exception of the illuminated square in the ceiling, the room was plunged in darkness and the voice added these six words: "This is the despatch from Mars;" and thereupon the following symbols appeared on the plate of the telephonoscope:

As this picture could only be seen by holding the head in a very fatiguing position, the president touched a bell and an assistant appeared, who by means of a projector and mirror transferred these hieroglyphics to a screen on the wall behind the desk, so that every one could readily see and analyze them at their leisure. Their interpretation was easy; nothing indeed could be more simple. The figure representing the comet needed no explanation. The arrow indicates the motion of the comet towards a heavenly body, which as seen from Mars presents phases, and sparkles like a star; this means the earth, naturally so delineated by the Martians, for their eyes, developed in a medium less luminous than ours, are somewhat more sensitive and distinguish the phases of the Earth, and this the more readily because their atmosphere is rarer and more transparent. (For us the phases of Venus are just on the limit of visibility.)

The double globe represents Mars looking at the Kaiser sea, the most characteristic feature of Martian geography, and indicates a velocity for the comet double the orbital velocity, or a little less, for the line does not quite reach the edge. The flames indicate the transformation of motion into heat; the aurora borealis and the lightning which follow, the transformation into electric and magnetic force. Finally, we recognize the boot of Italy, visible from Mars, and the black spot marks the locality threatened, according to their calculation, by one of the most dangerous fragments of the head of the comet; while the four arrows radiating in the direction of the four cardinal points of the compass seem to counsel removal from the point menaced.

The photophonic message from the Martians was much longer and far more complicated. The astronomers on Mt. Gaurisankar had previously received several such, and had discovered that they were sent from a very important, intellectual and scientific center situated in the equatorial zone not far from Meridian bay. The last message, whose general meaning is given above, was the most important. The remainder of it had not been transmitted, as it was obscure and it was not certain that its exact meaning had been made out.

The president rang his bell for order. He was about to sum up what had been said, before adjourning the meeting.

"Gentlemen," he began, "although it is after midnight, it will be of interest, before we separate, to summarize what has been told us in these two solemn sessions.

"The last despatch from Gaurisankar may well impress you. It seems clear that the inhabitants of Mars are farther advanced in science than ourselves, and this is not surprising, for they are a far older race and have had centuries innumerable in which to achieve this progress. Moreover, they may be much more highly organized than we are, they may possess better eyes, instruments of greater perfection, and intellectual faculties of a higher order. We observe, too, that their calculations, while in accord with ours as to the collision, are more precise, for they designate the very point which is to receive the greatest shock. The advice to flee from Italy should therefore be followed, and I shall at once telephone the Pope, who at this very moment is assembling the prelates of entire Christendom.

"So the comet will collide with the earth, and no one can yet foresee the consequences. But in all probability the disturbance will be local and the world will not be destroyed. The carbonic-oxide is not likely to penetrate the respirable portions of the atmosphere, but there will be an enormous development of heat.

"As to the veritable end of the world, of all the hypotheses which today permit us to forecast that event the most probable is the last – that explained to us by the learned chancellor of the Columbian academy: the life of the planet depends upon the sun; so long as the sun shines humanity is safe, unless indeed the diminution of the atmosphere and aqueous vapor should usher in before that time the reign of cold. In the former case we have yet before us twenty million years of life; in the latter only ten.

"Let us then await the night of July 13–14 without despair. I advise those who can to pass these fête days in Chicago, or better still in San Francisco, Honolulu or Noumea. The trans-Atlantic electric air-ships are so numerous and well managed that millions of travellers may make the journey before Saturday night."

Chapter V

WHILE THE ABOVE scientific discussions were taking place at Paris, meetings of a similar character were being held at London, Chicago, St. Petersburg, Yokohama, Melbourne, New York, and in all the principal cities of the world, in which every effort was made to throw light upon the great problem which so universally preoccupied the attention of humanity. At Oxford a theological council of the Reformed church was convened, in which religious traditions and interpretations were discussed at great length. To recite, or even to summarize here the proceedings of all these congresses would be an endless task, but we cannot omit reference to that of the Vatican as the most important from a religious point of view, just as that of the Institute of Paris was from a scientific one.

The council had been divided into a certain number of sections or committees, and the then often discussed question of the end of the world had been referred to one of these committees. Our duty here is to reproduce as accurately as possible the physiognomy of the main session, devoted to the discussion of this problem.

The patriarch of Jerusalem, a man of great piety and profound faith, was the first to speak in Latin. "Venerable fathers," he began, "I cannot do better than to open before you the Holy Gospel. Permit me to quote literally." He then read the words of the evangelists describing the last days of the earth, and went on:

"These words are taken verbatim from the Gospels, and you know that on this point the evangelists are in perfect accord.

"You also know, most reverend fathers, that the last great day is pictured in still more striking language in the Apocalypse of St. John. But every word of the Scriptures is known to you, and, in the presence of so learned an audience, it seems to me superfluous, if not out of place, to make further citations from what is upon every lip."

Such was the beginning of the address of the patriarch of Jerusalem. His remarks were divided under three heads: First, the teachings of Christ; second, the traditions of the Church; third, the dogma of the resurrection of the body, and of the last judgment. Taking first the form of an historical statement, the address soon became a sort of sermon, of vast range; and when the orator, passing from St. Paul to Clement of Alexandria, Tertulian and Origen, reached the council of Nice and the dogma of universal resurrection, he was carried away by his subject in such a flight of eloquence as to move the heart of every prelate before him. Several, who had renounced the apostolic faith of the earlier centuries, felt themselves again under its spell. It must be said that the surroundings lent themselves marvellously to the occasion. The assembly took place in the Sistine chapel. The immense and imposing painting of Michael Angelo, like a new apocalyptic heaven, was before every eye. The awful mingling of bodies, arms and legs, so forcibly and strangely foreshortened; Christ, the judge of the world; the damned borne struggling away by hideous devils; the dead issuing from their tombs; the skeletons returning to life and reclothing themselves with flesh; the frightful terror of humanity trembling in the presence of the wrath of God – all seemed to give a vividness, a reality, to the magnificent periods of the patriarch's oratory, and at times, in certain effects of light, one might almost hear the advancing trumpet sounding from heaven the call of judgment, and see between earth and sky the moving hosts of the resurrection.

Scarcely had the patriarch of Jerusalem finished his speech, when an independent bishop, one of the most ardent dissenters of the council, the learned Mayerstross, rushed to the tribune, and began to insist that nothing in the Gospel, or the traditions of the Church, should be taken literally.

"The letter kills," he cried, "the spirit vivifies! Everything is subject to the law of progress and change. The world moves. Enlightened Christians cannot any longer admit the resurrection of the body. All these images," he added, "were good for the days of the catacombs. For a long time no one has believed in them. Such ideas are opposed to science, and, most reverend fathers you know, as well as I do, that we must be in accord with science, which has ceased to be, as in the time of Galileo, the humble servant of theology: theologiæ humilis ancilla.

"The body cannot be reconstituted, even by a miracle, so long as its molecules return to nature and are appropriated, successively, by so many beings – human, animal and vegetable. We are formed of the dust of the dead, and, in the future, the molecules of oxygen, hydrogen, nitrogen, carbon, phosphorus, sulphur, or iron, which make up our flesh and our bones, will be incorporated in other human organisms. This change is perpetual, even during life. One human being dies every second; that is more than 86,000 each day, more than 30,000,000 each year, more than three milliards each century. In a hundred centuries – not a long period in the history of a planet, the number of the resurrected would be three hundred milliards. If the human race lived but a 100,000 years – and no one here is ignorant of the fact that geological and astronomical periods are estimated by millions of years – there would be gathered before the judgment throne something like three thousand milliards of men, women and children. My estimate is a modest one, because I take no account of the secular increase in population. You may reply to me, that only the saved will rise! What, then, will become of the others? Two weights and two measures! Death and life! Night and day, good and evil! Divine injustice and good-will, reigning together over creation! But, no, you will not accept such a solution. The eternal law is the same for all. Well! What will you do with these thousands of milliards? Show me the valley of Jehoshaphat vast enough to contain them. Will you spread them over the surface of the globe, do away with the oceans and the icefields of the poles, and cover the world with a forest of human bodies? So be it! And afterwards? What will become of this immense host? No, most holy fathers, our beliefs must not, cannot, be taken literally. Would that there were here no theologians with closed eyes, that look only within, but astronomers with open eyes, that look without."

These words had been uttered in the midst of an indescribable tumult; several times they wished to silence the Croatian bishop, gesticulating violently and denouncing him as schismatic; but the rules did not permit this, for the greatest liberty was allowed in the discussion. An Irish cardinal called down upon him the thunders of the Church, and spoke of excommunication and anathema; then, a distinguished prelate of the Gallican church, no less a person than the archbishop of Paris himself, ascended the rostrum and declared that the dogma of the resurrection of the dead might be discussed without incurring any canonical blame, and that it might be interpreted in entire harmony with reason and faith. According to him one might admit the dogma, and at the same time recognize the rational impossibility of a resurrection of the body!

"The Doctor Angelicus," he said, speaking of St. Thomas, "maintained that the complete dissolution of every human body by fire would take place before the resurrection. (Summa theologica, III.) I readily concede with Calmet (on the resurrection of the dead) that to the omnipotence of the Creator it would not be impossible to reassemble the scattered molecules in such a way that the resurrected body should not contain a single one which did not belong to it at some time during its mortal life. But such a miracle is not necessary. St. Thomas has himself shown (loco citato) that this complete material identity is by no means indispensable to establish the perfect identity of the resurrected body with the body destroyed by death. I also think, therefore, that the letter should give way to the spirit.

"What is the principle of identity in a living body? Assuredly it does not consist in the complete and persistent identity of its *matter*. For in this continual change and renewal, which is the very essence of physiological life, the elements, which have belonged successively from infancy to old age to the same human being, would form a colossal body. In this torrent of life the elements pass and change ceaselessly; but the organism remains the same, notwithstanding the modifications in its size, its form and its constitution. Does the growing stem of the oak, hidden between its two cotyledons, cease to be the same plant when it has become a mighty oak? Is the embryo of the caterpillar, while yet in the egg, no longer the same insect when it becomes a caterpillar, and then a chrysalis, and then a butterfly? Is individuality lost as the child passes through manhood to old age? Assuredly not. But in the case of the oak, the butterfly, and the man, is there a single remaining molecule of those which constituted the growing stem of the oak, the egg of the caterpillar or the human embryo? What then is the principle which persists through all these changes? This principle is a reality, not a fiction. It is not the soul, for the plants have life, and yet no souls, in the meaning of the word as we use it. Nevertheless, it must be an imponderable agent. Does it survive the body? It is possible. St. Gregory of Nyssus believed so. If it remains united to the soul, it may be invoked to furnish it with a new body identical with that which death has destroyed, even though this body should not possess *a single molecule* which it possessed at any period of its terrestrial life, and this would be as truly our body as that which we had when five, fifteen, or thirty, or sixty years of age.

"Such a conception agrees perfectly with the expressions of holy writ, according to which it is certain that after a period of separation the soul will again take on the body forever.

"In addition to St. Gregory of Nyssus, permit me, most reverend fathers, to cite a philosopher Leibnitz, who held the opinion that the physiological principle of life was imponderable but not incorporeal, and that the soul remains united to this principle, although separated from the ponderable and visible body. I do not pretend to either accept or reject this hypothesis. I only note that it may serve to explain the dogma of the resurrection, in which every Christian should firmly believe."

"This effort to conciliate reason and faith," interrupted the Croatian bishop, "is worthy of praise, but it seems to me more ingenious than probable. Are these bodies, bodies like our own? If they are perfect, incorruptible, fitted to their new conditions, they must not possess any organ for which there is no use. Why a mouth, if they do not eat? Why legs, if they do not walk? Why arms, if they do not work? One of the fathers of the early church, Origen, whose personal sacrifice is not forgotten, thought these bodies must be perfect spheres. That would be logical but not very beautiful or interesting."

"It is better to admit with St. Gregory of Nyssus and St. Augustin," replied the archbishop, "that the resurrected body will have the human form, a transparent veil of the beauty of the soul."

Thus was the modern theory of the Church on the resurrection of the body summed up by the French cardinal. As to the objections on the score of the locality of the resurrection, the number of the resurrected, the insufficiency of surface on the globe, the final abode of the elect and the damned, it was impossible to come to any common understanding for the contradictions were irreconcilable. The resultant impression was, however, that these matters also should be understood figuratively, that neither the heaven or the hell of the theologian represented any definite place, but rather states of the soul, of happiness or of misery, and that life, whatever its form, would be perpetuated on the countless worlds which people infinite space. And so it appeared that Christian thought had gradually become transformed, among the enlightened, and followed the progress of astronomy and the other sciences.

The council had been held on Tuesday evening, that is to say on the day following the two meetings of the Institute, of which an account has been given above. The Pope had made public the advice of the president of the Institute to leave Italy on the fatal day, but no attention had been paid to it, partly because death is a deliverance for every believer, and partly because most theologians denied the existence even of inhabitants upon Mars.

Chapter VI

IT IS NOW TIME to pause, amid the eventful scenes through which we are passing, in order to consider this new fear of the end of the world with others which have preceded it, and to pass rapidly in review the remarkable history of this idea, which has reappeared again and again in the past. At the time of which we are speaking, this subject was the sole theme of conversation in every land and in every tongue.

As to the dogma "Credo Resurrectionem Carnis," the addresses of the fathers of the Church before the council assembled in the Sistine chapel at Rome, were, on the whole, in accord with the opinion expressed by the cardinal archbishop of Paris. The clause "et vitam æternam" was tacitly ignored, in view of the possible discoveries of astronomy and psychology. These addresses epitomized, as it were, the history of the doctrine of the end of the world as held by the Christian Church in all ages.

This history is interesting, for it is also the history of the human mind face to face with its own destiny, and we believe it of sufficient importance to devote to it a separate chapter. For the time being, therefore, we abandon our role as the chronicler of the twenty-fourth century, and return to our own times, in order to consider this doctrine from an historical point of view.

The existence of a profound and tenacious faith is as old as the centuries, and it is a notable fact that all religions, irrespective of Christian dogma, have opened the same door from this mortal life upon the unknown which lies beyond, it is the door of the Divine Comedy of Dante, although the conceptions of paradise, hell and purgatory peculiar to the Christian Church, are not universal.

Zoroaster and the Zend-Avesta taught that the world would perish by fire. The same idea is found in the Epistle of St. Peter. It seems that the traditions of Noah and of Deucalion, according to which the first great disaster to humanity came by flood, indicated that the second great disaster would be of an exactly opposite character.

The apostles Peter and Paul died, probably, in the year 64, during the horrible slaughter ordered by Nero after the burning of Rome, which had been fired at his command and whose destruction he attributed to the Christians in order that he might have a pretext for new persecutions. St. John wrote the Apocalypse in the year 69. The reign of Nero was a bloody one, and martyrdom seemed to be the natural consequence of a virtuous life. Prodigies appeared on every hand; there were comets, falling stars, eclipses, showers of blood, monsters, earthquakes, famines, pestilences, and above all, there was the Jewish war and the destruction of Jerusalem. Never, perhaps, were so many horrors, so much cruelty and madness, so many catastrophes, crowded into so short a period as in the years 64–69 A.D. The little church of Christ was apparently dispersed. It was impossible to remain in Jerusalem. The horrors of the reign of terror of 1793, and of the Commune of 1871, were as nothing in comparison with those of the Jewish civil war. The family of Jesus was obliged to leave the holy city and to seek safety in flight. False prophets appeared, thus verifying former prophecies. Vesuvius was preparing the terrible eruption of the year 79, and already, in 63, Pompeii had been destroyed by an earthquake.

There was every indication that the end of the world was at hand. Nothing was wanting. The Apocalypse announced it.

But a calm followed the storm. The terrible Jewish war came to an end; Nero fell before Galba; under Vespasian and Titus, peace (71) succeeded war, and – the end of the world was not yet.

Once more it became necessary to interpret anew the words of the evangelists. The coming of Christ was put off until after the fall of the Roman empire, and thus considerable margin was given to the commentator. A firm belief in a final and even an imminent catastrophe persisted, but it was couched in vague terms, which robbed the spirit as well as the letter of the prophecy of all precision. Still, the conviction remained.

St. Augustine devotes the XXth book of the City of God (426) to the regeneration of the world, the resurrection, the last judgment, and the New Jerusalem; in the XXIst book he describes the everlasting torments of hell-fire. A witness to the fall of Rome and the empire, the bishop of Carthage believed these events to be the first act of the drama. But the reign of God was to continue a thousand years before the coming of Satan.

St. Gregory, bishop of Tours (573), the first historian of the Franks, began his history as follows: "As I am about to relate the wars of the kings with hostile nations, I feel impelled to declare my belief. The terror with which men await the end of the world decides me to chronicle the years already passed, that thus one may know exactly how many have elapsed since the beginning of the world."

This tradition was perpetuated from year to year and from century to century, notwithstanding that nature failed to confirm it. Every catastrophe, earthquake, epidemic, famine and flood, every phenomenon, eclipse, comet, storm, sudden darkness and tempest, was looked upon as the forerunner and herald of the final cataclysm. Trembling like leaves in the blast, the faithful awaited the coming judgment; and preachers successfully worked upon this dread apprehension, so deeply rooted in every heart.

But, as generation after generation passed, it became necessary to define again the widespread tradition, and about this time the idea of a millennium took form in the minds of commentators. There were many sects which believed that Christ would reign with the saints a thousand years before the day of judgment. St. Irenus, St. Papias, and St. Sulpicius Severus shared this belief, which acquired an exaggerated and sensual form in the minds of many, who looked forward to a day of general rejoicing for the elect and a reign of pleasure. St. Jerome and St. Augustine did much to discredit these views, but did not attack the central doctrine of a resurrection. Commentators on the Apocalypse continued to flourish through the somber night of the middle ages, and in the tenth century especially the belief gained ground that the year 1000 was to usher in the great change.

This conviction of an approaching end of the world, if not universal, was at least very general. Several charters of the period began with this sentence: Termino mundi appropinquante: "The end of the world drawing near." In spite of some exceptions, it seems difficult not to share the opinion of historians, notably of Michelet, Henry Martin, Guizot, and Duruy, regarding the prevalence of this belief throughout Christendom. Doubtless, neither the French monk Gerbert, at that time Pope Sylvester II., nor King Robert of France, regulated their lives by their superstition, but it had none the less penetrated the conscience of the faint-hearted, and many a sermon was preached from this text of the Apocalypse:

"And when the thousand years are expired, Satan shall be loosed out of his prison, and shall go out to deceive the nations which are in the four quarters of the earth...and another book was opened, which is the Book of Life...and the sea gave up the dead which were in it: and death and hell gave up the dead which were in them: and they were judged every man according to his works...and I saw a new heaven and a new earth."

Bernard, a hermit of Thuringia, had taken these very words of Revelation as the text of his preaching, and in about the year 960 he publicly announced that the end of the world was at hand. He even fixed the fatal day itself, as that on which "The Annunciation" and Holy Friday should fall on the same day, a coincidence which really occurred in 992.

Druthmar, a monk of Corbie, prophesied the end of the world for the 24th of March in the year 1000. In many cities popular terror was so great on that day that the people sought refuge in the churches, remaining until midnight, prostrate before the relics of the saints, in order to await there the last trump and to die at the foot of the cross.

From this epoch date many gifts to the Church. Lands and goods were given to the monasteries. Indeed, an authentic and very curious document is preserved, written in the year 1000 by a certain monk, Raoul Glaber, on whose first pages we find: "Satan will soon be unloosed, as prophesied by St. John, *the thousand years having been accomplished*. It is of these years that we are to speak."

The end of the tenth century and the beginning of the eleventh century was a truly strange and fearful period. From 980 to 1040 it seemed as if the angel of death had spread his wings over the world. Famine and pestilence desolated the length and breadth of Europe. There was in the first place the "mal des ardents," the flesh of its victims decaying and falling from the bones, was consumed as by fire, and the members themselves were destroyed and fell away. Wretches thus afflicted thronged the roads leading to the shrines and besieged the churches, filling them with terrible odors, and dying before the relics of the saints. The fearful pest made more than forty thousand victims in Acquitania, and devastated the southern portions of France.

Then came famine, ravaging a large part of Christendom. Of the seventy-three years between 987 and 1060, forty-eight were years of famine and pestilence. The invasion of the Huns, between 910 and 945, revived the horrors of Attila, and the soil was so laid waste by wars between domains and provinces that it ceased to be cultivated. For three years rain fell continuously; it was impossible either to sow or to reap. The earth became barren and was abandoned. "The price of a 'muid' of wheat," writes Raoul Glaber, "rose to sixty gold sous; the rich waxed thin and pale; the poor gnawed the roots of trees, and many were in such extremity as to devour human flesh. The strong fell upon the weak in the public highways, tore them in pieces, and roasted them for food. Children were enticed by an egg or some fruit into byways, where they were devoured. This frenzy of hunger was such that the beast was safer than man. Famished children killed their parents, and mothers feasted upon their children. One person exposed human flesh for sale in the market place of Tournus, as if it were a staple article of food. He did not deny the fact and was burned at the stake. Another, stealing this flesh by night from the spot where it had been buried, was also burned alive."

This testimony is that of one who lived at the time and in many cases was an eye witness to what he relates. On every side people were perishing of hunger, and did not scruple to eat reptiles, unclean animals, and even human flesh. In the depths of the forest of Mâcon, in the vicinity of a church dedicated to St. John, a wretch had built a hut in which he strangled pilgrims and wayfarers. One day a traveller entering the hut with his wife to seek rest, saw in a corner the heads of men, women and children. Attempting to fly, they were prevented by their host. They succeeded, however, in escaping, and on reaching Mâcon, related what they had seen. Soldiers were sent to the bloody spot, where they counted forty-eight human heads. The murderer was dragged to the town and burned alive. The hut and the ashes of the funeral pile were seen by Raoul Glaber. So numerous were the corpses that burial was impossible, and disease followed close upon famine. Hordes of wolves preyed upon the unburied. Never before had such misery been known.

War and pillage were the universal rule, but these scourges from heaven made men somewhat more reasonable. The bishops came together, and it was agreed to establish a truce for four days of each week, from Wednesday night to Monday morning. This was known as the truce of God.

It is not strange that the end of so miserable a world was both the hope and the terror of this mournful period.

The year 1000, however, passed like its predecessors, and the world continued to exist. Were the prophets wrong again, or did the thousand years of Christendom point to the year 1033? The world waited and hoped. In that very year occurred a total eclipse of the sun; "The great source of light became saffron colored; gazing into each others faces men saw that they were pale as death; every object presented a livid appearance; stupor seized upon every heart and a general catastrophe was expected." But the end of the world was not yet.

It was to this critical period that we owe the construction of the magnificent cathedrals which have survived the ravages of time and excited the wonder of centuries. Immense wealth had been lavished upon the clergy, and their riches increased by donations and inheritance. A new era seemed to be at hand. "After the year 1000," continues Raoul Glaber, "the holy basilicas throughout the world were entirely renovated, especially in Italy and Gaul, although for the most part they were in no need of repair. Christian nations vied with each other in the erection of magnificent churches. It seemed as if the entire world, animated by a common impulse, shook off the rags of the past to put on a new garment; and the faithful were not content to rebuild nearly all the episcopal churches, but also embellished the monasteries dedicated to the various saints, and even the chapels in the smaller villages."

The somber year 1000 had followed the vanished centuries into the past, but through what troubled times the Church had passed! The popes were the puppets of the rival Saxon emperors and the princes of Latium. All Christendom was in arms. The crisis had passed, but the problem of the end of the world remained, and credence in this dread event, though uncertain and vague, – was fostered by that profound belief in the devil and in prodigies which was yet to endure for centuries in the popular mind. The final scene of the last judgment was sculptured over the portals of every cathedral, and on entering the sanctuary of the church one passed under the balance of the archangel, on whose left writhed the bodies of the devils and the damned, delivered over to the eternal flames of hell.

But the idea that the world was to end was not confined to the Church. In the twelfth century astrologers terrified Europe by the announcement of a conjunction of all the planets in the constellation of the scales. This conjunction indeed, occurred, for on September 15th all the planets were found between the 180th and 190th degrees of longitude. But the end of the world did not come.

The celebrated alchemist, Arnauld de Villeneuve, foretold it again for the year 1335. In 1406, under Charles VI, an eclipse of the sun, occurring on June 16th, produced a general panic, which is chronicled by Juvénal of the Ursuline Order: "It is a pitiable sight," he says, "to see people taking refuge in the churches as if the world were about to perish." In 1491 St. Vincent Ferrier wrote a treatise entitled, "De la Fin du Monde et de la Science Spirituelle." He allows Christendom as many years of life as there are verses in the psalter, namely, 2537. Then a German astrologer, one Stoffler, predicted that on February 20, 1524, a general deluge would result from a conjunction of the planets. He was very generally believed, and the panic was extreme. Property situated in valleys, along river banks, or near the sea, was sold to the less credulous for a mere nothing. A certain doctor, Auriol, of Toulouse, had an ark built for himself, his family and his friends, and Bodin asserts that he was not the only one who took this precaution.

There were few sceptics. The grand chancellor of Charles V. sought the advice of Pierre Martyr, who told him that the event would not be as fatal as was feared, but that the conjunction of the planets would doubtless occasion grave disasters. The fatal day arrived...and never had the month of February been so dry! But this did not prevent new predictions for the year 1532, by the astrologer of the elector of Brandenburg, Jean Carion; and again for the year 1584, by the astrologer Cyprian Lëowitz. It was again a question of a deluge, due to planetary conjunctions.

"The terror of the populace," writes a contemporary, Louis Guyon, "was extreme, and the churches could not hold the multitudes which fled to them for refuge; many made their wills without stopping to think that this availed little if the world was really to perish; others donated their goods to the clergy, in the hope that their prayers would put off the day of judgment."

In 1588 there was another astrological prediction, couched in apocalyptic language, as follows: "The eighth year following the fifteen hundred and eightieth anniversary of the birth of Christ will be a year of prodigies and terror. If in this terrible year the globe be not dissolved in dust, and the land and the sea be not destroyed, every kingdom will be overthrown and humanity will travail in pain."

As might be expected, the celebrated soothsayer, Nostradamus, is found among these prophets of evil. In his book of rhymed prophecies, entitled Centuries, we find the following quatrain, which excited much speculation:

Quand Georges Dieu crucifiera,
Que Marc le ressuscitera,
Et que St. Jean le portera,
La fin du monde arrivera.

The meaning of which is, that when Easter falls on the twenty-fifth of April (St. Mark's day), Holy Friday will fall on the twenty-third (St. George's day), and Corpus Christi on the twenty-fourth of June (St. John's day), and the end of the world will come. This verse was not without malice, for at this time (Nostradamus died in 1556) the calendar had not been reformed; this was not done until 1582, and it was impossible for Easter to fall on the twenty-fifth of April. In the sixteenth century, the twenty-fifth of April corresponded to the fifteenth; the day following November 4, 1582, was called the fifteenth. After the introduction of the Gregorian calendar, Easter might fall on the twenty-fifth of April, its latest possible date, and this was the case in 1666, 1734, 1886, as it will be again in 1942, 2038, 2190, etc., the end of the world, however, not being a necessary consequence of this coincidence.

Planetary conjunctions, eclipses and comets were alike the basis for prophecies of evil. Among the comets recorded in history we may mention, as the most remarkable from this point of view, that of William the Conqueror, which appeared in 1066, and which is pictured on the tapestry of Queen Matilda, at Bayeux; that of 1264, which, it is said, disappeared the very day of the death of Pope Urban IV; that of 1327, one of the largest and most imposing ever seen, which "presaged" the death of Frederick, king of Sicily; that of 1399, which Juvénal, the Ursuline, described as "the harbinger of coming evil;" that of 1402, to which was ascribed the death of Gian Galeazzo, Visconti, duke of Milan; that of 1456, which filled all Christendom with terror, under Pope Calixtus III, during the war with the Turks, and which is associated with the history of the Angelus; and that of 1472, which preceded the death of the brother of Louis XI. There were others, also, associated like the preceding, with catastrophes and wars, and especially with the dreaded last hours of the race. That of 1527 is described by Ambroise Paré, and by Simon Goulart, as formed of severed heads, poignards and bloody clouds. The comet of 1531 was thought to herald the death of Louise of Savoy, mother of Francis I, and this princess shared the popular superstition in reference to evil stars: "Behold!" she exclaimed from her bed, on perceiving the comet through the window, "behold an omen which is not given to one of low degree. God sends it as a warning to us. Let us prepare to meet death." Three days after, she died. But the famous comet of Charles V, appearing in 1556, was perhaps the most memorable of all. It had been identified as the comet of 1264, and its return was announced for 1848. But it did not reappear.

The comets of 1577, 1607, 1652 and 1665 were the subjects of endless commentaries, forming a library by themselves. At the last of these Alphonso VI, king of Portugal, angrily discharged his pistol, with the most grotesque defiance. Pierre Petit, by order of Louis XIV, published a work designed to counteract the foolish, and political, apprehensions excited by comets. This illustrious king desired to be without a rival, the only sun, "Nec pluribus impar!" and would not admit the supposition that the glory of France could be imperilled even by a celestial phenomenon.

One of the greatest comets which ever struck the imagination of men was assuredly the famous comet of 1680, to which Newton devoted so much attention. "It issued," said Lemonnier, "with a frightful velocity from the depths of space and seemed falling directly into the sun and was seen to vanish with an equal velocity. It was visible for four months. It approached quite near to the earth, and Whiston ascribed the deluge to its former appearance." Bayle wrote a treatise to prove the absurdity of beliefs founded on these portents. Madame de Sévigné writing to her cousin, Count de Bussy-Rabutin, says: "We have a comet of enormous size; its tail is the most beautiful object conceivable. Every person of note is alarmed and believes that heaven, interested in their fate, sends them a warning in this comet. They say that the courtiers of Cardinal Mazarin, who is despaired of by his physicians believe this prodigy is in honor of his passing away, and tell him of the terror with which it has inspired them. He had the sense to laugh at them, and to reply facetiously that the comet did him too much honor. In truth we ought all to agree with him, for human pride assumes too much when it believes that death is attended by such signs from heaven."

We see that comets were gradually losing their prestige. Yet we read in a treatise of the astronomer Bernouilli this singular remark: "If the head of the comet be not a visible sign of the anger of God, *the tail may well be*."

Fear of the end of the world was reawakened by the appearance of comets in 1773; a great panic spread throughout Europe, and Paris itself was alarmed. Here is an extract from the memoirs of Bachaumont, accessible to every reader:

"May 6th, 1773. In the last public meeting of the Academy of Sciences, M. de Lalande was to read by far the most interesting paper of all; this, however, he was not able to do, for lack of time. It concerned the comets which, by approaching the earth, may cause revolutions, and dealt especially with that one whose return is expected in eighteen years. But although he affirmed that it was not one of those which would harm the earth, and that, moreover, he had observed that one could not fix, with any exactness, the order of such occurrences, there exists, nevertheless, a very general anxiety.

"May 9th. The cabinet of M. de Lalande is filled with the curious who come to question him concerning the above memoir, and, in order to reassure those who have been alarmed by the exaggerated rumors circulated about it, he will doubtless be forced to make it public. The excitement has been so great that some ignorant fanatics have besought the archbishop to institute prayers for forty hours, in order to avert the deluge which menaces us; and this prelate would have authorized these prayers, had not the Academy shown him the ridicule which such a step would produce.

"May 14th. The memoir of M. de Lalande has appeared. He says that it is his opinion that, of the sixty known comets, eight, by their near approach to the earth, might produce a pressure such that the sea would leave its bed and cover a part of the world."

In time, the excitement died away. The fear of comets assumed a new form. They were no longer regarded as indications of the anger of God, but their collision with the earth was discussed from a scientific point of view, and these collisions were not considered free of danger. At the close of the last century, Laplace stated his views on this question, in the forcible language which we have quoted in Chapter II.

In this century, predictions concerning the end of the world have several times been associated with the appearance of comets. It was announced that the comet of Biela, for example, would intersect the earth's orbit on October 29, 1832, which it did, as predicted. There was great excitement. Once more the end of things was declared at hand. Humanity was threatened. What was going to happen?

The orbit, that is to say the path, of the earth had been confounded with the earth itself. The latter was not to reach that point of its orbit traversed by the comet until November 30th, more than a month after the comet's passage, and the latter was at no time to be within 20,000,000 leagues of us. Once more we got off with a fright.

It was the same in 1857. Some prophet of ill omen had declared that the famous comet of Charles V., whose periodic time was thought to be three centuries, would return on the 13th of June of that year. More than one timid soul was rendered anxious, and the confessionals of Paris were more than usually crowded with penitents. Another prediction was made public in 1872, in the name of an astronomer, who, however, was not responsible for it – M. Plantamour, director of the Geneva observatory.

As in the case of comets, so with other unusual phenomena, such as total solar eclipses, mysterious suns appearing suddenly in the skies, showers of shooting stars, great volcanic eruptions accompanied with the darkness of night and seeming to threaten the burial of the world in ashes, earthquakes overthrowing and engulfing houses and cities – all these grand and terrible events have been connected with the fear of an immediate and universal end of men and things.

The history of eclipses alone would suffice to fill a volume, no less interesting than the history of comets. Confining our attention to a modern example, one of the last total eclipses of the sun, visible in France, that of August 12, 1654, had been foretold by astronomers, and its announcement had produced great alarm. For some it meant the overthrow of states and the fall of Rome; for others it signified a new deluge; there were those who believed that nothing less than the destruction of the world by fire was inevitable; while the more collected anticipated the poisoning of the atmosphere. Belief in these dreaded results were so widespread, that, in order to escape them, and by the express order of physicians, many terrified people shut themselves up in closed cellars, warmed and perfumed. We refer the reader, especially, to the second evening of Les Mondes of Fontenelle. Another writer of the same century, Petit, to whom we referred a moment ago, in his Dissertation on the Nature of Comets says, that the consternation steadily increased up to the fatal day, and that a country curate, unable to confess all who believed their last hour was at hand, at sermon time told his parishioners not to be in such haste, for the eclipse had been put off for a fortnight; and these good people were as ready to believe in the postponement of the eclipse as they had been in its malign influence.

At the time of the last total solar eclipses visible in France, namely, those of May 12, 1706; May 22, 1724, and July 8, 1842, as also of the partial ones of October 9, 1847; July 28, 1851; March 15, 1858; July 18, 1860, and December 22, 1870, there was more or less apprehension on the part of the timid; at least, we know, from trustworthy sources, that in each of these cases these natural phenomena were interpreted by a certain class in Europe as possible signs of divine wrath, and in several religious educational establishments the pupils were requested to offer up prayers as the time of the eclipse drew near. This mystical interpretation of the order of nature is slowly disappearing among enlightened nations, and the next total eclipse of the sun, visible in southern France on May 28, 1900, will probably inspire no fear on the French side of the Pyrenees; but it might be premature to make the same statement regarding those who will observe it from the Spanish side of the mountains.

Among uncivilized people these phenomena excite today the same terror which they once did among us. This fact is frequently attested by travellers, especially in Africa. During the eclipse of July 18, 1860, in Algeria, men and women resorted to prayer or fled affrighted to their homes. During the eclipse of July 29, 1878, which was total in the United States, a negro, suddenly crazed with terror, and persuaded that the end of the world was coming, cut the throats of his wife and children.

It must be admitted that such phenomena are well calculated to overwhelm the imagination. The sun, the god of day, the star upon whose light we are dependent, grows dim; and, just before it becomes extinguished, takes on a sickly and mournful hue. The light of the sky pales, the animal creation is stricken with terror, the beast of burden falters at his task, the dog flees to its master, the hen retreats with her brood to the coop, the birds cease their songs, and have been seen even to drop dead with fright. Arago relates that during the total eclipse of the sun at Perpignan, on July 8, 1842, twenty thousand spectators were assembled, forming an impressive spectacle. "When the solar disc was nearly obscured, an irresistible anxiety took possession of everybody; each felt the need of sharing his impressions with his neighbor. A deep murmur arose, like that of the far away sea after a storm. This murmur deepened as the crescent of light grew less, and when it had disappeared and sudden darkness had supervened, the silence which ensued marked this phase of the eclipse as accurately as the pendulum of our astronomical clock. The magnificence of the spectacle triumphed over the petulance of youth, over the frivolity which some people mistake for a sign of superiority, over the indifference which the soldier frequently assumes. A profound silence reigned also in the sky: the birds had ceased their songs. After a solemn interval of about two minutes, joyous transports and frantic applause greeted with the same spontaneity the first reappearance of the solar rays, and the melancholy and indefinable sense of depression gave way to a deep and unfeigned exultation which no one sought to moderate or repress."

Every one who witnessed this phenomenon, one of the most sublime which nature offers, was profoundly moved, and took away with him an impression never to be forgotten. The peasants especially were terrified by the darkness, as they believed that they were losing their sight. A poor child, tending his flock, completely ignorant of what was coming, saw the sun slowly growing dim in a cloudless sky. When its light had entirely disappeared the poor child, completely carried away by terror, began to cry and call for help. His tears flowed again when the first ray of light reappeared. Reassured, he clasped his hands, crying, "O, beautiful sun!"

Is not the cry of this child the cry of humanity?

So long as eclipses were not known to be the natural consequences of the motion of the moon about the earth, and before it was understood that their occurrence could be predicted with the utmost precision, it was natural that they should have produced a deep impression and been associated with the idea of the end of the world. The same is true of other celestial phenomena and notably of the sudden appearance of unknown suns, an event much rarer than an eclipse.

The most celebrated of these appearances was that of 1572. On the 11th of November of that year, about a month after the massacre of St. Bartholomew, a brilliant star of the first magnitude suddenly appeared in the constellation of Cassiopeia. The stupefaction was general, not only on the part of the public, to which it was visible every night in the sky, but also on the part of scientists, who could not explain its appearance. Astrologers found a solution of the enigma in the assertion that it was the star of the Magi, whose reappearance announced the return of the Son of God, the last judgment and the resurrection. This statement made a deep impression upon all classes of society. The star gradually diminished in splendor, and at the end of about eighteen months went out, without having caused any other disaster than that which human folly itself adds to the misery of a none too prosperous planet. Science records several apparitions of this nature, but the above was the most remarkable. A like agitation has accompanied all the grand phenomena of nature, especially those which have been unforeseen. In the chronicles of the middle ages, and even in more recent memoirs, we read of the terror which the aurora borealis, showers of shooting stars and the fall of meteorites have produced among the alarmed spectators. Recently, during the meteor shower of November 27, 1872, when the sky was filled with more than forty thousand meteorites belonging to the dispersed comet of Biela, women of the lower classes, at Nice especially, as also at Rome, in their excitement sought information of those whom they thought able to explain the cause of these celestial fire-works, which they had at once associated with the end of the world and with the fall of the stars, which it was foretold would usher in that last great event.

Earthquakes and volcanic eruptions have sometimes attained such proportions as to lead to the fear that the end of the world was at hand. Imagine the state of mind of the inhabitants of Herculaneum and of Pompeii when the eruption of Vesuvius buried them in showers of ashes! Was not this for them the end of the world? And more recently, were not those who witnessed the eruption of Krakatoa of the same opinion? Impenetrable darkness lasting eighteen hours, an atmosphere like a furnace, filling the eyes, nose and ears with ashes, the deep and incessant cannonade of the volcano, the falling of pumice stones from the black sky, the terrible scene illuminated only at intervals by the lurid lightning or the fire-balls on the spars and rigging of vessels, the thunder echoing from cloud and sea with an infernal musketry, the shower of ashes turning into a deluge of mud – this was the experience of the passengers of a Java vessel during the night of eighteen hours, from the 26th to the 28th of August, 1883, when a portion of the island of Krakatoa was hurled into the air, and the sea, after having first retreated, swept upon the shore to a height of thirty-five meters and to a distance of from one to ten kilometers over a coast-line of five hundred kilometers, and in the reflux carried away with it the four cities, Tjiringin, Mérak, Telok-Bétong and Anjer, and the entire population of the region, more than forty thousand souls. For a long time the progress of vessels was hindered by floating bodies inextricably interlaced; and human fingers, with their nails, and fragments of heads, with their hair were found in the stomachs of fishes. Those who escaped, or who saw the catastrophe from some vessel, and lived to welcome again the light of day, which had seemed forever extinguished, relate in terror with what resignation they expected the end of the world, persuaded that its very foundations were giving way and that the knell of a universal doom had sounded. One eye-witness assures us that he would not again pass through such an experience for all the wealth that could be imagined. The sun was extinguished and death seemed to reign sovereign over nature. This eruption, moreover, was of such terrific violence that it was heard through the earth at the antipodes; it reached an altitude of twenty thousand meters, producing an atmospheric disturbance which made the circuit of the entire globe in thirty-five hours (the barometer fell four millimeters in Paris even), and left for more than a year in the upper layers of the atmosphere a fine dust, which, illumined by the sun, gave rise to those magnificent twilight displays admired so much throughout the world.

These are formidable disturbances, partial ends of the world. Certain earthquakes deserve citation with these terrible volcanic eruptions, so disastrous have been their consequences. In the earthquake of Lisbon, November 1, 1755, thirty thousand persons perished; the shock was felt over an area four times as large as that of Europe. When Lima was destroyed, October 28, 1724, the sea rose twenty-seven meters above its ordinary level, rushed upon the city and erased it so completely that not a single house was left. Vessels were found in the fields several kilometers from the shore. On December 10, 1869, the inhabitants of the city of Onlah, in Asia Minor, alarmed by subterranean noises and a first violent trembling of the earth, took refuge on a neighboring hilltop, whence, to their stupefaction, they saw several crevasses open in the city which within a few moments entirely disappeared in the bowels of the earth. We have direct evidence that under circumstances far less dramatic, as for example on the occasion of the earthquake at Nice, February 23, 1887, the idea of the end of the world was the very first which presented itself to the mind.

The history of the earth furnishes a remarkable number of like dramas, catastrophes of a partial character, threatening the world's final destruction. It is fitting that we should devote a moment to the consideration of these great phenomena, as also to the history of that belief in the end of the world which has appeared in every age, though modified by the progress of human knowledge. Faith has in part disappeared; mystery and superstition, which struck the imagination of our ancestors, and which has been so curiously represented in the portals of our great cathedrals, and in the sculpture and painting inspired by Christian traditions, this theological aspect of the last great day, has given place to the scientific study of the probable life of the solar system to which we belong. The geocentric and anthropocentric conception of the universe, which makes man the center and end of creation, has become gradually transformed and has at last disappeared; for we know that our humble planet is but an island in the infinite, that human history has thus far been founded on pure illusions, and that the dignity of man consists in his intellectual and moral worth. Is not the destiny and sovereign end of the human mind the exact knowledge of things, the search after truth?

During the nineteenth century, evil prophets, more or less sincere, have twenty-five times announced the end of the world, basing their prophecies upon cabalistic calculations destitute of serious foundation. Like predictions will recur so long as the race exists.

But this historic interlude, although opportune, has for a moment interrupted our narrative. Let us hasten to return to the twenty-fifth century, for we have reached its most critical moment.

Chapter VII

INEXORABLY, WITH A FATALITY no power could arrest, like a projectile speeding from the mouth of a cannon toward the target, the comet continued to advance, following its appointed path, and hurrying, with an ever-increasing velocity, toward the point in space at which the earth would be found on the night of July 14–15. The final calculations were absolutely without error. These two heavenly bodies – the earth and the comet – were to meet like two trains, rushing headlong upon each other, with resistless momentum, as if impelled to mutual destruction by an insatiable rage. But in the present instance the velocity of shock would be 865 times that of two express trains having each a speed of one hundred kilometers per hour.

During the night of July 13–14, the comet spread over nearly the entire sky, and whirlwinds of fire could be seen by the naked eye, eddying about an axis oblique to the zenith. The appearance was that of an army of flaming meteors, in whose midst the flashing lightning produced the effect of a furious combat. The burning star had a revolution of its own, and seemed to be convulsed with pain, like a living thing. Immense jets of flame issued from various centers, some of a greenish hue, others red as blood, while the most brilliant were of a dazzling whiteness. It was evident that the sun was acting powerfully upon this whirlpool of gases, decomposing certain of them, forming detonating compounds, electrifying the nearer portions, and repelling the smoke from about the immense nucleus which was bearing down upon the world. The comet itself emitted a light far different from the sunlight reflected by the enveloping vapors; and its flames, shooting forth in ever-increasing volume, gave it the appearance of a monster, precipitating itself upon the earth to devour it. Perhaps the most striking feature of this spectacle was the absence of all sound. At Paris, as elsewhere, during that eventful night, the crowd instinctively maintained silence, spellbound by an indescribable fascination, endeavoring to catch some echo of the celestial thunder – but not a sound was heard.

The moon rose full, showing green upon the fiery background of the sky, but without brilliancy and casting no shadows. The night was no more night, for the stars had disappeared, and the sky glowed with an intense light.

The comet was approaching the earth with a velocity of 41,000 meters per second, or 2460 kilometers per minute, that is, 147,600 kilometers per hour; and the earth was itself travelling through space, from west to east, at the rate of 29,000 meters per second, 1740 kilometers per minute, or 104,400 kilometers per hour, in a direction oblique to the orbit of the comet, which for any meridian appeared at midnight in the northeast. Thus, in virtue of their velocities, these two celestial bodies were nearing each other at the rate of 173,000 kilometers per hour. When observation, which was in entire accord with the computations previously made, established the fact that the nucleus of the comet was at a distance no greater than that of the moon, everyone knew that two hours later the first phenomena of the coming shock would begin.

Contrary to all expectation, Friday and Saturday, the 13th and 14th of July were, like the preceding days, wonderfully beautiful; the sun shone in a cloudless sky, the air was tranquil, the temperature rather high, but cooled by a light, refreshing breeze. Nature was in a joyous mood, the country was luxuriant with beauty, the streams murmured in the valleys, the birds sang in the woods; but the dwelling places of man were heartrendingly sad. Humanity was prostrated with terror, and the impassible calm of nature stood over against the agonizing fear of the human heart in painful and harrowing contrast.

Two millions of people had fled to Australia from Paris, London, Vienna, Berlin, St. Petersburg, Rome and Madrid. As the day of collision approached, the Trans-Atlantic Navigation company had been obliged to increase threefold, fourfold, and even tenfold, the number of air-ships, which settled like flocks of birds upon San Francisco, Honolulu, Noumea, and the Australian cities of Melbourne, Sidney and Pax. But this exodus of millions represented only the fortunate minority, and their absence was scarcely noticed in the towns and villages, swarming with restless and anxious life.

Haunted by the fear of unknown perils, for several nights no one had been able to close their eyes, or even dared to go to bed. To do so, seemed to court the last sleep and to abandon all hope of awakening again. Every face was livid with terror, every eye was sunken; the hair was dishevelled, the countenance haggard and stamped with the impress of the most frightful anguish which had ever preyed upon the human soul.

The atmosphere was growing drier and warmer. Since the evening before, no one had bethought himself of food, and the stomach, usually so imperious in its demands, craved for nothing. A burning thirst was the first physiological effect of the dryness of the atmosphere, and the most self-restrained sought, in every possible way, to quench it, though without success. Physical pain had begun its work, and was soon to dominate mental suffering. Hour by hour, respiration became more difficult, more exhausting and more painful. Little children, in the presence of this new suffering, appealed in tears to their mothers.

At Paris, London, Rome and St. Petersburg, in every capital, in every city, in every village, the terrified population wandered about distractedly, like ants when their habitations are disturbed. All the business of ordinary life was neglected, abandoned, forgotten; every project was set aside. No one cared any longer for anything, for his house, his family, his life. There existed a moral prostration and dejection, more complete than even that which is produced by sea-sickness. Some few, abandoning themselves to the exaltation of love, seemed to live only for each other, strangers to the universal panic.

Catholic and Protestant churches, Jewish synagogues, Greek chapels, Mohammedan mosques and Buddhist temples, the sanctuaries of the new Gallican religion – in short, the places of assembly of every sect into which the idiosyncrasies of belief had divided mankind, were thronged by the faithful on that memorable day of Friday, July 13th; and even at Paris the crowds besieging the portals were such that no one could get near the churches, within which were to be seen vast multitudes, all prostrate upon the ground. Prayers were muttered in low tones, but no chant, no organ, no bell was to be heard. The confessionals were surrounded by penitents, waiting their turn, as in those early days of sincere and naïve faith described by the historians of the middle ages.

Everywhere on the streets and on the boulevards the same silence reigned; not a sound disturbed the hush, nothing was sold, no paper was printed; aviators, aeroplanes, dirigible balloons were no more to be seen; the only vehicles passing were the hearses bearing to the crematories the first victims of the comet, already numerous. The days of July 13th and 14th had passed without incident, but with what anxiety the fateful night was awaited! Never, perhaps, had there been so magnificent a sunset, never a sky so pure! The orb of day seemed to go down in a sea of gold and purple; its red disc disappeared below the horizon, but the stars did not rise – and night did not come! To the daylight succeeded a day of cometary and lunar splendor, illuminated by a dazzling light, recalling that of the aurora borealis, but more intense, emanating from an immense blazing focus, which had not been visible during the day because it had been below the horizon, but which would certainly have rivalled the sun in brilliancy. Amid the universal plaint of nature, this luminous center rose in the west almost at the same time with the full moon, which climbed the sky with it like a sacrificial victim ascending the funeral pyre. The moon paled as it mounted higher, but the comet increased in brightness as the sun sank below the western horizon, and now, when the hour of night had come, it reigned supreme, a vaporous, scarlet sun, with flames of yellow and green, like immense extended wings. To the terrified spectator it seemed some enormous giant, taking sovereign possession of earth and sky.

Already the cometary fringes had invaded the lunar orbit. At any moment they would reach the rarer limits of the earth's atmosphere, only two hundred kilometers away.

Then everyone beheld, as it were, a vast conflagration, kindled over the whole extent of the horizon, throwing skyward little violet flames, and almost immediately the brilliancy of the comet diminished, doubtless because just before touching the earth it had entered into the shadow of the planet and had lost that part of its light which came from the sun. This apparent decrease in brilliancy was chiefly due to contrast, for when the eye, less dazzled, had become accustomed to this new light, it seemed almost as intense as the former, but of a sickly, lurid, sepulchral hue. Never before had the earth been bathed in such a light, which at first seemed to be colorless, emitting lightning flashes from its pale and wan depths. The dryness of the air, hot as the breath of a furnace, became intolerable, and a horrible odor of sulphur, probably due to the super-electrified ozone, poisoned the atmosphere. Everyone believed his last hour was at hand. A terrible cry dominated every other sound. The earth is on fire! The earth is on fire! Indeed, the entire horizon was now illuminated by a ring of bluish flame, surrounding the earth like the flames of a funeral pile. This, as had been predicted, was the carbonic-oxide, whose combustion in the air produced carbonic-anhydride.

Suddenly, as the terrified spectator gazed silent and awestruck, holding his very breath in a stupor of fear, the vault of heaven seemed rent asunder from zenith to horizon, and from this yawning chasm, as from an enormous mouth, was vomited forth jets of dazzling greenish flame, enveloping the earth in a glare so blinding, that all who had not already sought shelter, men and women, the old and the young, the bold as well as the timid, all rushed with the impetuosity of an avalanche to the cellarways, already choked with people. Many were crushed to death, or succumbed to apoplexy, aneurismal ruptures, and wild delirium resulting in brain fever.

On the terraces and in the observatories, however, the astronomers had remained at their posts, and several had succeeded in taking an uninterrupted series of photographs of the sky changes; and from this time, but for a very brief interval, with the exception of a few courageous spirits, who dared to gaze upon the awful spectacle from behind the windows of some upper apartment, they were the sole witnesses of the collision.

Computation had indicated that the earth would penetrate the heart of the comet as a bullet would penetrate a cloud, and that the transit, reckoning from the first instant of contact of the outer zones of the comet's atmosphere with those of the earth, would consume four and one-half hours, – a fact easily established, inasmuch as the comet, having a diameter about sixty-five times that of the earth, would be traversed, not centrally, but at one-quarter of the distance from the center, with a velocity of about 173,000 kilometers per hour. Nearly forty minutes after the first instant of contact, the heat of this incandescent furnace, and the horrible odor of sulphur, became so suffocating that a few moments more of such torture would have sufficed to destroy every vestige of life. Even the astronomers crept painfully from room to room within the observatories which they had endeavored to close hermetically, and sought shelter in the cellars; and the young computor, whose acquaintance we have already made, was the last to remain on the terrace, at Paris, – a few seconds only, but long enough to witness the explosion of a formidable bolide, which was rushing southward with the velocity of lightning. But strength was lacking for further observations. One could breathe no longer. Besides the heat and the dryness, so destructive to every vital function, there was the carbonic-oxide which was already beginning to poison the atmosphere. The ears were filled with a dull, roaring sound, the heart beat ever more and more violently; and still this choking odor of sulphur! At the same time a fiery rain fell from every quarter of the sky, a rain of shooting stars, the immense majority of which did not reach the earth, although many fell upon the roofs, and the fires which they kindled could be seen in every direction. To these fires from heaven the fires of earth now made answer, and the world was surrounded with electric flashes, as by an army. Everyone, without thinking for an instant of flight, had abandoned all hope, expecting every moment to be buried in the ruins of the world, and those who still clung to each other, and whose only consolation was that of dying together, clung closer, in a last embrace.

But the main body of the celestial army had passed, and a sort of rarefaction, of vacuum, was produced in the atmosphere, perhaps as the result of meteoric explosions; for suddenly the windows were shattered, blown outwards, and the doors opened of themselves. A violent wind arose, adding fury to the conflagration. Then the rain fell in torrents, but reanimating at the same time the extinguished hope of life, and waking mankind from its nightmare.

"The XXVth Century! Death of the Pope and all the bishops! Fall of the comet at Rome! Paper, sir?"

Scarcely a half hour had passed before people began to issue from their cellars, feeling again the joy of living, and recovering gradually from their apathy. Even before one had really begun to take any account of the fires which were still raging, notwithstanding the deluge or rain, the scream of the newsboy was heard in the hardly awakened streets. Everywhere, at Paris, Marseilles, Brussels, London, Vienna, Turin and Madrid, the same news was being shouted, and before caring for the fires which were spreading on every side, everyone bought the popular one-cent sheet, with its sixteen illustrated pages fresh from the press.

"The Pope and the cardinals crushed to death! The sacred college destroyed by the comet! Extra! Extra!"

The newsboys drove a busy trade, for everyone was anxious to know the truth of these announcements, and eagerly bought the great popular socialistic paper.

This is what had taken place. The American Hebrew, to whom we have already referred, and who, on the preceding Tuesday, had managed to make several millions by the reopening of the Paris and Chicago exchanges, had not for a moment yielded to despair, and, as in other days, the monasteries had accepted bequests made in view of the end of the world, so our indefatigable speculator had thought best to remain at his telephone, which he had caused to be taken down for the nonce into a vast subterranean gallery, hermetically closed. Controlling special wires uniting Paris with the principal cities of the world, he was in constant communication with them. The nucleus of the comet had contained within its mass of incandescent gas a certain number of solid uranolites, some of which measured several kilometers in diameter. One of these masses had struck the earth not far from Rome, and the Roman correspondent had sent the following news by phonogram:

"All the cardinals and prelates of the council were assembled in solemn fête under the dome of St. Peter. In this grandest temple of Christendom, splendidly illuminated at the solemn hour of midnight, amid the pious invocations of the chanting brotherhoods, the altars smoking with the perfumed incense, and the organs filling the recesses of the immense church with their tones of thunder, the Pope, seated upon his throne, saw prostrate at his feet his faithful people from every quarter of the world; but as he rose to pronounce the final benediction a mass of iron, half as large as the city itself, falling from the sky with the rapidity of lightning, crushed the assembled multitudes, precipitating them into an abyss of unknown depth, a veritable pit of hell. All Italy was shaken, and the roar of the thunder was heard at Marseilles."

The bolide had been seen in every city throughout Italy, through the showers of meteorites and the burning atmosphere. It had illumined the earth like a new sun with a brilliant red light, and a terrible rending had followed its fall, as if the sky had really been split from top to bottom. (This was the bolide which the young calculator of the observatory of Paris had observed when, in spite of her zeal, the suffocating fumes had driven her from the terrace.)

Seated at his telephone, our speculator received his despatches and gave his orders, dictating sensational news to his journal, which was printed simultaneously in all the principal cities of the world. A quarter of an hour later these despatches appeared on the first page of the XXVth Century, in New York, St. Petersburg and Melbourne, as also in the capitals nearer Paris; an hour after the first edition a second was announced.

"Paris in flames! The cities of Europe destroyed! Rome in ashes! Here's your XXVth Century, second edition!"

And in this new edition there was a very closely written article, from the pen of an accomplished correspondent, dealing with the consequences of the destruction of the sacred college.

"Twenty-fifth Century, fourth edition! New volcano in Italy! Revolution in Naples! Paper, sir?"

The second had been followed by the fourth edition without any regard to a third. It told how a bolide, weighing ten thousand tons, or perhaps more, had fallen with the velocity above stated upon the solfatara of Pozzuoli, penetrating and breaking in the light and hollow crust of the ancient crater. The flames below had burst forth in a new volcano, which, with Vesuvius, illuminated the Elysian fields.

"Twenty-fifth Century, sixth edition! New island in the Mediterranean! Conquests of England!"

A fragment of the head of the comet had fallen into the Mediterranean to the west of Rome, forming an irregular island, fifteen hundred meters in length by seven hundred in width, with an altitude of about two hundred meters. The sea had boiled about it, and huge tidal waves had swept the shores. But there happened to be an Englishman nearby, whose first thought was to land in a creek of the newly formed island, and scaling a rock, to plant the British flag upon its highest peak.

Millions of copies of the journal of the famous speculator were distributed broadcast over the world during this night of July 14th, with accounts of the disaster, dictated by telephone from the office of its director, who had taken measures to monopolize every item of news. Everywhere these editions were eagerly read, even before the necessary precautions were taken to extinguish the conflagrations still raging. From the outset, the rain had afforded unexpected succor, yet the material losses were immense, notwithstanding the prevailing use of iron in building construction.

"Twenty-fifth Century, tenth edition! Great miracle at Rome!"

What miracle, it was easy enough to explain. In this latest edition, the XXVth Century announced that its correspondent at Rome had given circulation to a rumor which proved to be without foundation; that the bolide had not destroyed Rome at all, but had fallen quite a distance outside the city. St. Peter and the Vatican had been miraculously preserved. But hundreds of millions of copies were sold in every country of the world. It was an excellent stroke of business.

The crisis had passed. Little by little, men recovered their self-possession, rejoicing in the mere fact of living.

Throughout the night, the sky overhead was illuminated by the lurid light of the comet, and by the meteorites which still fell in showers, kindled on every side new conflagrations. When day came, about half past three in the morning, more than three hours had passed since the head of the comet had collided with the earth; the nucleus had passed in a southwesterly direction, and the earth was still entirely buried in the tail. The shock had taken place at eighteen minutes after midnight; that is to say, fifty-eight minutes after midnight, Paris time, exactly as predicted by the president of the Astronomical society of France, whose statement our readers may remember.

Although, at the instant of collision, the greater part of the hemisphere on the side of the comet had been effected by the constricting dryness, the suffocating heat and the poisonous sulphurous odors, as well as by deadening stupor, due to the resistance encountered by the comet in traversing the atmosphere, the supersaturation of the ozone with electricity, and the mixture of nitrogen protoxide with the upper air, the other hemisphere had experienced no other disturbance than that which followed inevitably from the destroyed atmospheric equilibrium. Fortunately, the comet had only skimmed the earth, and the shock had not been central. Doubtless, also, the attraction of the earth had had much to do with the fall of the bolides in Italy and the Mediterranean. At all events, the orbit of the comet had been entirely altered by this perturbation, while the earth and the moon continued tranquilly on their way about the sun, as if nothing had happened. The orbit of the comet had been changed by the earth's attraction from a parabola to an ellipse, its aphelion being situated near the ecliptic. When later statistics of the comet's victims were obtained, it was found that the number of the dead was one-fortieth of the population of Europe. In Paris alone, which extended over a part of the departments formerly known as the Seine and Seine-et-Oise, and which contained nine million inhabitants, there was more than two hundred thousand deaths.

Prior to the fatal week, the mortality had increased threefold, and on the 10th fourfold. This rate of increase had been arrested by the confidence produced by the sessions of the Institute, and had even diminished sensibly during Wednesday. Unfortunately, as the threatening star drew near, the panic had resumed its sway. On the following Thursday the normal mortality rate had increased fivefold, and those of weak constitution had succumbed. On Friday, the 13th, the day before the disaster, owing to privations of every kind, the absence of food and sleep, the heat and feverish condition which it induced, the effect of the excitement upon the heart and brain, the mortality at Paris had reached the hitherto unheard of figure of ten thousand! On the eventful night of the 14th, owing to the crowded condition of the cellars, the vitiation of the atmosphere by the carbonic-oxide gas, and suffocation due to the drying up of the lining membrane of the throat, pulmonary congestion, anæsthesia, and arrest of the circulation, the victims were more numerous than those of the battles of former times, the total for that day reaching the enormous sum of more than one hundred thousand. Some of those mortally effected lived until the following day, and a certain number survived longer, but in a hopeless condition. Not until a week had elapsed was the normal death-rate re-established. During this disastrous month 17,500 children were born at Paris, but nearly all died. Medical statistics, subtracting from the general total the normal mean, based upon a death-rate of twenty for every one thousand inhabitants, that is, 492 per day, or 15,252 for the month, which represents the number of those who would have died independently of the comet, ascribed to the latter the difference between these two numbers, namely, 222,633; of these, more than one-half, or more than one hundred thousand, died of fear, by syncope, aneurisms or cerebral congestions.

But this cataclysm did not bring about the end of the world. The losses were made good by an apparent increase in human vitality, such as had been observed formerly after destructive wars; the earth continued to revolve in the light of the sun, and humanity to advance toward a still higher destiny.

The comet had, above all, been the pretext for the discussion of every possible phase of this great and important subject – the end of the world.

The House on the Borderland

William Hope Hodgson

Chapter I
The Finding of the Manuscript

RIGHT AWAY in the west of Ireland lies a tiny hamlet called Kraighten. It is situated, alone, at the base of a low hill. Far around there spreads a waste of bleak and totally inhospitable country; where, here and there at great intervals, one may come upon the ruins of some long desolate cottage – unthatched and stark. The whole land is bare and unpeopled, the very earth scarcely covering the rock that lies beneath it, and with which the country abounds, in places rising out of the soil in wave-shaped ridges.

Yet, in spite of its desolation, my friend Tonnison and I had elected to spend our vacation there. He had stumbled on the place by mere chance the year previously, during the course of a long walking tour, and discovered the possibilities for the angler in a small and unnamed river that runs past the outskirts of the little village.

I have said that the river is without name; I may add that no map that I have hitherto consulted has shown either village or stream. They seem to have entirely escaped observation: indeed, they might never exist for all that the average guide tells one. Possibly this can be partly accounted for by the fact that the nearest railway station (Ardrahan) is some forty miles distant.

It was early one warm evening when my friend and I arrived in Kraighten. We had reached Ardrahan the previous night, sleeping there in rooms hired at the village post office, and leaving in good time on the following morning, clinging insecurely to one of the typical jaunting cars.

It had taken us all day to accomplish our journey over some of the roughest tracks imaginable, with the result that we were thoroughly tired and somewhat bad tempered. However, the tent had to be erected and our goods stowed away before we could think of food or rest. And so we set to work, with the aid of our driver, and soon had the tent up upon a small patch of ground just outside the little village, and quite near to the river.

Then, having stored all our belongings, we dismissed the driver, as he had to make his way back as speedily as possible, and told him to come across to us at the end of a fortnight. We had brought sufficient provisions to last us for that space of time, and water we could get from the stream. Fuel we did not need, as we had included a small oil-stove among our outfit, and the weather was fine and warm.

It was Tonnison's idea to camp out instead of getting lodgings in one of the cottages. As he put it, there was no joke in sleeping in a room with a numerous family of healthy Irish in one corner and the pigsty in the other, while overhead a ragged colony of roosting fowls distributed their blessings impartially, and the whole place so full of peat smoke that it made a fellow sneeze his head off just to put it inside the doorway.

Tonnison had got the stove lit now and was busy cutting slices of bacon into the frying pan; so I took the kettle and walked down to the river for water. On the way, I had to pass close to a little group of the village people, who eyed me curiously, but not in any unfriendly manner, though none of them ventured a word.

As I returned with my kettle filled, I went up to them and, after a friendly nod, to which they replied in like manner, I asked them casually about the fishing; but, instead of answering, they just shook their heads silently, and stared at me. I repeated the question, addressing more particularly a great, gaunt fellow at my elbow; yet again I received no answer. Then the man turned to a comrade and said something rapidly in a language that I did not understand; and, at once, the whole crowd of them fell to jabbering in what, after a few moments, I guessed to be pure Irish. At the same time they cast many glances in my direction. For a minute, perhaps, they spoke among themselves thus; then the man I had addressed faced 'round at me and said something. By the expression of his face I guessed that he, in turn, was questioning me; but now I had to shake my head, and indicate that I did not comprehend what it was they wanted to know; and so we stood looking at one another, until I heard Tonnison calling to me to hurry up with the kettle. Then, with a smile and a nod, I left them, and all in the little crowd smiled and nodded in return, though their faces still betrayed their puzzlement.

It was evident, I reflected as I went toward the tent, that the inhabitants of these few huts in the wilderness did not know a word of English; and when I told Tonnison, he remarked that he was aware of the fact, and, more, that it was not at all uncommon in that part of the country, where the people often lived and died in their isolated hamlets without ever coming in contact with the outside world.

"I wish we had got the driver to interpret for us before he left," I remarked, as we sat down to our meal. "It seems so strange for the people of this place not even to know what we've come for."

Tonnison grunted an assent, and thereafter was silent for a while.

Later, having satisfied our appetites somewhat, we began to talk, laying our plans for the morrow; then, after a smoke, we closed the flap of the tent, and prepared to turn in.

"I suppose there's no chance of those fellows outside taking anything?" I asked, as we rolled ourselves in our blankets.

Tonnison said that he did not think so, at least while we were about; and, as he went on to explain, we could lock up everything, except the tent, in the big chest that we had brought to hold our provisions. I agreed to this, and soon we were both asleep.

Next morning, early, we rose and went for a swim in the river; after which we dressed and had breakfast. Then we roused out our fishing tackle and overhauled it, by which time, our breakfasts having settled somewhat, we made all secure within the tent and strode off in the direction my friend had explored on his previous visit.

During the day we fished happily, working steadily upstream, and by evening we had one of the prettiest creels of fish that I had seen for a long while. Returning to the village, we made a good feed off our day's spoil, after which, having selected a few of the finer fish for our breakfast, we presented the remainder to the group of villagers who had assembled at a respectful distance to watch our doings. They seemed wonderfully grateful, and heaped mountains of what I presumed to be Irish blessings upon our heads.

Thus we spent several days, having splendid sport, and first-rate appetites to do justice upon our prey. We were pleased to find how friendly the villagers were inclined to be, and that there was no evidence of their having ventured to meddle with our belongings during our absences.

It was on a Tuesday that we arrived in Kraighten, and it would be on the Sunday following that we made a great discovery. Hitherto we had always gone up-stream; on that day, however, we laid aside our rods, and, taking some provisions, set off for a long ramble in the opposite direction. The day was warm, and we trudged along leisurely enough, stopping about mid-day to eat our lunch upon a great flat rock near the riverbank. Afterward we sat and smoked awhile, resuming our walk only when we were tired of inaction.

For perhaps another hour we wandered onward, chatting quietly and comfortably on this and that matter, and on several occasions stopping while my companion – who is something of an artist – made rough sketches of striking bits of the wild scenery.

And then, without any warning whatsoever, the river we had followed so confidently, came to an abrupt end – vanishing into the earth.

"Good Lord!" I said, "who ever would have thought of this?"

And I stared in amazement; then I turned to Tonnison. He was looking, with a blank expression upon his face, at the place where the river disappeared.

In a moment he spoke.

"Let us go on a bit; it may reappear again – anyhow, it is worth investigating."

I agreed, and we went forward once more, though rather aimlessly; for we were not at all certain in which direction to prosecute our search. For perhaps a mile we moved onward; then Tonnison, who had been gazing about curiously, stopped and shaded his eyes.

"See!" he said, after a moment, "isn't that mist or something, over there to the right – away in a line with that great piece of rock?" And he indicated with his hand.

I stared, and, after a minute, seemed to see something, but could not be certain, and said so.

"Anyway," my friend replied, "we'll just go across and have a glance." And he started off in the direction he had suggested, I following. Presently, we came among bushes, and, after a time, out upon the top of a high, boulder-strewn bank, from which we looked down into a wilderness of bushes and trees.

"Seems as though we had come upon an oasis in this desert of stone," muttered Tonnison, as he gazed interestedly. Then he was silent, his eyes fixed; and I looked also; for up from somewhere about the center of the wooded lowland there rose high into the quiet air a great column of hazelike spray, upon which the sun shone, causing innumerable rainbows.

"How beautiful!" I exclaimed.

"Yes," answered Tonnison, thoughtfully. "There must be a waterfall, or something, over there. Perhaps it's our river come to light again. Let's go and see."

Down the sloping bank we made our way, and entered among the trees and shrubberies. The bushes were matted, and the trees overhung us, so that the place was disagreeably gloomy; though not dark enough to hide from me the fact that many of the trees were fruit trees, and that, here and there, one could trace indistinctly, signs of a long departed cultivation. Thus it came to me that we were making our way through the riot of a great and ancient garden. I said as much to Tonnison, and he agreed that there certainly seemed reasonable grounds for my belief.

What a wild place it was, so dismal and somber! Somehow, as we went forward, a sense of the silent loneliness and desertion of the old garden grew upon me, and I felt shivery. One could imagine things lurking among the tangled bushes; while, in the very air of the place, there seemed something uncanny. I think Tonnison was conscious of this also, though he said nothing.

Suddenly, we came to a halt. Through the trees there had grown upon our ears a distant sound. Tonnison bent forward, listening. I could hear it more plainly now; it was continuous and harsh – a sort of droning roar, seeming to come from far away. I experienced a queer, indescribable, little feeling of nervousness. What sort of place was it into which we had got? I looked at my companion, to see what he thought of the matter; and noted that there was only puzzlement in his face; and then, as I watched his features, an expression of comprehension crept over them, and he nodded his head.

"That's a waterfall," he exclaimed, with conviction. "I know the sound now." And he began to push vigorously through the bushes, in the direction of the noise.

As we went forward, the sound became plainer continually, showing that we were heading straight toward it. Steadily, the roaring grew louder and nearer, until it appeared, as I remarked to Tonnison, almost to come from under our feet – and still we were surrounded by the trees and shrubs.

"Take care!" Tonnison called to me. "Look where you're going." And then, suddenly, we came out from among the trees, on to a great open space, where, not six paces in front of us, yawned the mouth of a tremendous chasm, from the depths of which the noise appeared to rise, along with the continuous, mistlike spray that we had witnessed from the top of the distant bank.

For quite a minute we stood in silence, staring in bewilderment at the sight; then my friend went forward cautiously to the edge of the abyss. I followed, and, together, we looked down through a boil of spray at a monster cataract of frothing water that burst, spouting, from the side of the chasm, nearly a hundred feet below.

"Good Lord!" said Tonnison.

I was silent, and rather awed. The sight was so unexpectedly grand and eerie; though this latter quality came more upon me later.

Presently, I looked up and across to the further side of the chasm. There, I saw something towering up among the spray: it looked like a fragment of a great ruin, and I touched Tonnison on the shoulder. He glanced 'round, with a start, and I pointed toward the thing. His gaze followed my finger, and his eyes lighted up with a sudden flash of excitement, as the object came within his field of view.

"Come along," he shouted above the uproar. "We'll have a look at it. There's something queer about this place; I feel it in my bones." And he started off, 'round the edge of the craterlike abyss. As we neared this new thing, I saw that I had not been mistaken in my first impression. It was undoubtedly a portion of some ruined building; yet now I made out that it was not built upon the edge of the chasm itself, as I had at first supposed; but perched almost at the extreme end of a huge spur of rock that jutted out some fifty or sixty feet over the abyss. In fact, the jagged mass of ruin was literally suspended in midair.

Arriving opposite it, we walked out on to the projecting arm of rock, and I must confess to having felt an intolerable sense of terror as I looked down from that dizzy perch into the unknown depths below us – into the deeps from which there rose ever the thunder of the falling water and the shroud of rising spray.

Reaching the ruin, we clambered 'round it cautiously, and, on the further side, came upon a mass of fallen stones and rubble. The ruin itself seemed to me, as I proceeded now to examine it minutely, to be a portion of the outer wall of some prodigious structure, it was so thick and substantially built; yet what it was doing in such a position I could by no means conjecture. Where was the rest of the house, or castle, or whatever there had been?

I went back to the outer side of the wall, and thence to the edge of the chasm, leaving Tonnison rooting systematically among the heap of stones and rubbish on the outer side. Then I commenced to examine the surface of the ground, near the edge of the abyss, to see whether there were not left other remnants of the building to which the fragment of ruin evidently belonged. But though I scrutinized the earth with the greatest care, I could see no signs of anything to show that there had ever been a building erected on the spot, and I grew more puzzled than ever.

Then, I heard a cry from Tonnison; he was shouting my name, excitedly, and without delay I hurried along the rocky promontory to the ruin. I wondered whether he had hurt himself, and then the thought came, that perhaps he had found something.

I reached the crumbled wall and climbed 'round. There I found Tonnison standing within a small excavation that he had made among the *débris*: he was brushing the dirt from something that looked like a book, much crumpled and dilapidated; and opening his mouth, every second or two, to bellow my name. As soon as he saw that I had come, he handed his prize to me, telling me to put it into my satchel so as to protect it from the damp, while he continued his explorations. This I did, first, however, running the pages through my fingers, and noting that they were closely filled with neat, old-fashioned writing which was quite legible, save in one portion, where many of the pages were almost destroyed, being muddied and crumpled, as though the book had been doubled back at that part. This, I found out from Tonnison, was actually as he had discovered it, and the damage was due, probably, to the fall of masonry upon the opened part. Curiously enough, the book was fairly dry, which I attributed to its having been so securely buried among the ruins.

Having put the volume away safely, I turned-to and gave Tonnison a hand with his self-imposed task of excavating; yet, though we put in over an hour's hard work, turning over the whole of the upheaped stones and rubbish, we came upon nothing more than some fragments of broken wood, that might have been parts of a desk or table; and so we gave up searching, and went back along the rock, once more to the safety of the land.

The next thing we did was to make a complete tour of the tremendous chasm, which we were able to observe was in the form of an almost perfect circle, save for where the ruin-crowned spur of rock jutted out, spoiling its symmetry.

The abyss was, as Tonnison put it, like nothing so much as a gigantic well or pit going sheer down into the bowels of the earth.

For some time longer, we continued to stare about us, and then, noticing that there was a clear space away to the north of the chasm, we bent our steps in that direction.

Here, distant from the mouth of the mighty pit by some hundreds of yards, we came upon a great lake of silent water – silent, that is, save in one place where there was a continuous bubbling and gurgling.

Now, being away from the noise of the spouting cataract, we were able to hear one another speak, without having to shout at the tops of our voices, and I asked Tonnison what he thought of the place – I told him that I didn't like it, and that the sooner we were out of it the better I should be pleased.

He nodded in reply, and glanced at the woods behind furtively. I asked him if he had seen or heard anything. He made no answer; but stood silent, as though listening, and I kept quiet also.

Suddenly, he spoke.

"Hark!" he said, sharply. I looked at him, and then away among the trees and bushes, holding my breath involuntarily. A minute came and went in strained silence; yet I could hear nothing, and I turned to Tonnison to say as much; and then, even as I opened my lips to speak, there came a strange wailing noise out of the wood on our left.... It appeared to float through the trees, and there was a rustle of stirring leaves, and then silence.

All at once, Tonnison spoke, and put his hand on my shoulder. "Let us get out of here," he said, and began to move slowly toward where the surrounding trees and bushes seemed thinnest. As I followed him, it came to me suddenly that the sun was low, and that there was a raw sense of chilliness in the air.

Tonnison said nothing further, but kept on steadily. We were among the trees now, and I glanced around, nervously; but saw nothing, save the quiet branches and trunks and the tangled bushes. Onward we went, and no sound broke the silence, except the occasional snapping of a twig under our feet, as we moved forward. Yet, in spite of the quietness, I had a horrible feeling that we were not alone; and I kept so close to Tonnison that twice I kicked his heels clumsily, though he said nothing. A minute, and then another, and we reached the confines of the wood coming out at last upon the bare rockiness of the countryside. Only then was I able to shake off the haunting dread that had followed me among the trees.

Once, as we moved away, there seemed to come again a distant sound of wailing, and I said to myself that it was the wind – yet the evening was breathless.

Presently, Tonnison began to talk.

"Look you," he said with decision, "I would not spend the night in *that* place for all the wealth that the world holds. There is something unholy – diabolical – about it. It came to me all in a moment, just after you spoke. It seemed to me that the woods were full of vile things – you know!"

"Yes," I answered, and looked back toward the place; but it was hidden from us by a rise in the ground.

"There's the book," I said, and I put my hand into the satchel.

"You've got it safely?" he questioned, with a sudden access of anxiety.

"Yes," I replied.

"Perhaps," he continued, "we shall learn something from it when we get back to the tent. We had better hurry, too; we're a long way off still, and I don't fancy, now, being caught out here in the dark."

It was two hours later when we reached the tent; and, without delay, we set to work to prepare a meal; for we had eaten nothing since our lunch at midday.

Supper over, we cleared the things out of the way, and lit our pipes. Then Tonnison asked me to get the manuscript out of my satchel. This I did, and then, as we could not both read from it at the same time, he suggested that I should read the thing out loud. "And mind," he cautioned, knowing my propensities, "don't go skipping half the book."

Yet, had he but known what it contained, he would have realized how needless such advice was, for once at least. And there seated in the opening of our little tent, I began the strange tale of *The House on the Borderland* (for such was the title of the MS.); this is told in the following pages.

Chapter II
The Plain of Silence

I AM AN old man. I live here in this ancient house, surrounded by huge, unkempt gardens.

The peasantry, who inhabit the wilderness beyond, say that I am mad. That is because I will have nothing to do with them. I live here alone with my old sister, who is also my housekeeper. We keep no servants – I hate them. I have one friend, a dog; yes, I would sooner have old Pepper than the rest of Creation together. He, at least, understands me – and has sense enough to leave me alone when I am in my dark moods.

I have decided to start a kind of diary; it may enable me to record some of the thoughts and feelings that I cannot express to anyone; but, beyond this, I am anxious to make some record of the strange things that I have heard and seen, during many years of loneliness, in this weird old building.

For a couple of centuries, this house has had a reputation, a bad one, and, until I bought it, for more than eighty years no one had lived here; consequently, I got the old place at a ridiculously low figure.

I am not superstitious; but I have ceased to deny that things happen in this old house – things that I cannot explain; and, therefore, I must needs ease my mind, by writing down an account of them, to the best of my ability; though, should this, my diary, ever be read when I am gone, the readers will but shake their heads, and be the more convinced that I was mad.

This house, how ancient it is! though its age strikes one less, perhaps, than the quaintness of its structure, which is curious and fantastic to the last degree. Little curved towers and pinnacles, with outlines suggestive of leaping flames, predominate; while the body of the building is in the form of a circle.

I have heard that there is an old story, told amongst the country people, to the effect that the devil built the place. However, that is as may be. True or not, I neither know nor care, save as it may have helped to cheapen it, ere I came.

I must have been here some ten years before I saw sufficient to warrant any belief in the stories, current in the neighborhood, about this house. It is true that I had, on at least a dozen occasions, seen, vaguely, things that puzzled me, and, perhaps, had felt more than I had seen. Then, as the years passed, bringing age upon me, I became often aware of something unseen, yet unmistakably present, in the empty rooms and corridors. Still, it was as I have said many years before I saw any real manifestations of the so-called supernatural.

It was not Halloween. If I were telling a story for amusement's sake, I should probably place it on that night of nights; but this is a true record of my own experiences, and I would not put pen to paper to amuse anyone. No. It was after midnight on the morning of the twenty-first day of January. I was sitting reading, as is often my custom, in my study. Pepper lay, sleeping, near my chair.

Without warning, the flames of the two candles went low, and then shone with a ghastly green effulgence. I looked up, quickly, and as I did so I saw the lights sink into a dull, ruddy tint; so that the room glowed with a strange, heavy, crimson twilight that gave the shadows behind the chairs and tables a double depth of blackness; and wherever the light struck, it was as though luminous blood had been splashed over the room.

Down on the floor, I heard a faint, frightened whimper, and something pressed itself in between my two feet. It was Pepper, cowering under my dressing gown. Pepper, usually as brave as a lion!

It was this movement of the dog's, I think, that gave me the first twinge of *real* fear. I had been considerably startled when the lights burnt first green and then red; but had been momentarily under the impression that the change was due to some influx of noxious gas into the room. Now, however, I saw that it was not so; for the candles burned with a steady flame, and showed no signs of going out, as would have been the case had the change been due to fumes in the atmosphere.

I did not move. I felt distinctly frightened; but could think of nothing better to do than wait. For perhaps a minute, I kept my glance about the room, nervously. Then I noticed that the lights had commenced to sink, very slowly; until presently they showed minute specks of red fire, like the gleamings of rubies in the darkness. Still, I sat watching; while a sort of dreamy indifference seemed to steal over me; banishing altogether the fear that had begun to grip me.

Away in the far end of the huge old-fashioned room, I became conscious of a faint glow. Steadily it grew, filling the room with gleams of quivering green light; then they sank quickly, and changed – even as the candle flames had done – into a deep, somber crimson that strengthened, and lit up the room with a flood of awful glory.

The light came from the end wall, and grew ever brighter until its intolerable glare caused my eyes acute pain, and involuntarily I closed them. It may have been a few seconds before I was able to open them. The first thing I noticed was that the light had decreased, greatly; so that it no longer tried my eyes. Then, as it grew still duller, I was aware, all at once, that, instead of looking at the redness, I was staring through it, and through the wall beyond.

Gradually, as I became more accustomed to the idea, I realized that I was looking out on to a vast plain, lit with the same gloomy twilight that pervaded the room. The immensity of this plain scarcely can be conceived. In no part could I perceive its confines. It seemed to broaden and spread out, so that the eye failed to perceive any limitations. Slowly, the details of the nearer portions began to grow clear; then, in a moment almost, the light died away, and the vision – if vision it were – faded and was gone.

Suddenly, I became conscious that I was no longer in the chair. Instead, I seemed to be hovering above it, and looking down at a dim something, huddled and silent. In a little while, a cold blast struck me, and I was outside in the night, floating, like a bubble, up through the darkness. As I moved, an icy coldness seemed to enfold me, so that I shivered.

After a time, I looked to right and left, and saw the intolerable blackness of the night, pierced by remote gleams of fire. Onward, outward, I drove. Once, I glanced behind, and saw the earth, a small crescent of blue light, receding away to my left. Further off, the sun, a splash of white flame, burned vividly against the dark.

An indefinite period passed. Then, for the last time, I saw the earth – an enduring globule of radiant blue, swimming in an eternity of ether. And there I, a fragile flake of soul dust, flickered silently across the void, from the distant blue, into the expanse of the unknown.

A great while seemed to pass over me, and now I could nowhere see anything. I had passed beyond the fixed stars and plunged into the huge blackness that waits beyond. All this time I had experienced little, save a sense of lightness and cold discomfort. Now however the atrocious darkness seemed to creep into my soul, and I became filled with fear and despair. What was going to become of me? Where was I going? Even as the thoughts were formed, there grew against the impalpable blackness that wrapped me a faint tinge of blood. It seemed extraordinarily remote, and mistlike; yet, at once, the feeling of oppression was lightened, and I no longer despaired.

Slowly, the distant redness became plainer and larger; until, as I drew nearer, it spread out into a great, somber glare – dull and tremendous. Still, I fled onward, and, presently, I had come so close, that it seemed to stretch beneath me, like a great ocean of somber red. I could see little, save that it appeared to spread out interminably in all directions.

In a further space, I found that I was descending upon it; and, soon, I sank into a great sea of sullen, red-hued clouds. Slowly, I emerged from these, and there, below me, I saw the stupendous plain that I had seen from my room in this house that stands upon the borders of the Silences.

Presently, I landed, and stood, surrounded by a great waste of loneliness. The place was lit with a gloomy twilight that gave an impression of indescribable desolation.

Afar to my right, within the sky, there burnt a gigantic ring of dull-red fire, from the outer edge of which were projected huge, writhing flames, darted and jagged. The interior of this ring was black, black as the gloom of the outer night. I comprehended, at once, that it was from this extraordinary sun that the place derived its doleful light.

From that strange source of light, I glanced down again to my surroundings. Everywhere I looked, I saw nothing but the same flat weariness of interminable plain. Nowhere could I descry any signs of life; not even the ruins of some ancient habitation.

Gradually, I found that I was being borne forward, floating across the flat waste. For what seemed an eternity, I moved onward. I was unaware of any great sense of impatience; though some curiosity and a vast wonder were with me continually. Always, I saw around me the breadth of that enormous plain; and, always, I searched for some new thing to break its monotony; but there was no change – only loneliness, silence, and desert.

Presently, in a half-conscious manner, I noticed that there was a faint mistiness, ruddy in hue, lying over its surface. Still, when I looked more intently, I was unable to say that it was really mist; for it appeared to blend with the plain, giving it a peculiar unrealness, and conveying to the senses the idea of unsubstantiality.

Gradually, I began to weary with the sameness of the thing. Yet, it was a great time before I perceived any signs of the place, toward which I was being conveyed.

"At first, I saw it, far ahead, like a long hillock on the surface of the Plain. Then, as I drew nearer, I perceived that I had been mistaken; for, instead of a low hill, I made out, now, a chain of great mountains, whose distant peaks towered up into the red gloom, until they were almost lost to sight."

Chapter III
The House in the Arena

AND SO, AFTER A TIME, I came to the mountains. Then, the course of my journey was altered, and I began to move along their bases, until, all at once, I saw that I had come opposite to a vast rift, opening into the mountains. Through this, I was borne, moving at no great speed. On either side of me, huge, scarped walls of rocklike substance rose sheer. Far overhead, I discerned a thin ribbon of red, where the mouth of the chasm opened, among inaccessible peaks. Within, was gloom, deep and somber, and chilly silence. For a while, I went onward steadily, and then, at last, I saw, ahead, a deep, red glow, that told me I was near upon the further opening of the gorge.

A minute came and went, and I was at the exit of the chasm, staring out upon an enormous amphitheatre of mountains. Yet, of the mountains, and the terrible grandeur of the place, I recked nothing; for I was confounded with amazement to behold, at a distance of several miles and occupying the center of the arena, a stupendous structure built apparently of green jade. Yet, in itself, it was not the discovery of the building that had so astonished me; but the fact, which became every moment more apparent, that in no particular, save in color and its enormous size, did the lonely structure vary from this house in which I live.

For a while, I continued to stare, fixedly. Even then, I could scarcely believe that I saw aright. In my mind, a question formed, reiterating incessantly: 'What does it mean?' 'What does it mean?' and I was unable to make answer, even out of the depths of my imagination. I seemed capable only of wonder and fear. For a time longer, I gazed, noting continually some fresh point of resemblance that attracted me. At last, wearied and sorely puzzled, I turned from it, to view the rest of the strange place on to which I had intruded.

Hitherto, I had been so engrossed in my scrutiny of the House, that I had given only a cursory glance 'round. Now, as I looked, I began to realize upon what sort of a place I had come. The arena, for so I have termed it, appeared a perfect circle of about ten to twelve miles in diameter, the House, as I have mentioned before, standing in the center. The surface of the place, like to that of the Plain, had a peculiar, misty appearance, that was yet not mist.

From a rapid survey, my glance passed quickly upward along the slopes of the circling mountains. How silent they were. I think that this same abominable stillness was more trying to me than anything that I had so far seen or imagined. I was looking up, now, at the great crags, towering so loftily. Up there, the impalpable redness gave a blurred appearance to everything.

And then, as I peered, curiously, a new terror came to me; for away up among the dim peaks to my right, I had descried a vast shape of blackness, giantlike. It grew upon my sight. It had an enormous equine head, with gigantic ears, and seemed to peer steadfastly down into the arena. There was that about the pose that gave me the impression of an eternal watchfulness – of having warded that dismal place, through unknown eternities. Slowly, the monster became plainer to me; and then, suddenly, my gaze sprang from it to something further off and higher among the crags. For a long minute, I gazed, fearfully. I was strangely conscious of something not altogether unfamiliar – as though something stirred in the back of my mind. The thing was black, and had four grotesque arms. The features showed indistinctly, 'round the neck, I made out several light-colored objects. Slowly, the details came to me, and I realized, coldly, that they were skulls. Further down the body was another circling belt, showing less dark against the black trunk. Then, even as I puzzled to know what the thing was, a memory slid into my mind, and straightway, I knew that I was looking at a monstrous representation of Kali, the Hindu goddess of death.

Other remembrances of my old student days drifted into my thoughts. My glance fell back upon the huge beast-headed Thing. Simultaneously, I recognized it for the ancient Egyptian god Set, or Seth, the Destroyer of Souls. With the knowledge, there came a great sweep of questioning – 'Two of the – !' I stopped, and endeavored to think. Things beyond my imagination peered into my frightened mind. I saw, obscurely. 'The old gods of mythology!' I tried to comprehend to what it was all pointing. My gaze dwelt, flickeringly, between the two. 'If—'

An idea came swiftly, and I turned, and glanced rapidly upward, searching the gloomy crags, away to my left. Something loomed out under a great peak, a shape of greyness. I wondered I had not seen it earlier, and then remembered I had not yet viewed that portion. I saw it more plainly now. It was, as I have said, grey. It had a tremendous head; but no eyes. That part of its face was blank.

Now, I saw that there were other things up among the mountains. Further off, reclining on a lofty ledge, I made out a livid mass, irregular and ghoulish. It seemed without form, save for an unclean, half-animal face, that looked out, vilely, from somewhere about its middle. And then I saw others – there were hundreds of them. They seemed to grow out of the shadows. Several I recognized almost immediately as mythological deities; others were strange to me, utterly strange, beyond the power of a human mind to conceive.

On each side, I looked, and saw more, continually. The mountains were full of strange things – Beast-gods, and Horrors so atrocious and bestial that possibility and decency deny any further attempt to describe them. And I – I was filled with a terrible sense of overwhelming horror and fear and repugnance; yet, spite of these, I wondered exceedingly. Was there then, after all, something in the old heathen worship, something more than the mere deifying of men, animals, and elements? The thought gripped me – was there?

Later, a question repeated itself. What were they, those Beast-gods, and the others? At first, they had appeared to me just sculptured Monsters placed indiscriminately among the inaccessible peaks and precipices of the surrounding mountains. Now, as I scrutinized them with greater intentness, my mind began to reach out to fresh conclusions. There was something about them, an indescribable sort of silent vitality that suggested, to my broadening consciousness, a state of life-in-death – a something that was by no means life, as we understand it; but rather an inhuman form of existence, that well might be likened to a deathless trance – a condition in which it was possible to imagine their continuing, eternally. 'Immortal!' the word rose in my thoughts unbidden; and, straightway, I grew to wondering whether this might be the immortality of the gods.

And then, in the midst of my wondering and musing, something happened. Until then, I had been staying just within the shadow of the exit of the great rift. Now, without volition on my part, I drifted out of the semi-darkness and began to move slowly across the arena – toward the House. At this, I gave up all thoughts of those prodigious Shapes above me – and could only stare, frightenedly, at the tremendous structure toward which I was being conveyed so remorselessly. Yet, though I searched earnestly, I could discover nothing that I had not already seen, and so became gradually calmer.

Presently, I had reached a point more than halfway between the House and the gorge. All around was spread the stark loneliness of the place, and the unbroken silence. Steadily, I neared the great building. Then, all at once, something caught my vision, something that came 'round one of the huge buttresses of the House, and so into full view. It was a gigantic thing, and moved with a curious lope, going almost upright, after the manner of a man. It was quite unclothed, and had a remarkable luminous appearance. Yet it was the face that attracted and frightened me the most. It was the face of a swine.

Silently, intently, I watched this horrible creature, and forgot my fear, momentarily, in my interest in its movements. It was making its way, cumbrously 'round the building, stopping as it came to each window to peer in and shake at the bars, with which – as in this house – they were protected; and whenever it came to a door, it would push at it, fingering the fastening stealthily. Evidently, it was searching for an ingress into the House.

I had come now to within less than a quarter of a mile of the great structure, and still I was compelled forward. Abruptly, the Thing turned and gazed hideously in my direction. It opened its mouth, and, for the first time, the stillness of that abominable place was broken, by a deep, booming note that sent an added thrill of apprehension through me. Then, immediately, I became aware that it was coming toward me, swiftly and silently. In an instant, it had covered half the distance that lay between. And still, I was borne helplessly to meet it. Only a hundred yards, and the brutish ferocity of the giant face numbed me with a feeling of unmitigated horror. I could have screamed, in the supremeness of my fear; and then, in the very moment of my extremity and despair, I became conscious that I was looking down upon the arena, from a rapidly increasing height. I was rising, rising. In an inconceivably short while, I had reached an altitude of many hundred feet. Beneath me, the spot that I had just left, was occupied by the foul Swine-creature. It had gone down on all fours and was snuffing and rooting, like a veritable hog, at the surface of the arena. A moment and it rose to its feet, clutching upward, with an expression of desire upon its face such as I have never seen in this world.

Continually, I mounted higher. A few minutes, it seemed, and I had risen above the great mountains – floating, alone, afar in the redness. At a tremendous distance below, the arena showed, dimly; with the mighty House looking no larger than a tiny spot of green. The Swine-thing was no longer visible.

Presently, I passed over the mountains, out above the huge breadth of the plain. Far away, on its surface, in the direction of the ring-shaped sun, there showed a confused blur. I looked toward it, indifferently. It reminded me, somewhat, of the first glimpse I had caught of the mountain-amphitheatre.

With a sense of weariness, I glanced upward at the immense ring of fire. What a strange thing it was! Then, as I stared, out from the dark center, there spurted a sudden flare of extraordinary vivid fire. Compared with the size of the black center, it was as naught; yet, in itself, stupendous. With awakened interest, I watched it carefully, noting its strange boiling and glowing. Then, in a moment, the whole thing grew dim and unreal, and so passed out of sight. Much amazed, I glanced down to the Plain from which I was still rising. Thus, I received a fresh surprise. The Plain – everything had vanished, and only a sea of red mist was spread far below me. Gradually as I stared this grew remote, and died away into a dim far mystery of red against an unfathomable night. A while, and even this had gone, and I was wrapped in an impalpable, lightless gloom.

Chapter IV
The Earth

THUS I WAS, and only the memory that I had lived through the dark, once before, served to sustain my thoughts. A great time passed – ages. And then a single star broke its way through the darkness. It was the first of one of the outlying clusters of this universe. Presently, it was far behind, and all about me shone the splendor of the countless stars. Later, years it seemed, I saw the sun, a clot of flame. Around it, I made out presently several remote specks of light – the planets of the Solar system. And so I saw the earth again, blue and unbelievably minute. It grew larger, and became defined.

A long space of time came and went, and then at last I entered into the shadow of the world – plunging headlong into the dim and holy earth night. Overhead were the old constellations, and there was a crescent moon. Then, as I neared the earth's surface, a dimness swept over me, and I appeared to sink into a black mist.

For a while, I knew nothing. I was unconscious. Gradually, I became aware of a faint, distant whining. It became plainer. A desperate feeling of agony possessed me. I struggled madly for breath, and tried to shout. A moment, and I got my breath more easily. I was conscious that something was licking my hand. Something damp swept across my face. I heard a panting, and then again the whining. It seemed to come to my ears, now, with a sense of familiarity, and I opened my eyes. All was dark; but the feeling of oppression had left me. I was seated, and something was whining piteously, and licking me. I felt strangely confused, and, instinctively, tried to ward off the thing that licked. My head was curiously vacant, and, for the moment, I seemed incapable of action or thought. Then, things came back to me, and I called 'Pepper,' faintly. I was answered by a joyful bark, and renewed and frantic caresses.

In a little while, I felt stronger, and put out my hand for the matches. I groped about, for a few moments, blindly; then my hands lit upon them, and I struck a light, and looked confusedly around. All about me, I saw the old, familiar things. And there I sat, full of dazed wonders, until the flame of the match burnt my finger, and I dropped it; while a hasty expression of pain and anger, escaped my lips, surprising me with the sound of my own voice.

After a moment, I struck another match, and, stumbling across the room, lit the candles. As I did so, I observed that they had not burned away, but had been put out.

As the flames shot up, I turned, and stared about the study; yet there was nothing unusual to see; and, suddenly, a gust of irritation took me. What had happened? I held my head, with both hands, and tried to remember. Ah! the great, silent Plain, and the ring-shaped sun of red fire. Where were they? Where had I seen them? How long ago? I felt dazed and muddled. Once or twice, I walked up and down the room, unsteadily. My memory seemed dulled, and, already, the thing I had witnessed came back to me with an effort.

I have a remembrance of cursing, peevishly, in my bewilderment. Suddenly, I turned faint and giddy, and had to grasp at the table for support. During a few moments, I held on, weakly; and then managed to totter sideways into a chair. After a little time, I felt somewhat better, and succeeded in reaching the cupboard where, usually, I keep brandy and biscuits. I poured myself out a little of the stimulant, and drank it off. Then, taking a handful of biscuits, I returned to my chair, and began to devour them, ravenously. I was vaguely surprised at my hunger. I felt as though I had eaten nothing for an uncountably long while.

As I ate, my glance roved about the room, taking in its various details, and still searching, though almost unconsciously, for something tangible upon which to take hold, among the invisible mysteries that encompassed me. 'Surely,' I thought, 'there must be something—' And, in the same instant, my gaze dwelt upon the face of the clock in the opposite corner. Therewith, I stopped eating, and just stared. For, though its ticking indicated most certainly that it was still going, the hands were pointing to a little *before* the hour of midnight; whereas it was, as well I knew, considerably *after* that time when I had witnessed the first of the strange happenings I have just described.

For perhaps a moment I was astounded and puzzled. Had the hour been the same as when I had last seen the clock, I should have concluded that the hands had stuck in one place, while the internal mechanism went on as usual; but that would, in no way, account for the hands having traveled backward. Then, even as I turned the matter over in my wearied brain, the thought flashed upon me that it was now close upon the morning of the twenty-second, and that I had been unconscious to the visible world through the greater portion of the last twenty-four hours. The thought occupied my attention for a full minute; then I commenced to eat again. I was still very hungry.

During breakfast, next morning, I inquired casually of my sister regarding the date, and found my surmise correct. I had, indeed, been absent – at least in spirit – for nearly a day and a night.

My sister asked me no questions; for it is not by any means the first time that I have kept to my study for a whole day, and sometimes a couple of days at a time, when I have been particularly engrossed in my books or work.

And so the days pass on, and I am still filled with a wonder to know the meaning of all that I saw on that memorable night. Yet, well I know that my curiosity is little likely to be satisfied.

Chapter V
The Thing in the Pit

THIS HOUSE IS, as I have said before, surrounded by a huge estate, and wild and uncultivated gardens.

Away at the back, distant some three hundred yards, is a dark, deep ravine – spoken of as the 'Pit,' by the peasantry. At the bottom runs a sluggish stream so overhung by trees as scarcely to be seen from above.

In passing, I must explain that this river has a subterranean origin, emerging suddenly at the East end of the ravine, and disappearing, as abruptly, beneath the cliffs that form its Western extremity.

It was some months after my vision (if vision it were) of the great Plain that my attention was particularly attracted to the Pit.

I happened, one day, to be walking along its Southern edge, when, suddenly, several pieces of rock and shale were dislodged from the face of the cliff immediately beneath me, and fell with a sullen crash through the trees. I heard them splash in the river at the bottom; and then silence. I should not have given this incident more than a passing thought, had not Pepper at once begun to bark savagely; nor would he be silent when I bade him, which is most unusual behavior on his part.

Feeling that there must be someone or something in the Pit, I went back to the house, quickly, for a stick. When I returned, Pepper had ceased his barks and was growling and smelling, uneasily, along the top.

Whistling to him to follow me, I started to descend cautiously. The depth to the bottom of the Pit must be about a hundred and fifty feet, and some time as well as considerable care was expended before we reached the bottom in safety.

Once down, Pepper and I started to explore along the banks of the river. It was very dark there due to the overhanging trees, and I moved warily, keeping my glance about me and my stick ready.

Pepper was quiet now and kept close to me all the time. Thus, we searched right up one side of the river, without hearing or seeing anything. Then, we crossed over – by the simple method of jumping – and commenced to beat our way back through the underbrush.

We had accomplished perhaps half the distance, when I heard again the sound of falling stones on the other side – the side from which we had just come. One large rock came thundering down through the treetops, struck the opposite bank, and bounded into the river, driving a great jet of water right over us. At this, Pepper gave out a deep growl; then stopped, and pricked up his ears. I listened, also.

A second later, a loud, half-human, half-piglike squeal sounded from among the trees, apparently about halfway up the South cliff. It was answered by a similar note from the bottom of the Pit. At this, Pepper gave a short, sharp bark, and, springing across the little river, disappeared into the bushes.

Immediately afterward, I heard his barks increase in depth and number, and in between there sounded a noise of confused jabbering. This ceased, and, in the succeeding silence, there rose a semi-human yell of agony. Almost immediately, Pepper gave a long-drawn howl of pain, and then the shrubs were violently agitated, and he came running out with his tail down, and glancing as he ran over his shoulder. As he reached me, I saw that he was bleeding from what appeared to be a great claw wound in the side that had almost laid bare his ribs.

Seeing Pepper thus mutilated, a furious feeling of anger seized me, and, whirling my staff, I sprang across, and into the bushes from which Pepper had emerged. As I forced my way through, I thought I heard a sound of breathing. Next instant, I had burst into a little clear space, just in time to see something, livid white in color, disappear among the bushes on the opposite side. With a shout, I ran toward it; but, though I struck and probed among the bushes with my stick, I neither saw nor heard anything further; and so returned to Pepper. There, after bathing his wound in the river, I bound my wetted handkerchief 'round his body; having done which, we retreated up the ravine and into the daylight again.

On reaching the house, my sister inquired what had happened to Pepper, and I told her he had been fighting with a wildcat, of which I had heard there were several about.

I felt it would be better not to tell her how it had really happened; though, to be sure, I scarcely knew myself; but this I did know, that the thing I had seen run into the bushes was no wildcat. It was much too big, and had, so far as I had observed, a skin like a hog's, only of a dead, unhealthy white color. And then – it had run upright, or nearly so, upon its hind feet, with a motion somewhat resembling that of a human being. This much I had noticed in my brief glimpse, and, truth to tell, I felt a good deal of uneasiness, besides curiosity as I turned the matter over in my mind.

It was in the morning that the above incident had occurred.

Then, it would be after dinner, as I sat reading, that, happening to look up suddenly, I saw something peering in over the window ledge the eyes and ears alone showing.

'A pig, by Jove!' I said, and rose to my feet. Thus, I saw the thing more completely; but it was no pig – God alone knows what it was. It reminded me, vaguely, of the hideous Thing that had haunted the great arena. It had a grotesquely human mouth and jaw; but with no chin of which to speak. The nose was prolonged into a snout; thus it was that with the little eyes and queer ears, gave it such an extraordinarily swinelike appearance. Of forehead there was little, and the whole face was of an unwholesome white color.

For perhaps a minute, I stood looking at the thing with an ever growing feeling of disgust, and some fear. The mouth kept jabbering, inanely, and once emitted a half-swinish grunt. I think it was the eyes that attracted me the most; they seemed to glow, at times, with a horribly human intelligence, and kept flickering away from my face, over the details of the room, as though my stare disturbed it.

It appeared to be supporting itself by two clawlike hands upon the windowsill. These claws, unlike the face, were of a clayey brown hue, and bore an indistinct resemblance to human hands, in that they had four fingers and a thumb; though these were webbed up to the first joint, much as are a duck's. Nails it had also, but so long and powerful that they were more like the talons of an eagle than aught else.

As I have said, before, I felt some fear; though almost of an impersonal kind. I may explain my feeling better by saying that it was more a sensation of abhorrence; such as one might expect to feel, if brought in contact with something superhumanly foul; something unholy – belonging to some hitherto undreamt of state of existence.

I cannot say that I grasped these various details of the brute at the time. I think they seemed to come back to me, afterward, as though imprinted upon my brain. I imagined more than I saw as I looked at the thing, and the material details grew upon me later.

For perhaps a minute I stared at the creature; then as my nerves steadied a little I shook off the vague alarm that held me, and took a step toward the window. Even as I did so, the thing ducked and vanished. I rushed to the door and looked 'round hurriedly; but only the tangled bushes and shrubs met my gaze.

I ran back into the house, and, getting my gun, sallied out to search through the gardens. As I went, I asked myself whether the thing I had just seen was likely to be the same of which I had caught a glimpse in the morning. I inclined to think it was.

I would have taken Pepper with me; but judged it better to give his wound a chance to heal. Besides, if the creature I had just seen was, as I imagined, his antagonist of the morning, it was not likely that he would be of much use.

I began my search, systematically. I was determined, if it were possible, to find and put an end to that swine-thing. This was, at least, a material Horror!

At first, I searched, cautiously; with the thought of Pepper's wound in my mind; but, as the hours passed, and not a sign of anything living, showed in the great, lonely gardens, I became less apprehensive. I felt almost as though I would welcome the sight of it. Anything seemed better than this silence, with the ever-present feeling that the creature might be lurking in every bush I passed. Later, I grew careless of danger, to the extent of plunging right through the bushes, probing with my gun barrel as I went.

At times, I shouted; but only the echoes answered back. I thought thus perhaps to frighten or stir the creature to showing itself; but only succeeded in bringing my sister Mary out, to know what was the matter. I told her, that I had seen the wildcat that had wounded Pepper, and that I was trying to hunt it out of the bushes. She seemed only half satisfied, and went back into the house, with an expression of doubt upon her face. I wondered whether she had seen or guessed anything. For the rest of the afternoon, I prosecuted the search anxiously. I felt that I should be unable to sleep, with that bestial thing haunting the shrubberies, and yet, when evening fell, I had seen nothing. Then, as I turned homeward, I heard a short, unintelligible noise, among the bushes to my right. Instantly, I turned, and, aiming quickly, fired in the direction of the sound. Immediately afterward, I heard something scuttling away among the bushes. It moved rapidly, and in a minute had gone out of hearing. After a few steps I ceased my pursuit, realizing how futile it must be in the fast gathering gloom; and so, with a curious feeling of depression, I entered the house.

That night, after my sister had gone to bed, I went 'round to all the windows and doors on the ground floor; and saw to it that they were securely fastened. This precaution was scarcely necessary as regards the windows, as all of those on the lower storey are strongly barred; but with the doors – of which there are five – it was wisely thought, as not one was locked.

Having secured these, I went to my study, yet, somehow, for once, the place jarred upon me; it seemed so huge and echoey. For some time I tried to read; but at last finding it impossible I carried my book down to the kitchen where a large fire was burning, and sat there.

I dare say, I had read for a couple of hours, when, suddenly, I heard a sound that made me lower my book, and listen, intently. It was a noise of something rubbing and fumbling against the back door. Once the door creaked, loudly; as though force were being applied to it. During those few, short moments, I experienced an indescribable feeling of terror, such as I should have believed impossible. My hands shook; a cold sweat broke out on me, and I shivered violently.

Gradually, I calmed. The stealthy movements outside had ceased.

Then for an hour I sat silent and watchful. All at once the feeling of fear took me again. I felt as I imagine an animal must, under the eye of a snake. Yet now I could hear nothing. Still, there was no doubting that some unexplained influence was at work.

Gradually, imperceptibly almost, something stole on my ear – a sound that resolved itself into a faint murmur. Quickly it developed and grew into a muffled but hideous chorus of bestial shrieks. It appeared to rise from the bowels of the earth.

I heard a thud, and realized in a dull, half comprehending way that I had dropped my book. After that, I just sat; and thus the daylight found me, when it crept wanly in through the barred, high windows of the great kitchen.

With the dawning light, the feeling of stupor and fear left me; and I came more into possession of my senses.

Thereupon I picked up my book, and crept to the door to listen. Not a sound broke the chilly silence. For some minutes I stood there; then, very gradually and cautiously, I drew back the bolt and opening the door peeped out.

My caution was unneeded. Nothing was to be seen, save the grey vista of dreary, tangled bushes and trees, extending to the distant plantation.

With a shiver, I closed the door, and made my way, quietly, up to bed.

Chapter VI
The Swine-Things

IT WAS EVENING, a week later. My sister sat in the garden, knitting. I was walking up and down, reading. My gun leant up against the wall of the house; for, since the advent of that strange thing in the gardens, I had deemed it wise to take precautions. Yet, through the whole week, there had been nothing to alarm me, either by sight or sound; so that I was able to look back, calmly, to the incident; though still with a sense of unmitigated wonder and curiosity.

I was, as I have just said, walking up and down, and somewhat engrossed in my book. Suddenly, I heard a crash, away in the direction of the Pit. With a quick movement, I turned and saw a tremendous column of dust rising high into the evening air.

My sister had risen to her feet, with a sharp exclamation of surprise and fright.

Telling her to stay where she was, I snatched up my gun, and ran toward the Pit. As I neared it, I heard a dull, rumbling sound, that grew quickly into a roar, split with deeper crashes, and up from the Pit drove a fresh volume of dust.

The noise ceased, though the dust still rose, tumultuously.

I reached the edge, and looked down; but could see nothing save a boil of dust clouds swirling hither and thither. The air was so full of the small particles, that they blinded and choked me; and, finally, I had to run out from the smother, to breathe.

Gradually, the suspended matter sank, and hung in a panoply over the mouth of the Pit.

I could only guess at what had happened.

That there had been a land-slip of some kind, I had little doubt; but the cause was beyond my knowledge; and yet, even then, I had half imaginings; for, already, the thought had come to me, of those falling rocks, and that Thing in the bottom of the Pit; but, in the first minutes of confusion, I failed to reach the natural conclusion, to which the catastrophe pointed.

Slowly, the dust subsided, until, presently, I was able to approach the edge, and look down.

For a while, I peered impotently, trying to see through the reek. At first, it was impossible to make out anything. Then, as I stared, I saw something below, to my left, that moved. I looked intently toward it, and, presently, made out another, and then another – three dim shapes that appeared to be climbing up the side of the Pit. I could see them only indistinctly. Even as I stared and wondered, I heard a rattle of stones, somewhere to my right. I glanced across; but could see nothing. I leant forward, and peered over, and down into the Pit, just beneath where I stood; and saw no further than a hideous, white swine-face, that had risen to within a couple of yards of my feet. Below it, I could make out several others. As the Thing saw me, it gave a sudden, uncouth squeal, which was answered from all parts of the Pit. At that, a gust of horror and fear took me, and, bending down, I discharged my gun right into its face. Straightway, the creature disappeared, with a clatter of loose earth and stones.

There was a momentary silence, to which, probably, I owe my life; for, during it, I heard a quick patter of many feet, and, turning sharply, saw a troop of the creatures coming toward me, at a run. Instantly, I raised my gun and fired at the foremost, who plunged head-long, with a hideous howling. Then, I turned to run. More than halfway from the house to the Pit, I saw my sister – she was coming toward me. I could not see her face, distinctly, as the dusk had fallen; but there was fear in her voice as she called to know why I was shooting.

'Run!' I shouted in reply. 'Run for your life!'

Without more ado, she turned and fled – picking up her skirts with both hands. As I followed, I gave a glance behind. The brutes were running on their hind legs – at times dropping on all fours.

I think it must have been the terror in my voice, that spurred Mary to run so; for I feel convinced that she had not, as yet, seen those hell creatures that pursued.

On we went, my sister leading.

Each moment, the nearing sounds of the footsteps, told me that the brutes were gaining on us, rapidly. Fortunately, I am accustomed to live, in some ways, an active life. As it was, the strain of the race was beginning to tell severely upon me.

Ahead, I could see the back door – luckily it was open. I was some half-dozen yards behind Mary, now, and my breath was sobbing in my throat. Then, something touched my shoulder. I wrenched my head 'round, quickly, and saw one of those monstrous, pallid faces close to mine. One of the creatures, having outrun its companions, had almost overtaken me. Even as I turned, it made a fresh grab. With a sudden effort, I sprang to one side, and, swinging my gun by the barrel, brought it crashing down upon the foul creature's head. The Thing dropped, with an almost human groan.

Even this short delay had been nearly sufficient to bring the rest of the brutes down upon me; so that, without an instant's waste of time, I turned and ran for the door.

Reaching it, I burst into the passage; then, turning quickly, slammed and bolted the door, just as the first of the creatures rushed against it, with a sudden shock.

My sister sat, gasping, in a chair. She seemed in a fainting condition; but I had no time then to spend on her. I had to make sure that all the doors were fastened. Fortunately, they were. The one leading from my study into the gardens, was the last to which I went. I had just had time to note that it was secured, when I thought I heard a noise outside. I stood perfectly silent, and listened. Yes! Now I could distinctly hear a sound of whispering, and something slithered over the panels, with a rasping, scratchy noise. Evidently, some of the brutes were feeling with their claw-hands, about the door, to discover whether there were any means of ingress.

That the creatures should so soon have found the door was – to me – a proof of their reasoning capabilities. It assured me that they must not be regarded, by any means, as mere animals. I had felt something of this before, when that first Thing peered in through my window. Then I had applied the term superhuman to it, with an almost instinctive knowledge that the creature was something different from the brute-beast. Something beyond human; yet in no good sense; but rather as something foul and hostile to the *great* and *good* in humanity. In a word, as something intelligent, and yet inhuman. The very thought of the creatures filled me with revulsion.

Now, I bethought me of my sister, and, going to the cupboard, I got out a flask of brandy, and a wine-glass. Taking these, I went down to the kitchen, carrying a lighted candle with me. She was not sitting in the chair, but had fallen out, and was lying upon the floor, face downward.

Very gently, I turned her over, and raised her head somewhat. Then, I poured a little of the brandy between her lips. After a while, she shivered slightly. A little later, she gave several gasps, and opened her eyes. In a dreamy, unrealizing way, she looked at me. Then her eyes closed, slowly, and I gave her a little more of the brandy. For, perhaps a minute longer, she lay silent, breathing quickly. All at once, her eyes opened again, and it seemed to me, as I looked, that the pupils were dilated, as though fear had come with returning consciousness. Then, with a movement so unexpected that I started backward, she sat up. Noticing that she seemed giddy, I put out my hand to steady her. At that, she gave a loud scream, and, scrambling to her feet, ran from the room.

For a moment, I stayed there – kneeling and holding the brandy flask. I was utterly puzzled and astonished.

Could she be afraid of me? But no! Why should she? I could only conclude that her nerves were badly shaken, and that she was temporarily unhinged. Upstairs, I heard a door bang, loudly, and I knew that she had taken refuge in her room. I put the flask down on the table. My attention was distracted by a noise in the direction of the back door. I went toward it, and listened. It appeared to be shaken, as though some of the creatures struggled with it, silently; but it was far too strongly constructed and hung to be easily moved.

Out in the gardens rose a continuous sound. It might have been mistaken, by a casual listener, for the grunting and squealing of a herd of pigs. But, as I stood there, it came to me that there was sense and meaning to all those swinish noises. Gradually, I seemed able to trace a semblance in it to human speech – glutinous and sticky, as though each articulation were made with difficulty: yet, nevertheless, I was becoming convinced that it was no mere medley of sounds; but a rapid interchange of ideas.

By this time, it had grown quite dark in the passages, and from these came all the varied cries and groans of which an old house is so full after nightfall. It is, no doubt, because things are then quieter, and one has more leisure to hear. Also, there may be something in the theory that the sudden change of temperature, at sundown, affects the structure of the house, somewhat – causing it to contract and settle, as it were, for the night. However, this is as may be; but, on that night in particular, I would gladly have been quit of so many eerie noises. It seemed to me, that each crack and creak was the coming of one of those Things along the dark corridors; though I knew in my heart that this could not be, for I had seen, myself, that all the doors were secure.

Gradually, however, these sounds grew on my nerves to such an extent that, were it only to punish my cowardice, I felt I must make the 'round of the basement again, and, if anything were there, face it. And then, I would go up to my study, for I knew sleep was out of the question, with the house surrounded by creatures, half beasts, half something else, and entirely unholy.

Taking the kitchen lamp down from its hook, I made my way from cellar to cellar, and room to room; through pantry and coal-hole – along passages, and into the hundred-and-one little blind alleys and hidden nooks that form the basement of the old house. Then, when I knew I had been in every corner and cranny large enough to conceal aught of any size, I made my way to the stairs.

With my foot on the first step, I paused. It seemed to me, I heard a movement, apparently from the buttery, which is to the left of the staircase. It had been one of the first places I searched, and yet, I felt certain my ears had not deceived me. My nerves were strung now, and, with hardly any hesitation, I stepped up to the door, holding the lamp above my head. In a glance, I saw that the place was empty, save for the heavy, stone slabs, supported by brick pillars; and I was about to leave it, convinced that I had been mistaken; when, in turning, my light was flashed back from two bright spots outside the window, and high up. For a few moments, I stood there, staring. Then they moved – revolving slowly, and throwing out alternate scintillations of green and red; at least, so it appeared to me. I knew then that they were eyes.

Slowly, I traced the shadowy outline of one of the Things. It appeared to be holding on to the bars of the window, and its attitude suggested climbing. I went nearer to the window, and held the light higher. There was no need to be afraid of the creature; the bars were strong, and there was little danger of its being able to move them. And then, suddenly, in spite of the knowledge that the brute could not reach to harm me, I had a return of the horrible sensation of fear, that had assailed me on that night, a week previously. It was the same feeling of helpless, shuddering fright. I realized, dimly, that the creature's eyes were looking into mine with a steady, compelling stare. I tried to turn away; but could not. I seemed, now, to see the window through a mist. Then, I thought other eyes came and peered, and yet others; until a whole galaxy of malignant, staring orbs seemed to hold me in thrall.

My head began to swim, and throb violently. Then, I was aware of a feeling of acute physical pain in my left hand. It grew more severe, and forced, literally forced, my attention. With a tremendous effort, I glanced down; and, with that, the spell that had held me was broken. I realized, then, that I had, in my agitation, unconsciously caught hold of the hot lamp-glass, and burnt my hand, badly. I looked up to the window, again. The misty appearance had gone, and, now, I saw that it was crowded with dozens of bestial faces. With a sudden access of rage, I raised the lamp, and hurled it, full at the window. It struck the glass (smashing a pane), and passed between two of the bars, out into the garden, scattering burning oil as it went. I heard several loud cries of pain, and, as my sight became accustomed to the dark, I discovered that the creatures had left the window.

Pulling myself together, I groped for the door, and, having found it, made my way upstairs, stumbling at each step. I felt dazed, as though I had received a blow on the head. At the same time, my hand smarted badly, and I was full of a nervous, dull rage against those Things.

Reaching my study, I lit the candles. As they burnt up, their rays were reflected from the rack of firearms on the sidewall. At the sight, I remembered that I had there a power, which, as I had proved earlier, seemed as fatal to those monsters as to more ordinary animals; and I determined I would take the offensive.

First of all, I bound up my hand; for the pain was fast becoming intolerable. After that, it seemed easier, and I crossed the room, to the rifle stand. There, I selected a heavy rifle – an old and tried weapon; and, having procured ammunition, I made my way up into one of the small towers, with which the house is crowned.

From there, I found that I could see nothing. The gardens presented a dim blur of shadows – a little blacker, perhaps, where the trees stood. That was all, and I knew that it was useless to shoot down into all that darkness. The only thing to be done, was to wait for the moon to rise; then, I might be able to do a little execution.

In the meantime, I sat still, and kept my ears open. The gardens were comparatively quiet now, and only an occasional grunt or squeal came up to me. I did not like this silence; it made me wonder on what devilry the creatures were bent. Twice, I left the tower, and took a walk through the house; but everything was silent.

Once, I heard a noise, from the direction of the Pit, as though more earth had fallen. Following this, and lasting for some fifteen minutes, there was a commotion among the denizens of the gardens. This died away, and, after that all was again quiet.

About an hour later, the moon's light showed above the distant horizon. From where I sat, I could see it over the trees; but it was not until it rose clear of them, that I could make out any of the details in the gardens below. Even then, I could see none of the brutes; until, happening to crane forward, I saw several of them lying prone, up against the wall of the house. What they were doing, I could not make out. It was, however, a chance too good to be ignored; and, taking aim, I fired at the one directly beneath. There was a shrill scream, and, as the smoke cleared away, I saw that it had turned on its back, and was writhing, feebly. Then, it was quiet. The others had disappeared.

Immediately after this, I heard a loud squeal, in the direction of the Pit. It was answered, a hundred times, from every part of the garden. This gave me some notion of the number of the creatures, and I began to feel that the whole affair was becoming even more serious than I had imagined.

As I sat there, silent and watchful, the thought came to me – Why was all this? What were these Things? What did it mean? Then my thoughts flew back to that vision (though, even now, I doubt whether it was a vision) of the Plain of Silence. What did that mean? I wondered – And that Thing in the arena? Ugh! Lastly, I thought of the house I had seen in that far-away place. That house, so like this in every detail of external structure, that it might have been modeled from it; or this from that. I had never thought of that—

At this moment, there came another long squeal, from the Pit, followed, a second later, by a couple of shorter ones. At once, the garden was filled with answering cries. I stood up, quickly, and looked over the parapet. In the moonlight, it seemed as though the shrubberies were alive. They tossed hither and thither, as though shaken by a strong, irregular wind; while a continuous rustling, and a noise of scampering feet, rose up to me. Several times, I saw the moonlight gleam on running, white figures among the bushes, and, twice, I fired. The second time, my shot was answered by a short squeal of pain.

A minute later, the gardens lay silent. From the Pit, came a deep, hoarse Babel of swine-talk. At times, angry cries smote the air, and they would be answered by multitudinous gruntings. It occurred to me, that they were holding some kind of a council, perhaps to discuss the problem of entering the house. Also, I thought that they seemed much enraged, probably by my successful shots.

It occurred to me, that now would be a good time to make a final survey of our defenses. This, I proceeded to do at once; visiting the whole of the basement again, and examining each of the doors. Luckily, they are all, like the back one, built of solid, iron-studded oak. Then, I went upstairs to the study. I was more anxious about this door. It is, palpably, of a more modern make than the others, and, though a stout piece of work, it has little of their ponderous strength.

I must explain here, that there is a small, raised lawn on this side of the house, upon which this door opens – the windows of the study being barred on this account. All the other entrances – excepting the great gateway which is never opened – are in the lower storey.

Chapter VII
The Attack

I SPENT SOME TIME, puzzling how to strengthen the study door. Finally, I went down to the kitchen, and with some trouble, brought up several heavy pieces of timber. These, I wedged up, slantwise, against it, from the floor, nailing them top and bottom. For half-an-hour, I worked hard, and, at last, got it shored to my mind.

Then, feeling easier, I resumed my coat, which I had laid aside, and proceeded to attend to one or two matters before returning to the tower. It was whilst thus employed, that I heard a fumbling at the door, and the latch was tried. Keeping silence, I waited. Soon, I heard several of the creatures outside. They were grunting to one another, softly. Then, for a minute, there was quietness. Suddenly, there sounded a quick, low grunt, and the door creaked under a tremendous pressure. It would have burst inward; but for the supports I had placed. The strain ceased, as quickly as it had begun, and there was more talk.

Presently, one of the Things squealed, softly, and I heard the sound of others approaching. There was a short confabulation; then again, silence; and I realized that they had called several more to assist. Feeling that now was the supreme moment, I stood ready, with my rifle presented. If the door gave, I would, at least, slay as many as possible.

Again came the low signal; and, once more, the door cracked, under a huge force. For, a minute perhaps, the pressure was kept up; and I waited, nervously; expecting each moment to see the door come down with a crash. But no; the struts held, and the attempt proved abortive. Then followed more of their horrible, grunting talk, and, whilst it lasted, I thought I distinguished the noise of fresh arrivals.

After a long discussion, during which the door was several times shaken, they became quiet once more, and I knew that they were going to make a third attempt to break it down. I was almost in despair. The props had been severely tried in the two previous attacks, and I was sorely afraid that this would prove too much for them.

At that moment, like an inspiration, a thought flashed into my troubled brain. Instantly, for it was no time to hesitate, I ran from the room, and up stair after stair. This time, it was not to one of the towers, that I went; but out on to the flat, leaded roof itself. Once there, I raced across to the parapet, that walls it 'round, and looked down. As I did so, I heard the short, grunted signal, and, even up there, caught the crying of the door under the assault.

There was not a moment to lose, and, leaning over, I aimed, quickly, and fired. The report rang sharply, and, almost blending with it, came the loud splud of the bullet striking its mark. From below, rose a shrill wail; and the door ceased its groaning. Then, as I took my weight from off the parapet, a huge piece of the stone coping slid from under me, and fell with a crash among the disorganized throng beneath. Several horrible shrieks quavered through the night air, and then I heard a sound of scampering feet. Cautiously, I looked over. In the moonlight, I could see the great copingstone, lying right across the threshold of the door. I thought I saw something under it – several things, white; but I could not be sure.

And so a few minutes passed.

As I stared, I saw something come 'round, out of the shadow of the house. It was one of the Things. It went up to the stone, silently, and bent down. I was unable to see what it did. In a minute it stood up. It had something in its talons, which it put to its mouth and tore at....

For the moment, I did not realize. Then, slowly, I comprehended. The Thing was stooping again. It was horrible. I started to load my rifle. When I looked again, the monster was tugging at the stone – moving it to one side. I leant the rifle on the coping, and pulled the trigger. The brute collapsed, on its face, and kicked, slightly.

Simultaneously, almost, with the report, I heard another sound – that of breaking glass. Waiting, only to recharge my weapon, I ran from the roof, and down the first two flights of stairs.

Here, I paused to listen. As I did so, there came another tinkle of falling glass. It appeared to come from the floor below. Excitedly, I sprang down the steps, and, guided by the rattle of the window-sash, reached the door of one of the empty bedrooms, at the back of the house. I thrust it open. The room was but dimly illuminated by the moonlight; most of the light being blotted out by moving figures at the window. Even as I stood, one crawled through, into the room. Leveling my weapon, I fired point-blank at it – filling the room with a deafening bang. When the smoke cleared, I saw that the room was empty, and the window free. The room was much lighter. The night air blew in, coldly, through the shattered panes. Down below, in the night, I could hear a soft moaning, and a confused murmur of swine-voices.

Stepping to one side of the window, I reloaded, and then stood there, waiting. Presently, I heard a scuffling noise. From where I stood in the shadow, I could see, without being seen.

Nearer came the sounds, and then I saw something come up above the sill, and clutch at the broken window-frame. It caught a piece of the woodwork; and, now, I could make out that it was a hand and arm. A moment later, the face of one of the Swine-creatures rose into view. Then, before I could use my rifle, or do anything, there came a sharp crack – cr-ac-k; and the window-frame gave way under the weight of the Thing. Next instant, a squashing thud, and a loud outcry, told me that it had fallen to the ground. With a savage hope that it had been killed, I went to the window. The moon had gone behind a cloud, so that I could see nothing; though a steady hum of jabbering, just beneath where I stood, indicated that there were several more of the brutes close at hand.

As I stood there, looking down, I marveled how it had been possible for the creatures to climb so far; for the wall is comparatively smooth, while the distance to the ground must be, at least, eighty feet.

All at once, as I bent, peering, I saw something, indistinctly, that cut the grey shadow of the house-side, with a black line. It passed the window, to the left, at a distance of about two feet. Then, I remembered that it was a gutter-pipe, that had been put there some years ago, to carry off the rainwater. I had forgotten about it. I could see, now, how the creatures had managed to reach the window. Even as the solution came to me, I heard a faint slithering, scratching noise, and knew that another of the brutes was coming. I waited some odd moments; then leant out of the window and felt the pipe. To my delight, I found that it was quite loose, and I managed, using the rifle-barrel as a crowbar, to lever it out from the wall. I worked quickly. Then, taking hold with both bands, I wrenched the whole concern away, and hurled it down – with the Thing still clinging to it – into the garden.

For a few minutes longer, I waited there, listening; but, after the first general outcry, I heard nothing. I knew, now, that there was no more reason to fear an attack from this quarter. I had removed the only means of reaching the window, and, as none of the other windows had any adjacent water pipes, to tempt the climbing powers of the monsters, I began to feel more confident of escaping their clutches.

Leaving the room, I made my way down to the study. I was anxious to see how the door had withstood the test of that last assault. Entering, I lit two of the candles, and then turned to the door. One of the large props had been displaced, and, on that side, the door had been forced inward some six inches.

It was Providential that I had managed to drive the brutes away just when I did! And that copingstone! I wondered, vaguely, how I had managed to dislodge it. I had not noticed it loose, as I took my shot; and then, as I stood up, it had slipped away from beneath me…I felt that I owed the dismissal of the attacking force, more to its timely fall than to my rifle. Then the thought came, that I had better seize this chance to shore up the door, again. It was evident that the creatures had not returned since the fall of the copingstone; but who was to say how long they would keep away?

There and then, I set-to, at repairing the door – working hard and anxiously. First, I went down to the basement, and, rummaging 'round, found several pieces of heavy oak planking. With these, I returned to the study, and, having removed the props, placed the planks up against the door. Then, I nailed the heads of the struts to these, and, driving them well home at the bottoms, nailed them again there.

Thus, I made the door stronger than ever; for now it was solid with the backing of boards, and would, I felt convinced, stand a heavier pressure than hitherto, without giving way.

After that, I lit the lamp which I had brought from the kitchen, and went down to have a look at the lower windows.

Now that I had seen an instance of the strength the creatures possessed, I felt considerable anxiety about the windows on the ground floor – in spite of the fact that they were so strongly barred.

I went first to the buttery, having a vivid remembrance of my late adventure there. The place was chilly, and the wind, soughing in through the broken glass, produced an eerie note. Apart from the general air of dismalness, the place was as I had left it the night before. Going up to the window, I examined the bars, closely; noting, as I did so, their comfortable thickness. Still, as I looked more intently, it seemed to me, that the middle bar was bent slightly from the straight; yet it was but trifling, and it might have been so for years. I had never, before, noticed them particularly.

I put my hand through the broken window, and shook the bar. It was as firm as a rock. Perhaps the creatures had tried to 'start' it, and, finding it beyond their power, ceased from the effort. After that, I went 'round to each of the windows, in turn; examining them with careful attention; but nowhere else could I trace anything to show that there had been any tampering. Having finished my survey, I went back to the study, and poured myself out a little brandy. Then to the tower to watch.

Chapter VIII
After the Attack

IT WAS NOW about three a.m., and, presently, the Eastern sky began to pale with the coming of dawn. Gradually, the day came, and, by its light, I scanned the gardens, earnestly; but nowhere could I see any signs of the brutes. I leant over, and glanced down to the foot of the wall, to see whether the body of the Thing I had shot the night before was still there. It was gone. I supposed that others of the monsters had removed it during the night.

Then, I went down on to the roof, and crossed over to the gap from which the coping stone had fallen. Reaching it, I looked over. Yes, there was the stone, as I had seen it last; but there was no appearance of anything beneath it; nor could I see the creatures I had killed, after its fall. Evidently, they also had been taken away. I turned, and went down to my study. There, I sat down, wearily. I was thoroughly tired. It was quite light now; though the sun's rays were not, as yet, perceptibly hot. A clock chimed the hour of four.

I awoke, with a start, and looked 'round, hurriedly. The clock in the corner, indicated that it was three o'clock. It was already afternoon. I must have slept for nearly eleven hours.

With a jerky movement, I sat forward in the chair, and listened. The house was perfectly silent. Slowly, I stood up, and yawned. I felt desperately tired, still, and sat down again; wondering what it was that had waked me.

It must have been the clock striking, I concluded, presently; and was commencing to doze off, when a sudden noise brought me back, once more, to life. It was the sound of a step, as of a person moving cautiously down the corridor, toward my study. In an instant, I was on my feet, and grasping my rifle. Noiselessly, I waited. Had the creatures broken in, whilst I slept? Even as I questioned, the steps reached my door, halted momentarily, and then continued down the passage. Silently, I tiptoed to the doorway, and peeped out. Then, I experienced such a feeling of relief, as must a reprieved criminal – it was my sister. She was going toward the stairs.

I stepped into the hall, and was about to call to her, when it occurred to me, that it was very queer she should have crept past my door, in that stealthy manner. I was puzzled, and, for one brief moment, the thought occupied my mind, that it was not she, but some fresh mystery of the house. Then, as I caught a glimpse of her old petticoat, the thought passed as quickly as it had come, and I half laughed. There could be no mistaking that ancient garment. Yet, I wondered what she was doing; and, remembering her condition of mind, on the previous day, I felt that it might be best to follow, quietly – taking care not to alarm her – and see what she was going to do. If she behaved rationally, well and good; if not, I should have to take steps to restrain her. I could run no unnecessary risks, under the danger that threatened us.

Quickly, I reached the head of the stairs, and paused a moment. Then, I heard a sound that sent me leaping down, at a mad rate – it was the rattle of bolts being unshot. That foolish sister of mine was actually unbarring the back door.

Just as her hand was on the last bolt, I reached her. She had not seen me, and, the first thing she knew, I had hold of her arm. She glanced up quickly, like a frightened animal, and screamed aloud.

'Come, Mary!' I said, sternly, 'what's the meaning of this nonsense? Do you mean to tell me you don't understand the danger, that you try to throw our two lives away in this fashion!'

To this, she replied nothing; only trembled, violently, gasping and sobbing, as though in the last extremity of fear.

Through some minutes, I reasoned with her; pointing out the need for caution, and asking her to be brave. There was little to be afraid of now, I explained – and, I tried to believe that I spoke the truth – but she must be sensible, and not attempt to leave the house for a few days.

At last, I ceased, in despair. It was no use talking to her; she was, obviously, not quite herself for the time being. Finally, I told her she had better go to her room, if she could not behave rationally.

Still, she took not any notice. So, without more ado, I picked her up in my arms, and carried her there. At first, she screamed, wildly; but had relapsed into silent trembling, by the time I reached the stairs.

Arriving at her room, I laid her upon the bed. She lay there quietly enough, neither speaking nor sobbing – just shaking in a very ague of fear. I took a rug from a chair near by, and spread it over her. I could do nothing more for her, and so, crossed to where Pepper lay in a big basket. My sister had taken charge of him since his wound, to nurse him, for it had proved more severe than I had thought, and I was pleased to note that, in spite of her state of mind, she had looked after the old dog, carefully. Stooping, I spoke to him, and, in reply, he licked my hand, feebly. He was too ill to do more.

Then, going to the bed, I bent over my sister, and asked her how she felt; but she only shook the more, and, much as it pained me, I had to admit that my presence seemed to make her worse.

And so, I left her – locking the door, and pocketing the key. It seemed to be the only course to take.

The rest of the day, I spent between the tower and my study. For food, I brought up a loaf from the pantry, and on this, and some claret, I lived for that day.

What a long, weary day it was. If only I could have gone out into the gardens, as is my wont, I should have been content enough; but to be cooped in this silent house, with no companion, save a mad woman and a sick dog, was enough to prey upon the nerves of the hardiest. And out in the tangled shrubberies that surrounded the house, lurked – for all I could tell – those infernal Swine-creatures waiting their chance. Was ever a man in such straits?

Once, in the afternoon, and again, later, I went to visit my sister. The second time, I found her tending Pepper; but, at my approach, she slid over, unobtrusively, to the far corner, with a gesture that saddened me beyond belief. Poor girl! her fear cut me intolerably, and I would not intrude on her, unnecessarily. She would be better, I trusted, in a few days; meanwhile, I could do nothing; and I judged it still needful – hard as it seemed – to keep her confined to her room. One thing there was that I took for encouragement: she had eaten some of the food I had taken to her, on my first visit.

And so the day passed.

As the evening drew on, the air grew chilly, and I began to make preparations for passing a second night in the tower – taking up two additional rifles, and a heavy ulster. The rifles I loaded, and laid alongside my other; as I intended to make things warm for any of the creatures who might show, during the night. I had plenty of ammunition, and I thought to give the brutes such a lesson, as should show them the uselessness of attempting to force an entrance.

After that, I made the 'round of the house again; paying particular attention to the props that supported the study door. Then, feeling that I had done all that lay in my power to insure our safety, I returned to the tower; calling in on my sister and Pepper, for a final visit, on the way. Pepper was asleep; but woke, as I entered, and wagged his tail, in recognition. I thought he seemed slightly better. My sister was lying on the bed; though whether asleep or not, I was unable to tell; and thus I left them.

Reaching the tower, I made myself as comfortable as circumstances would permit, and settled down to watch through the night. Gradually, darkness fell, and soon the details of the gardens were merged into shadows. During the first few hours, I sat, alert, listening for any sound that might help to tell me if anything were stirring down below. It was far too dark for my eyes to be of much use.

Slowly, the hours passed; without anything unusual happening. And the moon rose, showing the gardens, apparently empty, and silent. And so, through the night, without disturbance or sound.

Toward morning, I began to grow stiff and cold, with my long vigil; also, I was getting very uneasy, concerning the continued quietness on the part of the creatures. I mistrusted it, and would sooner, far, have had them attack the house, openly. Then, at least, I should have known my danger, and been able to meet it; but to wait like this, through a whole night, picturing all kinds of unknown devilment, was to jeopardize one's sanity. Once or twice, the thought came to me, that, perhaps, they had gone; but, in my heart, I found it impossible to believe that it was so.

Chapter IX
In the Cellars

AT LAST, what with being tired and cold, and the uneasiness that possessed me, I resolved to take a walk through the house; first calling in at the study, for a glass of brandy to warm me. This, I did, and, while there, I examined the door, carefully; but found all as I had left it the night before.

The day was just breaking, as I left the tower; though it was still too dark in the house to be able to see without a light, and I took one of the study candles with me on my 'round. By the time I had finished the ground floor, the daylight was creeping in, wanly, through the barred windows. My search had shown me nothing fresh. Everything appeared to be in order, and I was on the point of extinguishing my candle, when the thought suggested itself to me to have another glance 'round the cellars. I had not, if I remember rightly, been into them since my hasty search on the evening of the attack.

For, perhaps, the half of a minute, I hesitated. I would have been very willing to forego the task – as, indeed, I am inclined to think any man well might – for of all the great, awe-inspiring rooms in this house, the cellars are the hugest and weirdest. Great, gloomy caverns of places, unlit by any ray of daylight. Yet, I would not shirk the work. I felt that to do so would smack of sheer cowardice. Besides, as I reassured myself, the cellars were really the most unlikely places in which to come across anything dangerous; considering that they can be entered, only through a heavy oaken door, the key of which, I carry always on my person.

It is in the smallest of these places that I keep my wine; a gloomy hole close to the foot of the cellar stairs; and beyond which, I have seldom proceeded. Indeed, save for the rummage 'round, already mentioned, I doubt whether I had ever, before, been right through the cellars.

As I unlocked the great door, at the top of the steps, I paused, nervously, a moment, at the strange, desolate smell that assailed my nostrils. Then, throwing the barrel of my weapon forward, I descended, slowly, into the darkness of the underground regions.

Reaching the bottom of the stairs, I stood for a minute, and listened. All was silent, save for a faint drip, drip of water, falling, drop-by-drop, somewhere to my left. As I stood, I noticed how quietly the candle burnt; never a flicker nor flare, so utterly windless was the place.

Quietly, I moved from cellar to cellar. I had but a very dim memory of their arrangement. The impressions left by my first search were blurred. I had recollections of a succession of great cellars, and of one, greater than the rest, the roof of which was upheld by pillars; beyond that my mind was hazy, and predominated by a sense of cold and darkness and shadows. Now, however, it was different; for, although nervous, I was sufficiently collected to be able to look about me, and note the structure and size of the different vaults I entered.

Of course, with the amount of light given by my candle, it was not possible to examine each place, minutely, but I was enabled to notice, as I went along, that the walls appeared to be built with wonderful precision and finish; while here and there, an occasional, massive pillar shot up to support the vaulted roof.

Thus, I came, at last, to the great cellar that I remembered. It is reached, through a huge, arched entrance, on which I observed strange, fantastic carvings, which threw queer shadows under the light of my candle. As I stood, and examined these, thoughtfully, it occurred to me how strange it was, that I should be so little acquainted with my own house. Yet, this may be easily understood, when one realizes the size of this ancient pile, and the fact that only my old sister and I live in it, occupying a few of the rooms, such as our wants decide.

Holding the light high, I passed on into the cellar, and, keeping to the right, paced slowly up, until I reached the further end. I walked quietly, and looked cautiously about, as I went. But, so far as the light showed, I saw nothing unusual.

At the top, I turned to the left, still keeping to the wall, and so continued, until I had traversed the whole of the vast chamber. As I moved along, I noticed that the floor was composed of solid rock, in places covered with a damp mould, in others bare, or almost so, save for a thin coating of light-grey dust.

I had halted at the doorway. Now, however, I turned, and made my way up the center of the place; passing among the pillars, and glancing to right and left, as I moved. About halfway up the cellar, I stubbed my foot against something that gave out a metallic sound. Stooping quickly, I held the candle, and saw that the object I had kicked, was a large, metal ring. Bending lower, I cleared the dust from around it, and, presently, discovered that it was attached to a ponderous trap door, black with age.

Feeling excited, and wondering to where it could lead, I laid my gun on the floor, and, sticking the candle in the trigger guard, took the ring in both hands, and pulled. The trap creaked loudly – the sound echoing, vaguely, through the huge place – and opened, heavily.

Propping the edge on my knee, I reached for the candle, and held it in the opening, moving it to right and left; but could see nothing. I was puzzled and surprised. There were no signs of steps, nor even the appearance of there ever having been any. Nothing; save an empty blackness. I might have been looking down into a bottomless, sideless well. Then, even as I stared, full of perplexity, I seemed to hear, far down, as though from untold depths, a faint whisper of sound. I bent my head, quickly, more into the opening, and listened, intently. It may have been fancy; but I could have sworn to hearing a soft titter, that grew into a hideous, chuckling, faint and distant. Startled, I leapt backward, letting the trap fall, with a hollow clang, that filled the place with echoes. Even then, I seemed to hear that mocking, suggestive laughter; but this, I knew, must be my imagination. The sound, I had heard, was far too slight to penetrate through the cumbrous trap.

For a full minute, I stood there, quivering – glancing, nervously, behind and before; but the great cellar was silent as a grave, and, gradually, I shook off the frightened sensation. With a calmer mind, I became again curious to know into what that trap opened; but could not, then, summon sufficient courage to make a further investigation. One thing I felt, however, was that the trap ought to be secured. This, I accomplished by placing upon it several large pieces of 'dressed' stone, which I had noticed in my tour along the East wall.

Then, after a final scrutiny of the rest of the place, I retraced my way through the cellars, to the stairs, and so reached the daylight, with an infinite feeling of relief, that the uncomfortable task was accomplished.

Chapter X
The Time of Waiting

THE SUN was now warm, and shining brightly, forming a wondrous contrast to the dark and dismal cellars; and it was with comparatively light feelings, that I made my way up to the tower, to survey the gardens. There, I found everything quiet, and, after a few minutes, went down to Mary's room.

Here, having knocked, and received a reply, I unlocked the door. My sister was sitting, quietly, on the bed; as though waiting. She seemed quite herself again, and made no attempt to move away, as I approached; yet, I observed that she scanned my face, anxiously, as though in doubt, and but half assured in her mind that there was nothing to fear from me.

To my questions, as to how she felt, she replied, sanely enough, that she was hungry, and would like to go down to prepare breakfast, if I did not mind. For a minute, I meditated whether it would be safe to let her out. Finally, I told her she might go, on condition that she promised not to attempt to leave the house, or meddle with any of the outer doors. At my mention of the doors, a sudden look of fright crossed her face; but she said nothing, save to give the required promise, and then left the room, silently.

Crossing the floor, I approached Pepper. He had waked as I entered; but, beyond a slight yelp of pleasure, and a soft rapping with his tail, had kept quiet. Now, as I patted him, he made an attempt to stand up, and succeeded, only to fall back on his side, with a little yowl of pain.

I spoke to him, and bade him lie still. I was greatly delighted with his improvement, and also with the natural kindness of my sister's heart, in taking such good care of him, in spite of her condition of mind. After a while, I left him, and went downstairs, to my study.

In a little time, Mary appeared, carrying a tray on which smoked a hot breakfast. As she entered the room, I saw her gaze fasten on the props that supported the study door; her lips tightened, and I thought she paled, slightly; but that was all. Putting the tray down at my elbow, she was leaving the room, quietly, when I called her back. She came, it seemed, a little timidly, as though startled; and I noted that her hand clutched at her apron, nervously.

'Come, Mary,' I said. 'Cheer up! Things look brighter. I've seen none of the creatures since yesterday morning, early.'

She looked at me, in a curiously puzzled manner; as though not comprehending. Then, intelligence swept into her eyes, and fear; but she said nothing, beyond an unintelligible murmur of acquiescence. After that, I kept silence; it was evident that any reference to the Swine-things, was more than her shaken nerves could bear.

Breakfast over, I went up to the tower. Here, during the greater part of the day, I maintained a strict watch over the gardens. Once or twice, I went down to the basement, to see how my sister was getting along. Each time, I found her quiet, and curiously submissive. Indeed, on the last occasion, she even ventured to address me, on her own account, with regard to some household matter that needed attention. Though this was done with an almost extraordinary timidity, I hailed it with happiness, as being the first word, voluntarily spoken, since the critical moment, when I had caught her unbarring the back door, to go out among those waiting brutes. I wondered whether she was aware of her attempt, and how near a thing it had been; but refrained from questioning her, thinking it best to let well alone.

That night, I slept in a bed; the first time for two nights. In the morning, I rose early, and took a walk through the house. All was as it should be, and I went up to the tower, to have a look at the gardens. Here, again, I found perfect quietness.

At breakfast, when I met Mary, I was greatly pleased to see that she had sufficiently regained command over herself, to be able to greet me in a perfectly natural manner. She talked sensibly and quietly; only keeping carefully from any mention of the past couple of days. In this, I humored her, to the extent of not attempting to lead the conversation in that direction.

Earlier in the morning, I had been to see Pepper. He was mending, rapidly; and bade fair to be on his legs, in earnest, in another day or two. Before leaving the breakfast table, I made some reference to his improvement. In the short discussion that followed, I was surprised to gather, from my sister's remarks, that she was still under the impression that his wound had been given by the wildcat, of my invention. It made me feel almost ashamed of myself for deceiving her. Yet, the lie had been told to prevent her from being frightened. And then, I had been sure that she must have known the truth, later, when those brutes had attacked the house.

During the day, I kept on the alert; spending much of my time, as on the previous day, in the tower; but not a sign could I see of the Swine-creatures, nor hear any sound. Several times, the thought had come to me, that the Things had, at last, left us; but, up to this time, I had refused to entertain the idea, seriously; now, however, I began to feel that there was reason for hope. It would soon be three days since I had seen any of the Things; but still, I intended to use the utmost caution. For all that I could tell, this protracted silence might be a ruse to tempt me from the house – perhaps right into their arms. The thought of such a contingency, was, alone, sufficient to make me circumspect.

So it was, that the fourth, fifth and sixth days went by, quietly, without my making any attempt to leave the house.

On the sixth day, I had the pleasure of seeing Pepper, once more, upon his feet; and, though still very weak, he managed to keep me company during the whole of that day.

Chapter XI
The Searching of the Gardens

HOW SLOWLY the time went; and never a thing to indicate that any of the brutes still infested the gardens.

It was on the ninth day that, finally, I decided to run the risk, if any there were, and sally out. With this purpose in view, I loaded one of the shotguns, carefully – choosing it, as being more deadly than a rifle, at close quarters; and then, after a final scrutiny of the grounds, from the tower, I called Pepper to follow me, and made my way down to the basement.

At the door, I must confess to hesitating a moment. The thought of what might be awaiting me among the dark shrubberies, was by no means calculated to encourage my resolution. It was but a second, though, and then I had drawn the bolts, and was standing on the path outside the door.

Pepper followed, stopping at the doorstep to sniff, suspiciously; and carrying his nose up and down the jambs, as though following a scent. Then, suddenly, he turned, sharply, and started to run here and there, in semicircles and circles, all around the door; finally returning to the threshold. Here, he began again to nose about.

Hitherto, I had stood, watching the dog; yet, all the time, with half my gaze on the wild tangle of gardens, stretching 'round me. Now, I went toward him, and, bending down, examined the surface of the door, where he was smelling. I found that the wood was covered with a network of scratches, crossing and recrossing one another, in inextricable confusion. In addition to this, I noticed that the doorposts, themselves, were gnawed in places. Beyond these, I could find nothing; and so, standing up, I began to make the tour of the house wall.

Pepper, as soon as I walked away, left the door, and ran ahead, still nosing and sniffing as he went along. At times, he stopped to investigate. Here, it would be a bullet-hole in the pathway, or, perhaps, a powder stained wad. Anon, it might be a piece of torn sod, or a disturbed patch of weedy path; but, save for such trifles, he found nothing. I observed him, critically, as he went along, and could discover nothing of uneasiness, in his demeanor, to indicate that he felt the nearness of any of the creatures. By this, I was assured that the gardens were empty, at least for the present, of those hateful Things. Pepper could not be easily deceived, and it was a relief to feel that he would know, and give me timely warning, if there were any danger.

Reaching the place where I had shot that first creature, I stopped, and made a careful scrutiny; but could see nothing. From there, I went on to where the great copingstone had fallen. It lay on its side, apparently just as it had been left when I shot the brute that was moving it. A couple of feet to the right of the nearer end, was a great dent in the ground; showing where it had struck. The other end was still within the indentation – half in, and half out. Going nearer, I looked at the stone, more closely. What a huge piece of masonry it was! And that creature had moved it, single-handed, in its attempt to reach what lay below.

I went 'round to the further end of the stone. Here, I found that it was possible to see under it, for a distance of nearly a couple of feet. Still, I could see nothing of the stricken creatures, and I felt much surprised. I had, as I have before said, guessed that the remains had been removed; yet, I could not conceive that it had been done so thoroughly as not to leave some certain sign, beneath the stone, indicative of their fate. I had seen several of the brutes struck down beneath it, with such force that they must have been literally driven into the earth; and now, not a vestige of them was to be seen – not even a bloodstain.

I felt more puzzled, than ever, as I turned the matter over in my mind; but could think of no plausible explanation; and so, finally, gave it up, as one of the many things that were unexplainable.

From there, I transferred my attention to the study door. I could see, now, even more plainly, the effects of the tremendous strain, to which it had been subjected; and I marveled how, even with the support afforded by the props, it had withstood the attacks, so well. There were no marks of blows – indeed, none had been given – but the door had been literally riven from its hinges, by the application of enormous, silent force. One thing that I observed affected me profoundly – the head of one of the props had been driven right through a panel. This was, of itself, sufficient to show how huge an effort the creatures had made to break down the door, and how nearly they had succeeded.

Leaving, I continued my tour 'round the house, finding little else of interest; save at the back, where I came across the piece of piping I had torn from the wall, lying among the long grass underneath the broken window.

Then, I returned to the house, and, having re-bolted the back door, went up to the tower. Here, I spent the afternoon, reading, and occasionally glancing down into the gardens. I had determined, if the night passed quietly, to go as far as the Pit, on the morrow. Perhaps, I should be able to learn, then, something of what had happened. The day slipped away, and the night came, and went much as the last few nights had gone.

When I rose the morning had broken, fine and clear; and I determined to put my project into action. During breakfast, I considered the matter, carefully; after which, I went to the study for my shotgun. In addition, I loaded, and slipped into my pocket, a small, but heavy, pistol. I quite understood that, if there were any danger, it lay in the direction of the Pit and I intended to be prepared.

Leaving the study, I went down to the back door, followed by Pepper. Once outside, I took a quick survey of the surrounding gardens, and then set off toward the Pit. On the way, I kept a sharp outlook, holding my gun, handily. Pepper was running ahead, I noticed, without any apparent hesitation. From this, I augured that there was no imminent danger to be apprehended, and I stepped out more quickly in his wake. He had reached the top of the Pit, now, and was nosing his way along the edge.

A minute later, I was beside him, looking down into the Pit. For a moment, I could scarcely believe that it was the same place, so greatly was it changed. The dark, wooded ravine of a fortnight ago, with a foliage-hidden stream, running sluggishly, at the bottom, existed no longer. Instead, my eyes showed me a ragged chasm, partly filled with a gloomy lake of turbid water. All one side of the ravine was stripped of underwood, showing the bare rock.

A little to my left, the side of the Pit appeared to have collapsed altogether, forming a deep V-shaped cleft in the face of the rocky cliff. This rift ran, from the upper edge of the ravine, nearly down to the water, and penetrated into the Pit side, to a distance of some forty feet. Its opening was, at least, six yards across; and, from this, it seemed to taper into about two. But, what attracted my attention, more than even the stupendous split itself, was a great hole, some distance down the cleft, and right in the angle of the V. It was clearly defined, and not unlike an arched doorway in shape; though, lying as it did in the shadow, I could not see it very distinctly.

The opposite side of the Pit, still retained its verdure; but so torn in places, and everywhere covered with dust and rubbish, that it was hardly distinguishable as such.

My first impression, that there had been a land slip, was, I began to see, not sufficient, of itself, to account for all the changes I witnessed. And the water – ? I turned, suddenly; for I had become aware that, somewhere to my right, there was a noise of running water. I could see nothing; but, now that my attention had been caught, I distinguished, easily, that it came from somewhere at the East end of the Pit.

Slowly, I made my way in that direction; the sound growing plainer as I advanced, until in a little, I stood right above it. Even then, I could not perceive the cause, until I knelt down, and thrust my head over the cliff. Here, the noise came up to me, plainly; and I saw, below me, a torrent of clear water, issuing from a small fissure in the Pit side, and rushing down the rocks, into the lake beneath. A little further along the cliff, I saw another, and, beyond that again, two smaller ones. These, then, would help to account for the quantity of water in the Pit; and, if the fall of rock and earth had blocked the outlet of the stream at the bottom, there was little doubt but that it was contributing a very large share.

Yet, I puzzled my head to account for the generally *shaken* appearance of the place – these streamlets, and that huge cleft, further up the ravine! It seemed to me, that more than the landslip was necessary to account for these. I could imagine an earthquake, or a great *explosion*, creating some such condition of affairs as existed; but, of these, there had been neither. Then, I stood up, quickly, remembering that crash, and the cloud of dust that had followed, directly, rushing high into the air. But I shook my head, unbelievingly. No! It must have been the noise of the falling rocks and earth, I had heard; of course, the dust would fly, naturally. Still, in spite of my reasoning, I had an uneasy feeling, that this theory did not satisfy my sense of the probable; and yet, was any other, that I could suggest, likely to be half so plausible? Pepper had been sitting on the grass, while I conducted my examination. Now, as I turned up the North side of the ravine, he rose and followed.

Slowly, and keeping a careful watch in all directions, I made the circuit of the Pit; but found little else, that I had not already seen. From the West end, I could see the four waterfalls, uninterruptedly. They were some considerable distance up from the surface of the lake – about fifty feet, I calculated.

For a little while longer, I loitered about; keeping my eyes and ears open, but still, without seeing or hearing anything suspicious. The whole place was wonderfully quiet; indeed, save for the continuous murmur of the water, at the top end, no sound, of any description, broke the silence.

All this while, Pepper had shown no signs of uneasiness. This seemed, to me, to indicate that, for the time being, at least, there was none of the Swine-creatures in the vicinity. So far as I could see, his attention appeared to have been taken, chiefly, with scratching and sniffing among the grass at the edge of the Pit. At times, he would leave the edge, and run along toward the house, as though following invisible tracks; but, in all cases, returning after a few minutes. I had little doubt but that he was really tracing out the footsteps of the Swine-things; and the very fact that each one seemed to lead him back to the Pit, appeared to me, a proof that the brutes had all returned whence they came.

At noon, I went home, for dinner. During the afternoon, I made a partial search of the gardens, accompanied by Pepper; but, without coming upon anything to indicate the presence of the creatures.

Once, as we made our way through the shrubberies, Pepper rushed in among some bushes, with a fierce yelp. At that, I jumped back, in sudden fright, and threw my gun forward, in readiness; only to laugh, nervously, as Pepper reappeared, chasing an unfortunate cat. Toward evening, I gave up the search, and returned to the house. All at once, as we were passing a great clump of bushes, on our right, Pepper disappeared, and I could hear him sniffing and growling among them, in a suspicious manner. With my gun barrel, I parted the intervening shrubbery, and looked inside. There was nothing to be seen, save that many of the branches were bent down, and broken; as though some animal had made a lair there, at no very previous date. It was probably, I thought, one of the places occupied by some of the Swine-creatures, on the night of the attack.

Next day, I resumed my search through the gardens; but without result. By evening, I had been right through them, and now, I knew, beyond the possibility of doubt, that there were no longer any of the Things concealed about the place. Indeed, I have often thought since, that I was correct in my earlier surmise, that they had left soon after the attack.

Chapter XII
The Subterranean Pit

ANOTHER WEEK came and went, during which I spent a great deal of my time about the Pit mouth. I had come to the conclusion a few days earlier, that the arched hole, in the angle of the great rift, was the place through which the Swine-things had made their exit, from some unholy place in the bowels of the world. How near the probable truth this went, I was to learn later.

It may be easily understood, that I was tremendously curious, though in a frightened way, to know to what infernal place that hole led; though, so far, the idea had not struck me, seriously, of making an investigation. I was far too much imbued with a sense of horror of the

Swine-creatures, to think of venturing, willingly, where there was any chance of coming into contact with them.

Gradually, however, as time passed, this feeling grew insensibly less; so that when, a few days later, the thought occurred to me that it might be possible to clamber down and have a look into the hole, I was not so exceedingly averse to it, as might have been imagined. Still, I do not think, even then, that I really intended to try any such foolhardy adventure. For all that I could tell, it might be certain death, to enter that doleful looking opening. And yet, such is the pertinacity of human curiosity, that, at last, my chief desire was but to discover what lay beyond that gloomy entrance.

Slowly, as the days slid by, my fear of the Swine-things became an emotion of the past – more an unpleasant, incredible memory, than aught else.

Thus, a day came, when, throwing thoughts and fancies adrift, I procured a rope from the house, and, having made it fast to a stout tree, at the top of the rift, and some little distance back from the Pit edge, let the other end down into the cleft, until it dangled right across the mouth of the dark hole.

Then, cautiously, and with many misgivings as to whether it was not a mad act that I was attempting, I climbed slowly down, using the rope as a support, until I reached the hole. Here, still holding on to the rope, I stood, and peered in. All was perfectly dark, and not a sound came to me. Yet, a moment later, it seemed that I could hear something. I held my breath, and listened; but all was silent as the grave, and I breathed freely once more. At the same instant, I heard the sound again. It was like a noise of labored breathing – deep and sharp-drawn. For a short second, I stood, petrified; not able to move. But now the sounds had ceased again, and I could hear nothing.

As I stood there, anxiously, my foot dislodged a pebble, which fell inward, into the dark, with a hollow chink. At once, the noise was taken up and repeated a score of times; each succeeding echo being fainter, and seeming to travel away from me, as though into remote distance. Then, as the silence fell again, I heard that stealthy breathing. For each respiration I made, I could hear an answering breath. The sounds appeared to be coming nearer; and then, I heard several others; but fainter and more distant. Why I did not grip the rope, and spring up out of danger, I cannot say. It was as though I had been paralyzed. I broke out into a profuse sweat, and tried to moisten my lips with my tongue. My throat had gone suddenly dry, and I coughed, huskily. It came back to me, in a dozen, horrible, throaty tones, mockingly. I peered, helplessly, into the gloom; but still nothing showed. I had a strange, choky sensation, and again I coughed, dryly. Again the echo took it up, rising and falling, grotesquely, and dying slowly into a muffled silence.

Then, suddenly, a thought came to me, and I held my breath. The other breathing stopped. I breathed again, and, once more, it re-commenced. But now, I no longer feared. I knew that the strange sounds were not made by any lurking Swine-creature; but were simply the echo of my own respirations.

Yet, I had received such a fright, that I was glad to scramble up the rift, and haul up the rope. I was far too shaken and nervous to think of entering that dark hole then, and so returned to the house. I felt more myself next morning; but even then, I could not summon up sufficient courage to explore the place.

All this time, the water in the Pit had been creeping slowly up, and now stood but a little below the opening. At the rate at which it was rising, it would be level with the floor in less than another week; and I realized that, unless I carried out my investigations soon, I should probably never do so at all; as the water would rise and rise, until the opening, itself, was submerged.

It may have been that this thought stirred me to act; but, whatever it was, a couple of days later, saw me standing at the top of the cleft, fully equipped for the task.

This time, I was resolved to conquer my shirking, and go right through with the matter. With this intention, I had brought, in addition to the rope, a bundle of candles, meaning to use them as a torch; also my double-barreled shotgun. In my belt, I had a heavy horse-pistol, loaded with buckshot.

As before, I fastened the rope to the tree. Then, having tied my gun across my shoulders, with a piece of stout cord, I lowered myself over the edge of the Pit. At this movement, Pepper, who had been eyeing my actions, watchfully, rose to his feet, and ran to me, with a half bark, half wail, it seemed to me, of warning. But I was resolved on my enterprise, and bade him lie down. I would much have liked to take him with me; but this was next to impossible, in the existing circumstances. As my face dropped level with the Pit edge, he licked me, right across the mouth; and then, seizing my sleeve between his teeth, began to pull back, strongly. It was very evident that he did not want me to go. Yet, having made up my mind, I had no intention of giving up the attempt; and, with a sharp word to Pepper, to release me, I continued my descent, leaving the poor old fellow at the top, barking and crying like a forsaken pup.

Carefully, I lowered myself from projection to projection. I knew that a slip might mean a wetting.

Reaching the entrance, I let go the rope, and untied the gun from my shoulders. Then, with a last look at the sky – which I noticed was clouding over, rapidly – I went forward a couple of paces, so as to be shielded from the wind, and lit one of the candles. Holding it above my head, and grasping my gun, firmly, I began to move on, slowly, throwing my glances in all directions.

For the first minute, I could hear the melancholy sound of Pepper's howling, coming down to me. Gradually, as I penetrated further into the darkness, it grew fainter; until, in a little while, I could hear nothing. The path tended downward somewhat, and to the left. Thence it kept on, still running to the left, until I found that it was leading me right in the direction of the house.

Very cautiously, I moved onward, stopping, every few steps, to listen. I had gone, perhaps, a hundred yards, when, suddenly, it seemed to me that I caught a faint sound, somewhere along the passage behind. With my heart thudding heavily, I listened. The noise grew plainer, and appeared to be approaching, rapidly. I could hear it distinctly, now. It was the soft padding of running feet. In the first moments of fright, I stood, irresolute; not knowing whether to go forward or backward. Then, with a sudden realization of the best thing to do, I backed up to the rocky wall on my right, and, holding the candle above my head, waited – gun in hand – cursing my foolhardy curiosity, for bringing me into such a strait.

I had not long to wait, but a few seconds, before two eyes reflected back from the gloom, the rays of my candle. I raised my gun, using my right hand only, and aimed quickly. Even as I did so, something leapt out of the darkness, with a blustering bark of joy that woke the echoes, like thunder. It was Pepper. How he had contrived to scramble down the cleft, I could not conceive. As I brushed my hand, nervously, over his coat, I noticed that he was dripping; and concluded that he must have tried to follow me, and fallen into the water; from which he would not find it very difficult to climb.

Having waited a minute, or so, to steady myself, I proceeded along the way, Pepper following, quietly. I was curiously glad to have the old fellow with me. He was company, and, somehow, with him at my heels, I was less afraid. Also, I knew how quickly his keen ears would detect the presence of any unwelcome creature, should there be such, amid the darkness that wrapped us.

For some minutes we went slowly along; the path still leading straight toward the house. Soon, I concluded, we should be standing right beneath it, did the path but carry far enough. I led the way, cautiously, for another fifty yards, or so. Then, I stopped, and held the light high; and reason enough I had to be thankful that I did so; for there, not three paces forward, the path vanished, and, in place, showed a hollow blackness, that sent sudden fear through me.

Very cautiously, I crept forward, and peered down; but could see nothing. Then, I crossed to the left of the passage, to see whether there might be any continuation of the path. Here, right against the wall, I found that a narrow track, some three feet wide, led onward. Carefully, I stepped on to it; but had not gone far, before I regretted venturing thereon. For, after a few paces, the already narrow way, resolved itself into a mere ledge, with, on the one side the solid, unyielding rock, towering up, in a great wall, to the unseen roof, and, on the other, that yawning chasm. I could not help reflecting how helpless I was, should I be attacked there, with no room to turn, and where even the recoil of my weapon might be sufficient to drive me headlong into the depths below.

To my great relief, a little further on, the track suddenly broadened out again to its original breadth. Gradually, as I went onward, I noticed that the path trended steadily to the right, and so, after some minutes, I discovered that I was not going forward; but simply circling the huge abyss. I had, evidently, come to the end of the great passage.

Five minutes later, I stood on the spot from which I had started; having been completely 'round, what I guessed now to be a vast pit, the mouth of which must be at least a hundred yards across.

For some little time, I stood there, lost in perplexing thought. 'What does it all mean?' was the cry that had begun to reiterate through my brain.

A sudden idea struck me, and I searched 'round for a piece of stone. Presently, I found a bit of rock, about the size of a small loaf. Sticking the candle upright in a crevice of the floor, I went back from the edge, somewhat, and, taking a short run, launched the stone forward into the chasm – my idea being to throw it far enough to keep it clear of the sides. Then, I stooped forward, and listened; but, though I kept perfectly quiet, for at least a full minute, no sound came back to me from out of the dark.

I knew, then, that the depth of the hole must be immense; for the stone, had it struck anything, was large enough to have set the echoes of that weird place, whispering for an indefinite period. Even as it was, the cavern had given back the sounds of my footfalls, multitudinously. The place was awesome, and I would willingly have retraced my steps, and left the mysteries of its solitudes unsolved; only, to do so, meant admitting defeat.

Then, a thought came, to try to get a view of the abyss. It occurred to me that, if I placed my candles 'round the edge of the hole, I should be able to get, at least, some dim sight of the place.

I found, on counting, that I had brought fifteen candles, in the bundle – my first intention having been, as I have already said, to make a torch of the lot. These, I proceeded to place 'round the Pit mouth, with an interval of about twenty yards between each.

Having completed the circle, I stood in the passage, and endeavored to get an idea of how the place looked. But I discovered, immediately, that they were totally insufficient for my purpose. They did little more than make the gloom visible. One thing they did, however, and that was, they confirmed my opinion of the size of the opening; and, although they showed me nothing that I wanted to see; yet the contrast they afforded to the heavy darkness, pleased me, curiously. It was as though fifteen tiny stars shone through the subterranean night.

Then, even as I stood, Pepper gave a sudden howl, that was taken up by the echoes, and repeated with ghastly variations, dying away, slowly. With a quick movement, I held aloft the one candle that I had kept, and glanced down at the dog; at the same moment, I seemed to hear a noise, like a diabolical chuckle, rise up from the hitherto, silent depths of the Pit. I started; then, I recollected that it was, probably, the echo of Pepper's howl.

Pepper had moved away from me, up the passage, a few steps; he was nosing along the rocky floor; and I thought I heard him lapping. I went toward him, holding the candle low. As I moved, I heard my boot go sop, sop; and the light was reflected from something that glistened, and crept past my feet, swiftly toward the Pit. I bent lower, and looked; then gave vent to an expression of surprise. From somewhere, higher up the path, a stream of water was running quickly in the direction of the great opening, and growing in size every second.

Again, Pepper gave vent to that deep-drawn howl, and, running at me, seized my coat, and attempted to drag me up the path toward the entrance. With a nervous gesture, I shook him off, and crossed quickly over to the left-hand wall. If anything were coming, I was going to have the wall at my back.

Then, as I stared anxiously up the pathway, my candle caught a gleam, far up the passage. At the same moment, I became conscious of a murmurous roar, that grew louder, and filled the whole cavern with deafening sound. From the Pit, came a deep, hollow echo, like the sob of a giant. Then, I had sprung to one side, on to the narrow ledge that ran 'round the abyss, and, turning, saw a great wall of foam sweep past me, and leap tumultuously into the waiting chasm. A cloud of spray burst over me, extinguishing my candle, and wetting me to the skin. I still held my gun. The three nearest candles went out; but the further ones gave only a short flicker. After the first rush, the flow of water eased down to a steady stream, maybe a foot in depth; though I could not see this, until I had procured one of the lighted candles, and, with it, started to reconnoiter. Pepper had, fortunately, followed me as I leapt for the ledge, and now, very much subdued, kept close behind.

A short examination showed me that the water reached right across the passage, and was running at a tremendous rate. Already, even as I stood there, it had deepened. I could make only a guess at what had happened. Evidently, the water in the ravine had broken into the passage, by some means. If that were the case, it would go on increasing in volume, until I should find it impossible to leave the place. The thought was frightening. It was evident that I must make my exit as hurriedly as possible.

Taking my gun by the stock, I sounded the water. It was a little under knee-deep. The noise it made, plunging down into the Pit, was deafening. Then, with a call to Pepper, I stepped out into the flood, using the gun as a staff. Instantly, the water boiled up over my knees, and nearly to the tops of my thighs, with the speed at which it was racing. For one short moment, I nearly lost my footing; but the thought of what lay behind, stimulated me to a fierce endeavor, and, step-by-step, I made headway.

Of Pepper, I knew nothing at first. I had all I could do to keep on my legs; and was overjoyed, when he appeared beside me. He was wading manfully along. He is a big dog, with longish thin legs, and I suppose the water had less grasp on them, than upon mine. Anyway, he managed a great deal better than I did; going ahead of me, like a guide, and wittingly – or otherwise – helping, somewhat, to break the force of the water. On we went, step by step, struggling and gasping, until somewhere about a hundred yards had been safely traversed. Then, whether it was because I was taking less care, or that there was a slippery place on the rocky floor, I cannot say; but, suddenly, I slipped, and fell on my face. Instantly, the water leapt over me in a cataract, hurling me down, toward that bottomless hole, at a frightful speed. Frantically I struggled; but it was impossible to get a footing. I was helpless, gasping and drowning. All at once, something gripped my coat, and brought me to a standstill. It was Pepper. Missing me, he must have raced back, through the dark turmoil, to find me, and then caught, and held me, until I was able to get to my feet.

I have a dim recollection of having seen, momentarily, the gleams of several lights; but, of this, I have never been quite sure. If my impressions are correct, I must have been washed down to the very brink of that awful chasm, before Pepper managed to bring me to a standstill. And the lights, of course, could only have been the distant flames of the candles, I had left burning. But, as I have said, I am not by any means sure. My eyes were full of water, and I had been badly shaken.

And there was I, without my helpful gun, without light, and sadly confused, with the water deepening; depending solely upon my old friend Pepper, to help me out of that hellish place.

I was facing the torrent. Naturally, it was the only way in which I could have sustained my position a moment; for even old Pepper could not have held me long against that terrific strain, without assistance, however blind, from me.

Perhaps a minute passed, during which it was touch and go with me; then, gradually I recommenced my tortuous way up the passage. And so began the grimmest fight with death, from which ever I hope to emerge victorious. Slowly, furiously, almost hopelessly, I strove; and that faithful Pepper led me, dragged me, upward and onward, until, at last, ahead I saw a gleam of blessed light. It was the entrance. Only a few yards further, and I reached the opening, with the water surging and boiling hungrily around my loins.

And now I understood the cause of the catastrophe. It was raining heavily, literally in torrents. The surface of the lake was level with the bottom of the opening – nay! more than level, it was above it. Evidently, the rain had swollen the lake, and caused this premature rise; for, at the rate the ravine had been filling, it would not have reached the entrance for a couple more days.

Luckily, the rope by which I had descended, was streaming into the opening, upon the inrushing waters. Seizing the end, I knotted it securely 'round Pepper's body, then, summoning up the last remnant of my strength, I commenced to swarm up the side of the cliff. I reached the Pit edge, in the last stage of exhaustion. Yet, I had to make one more effort, and haul Pepper into safety.

Slowly and wearily, I hauled on the rope. Once or twice, it seemed that I should have to give up; for Pepper is a weighty dog, and I was utterly done. Yet, to let go, would have meant certain death to the old fellow, and the thought spurred me to greater exertions. I have but a very hazy remembrance of the end. I recall pulling, through moments that lagged strangely. I have also some recollection of seeing Pepper's muzzle, appearing over the Pit edge, after what seemed an indefinite period of time. Then, all grew suddenly dark.

Chapter XIII
The Trap in the Great Cellar

I SUPPOSE I must have swooned; for, the next thing I remember, I opened my eyes, and all was dusk. I was lying on my back, with one leg doubled under the other, and Pepper was licking my ears. I felt horribly stiff, and my leg was numb, from the knee, downward. For a few minutes, I lay thus, in a dazed condition; then, slowly, I struggled to a sitting position, and looked about me.

It had stopped raining, but the trees still dripped, dismally. From the Pit, came a continuous murmur of running water. I felt cold and shivery. My clothes were sodden, and I ached all over. Very slowly, the life came back into my numbed leg, and, after a little, I essayed to stand up. This, I managed, at the second attempt; but I was very tottery, and peculiarly weak. It seemed to me, that I was going to be ill, and I made shift to stumble my way toward the house. My steps were erratic, and my head confused. At each step that I took, sharp pains shot through my limbs.

I had gone, perhaps, some thirty paces, when a cry from Pepper, drew my attention, and I turned, stiffly, toward him. The old dog was trying to follow me; but could come no further, owing to the rope, with which I had hauled him up, being still tied 'round his body, the other end not having been unfastened from the tree. For a moment, I fumbled with the knots, weakly; but they were wet and hard, and I could do nothing. Then, I remembered my knife, and, in a minute, the rope was cut.

How I reached the house, I scarcely know, and, of the days that followed, I remember still less. Of one thing, I am certain, that, had it not been for my sister's untiring love and nursing, I had not been writing at this moment.

When I recovered my senses, it was to find that I had been in bed for nearly two weeks. Yet another week passed, before I was strong enough to totter out into the gardens. Even then, I was not able to walk so far as the Pit. I would have liked to ask my sister, how high the water had risen; but felt it was wiser not to mention the subject to her. Indeed, since then, I have made a rule never to speak to her about the strange things, that happen in this great, old house.

It was not until a couple of days later, that I managed to get across to the Pit. There, I found that, in my few weeks' absence, there had been wrought a wondrous change. Instead of the three-parts filled ravine, I looked out upon a great lake, whose placid surface, reflected the light, coldly. The water had risen to within half a dozen feet of the Pit edge. Only in one part was the lake disturbed, and that was above the place where, far down under the silent waters, yawned the entrance to the vast, underground Pit. Here, there was a continuous bubbling; and, occasionally, a curious sort of sobbing gurgle would find its way up from the depth. Beyond these, there was nothing to tell of the things that were hidden beneath. As I stood there, it came to me how wonderfully things had worked out. The entrance to the place whence the Swine-creatures had come, was sealed up, by a power that made me feel there was nothing more to fear from them. And yet, with the feeling, there was a sensation that, now, I should never learn anything further, of the place from which those dreadful Things had come. It was completely shut off and concealed from human curiosity forever.

Strange – in the knowledge of that underground hell-hole – how apposite has been the naming of the Pit. One wonders how it originated, and when. Naturally, one concludes that the shape and depth of the ravine would suggest the name 'Pit.' Yet, is it not possible that it has, all along, held a deeper significance, a hint – could one but have guessed – of the greater, more stupendous Pit that lies far down in the earth, beneath this old house? Under this house! Even now, the idea is strange and terrible to me. For I have proved, beyond doubt, that the Pit yawns right below the house, which is evidently supported, somewhere above the center of it, upon a tremendous, arched roof, of solid rock.

It happened in this wise, that, having occasion to go down to the cellars, the thought occurred to me to pay a visit to the great vault, where the trap is situated; and see whether everything was as I had left it.

Reaching the place, I walked slowly up the center, until I came to the trap. There it was, with the stones piled upon it, just as I had seen it last. I had a lantern with me, and the idea came to me, that now would be a good time to investigate whatever lay under the great, oak slab. Placing the lantern on the floor, I tumbled the stones off the trap, and, grasping the ring, pulled the door open. As I did so, the cellar became filled with the sound of a murmurous thunder, that rose from far below. At the same time, a damp wind blew up into my face, bringing with it a load of fine spray. Therewith, I dropped the trap, hurriedly, with a half frightened feeling of wonder.

For a moment, I stood puzzled. I was not particularly afraid. The haunting fear of the Swine-things had left me, long ago; but I was certainly nervous and astonished. Then, a sudden thought possessed me, and I raised the ponderous door, with a feeling of excitement. Leaving it standing upon its end, I seized the lantern, and, kneeling down, thrust it into the opening. As I did so, the moist wind and spray drove in my eyes, making me unable to see, for a few moments. Even when my eyes were clear, I could distinguish nothing below me, save darkness, and whirling spray.

Seeing that it was useless to expect to make out anything, with the light so high, I felt in my pockets for a piece of twine, with which to lower it further into the opening. Even as I fumbled, the lantern slipped from my fingers, and hurtled down into the darkness. For a brief instant, I watched its fall, and saw the light shine on a tumult of white foam, some eighty or a hundred feet below me. Then it was gone. My sudden surmise was correct, and now, I knew the cause of the wet and noise. The great cellar was connected with the Pit, by means of the trap, which opened right above it; and the moisture, was the spray, rising from the water, falling into the depths.

In an instant, I had an explanation of certain things, that had hitherto puzzled me. Now, I could understand why the noises – on the first night of the invasion – had seemed to rise directly from under my feet. And the chuckle that had sounded when first I opened the trap! Evidently, some of the Swine-things must have been right beneath me.

Another thought struck me. Were the creatures all drowned? Would they drown? I remembered how unable I had been to find any traces to show that my shooting had been really fatal. Had they life, as we understand life, or were they ghouls? These thoughts flashed through my brain, as I stood in the dark, searching my pockets for matches. I had the box in my hand now, and, striking a light, I stepped to the trap door, and closed it. Then, I piled the stones back upon it; after which, I made my way out from the cellars.

And so, I suppose the water goes on, thundering down into that bottomless hell-pit. Sometimes, I have an inexplicable desire to go down to the great cellar, open the trap, and gaze into the impenetrable, spray-damp darkness. At times, the desire becomes almost overpowering, in its intensity. It is not mere curiosity, that prompts me; but more as though some unexplained influence were at work. Still, I never go; and intend to fight down the strange longing, and crush it; even as I would the unholy thought of self-destruction.

This idea of some intangible force being exerted, may seem reasonless. Yet, my instinct warns me, that it is not so. In these things, reason seems to me less to be trusted than instinct.

One thought there is, in closing, that impresses itself upon me, with ever growing insistence. It is, that I live in a very strange house; a very awful house. And I have begun to wonder whether I am doing wisely in staying here. Yet, if I left, where could I go, and still obtain the solitude, and the sense of her presence,[1] that alone make my old life bearable?

Chapter XIV
The Sea of Sleep

FOR A CONSIDERABLE period after the last incident which I have narrated in my diary, I had serious thoughts of leaving this house, and might have done so; but for the great and wonderful thing, of which I am about to write.

How well I was advised, in my heart, when I stayed on here – spite of those visions and sights of unknown and unexplainable things; for, had I not stayed, then I had not seen again the face of her I loved. Yes, though few know it, none now save my sister Mary, I have loved and, ah! me – lost.

I would write down the story of those sweet, old days; but it would be like the tearing of old wounds; yet, after that which has happened, what need have I to care? For she has come to me out of the unknown. Strangely, she warned me; warned me passionately against this house; begged me to leave it; but admitted, when I questioned her, that she could not have come to me, had I been elsewhere. Yet, in spite of this, still she warned me, earnestly; telling me that it was a place, long ago given over to evil, and under the power of grim laws, of which none here have knowledge. And I – I just asked her, again, whether she would come to me elsewhere, and she could only stand, silent.

It was thus, that I came to the place of the Sea of Sleep – so she termed it, in her dear speech with me. I had stayed up, in my study, reading; and must have dozed over the book. Suddenly, I awoke and sat upright, with a start. For a moment, I looked 'round, with a puzzled sense of something unusual. There was a misty look about the room, giving a curious softness to each table and chair and furnishing.

Gradually, the mistiness increased; growing, as it were, out of nothing. Then, slowly, a soft, white light began to glow in the room. The flames of the candles shone through it, palely. I looked from side to side, and found that I could still see each piece of furniture; but in a strangely unreal way, more as though the ghost of each table and chair had taken the place of the solid article.

Gradually, as I looked, I saw them fade and fade; until, slowly, they resolved into nothingness. Now, I looked again at the candles. They shone wanly, and, even as I watched, grew more unreal, and so vanished. The room was filled, now, with a soft, yet luminous, white twilight, like a gentle mist of light. Beyond this, I could see nothing. Even the walls had vanished.

Presently, I became conscious that a faint, continuous sound, pulsed through the silence that wrapped me. I listened intently. It grew more distinct, until it appeared to me that I harked to the breathings of some great sea. I cannot tell how long a space passed thus; but, after a while, it seemed that I could see through the mistiness; and, slowly, I became aware that I was standing upon the shore of an immense and silent sea. This shore was smooth and long, vanishing to right and left of me, in extreme distances. In front, swam a still immensity of sleeping ocean. At times, it seemed to me that I caught a faint glimmer of light, under its surface; but of this, I could not be sure. Behind me, rose up, to an extraordinary height, gaunt, black cliffs.

Overhead, the sky was of a uniform cold grey color – the whole place being lit by a stupendous globe of pale fire, that swam a little above the far horizon, and shed a foamlike light above the quiet waters.

Beyond the gentle murmur of the sea, an intense stillness prevailed. For a long while, I stayed there, looking out across its strangeness. Then, as I stared, it seemed that a bubble of white foam floated up out of the depths, and then, even now I know not how it was, I was looking upon, nay, looking *into* the face of Her – aye! into her face – into her soul; and she looked back at me, with such a commingling of joy and sadness, that I ran toward her, blindly; crying strangely to her, in a very agony of remembrance, of terror, and of hope, to come to me. Yet, spite of my crying, she stayed out there upon the sea, and only shook her head, sorrowfully; but, in her eyes was the old earth-light of tenderness, that I had come to know, before all things, ere we were parted.

"At her perverseness, I grew desperate, and essayed to wade out to her; yet, though I would, I could not. Something, some invisible barrier, held me back, and I was fain to stay where I was, and cry out to her in the fullness of my soul, 'O, my Darling, my Darling—' but could say no more, for very intensity. And, at that, she came over, swiftly, and touched me and it was as though heaven had opened. Yet, when I reached out my hands to her, she put me from her with tenderly stern hands, and I was abashed—"

The Fragments[2]
The Legible Portions of the Mutilated Leaves

...through tears...noise of eternity in my ears, we parted... She whom I love. O, my God...!

I was a great time dazed, and then I was alone in the blackness of the night. I knew that I journeyed back, once more, to the known universe. Presently, I emerged from that enormous darkness. I had come among the stars...vast time...the sun, far and remote.

I entered into the gulf that separates our system from the outer suns. As I sped across the dividing dark, I watched, steadily, the ever-growing brightness and size of our sun. Once, I glanced back to the stars, and saw them shift, as it were, in my wake, against the mighty background of night, so vast was the speed of my passing spirit.

I drew nigher to our system, and now I could see the shine of Jupiter. Later, I distinguished the cold, blue gleam of the earthlight.... I had a moment of bewilderment. All about the sun there seemed to be bright, objects, moving in rapid orbits. Inward, nigh to the savage glory of the sun, there circled two darting points of light, and, further off, there flew a blue, shining speck, that I knew to be the earth. It circled the sun in a space that seemed to be no more than an earth-minute.

... nearer with great speed. I saw the radiances of Jupiter and Saturn, spinning, with incredible swiftness, in huge orbits. And ever I drew more nigh, and looked out upon this strange sight – the visible circling of the planets about the mother sun. It was as though time had been annihilated for me; so that a year was no more to my unfleshed spirit, than is a moment to an earth-bound soul.

The speed of the planets, appeared to increase; and, presently, I was watching the sun, all ringed about with hairlike circles of different colored fire – the paths of the planets, hurtling at mighty speed, about the central flame....

"...the sun grew vast, as though it leapt to meet me.... And now I was within the circling of the outer planets, and flitting swiftly, toward the place where the earth, glimmering through the blue splendor of its orbit, as though a fiery mist, circled the sun at a monstrous speed...." [3]

Chapter XV
The Noise in the Night

AND NOW, I come to the strangest of all the strange happenings that have befallen me in this house of mysteries. It occurred quite lately – within the month; and I have little doubt but that what I saw was in reality the end of all things. However, to my story.

I do not know how it is; but, up to the present, I have never been able to write these things down, directly they happened. It is as though I have to wait a time, recovering my just balance, and digesting – as it were – the things I have heard or seen. No doubt, this is as it should be; for, by waiting, I see the incidents more truly, and write of them in a calmer and more judicial frame of mind. This by the way.

It is now the end of November. My story relates to what happened in the first week of the month.

It was night, about eleven o'clock. Pepper and I kept one another company in the study – that great, old room of mine, where I read and work. I was reading, curiously enough, the Bible. I have begun, in these later days, to take a growing interest in that great and ancient book. Suddenly, a distinct tremor shook the house, and there came a faint and distant, whirring buzz, that grew rapidly into a far, muffled screaming. It reminded me, in a queer, gigantic way, of the noise that a clock makes, when the catch is released, and it is allowed to run down. The sound appeared to come from some remote height – somewhere up in the night. There was no repetition of the shock. I looked across at Pepper. He was sleeping peacefully.

Gradually, the whirring noise decreased, and there came a long silence.

All at once, a glow lit up the end window, which protrudes far out from the side of the house, so that, from it, one may look both East and West. I felt puzzled, and, after a moment's hesitation, walked across the room, and pulled aside the blind. As I did so, I saw the Sun rise, from behind the horizon. It rose with a steady, perceptible movement. I could see it travel upward. In a minute, it seemed, it had reached the tops of the trees, through which I had watched it. Up, up – It was broad daylight now. Behind me, I was conscious of a sharp, mosquitolike buzzing. I glanced 'round, and knew that it came from the clock. Even as I looked, it marked off an hour. The minute hand was moving 'round the dial, faster than an ordinary second-hand. The hour hand moved quickly from space to space. I had a numb sense of astonishment. A moment later, so it seemed, the two candles went out, almost together. I turned swiftly back to the window; for I had seen the shadow of the window-frames, traveling along the floor toward me, as though a great lamp had been carried up past the window.

I saw now, that the sun had risen high into the heavens, and was still visibly moving. It passed above the house, with an extraordinary sailing kind of motion. As the window came into shadow, I saw another extraordinary thing. The fine-weather clouds were not passing, easily, across the sky – they were scampering, as though a hundred-mile-an-hour wind blew. As they passed, they changed their shapes a thousand times a minute, as though writhing with a strange life; and so were gone. And, presently, others came, and whisked away likewise.

To the West, I saw the sun, drop with an incredible, smooth, swift motion. Eastward, the shadows of every seen thing crept toward the coming greyness. And the movement of the shadows was visible to me – a stealthy, writhing creep of the shadows of the wind-stirred trees. It was a strange sight.

Quickly, the room began to darken. The sun slid down to the horizon, and seemed, as it were, to disappear from my sight, almost with a jerk. Through the greyness of the swift evening, I saw the silver crescent of the moon, falling out of the Southern sky, toward the West. The evening seemed to merge into an almost instant night. Above me, the many constellations passed in a strange, 'noiseless' circling, Westward. The moon fell through that last thousand fathoms of the night-gulf, and there was only the starlight….

About this time, the buzzing in the corner ceased; telling me that the clock had run down. A few minutes passed, and I saw the Eastward sky lighten. A grey, sullen morning spread through all the darkness, and hid the march of the stars. Overhead, there moved, with a heavy, everlasting rolling, a vast, seamless sky of grey clouds – a cloud-sky that would have seemed motionless, through all the length of an ordinary earth-day. The sun was hidden from me; but, from moment to moment, the world would brighten and darken, brighten and darken, beneath waves of subtle light and shadow....

The light shifted ever Westward, and the night fell upon the earth. A vast rain seemed to come with it, and a wind of a most extraordinary loudness – as though the howling of a nightlong gale, were packed into the space of no more than a minute.

This noise passed, almost immediately, and the clouds broke; so that, once more, I could see the sky. The stars were flying Westward, with astounding speed. It came to me now, for the first time, that, though the noise of the wind had passed, yet a constant 'blurred' sound was in my ears. Now that I noticed it, I was aware that it had been with me all the time. It was the world-noise.

And then, even as I grasped at so much comprehension, there came the Eastward light. No more than a few heartbeats, and the sun rose, swiftly. Through the trees, I saw it, and then it was above the trees. Up – up, it soared and all the world was light. It passed, with a swift, steady swing to its highest altitude, and fell thence, Westward. I saw the day roll visibly over my head. A few light clouds flittered Northward, and vanished. The sun went down with one swift, clear plunge, and there was about me, for a few seconds, the darker growing grey of the gloaming.

Southward and Westward, the moon was sinking rapidly. The night had come, already. A minute it seemed, and the moon fell those remaining fathoms of dark sky. Another minute, or so, and the Eastward sky glowed with the coming dawn. The sun leapt upon me with a frightening abruptness, and soared ever more swiftly toward the zenith. Then, suddenly, a fresh thing came to my sight. A black thundercloud rushed up out of the South, and seemed to leap all the arc of the sky, in a single instant. As it came, I saw that its advancing edge flapped, like a monstrous black cloth in the heaven, twirling and undulating rapidly, with a horrid suggestiveness. In an instant, all the air was full of rain, and a hundred lightning flashes seemed to flood downward, as it were in one great shower. In the same second of time, the world-noise was drowned in the roar of the wind, and then my ears ached, under the stunning impact of the thunder.

And, in the midst of this storm, the night came; and then, within the space of another minute, the storm had passed, and there was only the constant 'blur' of the world-noise on my hearing. Overhead, the stars were sliding quickly Westward; and something, mayhaps the particular speed to which they had attained, brought home to me, for the first time, a keen realization of the knowledge that it was the world that revolved. I seemed to see, suddenly, the world – a vast, dark mass – revolving visibly against the stars.

The dawn and the sun seemed to come together, so greatly had the speed of the world-revolution increased. The sun drove up, in one long, steady curve; passed its highest point, and swept down into the Western sky, and disappeared. I was scarcely conscious of evening, so brief was it. Then I was watching the flying constellations, and the Westward hastening moon. In but a space of seconds, so it seemed, it was sliding swiftly downward through the night-blue, and then was gone. And, almost directly, came the morning.

And now there seemed to come a strange acceleration. The sun made one clean, clear sweep through the sky, and disappeared behind the Westward horizon, and the night came and went with a like haste.

As the succeeding day, opened and closed upon the world, I was aware of a sweat of snow, suddenly upon the earth. The night came, and, almost immediately, the day. In the brief leap of the sun, I saw that the snow had vanished; and then, once more, it was night.

Thus matters were; and, even after the many incredible things that I have seen, I experienced all the time a most profound awe. To see the sun rise and set, within a space of time to be measured by seconds; to watch (after a little) the moon leap – a pale, and ever growing orb

– up into the night sky, and glide, with a strange swiftness, through the vast arc of blue; and, presently, to see the sun follow, springing out of the Eastern sky, as though in chase; and then again the night, with the swift and ghostly passing of starry constellations, was all too much to view believingly. Yet, so it was – the day slipping from dawn to dusk, and the night sliding swiftly into day, ever rapidly and more rapidly.

The last three passages of the sun had shown me a snow-covered earth, which, at night, had seemed, for a few seconds, incredibly weird under the fast-shifting light of the soaring and falling moon. Now, however, for a little space, the sky was hidden, by a sea of swaying, leaden-white clouds, which lightened and blackened, alternately, with the passage of day and night.

The clouds rippled and vanished, and there was once more before me, the vision of the swiftly leaping sun, and nights that came and went like shadows.

Faster and faster, spun the world. And now each day and night was completed within the space of but a few seconds; and still the speed increased.

It was a little later, that I noticed that the sun had begun to have the suspicion of a trail of fire behind it. This was due, evidently, to the speed at which it, apparently, traversed the heavens. And, as the days sped, each one quicker than the last, the sun began to assume the appearance of a vast, flaming comet[4] flaring across the sky at short, periodic intervals. At night, the moon presented, with much greater truth, a cometlike aspect; a pale, and singularly clear, fast traveling shape of fire, trailing streaks of cold flame. The stars showed now, merely as fine hairs of fire against the dark.

Once, I turned from the window, and glanced at Pepper. In the flash of a day, I saw that he slept, quietly, and I moved once more to my watching.

The sun was now bursting up from the Eastern horizon, like a stupendous rocket, seeming to occupy no more than a second or two in hurling from East to West. I could no longer perceive the passage of clouds across the sky, which seemed to have darkened somewhat. The brief nights, appeared to have lost the proper darkness of night; so that the hairlike fire of the flying stars, showed but dimly. As the speed increased, the sun began to sway very slowly in the sky, from South to North, and then, slowly again, from North to South.

So, amid a strange confusion of mind, the hours passed.

All this while had Pepper slept. Presently, feeling lonely and distraught, I called to him, softly; but he took no notice. Again, I called, raising my voice slightly; still he moved not. I walked over to where he lay, and touched him with my foot, to rouse him. At the action, gentle though it was, he fell to pieces. That is what happened; he literally and actually crumbled into a mouldering heap of bones and dust.

For the space of, perhaps a minute, I stared down at the shapeless heap, that had once been Pepper. I stood, feeling stunned. What can have happened? I asked myself; not at once grasping the grim significance of that little hill of ash. Then, as I stirred the heap with my foot, it occurred to me that this could only happen in a great space of time. Years – and years.

Outside, the weaving, fluttering light held the world. Inside, I stood, trying to understand what it meant – what that little pile of dust and dry bones, on the carpet, meant. But I could not think, coherently.

I glanced away, 'round the room, and now, for the first time, noticed how dusty and old the place looked. Dust and dirt everywhere; piled in little heaps in the corners, and spread about upon the furniture. The very carpet, itself, was invisible beneath a coating of the same, all pervading, material. As I walked, little clouds of the stuff rose up from under my footsteps, and assailed my nostrils, with a dry, bitter odor that made me wheeze, huskily.

Suddenly, as my glance fell again upon Pepper's remains, I stood still, and gave voice to my confusion – questioning, aloud, whether the years were, indeed, passing; whether this, which I had taken to be a form of vision, was, in truth, a reality. I paused. A new thought had struck me. Quickly, but with steps which, for the first time, I noticed, tottered, I went across the room to the great pier-glass, and looked in. It was too covered with grime, to give back any reflection, and, with trembling hands, I began to rub off the dirt. Presently, I could see myself. The thought that had come to me, was confirmed. Instead of the great, hale man, who scarcely looked fifty, I was looking at a bent, decrepit man, whose shoulders stooped, and whose face was wrinkled with the years of a century. The hair – which a few short hours ago had been nearly coal black – was now silvery white. Only the eyes were bright. Gradually, I traced, in that ancient man, a faint resemblance to my self of other days.

I turned away, and tottered to the window. I knew, now, that I was old, and the knowledge seemed to confirm my trembling walk. For a little space, I stared moodily out into the blurred vista of changeful landscape. Even in that short time, a year passed, and, with a petulant gesture, I left the window. As I did so, I noticed that my hand shook with the palsy of old age; and a short sob choked its way through my lips.

For a little while, I paced, tremulously, between the window and the table; my gaze wandering hither and thither, uneasily. How dilapidated the room was. Everywhere lay the thick dust – thick, sleepy, and black. The fender was a shape of rust. The chains that held the brass clock-weights, had rusted through long ago, and now the weights lay on the floor beneath; themselves two cones of verdigris.

As I glanced about, it seemed to me that I could see the very furniture of the room rotting and decaying before my eyes. Nor was this fancy, on my part; for, all at once, the bookshelf, along the sidewall, collapsed, with a cracking and rending of rotten wood, precipitating its contents upon the floor, and filling the room with a smother of dusty atoms.

How tired I felt. As I walked, it seemed that I could hear my dry joints, creak and crack at every step. I wondered about my sister. Was she dead, as well as Pepper? All had happened so quickly and suddenly. This must be, indeed, the beginning of the end of all things! It occurred to me, to go to look for her; but I felt too weary. And then, she had been so queer about these happenings, of late. Of late! I repeated the words, and laughed, feebly – mirthlessly, as the realization was borne in upon me that I spoke of a time, half a century gone. Half a century! It might have been twice as long!

I moved slowly to the window, and looked out once more across the world. I can best describe the passage of day and night, at this period, as a sort of gigantic, ponderous flicker. Moment by moment, the acceleration of time continued; so that, at nights now, I saw the moon, only as a swaying trail of palish fire, that varied from a mere line of light to a nebulous path, and then dwindled again, disappearing periodically.

The flicker of the days and nights quickened. The days had grown perceptibly darker, and a queer quality of dusk lay, as it were, in the atmosphere. The nights were so much lighter, that the stars were scarcely to be seen, saving here and there an occasional hairlike line of fire, that seemed to sway a little, with the moon.

Quicker, and ever quicker, ran the flicker of day and night; and, suddenly it seemed, I was aware that the flicker had died out, and, instead, there reigned a comparatively steady light, which was shed upon all the world, from an eternal river of flame that swung up and down, North and South, in stupendous, mighty swings.

The sky was now grown very much darker, and there was in the blue of it a heavy gloom, as though a vast blackness peered through it upon the earth. Yet, there was in it, also, a strange and awful clearness, and emptiness. Periodically, I had glimpses of a ghostly track of fire that swayed thin and darkly toward the sun-stream; vanished and reappeared. It was the scarcely visible moon-stream.

Looking out at the landscape, I was conscious again, of a blurring sort of 'flitter,' that came either from the light of the ponderous-swinging sun-stream, or was the result of the incredibly rapid changes of the earth's surface. And every few moments, so it seemed, the snow would lie suddenly upon the world, and vanish as abruptly, as though an invisible giant 'flitted' a white sheet off and on the earth.

Time fled, and the weariness that was mine, grew insupportable. I turned from the window, and walked once across the room, the heavy dust deadening the sound of my footsteps. Each step that I took, seemed a greater effort than the one before. An intolerable ache, knew me in every joint and limb, as I trod my way, with a weary uncertainty.

By the opposite wall, I came to a weak pause, and wondered, dimly, what was my intent. I looked to my left, and saw my old chair. The thought of sitting in it brought a faint sense of comfort to my bewildered wretchedness. Yet, because I was so weary and old and tired, I would scarcely brace my mind to do anything but stand, and wish myself past those few yards. I rocked, as I stood. The floor, even, seemed a place for rest; but the dust lay so thick and sleepy and black. I turned, with a great effort of will, and made toward my chair. I reached it, with a groan of thankfulness. I sat down.

Everything about me appeared to be growing dim. It was all so strange and unthought of. Last night, I was a comparatively strong, though elderly man; and now, only a few hours later – ! I looked at the little dust-heap that had once been Pepper. Hours! and I laughed, a feeble, bitter laugh; a shrill, cackling laugh, that shocked my dimming senses.

For a while, I must have dozed. Then I opened my eyes, with a start. Somewhere across the room, there had been a muffled noise of something falling. I looked, and saw, vaguely, a cloud of dust hovering above a pile of *débris*. Nearer the door, something else tumbled, with a crash. It was one of the cupboards; but I was tired, and took little notice. I closed my eyes, and sat there in a state of drowsy, semi-unconsciousness. Once or twice – as though coming through thick mists – I heard noises, faintly. Then I must have slept.

Chapter XVI
The Awakening

I AWOKE, with a start. For a moment, I wondered where I was. Then memory came to me....

The room was still lit with that strange light – half-sun, half-moon, light. I felt refreshed, and the tired, weary ache had left me. I went slowly across to the window, and looked out. Overhead, the river of flame drove up and down, North and South, in a dancing semi-circle of fire. As a mighty sleigh in the loom of time it seemed – in a sudden fancy of mine – to be beating home the picks of the years. For, so vastly had the passage of time been accelerated, that there was no longer any sense of the sun passing from East to West. The only apparent movement was the North and South beat of the sun-stream, that had become so swift now, as to be better described as a *quiver*.

As I peered out, there came to me a sudden, inconsequent memory of that last journey among the Outer worlds. I remembered the sudden vision that had come to me, as I neared the Solar System, of the fast whirling planets about the sun – as though the governing quality of time had been held in abeyance, and the Machine of a Universe allowed to run down an eternity, in a few moments or hours. The memory passed, along with a, but partially comprehended, suggestion that I had been permitted a glimpse into further time spaces. I stared out again, seemingly, at the quake of the sun-stream. The speed seemed to increase, even as I looked. Several lifetimes came and went, as I watched.

Suddenly, it struck me, with a sort of grotesque seriousness, that I was still alive. I thought of Pepper, and wondered how it was that I had not followed his fate. He had reached the time of his dying, and had passed, probably through sheer length of years. And here was I, alive, hundreds of thousands of centuries after my rightful period of years.

For, a time, I mused, absently. 'Yesterday—' I stopped, suddenly. Yesterday! There was no yesterday. The yesterday of which I spoke had been swallowed up in the abyss of years, ages gone. I grew dazed with much thinking.

Presently, I turned from the window, and glanced 'round the room. It seemed different – strangely, utterly different. Then, I knew what it was that made it appear so strange. It was bare: there was not a piece of furniture in the room; not even a solitary fitting of any sort. Gradually, my amazement went, as I remembered, that this was but the inevitable end of that process of decay, which I had witnessed commencing, before my sleep. Thousands of years! Millions of years!

Over the floor was spread a deep layer of dust, that reached half way up to the window-seat. It had grown immeasurably, whilst I slept; and represented the dust of untold ages. Undoubtedly, atoms of the old, decayed furniture helped to swell its bulk; and, somewhere among it all, mouldered the long-ago-dead Pepper.

All at once, it occurred to me, that I had no recollection of wading knee-deep through all that dust, after I awoke. True, an incredible age of years had passed, since I approached the window; but that was evidently as nothing, compared with the countless spaces of time that, I conceived, had vanished whilst I was sleeping. I remembered now, that I had fallen asleep, sitting in my old chair. Had it gone…? I glanced toward where it had stood. Of course, there was no chair to be seen. I could not satisfy myself, whether it had disappeared, after my waking, or before. If it had mouldered under me, surely, I should have been waked by the collapse. Then I remembered that the thick dust, which covered the floor, would have been sufficient to soften my fall; so that it was quite possible, I had slept upon the dust for a million years or more.

As these thoughts wandered through my brain, I glanced again, casually, to where the chair had stood. Then, for the first time, I noticed that there were no marks, in the dust, of my footprints, between it and the window. But then, ages of years had passed, since I had awaked – tens of thousands of years!

My look rested thoughtfully, again upon the place where once had stood my chair. Suddenly, I passed from abstraction to intentness; for there, in its standing place, I made out a long undulation, rounded off with the heavy dust. Yet it was not so much hidden, but that I could tell what had caused it. I knew – and shivered at the knowledge – that it was a human body, ages-dead, lying there, beneath the place where I had slept. It was lying on its right side, its back turned toward me. I could make out and trace each curve and outline, softened, and moulded, as it were, in the black dust. In a vague sort of way, I tried to account for its presence there. Slowly, I began to grow bewildered, as the thought came to me that it lay just about where I must have fallen when the chair collapsed.

Gradually, an idea began to form itself within my brain; a thought that shook my spirit. It seemed hideous and insupportable; yet it grew upon me, steadily, until it became a conviction. The body under that coating, that shroud of dust, was neither more nor less than my own dead shell. I did not attempt to prove it. I knew it now, and wondered I had not known it all along. I was a bodiless thing.

Awhile, I stood, trying to adjust my thoughts to this new problem. In time – how many thousands of years, I know not – I attained to some degree of quietude – sufficient to enable me to pay attention to what was transpiring around me.

Now, I saw that the elongated mound had sunk, collapsed, level with the rest of the spreading dust. And fresh atoms, impalpable, had settled above that mixture of grave-powder, which the aeons had ground. A long while, I stood, turned from the window. Gradually, I grew more collected, while the world slipped across the centuries into the future.

Presently, I began a survey of the room. Now, I saw that time was beginning its destructive work, even on this strange old building. That it had stood through all the years was, it seemed to me, proof that it was something different from any other house. I do not think, somehow, that I had thought of its decaying. Though, why, I could not have said. It was not until I had meditated upon the matter, for some considerable time, that I fully realized that the extraordinary space of time through which it had stood, was sufficient to have utterly pulverized the very stones of which it was built, had they been taken from any earthly quarry. Yes, it was undoubtedly mouldering now. All the plaster had gone from the walls; even as the woodwork of the room had gone, many ages before.

While I stood, in contemplation, a piece of glass, from one of the small, diamond-shaped panes, dropped, with a dull tap, amid the dust upon the sill behind me, and crumbled into a little heap of powder. As I turned from contemplating it, I saw light between a couple of the stones that formed the outer wall. Evidently, the mortar was falling away....

After awhile, I turned once more to the window, and peered out. I discovered, now, that the speed of time had become enormous. The lateral quiver of the sun-stream, had grown so swift as to cause the dancing semi-circle of flame to merge into, and disappear in, a sheet of fire that covered half the Southern sky from East to West.

From the sky, I glanced down to the gardens. They were just a blur of a palish, dirty green. I had a feeling that they stood higher, than in the old days; a feeling that they were nearer my window, as though they had risen, bodily. Yet, they were still a long way below me; for the rock, over the mouth of the pit, on which this house stands, arches up to a great height.

It was later, that I noticed a change in the constant color of the gardens. The pale, dirty green was growing ever paler and paler, toward white. At last, after a great space, they became greyish-white, and stayed thus for a very long time. Finally, however, the greyness began to fade, even as had the green, into a dead white. And this remained, constant and unchanged. And by this I knew that, at last, snow lay upon all the Northern world.

And so, by millions of years, time winged onward through eternity, to the end – the end, of which, in the old-earth days, I had thought remotely, and in hazily speculative fashion. And now, it was approaching in a manner of which none had ever dreamed.

I recollect that, about this time, I began to have a lively, though morbid, curiosity, as to what would happen when the end came – but I seemed strangely without imaginings.

All this while, the steady process of decay was continuing. The few remaining pieces of glass, had long ago vanished; and, every now and then, a soft thud, and a little cloud of rising dust, would tell of some fragment of fallen mortar or stone.

I looked up again, to the fiery sheet that quaked in the heavens above me and far down into the Southern sky. As I looked, the impression was borne in upon me, that it had lost some of its first brilliancy – that it was duller, deeper hued.

I glanced down, once more, to the blurred white of the worldscape. Sometimes, my look returned to the burning sheet of dulling flame, that was, and yet hid, the sun. At times, I glanced behind me, into the growing dusk of the great, silent room, with its aeon-carpet of sleeping dust....

So, I watched through the fleeting ages, lost in soul-wearing thoughts and wonderings, and possessed with a new weariness.

Chapter XVII
The Slowing Rotation

IT MIGHT HAVE BEEN a million years later, that I perceived, beyond possibility of doubt, that the fiery sheet that lit the world, was indeed darkening.

Another vast space went by, and the whole enormous flame had sunk to a deep, copper color. Gradually, it darkened, from copper to copper-red, and from this, at times, to a deep, heavy, purplish tint, with, in it, a strange loom of blood.

Although the light was decreasing, I could perceive no diminishment in the apparent speed of the sun. It still spread itself in that dazzling veil of speed.

The world, so much of it as I could see, had assumed a dreadful shade of gloom, as though, in very deed, the last day of the worlds approached.

The sun was dying; of that there could be little doubt; and still the earth whirled onward, through space and all the aeons. At this time, I remember, an extraordinary sense of bewilderment took me. I found myself, later, wandering, mentally, amid an odd chaos of fragmentary modern theories and the old Biblical story of the world's ending.

Then, for the first time, there flashed across me, the memory that the sun, with its system of planets, was, and had been, traveling through space at an incredible speed. Abruptly, the question rose – *Where?* For a very great time, I pondered this matter; but, finally, with a certain sense of the futility of my puzzlings, I let my thoughts wander to other things. I grew to wondering, how much longer the house would stand. Also, I queried, to myself, whether I should be doomed to stay, bodiless, upon the earth, through the dark-time that I knew was coming. From these thoughts, I fell again to speculations upon the possible direction of the sun's journey through space.... And so another great while passed.

Gradually, as time fled, I began to feel the chill of a great winter. Then, I remembered that, with the sun dying, the cold must be, necessarily, extraordinarily intense. Slowly, slowly, as the aeons slipped into eternity, the earth sank into a heavier and redder gloom. The dull flame in the firmament took on a deeper tint, very somber and turbid.

Then, at last, it was borne upon me that there was a change. The fiery, gloomy curtain of flame that hung quaking overhead, and down away into the Southern sky, began to thin and contract; and, in it, as one sees the fast vibrations of a jarred harp-string, I saw once more the sun-stream quivering, giddily, North and South.

Slowly, the likeness to a sheet of fire, disappeared, and I saw, plainly, the slowing beat of the sun-stream. Yet, even then, the speed of its swing was inconceivably swift. And all the time, the brightness of the fiery arc grew ever duller. Underneath, the world loomed dimly – an indistinct, ghostly region.

Overhead, the river of flame swayed slower, and even slower; until, at last, it swung to the North and South in great, ponderous beats, that lasted through seconds. A long space went by, and now each sway of the great belt lasted nigh a minute; so that, after a great while, I ceased to distinguish it as a visible movement; and the streaming fire ran in a steady river of dull flame, across the deadly-looking sky.

An indefinite period passed, and it seemed that the arc of fire became less sharply defined. It appeared to me to grow more attenuated, and I thought blackish streaks showed, occasionally. Presently, as I watched, the smooth onward-flow ceased; and I was able to perceive that there came a momentary, but regular, darkening of the world. This grew until, once more, night descended, in short, but periodic, intervals upon the wearying earth.

Longer and longer became the nights, and the days equaled them; so that, at last, the day and the night grew to the duration of seconds in length, and the sun showed, once more, like an almost invisible, coppery-red colored ball, within the glowing mistiness of its flight. Corresponding to the dark lines, showing at times in its trail, there were now distinctly to be seen on the half-visible sun itself, great, dark belts.

Year after year flashed into the past, and the days and nights spread into minutes. The sun had ceased to have the appearance of a tail; and now rose and set – a tremendous globe of a glowing copper-bronze hue; in parts ringed with blood-red bands; in others, with the dusky ones, that I have already mentioned. These circles – both red and black – were of varying thicknesses. For a time, I was at a loss to account for their presence. Then it occurred to me, that it was scarcely likely that the sun would cool evenly all over; and that these markings were due, probably, to differences in temperature of the various areas; the red representing those parts where the heat was still fervent, and the black those portions which were already comparatively cool.

It struck me, as a peculiar thing, that the sun should cool in evenly defined rings; until I remembered that, possibly, they were but isolated patches, to which the enormous rotatory speed of the sun had imparted a beltlike appearance. The sun, itself, was very much greater than the sun I had known in the old-world days; and, from this, I argued that it was considerably nearer.

At nights, the moon[5] still showed; but small and remote; and the light she reflected was so dull and weak that she seemed little more than the small, dim ghost of the olden moon, that I had known.

Gradually, the days and nights lengthened out, until they equaled a space somewhat less than one of the old-earth hours; the sun rising and setting like a great, ruddy bronze disk, crossed with ink-black bars. About this time, I found myself, able once more, to see the gardens, with clearness. For the world had now grown very still, and changeless. Yet, I am not correct in saying, 'gardens'; for there were no gardens – nothing that I knew or recognized. In place thereof, I looked out upon a vast plain, stretching away into distance. A little to my left, there was a low range of hills. Everywhere, there was a uniform, white covering of snow, in places rising into hummocks and ridges.

It was only now, that I recognized how really great had been the snowfall. In places it was vastly deep, as was witnessed by a great, upleaping, wave-shaped hill, away to my right; though it is not impossible, that this was due, in part, to some rise in the surface of the ground. Strangely enough, the range of low hills to my left – already mentioned – was not entirely covered with the universal snow; instead, I could see their bare, dark sides showing in several places. And everywhere and always there reigned an incredible death-silence and desolation. The immutable, awful quiet of a dying world.

All this time, the days and nights were lengthening, perceptibly. Already, each day occupied, maybe, some two hours from dawn to dusk. At night, I had been surprised to find that there were very few stars overhead, and these small, though of an extraordinary brightness; which I attributed to the peculiar, but clear, blackness of the nighttime.

Away to the North, I could discern a nebulous sort of mistiness; not unlike, in appearance, a small portion of the Milky Way. It might have been an extremely remote star-cluster; or – the thought came to me suddenly – perhaps it was the sidereal universe that I had known, and now left far behind, forever – a small, dimly glowing mist of stars, far in the depths of space.

Still, the days and nights lengthened, slowly. Each time, the sun rose duller than it had set. And the dark belts increased in breadth.

About this time, there happened a fresh thing. The sun, earth, and sky were suddenly darkened, and, apparently, blotted out for a brief space. I had a sense, a certain awareness (I could learn little by sight), that the earth was enduring a very great fall of snow. Then, in an instant, the veil that had obscured everything, vanished, and I looked out, once more. A marvelous sight met my gaze. The hollow in which this house, with its gardens, stands, was brimmed with snow.[6] It lipped over the sill of my window. Everywhere, it lay, a great level stretch of white, which caught and reflected, gloomily, the somber coppery glows of the dying sun. The world had become a shadowless plain, from horizon to horizon.

I glanced up at the sun. It shone with an extraordinary, dull clearness. I saw it, now, as one who, until then, had seen it, only through a partially obscuring medium. All about it, the sky had become black, with a clear, deep blackness, frightful in its nearness, and its unmeasured deep, and its utter unfriendliness. For a great time, I looked into it, newly, and shaken and fearful. It was so near. Had I been a child, I might have expressed some of my sensation and distress, by saying that the sky hád lost its roof.

Later, I turned, and peered about me, into the room. Everywhere, it was covered with a thin shroud of the all-pervading white. I could see it but dimly, by reason of the somber light that now lit the world. It appeared to cling to the ruined walls; and the thick, soft dust of the years, that covered the floor knee-deep, was nowhere visible. The snow must have blown in through the open framework of the windows. Yet, in no place had it drifted; but lay everywhere about the great, old room, smooth and level. Moreover, there had been no wind these many thousand years. But there was the snow,[7] as I have told.

And all the earth was silent. And there was a cold, such as no living man can ever have known.

The earth was now illuminated, by day, with a most doleful light, beyond my power to describe. It seemed as though I looked at the great plain, through the medium of a bronze-tinted sea.

It was evident that the earth's rotatory movement was departing, steadily.

The end came, all at once. The night had been the longest yet; and when the dying sun showed, at last, above the world's edge, I had grown so wearied of the dark, that I greeted it as a friend. It rose steadily, until about twenty degrees above the horizon. Then, it stopped suddenly, and, after a strange retrograde movement, hung motionless – a great shield in the sky.[8] Only the circular rim of the sun showed bright – only this, and one thin streak of light near the equator.

Gradually, even this thread of light died out; and now, all that was left of our great and glorious sun, was a vast dead disk, rimmed with a thin circle of bronze-red light.

Chapter XVIII
The Green Star

THE WORLD was held in a savage gloom – cold and intolerable. Outside, all was quiet – quiet! From the dark room behind me, came the occasional, soft thud[9] of falling matter – fragments of rotting stone. So time passed, and night grasped the world, wrapping it in wrappings of impenetrable blackness.

There was no night-sky, as we know it. Even the few straggling stars had vanished, conclusively. I might have been in a shuttered room, without a light; for all that I could see. Only, in the impalpableness of gloom, opposite, burnt that vast, encircling hair of dull fire. Beyond this, there was no ray in all the vastitude of night that surrounded me; save that, far in the North, that soft, mistlike glow still shone.

Silently, years moved on. What period of time passed, I shall never know. It seemed to me, waiting there, that eternities came and went, stealthily; and still I watched. I could see only the glow of the sun's edge, at times; for now, it had commenced to come and go – lighting up a while, and again becoming extinguished.

All at once, during one of these periods of life, a sudden flame cut across the night – a quick glare that lit up the dead earth, shortly; giving me a glimpse of its flat lonesomeness. The light appeared to come from the sun – shooting out from somewhere near its center, diagonally. A moment, I gazed, startled. Then the leaping flame sank, and the gloom fell again. But now it was not so dark; and the sun was belted by a thin line of vivid, white light. I stared, intently. Had a volcano broken out on the sun? Yet, I negatived the thought, as soon as formed. I felt that the light had been far too intensely white, and large, for such a cause.

Another idea there was, that suggested itself to me. It was, that one of the inner planets had fallen into the sun – becoming incandescent, under that impact. This theory appealed to me, as being more plausible, and accounting more satisfactorily for the extraordinary size and brilliance of the blaze, that had lit up the dead world, so unexpectedly.

Full of interest and emotion, I stared, across the darkness, at that line of white fire, cutting the night. One thing it told to me, unmistakably: the sun was yet rotating at an enormous speed.[10] Thus, I knew that the years were still fleeting at an incalculable rate; though so far as the earth was concerned, life, and light, and time, were things belonging to a period lost in the long gone ages.

After that one burst of flame, the light had shown, only as an encircling band of bright fire. Now, however, as I watched, it began slowly to sink into a ruddy tint, and, later, to a dark, copper-red color; much as the sun had done. Presently, it sank to a deeper hue; and, in a still further space of time, it began to fluctuate; having periods of glowing, and anon, dying. Thus, after a great while, it disappeared.

Long before this, the smoldering edge of the sun had deadened into blackness. And so, in that supremely future time, the world, dark and intensely silent, rode on its gloomy orbit around the ponderous mass of the dead sun.

My thoughts, at this period, can be scarcely described. At first, they were chaotic and wanting in coherence. But, later, as the ages came and went, my soul seemed to imbibe the very essence of the oppressive solitude and dreariness, that held the earth.

With this feeling, there came a wonderful clearness of thought, and I realized, despairingly, that the world might wander for ever, through that enormous night. For a while, the unwholesome idea filled me, with a sensation of overbearing desolation; so that I could have cried like a child. In time, however, this feeling grew, almost insensibly, less, and an unreasoning hope possessed me. Patiently, I waited.

From time to time, the noise of dropping particles, behind in the room, came dully to my ears. Once, I heard a loud crash, and turned, instinctively, to look; forgetting, for the moment, the impenetrable night in which every detail was submerged. In a while, my gaze sought the heavens; turning, unconsciously, toward the North. Yes, the nebulous glow still showed. Indeed, I could have almost imagined that it looked somewhat plainer. For a long time, I kept my gaze fixed upon it; feeling, in my lonely soul, that its soft haze was, in some way, a tie with the past. Strange, the trifles from which one can suck comfort! And yet, had I but known – But I shall come to that in its proper time.

For a very long space, I watched, without experiencing any of the desire for sleep, that would so soon have visited me in the old-earth days. How I should have welcomed it; if only to have passed the time, away from my perplexities and thoughts.

Several times, the comfortless sound of some great piece of masonry falling, disturbed my meditations; and, once, it seemed I could hear whispering in the room, behind me. Yet it was utterly useless to try to see anything. Such blackness, as existed, scarcely can be conceived. It was palpable, and hideously brutal to the sense; as though something dead, pressed up against me – something soft, and icily cold.

Under all this, there grew up within my mind, a great and overwhelming distress of uneasiness, that left me, but to drop me into an uncomfortable brooding. I felt that I must fight against it; and, presently, hoping to distract my thoughts, I turned to the window, and looked up toward the North, in search of the nebulous whiteness, which, still, I believed to be the far and misty glowing of the universe we had left. Even as I raised my eyes, I was thrilled with a feeling of wonder; for, now, the hazy light had resolved into a single, great star, of vivid green.

As I stared, astonished, the thought flashed into my mind; that the earth must be traveling toward the star; not away, as I had imagined. Next, that it could not be the universe the earth had left; but, possibly, an outlying star, belonging to some vast star-cluster, hidden in the enormous depths of space. With a sense of commingled awe and curiosity, I watched it, wondering what new thing was to be revealed to me.

For a while, vague thoughts and speculations occupied me, during which my gaze dwelt insatiably upon that one spot of light, in the otherwise pitlike darkness. Hope grew up within me, banishing the oppression of despair, that had seemed to stifle me. Wherever the earth was traveling, it was, at least, going once more toward the realms of light. Light! One must spend an eternity wrapped in soundless night, to understand the full horror of being without it.

Slowly, but surely, the star grew upon my vision, until, in time, it shone as brightly as had the planet Jupiter, in the old-earth days. With increased size, its color became more impressive; reminding me of a huge emerald, scintillating rays of fire across the world.

Years fled away in silence, and the green star grew into a great splash of flame in the sky. A little later, I saw a thing that filled me with amazement. It was the ghostly outline of a vast crescent, in the night; a gigantic new moon, seeming to be growing out of the surrounding gloom. Utterly bemused, I stared at it. It appeared to be quite close – comparatively; and I puzzled to understand how the earth had come so near to it, without my having seen it before.

The light, thrown by the star, grew stronger; and, presently, I was aware that it was possible to see the earthscape again; though indistinctly. Awhile, I stared, trying to make out whether I could distinguish any detail of the world's surface, but I found the light insufficient. In a little, I gave up the attempt, and glanced once more toward the star. Even in the short space, that my attention had been diverted, it had increased considerably, and seemed now, to my bewildered sight, about a quarter of the size of the full moon. The light it threw, was extraordinarily powerful; yet its color was so abominably unfamiliar, that such of the world as I could see, showed unreal; more as though I looked out upon a landscape of shadow, than aught else.

All this time, the great crescent was increasing in brightness, and began, now, to shine with a perceptible shade of green. Steadily, the star increased in size and brilliancy, until it showed, fully as large as half a full moon; and, as it grew greater and brighter, so did the vast crescent throw out more and more light, though of an ever deepening hue of green. Under the combined blaze of their radiances, the wilderness that stretched before me, became steadily more visible. Soon, I seemed able to stare across the whole world, which now appeared, beneath the strange light, terrible in its cold and awful, flat dreariness.

It was a little later, that my attention was drawn to the fact, that the great star of green flame, was slowly sinking out of the North, toward the East. At first, I could scarcely believe that I saw aright; but soon there could be no doubt that it was so. Gradually, it sank, and, as it fell, the vast crescent of glowing green, began to dwindle and dwindle, until it became a mere arc of light, against the livid colored sky. Later it vanished, disappearing in the self-same spot from which I had seen it slowly emerge.

By this time, the star had come to within some thirty degrees of the hidden horizon. In size it could now have rivaled the moon at its full; though, even yet, I could not distinguish its disk. This fact led me to conceive that it was, still, an extraordinary distance away; and, this being so, I knew that its size must be huge, beyond the conception of man to understand or imagine.

Suddenly, as I watched, the lower edge of the star vanished – cut by a straight, dark line. A minute – or a century – passed, and it dipped lower, until the half of it had disappeared from sight. Far away out on the great plain, I saw a monstrous shadow blotting it out, and advancing swiftly. Only a third of the star was visible now. Then, like a flash, the solution of this extraordinary phenomenon revealed itself to me. The star was sinking behind the enormous mass of the dead sun. Or rather, the sun – obedient to its attraction – was rising toward it,[11] with the earth following in its trail. As these thoughts expanded in my mind, the star vanished; being completely hidden by the tremendous bulk of the sun. Over the earth there fell, once more, the brooding night.

With the darkness, came an intolerable feeling of loneliness and dread. For the first time, I thought of the Pit, and its inmates. After that, there rose in my memory the still more terrible Thing, that had haunted the shores of the Sea of Sleep, and lurked in the shadows of this old building. Where were they? I wondered – and shivered with miserable thoughts. For a time, fear held me, and I prayed, wildly and incoherently, for some ray of light with which to dispel the cold blackness that enveloped the world.

How long I waited, it is impossible to say – certainly for a very great period. Then, all at once, I saw a loom of light shine out ahead. Gradually, it became more distinct. Suddenly, a ray of vivid green, flashed across the darkness. At the same moment, I saw a thin line of livid flame, far in the night. An instant, it seemed, and it had grown into a great clot of fire; beneath which, the world lay bathed in a blaze of emerald green light. Steadily it grew, until, presently, the whole of the green star had come into sight again. But now, it could be scarcely called a star; for it had increased to vast proportions, being incomparably greater than the sun had been in the olden time.

"Then, as I stared, I became aware that I could see the edge of the lifeless sun, glowing like a great crescent-moon. Slowly, its lighted surface, broadened out to me, until half of its diameter was visible; and the star began to drop away on my right. Time passed, and the earth moved on, slowly traversing the tremendous face of the dead sun." [12]

Gradually, as the earth traveled forward, the star fell still more to the right; until, at last, it shone on the back of the house, sending a flood of broken rays, in through the skeletonlike walls. Glancing upward, I saw that much of the ceiling had vanished, enabling me to see that the upper storeys were even more decayed. The roof had, evidently, gone entirely; and I could see the green effulgence of the Starlight shining in, slantingly.

Chapter XIX
The End of the Solar System

FROM THE ABUTMENT, where once had been the windows, through which I had watched that first, fatal dawn, I could see that the sun was hugely greater, than it had been, when first the Star lit the world. So great was it, that its lower edge seemed almost to touch the far horizon.

Even as I watched, I imagined that it drew closer. The radiance of green that lit the frozen earth, grew steadily brighter.

Thus, for a long space, things were. Then, on a sudden, I saw that the sun was changing shape, and growing smaller, just as the moon would have done in past time. In a while, only a third of the illuminated part was turned toward the earth. The Star bore away on the left.

Gradually, as the world moved on, the Star shone upon the front of the house, once more; while the sun showed, only as a great bow of green fire. An instant, it seemed, and the sun had vanished. The Star was still fully visible. Then the earth moved into the black shadow of the sun, and all was night – Night, black, starless, and intolerable.

Filled with tumultuous thoughts, I watched across the night – waiting. Years, it may have been, and then, in the dark house behind me, the clotted stillness of the world was broken. I seemed to hear a soft padding of many feet, and a faint, inarticulate whisper of sound, grew on my sense. I looked 'round into the blackness, and saw a multitude of eyes. As I stared, they increased, and appeared to come toward me. For an instant, I stood, unable to move. Then a hideous swine-noise[13] rose up into the night; and, at that, I leapt from the window, out on to the frozen world. I have a confused notion of having run awhile; and, after that, I just waited – waited. Several times, I heard shrieks; but always as though from a distance. Except for these sounds, I had no idea of the whereabouts of the house. Time moved onward. I was conscious of little, save a sensation of cold and hopelessness and fear.

An age, it seemed, and there came a glow, that told of the coming light. It grew, tardily. Then – with a loom of unearthly glory – the first ray from the Green Star, struck over the edge of the dark sun, and lit the world. It fell upon a great, ruined structure, some two hundred yards away. It was the house. Staring, I saw a fearsome sight – over its walls crawled a legion of unholy things, almost covering the old building, from tottering towers to base. I could see them, plainly; they were the Swine-creatures.

The world moved out into the light of the Star, and I saw that, now, it seemed to stretch across a quarter of the heavens. The glory of its livid light was so tremendous, that it appeared to fill the sky with quivering flames. Then, I saw the sun. It was so close that half of its diameter lay below the horizon; and, as the world circled across its face, it seemed to tower right up into the sky, a stupendous dome of emerald colored fire. From time to time, I glanced toward the house; but the Swine-things seemed unaware of my proximity.

Years appeared to pass, slowly. The earth had almost reached the center of the sun's disk. The light from the Green *Sun* – as now it must be called – shone through the interstices, that gapped the mouldered walls of the old house, giving them the appearance of being wrapped in green flames. The Swine-creatures still crawled about the walls.

Suddenly, there rose a loud roar of swine-voices, and, up from the center of the roofless house, shot a vast column of blood-red flame. I saw the little, twisted towers and turrets flash into fire; yet still preserving their twisted crookedness. The beams of the Green Sun, beat upon the house, and intermingled with its lurid glows; so that it appeared a blazing furnace of red and green fire.

Fascinated, I watched, until an overwhelming sense of coming danger, drew my attention. I glanced up, and, at once, it was borne upon me, that the sun was closer; so close, in fact, that it seemed to overhang the world. Then – I know not how – I was caught up into strange heights – floating like a bubble in the awful effulgence.

Far below me, I saw the earth, with the burning house leaping into an ever growing mountain of flame, 'round about it, the ground appeared to be glowing; and, in places, heavy wreaths of yellow smoke ascended from the earth. It seemed as though the world were becoming ignited from that one plague-spot of fire. Faintly, I could see the Swine-things. They appeared quite unharmed. Then the ground seemed to cave in, suddenly, and the house, with its load of foul creatures, disappeared into the depths of the earth, sending a strange, blood colored cloud into the heights. I remembered the hell Pit under the house.

In a while, I looked 'round. The huge bulk of the sun, rose high above me. The distance between it and the earth, grew rapidly less. Suddenly, the earth appeared to shoot forward. In a moment, it had traversed the space between it and the sun. I heard no sound; but, out from the sun's face, gushed an ever-growing tongue of dazzling flame. It seemed to leap, almost to the distant Green Sun – shearing through the emerald light, a very cataract of blinding fire. It reached its limit, and sank; and, on the sun, glowed a vast splash of burning white – the grave of the earth.

The sun was very close to me, now. Presently, I found that I was rising higher; until, at last, I rode above it, in the emptiness. The Green Sun was now so huge that its breadth seemed to fill up all the sky, ahead. I looked down, and noted that the sun was passing directly beneath me.

A year may have gone by – or a century – and I was left, suspended, alone. The sun showed far in front – a black, circular mass, against the molten splendor of the great, Green Orb. Near one edge, I observed that a lurid glow had appeared, marking the place where the earth had fallen. By this, I knew that the long-dead sun was still revolving, though with great slowness.

Afar to my right, I seemed to catch, at times, a faint glow of whitish light. For a great time, I was uncertain whether to put this down to fancy or not. Thus, for a while, I stared, with fresh wonderings; until, at last, I knew that it was no imaginary thing; but a reality. It grew brighter; and, presently, there slid out of the green, a pale globe of softest white. It came nearer, and I saw that it was apparently surrounded by a robe of gently glowing clouds. Time passed....

I glanced toward the diminishing sun. It showed, only as a dark blot on the face of the Green Sun. As I watched, I saw it grow smaller, steadily, as though rushing toward the superior orb, at an immense speed. Intently, I stared. What would happen? I was conscious of extraordinary emotions, as I realized that it would strike the Green Sun. It grew no bigger than a pea, and I looked, with my whole soul, to witness the final end of our System – that system which had borne the world through so many aeons, with its multitudinous sorrows and joys; and now—

Suddenly, something crossed my vision, cutting from sight all vestige of the spectacle I watched with such soul-interest. What happened to the dead sun, I did not see; but I have no reason – in the light of that which I saw afterward – to disbelieve that it fell into the strange fire of the Green Sun, and so perished.

And then, suddenly, an extraordinary question rose in my mind, whether this stupendous globe of green fire might not be the vast Central Sun – the great sun, 'round which our universe and countless others revolve. I felt confused. I thought of the probable end of the dead sun, and another suggestion came, dumbly – Do the dead stars make the Green Sun their grave? The idea appealed to me with no sense of grotesqueness; but rather as something both possible and probable.

Chapter XX
The Celestial Globes

FOR A WHILE, many thoughts crowded my mind, so that I was unable to do aught, save stare, blindly, before me. I seemed whelmed in a sea of doubt and wonder and sorrowful remembrance.

It was later, that I came out of my bewilderment. I looked about, dazedly. Thus, I saw so extraordinary a sight that, for a while, I could scarcely believe I was not still wrapped in the visionary tumult of my own thoughts. Out of the reigning green, had grown a boundless river of softly shimmering globes – each one enfolded in a wondrous fleece of pure cloud. They reached, both above and below me, to an unknown distance; and, not only hid the shining of the Green Sun; but supplied, in place thereof, a tender glow of light, that suffused itself around me, like unto nothing I have ever seen, before or since.

In a little, I noticed that there was about these spheres, a sort of transparency, almost as though they were formed of clouded crystal, within which burned a radiance – gentle and subdued. They moved on, past me, continually, floating onward at no great speed; but rather as though they had eternity before them. A great while, I watched, and could perceive no end to them. At times, I seemed to distinguish faces, amid the cloudiness; but strangely indistinct, as though partly real, and partly formed of the mistiness through which they showed.

For a long time, I waited, passively, with a sense of growing content. I had no longer that feeling of unutterable loneliness; but felt, rather, that I was less alone, than I had been for kalpas of years. This feeling of contentment, increased, so that I would have been satisfied to float in company with those celestial globules, forever.

Ages slipped by, and I saw the shadowy faces, with increased frequency, also with greater plainness. Whether this was due to my soul having become more attuned to its surroundings, I cannot tell – probably it was so. But, however this may be, I am assured now, only of the fact that I became steadily more conscious of a new mystery about me, telling me that I had, indeed, penetrated within the borderland of some unthought-of region – some subtle, intangible place, or form, of existence.

The enormous stream of luminous spheres continued to pass me, at an unvarying rate – countless millions; and still they came, showing no signs of ending, nor even diminishing.

Then, as I was borne, silently, upon the unbuoying ether, I felt a sudden, irresistible, forward movement, toward one of the passing globes. An instant, and I was beside it. Then, I slid through, into the interior, without experiencing the least resistance, of any description. For a short while, I could see nothing; and waited, curiously.

All at once, I became aware that a sound broke the inconceivable stillness. It was like the murmur of a great sea at calm – a sea breathing in its sleep. Gradually, the mist that obscured my sight, began to thin away; and so, in time, my vision dwelt once again upon the silent surface of the Sea of Sleep.

For a little, I gazed, and could scarcely believe I saw aright. I glanced 'round. There was the great globe of pale fire, swimming, as I had seen it before, a short distance above the dim horizon. To my left, far across the sea, I discovered, presently, a faint line, as of thin haze, which I guessed to be the shore, where my Love and I had met, during those wonderful periods of soul-wandering, that had been granted to me in the old earth days.

Another, a troubled, memory came to me – of the Formless Thing that had haunted the shores of the Sea of Sleep. The guardian of that silent, echoless place. These, and other, details, I remembered, and knew, without doubt that I was looking out upon that same sea. With the assurance, I was filled with an overwhelming feeling of surprise, and joy, and shaken expectancy, conceiving it possible that I was about to see my Love, again. Intently, I gazed around; but could catch no sight of her. At that, for a little, I felt hopeless. Fervently, I prayed, and ever peered, anxiously.... How still was the sea!

Down, far beneath me, I could see the many trails of changeful fire, that had drawn my attention, formerly. Vaguely, I wondered what caused them; also, I remembered that I had intended to ask my dear One about them, as well as many other matters – and I had been forced to leave her, before the half that I had wished to say, was said.

My thoughts came back with a leap. I was conscious that something had touched me. I turned quickly. God, Thou wert indeed gracious – it was She! She looked up into my eyes, with an eager longing, and I looked down to her, with all my soul. I should like to have held her; but the glorious purity of her face, kept me afar. Then, out of the winding mist, she put her dear arms. Her whisper came to me, soft as the rustle of a passing cloud. 'Dearest!' she said. That was all; but I had heard, and, in a moment I held her to me – as I prayed – forever.

In a little, she spoke of many things, and I listened. Willingly, would I have done so through all the ages that are to come. At times, I whispered back, and my whispers brought to her spirit face, once more, an indescribably delicate tint – the bloom of love. Later, I spoke more freely, and to each word she listened, and made answer, delightfully; so that, already, I was in Paradise.

She and I; and nothing, save the silent, spacious void to see us; and only the quiet waters of the Sea of Sleep to hear us.

Long before, the floating multitude of cloud-enfolded spheres had vanished into nothingness. Thus, we looked upon the face of the slumberous deeps, and were alone. Alone, God, I would be thus alone in the hereafter, and yet be never lonely! I had her, and, greater than this, she had me. Aye, aeon-aged me; and on this thought, and some others, I hope to exist through the few remaining years that may yet lie between us.

Chapter XXI
The Dark Sun

HOW LONG our souls lay in the arms of joy, I cannot say; but, all at once, I was waked from my happiness, by a diminution of the pale and gentle light that lit the Sea of Sleep. I turned toward the huge, white orb, with a premonition of coming trouble. One side of it was curving inward, as though a convex, black shadow were sweeping across it. My memory went back. It was thus, that the darkness had come, before our last parting. I turned toward my Love, inquiringly. With a sudden knowledge of woe, I noticed how wan and unreal she had grown, even in that brief space. Her voice seemed to come to me from a distance. The touch of her hands was no more than the gentle pressure of a summer wind, and grew less perceptible.

Already, quite half of the immense globe was shrouded. A feeling of desperation seized me. Was she about to leave me? Would she have to go, as she had gone before? I questioned her, anxiously, frightenedly; and she, nestling closer, explained, in that strange, faraway voice, that it was imperative she should leave me, before the Sun of Darkness – as she termed it – blotted out the light. At this confirmation of my fears, I was overcome with despair; and could only look, voicelessly, across the quiet plains of the silent sea.

How swiftly the darkness spread across the face of the White Orb. Yet, in reality, the time must have been long, beyond human comprehension.

At last, only a crescent of pale fire, lit the, now dim, Sea of Sleep. All this while, she had held me; but, with so soft a caress, that I had been scarcely conscious of it. We waited there, together, she and I; speechless, for very sorrow. In the dimming light, her face showed, shadowy – blending into the dusky mistiness that encircled us.

Then, when a thin, curved line of soft light was all that lit the sea, she released me – pushing me from her, tenderly. Her voice sounded in my ears, 'I may not stay longer, Dear One.' It ended in a sob.

She seemed to float away from me, and became invisible. Her voice came to me, out of the shadows, faintly; apparently from a great distance:

'A little while—' It died away, remotely. In a breath, the Sea of Sleep darkened into night. Far to my left, I seemed to see, for a brief instant, a soft glow. It vanished, and, in the same moment, I became aware that I was no longer above the still sea; but once more suspended in infinite space, with the Green Sun – now eclipsed by a vast, dark sphere – before me.

Utterly bewildered, I stared, almost unseeingly, at the ring of green flames, leaping above the dark edge. Even in the chaos of my thoughts, I wondered, dully, at their extraordinary shapes. A multitude of questions assailed me. I thought more of her, I had so lately seen, than of the sight before me. My grief, and thoughts of the future, filled me. Was I doomed to be separated from her, always? Even in the old earth-days, she had been mine, only for a little while; then she had left me, as I thought, forever. Since then, I had seen her but these times, upon the Sea of Sleep.

A feeling of fierce resentment filled me, and miserable questionings. Why could I not have gone with my Love? What reason to keep us apart? Why had I to wait alone, while she slumbered through the years, on the still bosom of the Sea of Sleep? The Sea of Sleep! My thoughts turned, inconsequently, out of their channel of bitterness, to fresh, desperate questionings. Where was it? Where was it? I seemed to have but just parted from my Love, upon its quiet surface, and it had gone, utterly. It could not be far away! And the White Orb which I had seen hidden in the shadow of the Sun of Darkness! My sight dwelt upon the Green Sun – eclipsed. What had eclipsed it? Was there a vast, dead star circling it? Was the *Central* Sun – as I had come to regard it – a double star? The thought had come, almost unbidden; yet why should it not be so?

My thoughts went back to the White Orb. Strange, that it should have been – I stopped. An idea had come, suddenly. The White Orb and the Green Sun! Were they one and the same? My imagination wandered backward, and I remembered the luminous globe to which I had been so unaccountably attracted. It was curious that I should have forgotten it, even momentarily. Where were the others? I reverted again to the globe I had entered. I thought, for a time, and matters became clearer. I conceived that, by entering that impalpable globule, I had passed, at once, into some further, and, until then, invisible dimension; There, the Green Sun was still visible; but as a stupendous sphere of pale, white light – almost as though its ghost showed, and not its material part.

A long time, I mused on the subject. I remembered how, on entering the sphere, I had, immediately, lost all sight of the others. For a still further period, I continued to revolve the different details in my mind.

In a while, my thoughts turned to other things. I came more into the present, and began to look about me, seeingly. For the first time, I perceived that innumerable rays, of a subtle, violet hue, pierced the strange semi-darkness, in all directions. They radiated from the fiery rim of the Green Sun. They seemed to grow upon my vision, so that, in a little, I saw that they were countless. The night was filled with them – spreading outward from the Green Sun, fan-wise. I concluded that I was enabled to see them, by reason of the Sun's glory being cut off by the eclipse. They reached right out into space, and vanished.

Gradually, as I looked, I became aware that fine points of intensely brilliant light, traversed the rays. Many of them seemed to travel from the Green Sun, into distance. Others came out of the void, toward the Sun; but one and all, each kept strictly to the ray in which it traveled. Their speed was inconceivably great; and it was only when they neared the Green Sun, or as they left it, that I could see them as separate specks of light. Further from the sun, they became thin lines of vivid fire within the violet.

The discovery of these rays, and the moving sparks, interested me, extraordinarily. To where did they lead, in such countless profusion? I thought of the worlds in space.... And those sparks! Messengers! Possibly, the idea was fantastic; but I was not conscious of its being so. Messengers! Messengers from the Central Sun!

An idea evolved itself, slowly. Was the Green Sun the abode of some vast Intelligence? The thought was bewildering. Visions of the Unnamable rose, vaguely. Had I, indeed, come upon the dwelling-place of the Eternal? For a time, I repelled the thought, dumbly. It was too stupendous. Yet....

Huge, vague thoughts had birth within me. I felt, suddenly, terribly naked. And an awful Nearness, shook me.

And Heaven...! Was that an illusion?

My thoughts came and went, erratically. The Sea of Sleep – and she! Heaven.... I came back, with a bound, to the present. Somewhere, out of the void behind me, there rushed an immense, dark body – huge and silent. It was a dead star, hurling onward to the burying place of the stars. It drove between me and the Central Suns – blotting them out from my vision, and plunging me into an impenetrable night.

An age, and I saw again the violet rays. A great while later – aeons it must have been – a circular glow grew in the sky, ahead, and I saw the edge of the receding star, show darkly against it. Thus, I knew that it was nearing the Central Suns. Presently, I saw the bright ring of the Green Sun, show plainly against the night The star had passed into the shadow of the Dead Sun. After that, I just waited. The strange years went slowly, and ever, I watched, intently.

'The thing I had expected, came at last – suddenly, awfully. A vast flare of dazzling light. A streaming burst of white flame across the dark void. For an indefinite while, it soared outward – a gigantic mushroom of fire. It ceased to grow. Then, as time went by, it began to sink backward, slowly. I saw, now, that it came from a huge, glowing spot near the center of the Dark Sun. Mighty flames, still soared outward from this. Yet, spite of its size, the grave of the star was no more than the shining of Jupiter upon the face of an ocean, when compared with the inconceivable mass of the Dead Sun.

I may remark here, once more, that no words will ever convey to the imagination, the enormous bulk of the two Central Suns.

Chapter XXII
The Dark Nebula

YEARS MELTED into the past, centuries, aeons. The light of the incandescent star, sank to a furious red.

It was later, that I saw the dark nebula – at first, an impalpable cloud, away to my right. It grew, steadily, to a clot of blackness in the night. How long I watched, it is impossible to say; for time, as we count it, was a thing of the past. It came closer, a shapeless monstrosity of darkness – tremendous. It seemed to slip across the night, sleepily – a very hell-fog. Slowly, it slid nearer, and passed into the void, between me and the Central Suns. It was as though a curtain had been drawn before my vision. A strange tremor of fear took me, and a fresh sense of wonder.

The green twilight that had reigned for so many millions of years, had now given place to impenetrable gloom. Motionless, I peered about me. A century fled, and it seemed to me that I detected occasional dull glows of red, passing me at intervals.

Earnestly, I gazed, and, presently, seemed to see circular masses, that showed muddily red, within the clouded blackness. They appeared to be growing out of the nebulous murk. Awhile, and they became plainer to my accustomed vision. I could see them, now, with a fair amount of distinctness – ruddy-tinged spheres, similar, in size, to the luminous globes that I had seen, so long previously.

They floated past me, continually. Gradually, a peculiar uneasiness seized me. I became aware of a growing feeling of repugnance and dread. It was directed against those passing orbs, and seemed born of intuitive knowledge, rather than of any real cause or reason.

Some of the passing globes were brighter than others; and, it was from one of these, that a face looked, suddenly. A face, human in its outline; but so tortured with woe, that I stared, aghast. I had not thought there was such sorrow, as I saw there. I was conscious of an added sense of pain, on perceiving that the eyes, which glared so wildly, were sightless. A while longer, I saw it; then it had passed on, into the surrounding gloom. After this, I saw others – all wearing that look of hopeless sorrow; and blind.

A long time went by, and I became aware that I was nearer to the orbs, than I had been. At this, I grew uneasy; though I was less in fear of those strange globules, than I had been, before seeing their sorrowful inhabitants; for sympathy had tempered my fear.

Later, there was no doubt but that I was being carried closer to the red spheres, and, presently, I floated among them. In awhile, I perceived one bearing down upon me. I was helpless to move from its path. In a minute, it seemed, it was upon me, and I was submerged in a deep red mist. This cleared, and I stared, confusedly, across the immense breadth of the Plain of Silence. It appeared just as I had first seen it. I was moving forward, steadily, across its surface. Away ahead, shone the vast, blood-red ring[14] that lit the place. All around, was spread the extraordinary desolation of stillness, that had so impressed me during my previous wanderings across its starkness.

Presently, I saw, rising up into the ruddy gloom, the distant peaks of the mighty amphitheatre of mountains, where, untold ages before, I had been shown my first glimpse of the terrors that underlie many things; and where, vast and silent, watched by a thousand mute gods, stands the replica of this house of mysteries – this house that I had seen swallowed up in that hell-fire, ere the earth had kissed the sun, and vanished for ever.

Though I could see the crests of the mountain-amphitheatre, yet it was a great while before their lower portions became visible. Possibly, this was due to the strange, ruddy haze, that seemed to cling to the surface of the Plain. However, be this as it may, I saw them at last.

In a still further space of time, I had come so close to the mountains, that they appeared to overhang me. Presently, I saw the great rift, open before me, and I drifted into it; without volition on my part.

Later, I came out upon the breadth of the enormous arena. There, at an apparent distance of some five miles, stood the House, huge, monstrous and silent – lying in the very center of that stupendous amphitheatre. So far as I could see, it had not altered in any way; but looked as though it were only yesterday that I had seen it. Around, the grim, dark mountains frowned down upon me from their lofty silences.

Far to my right, away up among inaccessible peaks, loomed the enormous bulk of the great Beast-god. Higher, I saw the hideous form of the dread goddess, rising up through the red gloom, thousands of fathoms above me. To the left, I made out the monstrous Eyeless-Thing, grey and inscrutable. Further off, reclining on its lofty ledge, the livid Ghoul-Shape showed – a splash of sinister color, among the dark mountains.

Slowly, I moved out across the great arena – floating. As I went, I made out the dim forms of many of the other lurking Horrors that peopled those supreme heights.

Gradually, I neared the House, and my thoughts flashed back across the abyss of years. I remembered the dread Specter of the Place. A short while passed, and I saw that I was being wafted directly toward the enormous mass of that silent building.

About this time, I became aware, in an indifferent sort of way, of a growing sense of numbness, that robbed me of the fear, which I should otherwise have felt, on approaching that awesome Pile. As it was, I viewed it, calmly – much as a man views calamity through the haze of his tobacco smoke.

In a little while, I had come so close to the House, as to be able to distinguish many of the details about it. The longer I looked, the more was I confirmed in my long-ago impressions of its entire similitude to this strange house. Save in its enormous size, I could find nothing unlike.

Suddenly, as I stared, a great feeling of amazement filled me. I had come opposite to that part, where the outer door, leading into the study, is situated. There, lying right across the threshold, lay a great length of coping stone, identical – save in size and color – with the piece I had dislodged in my fight with the Pit-creatures.

I floated nearer, and my astonishment increased, as I noted that the door was broken partly from its hinges, precisely in the manner that my study door had been forced inward, by the assaults of the Swine-things. The sight started a train of thoughts, and I began to trace, dimly, that the attack on this house, might have a far deeper significance than I had, hitherto, imagined. I remembered how, long ago, in the old earth-days, I had half suspected that, in some unexplainable manner, this house, in which I live, was *en rapport* – to use a recognized term – with that other tremendous structure, away in the midst of that incomparable Plain.

Now, however, it began to be borne upon me, that I had but vaguely conceived what the realization of my suspicion meant. I began to understand, with a more than human clearness, that the attack I had repelled, was, in some extraordinary manner, connected with an attack upon that strange edifice.

With a curious inconsequence, my thoughts abruptly left the matter; to dwell, wonderingly, upon the peculiar material, out of which the House was constructed. It was – as I have mentioned, earlier – of a deep, green color. Yet, now that I had come so close to it, I perceived that it fluctuated at times, though slightly – glowing and fading, much as do the fumes of phosphorus, when rubbed upon the hand, in the dark.

Presently, my attention was distracted from this, by coming to the great entrance. Here, for the first time, I was afraid; for, all in a moment, the huge doors swung back, and I drifted in between them, helplessly. Inside, all was blackness, impalpable. In an instant, I had crossed the threshold, and the great doors closed, silently, shutting me in that lightless place.

For a while, I seemed to hang, motionless; suspended amid the darkness. Then, I became conscious that I was moving again; where, I could not tell. Suddenly, far down beneath me, I seemed to hear a murmurous noise of Swine-laughter. It sank away, and the succeeding silence appeared clogged with horror.

Then a door opened somewhere ahead; a white haze of light filtered through, and I floated slowly into a room, that seemed strangely familiar. All at once, there came a bewildering, screaming noise, that deafened me. I saw a blurred vista of visions, flaming before my sight. My senses were dazed, through the space of an eternal moment. Then, my power of seeing, came back to me. The dizzy, hazy feeling passed, and I saw, clearly.

Chapter XXIII
Pepper

I WAS SEATED in my chair, back again in this old study. My glance wandered 'round the room. For a minute, it had a strange, quivery appearance – unreal and unsubstantial. This disappeared, and I saw that nothing was altered in any way. I looked toward the end window – the blind was up.

I rose to my feet, shakily. As I did so, a slight noise, in the direction of the door, attracted my attention. I glanced toward it. For a short instant, it appeared to me that it was being closed, gently. I stared, and saw that I must have been mistaken – it seemed closely shut.

With a succession of efforts, I trod my way to the window, and looked out. The sun was just rising, lighting up the tangled wilderness of gardens. For, perhaps, a minute, I stood, and stared. I passed my hand, confusedly, across my forehead.

Presently, amid the chaos of my senses, a sudden thought came to me; I turned, quickly, and called to Pepper. There was no answer, and I stumbled across the room, in a quick access of fear.

As I went, I tried to frame his name; but my lips were numb. I reached the table, and stooped down to him, with a catching at my heart. He was lying in the shadow of the table, and I had not been able to see him, distinctly, from the window. Now, as I stooped, I took my breath, shortly. There was no Pepper; instead, I was reaching toward an elongated, little heap of grey, ashlike dust….

I must have remained, in that half-stooped position, for some minutes. I was dazed – stunned. Pepper had really passed into the land of shadows.

Chapter XXIV
The Footsteps in the Garden

PEPPER IS DEAD! Even now, at times, I seem scarcely able to realize that this is so. It is many weeks, since I came back from that strange and terrible journey through space and time. Sometimes, in my sleep, I dream about it, and go through, in imagination, the whole of that fearsome happening. When I wake, my thoughts dwell upon it. That Sun – those Suns, were they indeed the great Central Suns, 'round which the whole universe, of the unknown heavens, revolves? Who shall say? And the bright globules, floating forever in the light of the Green Sun! And the Sea of Sleep on which they float! How unbelievable it all is. If it were not for Pepper, I should, even after the many extraordinary things that I have witnessed, be inclined to imagine that it was but a gigantic dream. Then, there is that dreadful, dark nebula (with its multitudes of red spheres) moving always within the shadow of the Dark Sun, sweeping along on its stupendous orbit, wrapped eternally in gloom. And the faces that peered out at me! God, do they, and does such a thing really exist? … There is still that little heap of grey ash, on my study floor. I will not have it touched.

At times, when I am calmer, I have wondered what became of the outer planets of the Solar System. It has occurred to me, that they may have broken loose from the sun's attraction, and whirled away into space. This is, of course, only a surmise. There are so many things, about which I wonder.

Now that I am writing, let me record that I am certain, there is something horrible about to happen. Last night, a thing occurred, which has filled me with an even greater terror, than did the Pit fear. I will write it down now, and, if anything more happens, endeavor to make a note of it, at once. I have a feeling, that there is more in this last affair, than in all those others. I am shaky and nervous, even now, as I write. Somehow, I think death is not very far away. Not that I fear death – as death is understood. Yet, there is that in the air, which bids me fear – an intangible, cold horror. I felt it last night. It was thus:

Last night, I was sitting here in my study, writing. The door, leading into the garden, was half open. At times, the metallic rattle of a dog's chain, sounded faintly. It belongs to the dog I have bought, since Pepper's death. I will not have him in the house – not after Pepper. Still, I have felt it better to have a dog about the place. They are wonderful creatures.

I was much engrossed in my work, and the time passed, quickly. Suddenly, I heard a soft noise on the path, outside in the garden – pad, pad, pad, it went, with a stealthy, curious sound. I sat upright, with a quick movement, and looked out through the opened door. Again the noise came – pad, pad, pad. It appeared to be approaching. With a slight feeling of nervousness, I stared into the gardens; but the night hid everything.

Then the dog gave a long howl, and I started. For a minute, perhaps, I peered, intently; but could hear nothing. After a little, I picked up the pen, which I had laid down, and recommenced my work. The nervous feeling had gone; for I imagined that the sound I had heard, was nothing more than the dog walking 'round his kennel, at the length of his chain.

A quarter of an hour may have passed; then, all at once, the dog howled again, and with such a plaintively sorrowful note, that I jumped to my feet, dropping my pen, and inking the page on which I was at work.

'Curse that dog!' I muttered, noting what I had done. Then, even as I said the words, there sounded again that queer – pad, pad, pad. It was horribly close – almost by the door, I thought. I knew, now, that it could not be the dog; his chain would not allow him to come so near.

The dog's growl came again, and I noted, subconsciously, the taint of fear in it.

Outside, on the windowsill, I could see Tip, my sister's pet cat. As I looked, it sprang to its feet, its tail swelling, visibly. For an instant it stood thus; seeming to stare, fixedly, at something, in the direction of the door. Then, quickly, it began to back along the sill; until, reaching the wall at the end, it could go no further. There it stood, rigid, as though frozen in an attitude of extraordinary terror.

Frightened, and puzzled, I seized a stick from the corner, and went toward the door, silently; taking one of the candles with me. I had come to within a few paces of it, when, suddenly, a peculiar sense of fear thrilled through me – a fear, palpitant and real; whence, I knew not, nor why. So great was the feeling of terror, that I wasted no time; but retreated straight-way – walking backward, and keeping my gaze, fearfully, on the door. I would have given much, to rush at it, fling it to, and shoot the bolts; for I have had it repaired and strengthened, so that, now, it is far stronger than ever it has been. Like Tip, I continued my, almost unconscious, progress backward, until the wall brought me up. At that, I started, nervously, and glanced 'round, apprehensively. As I did so, my eyes dwelt, momentarily, on the rack of firearms, and I took a step toward them; but stopped, with a curious feeling that they would be needless. Outside, in the gardens, the dog moaned, strangely.

Suddenly, from the cat, there came a fierce, long screech. I glanced, jerkily, in its direction – Something, luminous and ghostly, encircled it, and grew upon my vision. It resolved into a glowing hand, transparent, with a lambent, greenish flame flickering over it. The cat gave a last, awful caterwaul, and I saw it smoke and blaze. My breath came with a gasp, and I leant against the wall. Over that part of the window there spread a smudge, green and fantastic. It hid the thing from me, though the glare of fire shone through, dully. A stench of burning, stole into the room.

Pad, pad, pad – Something passed down the garden path, and a faint, mouldy odor seemed to come in through the open door, and mingle with the burnt smell.

The dog had been silent for a few moments. Now, I heard him yowl, sharply, as though in pain. Then, he was quiet, save for an occasional, subdued whimper of fear.

A minute went by; then the gate on the West side of the gardens, slammed, distantly. After that, nothing; not even the dog's whine.

I must have stood there some minutes. Then a fragment of courage stole into my heart, and I made a frightened rush at the door, dashed it to, and bolted it. After that, for a full half-hour, I sat, helpless – staring before me, rigidly.

Slowly, my life came back into me, and I made my way, shakily, up-stairs to bed.

That is all.

Chapter XXV
The Thing from the Arena

THIS MORNING, early, I went through the gardens; but found everything as usual. Near the door, I examined the path, for footprints; yet, here again, there was nothing to tell me whether, or not, I dreamed last night.

It was only when I came to speak to the dog, that I discovered tangible proof, that something did happen. When I went to his kennel, he kept inside, crouching up in one corner, and I had to coax him, to get him out. When, finally, he consented to come, it was in a strangely cowed and subdued manner. As I patted him, my attention was attracted to a greenish patch, on his left flank. On examining it, I found, that the fur and skin had been apparently, burnt off; for the flesh showed, raw and scorched. The shape of the mark was curious, reminding me of the imprint of a large talon or hand.

I stood up, thoughtful. My gaze wandered toward the study window. The rays of the rising sun, shimmered on the smoky patch in the lower corner, causing it to fluctuate from green to red, oddly. Ah! that was undoubtedly another proof; and, suddenly, the horrible Thing I saw last night, rose in my mind. I looked at the dog, again. I knew the cause, now, of that hateful looking wound on his side – I knew, also, that, what I had seen last night, had been a real happening. And a great discomfort filled me. Pepper! Tip! And now this poor animal…! I glanced at the dog again, and noticed that he was licking at his wound.

'Poor brute!' I muttered, and bent to pat his head. At that, he got upon his feet, nosing and licking my hand, wistfully.

Presently, I left him, having other matters to which to attend.

After dinner, I went to see him, again. He seemed quiet, and disinclined to leave his kennel. From my sister, I have learnt that he has refused all food today. She appeared a little puzzled, when she told me; though quite unsuspicious of anything of which to be afraid.

The day has passed, uneventfully enough. After tea, I went, again, to have a look at the dog. He seemed moody, and somewhat restless; yet persisted in remaining in his kennel. Before locking up, for the night, I moved his kennel out, away from the wall, so that I shall be able to watch it from the small window, tonight. The thought came to me, to bring him into the house for the night; but consideration has decided me, to let him remain out. I cannot say that the house is, in any degree, less to be feared than the gardens. Pepper was in the house, and yet….

It is now two o'clock. Since eight, I have watched the kennel, from the small, side window in my study. Yet, nothing has occurred, and I am too tired to watch longer. I will go to bed….

During the night, I was restless. This is unusual for me; but, toward morning, I obtained a few hours' sleep.

I rose early, and, after breakfast, visited the dog. He was quiet; but morose, and refused to leave his kennel. I wish there was some horse doctor near here; I would have the poor brute looked to. All day, he has taken no food; but has shown an evident desire for water – lapping it up, greedily. I was relieved to observe this.

The evening has come, and I am in my study. I intend to follow my plan of last night, and watch the kennel. The door, leading into the garden, is bolted, securely. I am consciously glad there are bars to the windows….

Night: – Midnight has gone. The dog has been silent, up to the present. Through the side window, on my left, I can make out, dimly, the outlines of the kennel. For the first time, the dog moves, and I hear the rattle of his chain. I look out, quickly. As I stare, the dog moves again, restlessly, and I see a small patch of luminous light, shine from the interior of the kennel. It vanishes; then the dog stirs again, and, once more, the gleam comes. I am puzzled. The dog is quiet, and I can see the luminous thing, plainly. It shows distinctly. There is something familiar about the shape of it. For a moment, I wonder; then it comes to me, that it is not unlike the four fingers and thumb of a hand. Like a hand! And I remember the contour of that fearsome wound on the dog's side. It must be the wound I see. It is luminous at night – Why? The minutes pass. My mind is filled with this fresh thing….

Suddenly, I hear a sound, out in the gardens. How it thrills through me. It is approaching. Pad, pad, pad. A prickly sensation traverses my spine, and seems to creep across my scalp. The dog moves in his kennel, and whimpers, frightenedly. He must have turned 'round; for, now, I can no longer see the outline of his shining wound.

Outside, the gardens are silent, once more, and I listen, fearfully. A minute passes, and another; then I hear the padding sound, again. It is quite close, and appears to be coming down the graveled path. The noise is curiously measured and deliberate. It ceases outside the door; and I rise to my feet, and stand motionless. From the door, comes a slight sound – the latch is being slowly raised. A singing noise is in my ears, and I have a sense of pressure about the head—

The latch drops, with a sharp click, into the catch. The noise startles me afresh; jarring, horribly, on my tense nerves. After that, I stand, for a long while, amid an ever-growing quietness. All at once, my knees begin to tremble, and I have to sit, quickly.

An uncertain period of time passes, and, gradually, I begin to shake off the feeling of terror, that has possessed me. Yet, still I sit. I seem to have lost the power of movement. I am strangely tired, and inclined to doze. My eyes open and close, and, presently, I find myself falling asleep, and waking, in fits and starts.

It is some time later, that I am sleepily aware that one of the candles is guttering. When I wake again, it has gone out, and the room is very dim, under the light of the one remaining flame. The semi-darkness troubles me little. I have lost that awful sense of dread, and my only desire seems to be to sleep – sleep.

Suddenly, although there is no noise, I am awake – wide awake. I am acutely conscious of the nearness of some mystery, of some overwhelming Presence. The very air seems pregnant with terror. I sit huddled, and just listen, intently. Still, there is no sound. Nature, herself, seems dead. Then, the oppressive stillness is broken by a little eldritch scream of wind, that sweeps 'round the house, and dies away, remotely.

I let my gaze wander across the half-lighted room. By the great clock in the far corner, is a dark, tall shadow. For a short instant, I stare, frightenedly. Then, I see that it is nothing, and am, momentarily, relieved.

In the time that follows, the thought flashes through my brain, why not leave this house – this house of mystery and terror? Then, as though in answer, there sweeps up, across my sight, a vision of the wondrous Sea of Sleep, – the Sea of Sleep where she and I have been allowed to meet, after the years of separation and sorrow; and I know that I shall stay on here, whatever happens.

Through the side window, I note the somber blackness of the night. My glance wanders away, and 'round the room; resting on one shadowy object and another. Suddenly, I turn, and look at the window on my right; as I do so, I breathe quickly, and bend forward, with a frightened gaze at something outside the window, but close to the bars. I am looking at a vast, misty swine-face, over which fluctuates a flamboyant flame, of a greenish hue. It is the Thing from the arena. The quivering mouth seems to drip with a continual, phosphorescent slaver. The eyes are staring straight into the room, with an inscrutable expression. Thus, I sit rigidly – frozen.

The Thing has begun to move. It is turning, slowly, in my direction. Its face is coming 'round toward me. It sees me. Two huge, inhumanly human, eyes are looking through the dimness at me. I am cold with fear; yet, even now, I am keenly conscious, and note, in an irrelevant way, that the distant stars are blotted out by the mass of the giant face.

A fresh horror has come to me. I am rising from my chair, without the least intention. I am on my feet, and something is impelling me toward the door that leads out into the gardens. I wish to stop; but cannot. Some immutable power is opposed to my will, and I go slowly forward, unwilling and resistant. My glance flies 'round the room, helplessly, and stops at the window. The great swine-face has disappeared, and I hear, again, that stealthy pad, pad, pad. It stops outside the door – the door toward which I am being compelled….

There succeeds a short, intense silence; then there comes a sound. It is the rattle of the latch, being slowly lifted. At that, I am filled with desperation. I will not go forward another step. I make a vast effort to return; but it is, as though I press back, upon an invisible wall. I groan out loud, in the agony of my fear, and the sound of my voice is frightening. Again comes that rattle, and I shiver, clammily. I try – aye, fight and struggle, to hold back, *back*; but it is no use….

I am at the door, and, in a mechanical way, I watch my hand go forward, to undo the topmost bolt. It does so, entirely without my volition. Even as I reach up toward the bolt, the door is violently shaken, and I get a sickly whiff of mouldy air, which seems to drive in through the interstices of the doorway. I draw the bolt back, slowly, fighting, dumbly, the while. It comes out of its socket, with a click, and I begin to shake, aguishly. There are two more; one at the bottom of the door; the other, a massive affair, is placed about the middle.

For, perhaps a minute, I stand, with my arms hanging slackly, by my sides. The influence to meddle with the fastenings of the door, seems to have gone. All at once, there comes the sudden rattle of iron, at my feet. I glance down, quickly, and realize, with an unspeakable terror, that my foot is pushing back the lower bolt. An awful sense of helplessness assails me…. The bolt comes out of its hold, with a slight, ringing sound and I stagger on my feet, grasping at the great, central bolt, for support. A minute passes, an eternity; then another— My God, help me! I am being forced to work upon the last fastening. *I will not!* Better to die, than open to the Terror, that is on the other side of the door. Is there no escape…? God help me, I have jerked the bolt half out of its socket! My lips emit a hoarse scream of terror, the bolt is three parts drawn, now, and still my unconscious hands work toward my doom. Only a fraction of steel, between my soul and That. Twice, I scream out in the supreme agony of my fear; then, with a mad effort, I tear my hands away. My eyes seem blinded. A great blackness is falling upon me. Nature has come to my rescue. I feel my knees giving. There is a loud, quick thudding upon the door, and I am falling, falling….

I must have lain there, at least a couple of hours. As I recover, I am aware that the other candle has burnt out, and the room is in an almost total darkness. I cannot rise to my feet, for I am cold, and filled with a terrible cramp. Yet my brain is clear, and there is no longer the strain of that unholy influence.

Cautiously, I get upon my knees, and feel for the central bolt. I find it, and push it securely back into its socket; then the one at the bottom of the door. By this time, I am able to rise to my feet, and so manage to secure the fastening at the top. After that, I go down upon my knees, again, and creep away among the furniture, in the direction of the stairs. By doing this, I am safe from observation from the window.

I reach the opposite door, and, as I leave the study, cast one nervous glance over my shoulder, toward the window. Out in the night, I seem to catch a glimpse of something impalpable; but it may be only a fancy. Then, I am in the passage, and on the stairs.

Reaching my bedroom, I clamber into bed, all clothed as I am, and pull the bedclothes over me. There, after awhile, I begin to regain a little confidence. It is impossible to sleep; but I am grateful for the added warmth of the bedclothes. Presently, I try to think over the happenings of the past night; but, though I cannot sleep, I find that it is useless, to attempt consecutive thought. My brain seems curiously blank.

Toward morning, I begin to toss, uneasily. I cannot rest, and, after awhile, I get out of bed, and pace the floor. The wintry dawn is beginning to creep through the windows, and shows the bare discomfort of the old room. Strange, that, through all these years, it has never occurred to me how dismal the place really is. And so a time passes.

From somewhere down stairs, a sound comes up to me. I go to the bedroom door, and listen. It is Mary, bustling about the great, old kitchen, getting the breakfast ready. I feel little interest. I am not hungry. My thoughts, however; continue to dwell upon her. How little the weird happenings in this house seem to trouble her. Except in the incident of the Pit creatures, she has seemed unconscious of anything unusual occurring. She is old, like myself; yet how little we have to do with one another. Is it because we have nothing in common; or only that, being old, we care less for society, than quietness? These and other matters pass through my mind, as I meditate; and help to distract my attention, for a while, from the oppressive thoughts of the night.

After a time, I go to the window, and, opening it, look out. The sun is now above the horizon, and the air, though cold, is sweet and crisp. Gradually, my brain clears, and a sense of security, for the time being, comes to me. Somewhat happier, I go down stairs, and out into the garden, to have a look at the dog.

As I approach the kennel, I am greeted by the same mouldy stench that assailed me at the door last night. Shaking off a momentary sense of fear, I call to the dog; but he takes no heed, and, after calling once more, I throw a small stone into the kennel. At this, he moves, uneasily, and I shout his name, again; but do not go closer. Presently, my sister comes out, and joins me, in trying to coax him from the kennel.

In a little the poor beast rises, and shambles out lurching queerly. In the daylight he stands swaying from side to side, and blinking stupidly. I look and note that the horrid wound is larger, much larger, and seems to have a whitish, fungoid appearance. My sister moves to fondle him; but I detain her, and explain that I think it will be better not to go too near him for a few days; as it is impossible to tell what may be the matter with him; and it is well to be cautious.

A minute later, she leaves me; coming back with a basin of odd scraps of food. This she places on the ground, near the dog, and I push it into his reach, with the aid of a branch, broken from one of the shrubs. Yet, though the meat should be tempting, he takes no notice of it; but retires to his kennel. There is still water in his drinking vessel, so, after a few moments' talk, we go back to the house. I can see that my sister is much puzzled as to what is the matter with the animal; yet it would be madness, even to hint the truth to her.

The day slips away, uneventfully; and night comes on. I have determined to repeat my experiment of last night. I cannot say that it is wisdom; yet my mind is made up. Still, however, I have taken precautions; for I have driven stout nails in at the back of each of the three bolts, that secure the door, opening from the study into the gardens. This will, at least, prevent a recurrence of the danger I ran last night.

From ten to about two-thirty, I watch; but nothing occurs; and, finally, I stumble off to bed, where I am soon asleep.

Chapter XXVI
The Luminous Speck

I AWAKE SUDDENLY. It is still dark. I turn over, once or twice, in my endeavors to sleep again; but I cannot sleep. My head is aching, slightly; and, by turns I am hot and cold. In a little,

I give up the attempt, and stretch out my hand, for the matches. I will light my candle, and read, awhile; perhaps, I shall be able to sleep, after a time. For a few moments, I grope; then my hand touches the box; but, as I open it, I am startled, to see a phosphorescent speck of fire, shining amid the darkness. I put out my other hand, and touch it. It is on my wrist. With a feeling of vague alarm, I strike a light, hurriedly, and look; but can see nothing, save a tiny scratch.

'Fancy!' I mutter, with a half sigh of relief. Then the match burns my finger, and I drop it, quickly. As I fumble for another, the thing shines out again. I know, now, that it is no fancy. This time, I light the candle, and examine the place, more closely. There is a slight, greenish discoloration 'round the scratch. I am puzzled and worried. Then a thought comes to me. I remember the morning after the Thing appeared. I remember that the dog licked my hand. It was this one, with the scratch on it; though I have not been even conscious of the abasement, until now. A horrible fear has come to me. It creeps into my brain – the dog's wound, shines at night. With a dazed feeling, I sit down on the side of the bed, and try to think; but cannot. My brain seems numbed with the sheer horror of this new fear.

Time moves on, unheeded. Once, I rouse up, and try to persuade myself that I am mistaken; but it is no use. In my heart, I have no doubt.

Hour after hour, I sit in the darkness and silence, and shiver, hopelessly....

The day has come and gone, and it is night again.

This morning, early, I shot the dog, and buried it, away among the bushes. My sister is startled and frightened; but I am desperate. Besides, it is better so. The foul growth had almost hidden its left side. And I – the place on my wrist has enlarged, perceptibly. Several times, I have caught myself muttering prayers – little things learnt as a child. God, Almighty God, help me! I shall go mad.

Six days, and I have eaten nothing. It is night. I am sitting in my chair. Ah, God! I wonder have any ever felt the horror of life that I have come to know? I am swathed in terror. I feel ever the burning of this dread growth. It has covered all my right arm and side, and is beginning to creep up my neck. Tomorrow, it will eat into my face. I shall become a terrible mass of living corruption. There is no escape. Yet, a thought has come to me, born of a sight of the gun-rack, on the other side of the room. I have looked again – with the strangest of feelings. The thought grows upon me. God, Thou knowest, Thou must know, that death is better, aye, better a thousand times than This. This! Jesus, forgive me, but I cannot live, cannot, cannot! I dare not! I am beyond all help – there is nothing else left. It will, at least, spare me that final horror....

I think I must have been dozing. I am very weak, and oh! so miserable, so miserable and tired – tired. The rustle of the paper, tries my brain. My hearing seems preternaturally sharp. I will sit awhile and think....

"Hush! I hear something, down – down in the cellars. It is a creaking sound. My God, it is the opening of the great, oak trap. What can be doing that? The scratching of my pen deafens me... I must listen.... There are steps on the stairs; strange padding steps, that come up and nearer.... Jesus, be merciful to me, an old man. There is something fumbling at the door-handle. O God, help me now! Jesus – The door is opening – slowly. Somethi—"

That is all.[15]

Chapter XXVII
Conclusion

I PUT DOWN the Manuscript, and glanced across at Tonnison: he was sitting, staring out into the dark. I waited a minute; then I spoke.

"Well?" I said.

He turned, slowly, and looked at me. His thoughts seemed to have gone out of him into a great distance.

"Was he mad?" I asked, and indicated the MS., with a half nod.

Tonnison stared at me, unseeingly, a moment; then, his wits came back to him, and, suddenly, he comprehended my question.

"No!" he said.

I opened my lips, to offer a contradictory opinion; for my sense of the saneness of things, would not allow me to take the story literally; then I shut them again, without saying anything. Somehow, the certainty in Tonnison's voice affected my doubts. I felt, all at once, less assured; though I was by no means convinced as yet.

After a few moments' silence, Tonnison rose, stiffly, and began to undress. He seemed disinclined to talk; so I said nothing; but followed his example. I was weary; though still full of the story I had just read.

Somehow, as I rolled into my blankets, there crept into my mind a memory of the old gardens, as we had seen them. I remembered the odd fear that the place had conjured up in our hearts; and it grew upon me, with conviction, that Tonnison was right.

It was very late when we rose – nearly midday; for the greater part of the night had been spent in reading the MS.

Tonnison was grumpy, and I felt out of sorts. It was a somewhat dismal day, and there was a touch of chilliness in the air. There was no mention of going out fishing on either of our parts. We got dinner, and, after that, just sat and smoked in silence.

Presently, Tonnison asked for the Manuscript: I handed it to him, and he spent most of the afternoon in reading it through by himself.

It was while he was thus employed, that a thought came to me:

"What do you say to having another look at—?" I nodded my head down stream.

Tonnison looked up. "Nothing!" he said, abruptly; and, somehow, I was less annoyed, than relieved, at his answer.

After that, I left him alone.

A little before teatime, he looked up at me, curiously.

"Sorry, old chap, if I was a bit short with you just now;" (just now, indeed! he had not spoken for the last three hours) "but I would not go there again," and he indicated with his head, "for anything that you could offer me. Ugh!" and he put down that history of a man's terror and hope and despair.

The next morning, we rose early, and went for our accustomed swim: we had partly shaken off the depression of the previous day; and so, took our rods when we had finished breakfast, and spent the day at our favorite sport.

After that day, we enjoyed our holiday to the utmost; though both of us looked forward to the time when our driver should come; for we were tremendously anxious to inquire of him, and through him among the people of the tiny hamlet, whether any of them could give us information about that strange garden, lying away by itself in the heart of an almost unknown tract of country.

At last, the day came, on which we expected the driver to come across for us. He arrived early, while we were still abed; and, the first thing we knew, he was at the opening of the tent, inquiring whether we had had good sport. We replied in the affirmative; and then, both together, almost in the same breath, we asked the question that was uppermost in our minds: Did he know anything about an old garden, and a great pit, and a lake, situated some miles away, down the river; also, had he ever heard of a great house thereabouts?

No, he did not, and had not; yet, stay, he had heard a rumor, once upon a time, of a great, old house standing alone out in the wilderness; but, if he remembered rightly it was a place given over to the fairies; or, if that had not been so, he was certain that there had been something "quare" about it; and, anyway, he had heard nothing of it for a very long while – not since he was quite a gossoon. No, he could not remember anything particular about it; indeed, he did not know he remembered anything "at all, at all" until we questioned him.

"Look here," said Tonnison, finding that this was about all that he could tell us, "just take a walk 'round the village, while we dress, and find out something, if you can."

With a nondescript salute, the man departed on his errand; while we made haste to get into our clothes; after which, we began to prepare breakfast.

We were just sitting down to it, when he returned.

"It's all in bed the lazy divvils is, sor," he said, with a repetition of the salute, and an appreciative eye to the good things spread out on our provision chest, which we utilized as a table.

"Oh, well, sit down," replied my friend, "and have something to eat with us." Which the man did without delay.

After breakfast, Tonnison sent him off again on the same errand, while we sat and smoked. He was away some three-quarters of an hour, and, when he returned, it was evident that he had found out something. It appeared that he had got into conversation with an ancient man of the village, who, probably, knew more – though it was little enough – of the strange house, than any other person living.

The substance of this knowledge was, that, in the "ancient man's" youth – and goodness knows how long back that was – there had stood a great house in the center of the gardens, where now was left only that fragment of ruin. This house had been empty for a great while; years before his – the ancient man's – birth. It was a place shunned by the people of the village, as it had been shunned by their fathers before them. There were many things said about it, and all were of evil. No one ever went near it, either by day or night. In the village it was a synonym of all that is unholy and dreadful.

And then, one day, a man, a stranger, had ridden through the village, and turned off down the river, in the direction of the House, as it was always termed by the villagers. Some hours afterward, he had ridden back, taking the track by which he had come, toward Ardrahan. Then, for three months or so, nothing was heard. At the end of that time, he reappeared; but now, he was accompanied by an elderly woman, and a large number of donkeys, laden with various articles. They had passed through the village without stopping, and gone straight down the bank of the river, in the direction of the House.

Since that time, no one, save the man whom they had chartered to bring over monthly supplies of necessaries from Ardrahan, had ever seen either of them: and him, none had ever induced to talk; evidently, he had been well paid for his trouble.

The years had moved onward, uneventfully enough, in that little hamlet; the man making his monthly journeys, regularly.

One day, he had appeared as usual on his customary errand. He had passed through the village without exchanging more than a surly nod with the inhabitants and gone on toward the House. Usually, it was evening before he made the return journey. On this occasion, however, he had reappeared in the village, a few hours later, in an extraordinary state of excitement, and with the astounding information, that the House had disappeared bodily, and that a stupendous pit now yawned in the place where it had stood.

This news, it appears, so excited the curiosity of the villagers, that they overcame their fears, and marched *en masse* to the place. There, they found everything, just as described by the carrier.

This was all that we could learn. Of the author of the MS., who he was, and whence he came, we shall never know.

His identity is, as he seems to have desired, buried forever.

That same day, we left the lonely village of Kraighten. We have never been there since.

Sometimes, in my dreams, I see that enormous pit, surrounded, as it is, on all sides by wild trees and bushes. And the noise of the water rises upward, and blends – in my sleep – with other and lower noises; while, over all, hangs the eternal shroud of spray.

Grief[16]

Fierce hunger reigns within my breast,
I had not dreamt that this whole world,
Crushed in the hand of God, could yield
Such bitter essence of unrest,
Such pain as Sorrow now hath hurled
Out of its dreadful heart, unsealed!

Each sobbing breath is but a cry,
My heart-strokes knells of agony,
And my whole brain has but one thought
That nevermore through life shall I
(Save in ache of memory)
Touch hands with thee, who now art naught!

Through the whole void of night I search,
So dumbly crying out to thee;
But thou are not; and night's vast throne
Becomes an all stupendous church
With star-bells knelling unto me
Who in all space am most alone!

An hungered, to the shore I creep,
Perchance some comfort waits on me
From the old Sea's eternal heart;
But lo! from all the solemn deep,
Far voices out of mystery
Seem questioning why we are apart!

"Where'er I go I am alone
Who once, through thee, had all the world.
My breast is one whole raging pain
For that which was, and now is flown
Into the Blank where life is hurled
Where all is not, nor is again!"

Footnotes for 'The House on the Borderland'

1. An apparently unmeaning interpolation. I can find no previous reference in the MS. to this matter. It becomes clearer, however, in the light of succeeding incidents. – Ed.

2. Here, the writing becomes undecipherable, owing to the damaged condition of this part of the MS. Below I print such fragments as are legible. – Ed.

3. NOTE. – The severest scrutiny has not enabled me to decipher more of the damaged portion of the MS. It commences to be legible again with the chapter entitled 'The Noise in the Night.' – Ed.

4. The Recluse uses this as an illustration, evidently in the sense of the popular conception of a comet. – Ed.

5. No further mention is made of the moon. From what is said here, it is evident that our satellite had greatly increased its distance from the earth. Possibly, at a later age it may even have broken loose from our attraction. I cannot but regret that no light is shed on this point. – Ed.

6. Conceivably, frozen air. – Ed.

7. See previous footnote. This would explain the snow (?) within the room. – Ed.

8. I am confounded that neither here, nor later on, does the Recluse make any further mention of the continued north and south movement (apparent, of course,) of the sun from solstice to solstice. – Ed.

9. At this time the sound-carrying atmosphere must have been either incredibly attenuated, or – more probably – non-existent. In the light of this, it cannot be supposed that these, or any other, noises would have been apparent to living ears – to hearing, as we, in the material body, understand that sense. – Ed.

10. I can only suppose that the time of the earth's yearly journey had ceased to bear its present relative proportion to the period of the sun's rotation. – Ed.

11. A careful reading of the MS. suggests that, either the sun is traveling on an orbit of great eccentricity, or else that it was approaching the green star on a lessening orbit. And at this moment, I conceive it to be finally torn directly from its oblique course, by the gravitational pull of the immense star. – Ed.

12.. It will be noticed here that the earth was 'slowly traversing the tremendous face of the dead sun.' No explanation is given of this, and we must conclude, either that the speed of time had slowed, or else that the earth was actually progressing on its orbit at a rate, slow, when measured by existing standards. A careful study of the MS. however, leads me to conclude that the speed of time had been steadily decreasing for a very considerable period. – Ed.

13. See first footnote, Chapter 18.

14. Without doubt, the flame-edged mass of the Dead Central Sun, seen from another dimension. – Ed.

15. NOTE. – From the unfinished word, it is possible, on the MS., to trace a faint line of ink, which suggests that the pen has trailed away over the paper; possibly, through fright and weakness. – Ed.

16. These stanzas I found, in pencil, upon a piece of foolscap gummed in behind the fly-leaf of the MS. They have all the appearance of having been written at an earlier date than the Manuscript. – Ed.

The Rediscovery of Plants

E.E. King

She was born long after the war – long after environmental devastation had rendered natural human conception impossible. Radiation and its effects made selection necessary. We did not have the food, or space inside the dome, for useless eaters. We were accustomed to giving up the defectives: infants lacking sight or hearing, newborns tainted by fallout or fertility drugs. When survival is desperate, the unthinkable becomes commonplace.

We were starving. Most of our newborns lacked brains or faces. If we did not feed them, they died. If we did not dispose of them they rotted. They were dangerous, epidemic, worse than nothing. Modern Typhoid Marys'.

The defectives were so obviously lacking, so clearly nothing but a drain on scarce resources. Even the sentimentalists among us had no argument. The dome was built on cement. We had no place to bury, no way to burn. We combined disposal with nutrition. It was pure logic.

Now, the defects give back. They are welcomed into the world. Their cells are cloned to grow food, but it is a slow process.

To grow cultured meat, we anesthetized and dissected the defectives, utilizing the tissue with the most rapid rate of proliferation. Stem cells multiplied quickest, but were difficult to control. Fully developed muscle was ideal, but increased sluggishly. Even with all the cells from all the defectives reproducing in every lab beneath the dome, we only received meat once a year, on The Celebration of Survival.

We crowded together, fifty thousand strong, shoulder to shoulder and cheek to cheek, filling the central of the dome. It was the only space inside our protective bubble not filled with house cubies, machinery, meat plants, water desalination and electrolysis facilities. The one place where we could stand together, united in our determination to continuance. We raised our voices so loud, harmonies echoed from every wall:

"We will survive.
Give thanks to the sun.
We will continue.
Give thanks to water electrolysis.
We persevere.
Thanks to desalination
Our race is not done
We make up our lack
We give and give back
We live afresh
Eat of our flesh
No sacrifice is too great
To build our state."

Then we are each given sixty grams of meat. It is tender – our one luxury, our commitment to continuance. It is the same guarantee that an earlier age made when they took Communion: consuming the body of their beloved savior, drinking his holy blood, eating his sacred flesh. We have taken this promise to its rational conclusion and we are nothing if not rational. When survival is in doubt, fancies fade and faith dies quickly.

This is our one sacrament. The only time we come together without work. It is brief and powerful. It is vital.

Most of our nourishment comes from algae. It's healthy, but tasteless. Flavor is a luxury we can no longer afford. So, though we are in need of whole and healthy minds and bodies, defectives are welcomed, too.

My first baby, a boy, lacked eyes and ears. The abnormality was detected early on. In the days before meat cloning he would have been immediately aborted, but as it was, I had to carry it to term. I will not pretend it was easy, to be the bearer of food, but survival is never easy.

My second birth, a girl, was missing a small but vital fold in the cerebral cortex. I had no qualms about delivering her into the hands of the State.

While most defectives were obvious at birth, a few conditions did not reveal themselves until much later. That was harder.

Philicautotroph Syndrome, for example, is undetectable until the child is about age six. At first PS children seem normal, better than normal, as one the earliest traits observable, is an outsize ability to love.

"100% of Philicautotrophs are kind-spirited and 98% empathize with others' pain. Infants with Philicautotroph syndrome make frequent eye contact. Young children will often hug strangers. Individuals typically have high empathy, and are rarely aggressive. They excel in reading intentions, emotions, and mental states." – Hypatia Adair, Treatise on PS detection, 2314

Though I, Hypatia, am credited with discovering PS, in all fairness their attributes were first uncovered by their mothers who would not give their defects to the state, even though there was perfectly good meat on them. Some secreted their babes in basements. They died. Others concealed their children in window-lit attics. They thrived. Thus, we discovered they could not live without light.

"Each PS sufferer degenerates differently. In some, their eyes are the initial and primary organs affected. It is not so much a diminution of vision as a change of perspective. Their focus narrows. They become less responsive to dull colors.

"In others, audio changes are first. They smile and sway as though listening to music.

They cease to react to angry word or tone.

"In some, olfactory senses are initially effected." Hypatia Adair, PS Problems and Solutions, 2315

It was odd. PS patients seemed to react only to pleasant scents. It was dangerous, not having a warning system. A child who smelled air freshener, but not the sewage infiltrating the dome was imperiled.

As they soaked up the sunlight, listening to the rhythms in their heads, their appetites decreased They stopped responding to outside stimuli. Eventually, they ceased eating all together. They stayed where they were placed. Most did not respond to human touch, or voice. A few folded their hands when stroked, or curled their toes when tickled, but that was all. Their skin grew sallow, yellow gradually giving way to bright green.

It was from those few hidden children, some discovered when the disease was very far advanced, that I learned the secret of their foodless existence. I tested them. I dissected them. It is not as gruesome as it sounds. PS takes not only motion and sound, it takes everything – every nerve, muscle and neuron, every thought, idea and sentiment. By the time sufferers reach puberty, they are not human.

I worked on the program. Devising the best placement for each PS. Spreading them throughout the dome for maximum efficiency. Even though the children were no longer responsive, even though they were no longer really individuals, their mothers protested when I removed them. I did not understand: why a mother would cling so to her defective? Why would she care where they were placed? So many things I did not understand. I do now. I wish I didn't.

As those with PS grew, they turned light into sugar. They lived on sun beams, breathing in carbon monoxide and breathing out oxygen, enriching the air inside the dome. And so, we kept them.

I called her Gaia, my first perfect child. She had gazed into my eyes when I'd held her, searching so intently, I felt she could see into my soul. She made me want to suckle her, even though I had no milk, and even if I did, it would have been contaminated.

I was not prepared for the joy burying my face in the nape of her tiny neck gave me. I had never imagined she would smell of freshness, possibility, and hope. It was like breathing nineteen percent oxygen.

The air inside the dome fluctuated between fifteen and eleven percent. Maintaining adequate levels was one of our most difficult challenges. It had been easier to fill nutritional requirements in our algae tanks, even though we were always hungry. It had even been simpler to provide 1.7 liters of potable water per person daily from our desalination plants, though, despite our best efforts, the dryness was always there: a silent scream, a constant tickle in the back of every throat. The only benefit of the thirst, was that we rarely noticed the gnawing in our bellies.

The oxygen problem should have come as no surprise, after The Last War, the only surface to build on had been cement, and with almost fifty thousand people breathing in an enclosed space, it was a wonder we were able to keep up acceptable levels at all.

Water Electrolysis saved us. We poured seawater and diluted Hydrochloric Acid into a Hofmann Voltameter and passed electricity through it. Oxygen gathered on one end and was released into the dome. But even with the plants running at full capacity, we never got beyond fifteen percent.

Some whispered that the engineers had secret meetings in rooms filled with 22% oxygen, but I never believed it. In an earlier age, corruption was as ubiquitous as breathing, but since The Last War, shortages are too great. The only way we have survived is to depend on each other. Perhaps it is our silver lining: that having destroyed the feast, we must divide the scraps. Egalitarianism grown from deprivation. Altruism based on need.

Gaia walked and talked early. Her happiness was infectious. I, born after the war, when humanity struggled to survive inside our small domed city, had never considered things beyond endurance. We were too dehydrated, to be concerned with beauty. We were too hungry, to consider feeding the soul. But Gaia made the world seem full of possibilities. For her, every step was a dance, every word a poem.

Her voice, high and sweet, made me think of descriptions of birdsong. It was a sign, but I wasn't watching.

I had never expected to find wonder in the everyday; a visit to the algae tanks, a trip up a narrow ladder to adjust the solar panels, but she did, and I saw through her eyes. Every window to the outside became a portal to a magical realm. And I was drawn in, seeing unstable arcs of electromagnetic radiation outside the dome as rainbows, admiring the colors without worrying about what caused them. I was blinded by her light and never noticed the warnings.

She described the commonest things in words that made me look at them anew: the droplets of oil condensing on the dome's surface became tiny, iridescence replicas of our world, the reddish mists rising from the algae vaults transformed into clouds of glory.

"Language used by individuals with Philicautotroph syndrome differs notably from unaffected populations, including individuals matched for IQ. People with Philicautotroph syndrome use speech that is rich in emotional descriptors, high in prosody (exaggerated rhythm and emotional intensity), and features unusual terms and strange idioms." – Hypatia Adair, Further Discovers on Development in PS, 2315.

It was Gaia's strange idioms and fanciful metaphors that stopped first. Her speech grew simpler and more direct. I thought it was a sign of maturity and scolded myself for missing her curious sideway view of life. She had been born into a practical world with no room for illusions. So I tried not to mourn, never realizing it was a sign of degeneration.

Even if I had understood, what could I have done? I could not seek medical help. If she was a defective, she would be used for meat. Even as I considered the options, her cells were changing, each thin-walled cell division, metamorphosing from muscle and nerve into meristematic and permanent tissue.

She became less talkative, less gregarious, less adventurous. By the time she was eight, she had stopped dancing. By the time she was ten she had ceased walking. She liked to sit cross-legged on the floor in a corner soaking up the wan rays that permeated the dome, rocking slowly back and forth, softly humming to herself. I missed the birdsong of her voice and the rhythm of her skipping steps; but mostly I missed her laughter, that spontaneous burbling up of joy, that contagion of happiness.

Her vision was contracting until she could perceive only truth and goodness. She saw rainbows, but not the sea of trash below. She watched the love in my eyes, but not the trails of tears wearing grooves into my once-smooth skin. In this world, where beauty was so rare, she became blind.

I refused to believe. I brought her food. I read her books. I showed her pictures. I pleaded with her to respond. I shook her and yelled at her, but her eardrums were tuned only to pleasant sounds. She could hear harmonies, but not my sobbing. I slapped her non-responsive face. Her smile didn't even fade – not at first. But each day it grew dimmer, not because her mouth muscles were relaxing, but because her features were diminishing, retreating into blankness. My girl, my child, my joy – she was leaving me without moving.

I tell myself that I am fortunate. At least Gaia was born after we understood the benefits of PS. At least I will not lose her to the State, this daughter I love. And I wonder.

I wonder about movement and sentience. I wonder what Gaia, green head filled with light, is feeling? I wonder if she is thinking? Does she remember? Does she recall our games of hide and seek, our tales of magic and wonder? Does she still love me?

Man looks in the mirror and says, "That is beautiful. That is smart. I am the master of the universe."

I look at my small, motionless, verdant child. I think she's smiling but it's hard to be sure. I bury my nose in her flesh, trying to locate that fresh baby scent, but unearthing only a vegetable moistness. Her features are so indistinct, her face only a memory. Her brain has dissolved into meristematic tissue. In an earlier time, she would've provided food for animals and a place to live for birds. Even now, she cleanses our planet with each breath. And I wonder, which species is superior?

And I wonder, when she so clearly has a reason for being, why this is so hard? Why do I mourn this gift? Why do I feel I have lost her?

The Sun Takers

Michael Kortes

THE BUNKER'S hatch blew off its hinges with a titanic roar.

The explosion watered Wren's eyes with its stench of sulphur but it wouldn't stop her from scrambling down into the cloud of concrete dust. She could not hesitate. Four bullets and surprise would be all she had going for her. Still, she took one last glance up at the sun; or rather where it was supposed to be, now almost completely obscured by the haze of grey that had become the sky.

That glance provided her, she told herself, with her moral authority. The loss of the sun justified her choice to join a retrieval gang. Whatever was inside was not hers and would be tenaciously defended. If she wanted to steal it, she would have to take it with force.

She slid down the ladder into the blackness below. The bunker was an old missile silo. The countryside was full of them, perforating the badlands of North Dakota like a toddler gone mad with a drill on a wooden board. When the sun was lost to the haze, those that still had something left to protect, like food, took up residence. But once their shelter was found they became prey for the scavengers whose desperation was greater than their own.

Wren bent her knees to absorb the shock as her feet hit the concrete floor. Enshrouded in darkness she quickly pulled a cheap neon glow stick from her belt and cracked it against the wall of rusted steel, holding it high in one hand while she brandished her pistol with the other. The pale sphere of green revealed a central tube running in both directions before vanishing beyond the limits of her light.

This place was much bigger than she thought – and empty, or so it seemed. She called up to her partner Zan, sending him the all-clear. Zan always entered second. He outranked her in the Hungry Maw clan and wasn't shy about exercising his privilege.

"Keep going," he called down, waving her off. The blind tunnel exploration would fall to her. With the dust starting to dissipate she took a moment to remove the plastic swim goggles she used for protective eyewear and ran her fingers through her remaining patches of hair. Once, long ago, it had been long and blond. She remembered when it used to smell of Lavender and blue bubble gum, infused from her favourite shampoos. But her hair had fallen away after she fought through her first serious spate of starvation: first in strands, then in horrid soul-destroying clumps. She was much softer then. Much. Now, whenever she knew fear, she would give her stringy tuffs a tug and know she had overcome far worse. Both of them, hair and girl alike, were survivors.

She readied her pistol and, seeing no reason to choose otherwise, randomly advanced into the darkness to her right. As she scanned with her glow stick she saw there were cables affixed to the ceiling. Whatever hoarder lived down here, they might have had power at one time. No doubt any reservoir of gasoline for a generator would long since be depleted, so she doubted that whatever the cables attached to would still work. Still, it made sense to trace the columns of black stringy lines and see where they went.

She silently followed the cylindrical corridor around a second awkward bend until she spotted the telltale glow of electrical lighting, flickering from a low-ceilinged chamber beyond. Unexpected.

She quietly smothered her glow stick inside the fold of the rags of her tattered leather jacket, allowing her eyes to slowly adjust to the illumination creeping around the next corner. She squeezed the handle grip of her gun with both hands while she sucked in silent breaths, waiting. Then, gritting her teeth, she spun around the corner and pointed the barrel of her weapon, simultaneously crossing the threshold into a much larger chamber. Rows of file cabinets choked the room, awkwardly placed as they surrounded a large boardroom table that had obviously seen better days.

And there he was, sitting by himself in a chair with wide rubber wheels, his hands raised skyward.

"Don't move, hoarder!" Wren cried, her gun aimed straight at the dead center of his chest. Her eyes, however, cast about. He might not be alone. This had all the hallmarks of a trick. Hoarders didn't just surrender. Occasionally they killed themselves, fearing rape or cannibalism at the hands of a retrieval gang, but mostly they fought – tooth and nail.

"I'm unarmed," he said with a dissonant level of calm. "And it's just me down here." The warm disarming smile of the old bearded man had the opposite effect. Nothing about this felt right.

"The food is in the room off to the left," he continued, motioning with his chin. "The pantry's long been cleaned out, I'm afraid, but the hydroponics bay still has a decent harvest – if you can stomach vegetables."

Wren took a step forward and thrust her gun at the hoarder. With her diet consisting primarily of cockroaches, Wren had longed for the days she was still able to trap a sewer rat and suck the marrow from its bones. She had half a mind to just plug him now. Was he trolling her? A vegetable – a real vegetable – was beyond hope.

Still, the child within her wondered what kind it might be.

She suppressed it.

"Nobody has a garden," she said. "Not anymore."

"Ah!" said the old man with a glimmer in his eye, "There's a turbine two levels down, still powered by an underground stream. I can't get to it to service it anymore, but most days it still generates enough power to run the grow lights and keep the computers going."

Levels? Computers?

"What is this place?" She lowered her gun slowly. The old man appeared crippled. But even if it was a ruse she should be able to remove his head from his shoulders before he could close the gap between them.

"Why, it's a laboratory – or at least it was," he answered as though embarrassed by its sorry state.

"Naw, this is one of them missile silos."

"It was that too, and a telecom bunker. But my team moved in and repurposed the whole thing as a lab after the Obscuration." Something within her told Wren she needed to know more. But priorities.

"Show me the food."

And so the tour began. The talkative old man said his name was William. The others had been gone for some time. He was now the sole custodian.

The hydroponics bay was small, a room not much bigger than a walk-in closet. But the bounty rising from the tiered boxes of fertilizer under the soft white lights was the greatest

Wren had seen in years. Seconds later she was gnawing on a real honest to goodness carrot – orange and everything.

William offered her water and got her a plastic cup.

"Why're you being so nice?" It was more an accusation than a question. "You gone wrong in the head down here? You get what I am right?" She flashed her clan branding, showing him the puffy black scars that ran down her arms. Vaguely reminiscent of the incisor teeth of some predator, the stylized wounds marked her as property of the Hungry Maw, one of many sacrifices Wren had made to survive. "This stuff all belongs to the Maw now."

William nodded. "I understand. I have little need of it. I've been dying for a very long time."

"Yeah? What have you got cripple?"

"C1-82, corticobasal degeneration," he said from rote before adding, "something like Parkinson's."

"Sorry to hear it."

"Don't be, these days everyone left has it just as bad."

"Damn straight." He was right. What was she doing empathizing with a hoarder?

At that moment, just as Wren was helping herself to a second carrot, a bell went off: a soft chime, low and gentle in its pitch, its tone echoing from another chamber.

Wren's gun was raised again. "What trick is this?!"

"It's nothing," said William, his hands motioning to calm her. "Well it's not *nothing*, it's actually something rather extraordinary – harmless, but still extraordinary. It's an alert from the computer room."

"Take me," she commanded, gesturing with her gun. Where the heck was Zan? She would have expected him to have followed her in by now.

William pivoted his chair and exited the hydroponics bay traversing through yet another cramped tunnel of corrugated steel. Wren followed from behind as William began to push himself up a makeshift ramp of plywood covering the left-half of a small set of cement stairs.

He was slow. She lost her patience and moved to help, grabbing his handlebars as she wheeled him up to the higher level. To do so she had to return her gun to the hollow in the small of her back.

Along the way they passed a small chamber with a further cylindrical shaft jutting up to the surface. But rather than hosting a bolted ladder like the shaft through which Wren had entered, this time there was a long metal tube running up its length instead. At its base was a viewfinder with a pair of handles wrapped in electrical tape.

"That a—?"

"Periscope? Yes."

"You can see the outside from there?"

"Most days, when it doesn't rain. I check it daily, it's my only connection to the outside now."

Wren stopped William, pulling him back to the tube with the scope. She wondered where the top stuck out and how she had missed it. It must have been concealed somehow.

"Did you…?"

"…watch you watching me? Yes," he said. "For many days. I admired your tenacity."

Wren had staked out William's silo for four days and three nights, waiting for Zan to return with the explosives. He was late and her belly had ached with a fierceness that had become all too familiar as of late, but he had come.

"I thought you'd leave and go home."

"Naw," said Wren. "The Maw says to quit is to die." She entered the cement shaft to inspect the tube. She gave the periscope a try and was rewarded with a surprisingly clear view of the mud-crusted waste that was once the countryside. She did not, though, see Zan.

"I was sorely tempted to invite you inside, but I haven't been able to climb the ladder for well over a year now."

"You're lucky then. When a hoarder sticks his head out to get some air or dump a chamber pot, I pop 'em." She gestured to her gun.

"I see."

"It's my job."

"Then I'm lucky I dispose of waste in the river below by way of another shaft. I'll show you, c'mon!"

"Naw. Don't need to see the crapper. Take me to where the beep comes from."

A minute later they entered yet another cell of steel, once again with an uncomfortably low ceiling, only this time even more strangulated with thick electrical cords. A large black monitor bolted to the wall displayed a single digital number:

1278

"The number on the screen increased by one," explained William patiently. "Every time it happens it causes the bell to go off."

"What're you, some kind of scientist?"

"An engineer actually, or rather I was."

"Same thing." Wren almost spat. Many said it was the scientific community that invented the chemical haze that coated the sky outside.

She stepped in front of him so she could see his face instead of the back of his head. "If you're so smart then, you know who took the sun?" Everybody Wren met had their own opinion on the subject. Everyone blamed someone. Nuclear winter, global warming, God's displeasure.

"Nobody really knows for certain, I'm afraid. I can, of course, tell you what my colleagues and I believe. The reason all of this was built, actually."

"Yeah?"

"It's called a cosmic miasma. Our entire solar system is passing through it. It's like a galaxy-sized cloud. Mostly harmless, unless you need adequate sunlight which I'm afraid all living things do."

"Good," said Wren, pleased with his answer, even though she had heard variations of such a thing once or twice before. "Then when we pass out of this cloud of yours, things'll finally get better." She was a survivor; she could hold on. William seemed smarter than most people left. Maybe he knew what he was talking about.

"Oh child. I am so sorry. That *will* happen, just as you say, but if the readings I saw were accurate, it could take hundreds of years, if not thousands." His smile deserted him as he looked up at her. "This is an extinction event."

Wren chastised herself. She felt stupid for letting her hopes rise. Amateur. The world was pain. But getting your hopes dashed was pain you brought on yourself.

"What's your name," William asked her, finally breaking the silence.

"Wren."

"It's nice to meet you, Wren," he said solemnly. "Even if these are the end times."

"Then how come you're so chipper? The world's dying and you know I'm just gonna shoot you and strip this place."

"Because of that beep. Every time I hear it I know it's going to be OK. Not for me, but for them." He pointed to the monitor:

1278

"The sign? Who are they?"

"They," he repeated, "were only 984 when we started. We miniaturized them Wren. All of them. Absolutely tiny. Not microscopic, but even smaller. Those 984 people now exist in a single drop of water and spec of dirt."

Wren wrinkled her face.

"Earth is dying, Wren, but humanity has survived. Don't you see? We did it!" He took her to a safe in the wall, deftly playing with the circular tumblers until they fell open. Inside was a glass sphere, even smaller than a child's marble. It was nested in a black chassis.

"You're saying that you managed to put people in there? Nobody could live like that. How would they eat?"

"I actually don't know! I just know that they do! We sent them with a supply of livestock: pigs, chickens and a few malnourished cows – maybe some of the last ones on earth. So maybe, *probably*, they've got some kind of agrarian society. But I can't see them Wren, as much as I wish I could. So I really have no idea. They may well have discovered a completely new form of food down there. Maybe they hunt the local fauna, or eat some kind of plant too small to be detected by our imaging."

"Or maybe they're all just dead and you're crazy."

William pointed to his monitor. "Except that we can monitor their vitals. We know they're alive. We don't exactly know how, but we know that they are."

"Naw," said Wren, "They wouldn't have any sun either. They'd be just as screwed as you and me."

"True, true," said William excitedly. "We had to build them one and we can only guess at how well it works. The base here, under the sphere, is called a photonic simulator. It's my contribution to the program, actually. Their world is so small their sun can all be run off of a single battery. The battery is strong enough to power a flashlight for four years."

"So?"

"Or a single microscopic world for 10 Million years!"

"Decent battery then."

"After that, they're on their own. And if humanity can't get it right with a second go and 10 Million years, maybe we deserve to join the dinosaurs and let some other species take a try."

"You're insane, you know that? You've been down here too long." His brain had developed some kind of story, Wren decided. A story to cope with the destruction of his world, a fantasy in which he had somehow saved it personally, bestowing meaning to his meagre existence inside the isolated bunker of a hoarder.

"Sorry. Nobody survives in a snow globe – even if it has a battery attached."

"They're not just surviving, Wren. Remember the bell? They're multiplying. That's how I know. Whatever's going on down there, they're happy with it."

"Multiplying? How?"

William gave her a grin. "Wren, every time that bell goes off there's a new set of vitals detected, a soon-to-be-born baby."

Wren shot William a dark look. Babies had become a taboo subject long ago. Nobody tried to make babies anymore. They never lived. And the nutritional cost of a pregnancy usually spelled the end of the Mother for trying.

"You're saying there are babies in there…?"

"Yes, well over two hundred now. Though the first of them must have already grown into children by now."

Babies. *Children*. Wren remembered wanting a child once, back in the time when she still had golden hair. Her older sister in Texas had had one and dutifully sent her a photo every Christmas. Wren had truly meant to visit, but there was always something and she never did… And then the Obscuration came and the chaos soon after.

"Wait," she said suddenly. "Why are you showing me all of this? Why open the safe?" She hadn't asked him to.

"Because Wren, after you kill me and rummage through this place, I was rather hoping you wouldn't destroy the new world and throw it in the garbage. I figured if you knew what it was, you might leave it be."

"Makes sense." The pair stared at William's world in silence.

"I could kill you quickly," she suddenly offered. "Make it so it doesn't hurt. Much."

The old man gave a wry smile, "I'd take it as a kindness if you did."

Wren pulled up a rickety office chair and sat in it, her gaze irresistibly pulled to William's orb.

"You keep talking about others. But it's just you here. You bury your partners somewhere?"

William pointed to the tiny orb. "Only one of us needed to stay behind to initiate the miniaturization process."

"In there? They all left you?" She scrunched her face.

"My infirmity and lack of a family made me the obvious candidate to act as the custodian."

"But you're *dying*."

"A population of 1,278 tells me no more photonic adjustments are required. They're ready to exist on their own. They don't really need me, Wren, not anymore. "

"You really think things inside are that good? Food and water?"

"The ecosystem works. The water drop suspended inside the orb should be enough for thousands of generations – complete overkill actually. That small, the water might have physical properties we've never considered but the one thing we know is that there's enough of it. Maybe it floats in the air like a cloud or freezes at bizarre temperatures or has a hard skin that needs to be punctured or…." His voice trailed off as he suddenly clued in to where Wren's thoughts had taken her.

William quickly moved to stop her but her words had already begun.

"Do you think that I—?"

"I'm so sorry Wren. We can't miniaturize anymore. That level of power was long lost to us when the coastal grid collapsed. I wish I—"

"It's nothing!" she said, louder than she meant to. "Forget it. I've seen your toys. We're going back to the garden."

They travelled back in silence, William's chair having an easier time gliding downhill. Wren peered around the maze of shafts, gradually coming to realize that William's lab, this level at least, was actually much smaller than she first thought, just scattered with interconnected entrances and exits. In none of them though could she find Zan, who clearly should have been here by now. She resolved to grab a few more vegetables for herself and then go back for him. She recalled she had seen what looked to be a potato, still covered in wrinkly shoots.

Then she caught William wiping his eyes.

"What's with you?" she barked at him.

"I always knew one day I'd have to tell someone the tickets to paradise were all gone. I just didn't know it would be so damn hard."

Wren snorted and gave him a pat on the shoulder.

"It's okay. Like you said, you have no idea if things are really all that much better in there."

As if in refutation, the bunker suddenly echoed with another chime. Another baby.

Wren slammed her fist into the wall and swore. She grabbed William's wheelchair by the handles and spun him around. She leaned in, letting him see her few remaining teeth and how the Maw had filed them into points.

"You know what I don't get then? If you had all the answers and were sitting on some pot of gold, why didn't you just shrink everyone? Why keep it all secret?"

"*We couldn't!* We didn't know it would work, not for sure. We had to have a test colony. We said the…." He stopped himself, suddenly no longer willing to defend the indefensible. "No, maybe we couldn't have saved everybody. But we could have saved more – a lot more."

Wren stood up, somehow pushed by the force of his confession.

"I could have saved someone like you, Wren. You and so many others like you. The world died and we missed our chance to save it. There's no excuse for that."

She suddenly realized William had probably been asking himself that same question every day while he sat alone in his hole. She grabbed him roughly by the jaw with her hand. "Listen. This kind of talk won't do any good, not now. As the Hungry Maw says, 'the past is the past'. Instead, focus on 'where is the next meal'. That's all that matters now. It's the way to survive."

She bit into her raw potato, skin, eyes and all. "This," she said, brandishing it in front of her, "is what matters."

William nodded but they both knew he didn't agree.

"Damn straight!" came a voice.

It was Zan, standing outside the hydroponics bay. A half second later he brought his iron pipe down in a crushing blow. William was dead the instant it hit. But Zan dropped two more for good measure. Wren heard the echoing crack as the first blow split his skull. The second two sounded more like horrid slops as William's brain matter splashed out on to the walls of the hydroponics bay.

For Wren the shock subsided quickly. It was nothing she had not seen before.

"What are you talking to a hoarder for Wren?" said Zan shaking the skull fragments from his pipe. "You're better than that."

She bristled. "He was telling me where all his stuff was."

"Naw," he said. "Hoarder's just gonna trick you."

"You think I'm stupid?"

"I think you need to stop stuffing your face and pack this food up."

"Zan," she said. "It's a greenhouse. See the lights? If you leave it, it'll grow bigger and you can plant more. We can make food here!"

"We're not here to play house, Wren. You've got starving brothers and sisters back home who need their shares. Pack it up."

She bit her tongue and nodded. It was their way.

"There's a lot of stuff to pick through, Zan. This Hoarder had homegrown electricity."

"I know!" he said with a sudden lightening of his mood. "I found an actual battery I can use for my CD player when we get home. Haven't been able to play my tunes in a year."

"A battery" she repeated, suddenly fearful.

"Sitting in a safe. Hoarder left it wide open." He held it up. But Wren already knew what it would be. It was the power source for William's photonic simulator. The blood drained from her face.

"What?" he asked. "You don't know what a battery looks like no more?"

"I was just thinking was all."

"Thinking *what*?"

"That I finally know who took the sun."

"Whatever. Don't forget the Maw's teachings. Don't matter why. Only that it's gone."

"We took the sun, Zan, *we did*."

"Huh?"

And then she shot him. First in the stomach and then a second round to the chest to be sure.

Wren grabbed the battery from Zan's limp fingers. Without quite knowing why, she raced to William's computer room.

The counter read:

0

She found William's planet discarded in the corner of the room. The casing on the simulator was torn free. But the battery prongs were still there. She quickly inserted the battery – positive to positive, negative to negative.

"C'mon!" she cried.

The counter didn't make her wait. It blinked once and reproduced the number:

1279

What had it been like for them? Did they even notice? Did their lives flash before their eyes? Did the sun disappear? She found herself wishing she could have asked William. Gingerly cradling the orb in her palm she gently returned his world to the safe.

* * *

1286

Wren sat in William's wheelchair as she made note of the latest number. She had been the custodian of William's world for a month now and still beamed with pride every time there was an uptick. There had been losses: Wren discovered the computer had a tone for that too, but the gains had been an encouraging net positive.

She gnawed on her ration of carrot. Thus far, she had proven to be a poor farmer, but the turbine had yet to fail and she was determined to get the hang of it.

William and Zan had both been buried, though not together. Afterwards she had found a way to better disguise the broken hatch by covering it with a dead tree stump. She thought it was pretty convincing and thus far no one from the Hungry Maw who had come looking for them had discovered it. One day, she knew, someone would find her. No hoarder was ever safe forever.

But until then at least, there would be sun.

Scream and I'll Come to You

Raymond Little

"NOW IT'S YOUR turn." Beth Mackenzie popped the barrel from the revolver and let the bullets drop into her palm before passing the gun to her eight-year-old daughter.

"When am I going to learn how to shoot it?"

Beth glanced down from the porch at the long shadows cutting stripes across the dirt driveway. "Tomorrow. Don't forget the safety catch. Always check."

"I know." Megan ran a finger over the button, the way her mother had shown her a hundred times. "Safety on." She loaded the bullets one by one, the big revolver dipping under its own weight in her small hands.

"That's good. Now, where do we always keep it, until the day we might need it."

"In the pot under the sink."

"That's right." Beth forced a smile for her daughter and wondered once again how it could have come to this. "Come on honey," she said, "let's go and make something to eat."

Supper was simple – egg on toast using the bread she baked when they'd come to the farm – and they dined by candlelight.

"Are we going to live here forever?"

"I don't know. Maybe."

"But how will Daddy find us?"

Beth looked away. She knew the odds on Phil still being alive somewhere out there were more than remote. "He'll find a way if he can, sweetheart. Until then we'll just have to look out for each other."

* * *

Three came that night, in a dirty blue mini-bus. The screaming had woken Beth long before the hum of the approaching engine, enough warning for her to be ready. "Stay here," she told Megan as she led her to the back bedroom. "Lock the door behind me and don't open it for anyone else, no matter what they say."

The bus slowed and stopped ten feet short of where she stood, her pistol held out in both hands. The headlights blinked and faded as the motor switched off and the driver, lit silver by the full moon, stepped out.

"I suggest you get back in your van, sir, and drive back the way you came." She had to shout to be heard over the screaming coming from the back of the mini-bus, which helped to keep the tremble from her voice.

"Please," the man called. "I've been driving for hours, I need help." He stepped forward.

"Stay right where you are!" Beth fingered the safety.

"Please." The man's voice cracked and he held his face in his hands as his big shoulders jerked up and down.

"I'm sorry, there's nothing I can do for you. You may be infected. You have to go."

The man took a few moments to compose himself before wiping his sleeve across his face. "Let me have your gun, then. I'll take them away and..." He broke down, unable to finish the sentence.

"You know I can't do that."

"But they're suffering. You can't just turn us away!"

"I have to."

"Do it for me, then. Shoot them and I'll go. I promise."

"Who are they?"

"My wife. And my son."

Beth shook her head. "Don't ask me to do that." At the same time she thought of the pact she'd made with her daughter, the training she'd given the child in how exactly to shoot her own mother should the worst happen – and realised the hypocrisy of her answer to this poor man's request. Was she really incapable of doing to strangers what she intended to do to Megan if she became infected?

"Get back in the van and turn on the engine. Keep facing front and don't watch. When it's done, drive away. Don't ever come back and don't tell anyone else about this place."

She pulled a handkerchief from her pocket and held it over her nose and mouth as the man got behind the wheel and switched on the ignition. The electric window slid down as she approached and, no longer muffled, the screaming became unbearable. Beth looked in the back seat, illuminated by the dull, yellow internal light, and saw the man's wife slumped against the door, her face contorted with agony, fear and exhaustion. She turned her gaze on Beth, her eyes bulging, and screamed at the top of her lungs.

"Anne started screaming yesterday morning," the man said without turning. "Jack's had it for four days."

She looked at the boy in the far seat. His expression matched his mother's but no sound came from his wide open mouth; his vocal chords had been destroyed by his own exertions. He was near the end, his lips cracked and blistered from dehydration, his gasps shallow between his silent screams. He was emaciated, the skin stretched so thin across his cheekbones it had begun to split. Beth looked away, ashamed of her own revulsion at the sight of the crimson teardrops seeping from the corners of his eyes in mourning for his ruinous state.

"Do it," the man said. "Please, just do it."

Beth glanced at the farmhouse and prayed that Megan hadn't been tempted to leave the room at the back to see what was going on. "I'm sorry. Please forgive me," she said to the woman as she raised the gun. A change of expression, almost imperceptible, crossed the doomed woman's eyes. Later, as Beth replayed the scene over and over, she would tell herself it was gratitude.

"Make it quick," the man said over his shoulder.

Beth obeyed, and when it was done the man thanked her for killing his family.

* * *

No sleep would come that night.

"What did they want?" Megan asked as Beth settled her into the bed they shared.

"They wanted to stay here."

Megan clutched the sheets under her chin. "Did you shoot them?"

"They're gone now, honey. You don't have to worry about them."

"I heard two gunshots." Her voice trembled. "I was scared. I thought they might have had a gun. But the screaming stopped and I knew you were okay."

Beth felt her eyes begin to water as she fought away the vision of horror imprinted on her mind's eye. She'd taken their lives and surrendered her humanity; it seemed an unfair deal on both sides.

"I'm glad you shot them, Mummy." She lifted one arm from beneath her bedding and clutched her mother's hand. "They were in pain. I wouldn't want to suffer like that. I've been thinking, though. Maybe we can't catch the screams. A man on the telly said that some people were maroon."

"I think immune is what he said." Beth wiped a cuff across her damp cheeks and smiled.

"I miss the telly. Do you think it will come back?"

"One day, maybe. If there are people out there who know how to get the electricity back on." Even as she said it though, Beth doubted her own words. Getting any kind of power grid back in use would be a massive undertaking. From what she'd seen before they came to the farm she didn't believe there would be anywhere near enough survivors to organise such a task. "There are plenty of books, though."

"Will you read to me for a while?"

"Of course I will. I'll make us a hot drink."

Beth hugged her dressing gown around her shoulders as she waited down in the kitchen for the water to boil on the old wood stove. So much had changed in such a short time, but they'd coped. It was just three months since the first victim of the screams had been reported in the media. Not a long time for society to collapse.

That first case, a young man in France, had perplexed the doctors. Their initial diagnosis of a psychological condition had been crushed within days as similar cases broke out across Europe, then the world. All victims had the same single symptom, to suddenly start screaming for no apparent reason. The treatment of intravenous food and liquids – it was impossible to eat or drink – could not keep up with the rising number of cases. An untreated screamer could expect to survive no more than five or six days of the unbearable agony their condition brought. Their vocal chords would perish within two days, though they would still put all their effort into the silent scream that would no longer escape their gaping mouths. Exhaustion, dehydration and organ failure followed.

The first screamer Beth had seen, three days into the outbreak, was a teenage girl working at the local supermarket checkout. One moment she was scanning a tin of soup and making polite conversation, the next she was screaming as loud as she possibly could, her bulging eyeballs rolling from side to side in fear and confusion, searching the faces of her line of shoppers for some kind of help. The shop emptied within seconds, the customers running into the street for fear of contamination. By the end of that week the shops had begun to shut and board up as the emergency ration system began, the army and police patrolling the high streets for looters. Wearing a uniform held no immunity though, and as the forces numbers were depleted the streets began to resemble a battlefield. The real riots began in earnest by the third week, kick-started by the shocking leaked internet footage of the Prime Minister strapped down and screaming in a hospital bed.

Phil went missing just after that. Beth had begged him to stay in the house – they still had enough food and drink for another week – but he wouldn't listen, told her if he didn't get some supplies now they might not get another chance. And that was that. Beth knew when he didn't return that night that one of two things had happened; he'd become a victim of the street violence or he'd caught the screams. Either way, Beth didn't expect to see him again.

So she stayed at the house, managing to eke the supplies out for another fifteen days for her and Megan, in which time all government collapsed, media and power supplies crumbled, and the majority of the population became screamers. When at last she did venture out, it was quite safe. The town was quiet, the pavements and roads strewn with bodies and burnt out vehicles. Another week at the house and two more trips into town for supplies was enough for Beth to make up her mind. She would pack the car and head south into the countryside, away from the cloying stench of death. And so they came to the farm.

She lifted the old kettle from the wood stove and poured the drinks. Three months. She daren't let herself believe it, but maybe Megan was right. Maybe they were immune after all.

* * *

"Good girl, Daisy." Beth patted the cow and placed the half-full pail on the bench just inside the open barn door. "Come on girl," she said. "It's a lovely morning outside." Daisy flapped her tail but made no effort to leave the shady enclosure. "In your own time, then."

She stepped into the sunlight and glanced across at the farmhouse, wondering if Megan was out of bed. It was the first time her daughter had missed milking the cows since Beth had taught her how. She'd been withdrawn, quieter than usual since the mini-bus incident two nights before. Maybe it was one trauma too many after everything else. Or maybe, Beth thought, it was knowing that her mother had killed in cold blood. No, Megan was sensible, mature for her age. She'd even said she was glad Beth had put those poor souls out of their misery. "That's right," Beth muttered to herself as she crossed the yard. "You're a real sister of mercy."

She found Megan in the kitchen, sitting at the table. "You missed the milking, honey."

Megan shrugged her shoulders.

"Never mind." She took the seat opposite her daughter. "There's always tomorrow. I think Daisy missed you. She wouldn't go outside."

"Have we got any photos?"

Beth frowned. "Photos?"

"Yes. Of Dad. Of all of us, together."

She reached across the table top and gripped Megan's hand. "Of course we have. I brought them all. They're in a box, upstairs."

"That's good." She raised her gaze. "We're never going to see Daddy again, are we?"

Beth considered lying, saying there was a chance Megan's father had somehow survived, but she couldn't. Her daughter deserved more than that. She shook her head.

"He must be dead. If he was alive, he would have come home that night. Daddy would never have left us on our own."

"That's right darling. He loved us very much. If there had been any way of getting back home, he would have."

Megan slipped her hand from her mother's. "I'll fetch the milk."

Beth watched her leave the room and felt her shoulders slump. Megan had been through so much, and remained so strong. Maybe the acceptance of her father's death was the final hurdle. It wouldn't be easy, would take time, but they could move on now there were no more words left unsaid between them. With a sigh, Beth stood and began to cross to the window. The scream stopped her dead. She allowed herself no time to think, grabbing the gun and the bullets from beneath the sink. Loading them with trembling fingers just as she'd rehearsed so many times, she strode out into the yard.

The barn was dark as she passed from the sunlight, but she quickly picked out her daughter's shape from the direction of her screams. She raised the gun in both hands. "I love you, Megan. I'm sorry." Her voice cracked on that last word as she began to squeeze the trigger, but something was wrong, the scream was changing into words and Megan had one hand held out, aiming a finger at a point somewhere to the left of Beth.

"Mummy, no!"

Beth swung her arms, but her finger's pressure on the trigger was beyond return and the gunshot flashed in the dimness, its crack echoing in the confines of the barn. The rat, balancing on the rim of the milk pail, exploded against the wall. Beth dropped the smoking pistol to the floor and looked over at her daughter, silent now. "I, I almost…"

She stepped backward into the yard.

"It's okay," Megan said, "I'm alright. It was the rat, it scared me."

"Alright," Beth said, her voice flat. "You're alright." She felt sick, and horrified, and something else, something rising from deep inside, a rushing wave of unbearable terror, and she just had time to think, *is this it? Is this how it feels?* before opening her mouth wide and doing the only thing she could.

Megan stepped forward and picked up the pistol, checking there were at least two bullets in the barrel. "It's okay Mummy," she said. "I know what to do."

Mono no aware

Ken Liu

THE WORLD is shaped like the kanji for *umbrella*, only written so poorly, like my handwriting, that all the parts are out of proportion.

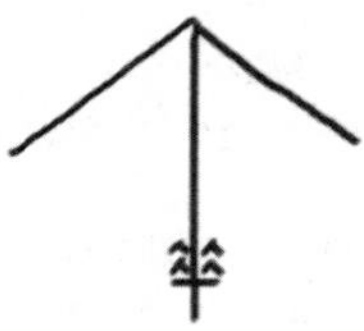

My father would be greatly ashamed at the childish way I still form my characters. Indeed, I can barely write many of them anymore. My formal schooling back in Japan ceased when I was only eight.

Yet for present purposes, this badly drawn character will do.

The canopy up there is the solar sail. Even that distorted kanji can only give you a hint of its vast size. A hundred times thinner than rice paper, the spinning disc fans out a thousand kilometers into space like a giant kite intent on catching every passing photon. It literally blocks out the sky.

Beneath it dangles a long cable of carbon nanotubes a hundred kilometers long: strong, light, and flexible. At the end of the cable hangs the heart of the *Hopeful*, the habitat module, a five-hundred-meter-tall cylinder into which all the 1,021 inhabitants of the world are packed.

The light from the sun pushes against the sail, propelling us on an ever widening, ever accelerating, spiraling orbit away from it. The acceleration pins all of us against the decks, gives everything weight.

Our trajectory takes us toward a star called 61 Virginis. You can't see it now because it is behind the canopy of the solar sail. The *Hopeful* will get there in about three hundred years, more or less. With luck, my great-great-great – I calculated how many "greats" I needed once, but I don't remember now – grandchildren will see it.

There are no windows in the habitat module, no casual view of the stars streaming past. Most people don't care, having grown bored of seeing the stars long ago. But I like looking through the cameras mounted on the bottom of the ship so that I can gaze at this view of the receding, reddish glow of our sun, our past.

* * *

"Hiroto," Dad said as he shook me awake. "Pack up your things. It's time."

My small suitcase was ready. I just had to put my Go set into it. Dad gave this to me when I was five, and the times we played were my favorite hours of the day.

The sun had not yet risen when Mom and Dad and I made our way outside. All the neighbors were standing outside their houses with their bags as well, and we greeted each other politely under the summer stars. As usual, I looked for the Hammer. It was easy. Ever since I could remember, the asteroid had been the brightest thing in the sky except for the moon, and every year it grew brighter.

A truck with loudspeakers mounted on top drove slowly down the middle of the street.

"Attention, citizens of Kurume! Please make your way in an orderly fashion to the bus stop. There will be plenty of buses to take you to the train station, where you can board the train for Kagoshima. Do not drive. You must leave the roads open for the evacuation buses and official vehicles!"

Every family walked slowly down the sidewalk.

"Mrs. Maeda," Dad said to our neighbor. "Why don't I carry your luggage for you?"

"I'm very grateful," the old woman said.

After ten minutes of walking, Mrs. Maeda stopped and leaned against a lamppost.

"It's just a little longer, Granny," I said. She nodded but was too out of breath to speak. I tried to cheer her. "Are you looking forward to seeing your grandson in Kagoshima? I miss Michi too. You will be able to sit with him and rest on the spaceships. They say there will be enough seats for everyone."

Mom smiled at me approvingly.

"How fortunate we are to be here," Dad said. He gestured at the orderly rows of people moving toward the bus stop, at the young men in clean shirts and shoes looking solemn, the middle-aged women helping their elderly parents, the clean, empty streets, and the quietness – despite the crowd, no one spoke above a whisper. The very air seemed to shimmer with the dense connections between all the people – families, neighbors, friends, colleagues – as invisible and strong as threads of silk.

I had seen on TV what was happening in other places around the world: looters screaming, dancing through the streets, soldiers and policemen shooting into the air and sometimes into crowds, burning buildings, teetering piles of dead bodies, generals shouting before frenzied crowds, vowing vengeance for ancient grievances even as the world was ending.

"Hiroto, I want you to remember this," Dad said. He looked around, overcome by emotion. "It is in the face of disasters that we show our strength as a people. Understand that we are not defined by our individual loneliness, but by the web of relationships in which we're enmeshed. A person must rise above his selfish needs so that all of us can live in harmony. The individual is small and powerless, but bound tightly together, as a whole, the Japanese nation is invincible."

* * *

"Mr. Shimizu," eight-year-old Bobby says, "I don't like this game."

The school is located in the very center of the cylindrical habitat module, where it can have the benefit of the most shielding from radiation. In front of the classroom hangs a large American flag to which the children say their pledge every morning. To the sides of the American flag are two rows of smaller flags belonging to other nations with survivors on the *Hopeful*. At the very end of the left side is a child's rendition of the Hinomaru, the corners of the white paper now curled and the once bright red rising sun faded to the orange of sunset. I drew it the day I came aboard the *Hopeful*.

I pull up a chair next to the table where Bobby and his friend, Eric, are sitting. "Why don't you like it?"

Between the two boys is a nineteen-by-nineteen grid of straight lines. A handful of black and white stones have been placed on the intersections.

Once every two weeks, I have the day off from my regular duties monitoring the status of the solar sail and come here to teach the children a little bit about Japan. I feel silly doing it sometimes. How can I be their teacher when I have only a boy's hazy memories of Japan?

But there is no other choice. All the non-American technicians like me feel it is our duty to participate in the cultural-enrichment program at the school and pass on what we can.

"All the stones look the same," Bobby says, "and they don't move. They're boring."

"What game do you like?" I ask.

"*Asteroid Defender*!" Eric says. "Now *that* is a good game. You get to save the world."

"I mean a game you do not play on the computer."

Bobby shrugs. "Chess, I guess. I like the queen. She's powerful and different from everyone else. She's a hero."

"Chess is a game of skirmishes," I say. "The perspective of Go is bigger. It encompasses entire battles."

"There are no heroes in Go," Bobby says, stubbornly.

I don't know how to answer him.

* * *

There was no place to stay in Kagoshima, so everyone slept outside along the road to the spaceport. On the horizon we could see the great silver escape ships gleaming in the sun.

Dad had explained to me that fragments that had broken off of the Hammer were headed for Mars and the Moon, so the ships would have to take us further, into deep space, to be safe.

"I would like a window seat," I said, imagining the stars steaming by.

"You should yield the window seat to those younger than you," Dad said. "Remember, we must all make sacrifices to live together."

We piled our suitcases into walls and draped sheets over them to form shelters from the wind and the sun. Every day inspectors from the government came by to distribute supplies and to make sure everything was all right.

"Be patient!" the government inspectors said. "We know things are moving slowly, but we're doing everything we can. There will be seats for everyone."

We were patient. Some of the mothers organized lessons for the children during the day, and the fathers set up a priority system so that families with aged parents and babies could board first when the ships were finally ready.

After four days of waiting, the reassurances from the government inspectors did not sound quite as reassuring. Rumors spread through the crowd.

"It's the ships. Something's wrong with them."

"The builders lied to the government and said they were ready when they weren't, and now the Prime Minister is too embarrassed to admit the truth."

"I hear that there's only one ship, and only a few hundred of the most important people will have seats. The other ships are only hollow shells, for show."

"They're hoping that the Americans will change their mind and build more ships for allies like us."

Mom came to Dad and whispered in his ear.

Dad shook his head and stopped her. "Do not repeat such things."

"But for Hiroto's sake—"

"No!" I'd never heard Dad sound so angry. He paused, swallowed. "We must trust each other, trust the Prime Minister and the Self-Defense Forces."

Mom looked unhappy. I reached out and held her hand. "I'm not afraid," I said.

"That's right," Dad said, relief in his voice. "There's nothing to be afraid of."

He picked me up in his arms – I was slightly embarrassed for he had not done such a thing since I was very little – and pointed at the densely packed crowd of thousands and thousands spread around us as far as the eye could see.

"Look at how many of us there are: grandmothers, young fathers, big sisters, little brothers. For anyone to panic and begin to spread rumors in such a crowd would be selfish and wrong, and many people could be hurt. We must keep to our places and always remember the bigger picture."

* * *

Mindy and I make love slowly. I like to breathe in the smell of her dark curly hair, lush, warm, tickling the nose like the sea, like fresh salt.

Afterwards we lie next to each other, gazing up at my ceiling monitor.

I keep looping on it a view of the receding star field. Mindy works in navigation, and she records the high-resolution cockpit video feed for me.

I like to pretend that it's a big skylight, and we're lying under the stars. I know some others like to keep their monitors showing photographs and videos of old Earth, but that makes me too sad.

"How do you say 'star' in Japanese?" Mindy asks.

"*Hoshi*," I tell her.

"And how do you say 'guest'?"

"*Okyakusan*."

"So we are *hoshi okyakusan*? Star guests?"

"It doesn't work like that," I say. Mindy is a singer, and she likes the sound of languages other than English. "It's hard to hear the music behind the words when their meanings get in the way," she told me once.

Spanish is Mindy's first language, but she remembers even less of it than I do of Japanese. Often, she asks me for Japanese words and weaves them into her songs.

I try to phrase it poetically for her, but I'm not sure if I'm successful. "*Wareware ha, hoshi no aida ni kyaku ni kite*." *We have come to be guests among the stars.*

"There are a thousand ways of phrasing everything," Dad used to say, "each appropriate to an occasion." He taught me that our language is full of nuances and supple grace, each sentence a poem. The language folds in on itself, the unspoken words as meaningful as the spoken, context within context, layer upon layer, like the steel in samurai swords.

I wish Dad were around so that I could ask him: How do you say "I miss you" in a way that is appropriate to the occasion of your twenty-fifth birthday, as the last survivor of your race?

"My sister was really into Japanese picture books. Manga."

Like me, Mindy is an orphan. It's part of what draws us together.

"Do you remember much about her?"

"Not really. I was only five or so when I came on board the ship. Before that, I only remember a lot of guns firing and all of us hiding in the dark and running and crying and stealing food. She was always there to keep me quiet by reading from the manga books. And then …"

I had watched the video only once. From our high orbit, the blue-and-white marble that was Earth seemed to wobble for a moment as the asteroid struck, and then, the silent, roiling waves of spreading destruction that slowly engulfed the globe.

I pull her to me and kiss her forehead, lightly, a kiss of comfort. "Let us not speak of sad things."

She wraps her arms around me tightly, as though she will never let go.

"The manga, do you remember anything about them?" I ask.

"I remember they were full of giant robots. I thought: *Japan is so powerful*."

I try to imagine it: heroic giant robots all over Japan, working desperately to save the people.

* * *

The Prime Minister's apology was broadcast through the loudspeakers. Some also watched it on their phones.

I remember very little of it except that his voice was thin and he looked very frail and old. He looked genuinely sorry. "I've let the people down."

The rumors turned out to be true. The shipbuilders had taken the money from the government but did not build ships that were strong enough or capable of what they promised. They kept up the charade until the very end. We found out the truth only when it was too late.

Japan was not the only nation that failed her people. The other nations of the world had squabbled over who should contribute how much to a joint evacuation effort when the Hammer was first discovered on its collision course with Earth. And then, when that plan had collapsed, most decided that it was better to gamble that the Hammer would miss and spend the money and lives on fighting with each other instead.

After the Prime Minister finished speaking, the crowd remained silent. A few angry voices shouted but soon quieted down as well. Gradually, in an orderly fashion, people began to pack up and leave the temporary campsites.

* * *

"The people just went home?" Mindy asks, incredulous.

"Yes."

"There was no looting, no panicked runs, no soldiers mutinying in the streets?"

"This was Japan," I tell her. And I can hear the pride in my voice, an echo of my father's.

"I guess the people were resigned," Mindy says. "They had given up. Maybe it's a culture thing."

"No!" I fight to keep the heat out of my voice. Her words irk me, like Bobby's remark about Go being boring. "That is not how it was."

* * *

"Who is Dad speaking to?" I asked.

"That is Dr. Hamilton," Mom said. "We – he and your father and I – went to college together, in America."

I watched Dad speak English on the phone. He seemed like a completely different person: it wasn't just the cadences and pitch of his voice; his face was more animated, his hand gestured more wildly. He looked like a foreigner.

He shouted into the phone.

"What is Dad saying?"

Mom shushed me. She watched Dad intently, hanging on every word.

"No," Dad said into the phone. "No!" I did not need that translated.

Afterwards Mom said, "He is trying to do the right thing, in his own way."

"He is as selfish as ever," Dad snapped.

"That's not fair," Mom said. "He did not call me in secret. He called you instead because he believed that if your positions were reversed, he would gladly give the woman he loved a chance to survive, even if it's with another man."

Dad looked at her. I had never heard my parents say "I love you" to each other, but some words did not need to be said to be true.

"I would never have said yes to him," Mom said, smiling. Then she went to the kitchen to make our lunch. Dad's gaze followed her.

"It's a fine day," Dad said to me. "Let us go on a walk."

We passed other neighbors walking along the sidewalks. We greeted each other, inquired after each other's health. Everything seemed normal. The Hammer glowed even brighter in the dusk overhead.

"You must be very frightened, Hiroto," he said.

"They won't try to build more escape ships?"

Dad did not answer. The late summer wind carried the sound of cicadas to us: *chirr, chirr, chirrrrrr.*

"*Nothing in the cry*
Of cicadas suggest they
Are about to die."

"Dad?"

"That is a poem by Basho. Do you understand it?"

I shook my head. I did not like poems much.

Dad sighed and smiled at me. He looked at the setting sun and spoke again:

"*The fading sunlight holds infinite beauty*
Though it is so close to the day's end."

I recited the lines to myself. Something in them moved me. I tried to put the feeling into words: "It is like a gentle kitten is licking the inside of my heart."

Instead of laughing at me, Dad nodded solemnly.

"That is a poem by the classical Tang poet Li Shangyin. Though he was Chinese, the sentiment is very much Japanese."

We walked on, and I stopped by the yellow flower of a dandelion. The angle at which the flower was tilted struck me as very beautiful. I got the kitten-tongue-tickling sensation in my heart again.

"The flower..." I hesitated. I could not find the right words.

Dad spoke,

"*The drooping flower*
As yellow as the moon beam
So slender tonight."

I nodded. The image seemed to me at once so fleeting and so permanent, like the way I had experienced time as a young child. It made me a little sad and glad at the same time.

"Everything passes, Hiroto," Dad said. "That feeling in your heart: it's called *mono no aware*. It is a sense of the transience of all things in life. The sun, the dandelion, the cicada, the Hammer, and all of us: we are all subject to the equations of James Clerk Maxwell and we are all ephemeral patterns destined to eventually fade, whether in a second or an eon."

I looked around at the clean streets, the slow-moving people, the grass, and the evening light, and I knew that everything had its place; everything was all right. Dad and I went on walking, our shadows touching.

Even though the Hammer hung right overhead, I was not afraid.

* * *

My job involves staring at the grid of indicator lights in front of me. It is a bit like a giant Go board.

It is very boring most of the time. The lights, indicating tension on various spots of the solar sail, course through the same pattern every few minutes as the sail gently flexes in the fading light of the distant sun. The cycling pattern of the lights is as familiar to me as Mindy's breathing when she's asleep.

We're already moving at a good fraction of the speed of light. Some years hence, when we're moving fast enough, we'll change our course for 61 Virginis and its pristine planets, and we'll leave the sun that gave birth to us behind like a forgotten memory.

But today, the pattern of the lights feels off. One of the lights in the southwest corner seems to be blinking a fraction of a second too fast.

"Navigation," I say into the microphone, "this is Sail Monitor Station Alpha, can you confirm that we're on course?"

A minute later Mindy's voice comes through my earpiece, tinged slightly with surprise. "I hadn't noticed, but there was a slight drift off course. What happened?"

"I'm not sure yet." I stare at the grid before me, at the one stubborn light that is out of sync, out of harmony.

* * *

Mom took me to Fukuoka, without Dad. "We'll be shopping for Christmas," she said. "We want to surprise you." Dad smiled and shook his head.

We made our way through the busy streets. Since this might be the last Christmas on Earth, there was an extra sense of gaiety in the air.

On the subway I glanced at the newspaper held up by the man sitting next to us. "USA Strikes Back!" was the headline. The big photograph showed the American president smiling triumphantly. Below that was a series of other pictures, some I had seen before: the first experimental American evacuation ship from years ago exploding on its test flight; the leader of some rogue nation claiming responsibility on TV; American soldiers marching into a foreign capital.

Below the fold was a smaller article: "American Scientists Skeptical of Doomsday Scenario." Dad had said that some people preferred to believe that a disaster was unreal rather than accept that nothing could be done.

I looked forward to picking out a present for Dad. But instead of going to the electronics district, where I had expected Mom to take me to buy him a gift, we went to a section of the city I had never been to before. Mom took out her phone and made a brief call, speaking in English. I looked up at her, surprised.

Then we were standing in front of a building with a great American flag flying over it. We went inside and sat down in an office. An American man came in. His face was sad, but he was working hard not to look sad.

"Rin." The man called my mother's name and stopped. In that one syllable I heard regret and longing and a complicated story.

"This is Dr. Hamilton," Mom said to me. I nodded and offered to shake his hand, as I had seen Americans do on TV.

Dr. Hamilton and Mom spoke for a while. She began to cry, and Dr. Hamilton stood awkwardly, as though he wanted to hug her but dared not.

"You'll be staying with Dr. Hamilton," Mom said to me.

"What?"

She held my shoulders, bent down, and looked into my eyes. "The Americans have a secret ship in orbit. It is the only ship they managed to launch into space before they got into this war. Dr. Hamilton designed the ship. He's my...old friend, and he can bring one person aboard with him. It's your only chance."

"No, I'm not leaving."

Eventually, Mom opened the door to leave. Dr. Hamilton held me tightly as I kicked and screamed.

We were all surprised to see Dad standing there.

Mom burst into tears.

Dad hugged her, which I'd never seen him do. It seemed a very American gesture.

"I'm sorry," Mom said. She kept saying "I'm sorry" as she cried.

"It's okay," Dad said. "I understand."

Dr. Hamilton let me go, and I ran up to my parents, holding on to both of them tightly.

Mom looked at Dad, and in that look she said nothing and everything.

Dad's face softened like a wax figure coming to life. He sighed and looked at me.

"You're not afraid, are you?" Dad asked.

I shook my head.

"Then it is okay for you to go," he said. He looked into Dr. Hamilton's eyes. "Thank you for taking care of my son."

Mom and I both looked at him, surprised.

"A dandelion
In late autumn's cooling breeze
Spreads seeds far and wide."

I nodded, pretending to understand.

Dad hugged me, fiercely, quickly.

"Remember that you're Japanese."

And they were gone.

* * *

"Something has punctured the sail," Dr. Hamilton says.

The tiny room holds only the most senior command staff – plus Mindy and me because we already know. There is no reason to cause a panic among the people.

"The hole is causing the ship to list to the side, veering off course. If the hole is not patched, the tear will grow bigger, the sail will soon collapse, and the *Hopeful* will be adrift in space."

"Is there anyway to fix it?" the Captain asks.

Dr. Hamilton, who has been like a father to me, shakes his headful of white hair. I have never seen him so despondent.

"The tear is several hundred kilometers from the hub of the sail. It will take many days to get someone out there because you can't move too fast along the surface of the sail – the risk of another tear is too great. And by the time we do get anyone out there, the tear will have grown too large to patch."

And so it goes. Everything passes.

I close my eyes and picture the sail. The film is so thin that if it is touched carelessly it will be punctured. But the membrane is supported by a complex system of folds and struts that give the sail rigidity and tension. As a child, I had watched them unfold in space like one of my mother's origami creations.

I imagine hooking and unhooking a tether cable to the scaffolding of struts as I skim along the surface of the sail, like a dragonfly dipping across the surface of a pond.

"I can make it out there in seventy-two hours," I say. Everyone turns to look at me. I explain my idea. "I know the patterns of the struts well because I have monitored them from afar for most of my life. I can find the quickest path."

Dr. Hamilton is dubious. "Those struts were never designed for a maneuver like that. I never planned for this scenario."

"Then we'll improvise," Mindy says. "We're Americans, damn it. We never just give up."

Dr. Hamilton looks up. "Thank you, Mindy."

We plan, we debate, we shout at each other, we work throughout the night.

* * *

The climb up the cable from the habitat module to the solar sail is long and arduous. It takes me almost twelve hours.

Let me illustrate for you what I look like with the second character in my name:

It means "to soar." See that radical on the left? That's me, tethered to the cable with a pair of antennae coming out of my helmet. On my back are the wings – or, in this case, booster rockets and extra fuel tanks that push me up and up toward the great reflective dome that blocks out the whole sky, the gossamer mirror of the solar sail.

Mindy chats with me on the radio link. We tell each other jokes, share secrets, speak of things we want to do in the future. When we run out of things to say, she sings to me. The goal is to keep me awake.

"*Wareware ha, hoshi no aida ni kyaku ni kite.*"

* * *

But the climb up is really the easy part. The journey across the sail along the network of struts to the point of puncture is far more difficult.

It has been thirty-six hours since I left the ship. Mindy's voice is now tired, flagging. She yawns.

"Sleep, baby," I whisper into the microphone. I'm so tired that I want to close my eyes just for a moment.

I'm walking along the road on a summer evening, my father next to me.

"We live in a land of volcanoes and earthquakes, typhoons and tsunamis, Hiroto. We have always faced a precarious existence, suspended in a thin strip on the surface of this planet between the fire underneath and the icy vacuum above."

And I'm back in my suit again, alone. My momentary loss of concentration causes me to bang my backpack against one of the beams of the sail, almost knocking one of the fuel tanks loose. I grab it just in time. The mass of my equipment has been lightened down to the last gram so that I can move fast, and there is no margin for error. I can't afford to lose anything.

I try to shake the dream and keep on moving.

"Yet it is this awareness of the closeness of death, of the beauty inherent in each moment, that allows us to endure. Mono no aware*, my son, is an empathy with the universe. It is the soul of our nation. It has allowed us to endure Hiroshima, to endure the occupation, to endure deprivation and the prospect of annihilation without despair."*

"Hiroto, wake up!" Mindy's voice is desperate, pleading. I jerk awake. I have not been able to sleep for how long now? Two days, three, four?

For the final fifty or so kilometers of the journey, I must let go of the sail struts and rely on my rockets alone to travel untethered, skimming over the surface of the sail while everything is moving at a fraction of the speed of light. The very idea is enough to make me dizzy.

And suddenly my father is next to me again, suspended in space below the sail. We're playing a game of Go.

"Look in the southwest corner. Do you see how your army has been divided in half? My white stones will soon surround and capture this entire group."

I look where he's pointing and I see the crisis. There is a gap that I missed. What I thought was my one army is in reality two separate groups with a hole in the middle. I have to plug the gap with my next stone.

I shake away the hallucination. I have to finish this, and then I can sleep.

There is a hole in the torn sail before me. At the speed we're traveling, even a tiny speck of dust that escaped the ion shields can cause havoc. The jagged edge of the hole flaps gently in space, propelled by solar wind and radiation pressure. While an individual photon is tiny, insignificant, without even mass, all of them together can propel a sail as big as the sky and push a thousand people along.

The universe is wondrous.

I lift a black stone and prepare to fill in the gap, to connect my armies into one.

The stone turns back into the patching kit from my backpack. I maneuver my thrusters until I'm hovering right over the gash in the sail. Through the hole I can see the stars beyond, the stars that no one on the ship has seen for many years. I look at them and imagine that around one of them, one day, the human race, fused into a new nation, will recover from near extinction, will start afresh and flourish again.

Carefully, I apply the bandage over the gash, and I turn on the heat torch. I run the torch over the gash, and I can feel the bandage melting to spread out and fuse with the hydrocarbon chains in the sail film. When that's done I'll vaporize and deposit silver atoms over it to form a shiny, reflective layer.

"It's working," I say into the microphone. And I hear the muffled sounds of celebration in the background.

"You're a hero," Mindy says.

I think of myself as a giant Japanese robot in a manga and smile.

The torch sputters and goes out.

"Look carefully," Dad says. "You want to play your next stone there to plug that hole. But is that what you really want?"

I shake the fuel tank attached to the torch. Nothing. This was the tank that I banged against one of the sail beams. The collision must have caused a leak and there isn't enough fuel left to finish the patch. The bandage flaps gently, only half attached to the gash.

"Come back now," Dr. Hamilton says. "We'll replenish your supplies and try again."

I'm exhausted. No matter how hard I push, I will not be able to make it back out here as fast. And by then who knows how big the gash will have grown? Dr. Hamilton knows this as well as I do. He just wants to get me back to the warm safety of the ship.

I still have fuel in my tank, the fuel that is meant for my return trip.

My father's face is expectant.

"I see," I speak slowly. "If I play my next stone in this hole, I will not have a chance to get back to the small group up in the northeast. You'll capture them."

"One stone cannot be in both places. You have to choose, son."

"Tell me what to do."

I look into my father's face for an answer.

"Look around you," Dad says. And I see Mom, Mrs. Maeda, the Prime Minister, all our neighbors from Kurume, and all the people who waited with us in Kagoshima, in Kyushu, in all the Four Islands, all over Earth and on the *Hopeful*. They look expectantly at me, for me to do something.

Dad's voice is quiet:

"The stars shine and blink.
We are all guests passing through,
A smile and a name."

"I have a solution," I tell Dr. Hamilton over the radio.

"I knew you'd come up with something," Mindy says, her voice proud and happy.

Dr. Hamilton is silent for a while. He knows what I'm thinking. And then: "Hiroto, thank you."

I unhook the torch from its useless fuel tank and connect it to the tank on my back. I turn it on. The flame is bright, sharp, a blade of light. I marshal photons and atoms before me, transforming them into a web of strength and light.

The stars on the other side have been sealed away again. The mirrored surface of the sail is perfect.

"Correct your course," I speak into the microphone. "It's done."

"Acknowledged," Dr. Hamilton says. His voice is that of a sad man trying not to sound sad.

"You have to come back first," Mindy says. "If we correct course now, you'll have nowhere to tether yourself."

"It's okay, baby," I whisper into the microphone. "I'm not coming back. There's not enough fuel left."

"We'll come for you!"

"You can't navigate the struts as quickly as I did," I tell her, gently. "No one knows their pattern as well as I do. By the time you get here, I will have run out of air."

I wait until she's quiet again. "Let us not speak of sad things. I love you."

Then I turn off the radio and push off into space so that they aren't tempted to mount a useless rescue mission. And I fall down, far, far below the canopy of the sail.

I watch as the sail turns away, unveiling the stars in their full glory. The sun, so faint now, is only one star among many, neither rising nor setting. I am cast adrift among them, alone and also at one with them.

A kitten's tongue tickles the inside of my heart.

* * *

I play the next stone in the gap.

Dad plays as I thought he would, and my stones in the northeast corner are gone, cast adrift.

But my main group is safe. They may even flourish in the future.

"Maybe there are heroes in Go," Bobby's voice says.

Mindy called me a hero. But I was simply a man in the right place at the right time. Dr. Hamilton is also a hero because he designed the *Hopeful*. Mindy is also a hero because she kept me awake. My mother is also a hero because she was willing to give me up so that I could survive. My father is also a hero because he showed me the right thing to do.

We are defined by the places we hold in the web of others' lives.

I pull my gaze back from the Go board until the stones fuse into larger patterns of shifting life and pulsing breath. "Individual stones are not heroes, but all the stones together are heroic."

"It is a beautiful day for a walk, isn't it?" Dad says.

And we walk together down the street, so that we can remember every passing blade of grass, every dewdrop, every fading ray of the dying sun, infinitely beautiful.

The Dream of Debs

Jack London

I AWOKE fully an hour before my customary time. This in itself was remarkable, and I lay very wide awake, pondering over it. Something was the matter, something was wrong – I knew not what. I was oppressed by a premonition of something terrible that had happened or was about to happen. But what was it? I strove to orient myself. I remembered that at the time of the Great Earthquake of 1906 many claimed they awakened some moments before the first shock and that during these moments they experienced strange feelings of dread. Was San Francisco again to be visited by earthquake?

I lay for a full minute, numbly expectant, but there occurred no reeling of walls nor shock and grind of falling masonry. All was quiet. That was it! The silence! No wonder I had been perturbed. The hum of the great live city was strangely absent. The surface cars passed along my street, at that time of day, on an average of one every three minutes; but in the ten succeeding minutes not a car passed. Perhaps it was a street-railway strike, was my thought; or perhaps there had been an accident and the power was shut off. But no, the silence was too profound. I heard no jar and rattle of waggon wheels, nor stamp of iron-shod hoofs straining up the steep cobble-stones.

Pressing the push-button beside my bed, I strove to hear the sound of the bell, though I well knew it was impossible for the sound to rise three stories to me even if the bell did ring. It rang all right, for a few minutes later Brown entered with the tray and morning paper. Though his features were impassive as ever, I noted a startled, apprehensive light in his eyes. I noted, also, that there was no cream on the tray.

"The Creamery did not deliver this morning," he explained; "nor did the bakery."

I glanced again at the tray. There were no fresh French rolls – only slices of stale graham bread from yesterday, the most detestable of bread so far as I was concerned.

"Nothing was delivered this morning, sir," Brown started to explain apologetically; but I interrupted him.

"The paper?"

"Yes, sir, it was delivered, but it was the only thing, and it is the last time, too. There won't be any paper tomorrow. The paper says so. Can I send out and get you some condensed milk?"

I shook my head, accepted the coffee black, and spread open the paper. The headlines explained everything – explained too much, in fact, for the lengths of pessimism to which the journal went were ridiculous. A general strike, it said, had been called all over the United States; and most foreboding anxieties were expressed concerning the provisioning of the great cities.

I read on hastily, skimming much and remembering much of labour troubles in the past. For a generation the general strike had been the dream of organized labour, which dream had arisen originally in the mind of Debs, one of the great labour leaders of thirty years before. I recollected that in my young college-settlement days I had even written an article on the subject for one of the magazines and that I had entitled it "The Dream of Debs." And I must confess that I had treated the idea very cavalierly and academically as a dream and nothing more. Time and the world had rolled on, Gompers was gone, the American Federation of Labour was gone, and gone was Debs with all his wild revolutionary ideas; but the dream had persisted, and here it was at last realized in fact. But I laughed, as I read, at the journal's gloomy outlook. I knew better. I had seen organized labour worsted in too many conflicts. It would be a matter only of days when the thing would be settled. This was a national strike, and it wouldn't take the Government long to break it.

I threw the paper down and proceeded to dress. It would certainly be interesting to be out in the streets of San Francisco when not a wheel was turning and the whole city was taking an enforced vacation.

"I beg your pardon, sir," Brown said, as he handed me my cigar-case, "but Mr. Harmmed has asked to see you before you go out."

"Send him in right away," I answered.

Harmmed was the butler. When he entered I could see he was labouring under controlled excitement. He came at once to the point.

"What shall I do, sir? There will be needed provisions, and the delivery drivers are on strike. And the electricity is shut off – I guess they're on strike, too."

"Are the shops open?" I asked.

"Only the small ones, sir. The retail clerks are out, and the big ones can't open; but the owners and their families are running the little ones themselves."

"Then take the machine," I said, "and go the rounds and make your purchases. Buy plenty of everything you need or may need. Get a box of candles – no, get half-a-dozen boxes. And, when you're done, tell Harrison to bring the machine around to the club for me – not later than eleven."

Harmmed shook his head gravely. "Mr. Harrison has struck along with the Chauffeurs' Union, and I don't know how to run the machine myself."

"Oh, ho, he has, has he?" said. "Well, when next Mister Harrison happens around you tell him that he can look elsewhere for a position."

"Yes, sir."

"You don't happen to belong to a Butlers' Union, do you, Harmmed?"

"No, sir," was the answer. "And even if I did I'd not desert my employer in a crisis like this. No, sir, I would—"

"All right, thank you," I said. "Now you get ready to accompany me. I'll run the machine myself, and we'll lay in a stock of provisions to stand a siege."

It was a beautiful first of May, even as May days go. The sky was cloudless, there was no wind, and the air was warm – almost balmy. Many autos were out, but the owners were driving them themselves. The streets were crowded but quiet. The working class, dressed in its Sunday best, was out taking the air and observing the effects of the strike. It was all so unusual, and withal so peaceful, that I found myself enjoying it. My nerves were tingling with mild excitement. It was a sort of placid adventure. I passed Miss Chickering. She was at the helm of her little runabout. She swung around and came after me, catching me at the corner.

"Oh, Mr. Corf!'" she hailed. "Do you know where I can buy candles? I've been to a dozen shops, and they're all sold out. It's dreadfully awful, isn't it?"

But her sparkling eyes gave the lie to her words. Like the rest of us, she was enjoying it hugely. Quite an adventure it was, getting those candles. It was not until we went across the city and down into the working-class quarter south of Market Street that we found small corner groceries that had not yet sold out. Miss Chickering thought one box was sufficient, but I persuaded her into taking four. My car was large, and I laid in a dozen boxes. There was no telling what delays might arise in the settlement of the strike. Also, I filled the car with sacks of flour, baking-powder, tinned goods, and all the ordinary necessaries of life suggested by Harmmed, who fussed around and clucked over the purchases like an anxious old hen.

The remarkable thing, that first day of the strike, was that no one really apprehended anything serious. The announcement of organized labour in the morning papers that it was prepared to stay out a month or three months was laughed at. And yet that very first day we might have guessed as much from the fact that the working class took practically no part in the great rush to buy provisions. Of course not. For weeks and months, craftily and secretly, the whole working class had been laying in private stocks of provisions. That was why we were permitted to go down and buy out the little groceries in the working-class neighbourhoods.

It was not until I arrived at the club that afternoon that I began to feel the first alarm. Everything was in confusion. There were no olives for the cocktails, and the service was by hitches and jerks. Most of the men were angry, and all were worried. A babel of voices greeted me as I entered. General Folsom, nursing his capacious paunch in a window-seat in the smoking-room was defending himself against half-a-dozen excited gentlemen who were demanding that he should do something.

"What can I do more than I have done?" he was saying. "There are no orders from Washington. If you gentlemen will get a wire through I'll do anything I am commanded to do. But I don't see what can be done. The first thing I did this morning, as soon as I learned of the strike, was to order in the troops from the Presidio – three thousand of them. They're guarding the banks, the Mint, the post office, and all the public buildings. There is no disorder whatever. The strikers are keeping the peace perfectly. You can't expect me to shoot them down as they walk along the streets with wives and children all in their best bib and tucker."

"I'd like to know what's happening on Wall Street," I heard Jimmy Wombold say as I passed along. I could imagine his anxiety, for I knew that he was deep in the big Consolidated-Western deal.

"Say, Corf," Atkinson bustled up to me, "is your machine running?"

"Yes," I answered, "but what's the matter with your own?"

"Broken down, and the garages are all closed. And my wife's somewhere around Truckee, I think, stalled on the overland. Can't get a wire to her for love or money. She should have arrived this evening. She may be starving. Lend me your machine."

"Can't get it across the bay," Halstead spoke up. "The ferries aren't running. But I tell you what you can do. There's Rollinson – oh, Rollinson, come here a moment. Atkinson wants to get a machine across the bay. His wife is stuck on the overland at Truckee. Can't you bring the Lurlette across from Tiburon and carry the machine over for him?"

The Lurlette was a two-hundred-ton, ocean-going schooner-yacht.

Rollinson shook his head. "You couldn't get a longshoreman to land the machine on board, even if I could get the Lurlette over, which I can't, for the crew are members of the Coast Seamen's Union, and they're on strike along with the rest."

"But my wife may be starving," I could hear Atkinson wailing as I moved on.

At the other end of the smoking-room I ran into a group of men bunched excitedly and angrily around Bertie Messener. And Bertie was stirring them up and prodding them in his cool, cynical way. Bertie didn't care about the strike. He didn't care much about anything. He was blase – at least in all the clean things of life; the nasty things had no attraction for him. He was worth twenty millions, all of it in safe investments, and he had never done a tap of productive work in his life – inherited it all from his father and two uncles. He had been everywhere, seen everything, and done everything but get married, and this last in the face of the grim and determined attack of a few hundred ambitious mammas. For years he had been the greatest catch, and as yet he had avoided being caught. He was disgracefully eligible. On top of his wealth he was young, handsome, and, as I said before, clean. He was a great athlete, a young blond god that did everything perfectly and admirably with the solitary exception of matrimony. And he didn't care about anything, had no ambitions, no passions, no desire to do the very things he did so much better than other men.

"This is sedition!" one man in the group was crying. Another called it revolt and revolution, and another called it anarchy.

"I can't see it," Bertie said. "I have been out in the streets all morning. Perfect order reigns. I never saw a more law-abiding populace. There's no use calling it names. It's not any of those things. It's just what it claims to be, a general strike, and it's your turn to play, gentlemen."

"And we'll play all right!" cried Garfield, one of the traction millionaires. "We'll show this dirt where its place is – the beasts! Wait till the Government takes a hand."

"But where is the Government?" Bertie interposed. "It might as well be at the bottom of the sea so far as you're concerned. You don't know what's happening at Washington. You don't know whether you've got a Government or not."

"Don't you worry about that," Garfield blurted out.

"I assure you I'm not worrying," Bertie smiled languidly. "But it seems to me it's what you fellows are doing. Look in the glass, Garfield."

Garfield did not look, but had he looked he would have seen a very excited gentleman with rumpled, iron-grey hair, a flushed face, mouth sullen and vindictive, and eyes wildly gleaming.

"It's not right, I tell you," little Hanover said; and from his tone I was sure that he had already said it a number of times.

"Now that's going too far, Hanover," Bertie replied. "You fellows make me tired. You're all open-shop men. You've eroded my eardrums with your endless gabble for the open shop and the right of a man to work. You've harangued along those lines for years. Labour is doing nothing wrong in going out on this general strike. It is violating no law of God nor man. Don't you talk, Hanover. You've been ringing the changes too long on the God-given right to work... or not to work; you can't escape the corollary. It's a dirty little sordid scrap, that's all the whole thing is. You've got labour down and gouged it, and now labour's got you down and is gouging you, that's all, and you're squealing."

Every man in the group broke out in indignant denials that labour had ever been gouged.

"No, sir!" Garfield was shouting. "We've done the best for labour. Instead of gouging it, we've given it a chance to live. We've made work for it. Where would labour be if it hadn't been for us?"

"A whole lot better off," Bertie sneered. "You've got labour down and gouged it every time you got a chance, and you went out of your way to make chances."

"No! No!" were the cries.

"There was the teamsters' strike, right here in San Francisco," Bertie went on imperturbably. "The Employers' Association precipitated that strike. You know that. And you know I know it, too, for I've sat in these very rooms and heard the inside talk and news of the fight. First you precipitated the strike, then you bought the Mayor and the Chief of Police and broke the strike. A pretty spectacle, you philanthropists getting the teamsters down and gouging them.

"Hold on, I'm not through with you. It's only last year that the labour ticket of Colorado elected a governor. He was never seated. You know why. You know how your brother philanthropists and capitalists of Colorado worked it. It was a case of getting labour down and gouging it. You kept the president of the South-western Amalgamated Association of Miners in jail for three years on trumped-up murder charges, and with him out of the way you broke up the association. That was gouging labour, you'll admit. The third time the graduated income tax was declared unconstitutional was a gouge. So was the eight-hour Bill you killed in the last Congress.

"And of all unmitigated immoral gouges, your destruction of the closed-shop principle was the limit. You know how it was done. You bought out Farburg, the last president of the old American Federation of Labour. He was your creature – or the creature of all the trusts and employers' associations, which is the same thing. You precipitated the big closed-shop strike. Farburg betrayed that strike. You won, and the old American Federation of Labour crumbled to pieces. You follows destroyed it, and by so doing undid yourselves; for right on top of it began the organization of the I.L.W. – the biggest and solidest organization of labour the United States has ever seen, and you are responsible for its existence and for the present general strike. You smashed all the old federations and drove labour into the I.L.W., and the I.L.W. called the general strike – still fighting for the closed shop. And then you have the effrontery to stand here face to face and tell me that you never got labour down and gouged it. Bah!"

This time there were no denials. Garfield broke out in self-defence—

"We've done nothing we were not compelled to do, if we were to win."

"I'm not saying anything about that," Bertie answered. "What I am complaining about is your squealing now that you're getting a taste of your own medicine. How many strikes have you won by starving labour into submission? Well, labour's worked out a scheme whereby to starve you into submission. It wants the closed shop, and, if it can get it by starving you, why, starve you shall."

"I notice that you have profited in the past by those very labour gouges you mention," insinuated Brentwood, one of the wiliest and most astute of our corporation lawyers. "The receiver is as bad as the thief," he sneered. "You had no hand in the gouging, but you took your whack out of the gouge."

"That is quite beside the question, Brentwood," Bertie drawled. "You're as bad as Hanover, intruding the moral element. I haven't said that anything is right or wrong. It's all a rotten game, I know; and my sole kick is that you fellows are squealing now that you're down and labour's taking a gouge out of you. Of course I've taken the profits from the gouging and, thanks to you, gentlemen, without having personally to do the dirty work. You did that for me – oh, believe me, not because I am more virtuous than you, but because my good father and his various brothers left me a lot of money with which to pay for the dirty work."

"If you mean to insinuate—" Brentwood began hotly.

"Hold on, don't get all-ruffled up," Bertie interposed insolently. "There's no use in playing hypocrites in this thieves' den. The high and lofty is all right for the newspapers, boys' clubs, and Sunday schools – that's part of the game; but for heaven's sake don't let's play it on one another. You know, and you know that I know just what jobbery was done in the building trades' strike last fall, who put up the money, who did the work, and who profited by it." (Brentwood flushed darkly.) "But we are all tarred with the same brush, and the best thing for us to do is to leave morality out of it. Again I repeat, play the game, play it to the last finish, but for goodness' sake don't squeal when you get hurt."

When I left the group Bertie was off on a new tack tormenting them with the more serious aspects of the situation, pointing out the shortage of supplies that was already making itself felt, and asking them what they were going to do about it. A little later I met him in the cloak-room, leaving, and gave him a lift home in my machine.

"It's a great stroke, this general strike," he said, as we bowled along through the crowded but orderly streets. "It's a smashing body-blow. Labour caught us napping and struck at our weakest place, the stomach. I'm going to get out of San Francisco, Corf. Take my advice and get out, too. Head for the country, anywhere. You'll have more chance. Buy up a stock of supplies and get into a tent or a cabin somewhere. Soon there'll be nothing but starvation in this city for such as we."

How correct Bertie Messener was I never dreamed. I decided that he was an alarmist. As for myself, I was content to remain and watch the fun. After I dropped him, instead of going directly home, I went on in a hunt for more food. To my surprise, I learned that the small groceries where I had bought in the morning were sold out. I extended my search to the Potrero, and by good luck managed to pick up another box of candles, two sacks of wheat flour, ten pounds of graham flour (which would do for the servants), a case of tinned corn, and two cases of tinned tomatoes. It did look as though there was going to be at least a temporary food shortage, and I hugged myself over the goodly stock of provisions I had laid in.

The next morning I had my coffee in bed as usual, and, more than the cream, I missed the daily paper. It was this absence of knowledge of what was going on in the world that I found the chief hardship. Down at the club there was little news. Rider had crossed from Oakland in his launch, and Halstead had been down to San Jose and back in his machine. They reported the same conditions in those places as in San Francisco. Everything was tied up by the strike. All grocery stocks had been bought out by the upper classes. And perfect order reigned. But what was happening over the rest of the country – in Chicago? New York? Washington? Most probably the same things that were happening with us, we concluded; but the fact that we did not know with absolute surety was irritating.

General Folsom had a bit of news. An attempt had been made to place army telegraphers in the telegraph offices, but the wires had been cut in every direction. This was, so far, the one unlawful act committed by labour, and that it was a concerted act he was fully convinced. He had communicated by wireless with the army post at Benicia, the telegraph lines were even then being patrolled by soldiers all the way to Sacramento. Once, for one short instant, they had got the Sacramento call, then the wires, somewhere, were cut again. General Folsom reasoned that similar attempts to open communication were being made by the authorities all the way across the continent, but he was non-committal as to whether or not he thought the attempt would succeed. What worried him was the wire-cutting; he could not but believe that it was an important part of the deep-laid labour conspiracy. Also, he regretted that the Government had not long since established its projected chain of wireless stations.

The days came and went, and for a while it was a humdrum time. Nothing happened. The edge of excitement had become blunted. The streets were not so crowded. The working class did not come uptown any more to see how we were taking the strike. And there were not so many automobiles running around. The repair-shops and garages were closed, and whenever a machine broke down it went out of commission. The clutch on mine broke, and neither love nor money could get it repaired. Like the rest, I was now walking. San Francisco lay dead, and we did not know what was happening over the rest of the country. But from the very fact that we did not know we could conclude only that the rest of the country lay as dead as San Francisco. From time to time the city was placarded with the proclamations of organized labour – these had been printed months before, and evidenced how thoroughly the I.L.W. had prepared for the strike. Every detail had been worked out long in advance. No violence had occurred as yet, with the exception of the shooting of a few wire-cutters by the soldiers, but the people of the slums were starving and growing ominously restless.

The business men, the millionaires, and the professional class held meetings and passed resolutions, but there was no way of making the proclamations public. They could not even get them printed. One result of these meetings, however, was that General Folsom was persuaded into taking military possession of the wholesale houses and of all the flour, grain, and food warehouses. It was high time, for suffering was becoming acute in the homes of the rich, and bread-lines were necessary. I knew that my servants were beginning to draw long faces, and it was amazing – the hole they made in my stock of provisions. In fact, as I afterward surmised, each servant was stealing from me and secreting a private stock of provisions for himself.

But with the formation of the bread-lines came new troubles. There was only so much of a food reserve in San Francisco, and at the best it could not last long. Organized labour, we knew, had its private supplies; nevertheless, the whole working class joined the bread-lines. As a result, the provisions General Folsom had taken possession of diminished with perilous rapidity. How were the soldiers to distinguish between a shabby middle-class man, a member of the I.L.W., or a slum dweller? The first and the last had to be fed, but the soldiers did not know all the I.L.W. men in the city, much less the wives and sons and daughters of the I.L.W. men. The employers helping, a few of the known union men were flung out of the bread-lines; but that amounted to nothing. To make matters worse, the Government tugs that had been hauling food from the army depots on Mare Island to Angel Island found no more food to haul. The soldiers now received their rations from the confiscated provisions, and they received them first.

The beginning of the end was in sight. Violence was beginning to show its face. Law and order were passing away, and passing away, I must confess, among the slum people and the upper classes. Organized labour still maintained perfect order. It could well afford to – it had plenty to eat. I remember the afternoon at the club when I caught Halstead and Brentwood whispering in a corner. They took me in on the venture. Brentwood's machine was still in running order, and they were going out cow-stealing. Halstead had a long butcher knife and a cleaver. We went out to the outskirts of the city. Here and there were cows grazing, but always they were guarded by their owners. We pursued our quest, following along the fringe of the city to the east, and on the hills near Hunter's Point we came upon a cow guarded by a little girl. There was also a young calf with the cow. We wasted no time on preliminaries. The little girl ran away screaming, while we slaughtered the cow. I omit the details, for they are not nice – we were unaccustomed to such work, and we bungled it.

But in the midst of it, working with the haste of fear, we heard cries, and we saw a number of men running toward us. We abandoned the spoils and took to our heels. To our surprise we were not pursued. Looking back, we saw the men hurriedly cutting up the cow. They had been on the same lay as ourselves. We argued that there was plenty for all, and ran back. The scene that followed beggars description. We fought and squabbled over the division like savages. Brentwood, I remember, was a perfect brute, snarling and snapping and threatening that murder would be done if we did not get our proper share.

And we were getting our share when there occurred a new irruption on the scene. This time it was the dreaded peace officers of the I.L.W. The little girl had brought them. They were armed with whips and clubs, and there were a score of them. The little girl danced up and down in anger, the tears streaming down her cheeks, crying: "Give it to 'em! Give it to 'em! That guy with the specs – he did it! Mash his face for him! Mash his face!" That guy with the specs was I, and I got my face mashed, too, though I had the presence of mind to take off my glasses at the first. My! but we did receive a trouncing as we scattered in all directions. Brentwood, Halstead, and I fled away for the machine. Brentwood's nose was bleeding, while Halstead's cheek was cut across with the scarlet slash of a black-snake whip.

And, lo, when the pursuit ceased and we had gained the machine, there, hiding behind it, was the frightened calf. Brentwood warned us to be cautious, and crept up on it like a wolf or tiger. Knife and cleaver had been left behind, but Brentwood still had his hands, and over and over on the ground he rolled with the poor little calf as he throttled it. We threw the carcass into the machine, covered it over with a robe, and started for home. But our misfortunes had only begun. We blew out a tyre. There was no way of fixing it, and twilight was coming on. We abandoned the machine, Brentwood pulling and staggering along in advance, the calf, covered by the robe, slung across his shoulders. We took turn about carrying that calf, and it nearly killed us. Also, we lost our way. And then, after hours of wandering and toil, we encountered a gang of hoodlums. They were not I.L.W. men, and I guess they were as hungry as we. At any rate, they got the calf and we got the thrashing. Brentwood raged like a madman the rest of the way home, and he looked like one, with his torn clothes, swollen nose, and blackened eyes.

There wasn't any more cow-stealing after that. General Folsom sent his troopers out and confiscated all the cows, and his troopers, aided by the militia, ate most of the meat. General Folsom was not to be blamed; it was his duty to maintain law and order, and he maintained it by means of the soldiers, wherefore he was compelled to feed them first of all.

It was about this time that the great panic occurred. The wealthy classes precipitated the flight, and then the slum people caught the contagion and stampeded wildly out of the city. General Folsom was pleased. It was estimated that at least 200,000 had deserted San Francisco, and by that much was his food problem solved. Well do I remember that day. In the morning I had eaten a crust of bread. Half of the afternoon I had stood in the bread-line; and after dark I returned home, tired and miserable, carrying a quart of rice and a slice of bacon. Brown met me at the door. His face was worn and terrified. All the servants had fled, he informed me. He alone remained. I was touched by his faithfulness and, when I learned that he had eaten nothing all day, I divided my food with him. We cooked half the rice and half the bacon, sharing it equally and reserving the other half for morning. I went to bed with my hunger, and tossed restlessly all night. In the morning I found Brown had deserted me, and, greater misfortune still, he had stolen what remained of the rice and bacon.

It was a gloomy handful of men that came together at the club that morning. There was no service at all. The last servant was gone. I noticed, too, that the silver was gone, and I learned where it had gone. The servants had not taken it, for the reason, I presume, that the club members got to it first. Their method of disposing of it was simple. Down south of Market Street, in the dwellings of the I.L.W., the housewives had given square meals in exchange for it. I went back to my house. Yes, my silver was gone – all but a massive pitcher. This I wrapped up and carried down south of Market Street.

I felt better after the meal, and returned to the club to learn if there was anything new in the situation. Hanover, Collins, and Dakon were just leaving. There was no one inside, they told me, and they invited me to come along with them. They were leaving the city, they said, on Dakon's horses, and there was a spare one for me. Dakon had four magnificent carriage horses that he wanted to save, and General Folsom had given him the tip that next morning all the horses that remained in the city were to be confiscated for food. There were not many horses left, for tens of thousands of them had been turned loose into the country when the hay and grain gave out during the first days. Birdall, I remember, who had great draying interests, had turned loose three hundred dray horses. At an average value of five hundred dollars, this had amounted to $150,000. He had hoped, at first, to recover most of the horses after the strike was over, but in the end he never recovered one of them. They were all eaten by the people that fled from San Francisco. For that matter, the killing of the army mules and horses for food had already begun.

Fortunately for Dakon, he had had a plentiful supply of hay and grain stored in his stable. We managed to raise four saddles, and we found the animals in good condition and spirited, withal unused to being ridden. I remembered the San Francisco of the great earthquake as we rode through the streets, but this San Francisco was vastly more pitiable. No cataclysm of nature had caused this, but, rather, the tyranny of the labour unions. We rode down past Union Square and through the theatre, hotel, and shopping districts. The streets were deserted. Here and there stood automobiles, abandoned where they had broken down or when the gasolene had given out. There was no sign of life, save for the occasional policemen and the soldiers guarding the banks and public buildings. Once we came upon an I.L.W. man pasting up the latest proclamation. We stopped to read. "We have maintained an orderly strike," it ran; "and we shall maintain order to the end. The end will come when our demands are satisfied, and our demands will be satisfied when we have starved our employers into submission, as we ourselves in the past have often been starved into submission."

"Messener's very words," Collins said. "And I, for one, am ready to submit, only they won't give me a chance to submit. I haven't had a full meal in an age. I wonder what horse-meat tastes like?"

We stopped to read another proclamation: "When we think our employers are ready to submit we shall open up the telegraphs and place the employers' associations of the United States in communication. But only messages relating to peace terms shall be permitted over the wires."

We rode on, crossed Market Street, and a little later were passing through the working-class district. Here the streets were not deserted. Leaning over the gates or standing in groups were the I.L.W. men. Happy, well-fed children were playing games, and stout housewives sat on the front steps gossiping. One and all cast amused glances at us. Little children ran after us, crying: "Hey, mister, ain't you hungry?" And one woman, nursing a child at her breast, called to Dakon: "Say, Fatty, I'll give you a meal for your skate – ham and potatoes, currant jelly, white bread, canned butter, and two cups of coffee."

"Have you noticed, the last few days," Hanover remarked to me, "that there's not been a stray dog in the streets?"

I had noticed, but I had not thought about it before. It was high time to leave the unfortunate city. We at last managed to connect with the San Bruno Road, along which we headed south. I had a country place near Menlo, and it was our objective. But soon we began to discover that the country was worse off and far more dangerous than the city. There the soldiers and the I.L.W. kept order; but the country had been turned over to anarchy. Two hundred thousand people had fled from San Francisco, and we had countless evidences that their flight had been like that of an army of locusts.

They had swept everything clean. There had been robbery and fighting. Here and there we passed bodies by the roadside and saw the blackened ruins of farm-houses. The fences were down, and the crops had been trampled by the feet of a multitude. All the vegetable patches had been rooted up by the famished hordes. All the chickens and farm animals had been slaughtered. This was true of all the main roads that led out of San Francisco. Here and there, away from the roads, farmers had held their own with shotguns and revolvers, and were still holding their own. They warned us away and refused to parley with us. And all the destruction and violence had been done by the slum-dwellers and the upper classes. The I.L.W. men, with plentiful food supplies, remained quietly in their homes in the cities.

Early in the ride we received concrete proof of how desperate was the situation. To the right of us we heard cries and rifle-shots. Bullets whistled dangerously near. There was a crashing in the underbrush; then a magnificent black truck-horse broke across the road in front of us and was gone. We had barely time to notice that he was bleeding and lame. He was followed by three soldiers. The chase went on among the trees on the left. We could hear the soldiers calling to one another. A fourth soldier limped out upon the road from the right, sat down on a boulder, and mopped the sweat from his face.

"Militia," Dakon whispered. "Deserters."

The man grinned up at us and asked for a match. In reply to Dakon's "What's the word?" he informed us that the militiamen were deserting. "No grub," he explained. "They're feedin' it all to the regulars." We also learned from him that the military prisoners had been released from Alcatraz Island because they could no longer be fed.

I shall never forget the next sight we encountered. We came upon it abruptly around a turn of the road. Overhead arched the trees. The sunshine was filtering down through the branches. Butterflies were fluttering by, and from the fields came the song of larks. And there it stood, a powerful touring car. About it and in it lay a number of corpses. It told its own tale. Its occupants, fleeing from the city, had been attacked and dragged down by a gang of slum dwellers – hoodlums. The thing had occurred within twenty-four hours. Freshly opened meat and fruit tins explained the reason for the attack. Dakon examined the bodies.

"I thought so," he reported. "I've ridden in that car. It was Perriton – the whole family. We've got to watch out for ourselves from now on."

"But we have no food with which to invite attack," I objected.

Dakon pointed to the horse I rode, and I understood.

Early in the day Dakon's horse had cast a shoe. The delicate hoof had split, and by noon the animal was limping. Dakon refused to ride it farther, and refused to desert it. So, on his solicitation, we went on. He would lead the horse and join us at my place. That was the last we saw of him; nor did we ever learn his end.

By one o'clock we arrived at the town of Menlo, or, rather, at the site of Menlo, for it was in ruins. Corpses lay everywhere. The business part of the town, as well as part of the residences, had been gutted by fire. Here and there a residence still held out; but there was no getting near them. When we approached too closely we were fired upon. We met a woman who was poking about in the smoking ruins of her cottage. The first attack, she told us had been on the stores, and as she talked we could picture that raging, roaring, hungry mob flinging itself on the handful of townspeople. Millionaires and paupers had fought side by side for the food, and then fought with one another after they got it. The town of Palo Alto and Stanford University had been sacked in similar fashion, we learned. Ahead of us lay a desolate, wasted land; and we thought we were wise in turning off to my place. It lay three miles to the west, snuggling among the first rolling swells of the foothills.

But as we rode along we saw that the devastation was not confined to the main roads. The van of the flight had kept to the roads, sacking the small towns as it went; while those that followed had scattered out and swept the whole countryside like a great broom. My place was built of concrete, masonry, and tiles, and so had escaped being burned, but it was gutted clean. We found the gardener's body in the windmill, littered around with empty shot-gun shells. He had put up a good fight. But no trace could we find of the two Italian labourers, nor of the house-keeper and her husband. Not a live thing remained. The calves, the colts, all the fancy poultry and thoroughbred stock, everything, was gone. The kitchen and the fireplaces, where the mob had cooked, were a mess, while many camp-fires outside bore witness to the large number that had fed and spent the night. What they had not eaten they had carried away. There was not a bite for us.

We spent the rest of the night vainly waiting for Dakon, and in the morning, with our revolvers, fought off half-a-dozen marauders. Then we killed one of Dakon's horses, hiding for the future what meat we did not immediately eat. In the afternoon Collins went out for a walk, but failed to return. This was the last straw to Hanover. He was for flight there and then, and I had great difficulty in persuading him to wait for daylight. As for myself, I was convinced that the end of the general strike was near, and I was resolved to return to San Francisco. So, in the morning, we parted company, Hanover heading south, fifty pounds of horse-meat strapped to his saddle, while I, similarly loaded, headed north. Little Hanover pulled through all right, and to the end of his life he will persist, I know, in boring everybody with the narrative of his subsequent adventures.

I got as far as Belmont, on the main road back, when I was robbed of my horse-meat by three militiamen. There was no change in the situation, they said, except that it was going from bad to worse. The I.L.W. had plenty of provisions hidden away and could last out for months. I managed to get as far as Baden, when my horse was taken away from me by a dozen men. Two of them were San Francisco policemen, and the remainder were regular soldiers. This was ominous. The situation was certainly extreme when the regulars were beginning to desert. When I continued my way on foot, they already had the fire started, and the last of Dakon's horses lay slaughtered on the ground.

As luck would have it, I sprained my ankle, and succeeded in getting no farther than South San Francisco. I lay there that night in an out-house, shivering with the cold and at the same time burning with fever. Two days I lay there, too sick to move, and on the third, reeling and giddy, supporting myself on an extemporized crutch, I tottered on toward San Francisco. I was weak as well, for it was the third day since food had passed my lips. It was a day of nightmare and torment. As in a dream I passed hundreds of regular soldiers drifting along in the opposite direction, and many policemen, with their families, organized in large groups for mutual protection.

As I entered the city I remembered the workman's house at which I had traded the silver pitcher, and in that direction my hunger drove me. Twilight was falling when I came to the place. I passed around by the alleyway and crawled up the black steps, on which I collapsed. I managed to reach out with the crutch and knock on the door. Then I must have fainted, for I came to in the kitchen, my face wet with water, and whisky being poured down my throat. I choked and spluttered and tried to talk. I began saying something about not having any more silver pitchers, but that I would make it up to them afterward if they would only give me something to eat. But the housewife interrupted me.

"Why, you poor man," she said, "haven't you heard? The strike was called off this afternoon. Of course we'll give you something to eat."

She bustled around, opening a tin of breakfast bacon and preparing to fry it.

"Let me have some now, please," I begged; and I ate the raw bacon on a slice of bread, while her husband explained that the demands of the I.L.W. had been granted. The wires had been opened up in the early afternoon, and everywhere the employers' associations had given in. There hadn't been any employers left in San Francisco, but General Folsom had spoken for them. The trains and steamers would start running in the morning, and so would everything else just as soon as system could be established.

And that was the end of the general strike. I never want to see another one. It was worse than a war. A general strike is a cruel and immoral thing, and the brain of man should be capable of running industry in a more rational way. Harrison is still my chauffeur. It was part of the conditions of the I.L.W. that all of its members should be reinstated in their old positions.

Brown never came back, but the rest of the servants are with me. I hadn't the heart to discharge them – poor creatures, they were pretty hard-pressed when they deserted with the food and silver. And now I can't discharge them. They have all been unionized by the I.L.W. The tyranny of organized labour is getting beyond human endurance. Something must be done.

And Fade Out Again

Thana Niveau

THE ONLY THING stronger than mankind's compulsion to destroy itself was the determination that it would endure. Like a virus, it adapted. It survived.

Stefani watched the colours, luminescent in the glow from the sun lamps. The light was artificial, but the surrounding coral didn't seem to mind. It was the only thing truly thriving in the poisoned ocean. If you didn't count the city.

By the time the human race had finally decided to stop killing each other, the planet was nearly uninhabitable. It was too late to reverse the effects of global warming. The polar ice caps were long gone and the seas had risen, drowning cities, countries and finally entire continents. Most of the land was gone, as were any hopes of escaping to the stars to find and colonise other worlds. The space program had drowned along with most of the planet.

Stefani couldn't imagine what it must have been like living above the surface. VR tech could approximate the experience of wandering through forests or deserts, but it all seemed so unnatural, and the animals that had once lived up there were terrifying and strange. She had never known life outside the maternal embrace of the superocean and the comforting womb of New Eden.

Once the world above had reached the point of no return, scientists and architects had focused their efforts on the world below. Or rather – the world that would soon *be* below. And the Eden Project in Cornwall was a perfect starting point.

The huge geodesic domes housed both a tropical rainforest and a Mediterranean environment. Over a period of months, the structures were essentially uprooted and a giant foundation constructed beneath them. At the same time, teams of underwater engineers and computer programmers combined their efforts in revolutionary 3D printing technology, constructing a giant bubble of metallic glass to form an underwater habitat. Detractors called it the Goldfish Bowl, and for a while the name stuck. But New Eden was the official name.

As the seas continued to rise, the British coast was devastated by flooding and erosion. The Doomsday Clock ticked away the dwindling time as the waves lapped closer and closer, engulfing the Cornish countryside. In a few short months, the bubble was completely submerged and a maze of corridors and rooms branched off in every direction. A titanium auger spiralled down through the centre of the habitat, anchoring it to the seabed, and the weight of the water provided all the energy the city needed. And at the top, the domes floated like manmade islands, their hexagonal panels reinforced to filter the deadly rays of the sun through the depleted atmosphere. The plants and trees within would have to sustain what remained of the human race.

The other major food was fish. Specifically, lionfish. The notoriously invasive species was once considered a major threat to marine ecosystems, and the lionfish's unchecked proliferation had altered the balance of life beneath the waves long before the catastrophic flooding that drowned the world. Thousands of other species had died out, and scientists could only speculate how widespread the lionfish were throughout the rest of the superocean. But until they overpopulated themselves out of existence, they provided an unlimited food source.

Once Britain had been fully subsumed by the ocean, the reef began to establish itself. First the coral covered the remaining features of the Eden Project – the visitor centre, restaurant and sculptures. Then it spread outward into the towns and villages, and finally the habitat, blanketing everything as it had once engulfed shipwrecks and other structures. It was a living organism as vibrant as the terrestrial forests and jungles once had been. It made a home of anything it found in the sea. Like humans, it colonised. And like humans, it learned and adapted.

The doomsayers fretted about structural collapse. The reef was consuming New Eden, they said. In time it would crush the entire habitat, level by level. And yes, the older parts of the structure were beginning to show signs of stress. But the printers worked day and night to keep extending the city. If and when the reef did overrun them, they had the rest of the ocean to spread out in. There were even plans to start a new city, one entirely independent of New Eden.

Stefani listened to the buzz of the printers as she ran through the routine systems check of the machines. The newest corridor was growing fast. A special airlock would keep it isolated from the water until it was completed. Then the structural engineers would move in, performing rigorous stress tests until the area was declared safe and could be opened to the population.

This particular corridor would lead to a new housing wing, where Stefani had reserved a place. Her apartment was in the oldest part of the city, but it was beginning to show its age. The surrounding glass was cloudy and scratched, and due to be recycled as soon as the new wing was completed. As much as she loved her view of the giant bee sculpture blanketed in coral, her view of the reef would be much better from one of the modern developments.

Many people found it oppressive on the seabed, but Stefani had never been claustrophobic. On the contrary, she felt safe, cocooned in the smaller rooms of the original construction. In this tiny corner of what was once the British Isles, mankind had made history. First with the Eden Project itself, and then with the city.

The vibrations of the machinery often attracted animals and today was no exception. The eel was back. Stefani watched as the gleaming yellow creature slithered past, its mouth opening to show rows of teeth. It paused to snap up a bright orange clownfish that had left the sanctuary of the coral. Stefani pressed a hand against the glass as she watched the eel. Supposedly there had once been similar animals on land, immense snakes that could swallow a person whole. She'd seen images of them, but to her they were like dinosaurs must have seemed to her forefathers. Beautiful, deadly animals one could scarcely even imagine.

A pride of lionfish was prowling nearby and for a moment the eel looked poised to attack. But the lionfish flared their venomous spines, making themselves appear larger than they were. The display was enough to change the eel's mind. With a flick of its golden tail, it was gone, away into the depths.

"Goodbye, Sunray," Stefani said. "Bring your family next time."

From behind her came a soft laugh. She turned to see Aren standing there, shaking his head.

"What?"

"Did you name all the lionfish too, Stef?"

She grinned at his teasing tone. "Not all of them. But then, they're not as friendly. Plus I don't like to eat the ones I chat to."

Aren looked out into the water and Stef followed his gaze into the vibrantly colourful reef. For a while they watched in silence as different fish darted in amongst the anemones and coral. Tiny moon jellyfish pulsed in the gentle current, transforming the void into a starry underwater sky.

"I never get tired of watching," Stef said.

Aren sighed. "I was sick of it after the first five minutes down here."

Stef stared at him in disbelief. "Really?"

"Really. Nothing ever changes. Same reef, same fish. Same bloody *lionfish*. I saw a shark once, but it didn't look anything like I expected. I thought they were supposed to be these huge monsters, vicious killers. It was smaller than me and it just swam by, as bored as I was."

For long moments Stef was at a loss for words. There was nothing at all boring about the reef or its inhabitants. But then, Aren normally worked in the rainforest. He'd told her before that fish weren't as interesting to a botanist as plants were. You couldn't interact with the reef the way you could with things in the dome.

She watched as he cupped his hands around his face, peering through the glass at the undersea world.

"Without diving gear," he said, "that's as close as you can get to the reef. In the dome you can climb trees, pick flowers, even let bees and butterflies clamber over you. You can talk to plants and see them respond. Down here you're just a watcher. Passive." He shook his head sadly.

Ah. Now she understood. What were they thinking, exiling someone like Aren to the lower decks?

"Do you name all the trees and bees and flowers up top?" she asked.

Aren turned away from the glass, the hint of a smile threatening to overtake his gloomy expression. "Nothing *ever* gets you down, does it?"

Stef blushed and looked back out into the water. "I don't know," she mumbled. "Maybe. Sometimes."

There was a ping as one of the printers finished a circuit of the corridor and reversed direction to begin another. Stef glanced at the readings on the wall screen.

"All good," she said cheerfully.

"Yeah, that's the problem down here," Aren said. "It's *always* good. Always the same. Like the reef. Nothing ever changes. Print, print, print. Another corridor. Start again. Another hatch. Another wing. And the *noise.*" He pressed his hands against his temples. "I just wish I could leave."

"Leave? You mean move to a new apartment? A new wing?"

"No. A new city. Above the water."

Stef frowned. The very thought was so alien, so *terrifying.*

"I just feel it pressing in," Aren continued. "The reef." His voice was low and conspiratorial, as though he was afraid of being overheard. "Every day it obscures more and more of the glass. It's like it wants to get inside. Crush this insignificant little bubble and rid the planet of the last of our industry. We weren't meant to be down here."

Stef shifted uncomfortably. It wasn't like Aren to be so morose. She'd been delighted when they'd first assigned him to work with her. Aren was like her – friendly and outgoing. But after only a handful of days on the seabed, his mood had changed. Now his words had an eerily familiar ring to them.

Her workstation sat against one curved wall of the little room. It was surrounded by coral, encrusted by the stony exoskeletons of millions of sea creatures. The divers had cleared away a large circular portion so she could see out into the water, and the area where she sat for most of the day gave the illusion of being part of the reef itself. It was beautiful, comforting. Not at all like the domes. Up there it was too bright. There was too much space, too much openness. You were too close to the sun up there, too close to its poisonous rays and heat.

"Look," she said, "I know there's always supposed to be two people here, but this isn't the right posting for you, even if it is only temporary. I can call for help if anything goes wrong. It's not fair to make you cover for someone in another station."

Aren dragged his fingers through his hair, shaking his head. "No, no," he said. "You know the rules. I can't leave you here by yourself."

"Yeah. I know the rules. And I'm telling you it's okay to break them. The printers have only slowed a little bit; they haven't stopped. And they won't. These new precautions are nothing but administrative overprotectiveness. I'm fine here on my own. I *like* it here."

Of course she knew the real reason he was reluctant to go. It was the same reason she found his sudden pessimism so disturbing. She met his eyes and added firmly, "I'm not like Dunkan. What happened to him would never happen to me."

Aren listened, then glanced out into the water again. Lionfish were swarming over a cluster of Gorgonian sea fans, darting in and out as they plucked tiny creatures from the delicate structures.

"Pygmy seahorses," she said, allowing a trace of wistfulness into her voice.

Aren winced and turned away.

Another printer signalled its completion, and the vibrations took on a higher tone as it began the more detailed work of constructing the door hatch.

Stef placed her hands on Aren's shoulders. "Go," she said. "I don't need help to keep an eye on the printers. And I don't need companionship. Solitude and monotony don't bother me. In fact, it's how I like it. Go tell your supervisor a robot could do my job."

He met that with a wry laugh. "Careful or you'll make yourself obsolete." His eyes flicked across to the sunroom, the little chamber he'd retreated to every hour for a dose of artificial sun. The real sunlight never reached this far down.

Stef registered the look and he noticed her noticing.

"All right," he said at last. "If you're sure…"

"I'm sure."

He cast one final look out at the reef, then turned to go. He hesitated at the door, then murmured "Thank you" before slipping away down the corridor and out of sight.

Stef was alone again. She sighed as she sat down. Already the room felt larger, emptier. She would miss Aren's company, but she couldn't stand to see him suffer. And he *was* suffering. Very few people were suited to life at the bottom of New Eden. She took trips up to the biomes from time to time. But she preferred the synthetic floor to the dirt, and the water to the sky. The habitat was all she'd ever known, and all she needed.

Unlike Stef, most people needed the bright world above. Some went mad without it. A flicker of disquiet ran through her and she tried to push the memory Aren had evoked to the back of her mind. But it came, unbidden.

* * *

She was running late. Her shower had stopped halfway through washing her hair and she'd had to scrub away the remaining soap with a towel. She tried to call the print lab, but there was no answer. When she finally arrived, ready with a breezy apology, there was no sign of Dunkan. She found him quickly enough, though, crouched in a corner, staring around wildly. He was murmuring to himself.

"Please," he whispered, "leave me alone. Stop following me. I'm sorry."

"Dunkan? What's wrong?"

He seemed not to hear her and kept up his frantic pleading for a few moments more.

Growing concerned, Stef knelt beside him. "Who are you talking to?"

He stared at her, his eyes wide, distraught. At last, he said in a whisper, "Mila."

Stef felt a chill at that and she glanced behind her in spite of herself.

"Dunkan," she said, her voice low and calm, "Mila's not here anymore."

But his expression of fear didn't change. "Don't you think I know that?"

Stef didn't want to ask, but she had to. "Where did you see her?"

Dunkan pointed a trembling finger towards the glass, towards the cleared window of coral. "Out there."

A wave of sadness and pity washed over Stef. There was nothing out there, nothing but the reef. Mila had drowned a week ago whilst clearing away more coral from the habitat.

"I sometimes think I see things in the water too. But it's just a trick of the light, fish swimming around, turtles." But she could see her reassurances were having no effect.

"No! It was *her*, Stef. It was Mila. But her body was… it was all *wrong*. Her *eyes*…" He lowered his voice. "I think she blames me."

Stef shook her head. "What are you talking about? Blames you for what?"

He covered his face with his hands. "I saw it. Saw *her*, I mean, when she…" He began to cry then, murmuring Mila's name over and over.

Stef didn't know what to say. She stood up, looking out into the water as she tried to imagine what Dunkan had seen. She supposed it was possible that Mila's body – or some of it – was still floating out there, but it wouldn't comfort Dunkan to be told that the sea and its inhabitants had most likely consumed her by now. He knew that anyway. Like everything else in New Eden, the dead were recycled, returned to the sea.

"I know what you're thinking, Stef."

"What?"

"That there's nothing left of her."

Stef turned back to him, unnerved that he seemed to have read her mind. But then, what else could she have been thinking? After a few moments of silence, she said, "It's true. There *can't* be anything left. You know that."

Dunkan nodded slowly, his expression darkening. "I know. The fish eat us and we eat the fish. We've become cannibals."

It was a sickening leap in logic. Even so, she felt her stomach lurch at the thought. "Dunkan…"

"And why not? We devoured everything else on the planet. We started as we meant to go on. We're like that ugly reef out there, taking over everything, grinding it down, destroying it."

"But we work *with* the reef," Stef protested. She was desperate to derail his morbid train of thought. "It's what keeps us alive. It *saved* us."

"No. It's killing us. Like it killed Mila." He paused, taking a long shuddering breath. "I saw her die."

Stef blinked. He hadn't said anything about that at the time. Only Ling, Mila's diving partner, had witnessed her fate. One of her hoses had snagged on the reef, trapping her behind Ling, who had only turned back at the last minute to see Mila struggling with her regulator. And by then it was too late. Her air was gone, leaked into the surrounding sea.

"Why didn't you tell anyone?" Stef asked softly.

Dunkan looked at her, misery etched on his face. "It didn't matter, did it? There was nothing I could have done. I stood right here and watched her drown."

Stef remembered the day well. If it had happened ten minutes earlier, she might have been the one to witness Mila's final moments instead. But she'd been topping up the thermoplastics in the printers, two rooms away.

Dunkan turned his head slowly, peering out into the reef again. "But now she's back."

The room felt chilly, and Stef wrapped her arms around herself as she stared into the murky water beyond the glass.

"If she truly is back," she ventured, choosing her words carefully, "then maybe she's telling you not to feel guilty."

The silence her words fell into was icy cold. And colder still was the look in Dunkan's eyes. He slowly got to his feet, glaring as he loomed over her. "Don't patronise me. I know what I saw."

For a moment it looked as if fury would triumph over fear, and Stef found herself edging away. But then his expression softened and he turned away, covering his face once more.

"She's out there," he whimpered. "She's coming back. They all are."

* * *

Dunkan had been taken to the infirmary, and that was the last anyone saw of him. By the time Stef went to visit him, he was gone. A notebook was later found in his quarters, filled with wild scribbling and repeated apologies, mostly to Mila. In between were frankly apocalyptic rantings, along with what the doctors called survivor's guilt. It wasn't difficult to guess what had happened.

A new rule was made that no one was to be left alone in the print lab. Stef had finally managed to push the incident to the back of her mind, but now Aren had brought it all racing back.

She closed her eyes, banishing the bad memories. She'd meant everything she said to Aren, that the solitude didn't bother her, that she was nothing like Dunkan. She wasn't prone to morbid preoccupations and she'd never seen anything in the water that shouldn't be there. Certainly not a ghost.

It was true that living below the surface wasn't natural for humans. But surely that was why they'd evolved intelligence over other species, to adapt to new and different surroundings. Before the destruction of the planet, hadn't they lived in shelters in even more challenging environments? Deserts, mountains. They'd even built a space station once.

Down here they enjoyed a symbiotic relationship with the reef. They had even begun to harvest the coral, adapting the printers to incorporate the new material. Perhaps one day new rooms would be made entirely of coral. The reef reinforced the structure of the habitat as well as providing them with food. Where Dunkan had felt trapped by it, Stef felt nurtured. The humans were doing the same thing as the reef – expanding and colonising.

The grinding of the printers was a pleasant background hum. To Stef it was the sound of life. But a sudden stutter in the mechanical droning shook her from her thoughts. She opened her eyes. And froze. Directly beyond her window was a curving arm of the reef, the same one she watched every day. It swept past the bee sculpture, up to the ruins of what had once been a concert stage. But now the coral was pushed tight against the glass. And for a moment she thought she saw a face within the waving fingers of anemone.

But it was only for a moment. Then the coral drifted away, moving on like a curious fish. Something must have broken off the piece she'd just been looking at. It happened sometimes. Storms on the surface affected the currents, even as far down as this.

She shook her head in annoyance. Aren's brooding had darkened her mood, that was all. He'd made her think of Dunkan. She turned back to the main console, pushing away her irritation before resentment could set in. It wasn't Aren's fault. But she made herself promise to be extra vigilant now that she was on her own here.

When Cassa and Min came to relieve her at the end of her shift, she decided not to tell them anything about what she'd seen. She'd only *thought* she'd seen it, after all, and it wouldn't benefit anyone to have some momentary trick of her eyes on record.

* * *

The next few days passed without incident, and Stef was beginning to settle into her new solitary routine, enjoying the peace and quiet of having the lab to herself. Just the way she liked it. The eel greeted her occasionally, as did prides of lionfish and other creatures.

She stood before the window, gazing out into the blue. A flash of movement caught her eye and she saw to her delight that it was an octopus. The shy animal wrapped its gracefully coiling arms around the reef as it pulled itself along, pausing to camouflage itself when a large fish came too close. Stef watched until it was out of sight and then went to check the progress of the new corridor.

The printers were fine, buzzing away as usual. The readings showed a slight fluctuation and, when she investigated further, she realised that one of the storage tanks was damaged, leaking a small amount of fluid into the ocean. It could only have just happened, so she didn't feel too guilty. She entered the repair order into the system and made her way back to the main lab.

She felt it instantly. Something had changed. The room was shockingly cold and she spied a small puddle of water beside her desk. That wasn't unusual. The habitat did leak from time to time. But that wasn't what made her skin prickle.

Reluctantly, she turned towards the coral window, and her eyes went wide. Dunkan was out there, his face pressed against the glass, peering in.

For long moments she stood frozen, staring and not believing what she saw.

"You're dead," she whispered at last. "Aren't you?"

Dunkan stared back, and his lips curled in mimicry of a smile. It was an awful sight, that smile. False and unnatural.

Then she noticed his arms. His hands were cupped around his face, as though he were simply standing outside and looking in. But a third arm dangled by his side, boneless and slightly too long.

Her body was…it was all wrong. *Her* eyes…

Stef screamed.

If Dunkan heard her, he didn't react. He merely drifted there, buffeted slightly by the current, the horrible smile unwavering as he continued to stare through the glass at her.

It was as though she'd ordered the printer to craft a replica of Dunkan and it had done the best it could with only the most limited information. And Stef's heart wrenched as she began to understand at last.

Dunkan *had* seen Mila. A *replica* of her. As the printers had learned from the coral, so too had the coral learned from the printers. Whatever the invading humans left in the sea, it was beginning to reproduce.

The reef was printing too.

She ran to the back room and wrenched open the airlock door. From there she had a better view of the leaking tank. It was encrusted with spiny corals and surrounded by lionfish. They appeared to be working together to widen a puncture in the tank. Liquid polymer and plastic streamed into the water from the breach, along with the coral that had been had harvested to supplement it.

We weren't meant to be down here.

Stef sank to her knees, unable to stand upright anymore. Not even the most fatalistic of scientists could have predicted this. She thought of what Aren had said about them becoming cannibals. But that wasn't entirely right. What they'd become was prey. No, it was even worse than that. They were a minor hurdle. Nothing more. The human race was simply in the way, as it always had been.

A thump sounded behind her and she slowly looked around. She wasn't surprised to see that Dunkan had followed her. He drifted just outside the airlock, his smile still frozen in place. And as she watched, he pointed towards the damaged tank with his new arm. It almost looked like he was laughing.

The End of the World
Retold Tales from the Eddas and Sagas

We shall see emerge
From the bright Ocean at our feet an earth
More fresh, more verdant than the last, with fruits
Self-springing, and a seed of man preserved,
Who then shall live in peace, as then in war.
Matthew Arnold, Balder Dead

BALDER WAS PURE OF HEART, and he represented goodness in every form. His life in Asgard was one of kindness and generosity, and while he lived the force of his righteousness would allow everyone in Asgard to enjoy peace from evil. But evil comes in many forms and not even the gods could be protected from its sinister influence forever. In Asgard, Loki was the evil that would burst the bauble of their happiness, and it was Loki who would bring about the end to the eternal conflict between virtue and corruption. It was an end that had been predicted since the earth was created, and its reality was as frightening as every prediction had suggested. Ragnarok would rid the world of evil, and leave a trail of ashes that blotted out the sun and all that had once glowed in their gilded world. But it is from ashes that new life springs, and the world of the Viking gods was no exception.

The Death of Balder

So on the floor lay Balder dead; and round
Lay thickly strewn swords, axes, darts, and spears,
Which all the Gods in sport had idly thrown
At Balder, whom no weapon pierced or clove;
But in his breast stood fixed the fatal bough
Of mistletoe, which Lok, the Accuser, gave
To Hoder, and unwitting Hoder threw –
'Gainst that alone had Balder's life no charm.
Matthew Arnold, Balder Dead

TO ODIN AND FRIGGA, we are told, were born twin sons as dissimilar in character and physical appearance as it was possible for two children to be. Hodur, god of darkness, was sombre, taciturn, and blind, like the obscurity of sin, which he was supposed to symbolise, while his brother Balder, the beautiful, was worshipped as the pure and radiant god of innocence and light. From his snowy brow and golden locks seemed to radiate beams of sunshine which gladdened the hearts of gods and men, by whom he was equally beloved. Each life that he touched glowed with goodness, and he was loved by all who knew him. Balder tended to his twin brother Hodur with every kindness and consideration. Hodur worshipped Balder, and would do nothing in his power to harm him.

The youthful Balder attained his full growth with marvellous rapidity, and was early admitted to the council of the gods. He took up his abode in the palace of Breidablik, whose silver roof rested upon golden pillars, and whose purity was such that nothing common or unclean was ever allowed within its precincts, and here he lived in perfect unity with his young wife Nanna (blossom), the daughter of Nip (bud), a beautiful and charming goddess.

The god of light was well versed in the science of runes, which were carved on his tongue; he knew the various virtues of simples, one of which, the camomile, was called "Balder's brow," because its flower was as immaculately pure as his forehead. The only thing hidden from Balder's radiant eyes was the perception of his own ultimate fate.

There came a morning when Balder woke with the dawn, his face tightened with fear and foresight. He had dreamed of his own death and he lay there petrified, aware, somehow, that the strength of this dream forecasted sinister things to come. So Balder travelled to see Odin, who listened carefully, and knew at once that the fears of his son were justified – for in his shining eyes there was no longer simply innocence; there was knowledge as well. Odin went at once to his throne at the top of Yggdrasill, and he prayed there for a vision to come to him. At once he saw the head of Vala the Seer come to him, and he knew he must travel to Hel's kingdom, to visit Vala's grave. Only then would he learn the truth of his favourite son's fate.

It was many long days before Odin reached the innermost graves on Hel's estate. He moved quietly so that Hel would not know of his coming, and he was disregarded by most of the workers in her lands, for they were intent on some celebrations, and were preparing the hall for the arrival of an esteemed guest. At last the mound of Vala's grave appeared, and he sat there on it, keeping his head low so that the prophetess would not catch a glimpse of his face. Vala was a seer of all things future, and all things past; there was nothing that escaped her bright eyes, and she could be called upon only by the magic of the runes to tell of her knowledge.

The grave was wreathed in shadows, and a mist hung uneasily over the tombstone. There was silence as Odin whispered to Vala to come forth, and then, at once, there was a grating and steaming that poured forth an odour that caused even the all-powerful Odin to gag and spit.

'Who disturbs me from my sleep,' said Vala with venom. Odin thought carefully before replying. He did not wish her to know that he was Odin, king of gods and men, for she may not wish to tell him of a future that would touch on his own. And so he responded:

'I am Vegtam, son of Valtam, and I wish to learn of the fate of Balder.'

'Balder's brother will slay him,' said Vala, and with that she withdrew into her grave.

Odin leapt up and cried out, 'With the power of the runes, you must tell me more. Tell me, Vala, which esteemed guest does Hel prepare for?'

'Balder,' she muttered from the depths of her grave, 'and I will say no more.'

Odin shook his head with concern. He could not see how it could be possible that Balder's brother would take his life; Balder and Hodur were the closest of brothers, and shared the same thoughts and indeed speech for much of the time. He returned to Asgard with his concerns still intact, and he discussed them there with Frigga, who listened carefully.

'I have a plan,' she announced, 'and I am certain you will agree that this is the best course of action for us all. I plan to travel through all nine lands, and I will seek the pledge of every living creature, every plant, every metal and stone, not to harm Balder.'

And Frigga was as good as her word, for on the morrow she set out and travelled far and wide, everywhere she went extracting with ease the promise of every living creature, and inanimate object, to love Balder, and to see that he was not injured in any way.

And so it was that Balder was immune to injury of any kind, and it became a game among the children of Asgard to aim their spears and arrows at him, and laugh as they bounced off, leaving him unharmed. Balder was adored throughout the worlds, and there was no one who did not smile when he spied him.

No one, that is except Loki, whose jealousy of Balder had reached an unbearable pitch. Each night he ruminated over the ways in which he could murder Balder, but he could think of none. Frigga had taken care to involve all possible dangers in her oath, and there was nothing now that would hurt him. But the scheming Loki was not unwise, and he soon came up with a plan. Transforming himself into a beggarwoman, he knocked on Frigga's door and requested a meal. Frigga was pleased to offer her hospitality, and she sat down to keep the beggar company as she ate.

Loki, in his disguise, chattered on about the handsome Balder, who he'd seen in the hall, and he mentioned his fears that Balder would be killed by one of the spears and arrows he had seen hurled at him. Frigga laughed, and explained that Balder was now invincible.

'Did everything swear an oath to you then?' asked Loki slyly.

'Oh, yes,' said Frigga, but then she paused, 'all, that is, except for a funny little plant which was growing at the base of the oak tree at Valhalla. Why I'd never before set eyes on such a little shoot of greenery and it was far too immature to swear to anything so important as my oath.'

'What's it called?' asked Loki again.

'Hmmm,' said Frigga, still unaware of the dangers her information might invoke, 'mistletoe. Yes, mistletoe.'

Loki thanked Frigga hastily for his meal, and left her palace, transforming at once into his mischievous self, and travelling to Valhalla as quickly as his feet would take him. He carefully plucked the budding mistletoe, and returned to Odin's hall, where Balder played with the younger gods and goddesses, as they shot him unsuccessfully with arms of every shape and size.

Hodur was standing frowning in the corner, and Loki whispered for him to come over.

'What is it, Hodur,' he asked.

'Nothing, really, just that I cannot join their games,' said Hodur quietly.

'Come with me,' said Loki, 'for I can help.' And leading Hodur to a position close to Balder, he placed in his hands a bow and arrow fashioned from the fleetest of fabrics. To the end of the arrow, he tied a small leaf of mistletoe, and topped the razor-sharp tip with a plump white berry. 'Now, shoot now,' he cried to Hodur, who pulled back the bow and let the arrow soar towards its target.

There was a sharp gasp, and then there was silence. Hodur shook his head with surprise – where were the happy shouts, where was the laughter telling him that his own arrow had hit its mark and failed to harm the victim? The silence spoke volumes, for Balder lay dead in a circle of admirers as pale and frightened as if they had seen Hel herself.

The agony spread across Asgard like a great wave. When it was discovered who had shot the fatal blow, Hodur was sent far from his family, and left alone in the wilderness. He had not yet had a moment to utter the name of the god who had encouraged him to perpetrate this grave crime, and his misery kept him silent.

Frigga was disconsolate with grief. She begged Hermod, the swiftest of her sons, to set out at once for Filheim, to beg Hel to release Balder to them all. And so he climbed upon Odin's finest steed, Sleipnir, and set out for the nine worlds of Hel, a task so fearsome that he shook uncontrollably.

In Asgard, Frigga and Odin carried their son's body to the sea, where a funeral pyre was created and lit. Nanna, Balder's wife, could bear it no longer, and before the pyre was set out on the tempestuous sea, she threw herself on the flames, and perished there with her only love. As a token of their great affection and esteem, the gods offered, one by one, their most prized possessions and laid them on the pyre as it set out for the wild seas. Odin produced his magic ring Draupnir, and the greatest gods of Asgard gathered to see the passing of Balder.

And so the blazing ship left the shore, will full sail set. And then darkness swallowed it, and Balder had gone.

Throughout this time, Hermod had been travelling at great speed towards Hel. He rode for nine days and nine nights, and never took a moment to sleep. He galloped on and on, bribing the watchman of each gate to let him past, and invoking the name of Balder as the reason for his journey. At last, he reached the hall of Hel, where he found Balder sitting easily with Nanna, in great comfort and looking quite content. Hel stood by his side, keeping a close watch on her newest visitor. She looked up at Hermod with disdain, for everyone knew that once a spirit had reached Hel it could not be released. But Hermod fell on one knee and begged the icy mistress to reconsider her hold over Balder.

'Please, Queen Hel, without Balder we cannot survive. There can be no future for Asgard without his presence,' he cried.

But Hel would not be moved. She held out for three days and three nights, while Hermod stayed right by her side, begging and pleading and offering every conceivable reason why Balder should be released. And finally the Queen of darkness gave in.

'Return at once to Asgard,' she said harshly, 'and if what you say is true, if everything – living and inanimate – in Asgard loves Balder and cannot live without him, then he will be released. But if there is even one dissenter, if there is even one stone in your land who does not mourn the passing of Balder, then he shall remain here with me.'

Hermod was gladdened by this news, for he knew that everyone – including Hodur who had sent the fatal arrow flying through the air – loved Balder. He agreed to these terms at once, and set off for Asgard, relaying himself and his news with speed that astonished all who saw him arrive.

Immediately, Odin sent messengers to all corners of the universe, asking for tears to be shed for Balder. And as they travelled, everyone and everything began to weep, until a torrent of water rushed across the tree of life. And after everyone had been approached, and each had shed his tears, the messengers made their way back to Odin's palace with glee. Balder would be released, there could be no doubt!

But it was not to be, for as the last messenger travelled back to the palace, he noticed the form of an old beggarwoman, hidden in the darkness of a cave. He approached her then, and bid her to cry for Balder, but she did not. Her eyes remained dry. The uproar was carried across to the palace, and Odin himself came to see 'dry eyes', whose inability to shed tears would cost him the life of his son. He stared into those eyes and he saw then what the messenger had failed to see, what Frigga had failed to see, and what had truly caused the death of Balder. For those eyes belonged to none other than Loki, and it was he who had murdered Balder as surely as if the arrow had left his own hands.

The sacred code of Asgard had been broken, for blood had been spilled by one of their own, in their own land. The end of the world was nigh – but first, Loki would be punished once and for all.

The Revenge of the Gods

Thee, on a rock's point,
With the entrails of thy ice-cold son,
The god will bind.
Benjamin Thorpe, Saemund's Edda

THE WRATH OF THE GODS was so great that Asgard shuddered and shook. As Odin looked down upon Loki in the form of the beggarwoman, and made the decision to punish him, Loki transformed himself into a fly and disappeared.

Although he was crafty, even his most supreme efforts to save himself were as nothing in the face of Odin's determination to trace him.

Loki travelled to far distant mountains, and on the peak of the most isolated of them all, he built a cabin, with windows and doors on all sides so that he could see the enemy approaching, and flee from any side before they reached him. By day, he haunted a pool by a rushing waterfall, taking the shape of a salmon. His life was uncomplicated, and although he was forced to live by his wits, and the fear of the god's revenge was great, Loki was not unhappy.

From his throne above the worlds, Odin watched, and waited. And when he saw that Loki had grown complacent, and no longer looked with quite such care from his many windows, he struck.

It was one particular evening that Loki sat weaving. He had just invented what we today call a fish net, and as he worked he hummed to himself, glancing every now and then from his great windows, and then back at his work. The gods were almost upon him when he first noticed them, and they were led by Kvasir, who was known amongst all gods for his wisdom and ability to unravel the tricks of even the most seasoned trickster. And as he saw them arriving, Loki fled from the back door, and transformed himself into a salmon, and leapt into the pond.

The gods stood in the doorway, surveying the room. Kvasir walked over to the fishing net and examined it closely. His keen eyes caught a glimmer of fish scales on the floor, and he nodded sagely.

'It is my assessment,' he said, 'that our Loki has become a fish. And,' he held up the fishing net, 'we will catch him with his own web.'

The gods made their way to the stream, and the pond which lay at the bottom of the waterfall. Throwing the net into the water, they waited for daybreak, when Loki the salmon would enter the waters and be caught in their net. Of course, Loki was too clever to be trapped so easily, and he swam beneath the net and far away from the part of the pond where the gods were fishing. Kvasir soon realized their mistake, and he ordered that rocks be placed at the bottom of the net, so that none could swim beneath it. And they waited.

Loki looked with amusement at the god's trap, and gracefully soared through the air above the net, his eyes glinting in the early morning light. And as his fins were just inches from the water, and when he was so close to escape that he had begun to plan his celebrations, two firm hands were thrust out, and he was lifted into the air.

He hardly dared look at his captor, and he began to tremble when he saw that it was none other than Thor who had moved so swiftly to catch him.

'I command you to take your own form, Loki,' he shouted, holding tight to the smooth scales of the salmon.

Loki knew he was beaten. Quietly he transformed himself once again into Loki, only to find himself hung by the heels over the rippling waters. And as Thor raised his great hammer to beat Loki to death, a hand reached out and stopped him. It was Odin, and he spoke gently, and with enormous purpose.

'Death is too good for this rodent,' he whispered. 'Take him at once to the Hel's worlds and tie him there for good.'

And so it was that Loki was taken to Filheim, where Thor grabbed three massive rocks and formed a platform for the hapless trickster. Then, Loki's two sons, Vali and Nari, were brought forth, and an enchantment was laid upon Vali so that he took the form of a wolf and attacked his brother Nari, tearing him to pieces in front of his anguished father. Gathering up Nari's entrails, which were now endowed with magic properties, he tied Loki's limbs so that he lay across the three rocks, unable to move. The entrails would tighten with every effort he made to escape, and to ensure that he could not use trickery to free himself, Thor placed the rocks on a precipice. One false move and he would be sent crashing to his death in the canyon below.

Finally, Skadi caught a poisonous snake, and trapped it by its tail so that it hung over Loki's face, dripping venom into his mouth so that he screamed with pain and terror. He began to convulse and was such a terrible sight that his wife Sigyn rushed forward and begged to be allowed to stay beside him, holding a bowl with which to collect the poison.

The work of the gods was done. They turned then and left, and Sigyn remained with her husband, ever true to her wedding vows. Every day or so she moved from her position at his side in order to empty her bowl, and Loki's convulsions brought an earthquake to Asgard that lasted just as long as it took her to return with her bowl. They would remain there until the end of time – for the gods, that is. The end of time was nigh, and it was Ragnarok.

Ragnarok

Brothers slay brothers;
Sisters' children
Shed each other's blood.
Hard is the world;
Sensual sin grows huge.
There are sword-ages, axe-ages;
Shields are cleft in twain;
Storm-ages, murder-ages;

Till the world falls dead,
And men no longer spare
Or pity one another.
R.B. Anderson, Norse Mythology

THE END OF THE WORLD had been prophesied from its beginning, and everyone across the world knew what to expect when Ragnarok fell upon them. For Ragnarok was the twilight of the gods, an end to the golden years of Asgard, an end to the palaces of delight, an end to the timeless world where nothing could interfere. It was the death of Balder that set the stage for the end of the world, and it was Loki's crimes which laid in place the main characters. And when the action had begun, there was no stopping it.

When evil entered Asgard, it tainted all nine worlds. Sol and Mani, high in the sky, paled with fright, and their chariots slowed as they moved with effort across the sky. They knew that the wolves would be soon upon them and that it would be only a matter of time before eternal darkness would fall once again. And when Sol and Mani had been devoured, there was no light to shine on the earth, and the terrible cold crept into the warm reaches of summer and drew from the soil what was growing there. Snow began to drift down upon the freezing land, and soon it snowed a little faster, and a little harder, until the earth was covered once again in a dark layer of ice.

Winter was upon them, and it did not cease. For three long, frozen seasons, it was winter, and then, after a thaw that melted only one single layer of ice, it was back for three more. With the cold and the darkness came evil, which rooted itself in the hearts of men. Soon crime was rampant, and all shreds of human kindness disappeared with the spring. At last, the stars were flung from the skies, causing the earth to tremble and shake. Loki and Fenris were freed from their manacles, and together they moved forward to wreak their revenge on the gods and men who had bound them so cruelly.

At the bottom of Yggdrasill, there was a groan that emanated the entire length of the tree, for at that moment, Nithog had gnawed through the root of the world tree, which quivered and shook from bottom to top. Fialar, the red cock who made his home above Valhalla shrieked out his cry, and then flew away from the tree as his call was echoed by Gullinkambi, the rooster in Midgard.

Heimdall knew at once what was upon them, and raising his mighty horn to his lips he blew the call that filled the hearts of all gods and mankind with terror. Ragnarok. The gods sprang from their beds, and thrust aside the finery that hung in their bed chambers. They armed themselves and mounted their horses, ready for the war that had been expected since the beginning of time. They moved quickly over the rainbow bridge and then they reached the field of Vigrid, where the last battle would be fought.

The turmoil on earth caused the seas to toss and twist with waves, and soon the world serpent Jormungander was woken from his deep sleep. The movement of the seas yanked his tail from his mouth, and it lashed around, sending waves crashing in every direction. And as he crawled out upon land for the first time, a tidal wave swelled across the earth, and set afloat Nagilfar, the ship of the dead, which had been constructed from the nails of the dead whose relatives had failed in their duties, and had neglected to pare the nails of the deceased when they were laid to rest. As the wind caught the blackened sail, Loki leapt aboard, and took her wheel – the ship of the undead captained by the personification of all evil. Loki called upon the fire-gods from Muspell, and they arrived in a conflagration of terrible glory.

Another ship had set out for Vigrid, and this was steered by Hrym and crewed by the frost-giants who had waited many centuries for this battle. Across the raging sea, both vessels made for the battlefield.

As they travelled, Hel, crept from her underground estate, bringing with her Nithog, and the hellhound Garm. From up above, there was a great crack, and Surtr, with sword blazing, leapt with his sons to the Bifrost bridge, and with one swoop they felled it, and sent the shimmering rainbow crashing to the depths below. Quickly, Odin escaped from the battlefield, and slipped one last time to the Urdar fountain, where the Norns sat quietly, accepting their fate. He leant over Mimir, and requested her wisdom, but for once the head would not talk to him, and he remounted Sleipnir and returned to the field, frightened and aware that he had no powers left with which to defend his people.

The opposing armies lined themselves on Vigrid field. On one side were the Aesir, the Vanir and the Einheriear – on the other, were the fire-giants led by Surtr, the frost-giants, the undead with Hel, and Loki with his children – Fenris and Jormungander. The air was filled with poison and the stench of evil from the opposing army, yet the gods held up their heads and prepared for a battle to end all time.

And so it was that the ancient enemies came to blows. Odin first met with the evil Fenris, and as he charged towards the fierce wolf, Fenris's massive jaws stretched open and Odin was flung deep into the red throat. Thor stopped in his tracks, the death of his father burning deep in his breast, and with renewed fury he lunged at the world serpent, engaging in a combat that would last for many hours. His hammer laid blow after blow on the serpent, and at last there was silence. Thor sat back in exhaustion, Jormungander dying at his side. But as Thor made to move forward, to carry on and support his kin in further battles, the massive serpent exhaled one last time, in a cloud of poison so vile that Thor fell at once, lifeless in the mist of the serpent's breath.

Tyr fought bravely with just one arm, but he, like his father, was swallowed whole, by the hellhound Garm, but as he passed through the gullet of the hound he struck out one last blow with his sword and pierced the heart of his enemy, dying in the knowledge that he had obtained his life's ambition.

Heimdall met Loki hand to hand, and the forces of good and evil engaged in the battle that had been raging for all time. Their flames engulfed one another; there was a flash of light. And then there was nothing.

The silent Vidar came rushing from a distant part of the plain to avenge the death of Odin, and he laid upon the jaw of Fenris a shoe which had been created for this day. With his arms and legs in motion he tore the wolf's head from his body, and then lay back in a pool of blood. Of all the gods, only Frey was left fighting. He battled valiantly, and as he laid down giant after giant, he felt a warmth on the back of his neck that meant only one thing. The heat burned and sizzled his skin, and as he turned he found himself face to face with Surtr. With a cry of rage that howled through the torn land, and shook the massive stem of the world ash, Yggdrasill, Surtr flung down bolts of fire that engulfed the golden palaces of the gods, and each of the worlds which lay beneath it. The heat caused the seas to bubble and to boil, and there came at once a wreath of smoke that blotted out the fire, and then, the world.

At last all was as it had been in the beginning. There was blackness. There was chaos. There was a nothingness that stretched as far as there was space.

The End of the World

All evil
Dies there an endless death, while goodness riseth
From that great world-fire, purified at last,
to a life far higher, better, nobler than the past.
R. B. Anderson, Viking Tales of the North

THE EARTH WAS PURGED by the fire and there was at once a new beginning. The sun rose in the sky, mounted on a chariot driven by the daughter of Sol, born before the wolf had eaten her father and her mother. Fresh green grass sprung up in the crevices, and flowers and fruits burst forth. Two new humans, Lif, a woman, and Lifthrasir, a man, emerged from Mimir's forest, where they had been reincarnated at the end of the world. Vali and Vidar, the forces of nature had survived the fiery battle, and they returned to the plan to be greeted by Thor's sons, Modi and Magni, who carried with them their father's hammer.

Hoenir had escaped from the Vanir, who had vanished forever, and from the deepest depths of the earth came Balder, renewed and as pure as he had ever been. Hodur rose with him, and the two brothers embraced, and greeted the new day. And so this small group of gods turned to face the scenes of destruction and devastation, and to witness the new life that was already curling up from the cloak of death and darkness. The land had become a refuge for the good. They looked up – they all looked way up – and there in front of them, stronger than ever was the world ash, Yggdrasill, which had trembled but not fallen.

There was a civilization to be created, and a small band of gods with whom it could be done. The gods had returned in a blaze of white light – a light as pure and virtuous as the new inhabitants of the earth – and in that light they brought forth our own world.

Free Air

John B. Rosenman

MORLEY'S WALK during his lunch period had taken him a half-dozen blocks from work. Now, surrounded by buildings, uniformly gray and lifeless, he found himself blinking at a sign that made no sense at all.

Free Air.

Free Air – what could it mean? Morley stood breathing from a hose that led to an oxygen tank on his back. Inhale, exhale. Each cycle took a slow 10.8 seconds; the even rhythm was the result of intensive childhood conditioning. One inhaled air and did not expel it until necessary. To do otherwise was to squander his meager oxygen reserves.

Free Air. The words were only half-visible in the sweltering atmosphere. Morley checked his watch. Twelve-thirty. He was due back at his post in twenty minutes and would have to hurry to make it. Still...

Curious, he went to the door beneath the sign. A small plaque over a doorbell read *Ring for Service. He* pressed it.

As soon as he did, he felt foolish. The unemployment rate was over forty percent, and it had required all his family's influence to get him the clerk's position at the Ministry of Records. There was a waiting list of hundreds who would do anything to have his job – a job he could lose if he were only a minute late. Yet he had taken this long walk, challenging his air reserves, to get away from Simon Wiseman's subtle bullying and the prison-like walls at work. And what was the result? Like a fool, he now stood outside some dismal relic of the previous century, waiting for—

The door opened and Morley forgot all about being late. His mouth dropped open.

Inside stood a plump, little man.

And the man had nothing – absolutely nothing – in his mouth.

Morley took a step forward and stopped, not hearing the door ring shut behind him. "You... don't have an oxygen tank!"

"Of course not," the man said. "Why should I? Your contaminated air can't enter, and there's only fresh air around us." He waved theatrically at his surroundings. "Fresh air, sir. Bounteous, plenteous, copious air. Here, let me help you with that."

Morley retreated, automatically guarding the hose, a device he had used since infancy. To be stripped of it was to die, choking in the rank sewage that passed for atmosphere. Even straying from the Ministry was dangerous. Despite the falling population, the inner cities were like jungles these days, swarming with outlaws who prowled the streets for unwary prey. Why, at today's prices, even the half-filled tank on his back would easily bring two hundred credits on the black market.

The little man recognized his mistake and stepped back. "I'm sorry. Working here, one forgets the plight that prevails beyond our portal." He smiled. "Please, if you'll just remove your mouthpiece, you'll find it quite safe."

Morley blinked. "Remove my mouthpiece?"

"Please. There's no greenhouse effect in here, no dangerously high levels of carbon dioxide or hydrocarbon." He raised his eyes beatifically to the ceiling. "Only fresh, clean, redolent air provided by Mother Nature herself."

The man's extravagant words confused Morley, but against his better judgment, he cautiously removed his mouthpiece. It must be some trick…

Air.

Sweet, heavenly air.

He almost choked on its richness. Unlike the sterile, canned variety he had breathed ever since he could remember, *this a*ir was alive with nuances and dimensions it would take a lifetime to know. Morley gazed at the man in disbelief.

"That's better." The plump man beamed in satisfaction. "But there's really no reason to breathe so slowly."

"Slowly?"

The man gestured at the arched chamber they stood in. "As you can see, you can have *all* you want."

Morley looked around. His unencumbered mouth felt foreign and unnatural. Yet the air was so sweet and fragrant, he felt he might faint from pleasure. And what had the man said? That there was so much of it he could breathe as rapidly as he wanted.

Against all his training, Morley forced himself to quicken his consumption. It wasn't easy. Thirty years of conditioning were against him. He found he had to concentrate, to *will* his lungs to inflate and deflate more quickly. Such prodigal waste disturbed him deeply. Not only did it violate the rights of others, but it was illegal as well. People had their air rations cut, were imprisoned – even executed for repeated offenses, yet here he was…

"Faster," the little man commanded.

Morley gaped at him. "Faster?"

"Yes. You've barely increased your intake. You need to breathe *much* faster."

Morley thought he'd been gulping it. He gazed incredulously at the man's smooth, soft features. Concentrating, he worked his lungs like bellows. In, out. Oxygen poured in, and he felt his entire body flood with vitality and well-being. Why, it was paradise, his most secret dream miraculously come true!

"How in the world…"

A smile. "If you'll just follow me, Mr…"

"Uh, Morley. George Morley."

"Yes. If you'll just follow me, Mr. Morley, I assure you, all your questions will be answered to your complete satisfaction."

Morley watched the man enter a hallway and drifted after him. Cool gusts of air laved his face, and it was as if his feet had wings.

The man opened a door and Morley followed him through it.

They stood on a gleaming white walkway that girdled an immense, domed enclosure. And beneath them were…

Morley sucked in his breath, not believing his eyes.

Trees.

He shook his head at the lush green expanse. "No, it can't be. Must be…some kind of mirage."

Soft laughter. "Oh, Mr. Morley, I assure you, they're no mirage." He pointed over the rail. "To your far right, you will observe cedar. Twenty of them. And next to them, twenty elm, twenty ash…"

But Morley was barely listening. He had found a stand of exquisite Lombardy poplars and watched dumbly as their tall, slender columns swayed gracefully in wind that came from nowhere.

"I thought they were extinct," he said.

"The poplars?" The other grew serious. "No, Mr. Morley. Thanks to botanical engineering and recent ecological breakthroughs, some species have been saved. True, it hasn't been easy. Today we have famine, water shortages, and a life expectancy of forty." He paused, and his voice softened as he gazed at the trees. "But this is proof that something *can* be done to save this dying planet. Life, Mr. Morley. Everything society lacks is symbolized before you, and one day we shall rejuvenate the world, fill it once again with clean, fresh air, no matter what sacrifices we have to make."

Morley no longer gazed at the trees, but at this odd, somehow compelling little man who barely reached his shoulder. Up to now he had acted like the effusive host of some mysterious party, but his speech had carried a messianic fervor and borne the stamp of a cause. Morley cleared his throat.

"But…" He couldn't continue. He knew from his work at the Ministry of Records that there were, at best, seven preserves remaining in North America, all of them paltry efforts that fell pitifully short of this…forest. Yet here it was. Why didn't the Government know of this miraculous experiment? Why hadn't they stepped in and seized it, as they had everything else? After all, it was operating almost in plain sight, and he had stumbled upon it without meaning to.

Morley moaned. The free air, the lush trees, this fantastic little man with his crazy talk. Trembling, Morley stepped forward and gripped the rail, half wishing that all he had experienced would vanish in a puff of smoke.

A hand with a large jade ring covered Morley's. "Come, I have something to discuss with you."

Suddenly Morley remembered that he was due back at the Ministry and consulted his watch. Seven minutes!

"My job—"

"Don't worry. It will be taken care of, I assure you."

"But if I'm late, I'll lose it. They'll give it to someone else. There are hundreds just waiting—"

"*Relax,* Mr. Morley." The small man patted Morley's shoulder. "I assure you, your position will be waiting for you when you return."

Morley's breath caught. Was it possible that the Government *did k*now of this experiment? That it actually sanctioned it? He tried to ask but found himself being led into a spacious and luxurious office. Lights gleamed in profusion, and its green carpet felt as soft as grass.

Dazed, his senses overloaded, he stumbled to a chair and sat down, not noticing that all the furniture was made of *wood.*

"Now, then." His host produced a sheet of paper. "Mr. Morley, I'd like to make you a proposition."

"Proposition?"

"Yes. A most excellent proposition, too. One that any of your friends would give a year's salary for."

"Really?" About him, air – sweet oceans of it – pressed against his lips and nostrils.

"Yes, Mr. Morley, *really.*" He smiled. "Now, what would you say if I told you that you could have all the air you wanted piped into your home, absolutely free?"

His head swam. "Free?"

"Yes, Mr. Morley, for free. Not one sou, not one yen, not one centime will be asked of you. You need only sign a simple agreement to enlist in our pilot program, and we'll make the necessary adjustments to your living quarters. From six in the evening to six in the morning, you can enjoy all the fresh air you want, free of charge."

"Free of charge." He nuzzled the words, trying to recover his usual skepticism. Free Air? In the blighted economy he had known all his life, a pound of real meat cost a week's salary and a single razor blade had to last months. *Nothing w*as free, certainly not air. Yet this man said he could have it every night.

There had to be a catch. "What do you want in return?"

The man beamed. "Ah, quid pro quo, something for something. Well, in a way you're right. But it isn't what you think. You see, Mr. Morley, the organization I represent is dedicated to replenishing our lost air reserves through the creation of plants and trees. Renewal, Mr. Morley, renewal is what we're all about." He paused. "And one day, Mr. Morley, the whole Earth will be green and fertile again, a vast garden, flourishing in a symbiotic relationship with man. We will breathe out carbon dioxide and nature will convert it to oxygen, just as God intended."

The speech swept Morley along, and he thought of preachers who had once overwhelmed multitudes. "You haven't told me—"

"What we want from you, Mr. Morley, is for you to simply try breathing fresh, untainted air in your apartment for twelve hours a day. Call it part of our program for gradually introducing it to society. You, and a few other fortunate individuals, will be in the vanguard that will prepare humanity for what is to come."

The man set the paper on a desk. A pen appeared in his hand. "Now, if you will be so good as to sign it, we can begin at once to make the necessary arrangements."

Morley blinked at the sheet, noticing several terms he didn't recognize. Maybe he should ask for clarification, take it home to examine.

But the thought of losing this opportunity...

"Please, I do have another appointment."

Aw hell, what was wrong with him? They were willing to transform his shabby dump into paradise, and he was studying the fine print. Why, anyone else would leap at the chance!

He took the pen and signed.

"Excellent!" His host snapped the paper up and pocketed the pen. "You've made a wise decision, Mr. Morley, and I think you'll find yourself very happy. Now..."

Quietly, not even asking why he hadn't received a copy of the agreement, Morley allowed himself to be led from the building. It was only when he was halfway through the front door, that the implausibility of the situation crashed down upon him. And one in particular—

"Hey," he shouted, removing his mouthpiece, "You didn't even tell me your name!"

The door slammed in his face. Ever so faintly, he heard receding footsteps.

* * *

Morley sat in his apartment, waiting.

As on the first two nights when they'd turned on the air, his heart beat excitedly. Breathing fresh, fragrant air, he had discovered, was not something he'd ever become used to or take for granted. It made the dull days at the office so much more bearable because he had something to look forward to. Tonight, if anything, he was more expectant than ever.

But would they turn on the air for a third straight night? He checked his watch. Five minutes to six. Gripped by suspense, he rose and stalked impatiently about, hating the feel of the mouthpiece between his lips.

In just a few minutes though he wouldn't even need it! He could have all the air he wanted. And it would be sweet air, unlike the flat kind that always smelled and tasted of plastic hose. He passed the meager water tank, whose meter was checked weekly, and stopped before a print on the wall. It was the only thing that enlivened the gray plaster, and it showed a line of Lombardy poplars whose branches pointed upward in slender, graceful columns. Recently, since the air had been turned on, he felt he could sometimes hear their leaves rustle in the wind.

Morley sat down and rechecked his watch. 5:59. He felt a surge of panic. What if they were only playing with him and wouldn't turn on the air anymore? The thought of returning to the way it was before filled him with horror. They couldn't be so cruel!

He stared at the vent on the wall. It was the most obvious change they'd made in his apartment. Sometimes, after they turned the air on, he'd lie on the floor and gulp from the vent like a glutton. Tonight, Morley watched the strips of cloth he'd tied to it. When the air was turned on…

He saw the streamers rise.

Morley forced himself not to rip off his mouthpiece. The night before, he had done that and almost drowned in a vacuum. Apparently, they had sucked all the poison out of the apartment and sealed it tight. To remove the mouthpiece now would be to breathe nothing.

So he forced himself to wait. The first night, after the air had been turned on, it had struck him as a cruel joke that he must spend half his twelve hours in mindless sleep, unaware of the ambrosia about him. But sleep had turned out to be the greatest blessing of all. How wonderful it was to lie down without being attached to an oxygen tank and mouthpiece! To wake in the night and savor the freedom of it, even rise and walk about if he wished. And above all, how glorious to wake up clear-eyed, refreshed, alive!

Morley looked at his watch. 6:05. It was time.

He removed his mouthpiece, and the air that poured into his lungs was like wine. His senses reeled, pirouetted in ecstasy. Then the room righted itself, and his delirium became something manageable, merely an exultant sense of well-being. He spread his arms, drinking the air like a drunkard.

Finally he rose, delighting in this precious new freedom. No mouthpiece. No air tank. He laughed in joy and spun about.

The doorbell rang.

He went and activated the screen. Outside his apartment, Simon Wiseman and Martin Edwards gazed back at him.

"It's true!" Edwards exclaimed. "See – he's not wearing a mouthpiece!"

He smiled. "Hi, guys."

"Simon, he wasn't lying," Edwards continued. "Look, he doesn't have an air tank!"

"I can see that," Simon said. He studied Morley, then peered behind him in search of some deception. Morley grinned back.

"See, Simon, I told you they were going to give me twelve hours of free air a day. Well, here's the proof!"

The other scoffed. "Must be some trick."

"Does it look like a trick?" Morley stepped closer to the screen, fighting down his hate and jealousy of Simon, a specialist who was three grades above him at the Ministry and always acted as if he knew everything. Staring directly at Simon's mouthpiece, Morley began to breathe in fast, prodigious gasps, rubbing their noses in his good fortune. "Look, Simon, all the air I want, and you wouldn't believe how rich and sweet it is!" He sneered. "It's not at all like that stale-tasting shit you have to suck on every eleven seconds."

Simon's eyes hardened; Edward's mouth opened in awe.

"Christ, Simon, he's telling the truth."

"There's got to be a gimmick." Simon scrutinized him. "You said you found this place about six blocks from the Ministry, and the sign said 'Free Air'?"

"Yup."

"And once inside, you didn't need a mouthpiece and actually saw *tall trees?*"

Morley felt a barb of irritation. "I already told you at work I did, didn't I? And like the man promised, they didn't even blink when I got back to the Ministry a half hour late. *You t*ry that sometime."

Simon paled. "Well, I don't believe it, especially about the trees. Everyone knows there isn't enough timber left in the world to cover more than a few acres." He frowned. "It must be some kind of Government operation. And if it is, you *know* something's wrong. They don't give *anything* away."

"But Simon, why?" Edwards asked.

"I don't know." Morley could tell Simon was trying hard to sustain his superior air, but the sight of Morley flaunting and wallowing in his gift was just too much. "There must be some Government link," Simon managed. "They set up an operation where you'd least expect it, to draw the first ones in. Then, after they've enticed enough people..."

He stopped, having nowhere to go. For the first time since Morley had known him, Simon was at a loss for words.

Morley laughed and motioned at the ocean of air around him. "Why don't you just admit I got lucky and fell into a windfall you'd sell your soul for? Admit that I'm ten golden rungs above you on the ladder?"

Simon's expression was all the victory Morley needed. Laughing in both their faces, he turned off the screen.

Returning to his chair, he sank into it with delight. At last, he had out-pointed Simon Wiseman, made him choke on his own arrogance! He threw his head back and laughed, determined to savor his triumph.

Abruptly, he stopped.

What was it? Morley frowned, feeling a strange tingling in his arms and legs. He rose, surprised at his sluggishness. Something was wrong. He felt different. After a moment he noticed something else.

He wasn't breathing the air.

With an effort, he moved into the bathroom. What he saw in the mirror made him recoil in horror. His face had changed. Trembling, no longer needing to breathe, he staggered into the living room, where he saw the plump man who had sold him the air.

"You!"

The man came forward and felt Morley's cheek, his jade ring pressing into his flesh.

"Good, it's starting," he said. "Evidently three nights' exposure to the gas is sufficient to trigger the mutation." He nodded at two uniformed figures. "You can take him now."

"What *is* this?" The strangeness in Morley's body was growing, and he pulled back. "What's *happening* to me?"

The man stayed the others with his hand. "Remember what I told you about renewal, Mr. Morley? About how we'd replenish our air reserves through the creation of plants and trees? Well, what I didn't tell you is that the most practical way to do it is by using people *while there's enough of them left.*"

"People?"

"Call it a conversion program of oxygen-breathing organisms to oxygen-*producing* ones." His eyes glinted. "You should be proud, Mr. Morley, for you are in the vanguard, the first of many who will be sacrificed so the few of us, the elite, can carry on."

"I don't understand..." Morley faltered, finding it difficult to speak.

Gently, the man turned Morley toward the picture of the poplars he had admired so often.

"But it's impossible!"

Triumphant laughter. "The Government had its doubts too, Mr. Morley. That's why the niggards forced us to operate under such stringent conditions. But ordinary people like you shall conquer their skepticism and make our vision viable."

"Vi-a..." Morley's lips struggled with the syllables. "It's *insane!*"

"No, it's not. Incredible as it may sound, the process is rather simple. You see, we're all made of basically the same stuff. People, trees, animals, plants: it's merely a matter of converting one form into a functional approximation of another."

A functional approximation of another. Morley stared at the poplars, horrified by the implications. People must be warned about this. *Everybody!*

"I wouldn't take it too hard," the man said. "If you're fortunate, you might even retain some faint degree of consciousness." He sighed. "I almost envy you, Mr. Morley. Imagine: having the opportunity to experience *two* states of being."

Morley saw the men come toward him. Panicking, he screamed and lurched toward the door, knowing it was his only chance to escape.

* * *

"It must be somewhere near here," Edwards said a week later.

Simon glanced about the sultry streets. Dust lay everywhere, and some windows, he was sure, had been broken for decades.

"There's no way to tell where it is. Most of the signs are down." He spat. "Morley made up the whole thing."

"But—"

"Yeah, I know. We saw him breathing air." He stopped, one foot resting on a rusty Coca-Cola sign. Here in the inner-city, they were practically begging someone to cut their throats for their air tanks.

Simon drew his gun. Damn Morley! The smug little pup had laughed right in his face.

Edwards pointed. "Look!"

Simon turned, seeing a sign. *Free Air.*

His excited intake of air was in clear violation of the 10.8-second cycle. "All right," Simon said reluctantly, "that much, at least, he was telling the truth about."

Edwards approached the doorbell incredulously. "I don't get it," he said. "Why aren't there more people here? Why isn't there a line stretching from here to the Ministry?"

"People aren't suckers, that's why. They know you don't get something for nothing. Besides, these streets are dangerous. If you're not careful—"

He stopped in disbelief.

"What is it, Simon?"

Simon only stared. After a moment he walked over until he stood right before it.

Beneath the clear plastic dome, the dozen saplings swayed in an artificial breeze. He saw tubes, spray nozzles, and soil – actual thick, rich, loamy soil.

Edwards sputtered beside him. "But how, Simon? Trees! I've seen a couple nurseries before. All they can grow is sickly stuff, scraggly dwarfs that are barely alive. These are *thriving.*" He pointed. "What's this one?"

Simon said, "Lombardy poplar."

The tree leaned forward as if to touch them. Yet there could only be a slight breeze inside the dome. Simon shifted his weight uneasily.

Edwards started to leave. "I'm going to give it a try," he said.

"Wait!" Simon stared at the poplar, which was leaning even closer now, its leaves trembling as if in excitement. "Maybe we'd better think it over."

"What's wrong with you, Simon? You want to pass up a once-in-a-lifetime opportunity?"

Sensing something wrong, Simon turned away. "Maybe we ought to come back another day," he said.

Edwards smirked, and Simon felt foolish. He forgot his misgivings and tried to act casual. "I suppose it wouldn't hurt to have a look," he said.

"Why not?" Edwards grinned. He took Simon's arm and led him to the building. Rang the doorbell. "You know something, Simon? You're a bright boy, but sometimes you have a tendency to look a gift horse in the mouth."

A Line Cutting Canvas

Sydney Rossman-Reich

I JAB my paintbrush into the acrylic canvas, pretending my brush is striking Ms. Preacher.

"Artisan. Artisan. Artisan," I snarl in rhythm with my thrusts.

The oily red on the tip of my brush splatters like blood on my smock. I wind my arm back and slice at the dripping canvas, the cheap wooden tool snapping in two.

I stare at my hands, stained in one layer of paint above another layer of blisters. At least I'll have calluses when Ms. Preacher and her precious *San Jose Drawn & Painted Arts Institute* send me to the *Line*.

I don't turn my head when the studio's thin metal door slides open and another student enters.

"Shit, Neha. You failed." Jojo, my assigned mentee, eases into my studio.

Jojo is only fourteen, nearly half my age. She has just started her rotation across the twenty official arts institutes. Even though attaining the Artisan designation is very difficult, Jojo will have many more chances.

The thought makes my stomach roil. "Obviously I failed! This was my last craft-defense."

Machines serve nearly every function in our overpopulated society. Without significant inheritance, my only options were to become an Artisan or be a government project – the new New Deal. Now I know what I am.

I clench my hands into fists, popping a few of the blisters on my palms. The pus joins the drying mess of red paint on the floor.

"I bet Preacher's already submitted her recommendation to the board. Of all people, you'd think she would have some sympathy. Preacher didn't earn her designation until her nineteenth institute." I want to strike my canvas again.

Jojo draws toward me, her arms open, then she jerks back. We haven't known each other long enough to really be friends.

But I know I should control myself. I am Jojo's mentor for one more day, and I need to give her hope for her own rotation. Too bad my resolve is already flotsam somewhere in the drying puddle on the floor.

Jojo's face twitches. "The *Line* isn't supposed to be bad. We don't need people to pave roads or monitor machines. It's just to keep everyone busy. You won't have to deal with the pressures of constantly creating like you do here. That's why so many drop out early. Think of how good it will feel being free of these institutes."

Jojo flushes, her own eyes water-colored with mounting tears. She continues, "My hope is that you will be so happy there."

Tears already paint my cheeks. "I *want* to create, to add value to the world. I don't care about the pressures. I want to be special."

Jojo wrings her hands and lies. "Neha, you are."

* * *

After a day of rushed goodbyes, I pack my bag and cab to the nearest *Line* registration office. I want to be sent as far away as possible and ask for out-of-state assignments. I am offered a few options: Everglades care in southern Florida, shipping automation supervision in Kansas, road maintenance in Arizona. When I ask the *Line* clerk which he'd choose, he picks Arizona, so that's where I go.

The next morning, I arrive at my assignment – a small, two-hundred-person crew outside of Scottsdale. The job itself is simple: road cleaning, paving, and painting for six hour shifts, five days a week. I don't look at the rusty paint cans and cracked rollers heaped onto the supply pile.

"Short and sweet." Rohan, my shift manager, beams. His hands are soft when they shake mine. Maybe I won't need my calluses after all.

"And what do we do with the rest of the time?" I grumble, displeased at how easily the crew welcomes me with their plastered smiles.

"I like reading, though the new originals on Streamvid are pretty good. Most others play video games, drink. . .get to know one another. Pop-control measures have a way of busting open the old relationship model, eh?" Rohan grins impossibly wide at that. "Life's pretty great here."

His words remind me of Jojo's encouragements, thin like a cheap veneer. My chest tightens.

"Does anyone do any art, even if it's when their shift is done?" I ask, venturing a glance at the paint cans.

Rohan shrugs. "You can use your off time how you want."

It's almost funny how this is meant to relieve me. I'm free from high standards and significance.

Rohan claps his hands, obviously misinterpreting my smirk as a sign he's assuaged my nerves. I suspect most of those who join the *Line* are like him, preferring the redundant labor and ample free time to the demands of the Artisan rotation.

But I am not one of them. I remember hours scratching at the ill-fitting words of my best poem and the smell of burnt loaves clinging to my jacket. I remember singing an out-of-tune song with my bunkmates and accidentally spotting red pigment on Jojo's clean canvas.

Over the next few weeks, I learn how to perform the basic road work and grow accustomed to the crew. I tolerate the games they play, the vids they watch, and the breezy nights they spend huddled around fires heating meal-packs. Yet I cannot forget what I was forced to leave behind: a chance to actually contribute to the world. The yearning rattles in my gut like the pea inside an empty spray can.

Jojo's enquiries do little to settle my frustrations. Her short texts taunt me from my rent-phone. *How are you?* she asks again and again.

I have yet to answer. She had been right in one respect – the *Line is* an easy life. But it's pointless. We steam-wash spotless roads, smooth over barely visible chinks in the asphalt, and brush dust to the curb that will blow back by the next day. I stencil my smiles to match the others' and hide my disdain beneath coats of superficial mirth. But I avoid any painting work: striping lines on pavement, retouching signs, dying concrete.

On nights when my façade wavers, I stare up at the squat ceiling of my mobile unit and pretend I'm in my studio. My body is light, my fingers move invisible paintbrushes across imaginary canvas, and I can take a full breath. But the fantasy flees, yielding to restless sleep and red-eyed mornings.

Only Rohan notices when a layer of my hardened lacquer peels. After a month, he knocks on my mobile door before bedtime and asks how I am. His question is the same as the one I've left unanswered from Jojo.

"How are you really, Neha?" Rohan pries, leaning through my doorway.

I am as sturdy as a sopping papier mâché.

"Not good," I finally admit out loud. "I miss the art institutes."

Rohan grimaces. "Most don't have a problem moving on."

"Why?" I haven't figured it out. "What drives all of you?"

Rohan reaches across the threshold and pats my shoulder. "You're too young to remember what happened when the tech took too many of the jobs. The protests, revolts, violence. Our society almost snapped from the tension. For those of us without money or 'essential' work or some creative talent, the New Deal was our only chance."

I frown. "Only chance? A machine could as easily do the infrastructure work we do. The only reason it doesn't is because our work is so unimportant. At least the Artisans create something new – do what no machine can. The Artisans actually have a purpose."

"I'm not explaining myself well." Rohan's eyes slather me in clumsy glances. "I mean I think what we do *is* important. We *are* creating something new."

"What?" I am desperate for the answer.

"We're building a future – sacrificing families to fix the population problem, jobs we might enjoy so the machines can do them better. After enough time the birthing restrictions will leave few enough people that anyone can do exactly what they want. Our sacrifices today ensure a future in which anyone can be an Artisan. A future in which what happened to you can never—"

I flick away Rohan's hand. His answer sounds like some official speech mocked up by a bumbling government official who shaped this New Deal. It's a glossy glaze that covers crap. I shouldn't have to make a sacrifice for some future I will never see.

Rohan ignores my gesture and steps closer, hugging me into his chest. "I promise these feelings will fade. It will get better." Rohan can't be sure. "At the very least, you'll find distraction."

Rohan's embrace tightens, and he rubs his cheek into my hair, inhaling my scent.

His concern for me is another thin glaze. I break away, my answer to his affection etched into the hard furrow of my brow. I don't want him.

Rohan misunderstands, nodding vigorously. "It's okay. I'll wait."

He turns before I can protest, leaving for his own mobile unit. When Rohan is out of sight, I close the door to my trailer and finally retrieve my rent-phone to respond to Jojo's texts. She should hear my confession too. I should admit the truth. I should.

Hi Jojo – sorry I'm just getting back to you. I'm doing great. Life here is as good as you said. Don't worry about me.

It is easier to lie than I expected.

Right away, I see dots flutter across the messaging screen. Jojo is already replying.

I am so glad to hear it! You don't know how happy that makes me. I think about you and the Line. It's exhausting here.

I see Jojo's smiling face, speckled with flecks of color from that day's project. A familiar ache curls in my gut.

The three dots flutter again then stop, start then stop. I wait, watching the starting and stopping of Jojo's typing.

Finally, she sends her message. *I passed the test. I'm officially a painter, designation and all. No Line for me...*

I type my reply quickly before I can do something rash.

That's such good news. I'm glad we're both doing so well.

* * *

Half a decade passes.

It turns out, I am far better at steam-cleaning pavement than I'd ever officially been at any art – not a welcome realization. Rohan promotes me to junior manager. I wonder if he hopes the position will bring us closer, but I do not risk asking.

Jojo continues to message me. She enquires about my life, asking how I spend my free hours, who I've befriended, the scenery I see as we move across the state.

Lying is as easy as paint-by-numbers. I tell Jojo about the video game tournaments I've never entered, the popcorn I've never thrown at the worst scenes in new movies, dances I've never waltzed around the campfire, and kisses I've never shared with other crew men and women. I also keep from her the few friends I have made, others who secretly feel wasted like me. We've begrudgingly started to accept our lot.

Jojo, for her part, does not ask if I still paint or cook or write or do any of the other arts. And I do not ask her about her days as a designated Artisan. Our conversations always end with an innocuous note from Jojo I leave unanswered. Months pass before Jojo is the one to inevitably pick up the thread again.

My worst nights are when I dream of the art institutes. I imagine spending all day in my studio. I present my craft-defense successfully, eliciting standing ovations from esteemed faculty. Ms. Preacher falls over herself to shake my hand. I paint grand murals, billboards as tall as skyscrapers ogled by every passer-by. My art persists through a hundred generations, my name forever marking history.

And I see Jojo – Jojo painting, Jojo smiling, Jojo contributing value to the world.

Then I wake, and the alternate history evaporates into nothing, Arizona dust drowning in the loud crank of cement machines and restless workers whining.

How are you, Neha? Jojo always asks when she attempts to lure me back into conversation.

Never better. You? I will eventually reply.

On the morning of my sixth anniversary of joining the crew, Rohan meets me outside my mobile home. He smiles at me, some lingering hope peeping through his expression like a dark base coat.

"Morning, Ro." I am always sullen on this day each year. And Rohan always tries to brighten my shade.

"New site today. New segment of road," he beams, excited whenever the crew moves further along our never-ending loop of highway.

"I can see that," I snap.

He flinches but recovers quickly. "There are a few billboards up a short walk from here. I radioed central. They say it's new – some grand government art project to decorate all the roads across the country, even our isolated bits. It's really good. Thought you'd appreciate it."

He turns, gesturing to a few small square dots in the distance. The land is flat, so no coverage hides where the billboards stand, but I can't make out the artworks' details. The anniversary marking my failure as an artist is not my ideal day for gazing at murals, but Rohan links his arm in mine and pulls me along. I am not in a mood to fight him.

"I know how much you like this stuff," Rohan says as we walk. "I mean real art. Not trashy dramas or shooter games like me."

My eyes are glued ahead.

Rohan's voice softens. "How are you, Neha?"

"Better," I wince, the acknowledgement feeling like another failure. "But I'm not sure the *Line* will ever be enough."

"I hear you, though it's hard to empathize. I dropped out of the institutes early."

Rohan had never revealed this to me. "Why did you drop out?"

"Didn't want to risk getting a designation and not being able to leave. As weird as it might sound, I always dreamed of the *Line.* Like this isn't a good fit for you, the high-pressure, high-expectation, lonely life of a creative wasn't for me. I wanted leisure and laughter and family."

"But Linemen can't have families."

Rohan shrugs. "My definition of family is a little less biologi—"

I grab Rohan's arm, my eyes going wide as the first mural's details come into view.

It is a giant art piece, a billboard beginning only a few yards off the ground and extending a hundred feet into the sky. The art displays a woman, dark-haired and broad, maybe just over thirty years old, laughing wildly as she signs up for a gaming tournament, the console's logo striped across the board's lower half. It is a commercial piece about a *Line* crew.

I rush forward, the next billboard almost in view.

"Wait, what's going on?" Rohan asks, worried. He chases after me.

The next billboard is another *Line* piece. This one shows the same woman, now reclined in a lounge chair, laughing at an upcoming movie's trailer flashing on the screen in front of her. She is throwing popcorn at the actors' faces.

I sprint to the next one. The woman dances at a campfire roasting a new meal-pack flavor.

The next, she kisses a man resembling Rohan as the sun sets behind them, Scottsdale in the distance.

"What's wrong?" Rohan huffs, finally catching me.

"This...this..." I stammer. "This is celebrating the *Line.*"

Rohan bends over his knees, catching his breath. "What? That's bad? It reminds me of us, our crew. The lady in all of them looks a lot like you."

That's because it is our crew. The woman is me.

Jojo did this.

I clench my fists, remembering the pain of popping blisters, a packed bag, and an empty studio. "Rohan?"

Rohan dabs his sweaty face with the ends of his shirt. "Yeah?"

"I want to take some time off."

"Uh...okay."

I peel myself away from the billboard and glare at my shift manager. "You were wrong before. *Line* workers have no purpose. We don't matter to any of them."

I abandon Rohan and march back to camp.

* * *

When my flight lands, I head straight to the *San Jose Drawn & Painted Arts Institute.* It's Saturday – visitors' day. When I arrive, the institute already prattles with activity. The other visitors wear designer suits and jewelry more extravagant than anything I've ever seen. Had they always looked like this? I don't see any other Linemen or Linewomen in the crowd. I have no people here.

"Where are the painters receiving guests today?" I ask a teenage boy fiddling his fingers behind the reception desk. He must be in the middle of his Artisan rotation.

"Who are you looking for?" he asks, eyeing me.

"Jojo…" I can't remember her last name. "Just Jojo."

The boy nods. "Oh yeah, she's a popular one. Takes visitors in her studio. All the way down the hallway ahead. Last door on the left."

I wince. That studio had been mine. I might throw up.

The boy continues, "If you need me to, I can walk you down there."

"No," a new voice interrupts. "I can take her."

I turn, recognizing the sharp tone of Ms. Preacher.

I expect to see my old instructor's sardonic gaze, but Preacher's expression is kind. She puts her hands on my shoulders and squeezes me gently.

"It's nice to see former students," she says without irony.

I shake myself free of her grasp. "I'm here to see Jojo."

"Of course." Preacher's grin reminds me of Rohan's. I don't like the sudden affinity I feel for this woman. "Jojo talks about you a lot. Neha's doing this. Neha's doing that. She says you're very happy."

Preacher arcs an eyebrow in question, waiting for my confirmation.

When I say nothing, her eyes darken.

Preacher sighs, "Well…that's disappointing. I'll admit I'd hoped you'd find happiness at the *Line* too. If not for your sake, then for…"

"Jojo's?" I finish. "She used me in her art. Did you know that? She transformed my suffering into fame for herself."

Preacher hesitates. "That's not what she did. Not at all. Neha, do you have any idea how Jojo is doing here? Why she's so invested in you?"

The ache is back. I don't know what Preacher expects from me, but whatever Jojo's dealing with is not my responsibility. When will it be my turn to matter?

"Don't make my visit about her. Jojo took advantage of me, and I have a right to be upset." I exhale slowly. "I should have been an Artisan. This was the only place that could make me happy."

Preacher bites her cheek. She looks concerned. "You're right. Your feelings matter too, but this is the way things are. There isn't enough money and too many people for everyone to be an Artisan. But that doesn't mean you don't have a purpose. When the pop falls enough, the New Deal will end. Your sacrifice is what makes that possible."

Another political speech meant to placate me. But I don't care about Preacher. Or Rohan. Or the officials who made my choices for me. I am not here for them. I'm here for Jojo, to tell her how she's wronged me by using my failure for her inspiration.

Before Preacher can act, I race down the hall. I fling open my old studio door, the emerging sounds of the chattering crowd drowning out Preacher's calls behind me. The small studio is packed with visitors inspecting the sketches that fill the room.

My face is in all of the them. Jojo has painted each and every one of my lies.

I force my way through the crowd.

"Jojo!" I shout, finally reaching the front.

Jojo glances up at me.

She is taller now, no longer a little girl. But her arms are still thin, skin freckled in accidental graffiti. She wears a smock similar to the one I'd used. Maybe it is the same one. When our eyes meet, Jojo smiles, but it isn't as light as I remember.

She walks up to me, clasping my face between her rough hands. There are dark bags under her eyes. Her breath is haggard, and her posture is bent. She is worn and used up.

My anger fades, and I am empty. How could all I've dreamed of left Jojo in such a state?

"You came," she whispers. "I hoped you would come."

I forget why I'm here, but I know the hole still stretches open inside me.

"Jojo..." I try.

Jojo is on the verge of crying. "All this art is for you and where you are, an homage to the *Line* and how great it is there. I've wanted to visit you, to see it. I dream about the *Line* most nights. I want so badly to..." tears streak her face. "Do you like my art?"

I pull back, escaping Jojo's grip. The crowd around us watches. I glance at their confused faces, so different from mine and Jojo's, crack-less, made-up, bright. Is Jojo the one who's wronged me? Was it these wealthy spectators and the progress they represent? Or something else entirely? Jojo's expression is more confused than all of those of the men and women around us.

"Yes," I say instinctually. "I like your art."

Her art is my stolen pain. It is offensive and false. But ripping it to shreds won't change what's become of us. And I'm used to lying to Jojo.

Jojo falters. "It's the truth? You like it. The *Line* – what you've told me is all real?" She bites her lip. "You don't look happy. How are you, Neha?"

I recognize the longing in Jojo's voice. My dream died when my Artisan rotation ended, but Jojo's had lived on. Now I understand – she wanted to join the *Line*. She had achieved her Artisan designation too fast, barring her option to drop out. What would Rohan have looked like, stuck in an institute he hated? Would he look like Jojo? Like I looked on the *Line?*

Jojo's tears still paint her cheeks, and my blisters have long faded.

I force a smile. "I am happy. Truly."

It is a small offering. Had I found Jojo happy here, my grief might have felt justified. It might have given me some closure. I won't get that now, but that doesn't mean I can't let Jojo have hers.

"Good luck," I whisper, hugging Jojo then turning to leave.

"Wait! Stay, please." Jojo grabs my arm. She wants me to comfort her further, to tell her more lies.

But that's not what I want. I can't have what I want and, in the end, Jojo won't have what she wants either.

I pull away, and I don't look at Jojo again. I scan the art-filled studio one final time. My old studio is what I should have come to see.

"Goodbye," I whisper, bending to skim my knuckles across the stained floor.

My fingers knock an easel leg, and a tiny paintbrush clatters to the tile. I grab it quickly and leave the studio. No one stops me, and I don't look back.

Outside in the sun, I grip my stolen paintbrush as tight as I can. The cheap wood is warm and the bristles are soft against my skin. I *won't* look back. But I'll remember the callouses, those behind me and those ahead.

I smile.

There are paint cans with my *Line* crew in Scottsdale and billboards along the highway in desperate need of serious revision.

I've made my last sacrifice, and this time I'll take a piece for myself. This time, I'll decide.

What Treasures We Store on Earth

Elizabeth Rubio

ZAKARIA held the letter in trembling hands.

> *Dear Mr. and Mrs. Carver,*
>
> *You have been selected to undergo sterilization reversal procedures. Please report to the Winnipeg Family Planning Authority office on or before September 17, 2081 to begin the family planning process. Failure to appear by the above date constitutes forfeiture of this opportunity.*

"Alden," Zakaria called.

"Yeah?" Alden didn't rise from his seat. He rarely did so in the evenings, after having worked twelve hours on his feet. Zakaria sank beside him onto the couch and handed him the paper.

He scanned it, his eyes traveling quickly over the words three times, as if he couldn't believe them. When he finally looked up at her again, they were brimming with tears.

"A baby," he breathed.

Zakaria nodded, and Alden gathered her into his arms. The sounds of the city faded into a distant hum as they clung to each other.

* * *

It took six days for Alden to get an afternoon off work so they could go to the FPA. Zakaria couldn't rightly afford the time off at all, as school would begin in two weeks, but she considered it a blessing that class wasn't yet in session and penciled in an extra couple of evenings in addition to her regular days to ensure she didn't fall behind. The day of their appointment she met him at noon outside the fulfillment center where he worked, and they walked together the six blocks to the rail station.

On the train they sat in silence, fingers intertwined in their clasped hands. Zakaria stared out the window as the city whipped by. As the train began to slow near the Broadway station, Zakaria gasped.

A bright green gallows stood on the lawn of the legislative building, four bodies swinging beneath it.

Alden pulled her away from the window. "Damn protestors," he muttered. "How do they even build those so fast? Surprised the cops didn't stop them."

Zakaria gulped. She'd heard about the rise in die-ins, of course, but this was the first she'd actually seen. The wind was high, making their feet sway like children on a macabre swing set.

"Come on, baby," Alden said, pulling her toward him as the gallows disappeared behind a building. "This is our stop."

Zakaria shoved the image of the swinging corpses into the back of her mind and she and Alden made their way from the train station to the FPA office.

In the office, Zakaria and Alden were escorted into a room where a pale woman with precisely coiffed hair and a golden nametag that read MICHELE sat behind a large desk. Michele greeted them and motioned for them to sit in the chair across from her.

"Mr. and Mrs. Carver, so pleased to see you. Congratulations on achieving the opportunity to grow your family!" Michele said this as if it were something Zakaria had accomplished, rather than a random drawing. She smiled, showing a bit of lipstick on her teeth, and pushed a brightly colored brochure across the desk. "You may take this brochure home to read at your leisure. Please note that there are no guarantees. The reversal process has a success rate of ninety percent for men and seventy percent for women."

Alden squeezed Zakaria's hand.

Michele leafed through a file. "Now, Mr. Carver, I understand you never underwent reversal in the first place, is that correct?"

"Correct."

"So Mrs. Carver, only you will need to have your procedure reversed. That's great, really increases the chances you two will conceive." Michele leafed through a file. "Now, Mr. Carver, it says here you are employed by Amwal fulfillment services?"

Alden nodded. "Yes, full time."

"And Mrs. Carver, you are an adjunct professor at University of Manitoba?"

"Yes, I'm in the English, Film, and Theater department."

Michele folded her hands and looked up. "I see you were naturalized under the Canadian Union Citizenry Resolution in 2076. Where are you from?"

Zakaria shifted in her chair and glanced at Alden. "Well," she said, "I lived in Tallahassee until '61. My family and I left because of Hurricane Julian. We evacuated to Atlanta, and we lived there until...." She cleared her throat. "I was in Atlanta in '66."

"Ah." Michele gave her a simpering smile that Zakaria took to be sympathetic. "When did you arrive in Winnipeg?"

"Just after that," Zakaria said. "I was granted asylum in '69, and resettled in Winnipeg that fall. Been here ever since."

Michele consulted her notes again. "It says here your household annual income is $78,000?"

"Yes, give or take," Alden answered.

"Then you qualify for the family assistance program. You'll need to meet with our assistance representative before you leave today."

Zakaria glanced at Alden. The corner of his mouth twitched, clearly trying to suppress a smile. If she was honest, the thought of some assistance was welcome, especially if they were going to take on all the expenses of a baby.

Michele finished their interview and led them down a sterile white hallway to a small room. A man with short dreads sat behind a cluttered desk. He greeted them warmly and closed the door as Michele left.

"My name is Erick. I'll be discussing the assistance programs you qualify for." Erick looked over the file Michele had left. "Based on your income, you should qualify for every program in the book."

Zakaria hoped he didn't mean that as a compliment.

Erick folded his hands. "Basically, it's like this: The government sees families with children as an investment. The birth rate has fallen in recent years, and that coupled with the...protest events has led to an increased need for more families."

Neither Zakaria nor Alden commented on his euphemism for people killing themselves en masse as a form of protest.

"So, because you have been selected for reversal, we wish to help you with all the necessities to ensure the welfare of your child and the stability of your household." Erick dug in a drawer and produced a notebook, which he opened and pushed toward them. "You qualify for housing assistance. Most families in your position choose the Child and Family housing, which are units specifically built to house new families. You won't pay rent, but you must continue to meet income requirements, and submit to a welfare inspection once every six months."

The notebook showed several pictures of spacious, well-furnished apartments. Each had a separate bedroom, some with cribs, others with small beds and toy chests. Zakaria grinned widely.

"We currently have available units in Crescentwood, Norwood, and Osborne Village. The sooner you choose, the more likely you are to get your first choice."

Alden sucked in a deep breath. Zakaria felt her pulse quicken. Those neighborhoods were home to houses with lawns, and some even had fences and gates.

"In addition to housing, you'll receive monthly food credits in the form of an EBT card. It should arrive in the mail in a couple of weeks. Mrs. Carver, you may begin using your card for prenatal needs, such as fresh produce and vitamins, as soon as a doctor confirms your pregnancy."

Zakaria's head swam.

"You'll also receive a yearly stipend of $10,000 for various expenses. This should cover the cost of clothing, school supplies, medications, and even toys." Erick smiled. "We want all of the Canadian Union's children to be happy and well cared for."

Zakaria gripped the arms of her chair, and Alden let out a long breath. "Ten thousand dollars per year? For how long?"

"Until your child turns 18." Erick sat back. "Now, I should also inform you that you may choose to forgo this payment and instead roll it into the non-sterilization penalty. The cost of the penalty is currently $150,000. This would leave you with three years' worth of payments, which you could activate at any point in your child's life."

Zarakia shot a glance at Alden. He was shaking his head. "I don't think we—"

"Thank you, Erick, we'll discuss it." Zakaria cut Alden off.

"Of course," Erick replied. "You don't have to make any decisions right away. But please do make housing arrangements as soon as possible. Moving can be very stressful, so it would be ideal for you to get settled in a new home before your pregnancy is very far along."

* * *

On the train back to their apartment, Zakaria and Alden looked through the brochures and handouts. The plain white paper with black text describing available apartments didn't offer images for Zakaria to pore over, but she could imagine it: crown molding in every room, shining new appliances, a tile backsplash in the kitchen, maybe even a soaking bathtub. She pictured a baby's room decked out in primary colors, with a white crib and a rocking chair.

"After your reversal, let's take a few days off and go look at apartments," Alden said. "We should request a unit soon so we get a good one."

"We can't afford a few days," Zakaria replied. "School is starting, and you'll lose your job if you take off more than two days in a month."

"So what? I'll find another job. And even if I don't, Zakaria, we'll have *ten thousand dollars a year*. We can afford to miss a paycheck or two."

Zakaria searched his face. "You want to just take the money."

His eyebrows rose. "You don't? Babe, it's ten K a year, no strings. And we won't have any rent, and we'll be getting groceries. Why wouldn't you want it?"

Zakaria clasped her hands over her belly. She didn't remember her sterilization procedure, of course; she had been only a baby, like everyone else. Everyone except the ones whose parents paid the penalty, like Alden. But the scar still marked her body, still reminded her of what had been taken from her, what she now stood to regain. "We could save our child from sterilization. Maybe have grandchildren."

Alden shifted away from her in his seat. "Grandchildren? We don't even have a child yet."

Zakaria sighed. "And our child likely won't have a child unless we pay the penalty. Or..." Zakaria's mind pushed an image into her thoughts. Celeste, their neighbor across the way, had gone to one of those back-alley quacks to try to take matters into her own hands. She had died nine days later. "The chances of our child winning this opportunity are so small."

Alden's expression became closed. "And if we don't take that money, the chances of our child breaking their back twelve hours a day for pennies are a hundred percent."

"Alden, I know this feels personal to you—"

"It is personal!" Heads turned their way. A vein pulsed in Alden's temple as he fought to regain control. "You think I don't remember what it was like? Having enough to eat, enough to drink? Hell, more than enough. We had leftovers, Zakaria. Leftovers! And we lost it all the moment I turned eighteen. Because my parents thought I'd be happier if I had the dream of kids of my own instead of the reality of enough to live on."

"And now you'll have both!" Zakaria reached for his hand but he pulled it away.

The train hissed into the station, and Zakaria stood and gathered her things. Alden slumped in his seat, looking out the window. "Aren't you coming?" she asked.

He shook his head, staring into the distance. "Gonna try to pick up another shift. Said it yourself, we need the money." Finally, he looked up at her, his eyes hard. "See you later."

Zakaria turned to hide her tears and stepped off the train.

* * *

Alden had not returned home by the time Zakaria left for work in the morning. She couldn't know without calling him whether he had succeeded in picking up a shift or two or had just spent the night wallowing in his troubles over whisky, and she didn't feel up to having an argument over the phone. Instead, she gathered her things and left, trying not to think about it.

But she couldn't help but wonder, as she walked to work, the sweat trickling down her back, what would happen if she and Alden couldn't agree. He couldn't know what it was like, knowing that your future was completely in the hands of someone else. Knowing that your only chance at your legacy turned on a twist of luck.

A wind stirred Zakaria's hair, but it was a hot wind, like the gust from an oven, rather than a refreshing breeze. Sweat dripped from her temples. She brushed it away, feeling as if she were back in Tallahassee, back when it still existed. Perhaps she didn't know what it was like either. The United States had never had any family assistance policies. She had never had enough to eat or drink. Perhaps having that taken from you was, indeed, harder than never having it at all.

Zakaria breathed a sigh of relief as she pushed open the door to her building, reveling in the cool air that surrounded her. But she stopped short when she laid eyes on the spectacle in the middle of the entryway.

A handmade gallows, painted brightly green, stood in the center of the entryway. From it hung a single man, the rope tight around his neck. His face had become purple, although the color was beginning to drain. His tongue lolled, and his glassy eyes stared blankly into nothing. Around his shoulders hung a hand-painted sign: BE THE CHANGE YOU WISH TO SEE IN THE WORLD.

Zakaria's breath caught in her throat. His distorted face was familiar, despite its odd color. The man was Claude, her colleague. He taught Medieval and European literature.

A wave of heat washed over Zakaria as someone pulled open the door behind her. They stepped around her and let out a gasp. The two of them stood rooted in horror, staring at the grisly sight, until Zakaria felt herself reach for her phone.

A feeling of unreality pervaded her as she dialed 911 and gave the details of the situation. She felt outside her body, as if she were a spectator witnessing a gruesome play. Only there was no hero, and the villain would not be vanquished. There was only another death, another body to add to the count.

An hour later, Zakaria sat in a small lounge with Rebecca, another adjunct professor. Both of them clutched paper cups of chicory. Zakaria's hands, wrapped around the cup, felt much too warm, but she relished the sensation. It reminded her that she was still alive.

"I don't understand," Rebecca said, her voice thick. "He didn't seem depressed."

"It's not about depression," Zakaria said. "It was a protest. With the green gallows movement. They're meant to make people take notice about human-induced climate change and carbon footprints."

Rebecca sighed. "Seems stupid. Hardly anybody even saw. Just, what, six or seven of us? What will that gain?"

Zakaria shrugged. "I guess that was a big enough statement for him. Claude isn't…wasn't a stupid man."

Claude hadn't seemed the type, now that she considered it. He was quiet, introspective, always clutching a stack of books. Sure, he'd grumbled about food shortages, wealth disparities, the increasing weather calamities, even the sterilization laws, but who hadn't? Wasn't grumbling about the general state of things what college campuses were for? Of all the people Zakaria could think to join a suicidal political movement, Claude was not one.

Perhaps she didn't know people as well as she thought.

"It's funny," Rebecca said, staring into her cup. "They kill themselves to reduce the number of people, right? But the government just opened the lottery again. They're just dying for no reason."

The corners of Zakaria's mouth tugged into a grin.

"What?" Rebecca said. "You think that's funny?"

"No, it's not that." Zakaria tried and failed to stop grinning. "I got selected."

Rebecca's expression darkened. "Congrats."

Right, she was almost 35. In a few months she would be ineligible. "I gotta get my lesson plans together." Zakaria stood, leaving her chicory on the table. "You can have my chicory if you want."

Rebecca only grunted. "See you."

* * *

Alden set down the last box and stretched. He had restricted Zakaria to carrying in pillows only, reminding her that physical stress could harm the baby she carried. Not that he had much to do; their new place was fully furnished, the furniture new and clean, not like the broken, stained castoffs they'd had in their tenement. She brought him a cold glass of water, marveling that clean, drinkable water would be delivered every week in their new apartment.

"Welcome home, love." She clinked her own glass against his, and they drank, smiles on both their faces.

"Can you believe this place?" Alden looked around, his face glowing. "Electricity 24 hours a day, water and food delivery, and check out these digs! It even smells clean in here!"

She laughed and kissed him. "A great place to raise the baby."

"Great indeed." He returned her kiss, and they retired to break in the new bedroom before unpacking.

The next morning, Alden sighed as he glanced through the paper. Zakaria peered over his shoulder. "Bad news?"

"More of those protestors." Alden folded the paper and set it aside. "I guess we should thank them, really. If not for the deaths, we wouldn't be having our baby.

Zakaria considered mentioning that the protestors' deaths wouldn't be necessary for their baby's conception if not for the sterilization laws, but chose not to start another argument. Instead, she pulled out a chair and sat. "So, you gonna go job hunting today?"

Alden set the paper down and leaned back. "Was actually thinking about going with you to the school."

"You were?" Zakaria asked.

"Thought I might see about..." Alden trailed off and picked at a spot under his fingernail. "You know, find out what their entrance requirements are. See if they'd let me in." He met her eyes. "As a student."

"Alden." Zakaria tried to keep her tone from being admonishing. "If you do that, we'll have to keep the money."

He reached across the table and took her hand. "I'm not saying I definitely will. But it's already November. If I don't enroll now, I'll miss my chance. I can always stop and get a job later."

"You can always get a job now and go back to school later." But she didn't let go of his hand.

He rubbed his thumb over her knuckles. "Think of it as an investment in our family. We'll put half the money every year into a savings account. And without rent and groceries, we'll have enough left for the baby and some besides. Plus we'll still have your salary, and I'll find something part time that I can work around classes." He swallowed hard. "And I mean..." His gaze was intense. "Think about those protestors. They find this world so intolerable, so unsalvageable, they'd rather die than stay here. What if our child joins them? What if looming poverty on their eighteenth birthday pushes them there?"

Zakaria took a shaky breath. "I guess it can't hurt for you to get some information." Together, they left the apartment.

* * *

A knock at the front door rang through the apartment. The baby's wails began immediately, filling the silence. "Oh, hell," Zakaria swore, pushing her chair back. She picked up the infant and rocked him against her chest as she unlocked the door.

"Mrs. Carver. So sorry to have disturbed your little one."

Zakaria managed not to roll her eyes, but only just. "It happens." She opened the door wider. "Come in, Mr. Bireaux."

This marked the third welfare visit from Guillame Bireaux, the FPA agent assigned to oversee the family's welfare for the duration of their child's life. Zakaria figured she might as well make the visits as smooth as possible. After all, he held the power to end their support at any time.

"You're looking well, Mrs. Carver. How is little Phillip doing?" He peered at the baby, whose mouth still quavered in a scream.

"Well, his lungs are working great, that's for sure." Zakaria smiled. "I'm sorry, he was having a nap. He might be fussy for a while."

"No matter, no matter." Bireaux waved a hand. "I'll be as brief as I can. Is your husband home?"

"No, he's in class."

"Ah, so he did enroll?"

Zakaria nodded.

"And you are still on maternity leave?"

"Yes, through the end of the semester. I'll go back in the spring."

"Who will look after your little one then?"

The little one had finally dialed down his screeches to a mere hiccuping whimper. "Alden is going to try to get night classes. He'll stay home during the day, I'll be home at night. If it comes down to it, we'll put Phillip in daycare, but we're really trying to stay with him as much as possible."

"Excellent, good to hear. Babies do tend to thrive most with their parents." Bireaux grinned at the baby, who waved a fist at him. "And I'll remind you, the deadline is approaching for little Phillip's procedure. If you wish to pay the penalty, you may do it at any time. Otherwise, we'll need to have him brought to the Children's Hospital between the sixth and nineteenth of November." Zakaria opened her mouth, but Bireaux waved a hand. "No need to tell me your decision. Many parents find they change their minds as the date approaches. Just pay the penalty or present your son for his procedure. He's male, so it's just a walk-in. You don't even need an appointment."

"Thanks for the reminder, Mr. Bireaux. Would you like a glass of water before you leave?"

"No, thank you, I have other appointments. See you in six months, Mrs. Carver."

As she peered through the curtains to watch Mr. Bireaux knock on her neighbor's door, Zakaria rocked Phillip gently. She wondered how many green gallows the government agent ever saw, privileged as he was to work and live in an area of government-sponsored wealth. She wondered if he had any children of his own, and whether he had paid exorbitant fees to keep their reproductive organs untouched by his fellow agents. She wondered whether her descendants would ever know that wealth and privilege, or whether there would even be a generation after the next one. She wondered if humanity had truly sealed its fate long ago, and was already strung up on its own gallows.

"Best put that money to use while we can then, eh Phillip?" She kissed his forehead, inhaling the sweet, powdery scent of his skin, and put him back in his crib. Perhaps she could not save him from all of society's evils. But if she gave him all she could, maybe Philip could make his own luck.

The Final Chapter of Marathon Mandy

Zach Shephard

HE TOLD ME if I stopped running, I would die.

So I ran.

I stayed close to the river. The land there was flat and easy to navigate. I might have been able to find a shorter path on the hillside to my right, but that place was full of trees and boulders and nasty things I didn't want to think about just then, so I stuck with my current course.

My boot sunk into a puddle and smashed a mirror that reflected gray skies. I stumbled and lost a step, and wondered if that would be the one that cost me.

No time to think about it. I shook the idea from my head and sprinted to make up for the difference.

"You're going too fast, Mandy – at that pace you'll tire out before you get here."

I didn't respond. Reaching for the call button on my communicator seemed like too much work just then, and I couldn't afford to lose my stride.

So I ran.

As everything crumbled around me I couldn't help but wonder where things had gone wrong. Life was supposed to be better here. I'd been promised a world without distractions – a place where I could read in quiet solitude, and embrace nature's beauty without feeling like an outsider. It wasn't supposed to be like this.

A tremor boiled the river and sent me sprawling. I hit the carpet of rounded stones and shot back to my feet before I had a chance to think about the new cut on my chin or the pain in my hip. Somewhere behind me, I heard an explosion that could have been a volcano erupting or more of our equipment malfunctioning – or possibly both, because one often led to another.

I didn't look back. There could have been a wave of lava or ash coming my way, but seeing it wouldn't change things. Craig had calculated my pace, and we both knew there was no way I'd get to base in time if I stopped to do any sightseeing.

So I ran.

Craig's voice called out over the cataclysmic rumbling and gave me a progress update that wasn't very uplifting. I gritted my teeth and cursed myself. For the first time in my history as a NASA camper, I wished I hadn't pitched my tent so far from base. You spend your whole life trying to get away from people, then just when you get what you want…

There was a loud crack like a branch snapping off a tree. I ignored it at first, figuring it was just another symptom of the world we'd killed. But when I heard it again and saw a puff of dirt explode on the ground in front of me, I knew I had a whole new problem on my hands.

I looked across the river. There, Gerrickson was sprinting just as hard as I was. Except he was doing it with a pistol in hand.

He fired two more shots and I ducked and hunched my shoulders. My pace slackened, and Craig noticed.

"Mandy! What's wrong? Why are you slowing down?"

This time, I felt like responding.

"Why the hell is Gerrickson shooting at me?"

I didn't hear another shot. Gerrickson must have been content with slowing me down. Now that he had a strong lead, he focused on racing toward base. I picked up my pace again, hoping Gerrickson wouldn't have time to cast a glance over his shoulder.

Craig's voice returned: "Listen – I need to level with you, Mandy. There's a reason the captain sent all the campers so far away from base on the last mission."

"You said we needed to cast a wider net; that we needed to gather more data to figure out why this moon was rejecting the terraform."

"I said what I was told to say. But that was then. Now, I don't care what the captain thinks. I'm telling you the truth."

He said something more, but I missed it when a rockslide rushed down the hill to my right. The billowing dust-wall came straight at me, and I felt like an ant scrambling under the shadow of a boot.

I tore my gaze from the oncoming disaster and kicked hard. My legs felt like they were going to rip right off my body. My heart was about to explode.

Somewhere behind me, the wave smothered my tracks and hissed into the river. I didn't bother looking back, because I didn't want to know how close it was.

I slowed from my sprint but kept moving at a strong pace. Gasping for breath, I reached for my communicator.

"Sorry," I said over the groans and growls of the dying moon, "but if you want to tell me the truth, you'll have to speak up."

Craig gave me another disappointing status update, then started his story over.

"You were right," he said. "It's true that we needed more data. But that information was being collected for the benefit of future expeditions. This moon was lost to us the moment it started rejecting the terraform so violently."

"Are you telling me—"

"We never intended to fix things here."

I felt my inner world collapse, just like the one around me.

"You sent me out here to die?"

"It's more complicated than that, Mandy."

"How does it get more complicated than—"

Gunshots. Apparently I'd caught up to Gerrickson. He was firing across the river again. I ducked behind a boulder.

"Mandy, you're slowing dow—"

"I don't need a progress report! Just tell me why Gerrickson is shooting at me!"

Craig sighed into the communicator. "There are a lot of supplies to be brought along when terraforming a moon. We're restricted by expenses and engineering. If we could bring everything we wanted, we would, but things never seem to work out that—"

"Get to the point!"

He swallowed. "It's the escape shuttle, Mandy. It's not big enough for all of us."

I didn't say anything. I couldn't. Rage had fused my teeth together.

"There's enough room for the main crew," Craig said, "but mission control decided that in the event of a disaster, the campers were expendable."

Of course we were. After all, we weren't the chemists or biologists or engineers. We were the guinea pigs who pitched their tents in the wilderness to see if the land was habitable; we were the survivalists who collected samples we didn't even understand, so the big brains back at base could have something to study.

A bullet ricocheted off the boulder and I sunk farther behind my cover. The river thrashed like a diamond-jeweled snake in the throes of death. Everything in the world sounded like a roaring jet engine. I didn't have to check my watch to know I was running out of time.

"You still haven't told me why Gerrickson is shooting at me," I said. "If you're leaving the campers to die, shouldn't he be saving those bullets for you?"

"He's just trying to increase his chances."

"What?"

"The engineering team tried to fix the problem, Mandy. We didn't want to abandon you. So when we saw that this place was rejecting us, we got to work modifying the escape craft. We tried to make room for everyone, but this thing was built with minimalism in mind to begin with – there's not much that can be removed if we want it to continue functioning. But we did make some progress, and..."

"And?"

"There's one seat left."

At that point I think something may have erupted nearby, but I was too angry to really notice.

"I'm sorry," Craig said. "It was supposed to be a secret – the campers weren't supposed to know. It should've been first come, first serve. But someone must like Gerrickson enough to have filled him in, because he realizes what's going on."

I pulled my pistol from its holster. I'd always liked Gerrickson, but he'd left me with no other choice.

Time was running out. Everything was falling apart. If I stayed behind that boulder any longer, the world was going to open up and swallow me.

So I ran.

Gerrickson was too far ahead for me to hit, but I shot anyway to slow him down. It worked, for a time – he panicked and flattened out on the ground, but popped back up and started running again as soon as he realized that waiting wasn't really an option.

"You lost a lot of time when you stopped back there," Craig said, "but you're faster than Gerrickson. You can push the pace longer than he can."

"Sounds like you're playing favorites."

"Maybe I am."

I didn't say anything, because I was hoping it would end at that. Craig had different ideas.

"Listen, Mandy, what happened at the landing party—"

"—is not important right now. I'm sort of busy at the moment."

"Fine. But before you shut me out again, at least let me tell you this – it might not matter that you're faster than Gerrickson. You lost too much time when you stopped for a breather."

"A *breather?* I wasn't resting, I was being shot at!"

"Whatever the reason, the result is the same – I've calculated your movement rate, and I'm not sure you'll get here before we launch."

"How close are the other campers?"

"We've lost contact with Janeway and Rosario. Their side of the moon was the first to go."

"So it's just Gerrickson I have to worry about."

"Just him and the clock."

Right on cue, a bullet skipped off the ground nearby. I fired a few shots on the run and Gerrickson went down.

He held his leg low, around the ankle. I saw red oozing between his fingers. For a brief moment, my instincts overpowered my brain and told me to go help him. I took a step toward the river, but stopped when Gerrickson started firing at me again. I turned away and continued toward base. He had no chance of catching me at that point, but I fired a few blind shots behind me anyway to scare him off. It must have worked, because he quit firing back.

My gun was empty and I didn't have another clip on me, so I tossed it aside. One less thing to carry.

Then I saw the bear.

It wasn't the type of Earth-bear you're thinking of, but that's the closest comparison I can make. The thing was like a grizzly with a line of stegosaurus plates down its back, wrapped in a coat of green-and-brown tiger fur. It descended the rumbling hill at full speed, on a path that was looking to cross my own.

Most animals you'd come across in that type of situation would be primarily concerned with escaping the chaos, but those bears were extremely territorial, and I had a feeling this one was trying to chase me off rather than save its own skin. I guess its motivation didn't matter either way, because I was in its path and there wasn't room for the both of us. My only options were to get ahead of it or hang behind and let it pass, and if I slowed even a little, I was a dead woman anyway.

So I ran.

The ball of muscle and fur barreled down the hill. When it hit flat land, it only got faster. At that point, there was no longer any question in my mind: the bear wasn't fleeing. It was coming after me.

It kicked across the riverbank stones and opened a mouth full of dripping teeth. The growl that came from its throat was somehow louder than the death of a moon.

The bear made its final lunge and I dove to the side. I rolled to a stop near the edge of the river, belly-down with my arms covering my head. I waited to feel the teeth and claws sink into my back, and wondered if my body would even notice the pain over all the fatigue and desperation.

When I looked up, I saw the bear sprawled out next to me. Its mouth was open and its tongue was lolling out. There was a hole in its head where Gerrickson had shot it.

Maybe he'd been aiming for me, but I prefer to think he realized he was out of the race and wanted at least one of us to survive. I once again found myself with the urge to go back and check on his ankle wound, but I was already behind schedule and didn't want his gesture to go to waste.

I got to my feet, ran three steps and fell over from exhaustion.

Getting up again was the hardest thing I'd ever done.

As I stumbled alongside the river, I clicked on my communicator.

"Craig," I said, "if you get a chance to patch through to Gerrickson, tell him—"

"He says you're welcome. And good luck."

I wish I could have looked back and waved. Especially now that I know how things ended up.

I got my second wind and sprinted toward camp. I passed a ravine that hadn't been there before and a bear that wasn't interested in me. My feet were bloody inside my boots, or at least they felt that way. My legs didn't feel like anything at all.

I saw a canoe up ahead near the bank of the river. Rosario had left it there about a month ago. I wasn't sure I'd be able to navigate the rapids when the river was trying to digest itself, but I also wasn't sure how long I'd be able to keep running. I hit the communicator and asked Craig to figure out my best option. No response. The canoe was getting closer, closer, closer…and then it was gone, receding into the Ragnarok that chased me. Even if Craig were to answer at that point, it was too late to backtrack and paddle my way home.

So I ran.

And then, just when I was getting close, I saw something rise above the trees and shoot into the ashen sky.

I tried to contact Craig. I tried to contact anyone else on the team. No one responded.

In hindsight, I shouldn't have been surprised.

I limped into base anyway, hoping that maybe there was a second ride waiting to depart. There wasn't. I was alone among a bunch of tents and panicked footprints.

I sat on a crate and watched the shuttle disappear, while somewhere in the distance a volcano ripped apart the sky.

I let my head hang and caught my breath, and thought about all the things I could have done differently.

It had seemed like the best deal anyone could ask for: I was given the opportunity to see the stars, to settle a new world where the touch of mankind was still faint and nature was something you didn't need a museum ticket to see. Ever since I was a little girl, I'd wanted to run away – from technology, from pollution, from the corrupting hand of man and from the people who raised me.

I shook my head and couldn't help but laugh at the situation. All my life, all I'd ever wanted was to be left alone. And now that I finally got my wish – now that I finally had a world all to myself – it was going to swallow me whole. Or maybe it would asphyxiate me, or just burn me to death. I guess I don't really know what the procedure is when a moon decides it isn't going to be terraformed. I hadn't exactly planned on that happening.

For the first time in my life, I didn't like being alone. Then I remembered that Gerrickson was still out there, stranded by the river.

So I ran.

My body hated me, but I didn't care. I probably wasn't going to be using it much longer anyway.

I ran through a world of ash and smoke. I stumbled across spider-web cracks in the ground that would probably be canyons if I passed that way again. I entered the calmest, narrowest bit of river I could find, and halfway to the other side, I nearly gave up and just sank to the bottom.

But I continued on, and after an eternity of pounding my heavy feet against the shaking ground, I found Gerrickson. He was right where I'd left him.

He was dead.

The wound on his ankle didn't look bad. The one on the side of his neck was much worse. And to think, firing those last blind shots as I escaped had seemed like such a good idea at the time.

I wanted to just sit there next to Gerrickson's body and wait it out. I wanted the end to come and take me, because I was too tired to continue on. But then I remembered one of the gadgets back at base, and knew I had one last journey to make before the world devoured me.

So I ran.

* * *

So here I am, hunched over this modern-day equivalent of a message in a bottle while a moon takes its last breaths around me. I'll launch the comm-capsule as soon as I've finished recording everything, and maybe some passing spacecraft will scoop it up and learn from our mistakes. Of course, you won't be getting any useful scientific analyses out of me – all you're getting is my story, because that's all I've got left.

I came to this moon to explore. I came here to lose myself in the woods, to spend time reading and writing and observing a new, wonderful world. And now, thanks to the budgetary concerns of some faceless politicians at mission control, I'm going to die.

But I guess that's just the way things go.

It's sort of funny. Even as my time dwindles away, the thing I regret most is leaving my book back at camp. When I got the call to return to base in a hurry, I didn't even think to take it with me. And now it's sitting there, alone, with my bookmark stuffed into its final chapter.

I can smell the forest fires in the air. The sky is dark with ash and it's getting harder to breathe. The world is ripping itself to pieces around me, and yet, all I can think about is that unfinished book.

My camp is miles away. Probably even farther now, since most of the old routes have likely been obliterated or buried. But even if that book was on the other side of this moon, I wouldn't care – I've got to get back to it. I've got to find out how the story ends. And as far as I can tell, there's only one way to make that happen.

So I'll run.

Communal

Shikhandin

COMMUNICATION *was not born from sound. Yet, in the past we used sound to communicate. Sound created in patterns and aural shapes. Not just us. All creatures that moved over the surface of our Earth. We were divided into those with tongues and those without, those who were rootless and those who weren't. Those whose movements were quick and visible and those who seemingly stayed still. The tongued and rootless earthlings had a hierarchy. We were the highest in that hierarchy. We ruled and decided everything, including the births and deaths of all that lived on Earth.*

Though we did not know it then, did not understand it or even dream of it, we were one family. Yes, we of the tongued and rootless clan and those of the silent and rooted ones came from the same womb. But that memory was lost in the meanderings of evolution. We did not remember our origins, and we did not respect our differences.

We were related, but did not live as one harmonious family. We were not a united family. We were not a considerate and caring family. We, the most powerful, did not rule wisely. We disobeyed Earth's circadian rhythm. We disrupted the paths of wind and water. We drowned everything in toxins. So immersed were we in our own sounds that we failed to hear the soundless communications we had been receiving. Blinded by our egos we did not see it coming.

Life is a powerful being. Yes life, that force we took for granted. Life, like us, is a child of earth, and friend to all things great and small. Life is the energy we believed we owned, and thought we were Gods of. No mother will tolerate the abuse of her child. No mother will stand by meek and helpless, watching the slaughter of her child. No mother is entirely unforgiving. No good mother is partial to only one child.

Mother, you did not forsake us. You took us, the prodigals, back. And here I am today, grown old, but so wondrously fulfilled. I had never imagined this life in my boyhood.

* * *

"Hey Bhagwan! Hey bhagwan!" Ma clamped her hand over her mouth and slammed her foot on the brakes.

Startled, I dropped my school tablet. My previous day's assignment blinked out of view. I looked up and froze. The traffic had come to a standstill. People were either looking at the news feeds set up at traffic booths or into their individual screens. The news feeds were screaming. Over and over and over again. The scene was replayed just as many times. It was the latest hot topic.

I had never seen such aggression before. But I am just a boy. No grownup had ever seen such aggression before either. Not ma, not bapu, not even dadi, who is more than a hundred years old.

Everyone seemed to be talking all at once. Terrorism! Wilful aggression, they said. Premeditated action. Danger to mankind! It was shocking, at first. The anger came later. When the enormity of what was happening sunk in. The impossible had happened. A strange, powerful and evil miracle had taken place. It was unbelievable. But the proof was there, staring at us from every screen. In Jaisalmer. In other cities. Across the world.

The things had brought an airship down. An entire jumbo airship packed with passengers and cargo!

I saw the clip shot by the drones on my way to school. The thirty second clip, with the warning "disturbing graphic content" flashing at the top right corner, played over and over again. And all around me I could see the grown-ups, my folks included, watching it continuously, as if they were mesmerised. Now there's a funny thing, the drones are never hurt. It's as if they know what contains bio-mass and what doesn't.

The things, I can't think of anything else to call them, looked like vines resembling pythons. Or maybe pythons that looked like vines. Pythons with leaves and fruit. They swung out to grab the sky, shoots and shoots and shoots of them. Like Jack's beanstalks gone crazy. They flung themselves at the airship with loud thwacks. It took them less than thirty seconds to cover it with a mass of writhing green. They twisted and turned, maybe twice or thrice, and went down just as suddenly as they had appeared. After that the sky became empty again. Just like that. Not even a bird in sight.

Of course the government announced an indefinite holiday for all schools and offices. The news feeds urged people to stock up on essentials and stay home. We knew what would happen next. Cutters would be deployed. A whole army of humongous robots made of steel, and powered by uranium. Completely automated, with nothing remotely organic in them. The older models used to be manned by drivers though, seated inside bulletproof see-through cabins fitted into the central portion of the cutters. These would lumber out, sweeping their long metallic arms rhythmically, and making pulp out of all living greens. Some of them still exist. Bapu has one, a smaller, family size machine. The fully automated cutters were much faster. They turned the world bare again within minutes.

Dadi used to tell me stories of how, before she was born, Muslims and Dalits alike would be thrashed and jailed or killed outright whenever stray cows disappeared. Afterwards, when she was a young girl, whole herds began to disappear. Not regularly but often enough to get noticed. These were the cattle let out to roam, because they were past their prime and nobody dared kill them for meat and skin. It was as if the animals had been spirited away overnight. An impossible feat, because even if they had been powerlifted and dumped inside cargo-hovers, someone would have noticed. Goats started to vanish too, and sheep, donkeys and camels. All grazing animals in fact. And then chickens, dogs and cats. And then humans, a few at a time, the kind nobody would miss - the poor, the outdoor sleepers, the homeless, the beggars and discards.

The sand was gone forever in Jaisalmer. Had gone, years before I was born. What existed in its place was a squishy kind of soil that seemed alive in places. Jaisalmer was green. The whole world was green. Not a grain of desert anywhere.

* * *

"The Thar Desert shrank right before our eyes," said dadi. "Not only the Thar, deserts all over the world. We were so happy. More forest meant more animals and birds. That's what we thought at first. But this was a strange kind of greening. More a curse than a blessing."

The disappearances didn't affect humans directly. Nor were they seen as a problem at first. Food was being grown in factories before Dadi's birth. Pure and clean food that adhered to our respective faiths. Halal for Muslims. Kosher for Jews. Untainted vegetarian for Brahmins like us, and Jains. And then there was the regular varieties for those who ate everything indiscriminately.

Animals existed to add to the scenic beauty. Forests were left intact as far as possible, with the department of forestry regulating the populations of all the species. Extinct ones had been successfully cloned. Some were even returned to the wild. So we were good. Humans were doing good, taking good care of the planet, a complete departure from how it used to be even until a century before dadi's birth.

Dadi had her own theories. She said that her parents would often lament about the changes, and that things were no longer the same. That something was brewing underfoot, and maybe this heralded the actual end of the world. The scriptures predicted the ends of epochs, of life. Dadi brought religion into everything, being old, and old-fashioned and all. Bapu didn't say anything to her face, but he found her theories childish. Ma, being the scientific sort openly pooh-poohed her.

I wasn't born when the animals began to disappear. Bapu told me that when the governments noticed, all countries got together. They held joint meetings. Engineers pooled all their knowledge and designed the cutters. Scientists from every field got together to build labs. They studied the phenomena, took notes, made tests and exchanged information. In the beginning it looked like humanity would win. We anyway had our food labs where we could grow anything from radish to lamb chops. Not that we needed the lamb chops. My family, like most people from Rajasthan and the Marwar region are pure vegetarian. The only animal products we consumed were milk and ghee and other things made from milk, created duly in sterile factories. Dadi was squeamish about eating root vegetables, like carrots. She said they reminded her of bones.

"Haddi," she said. "All root veggies are nothing but haddi, bones." But she wouldn't explain bones of what.

Ma and bapu had no such qualms. Bapu even encouraged us to eat eggs, saying milk and eggs were both animal products and if we could have milk we shouldn't have any issues with egg. But dadi wouldn't allow eggs into the house. So we would get to eat eggs only as a treat in restaurants.

Ma worked for a government lab. Her job was to test new mutations of the green things. She checked to see if they had in any way infected the lab grown food. She had a team under her working on keeping our food contamination-free round the clock. Ma had many degrees. Bapu wasn't as qualified as ma. But he had a keen business eye. He used to run a real estate business. He was good at it. Among the perks of his job was getting first-hand information on the best plots and deals available. That's how we got our haveli.

Dadi used to tell us about her young days in the Jaisalmer of old. According to her, Jaisalmer used to be a beautiful city, rising like a gem-studded tiara from the sand. The only time I ever saw sand was in a picture she had showed me. It was a photograph of her village, a cluster of small brick houses on the outskirts of Jaisalmer. Sand lapped like ocean waves against the porches, except that by the time I was born, the ocean waves were no longer blue, but a rich algal green. A few goats stood around in her photo. There also were a couple of disinterested dogs, lean and yellow like the sand. At the photos edge, I could see the city of Jaisalmer, its sandstone buildings shimmering like burnished gold. An elegant contrast against the yellow-white sand and hard candy blue sky. I can't believe it was that beautiful. The sky looked like an upturned and frozen sea, a mirage of the legendary arctic waters. The sand looked like the soft semolina halwa that Dadi used to make when things hadn't gotten quite so out of hand. There were camels too. Yes, camels!

I had drawn a camel once, based on Dadi's descriptions and the pictures I'd seen in my school tablet. The camels were extinct by the time I was born, but some cloned ones still existed, housed inside high security zoos. I pulled a copy of my camel anime-drawing from my art-screen and gave it to Dadi. I helped her set it up on a wall in her room. My camel was taller than the date palm in the picture and it was funny to see it reach down and pluck a few fronds to chew. Dadi laughed a lot, and said she loved her special camel. I drew some more animals, and Dadi wanted them all put up in her room. Soon dadi's room began to resemble a zoo-screen. I still hadn't learnt to add sound to my pictures, which is a blessing, because I doubt dadi would have been able to sleep with all that din around her.

When dadi was a little girl, she used to listen to the elders talk. At first the talks were stories and legends, but as the problems grew, the conversations became a long line of lament.

The vegetable crops, and the fields of bajra and mustard weren't turning out right. They were growing too fast and were too stringy. The date palms and thorny bushes were also proliferating. Yet birds and small animals like squirrels were hardly attracted. Small fauna seemed to be starving. The food they cooked took longer and longer, as if the vegetables and grain and acquired a greater resistance to being changed or killed, if that is the right term to use for vegetation. Dadi said her mother would gaze into the horizon at sundown and mutter to herself.

Soon there rose a clamour of complaints during the evening conversations. Complaints about the quality of food. How things had deteriorated so much that they could barely eat. And then, there were the disappearances too. Since nobody had a clue, the theories and conjectures were tossed fast and loose. Some were outright outlandish. Most had religious undertones. The elders conferred. Special pujas were done to propitiate the Gods. They said this was the cusp, the time when one epoch ended and another began. They said the transition period would bring with it much havoc and mayhem.

"The golden age will return after that," dadi told us with confidence. "Nothing to be afraid of. The act of creation is always preceded by destruction." She became distracted again, mumbling her prayers, and fingering her beads.

Dadi's faith made her unafraid and accepting. But ma and bapu were barely calm after the vine attack. Bittu was the only one whose presence seemed to soothe them. It was the same for me. Ma was always after us, during that time.

"Ankur," she'd yell, even though I had done nothing to annoy her. "Take you meds."

"I did."

"Don't argue. When did you last take them? The yellow round ones? Did you take them first?"

I would bring her my med-tray and show her the empty cavities with the dates marked against each. Only then would she be satisfied, but not for long. Ma would turn towards bapu and dadi after she was done with me, and go checking and rechecking Bittu's med-tray.

Ma also seemed to be on a perennial short fuse, and jumpy. Like the frogs I'd once caught, and put in the fish tank. She had made me wash my hands thoroughly, and then disinfected me, all of me, with a vile smelling spray. She had glared at me as I swallowed my tablets. All that fuss over a bunch of tiny frogs! I had looked at Dadi for support, but for once she had studiously avoided my eyes.

The day after the vine incident, Ma got busy piling up the trolley with all kinds of food stuffs. We'd stopped eating lab grown fresh vegetables and fruit. But at least I knew what they looked like. Bittu didn't remember. As for milk, there was no question of any animal milk, lab grown or not. We had turned into high-tech vegans. We only ate food manufactured in sterile factories, shut away inside big silo like buildings. Our earlier lab-growns or countertop-farm foods was discontinued at ma's insistence. Instead we now consumed food created in petri dishes, one cell at a time. Ma's distrust of nature had reached epic proportions!

I watched as ma threw the packets and cans into our trolley. It was already spilling over with food and household cleaners. She had even got one of those portable contraptions that made water from air. Looking at her go, you'd think the whole of Jaisalmer was about to shut down. The thought had possibly occurred to many people. The stores were super crowded. The other folks didn't appear to be paranoid though. Unless they were pretending. Like ma and dadi, chitchatting away with fellow shoppers, the friendlier ones, like it was business as usual. I caught the strained smile on some of their faces. Dadi grinned and nodded like a senile woman. Ma said something that was supposed to sound funny, as she put some more stuff on our trolley. Then we zigzagged our way to the till. Pushing through the crowd to be first. Nothing unusual. We are Indians after all.

Ma began to unload straightaway. She changed her mind about something and rushed off to replace it, motioning bapu to take over the unloading. Bapu protested softly. The queue behind us muttered. Some folks got restive. Ma returned at last, squeezing her way back past the queue. The glum looking girl with brown pimples on her chin at the counter shoved the bill-swipe at Ma. She blinked into the screen. It blinked back at her, flashing green. The girl turned towards the next customer without bothering to respond to ma's cheerful, "thanks, bye." The queue sighed. Ma obviously hadn't heard it. Or if she had, she simply didn't care. We raced towards the car park. Some cutters were already there, clearing away fresh growth.

Jaisalmer was relatively calm, except for sporadic bursts of panic. Other cities were bursting with growth and panicking humans. The roads had sprouted bumps with seams of green everywhere. Buildings undulated with verdant growth. Fields and farmlands were menacingly lush with no edible plants. Some blamed it on the past misdeeds of humans. Some blamed the government for setting up labs for mutant flora and fauna. That's what created the problem, they claimed. The government replied they couldn't watch people starve and do nothing. Activists were petitioning for the closure of unlicensed plant labs. But regular citizens preferred to trust the politicians and the news-feeds. Ma of course trusted no one. And bapu preferred to play it safe.

Some months ago, at ma's insistence, we shifted to our haveli. It was an early 20th century house with a swimming pool sized courtyard within and a wide garden encircling it outside. Bapu had bought it for a song, and turned it into a weekend home for us. But now, by the looks of ma's grocery shopping, we'd probably be there for much longer. A year maybe. It was a long way off from the city, far beyond the suburbs. When the roads were good though, returning wasn't a problem.

On the way back from the stores we picked up Bittu from his play school. Divya mausi came out waddling out holding Bittu against her chest. She was one of the last remaining teachers. Divya mausi didn't have to carry Bittu. He could walk, run in fact. But he became everybody's darling very quickly. Everyone loved to pick him up, squish him a bit, and smell his fresh baby smell. Bittu could get away with anything, from anyone. Except me. I'm the only one he really listened to. I mean, really as in really, really.

"You're picking him up so soon today Pavitra ji," said Divya mausi.

"I'll bring Bittu early tomorrow," Ma replied. She plucked him from Divya mausi's reluctant arms.

"Bai-bai Deeya maathee," said Bittu.

Divya mausi beamed and ran her fingers down his curls.

The traffic was snaggy on the way home, but we had a determined ma at the controls. Bittu pattered on about his day, and even though some of the words were gibberish, I nodded to show I was interested. Dadi had her eyes closed, like she was praying again. Bapu seemed distracted. Maybe he was waiting to see what mad thing ma was going to do next. He didn't have to wait long. The minute we reached home, she was ready to go back to town again.

"Stay home and fix the boys some dinner," she told him, sounding unusually authoritative. Dadi pursed her lips in disapproval, but bapu didn't react. "I'll finish the stockpiling."

"It's almost six," protested bapu gently. "The stores will be closed by the time you reach Pavi."

"I'll do the shortcut," said ma. And she was out before he could counter that the shortcuts had become virtually un-navigable.

Ma returned long past my bed time. Their voices woke me up so I crept out of my room to see.

"Pavi," I heard bapu say. "Pavi, this is madness." Bapu touched her cheek. "You're being paranoid."

"I'm not. It's begun already. Can't you see?" said ma. She sounded drained of both strength and hope.

"You're not going to let all that talk dictate our lives. Please Pavi," bapu pleaded. "You should know how paranoid all activists are. Always have been."

Ma began to weep. She sat down. Bapu shook his head, but stroked her hair as he spoke. "Hush now Pavi. It'll be ok." But ma only shook her head vigorously, her shoulders convulsing with fear and despair, as the tears rolled down unchecked.

Next morning both bapu and ma stayed home. Bapu cleared out the garden around the house. I heard his mini-cutter going chug-chug and thwack-thwack in a rhythmic cycle. It was barely seven in the morning. Bapu must have begun really early for I could see wide swatches of brown ground around the house. He poured some liquid on the cleared ground which hardened into a smooth synthetic surface after a while.

You have to have the right connections, to get a haveli like ours. Ma and bapu had worked hard for many years, and befriended all the right people. And they'd certainly intended to make the most of it. They'd planned on throwing parties for their friends and colleagues, birthday bashes for Bittu and me here. The idea was to make it a real old fashioned haveli. They had planned on having a pond and cow and dog clones, fruit tree and vegetable plant replicas, ma's favourite flowers and dadi's herbs. All lab-certified. I wanted a largish area especially designated for Bittu and myself. Bapu planned to add a swimming pool with simulated waves for us to go surfing when we felt like it. We had dreams for our haveli. Big dreams.

The cost of the inoculations that bapu, Bittu and I had to take – twelve each for the three of us - put all our plans on hold. Ma and dadi needed only four sets of inoculations each and a follow up. Women were apparently more resistant, but not entirely. And they could also be carriers themselves, unlike us men. That's what the doctor had told us. All of us had to take the same medicines though, every day, because prevention was the only cure, and we couldn't be too careful. That's what ma and dadi said over and over again. Activists of course pooh-poohed the medicines. But my parents weren't taking any chances. Bapu was thankful that we were well off. Nobody in our home spoke of the hundreds who had disappeared, because they didn't have the means to pay for prevention!

Soon after we settled in, a few folks from the village came over. They wanted jobs. Ma told them she'd let them know after we were settled in. She was wary of getting more mouths to feed. And, she didn't want strangers around our house. After two days of working nonstop bapu wanted his freedom back. He wanted to go back to his real job in Jaisalmer. But ma wouldn't let him.

"Who's going to pay for this," said bapu, extending his arms towards the dining hall which looked more like a warehouse of assorted things, mostly food items and water. "We're living on credit. We're in too much debt."

"Trust me," said ma. "Don't go. We need to fortify the house. Nobody understands yet, but when they do there'll be pandemonium, we'll be safe here. We'll be free of..." She didn't finish.

Ma scared me with her talk. Bittu was too small to be scared. But dadi, during those last days seemed to be with ma all the way.

"She's right Santosh," Dadi said to bapu when he finally lost his temper with ma. It was unlike dadi to argue with her son-in-law, he was the head of the family as far as she was concerned. In her time women didn't talk back; they simply obeyed the men.

Bapu on his part never argued back with dadi, who was an elder. He was old-fashioned that way. He picked up his toolbox quietly and went into the yard. By evening the fences were up. They were made of a kind of electro-magnetic metal mesh that you saw only at the military and ship landing areas. The kind that destroyed life, both of the plant and animal kind, on contact.

A week passed. We remained inside our oasis. It was boring without school. Not that we had much of that any more. So many streets had become unnavigable, and so many students had vanished. One by one they had dropped out from our communication screens too. Our shared conversations were over. I missed my friends. But Ma had forbidden me to hang out with anyone months ago.

Another week passed. Ma sprang into action. She had just realised that our medical supplies were running low. Bittu wanted to go as well when he saw her getting ready. He threw such a tantrum that she had to take him along. She returned hours later looking thoroughly exhausted, and fell asleep almost immediately, without even changing. Dadi took Bittu from her. She fed him and put him to bed. And then she was back again, all wild-eyed and trembling. She shook ma awake and spoke urgently. Ma stifled a scream. Bapu and I dropped what we were doing and rushed into Bittu's room. We peered at his sweet angel face in the cot. Dadi removed the coverlet. Ma started hitting her chest like he was dead already. She covered her mouth to stop the wail that threatened to roll out from her throat. Three little pimples, brown and hard, sat wickedly on Bittu's right thigh.

Ma stood like a petrified tree. Dadi wept into her sari pallu. Bapu held his head in his hands. When I looked into ma's face I saw the all terrible things she had refused to say out loud. We wouldn't be able to bear it. Even though we knew deep in our hearts that it was inevitable. But we had no knowledge of the process. The unknown terrified us.

There was one person on Earth though who loved Bittu as much as us, and who we could trust. The one person who was also as tough as nails, and a wise old woman, like dadi. Ma was taking Bittu to her.

Nobody stopped ma. Nobody said a word. We were all secretly thinking that no one should know our family had been hit. The government folks would be here in a jiffy. We'd be quarantined. We'd lose everything we owned. We would vanish. Everything we had would vanish. Would we be together or separated? We had no idea. Nobody really knew what was going on. There were whispers. But people mostly acted as if the government caught and took away renegades, not ordinary hardworking citizens like us.

People went about their daily lives, buying extra groceries, taking their meds and inoculations from the government approved clinics, acting like it was as normal as any other vaccine for any regular epidemic. Nobody raised a hue and cry when whole families disappeared. Nobody spoke of the roads covered with green growing things, the neglected houses as green as tropical hillocks. Nobody praised the weather, so moistly cool and fragrant, like an eternal spring, a season I had only read about in the old stories.

Ma strode out, a still sleepy Bittu on her hip. On the way out she said over her shoulder more out of habit, "I hope you remembered to take your pills, Ankur."

I nodded. My heart felt cold and hot at the same time. Maybe the baby dose hadn't been enough for Bittu. Babies were more vulnerable. I was already eleven years old, going on twelve. I was going to teach my kid brother to be tough like me. Years before he was even born I had already begun saving up my toys and books, looking forward to the day when I would share my things with my own sibling. Ma and bapu took so long to decide that I had almost given up hope.

I watched ma backing the hover-car out from its hangar. I couldn't see her beyond the gate because of the green invasion. The new ones were mutating every day. They were able to overcome many things that they couldn't tolerate at first, when they grew only on soil. Now they seemed to fear almost nothing. No one was safe from them anymore.

Bittu would be safe with Divya mausi. And she would be glad to care for Bittu. We would be spared from watching Bittu getting transformed right before our eyes. The idea of transformation frightened us. Once the process was complete, she would know exactly what to do. She would keep him hidden in her tiny garden until he grew strong enough to withstand being replanted. A matter of days, really. We would get him back then, let him grow wild and free in our haveli, our holiday home, our family get-together and hang-out place! We wouldn't be needing our doses after that. Oh no.

I had overheard ma, bapu and dadi discuss it.

"In the worst case scenario," Bapu had said. Over and over again. And Ma had stifled a sob. They had planned everything, down to the last detail. Maybe they had even discussed it with Divya mausi. She was there at our door, looking cheerfully pimply herself, carrying Bittu in a jar. His fronds waved excitedly from their glass prison. Divya mausi was of course a welcome member of our haveli then onwards. I was really glad. It was nice to have someone else to talk to.

Thereafter we carried on, as if nothing had happened, but with one small adjustment. We no longer took our meds. We had a private ceremony when we planted Bittu in the centre of our courtyard. Soon the courtyard became the central part of our house. It became the place where we ate our meals, of which we had less and less need as the days went by, as our bodies looked more to sun, air and water for sustenance. We sat in our courtyard chatting quietly, stroking Bittu's growing branches and trunk. Ma instructed us daily on what to do when only one of us remained human. We closed our haveli gates permanently. Families were supposed to stay together, no matter what. And that was what we were going to do, until the very end.

* * *

We don't mind the overcrowding. It is but natural. After we got over the initial shock of complete metamorphosis, we began to get used to the new silence. At first our thoughts merged with our soundless speech, and it was awkward. It was awkward too not to feel any particular and possessive love for those who were of our blood in the past. Relationships have new meaning now. It means I can intertwine with the green entity who had once in a long ago life-time birthed me. We were different then, and those old ethics no longer hold.

We clamber over each other, rejoicing in the touch of sun and rain. There is nothing to be afraid of. And why should there? Beneath the runnels of soil we speak to countless more, plant beings, who look no more like us than we do with respect to our previous forms. Our initial doubts were cleared by those who came before us. They gave us their nutrients when the time came for them to pass, merging into the soil or melting into the waters.

A distant memory makes me smile, but not in the way humans do. It's a sensation, and I can express it by physically expanding a little. In that other life, the entity I called ma, used to say that plants speak to each other. She was wrong. It's not just the plants, even stones and water droplets speak. Air molecules speak. The lava rivers deep within mother earth's womb speak.

We all speak to each other. We speak even when miles apart, to use a human term. We think and we feel and we strategize. But our timelines are different. Our measurements of space are different from that of humans. That is why it took us more than a millennium to regain our lost territories.

Be that as it may. There is no anger. No fear. No greed or hate. Nothing negative. Contentment and mutual benefaction drives us. Mother earth smiles a lot these days. She churns her womb and tickles our roots. She pulls at our genetic codes with the gentlest of tugs. We leak our DNA into her. Our mating rituals are ancient and prolonged.

Soon another transformation will take place. Beneath rock and upon ocean beds, new life as delicate as filaments will wriggle free. We will swoop down and add our gifts, welcoming the new children, who in turn will grow. Together we will dance the dance of life. And held in earth's bosom we will swim with her across the cosmos.

Ambassador to the Meek

Alex Shvartsman

MARY APPROACHED the compound, willing aside the memories of this place, fighting the uneasiness in her belly. A twelve-foot gray concrete wall extended in both directions from the heavy wooden gate. *No Trespassers!* was etched into the wood in neat block letters, each character a foot high. A smaller sign was written in red paint, a neat cursive at eye level. It declared: *Tax collectors will be shot on sight.*

"Hello?" She looked up at the guard tower that stood just inside the wall.

A head appeared at the top of the wall in a halo of unruly hair and beard.

"I want to talk to Randall Bryce," she said.

"No strangers. Keep moving."

Her colleagues had tried and were always turned away, even before things got really bad. The most persistent of them had a pair of bullets fired into the ground at his feet before he got the message and retreated.

"I'm not a stranger. Look." She pulled aside the strands of her hair, revealing an old tattoo at the base of her neck, below her left ear. Its color had faded with time and its shape had stretched, but its provenance was unmistakable.

The guard appeared to think it over.

"Anyone can get inked," he said, but there was less hostility in his voice.

"I was born here," she said. "Go find a paragon and tell them the daughter of Chloe Gaskell has returned."

Gusts of Wyoming autumn wind stung her face as she waited. Mary was only five the day she saw these walls for what she thought was the last time. Mostly she remembered the cold. She held her mother's hand as they walked away. Mom was carrying a sack of their belongings and they were both bundled in several layers of clothes, but the wind still got underneath and chilled her bones. Mary cried but kept pace as Mom held on tightly and ushered her along. Everyone they had ever known was left behind; dozens of people watched them go with opprobrium from atop the walls.

This time around she wore a weatherproof jacket and pants, insulated with synthetic-fiber clusters. The wind would not find its way in. Still, she felt small and scared, like the five-year-old girl, the memory of the bone-chilling wind piercing the jacket's material in the way the weather could not.

She'd never imagined returning.

The gate creaked as it was pulled ajar from the inside. She squeezed through to find several guards with rifles slung over their shoulders surrounding a shorter man in his thirties with a sun-icon tattoo above his left eyebrow identifying him as a paragon. He studied her and she stared back; he was rather young to have risen so high within the cult.

"So, you're Mary Gaskell?" he asked.

She nodded.

"The prodigal daughter returns." He smiled. "I'm Thomas. You probably don't remember, but we knew each other when we were kids."

Of course. She didn't recognize him, but she remembered a Thomas. A quiet boy. Helpful. Often more eager to assist adults with some chore or another than to play with the other kids. He was one of Randall Bryce's nephews, which would explain his position of authority.

She forced herself to smile back. "Hello, Thomas. It's good to see you again."

"To what do we owe the pleasure?" asked Thomas. "Have you finally seen the light, yearned to rejoin the righteous? Or are you merely crawling back because your world is ending, just as the Great Paragon has prophesized?"

She'd expected him to gloat. They all gloated: the Amish and the ultra-Orthodox Jews, the cultists and the survivalists. Especially the survivalists. Even so, most had the courtesy not to begin gloating before she even made it indoors.

"I'd like to speak to Randall," she said. "I have a proposition he'll want to hear."

"There's nothing your morally bankrupt and rotting society has to offer that we might need," said Thomas, loud enough for his men to hear.

"Guns. Tools. Medical supplies. All the things you can't make on your own that are about to become scarce," she said. "I can provide an ample supply."

She had seen that glint in the eyes of men she had dealt with often enough over the course of the past year to know that she had his attention.

* * *

She sat on a stool in front of Randall Bryce's house and waited. It seemed all the paragons were summoned. They assembled one by one, stepping past her as though the stool were empty. A few other denizens of the compound she saw also gave her a wide berth. Eventually, a man in his fifties, who also displayed a paragon tattoo on his forehead, approached her.

"Hello, Mary. I'm Jack. I knew your mom."

She didn't remember him.

"How is she?"

"She passed away eighteen months ago. Same reason as everyone else."

"I'm sorry," said Jack. "I was the one who convinced Randall and the others to let you two leave. Now I wish I hadn't. She'd probably still be with us."

"She never regretted her decision," Mary said curtly. "And neither do I."

His eyes widened. "Of course, you too.... For what it's worth, I really am sorry. I liked Chloe very much."

Mary wondered if this man might be her father. He was about the right age. Mom never told her who her father was, never told anyone. Having a child out of wedlock was not the sort of behavior the Grand Paragon condoned. The shaming and abuse that came with it was something the young Chloe seemed willing to suffer; it was her only way off the compound. Even so, it took over five years for these damned cultists to let Mom and her go. And they were the people she was now forced to deal with.

"Listen. Randall...is not how you remember him." Jack lowered his voice. "His health is failing him, and especially his memory. One day he's sharp as a needle, the next he barely knows his own name. Whatever you want, better explain it very thoroughly and hope he isn't having a really bad day."

So that explained all the other paragons. The Randall Bryce she'd known had ruled his followers with an iron fist, but he was well into his eighties now, and perhaps more of a figurehead. Was it him she would have to convince, or the others? Who was the power behind the throne?

"Thanks, Jack," she said. She caught herself searching for features in his face that she recognized in the mirror and forced herself to stop. This was not why she was here.

* * *

Randall Bryce, the Grand Paragon and leader of over four hundred people destined to survive the end of the world, stared past her, his gaze vacant. He was surrounded by eleven paragons of various ages, all men – the elders of the backward, ignorant commune her mother had worked so hard to escape.

Jack sat to his immediate left, Thomas second to his right. Was the power structure of the compound as unsubtle as that? This wasn't something Mary learned as a child, and her mother, understandably, did not talk much about her life as a Luddite.

As per Jack's advice, she started all the way at the beginning.

"Thirty years ago a new mode of transportation was made available for public use, a technology that allowed people and goods to be instantly transported to any receiving station within three thousand miles."

There was a murmur among the paragons. "Heresy," they said. Randall's followers believed it was a sin to use any technology complex enough to rely on microchips.

She soldiered on. "After a ten-year stretch of extensive testing and study it was deemed safe. Of course, we have since learned that it wasn't."

More murmurs. These backward lunatics would survive while the rest of the world perished. How they must've congratulated themselves when the news broke.

"It was eventually discovered that the technology causes inoperable and aggressive brain tumors to form in people twenty-eight to thirty-two years after the initial use, regardless of whether they used a transporter only once or rode the Gate system multiple times per day for decades."

They all knew this, except perhaps Randall himself. But they let her go on. It wasn't kindness, she realized. It was schadenfreude.

"The world as we know it is ending. We've lost close to fifty per cent of the global population already, and things are deteriorating fast. Most of the long-term survivors will be from communities like yours; people whose religious beliefs or economic circumstances kept them from becoming exposed to this deadly technology."

"Mathew 5:5," said Jack.

"Excuse me?" Mary turned to Jack, as did the other paragons.

"'Blessed are the meek, for they shall inherit the earth.' It's in the Bible."

Thomas looked askance at Jack. "What use have we for the Christian Bible, when the Grand Paragon himself predicted the demise of the heretics?" He turned his attention to Mary. "The sinners have defied the laws of nature and will now perish for it. But we're not the meek, far from it. We're the righteous, and the earth is ours for the taking!"

Jack leaned back in his chair. "Save the theatrics and the rhetoric for our flock, Thomas."

"You forget your place, Jack. You don't get to tell me what—"

Randall Bryce tapped the palm of his thin, wrinkled hand on the tabletop, and although it emitted only a gentle, barely audible *thump,* it was enough to command the attention of everyone in the room and to cut off Thomas's tirade mid-sentence. The Grand Paragon's gaze was focused now, his presence too large for the room.

"I remember when I was a child," said Randall. His deep baritone seemed to have fared better than his failing body; his voice was steady and honeyed, like that of a radio announcer. "They said cell phones would eventually give you brain cancer. Just about everyone was willing to take their chances anyway; human beings are terrible at considering anything but the most immediate implications of their actions." He looked at his lieutenants gathered around the table. "I always said: cigarettes, sugar and technology are bad for you."

Mary watched as the paragons nodded eagerly at their spiritual leader's words. She remembered the ludicrous things so-called teachers said to indoctrinate her and the other children. The misogyny, close-mindedness, and even occasional brutality of the everyday life at the compound. She knew the world would not be inherited by the meek but by the likes of them, and it was so unfair she wanted to scream.

Caught up in her thoughts Mary took a moment to notice that Randall and the others were all looking at her. They were waiting for her to continue.

"We've had a decade to prepare as best we could for the inevitable. Before the panic really set in, before the collapse of society, the government did everything possible to ensure the long-term survival of communities like yours. We prepared medicines, essential tools, and other supplies, items that might not be easily scavenged from the dead cities in years to come, and we would like to offer some of them to you."

This got their attention. The paragons looked to each other but waited for their leader's reaction before any of them would speak.

Randall stroked his chin. "What's the catch?"

"There is no catch," said Mary a little too quickly. "But there is a second part to my offer. There are children born after the lethal flaw in the transporter technology was discovered, but there are too many of them for people who were exposed to the effects of the transporters more recently to raise. Based on the size of your group, you should be able to accept seventy children aged three to six without putting an undue strain on your re—"

"So there is a catch," said Jack. "Let me guess, your offer of supplies is contingent on this… adoption scheme?"

Mary felt anxious and afraid, emotion crippling her in a way she had never quite experienced with any of the several dozen groups she had previously made this pitch to. Her job was condemning children to live with groups like these. But then, her mother had taught her it was always a braver choice to select the lesser of two evils than to do nothing. She had to get a grip and get her job done. She forced herself to mentally count to five before responding.

"We'll provide the supplies no matter what. Of course, the amount you'll receive is calculated based on your population, so those seventy children will certainly increase your allocation."

Randall frowned. "What you're asking is not feasible. Perhaps we could take on a dozen of the younger children. I fear the six-year-olds will have already been corrupted by your ways."

Mary wanted to scream. What sort of person would callously bargain over the lives and well-being of children? But she knew that to be the very reason such argument would not sway the octogenarian cult leader.

She forced herself to laugh.

"You misunderstand," she said. "This is a far more generous offer than the gift of supplies. In the next decade or two, the most precious resource won't be guns or tools; it will be people. Communities that can grow fastest will take over more territory and resources, will shape the future of humanity." She watched the paragons intently, knowing she had their attention. "So if you want to take on fewer healthy people, that's perfectly fine. Seventy isn't the minimum number of children we'd like you to adopt; it's the maximum we're willing to give you."

As she continued the pitch she could see the look in Randall's eyes she had seen in so many before him; she had him. Now it was only a matter of ironing out the details.

The meeting lasted for the better part of an hour.

* * *

Mary stepped out of the industrial-size transporter, back to the relative safety and comfort of the temporary base set up by her agency.

They operated out of a FEMA warehouse on the outskirts of Worland, WY. Supplies, carefully parceled out and packaged, were stored in dozens of M939 army trucks covered with green-vinyl tarps, parked in neat rows within the huge structure.

A gaggle of children were playing by the tents set up on the far side of the warehouse. They must've arrived while Mary was negotiating with the cultists. She didn't like rushing things like this; what if she had failed to convince Bryce to accept the kids? But things were turning for the worse rapidly now, with so many people dying every day. They had to act quickly and take chances.

Mary walked over and paused to listen to the laughter and shouting of children. The cacophony reassured her; she was doing the right thing, ensuring the future for these kids even if life at the compound wouldn't be all sunshine and rainbows.

Mary saw a girl of perhaps six sitting by herself on a plastic bench, watching her intently. When their eyes locked, the child looked away, staring down at the concrete floor. Mary walked over and sat next to her.

"What's your name?"

"Abigail," the girl said softly. She wouldn't look directly at Mary.

"Why aren't you playing with the others?"

"I'm scared," said Abigail.

"Scared of this place?"

"A little," said Abigail. "But I'm really scared because I heard one of the teachers say to another that the place we're going to live is not a nice place."

Mary sighed. The last thing these children needed was for some careless staffer to introduce doubt into their already upturned lives.

"I know how you feel," said Mary. "When I was little, I had to move to a different place, too. Everything was new, and strange, and a little scary."

Abigail said nothing, but she looked at Mary rather than at the ground.

"That new place was called Minnesota."

"Really?" Mary's eyes grew wide. "That's where I'm from!"

Mary and her mom had ended up in Ohio, but she knew where this group of children had come from. She thought back to how difficult the adjustment was, even though her new life was softer, more comfortable than her old one. And she had her mom.

"I'll tell you a secret," said Mary. "The place I lived originally was the same place you're going to live."

"Is it a nice place?" Abigail asked, hope in her voice.

"You'll like it," Mary lied. Then she added, "It may take some time for you to get used to it. Moving to a new place is scary, no matter what. But I promise, you'll be all right. You'll adjust to the life in Wyoming just like I adjusted to life in Minnesota."

Mary sat with Abigail for a few more minutes. By the time she left, the child was smiling.

Visiting her birthplace had taken a lot out of Mary. She conferred with colleagues briefly, ate some nutritious but tasteless slop dispensed at the commissary and retired to her tent for a nap.

* * *

She woke to the sound of distant gunfire.

Mary stole a glance at her watch as she got dressed; she had been asleep for just over three hours. She brushed her hands through her hair as she rushed to the makeshift command center in the suite of offices along one of the warehouse's walls. Camera feeds displayed images of the perimeter onto an array of monitors set up there.

"What's happening?" she demanded as she shouldered her way toward the monitors.

"Raiders of some kind," said Phillip, her second in command. "At least thirty or forty of them."

Only a dozen soldiers were guarding the perimeter, with twice as many civilians working inside the warehouse. She watched the monitor with trepidation as a group of armed men ran past a camera. She recognized one of them.

"These are Bryce's men! But how did they find us?"

"They couldn't have followed you." Phillip chewed his lip.

"Even if they had, I drove to the nearest transporter, then used the gate twice to get here. They would have lost me," said Mary. "Up until a few hours ago they didn't even know we existed."

After days of quiet in the deserted commercial neighborhood of a small town the sounds of a firefight seemed surreal.

"Have the soldiers pull back inside; we can't hold such a vast area against a larger force," said Mary. The best way for her to shake off the fear was to act. "Arm the staff. Anyone who doesn't want to stay, have them drive one of the supply trucks through the transporter network and deliver them to the Baton Rouge base."

"What about the kids?" asked Phillip.

Mary hesitated. The only way to get them to safety would be through the transporter, but that would limit their life spans to the maximum of the next thirty years. Worse yet, there was no guarantee she could find someone else to care for them. On the other hand, she had no idea what the raiders might do.... Her mother's admonition about the lesser evil popped unbidden into her mind. She had to decide quickly.

"They're not here for the children," she said, trying to convince herself as much as Phillip. "They want the supplies; we need to salvage as much as we can before they get inside or we'll have no bargaining chips left to negotiate with the next batch of psychopathic separatists."

To his credit, Phillip hesitated only briefly. He must've performed the same mental calculations as she had. He nodded grimly and issued orders through his headset while Mary got on her satellite phone to request help from Fort Bragg. She realized they probably would not mobilize in time even if someone approved military action by the thinly stretched army right away. More likely they would simply order them to retreat and leave the supplies behind.

* * *

Her people managed to save a handful of the trucks. A few staffers were even brave enough to return through the transporter to drive an additional vehicle each to safety. But it was not long before the raiders breached the warehouse itself.

Mary ordered all non-military personnel to leave. The few remaining defenders sniped at the enemy while taking cover behind the trucks. She had herded all the children into a patchwork of small offices, locked the door, and prayed the walls would be thick enough to stop any stray bullets.

She sat at the receptionist's desk, her hands atop its bare surface to show she was unarmed, when Thomas and Jack walked in. Both men had rifles slung over their shoulders and entered the room cautiously, handguns trained ahead.

"You didn't have to do this," she said, trying to keep her voice even. "We were going to provide you with sufficient supplies anyway."

"These supplies are the currency of the new world," said Jack. "There's never such thing as enough currency."

Thomas edged toward the door behind Mary, gun raised.

"Please put that away. All the children are in there, and no one else," said Mary.

Neither of the men replied, but Thomas stepped back.

"How did you find us?" she asked.

Jack's lips stretched into a thin smile. "I planted a tracker on you. A small sin for the sake of our community. The Grand Paragon has absolved me."

The sounds of gunfire outside intensified.

"Please…" Mary searched for the right words. "Everything I said about the value of these children is still true. Do not harm them."

"Randall reluctantly agrees with your assessment," said Jack. His expression turned somber. "We'll take the kids. You, on the other hand…. I'm sorry." He pointed the handgun at her.

The sound of two ear-splitting bangs filled the room. Jack crumpled to the ground, the side of his head devastated by a pair of point blank shots.

Mary stared in horror as Thomas put away his own pistol and gingerly picked up Jack's.

"Thank you," she whispered.

"It's unfortunate how one of the soldiers ambushed Jack, then escaped out the back," said Thomas. He looked Mary in the eye. "So long as we can agree on this version of events, there will be no need to use this on you." He waved Jack's pistol in his hand.

Mary struggled mightily to control her shaking. "Why?" she managed to ask.

"One of us is going to take over as the Grand Paragon eventually," said Thomas. "I get that it may not seem that way to an outsider, but trust me, these kids are better off if that's me. Even if it's only for the next fifteen years or so."

"Fifteen years?"

"I always wanted to see an ocean when I was a kid," said Thomas. "We had this family heirloom, a postcard of the Pacific from where my dad grew up, near San Diego. So as a teenager I snuck out for a day and used a transporter to visit his old digs." He tucked the second pistol into his belt. "So you see, none of us are without sin. Mine will come due in fifteen years time, but I can loosen the screws a little, leave our people better off than Randall has and still protect them from whatever dangers the end of the world might bring."

Mary nodded. She wasn't entirely sure how much of an improvement Thomas had envisioned for his people, but at least he sounded like he was willing to try. At least he hadn't murdered her in cold blood while he could have.

"Come back to the compound with us," said Thomas. "I can use someone more forward thinking than most of the paragons, and Randall and the rest will accept you as a sort of a prodigal-daughter-returning situation."

Mary hesitated. Life on the compound was not something she had ever considered returning to. In some ways, it might be worse than getting executed by Jack. "I have very little time left," she said. It had been thirty years since she used the transporter for the first time. "A year or two, at most."

"Do it for them." Thomas pointed toward the door. They could hear the faint wails of children crying on the other side. "Help them acclimate, for as long as you can. Who knows the ways of both societies like you do?"

Mary knew that Thomas wasn't being altruistic. To him, she was just another resource, another set of skills to further his agenda over the course of however much time she had left. She thought of Abigail, lonely and scared, trying to adjust to the life on the compound. She was only a little older than Mary was when she left there, but Mary had her mother. Abigail would have no one to look out for her interests.

For several years Mary had done all that she could to save children and ensure the future of humanity. She'd done the most good she could in that role, but it was a role others could fill. Protecting these children, easing their transition to the life on the compound, was something only she could do.

"Come on," said Thomas. "What was it Jack said? The society of the mighty may be in its death throes but the meek will need all the help they can get if they're to inherit the world."

Mary nodded. She always had enough courage to choose the lesser of the two evils.

Together, she and Thomas unlocked the door and set out to calm the children.

The Empire of the Necromancers

Clark Ashton Smith

THE LEGEND of Mmatmuor and Sodosma shall arise only in the latter cycles of Earth, when the glad legends of the prime have been forgotten. Before the time of its telling, many epochs shall have passed away, and the seas shall have fallen in their beds, and new continents shall have come to birth. Perhaps, in that day, it will serve to beguile for a little the black weariness of a dying race, grown hopeless of all but oblivion. I tell the tale as men shall tell it in Zothique, the last continent, beneath a dim sun and sad heavens where the stars come out in terrible brightness before eventide.

Chapter I

MMATMUOR and Sodosma were necromancers who came from the dark isle of Naat, to practise their baleful arts in Tinarath, beyond the shrunken seas. But they did not prosper in Tinarath: for death was deemed a holy thing by the people of that gray country; and the nothingness of the tomb was not lightly to be desecrated; and the raising up of the dead by necromancy was held in abomination.

So, after a short interval, Mmatmuor and Sodosma were driven forth by the anger of the inhabitants, and were compelled to flee toward Cincor, a desert of the south, which was peopled only by the bones and mummies of a race that the pestilence had slain in former time.

The land into which they went lay drear and leprous and ashen below the huge, ember-colored sun. Its crumbling rocks and deathly solitudes of sand would have struck terror to the hearts of common men; and, since they had been thrust out in that barren place without food or sustenance, the plight of the sorcerers might well have seemed a desperate one. But, smiling secretly, with the air of conquerors who tread the approaches of a long-coveted realm, Sodosma and Mmatmuor walked steadily on into Cincor

Unbroken before them, through fields devoid of trees and grass, and across the channels of dried-up rivers, there ran the great highway by which travelers had gone formerly betweea Cincor and Tinarath. Here they met no living thing; but soon they came to the skeletons of a horse and its rider, lying full in the road, and wearing still the sumptuous harness and raiment which they had worn in the flesh. And Mmatmuor aad Sodosma paused before the piteous bones, on which no shred of corruption remained; and they smiled evilly at each other.

"The steed shall be yours," said Mmatmuor, "since you are a little the elder of us two, and are thus entitled to precedence; and the rider shall serve us both and be the first to acknowledge fealty to us in Cincor."

Then, in the ashy sand by the wayside, they drew a threefold circle; and standing together at its center, they performed the abominable rites that compel the dead to arise from tranquil nothingness and obey henceforward, in all things, the dark will of the necromancer. Afterward they sprinkled a pinch of magic powder on the nostril-holes of the man and the horse; and the white bones, creaking mournfully, rose up from where they had lain and stood in readiness to serve their masters.

So, as had been agreed between them, Sodosma mounted the skeleton steed and took up the jeweled reins, and rode in an evil mockery of Death on his pale horse; while Mmatmuor trudged on beside him, leaning lightly on an ebon staff; and the skeleton of the man, with its rich raiment flapping loosely, followed behind the two like a servitor.

After a while, in the gray waste, they found the remnant of another horse and rider, which the jackals had spared and the sun had dried to the leanness of old mummies. These also they raised up from death; and Mmatmuor bestrode the withered charger; and the two magicians rode on in state, like errant emperors, with a lich and a skeleton to attend them. Other bones and charnel remnants of men and beasts, to which they came anon, were duly resurrected in like fashion; so that they gathered to themselves an everswelling train in their progress through Cincor.

Along the way, as they neared Yethlyreom, which had been the capital, they found numerous tombs and necropoli, inviolate still after many ages, and containing swathed mummies that had scarcely withered in death. All these they raised up and called from sepulchral night to do their bidding. Some they commanded to sow and till the desert fields and hoist water from the sunken wells; others they left at diverse tasks, such as the mummies had performed in life. The century-long silence was broken by the noise and tumult of myriad activities; and the lank liches of weavers toiled at their shuttles; and the corpses of plowmen followed their furrows behind carrion oxen.

Weary with their strange journey and their oft-repeated incantations, Mmatmuor and Sodosma saw before them at last, from a desert hill, the lofty spires and fair, unbroken domes of Yethlyreom, steeped in the darkening stagnant blood of ominous sunset.

"It is a goodly land," said Mmatmuor, "and you and I will share it between us, and hold dominion over all its dead, and be crowned as emperors on the morrow in Yethlyreom."

"Aye," replied Sodosma, "for there is none living to dis pute us here; and those that we have summoned from the tomb shall move and breathe only at our dictation, and may not rebel against us."

So, in the blood-red twilight that thickened with purple, they entered Yethlyreom and rode on among the lofty, lampless mansions, and installed themselves with their grisly retinue in that stately and abandoned palace, where the dynasty of Nimboth emperors had reigned for two thousand years with dominion over Cincor.

In the dusty golden halls, they lit the empty lamps of onyx by means of their cunning sorcery, and supped on royal viands, provided from past years, which they evoked in like manner. Ancient and imperial wines were poured for them in moonstone cups by the fleshless hands of their servitors; and they drank and feasted and revelled in fantasmagoric pomp, deferring till the morrow the resurrectiom of those who lay dead in Yethlyreom.

They rose betimes, in the dark crimson dawn, from the opulent palace-beds in which they had slept; for much remained to be done. Everywhere in that forgotten city, they went busily to and fro, working their spells on the people that had died in the last year of the pest and had lain unburied. And having accomplished this, they passed beyond Yethlyreom into that other city of high tombs and mighty mausoleums, in which lay the Nimboth emperors and the more consequential citizens and nobles of Cincor.

Here they bade their skeleton slaves to break in the sealed doors with hammers; and then, with their sinful, tyrannous incantations, they called forth the imperial mummies, even to the eldest of the dynasty, all of whom came walking stiffly, with lightless eyes, in rich swathings sewn with flame-bright jewels. And also, later, they brought forth to a semblance of life many generations of courtiers and dignitaries.

Moving in solemn pageant, with dark and haughty and hollow faces, the dead emperors and empresses of Cincor made obeisance to Mmatmuor and Sodosma, and attended them like a train of captives through all the streets of Yethlyreom. Afterward, in the immense throne-room of the palace, the necromancers mounted the high double throne, where the rightful rulers had sat with their consorts. Amid the assembled emperors, in gorgeous and funereal state, they were invested with sovereignty by the sere hands of the mummy of Hestaiyon, earliest of the Nimboth line, who had ruled in half-mythic years. Then all the descendants of Hestaiyon, crowding the room in a great throng, acclaimed with toneless, echo-like voices the dominion of Mmatmuor and Sodosma.

Thus did the outcast necromancers find for themselves an empire and a subject people in the desolate, barren land where the men of Tinarath had driven them forth to perish. Reignhg supreme over all the dead of Cincor, by virtue of their malign magic, they exercised a baleful despotism. Tribute was borne to them by fleshless porters from outlying realms; and plague-eaten corpses, and tall mummies scented with mortuary balsams, went to and fro upon their errands in Yethlyreom, or heaped before their greedy eyes, fmm inexhaustible vaults, the cobweb-blackened gold and dusty gems of antique time.

Dead laborers made their palace-gardens to bloom with long-perished flowers; liches and skeletons toiled for them in the mines, or reared superb, fantastic towers to the dying sun. Chamberlains and princes of old time were their cupbearers, and stringed instruments were plucked for their delight by the slim hands of empresses with golden hair that had come forth untarnished from the night of the tomb. Those that were fairest, whom the plague and the worm had not ravaged overmuch, they took for their lemans and made to serve their necrophilic lust.

Chapter II

IN ALL things, the people of Cincor performed the actions of life at the will of Mmatmuor and Sodosma. They spoke, they moved, they ate and drank as in life. They heard and saw and felt with a similitude of the senses that had been theirs before death; but their brains were enthralled by a dreadful necromancy. They recalled but dimly their former existence; and the state to which they had been summoned was empty and troublous and shadow-like. Their blood ran chill and sluggish, mingled with water of Lethe; and the vapors of Lethe clouded their eyes.

Dumbly they obeyed the dictates of their tyrannous lords, without rebellion or protest, but filled with a vague, illimitable weariness such as the dead must know, when having drunk of eternal sleep, they are called back once more to the bitterness of mortal being. They knew no passion or desire. or delight, only the black languor of their awakening from Lethe, and a gray, ceaseless longing to return to that interrupted slumber.

Youngest and last of the Nimboth emperors was Illeiro, who had died in the first month of the plague. and had lain in his high-built mausoleum for two hundred years before the coming of the necromancers.

Raised up with his people and his fathers to attend the tyrants, Illeiro had resumed the emptiness of existence without question and had felt no surprise. He had accepted his own resurrection and that of his ancestors as one accepts the indignities and marvels of a dream. He knew that he had come back to a faded sun, to a hollow and spectral world, to an order of things in which his place was merely that of an obedient shadow. But at first he was troubled only, like the others, by a dim weariness and pale hunger for the lost oblivion.

Drugged by the magic of his overlords, weak from the age-long nullity of death, he beheld like a somnambulist the enormities to which his fathers were subjected. Yet, somehow, after many days, a feeble spark awoke in the sodden twilight of his mind.

Like something lost and irretrievable, beyond prodigious gulfs, he recalled the pomp of his reign in Yethlyreom, and the golden pride and exultation that had been his in youth. And recalling it, he felt a vague stirring of revolt, a ghostly resentment against the magicians who had haled him forth to this calamitous mockery of life. Darkly he began to grieve for his fallen state, and the mournful plight of his ancestors and his people.

Day by day, as a cup-bearer in the halls where he had ruled aforetime, Illeiro saw the doings of Mmatmuor and Sodosma. He saw their caprices of cruelty and lust, their growing drunkenness and gluttony. He watched them wallow in their necromantic luxury, and become lax with indolence, gross with indulgence, They neglected the study of their art, they forgot many of their spells. But still they ruled, mighty and formidable; and, lolling on couches of purple and rose, they planned to lead an army of the dead against Tinarath.

Dreaming of conquest, and of vaster necromancies, they grew fat and slothful as worms that have installed themselves in a charnel rich with corruption. And pace by pace with their laxness and tyranny, the fire of rebellion mounted in the shadowy heart of Illeiro, like a flame that struggles with Lethean damps. And slowly, with the waxing of his wrath, there returned to him something of the strength and firmness that had been his in life. Seeing the turpitude of the oppressors, and knowing the wrong that had been done to the helpless dead, he heard in his brain the clamor of stifled voices demanding vengeance.

Among his fathers, through the palace-halls of Yethlyreom, Illeiro moved silently at the bidding of the masters, or stood awaiting their command. He poured in their cups of onyx the amber vintages, brought by wizardry from hills beneath a younger sun; he submitted to their contumelies and insults. And night by night he watched them nod in their drunkenness, till they fell asleep, flushed and gross, amid their arrogated splendor.

There was little speech among the living dead; and son and father, daughter and mother, lover and beloved, went to and fro without sign of recognition, making no comment on their evil lot. But at last, one midnight, when the tyrants lay in slumber, and the flames wavered in the necromantic lamps, Illeiro took counsel with Hestaiyon, his eldest ancestor, who had been famed as a great wizard in fable and was reputed to have known the secret lore of antiquity.

Hestaiyon stood apart from the others, in a corner of the shadowy hall. He was brown and withered in his crumbling mummy-cloths; and his lightless obsidian eyes appeared to gaze still upon nothingness. He seemed not to have heard the questions of Illeiro; but at length, in a dry, rustling whisper, he responded:

"I am old, and the night of the sepulcher was long, and I have forgotten much. Yet, groping backward across the void of death, it may be that I shall retrieve something of my former wisdom; and between us we shall devise a mode of deliverance." And Hestaiyon searched among the shreds of memory, as one who reaches into a place where the worm has been and the hidden archives of old time have rotted in their covers; till at last he remembered, and said:

"I recall that I was once a mighty wizard; and among other things, I knew the spells of necromancy; but employed them not, deeming their use and the raising up of the dead an abhorrent act. Also, I possessed other knowledge; and perhaps, among the remnants of that ancient lore, there is something which may serve to guide us now. For I recall a dim, dubitable prophecy, made in the primal years, at the founding of Yethlyreom and the empire of Cincor.

The prophecy was, that an evil greater than death would befall the emperors and the people of Cincor in future times; and that the first and the last of the Nimboth dynasty, conferring together, would effect a mode of release and the lifting of the doom. The evil was not named in the prophecy: but it was said that the two emperors would learn the solution of their problem by the breaking of an ancient clay image that guards the nethermost vault below the imperial palace in Yethlyreom."

Then, having heard this prophecy from the faded lips of his forefather, Illeiro mused a while, and said:

"I remember now an afternoon in early youth, when searching idly through the unused vaults of our palace, as a boy might do, I came to the last vault and found therein a dusty, uncouth image of clay, whose form and countenance were strange to me. And, knowing not the prophecy. I turned away in disappointment, and went back as idly as I had come, to seek the moted sunlight."

Then, stealing away from their heedless kinfolk, and carrying jeweled lamps they had taken from the hall, Hestaiyon and Illeiro went downward by subterranean stairs beneath the palace; and, threading like implacable furtive shadows the maze of nighted corridors, they came at last to the lowest crypt.

Here, in the black dust and clotted cobwebs of an immemorial past, they found, as had been decreed, the clay image, whose rude features were those of a forgotten earthly god. And Illeiro shattered the image with a fragment of stone; and he and Hestaiyon took from its hollow center a great sword of unrusted steel, and a heavy key of untarnished bronze, and tablets of bright brass on which were inscribed the various things to be done, so that Cincor should be rid of the dark reign of the necromancers and the people should win back to oblivious death.

So, with the key of untarnished bronze, Illeiro unlocked, as the tablets had instructed him to do, a low and narrow door at the end of the nethermost vault, beyond the broken image; and he and Hestaiyon saw, as had been prophesied, the coiling steps of somber stone that led downward to an undiscovered abyss, where the sunken fires of earth still burned. And leaving Illeiro to ward the open door, Hestaiyon took up the sword of unrusted steel in his thin hand, and went back to the hall where the necromancers slept, lying a-sprawl on their couches of rose and purple, with the wan, bloodless dead about them in patient ranks.

Upheld by the ancient prophecy and the lore of the bright tablets, Hestaiyon lifted the great sword and struck off the head of Mmatmuor and the head of Sodosma, each with a single blow. Then, as had been directed, he quartered the remains with mighty strokes. And the necromancers gave up their unclean lives, and lay supine, without movement, adding a deeper red to the rose and a brighter hue to the sad purple of their couches.

Then, to his kin, who stood silent and listless, hardly knowing their liberation, the venerable mummy of Hestaiyon spoke in sere murmurs, but authoritatively, as a king who issues commands to his children. The dead emperors and empresses stirred, like autumn leaves in a sudden wind, and a whisper passed among them and went forth from the palace, to be communicated at length, by devious ways, to all the dead of Cincor.

All that night, and during the blood-dark day that followed, by wavering torches or the light of the failing sun, an endless army of plague-eaten liches, of tattered skeletons, poured in a ghastly torrent through the streets of Yethlyreom and along the palace-hall where Hestaiyon stood guard above the slain necromancers. Unpausing, with vague, fixed eyes, they went on like driven shadows, to seek the subterraaean vaults below the palace, to pass through the open door where Illeiro waited in the last vault, and then to wend downward by a thousand

thousand steps to the verge of that gulf in which boiled the ebbing fires of earth. There, from the verge, they flung themselves to a second death and the clean annihilation of the bottomless flames.

But, after all had gone to their release, Hestaiyon still remained, alone in the fading sunset, beside the cloven corpses of Mmatmuor and Sodosma. There, as the tablets had directed him to do, he made trial of those spells of elder necromancy which he had known in his former wisdom, and cursed the dismembered bodies with that perpetual life-in-death which Mmatmuor and Sodosma had sought to inflict upon the people of Cincor. And maledictions came from the pale lips, and the heads rolled horribly with glaring eyes, and the limbs and torsos writhed on their imperial couches amid clotted blood. Then, with no backward look, knowing that all was done as had been ordained and predicted from the first, the mummy of Hestaiyon left the necromancers to their doom, and went wearily through the nighted labyrinth of vaults to rejoin Illeiro.

So, in tranquil silence, with no further need of words, Illeiro and Hestaiyon passed through the open door of the nether vault, and Illeiro locked the door behind them with its key of untarnished bronze. And thence, by the coiling stairs, they wended their way to the verge of the sunken flames and were one with their kinfolk and their people in the last, ultinate nothingness.

But of Mmatmuor and Sodosma, men say that their quartered bodies crawl to and fro to this day in Yethlyreom, finding no peace or respite from their doom of life-indeath. and seeking vainly through the black maze of nether vaults the door that was locked by Illeiro.

The Isle of the Torturers

Clark Ashton Smith

BETWEEN the sun's departure and return, the Silver Death had fallen upon Yoros. Its advent, however, had been foretold in many prophecies, both immemorial and recent. Astrologers had said that this mysterious malady, heretofore unknown on earth, would descend from the great star, Achernar, which presided balefully over all the lands of the southern continent of Zothique; and having sealed the flesh of a myriad men with its bright, metallic pallor, the plague would still go onward in time and space, borne by the dim currents of ether to other worlds.

Dire was the Silver Death; and none knew the secret of its contagion or the cure. Swift as the desert wind, it came into Yoros from the devastated realm of Tasuun, overtaking the very messengers who ran by night to give warning of its nearness. Those who were smitten felt an icy, freezing cold, an instant rigor, as if the outermost gulf had breathed upon them. Their faces and bodies whitened strangely, gleaming with a wan luster, and became stiff as long-dead corpses, all in an interim of minutes.

In the streets of Silpon and Siloar, and in Faraad, the capital of Yoros, the plague passed like an eery, glittering light from countenance to countenance under the golden lamps; and the victims fell where they were stricken; and the deathly brightness remained upon them.

The loud, tumultuous public carnivals were stifled by its passing, and the merry-makers were frozen in frolic attitudes. In proud mansions, the wine-flushed revelers grew pale amid their garish feasts, and reclined in their opulent chairs, still holding the half-emptied cups with rigid fingers. Merchants lay in their counting-houses on the heaped coins they had begun to reckon; and thieves, entering later, were unable to depart with their booty. Diggers died in the half completed graves they had dug for others; but no one came to dispute their possession.

There was no time to flee from the strange, inevitable scourge. Dreadfully and quickly, beneath the clear stars, it breathed upon Yoros; and few were they who awakened from slumber at dawn. Fulbra, the young king of Yoros, who had but newly suceeeded to the throne, was virtually a ruler without a people.

Fulbra had spent the night of the plague's advent on a high tower of his palace above Faraad: an observatory tower, equipped with astronomical appliances. A great heaviness had lain on his heart, and his thoughts were dulled with an opiate despair; but sleep was remote from his eye-lids. He knew the many predictions that foretold the Silver Death; and moreover he had read its imminent coming in the stars, with the aid of the old astrologer and sorcerer, Vemdeez. This latter knowledge he and Vemdeez had not cared to promulgate, knowing full well that the doom of Yoros was a thing decreed from all time by infinite destiny; and that no man could evade the doom, unless it were written that he should die in another way than this.

Now Vemdeez had cast the horoscope of Fulbra; and though he found therein certain ambiguities that his science could not resolve, it was nevertheless written plainly that the king would not die in Yoros. Where he would die, and in what manner, were alike doubtful. But Vemdeez, who had served Altath the father of Fulbra, and was no less devoted to the new ruler, had wrought by means of his magical art an enchanted ring that would protect Fulbra from the Silver Death in all times and places. The ring was made of a strange. red metal, darker than ruddy gold or copper, and was set with a black and oblong gem, not known to terrestrial lapidaries, that gave forth eternally a strong aromatic perfume. The sorcerer told Fulbra never to remove the ring from the middle finger on which he wore it — not even in lands afar from Yoros and in days after the passing of the Silver Death: for if once the plague had breathed upon Fulbra, he would bear its subtle contagion always in his flesh; and the contagion would assume its wonted virulence with the ring's removal. But Vemdeez did not tell the origin of the red metal and the dark gem, nor the price at which the protective magic had been purchased.

With a sad heart, Fulbra had accepted the ring and had worn it; and so it was that the Silver Death blew over him in the night and harmed him not. But waiting anxiously on the high tower, and watching the golden lights of Faraad rather than the white, implacable stars, he felt a light, passing chillness that belonged not to the summer air. And even as it passed the gay noises of the city ceased; and the moaning lutes faltered strangely and expired. A stillness crept on the carnival; and some of the lamps went out and were not re-lit. In the palace beneath him there was also silence; and he heard no more the laughter of his courtiers and chamberlains. And Vemdeez came not, as was his custom, to join Fulbra on the tower at midnight. So Fulbra knew himself for a realmless king; and the grief that he still felt for the noble Altath was swollen by a great sorrow for his perished people.

Hour by hour he sat motionless, too sorrowful for tears. The stars changed above him; and Achernar glared dovm perpetually like the bright, cruel eye of a mocking demon; and the heavy balsam of the black-jeweled ring arose to his nostrils and seemed to stifle him. And once the thought occurred to Fulbra, to cast the ring away and die as his people had died. But his despair was too heavy upon him even for this; and so, at length, the dawn came slowly in heavens pale as the Silver Death, and found him still on the tower.

In the dawn, King Fulbra rose and descended the coiled stairs of porphyry into his palace. And midway on the stairs he saw the fallen corpse of the old sorcerer Vemdeez, who had died even as he climbed to join his master. The wrinkled face of Vemdeez was like polished metal, and was whiter than his beard and hair; and his open eyes, which had been dark as sapphires, were frosted with the plague. Then, grieving greatly for the death of Vemdeez, whom he had loved, as a foster-father, the king went slowly on. And in the suites and halls below, he found the bodies of his courtiers and servants and guardsmen. And none remained alive, excepting three slaves who warded the green, brazen portals of the lower vaults, far beneath the palace.

Now Fulbra bethought him of the counsel of Vemdeez, who had urged him to flee from Yoros and to seek shelter in the southern isle of Cyntrom, which paid tribute to the kings of Yoros. And though he had no heart for this, nor for any course of action, Fulbra bade the three remaining slaves to gather food and such other supplies as were necessary for a voyage of some length, and to carry them aboard a royal barge of ebony that was moored at the palace porticoes on the river Voum.

Then, embarking with the slaves, he took the helm of the barge, and directed the slaves to unfurl the broad amber sail. And past the stately city of Faraad, whose streets were thronged with the silvery dead, they sailed on the widening jasper estuary of the Voum, and into the amaranth-colored gulf of the Indaskian Sea.

A favorable wind was behind them, blowing from the north over desolate Tasuun and Yoros, even as the Silver Death had blown in the night. And idly beside them, on the Voum, there floated seaward many vessels whose crews and captains had all died of the plague. And Faraad was still as a necropolis of old time; and nothing stirred on the estuary shores, excepting the plumy, fanshapen palms that swayed southward in the freshening wind. And soon the green strand of Yoros receded, gathering to itself the blueness and the dreams of distance.

Creaming with a winy foam, full of strange murmurous voices and vague tales of exotic things, the halcyon sea was about the voyagers now beneath the high-lifting summer sun. But the sea's enchanted voices and its long languorous, immeasurable cradling could not soothe the sorrow of Fulbra; and in his heart a despair abided, black as the gem that was set in the red ring af Vemdeez.

Howbeit, he held the great helm of the ebon barge, and steered as straightly as he could by the sun toward Cyntrom. The amber sail was taut with the favoring wind; and the barge sped onward all that day, cleaving the amaranth waters with its dark prow that reared in the carven form of an ebony goddess. And when the night came with familiar austral stars, Fulbra was able to correct such errors as he had made in reckoning the course.

For many days they flew southward; and the sun lowered a little in its circling behind them; and new stars climbed and clustered at evening about the black goddess of the prow. And Fulbra, who had once sailed to the isle of Cymtrom in boyhood days with his father Altath, thought to see ere long the lifting of its shores of camphor and sandalwood from the winy deep. But in his heart there was no gladness; and often now he was blinded by wild tears, remembering that other voyage with Altath.

Then, suddenly and at high noon, there fell an airless cabin, and the waters became as purple glass about the barge. The sky changed to a dome of beaten copper, arching close and low; and as if by some evil wizardry, the dome darkened with untimely night, and a tempest rose like the gathered breath of mighty devils and shaped the sea into vast ridges, and abysmal valleys. The mast of ebony snapped like a reed in the wind, and the sail was torn asunder, and the helpless vessel pitched headlong in the dark troughs and was hurled upward through veils of blinding foam to the giddy summits of the billows.

Fulbra clung to the useless helm, and the slaves, at his command, took shelter in the forward cabin. For countless hours they were borne onward at the will of the mad hurricane; and Fulbra could see naught in the lowering gloom, except the pale crests of the beetling waves; and he could tell no longer the direction of their course.

Then, in that lurid dusk, he beheld at intervals another vessel that rode the storm-driven sea, not far from the barge. He thought that the vessel was a galley such as might be used by merchants that voyaged among the southern isles, trading for incense and plumes and vermilion; but its oars were mostly broken, and the toppled mast and sail hung forward on the prow.

For a time the ships drove on together; till Fulbra saw, in a rifting of the gloom, the sharp and somber crags of an unknown shore, with sharper towers that lifted palely above them. He could not turn the helm; and the barge and its companion vessel were carried toward the looming rocks, till Fulbra thought that they would crash thereon. But, as if by some enchantment, even as it had risen, the sea fell abruptly in a windless calm; and quiet sunlight poured from a clearing sky; and the barge was left on a broad crescent of ochre-yellow sand between the crags and the lulling waters, with the galley beside it.

Dazed and marveling, Fulbra leaned on the helm, while his slaves crept timidly forth from the cabin, and men began to appear on the decks of the galley. And the king was about to hail these men, some of whom were dressed as humble sailors and others in the fashion of rich merchants. But he heard a laughter of strange voices, high and shrill and somehow evil, that seemed to fall from above; and looking up he saw that many people were descending a sort of stairway in the cliffs that enclosed the beach.

The people drew near, thronging about the barge and the galley. They wore fantastic turbans of blood-red, and were clad in closely fitting robes of vulturine black. Their faces and hands were yellow as saffron; their small and slaty eyes were set obliquely beneath lashless lids; and their thin lips, which smiled eternally, were crooked. as the blades of scimitars.

They bore sinister and wicked-looking weapons, in the form of saw-toothed swords and doubled-headed spears. Some of them bowed low before Fulbra and addressed him obsequiously, staring upon him all the while with an unblinking gaze that he could not fathom. Their speech was no less alien than their aspect; it was full of sharp and hissing sounds; and neither the king nor his slaves could comprehend it. But Fulbra bespoke the people courteously, in the mild and mellow-flowing tongue of Yoros, and inquired the name of this land whereon the barge had been cast by the tempest.

Certain of the people seemed to understand him, for a light came in their slaty eyes at his question; and one of them answered brokenly in the language of Yoros, saying that the land was the Isle of Uccastrog, Then, with something of covert evil in his smile, this person added that all shipwrecked mariners and seafarers would receive a goodly welcome from Ildrac, the king of the Isle.

At this, the heart of Fulbra sank within him; for he had heard numerous tales of Uccastrog in bygone years; and the tales were not such as would reassure a stranded traveler. Uccastrog, which lay far to the east of Cyntrom, was commonly known as the Isle of the Torturers; and men said that all who landed upon it unaware, or were cast thither by the seas, were imprisoned by the inhabitants and were subjected later to unending curious tortures whose infliction formed the chief delight of these cruel beings. No man, it was rumored, had ever escaped from Uccastrog; but many had lingered for years in its dungeons and hellish torture chambers, kept alive for the pleasure of King Ildrac and his followers. Also, it was believed that the Torturers were great magicians who could raise mighty storms with their enchantments, and could cause vessels to be carried far from the maritime routes, and then fling them ashore upon Uccastrog.

Seeing that the yellow people were all about the barge, and that no escape was possible, Fulbra asked them to take him at once before King Ildrac. To Ildrac he would announce his name and royal rank; and it seemed to him, in his simplicity, that one king, even though cruel-hearted, would scarcely torture another or keep him captive. Also, it might be that the inhabitants of Uccastrog had been somewhat maligned by the tales of travelers.

So Fulbra and his slaves were surrounded by certain of the throng and were led toward the palace of Ildrac, whose high, sharp towers crowned the crags beyond the beach, rising above those clustered abodes in which the island people dwelt. And while they were climbing the hewn steps in the cliff, Fulbra heard a loud outcry below and a clashing of steel against steel; and looking back, he saw that the crew of the stranded galley had drawn their swords and were fighting the islanders. But being outnumbered greatly, their resistance was borne down by the swarming Torturers; and most of them were taken alive. And Fulbra's heart misgave him sorely at this sight; and more and nore did he mistrust the yellow people.

Soon he came into the presence of Ildrac, who sat on a lofty brazen chair in a vast hall of the palace. Ildrac was taller by half a head than any of his followers; and his features were like a mask of evil wrought from some pale, gilded metal; and he was clad in vestments of a strange hue, like sea-purple brightened with fresh-flowing blood. About him were many guardsmen, armed with terrible scythe-like weapons; and the sullen, slant-eyed girls of the palace, in skirts of vermilion and breast-cups of lazuli, went to and fro among huge basaltic columns. About the hall stood numerous engineries of wood and stone and metal such as Fulbra had never beheld, and having a formidable aspect with their heavy chains, their beds of iron teeth and their cords and pulleys of fish-skin.

The young king of Yoros went forward with a royal and fearless bearing, and addressed Ildrac, who sat motionless and eyed him with a level, unwinking gaze. And Fulbra told Ildrac his name and station, and the calamity that had caused him to flee from Yoros; and he mentioned also his urgent desire to reach the Isle of Cyntrom.

"It is a long voyage to Cyntrom," said Ildrac, with a subtle smile. "Also, it is not our custom to permit guests to depart without having fully tasted the hospitality of the Isle of Uccastrog. Therefore, King Fulbra, I must beg you to curb your impatience. We have much to show you here, and many diversions to offer. My chamberlains will now conduct you to a room befitting your royal rank. But first I must ask you to leave with me the sword that you carry at your side; for swords are often sharp — and I do not wish my guests to suffer injury by their own hands."

So Fulbra's sword was taken from him by one of the palace guardsmen; and a small ruby-hilted dagger that he carried was also removed. Then several of the guards, hemming him in with their scythed weapons, led him from the hall and by many corridors and downward flights of stairs into the soft rock beneath the palace. And he knew not whither his three slaves were taken, or what disposition was made of the captured crew of the galley. And soon he passed from the daylight into cavernous halls illumed by sulfur-colored flames in copper cressets; and all around him, in hidden chambers, he heard the sound of dismal moans and loud, maniacal howlings that seemed to beat and die upon adamantine doors.

In one of these halls, Fulbra and his guardsnen met a young girl, fairer and less sullen of aspect than the others; and Fulbra thought that the girl smiled upon him compassionately as he went by; and it seemed that she murmured faintly in the language of Yoros: "Take heart, King Fulbra, for there is one who would help you." And her words apparently, were not heeded or understood by the guards, who knew only the harsh and hissing tongue of Uccastrog.

After descending many stairs, they came to a ponderous door of bronze; and the door was unlocked by one of the guards, and Fulbra was compelled to enter; and the door clanged dolorously behind him. The chamber into which he had been thrust was walled on three sides with the dark stone of the island, and was walled on the fourth with heavy, unbreakable glass. Beyond the glass he saw the blue-green, glimnering waters of the undersea, lit by the hanging cressets of the chamber; and in the waters were great devil-fish whose tentacles writhed along the wall; and huge pythonomorphs with fabulous golden coils receding in the gloom; and the floating corpses of men that stared in upon him with eyeballs from which the lids had been excised.

There was a couch in one comer of the dungeon, close to the wall of glass; and food and drink had been supplied for Fulbra in vessels of wood. The king laid himself down, weary and hopeless, without tasting the food. Then, lying with close-shut eyes while the dead men and sea-monsters peered in upon him by the glare of the cressets, he strove to forget his griefs and the dolorous doom that impended. And through his clouding terror and sorrow, he seemed to see the comely face of the girl who had smiled upon him compassionately, and who, alone of all that he had met in Uccastrog, had spoken to him with words of kindness. The face returned ever and anon, with a soft haunting, a gentle sorcery; and Fulbra felt, for the first time in many suns, the dim stirring of his buried youth and the vague, obscure desire of life. So, after a while, he slept; and the face of the girl came still before him in his dreams.

The cressets burned above him with undiminished flames when he awakened; and the sea beyond the wall of glass was thronged with the same monsters as before, or with others of like kind. But amid the floating corpses he now beheld the flayed bodies of his own slaves, who, after being tortured by the island people, had been cast forth into the submarine cavern that adjoined his dungeon, so that he might see them on awakening.

He sickened with new horror at the sight; but even as he stared at the dead faces, the door of bronze swung open with a sullen grinding, and his guards entered. Seeing that he had not consumed the food and water provided for him, they forced him to eat and drink a little, menacing him with their broad, crooked blades till he complied. And then they led him from the dungeon and took him before King Ildrac, in the great hall of tortures.

Fulbra saw, by the level golden light through the palace windows and the long shadows of the columns and machines of torment, that the time was early dawn. The hall was crowded with the Torturers and their women; and many seemed to look on while others, of both sexes, busied themselves with ominous preparations. And Fulbra saw that a tall brazen statue, with cruel and demonian visage, like some implacable god of the underworld, was now standing at the right hand of Ildrac where he sat aloft on his brazen chair.

Fulbra was thrust forward by his guards, and Ildrac greeted him briefly, with a wily smile that preceded the words and lingered after them. And when Ildrac had spoken, the brazen image also began to speak, addressing Fulbra in the language of Yoros, with strident and metallic tones, and telling him with full and minute circumstance the various infernal tortures to which he was to be subjected on that day.

When the statue had done speaking, Fulbra heard a soft whisper in his ear, and saw beside him the fair girl whom he had previously met in the nether corridors. And the girl, seemingly unheeded by the Torturers, said to him: "Be courageous, and endure bravely all that is inflicted; for I shall effect your release before another day, if this be possible."

Fulbra was cheered by the girl's assurance; and it seemed to him that she was fairer to look upon than before; and he thought that her eyes regarded him tenderly; and the twin desires of love and life were strangely resurrected in his heart, to fortify him against the tortures of Ildrac.

Of that which was done to Fulbra for the wicked pleasure of King Ildrac and his people, it were not well to speak fully. For the islanders of Uccastrog had designed innumerable torments, curious and subtle, wherewith to harry and excruciate the five senses; and they could harry the brain itself, driving it to extremes more terrible than madness; and could take away the dearest treasures of memory and leave unutterable foulness in their place.

On that day, however, they did not torture Fulbra to the uttermost. But they racked his ears with cacophonous sounds; with evil flutes that chilled the blood and curdled it upon his heart; with deep drums that seemed to ache in all his tissues; and thin tabors that wrenched his very bones. Then they compelled him to breathe the mounting fumes of braziers wherein the dried gall of dragons and the adipocere of dead cannibals were burned together with a fetid wood. Then, when the fire had died down, they freshened it with the oil of vampire bats; and Fulbra swooned, unable to bear the fetor any longer.

Later, they stripped away his kingly vestments and fastened about his body a silken girdle that had been freshly dipt in an acid carrosive only to human flesh; and the acid ate slowly, fretting his skin with infinite pangs.

Then, after removing the girdle lest it slay him, the Torturers brought in certain creatures that had the shape of elllong serpents, but were covered from head to tail with sable hairs like those of a caterpillar. And these creatures twined themselves tightly about the arms and legs of Fulbra; and though he fought wildly in his revulsion, he could not loosen them with his hands; and the hairs that covered their constringent coils began to pierce his limbs like a million tiny needles, till he screamed with the agony. And when his breath failed him and he could scream no longer, the baby serpents were induced to relinquish their hold by a languorous piping of which the islanders knew the secret. They dropped away and left him; but the mark of their coils was imprinted redly about his limbs; and around his body there burned the raw branding of the girdle.

King Ildrac and his people looked on with a dreadful gloating; for in such things they took their joy, and strove to pacify an implacable obscure desire. But seeing now that Fulbra could endure no more, and wishing to wreak their will upon him for many future days, they took him back to his dungeon.

Lying sick with remembered horror, feverish with pain, he longed not for the clemency of death, but hoped for the coming of the girl to release him as she had promised. The long hours passed with a half-delirious tedium; and the cressets, whose flames had been changed to crimson, appeared to fill his eyes with flowing blood; and the dead men and the sea-monsters swam as if in blood beyond the wall of glass. And the girl came not; and Fulbra had begun to despair. Then, at last, he heard the door open gently and not with the harsh clangor that had proclaimed the entrance of his guards.

Turning, he saw the girl, who stole swiftly to his couch with a lifted fingertip, enjoining silence. She told him with soft whispers that her plan had failed; but surely on the following night she would be able to drug the guards and obtain the keys of the outer gates; and Fulbra could escape from the palace to a hidden cove in which a boat with water and provisions lay ready for his use. She prayed him to endure for another day the torments of Ildrac; and to this, perforce, he consented. And he thought that the girl loved him; for tenderly she caressed his feverous brow, and rubbed his torture-burning limbs with a soothing ointment. He deemed that her eyes were soft with a compassion that was more than pity. So Fulbra believed the girl and trusted her, and took heart against the horror of the coming day. Her name, it seemed, was Ilvaa; and her mother was a woman of Yoros who had married one of the evil islanders, choosing this repugnant union as an alternative to the flaying-knives of Ildrac.

Too soon the girl went away, pleading the great danger of discovery, and closed the door softly upon Fulbra. And after a while the king slept; and Ilvaa returned to him anid the delirious abominations of his dreams, and sustained him against the terror of strange hells.

At dawn the guards came with their hooked weapons, and led him again before Ildrac. And again the brazen, demoniac statue, in a strident voice, announced the fearful ordeals that he was to undergo. And this time he saw that other captives, including the crew and merchants of the galley, were also awaiting the malefic ministrations of the Torturers in the vast hall.

Once more in the throng of watchers the girl Ilvaa pressed close to him, unreprimanded by his guards, and murmured words of comfort; so that Fulbra was enheartened against the enormities foretold by the brazen oracular image. And indeed a bold and hopeful heart was required to endure the ordeals of that day…

Among other things less goodly to be mentioned, the Torturers held before Fulbra a mirror of strange wizardry, wherein his own face was reflected as if seen after death. The rigid features, as he gazed upon them, became marked with the green and bluish marbling of corruption; and the withering flesh fell in on the sharp bones, and displayed the visible fretting of the worm. Hearing meanwhile the dolorous groans and agonizing cries of his fellow captives all about the hall, he beheld other faces, dead, swollen, lidless, and flayed, that seemed to approach him from behind and to throng about his own face in the mirror. Their looks were dank and dripping, like the hair of corpses recovered from the sea; and sea-weed was mingled with the locks. Then, turning at a cold and clammy touch, he found that these faces were no illusion but the actual reflection of cadavers drawn from the under-sea by a malign sorcery, that had entered the hall of Ildrac like living men and were peering over his shoulder.

His own slaves, with flesh that the sea-things had gnawed even to the bone, were among them. And the slaves came toward him with glaring eyes that saw only the voidness of death. And beneath the sorcerous control of Ildrac, their evilly animated corpses began to assail Fulbra, clawing at his face and raiment with half-eaten fingers. And Fulbra, faint with loathing, struggled against his dead slaves, who knew not the voice of their master and were deaf as the wheels and racks of torment used by Ildrac...

Anon the drowned and dripping corpses went away; and Fulbra was stripped by the Torturers and was laid supine on the palace floor, with iron rings that bound him closely to the flags at knee and wrist, at elbow and ankle. Then they brought in the disinterred body of a woman, nearly eaten, in which a myriad maggots swarmed on the uncovered bones and tatters of dark corruption; and this body they placed on the right hand of Fulbra. And also they fetched the carrion of a black goat that was newly touched with beginning decay; and they laid it down beside him on the left hand. Then, across Fulbra, from right to left, the hungry maggots crawled in a long and undulant wave...

After the consummation of this torture, there came many others that were equally ingenious and atrocious, and were well designed for the delectation of King Ildrac and his people. And Fulbra endured the tortures valiantly, upheld by the thought of Ilvaa.

Vainly, however, on the night that followed this day, he waited in his dungeon for the girl. The cressets burned with a bloodier crimson; and new corpses were among the flayed and floating dead in the sea-cavern; and strange double-bodied serpents of the nether deep arose with an endless squirming; and their horned heads appeared to bloat immeasurably against the crystal wall. Yet the girl Ilvaa came not to free him as she had promised; and the night passed. But though despair resumed its old dominion in the heart of Fulbra, and terror came with talons steeped in fresh venom, he refused to doubt Ilvaa, telling himself that she had been delayed or prevented by some unforeseen mishap.

At dawn of the third day, he was again taken before Ildrac. The brazen image, announcing the ordeals of the day, told him that he was to be bound on a wheel of adamant; and, lying on the wheel, was to drink a drugged wine that would steal away his royal memories for ever, and would conduct his naked soul on a long pilgrimage through monstrous and infamous hells before bringing it back to the hall of Ildrac and the broken body on the wheel.

Then certain women of the Torturers, laughing obscenely, came forward and bound King Fulbra to the adamantine wheel with thongs of dragon-gut. And after they had done this, the girl Ilvaa, smiling with the shameless exultation of open cruelty, appeared before Fulbra and stood close beside him, holding a golden cup that contained the drugged wine. She mocked him for his folly and credulity in trusting her promises; and the other women and the male Torturers, even to Ildrac on his brazen seat, laughed loudly and evilly at Fulbra, and praised Ilvaa for the perfidy she had practised upon him.

So Fulbra's heart grew sick with a darker despair then any he had yet known, The brief, piteous love that had been born amid sorrow and agony perished within him, leaving but ashes steeped in gall. Yet, gazing at Ilvaa with sad eyes, he uttered no word of reproach. He wished to live no longer; and yearning for a swift death, he bethought him of the wizard ring of Vemdeez and of that which Vemdeez had said would follow its removal from his finger. He still wore the ring. which the Torturers had deemed a bauble of small value. But his hands were bound tightly to the wheel, and he could not remove it. So, with a bitter cunning, knowing full well that the islanders would not take away the ring if he should offer it to them, he feigned a sudden madness and cried wildly:

"Steal my memories, if ye will, with your accursed wine -and send me through a thousand hells and bring me back again to Uccastrog: but take not the ring that I wear on my middle finger; for it is more precious to me than many kingdoms or the pale breasts of love."

Hearing this, King Ildrac rose from his brazen seat; and bidding IIvaa to delay the administration of the wine, he came forward and inspected curiously the ring of Vemdeez, which gleamed darkly, set with its rayless gem, on Fulbra's finger. And all the while, Fulbra cried out against him in a frenzy, as if fearing that he would take the ring.

So Ildrac, deeming that he could plague the prisoner thereby and could heighten his suffering a little, did the very thing for which Fulbra had planned. And the ring came easily from the shrunken finger; and Ildrac, wishing to mock the royal captive, placed it on his own middle digit.

Then, while Ildrac regarded the captive with a more deeply graven smile of evil on the pale, gilded mask of his face, there came to King Fulbra of Yoros the dreadful and longed-for thing. The Silver Death, that had slept so long in his body beneath the magical abeyance of the ring of Vemdeez, was made manifest even as he hung on the adamantine wheel. His limbs stiffened with another rigor than that of agony; and his face shone brightly with the coming of the Death; and so he died.

Then, to Ilvaa and to many of the Torturers who stood wondering about the wheel, the chill and instant contagion of the Silver Death was communicated. They fell even where they had stood; and the pestilence remained like a glittering light on the faces and the hands of the men and shone forth from the nude bodies of the women. And the plague passed along the immense hall; and the other captives of King Ildrac were released thereby from their various torments; and the Torturers found surcease from the dire longing that they could assuage only through the pain of their fellowmen. And through all the palace, and throughout the Isle of Uccastrog, the Death flew swiftly, visible in those upon whom it had breathed, but otherwise unseen and inpalpable.

But Ilrac, wearing the ring of Vemdeez, was immune. And guessing not the reason for his immunity, he beheld with consternation the doom that had overtaken his followers, and watched in stupefaction the freeing of his victims. Then, fearful of some inimic sorcery, he rushed from the hall; and standing in the early sun on a palace-terrace above the sea, he tore the ring of Vemdeez from his finger and hurled it to the foamy billows far below, deeming in his terror that the ring was perhaps the source or agent of the unknown hostile magic.

So Ildrac, in his turn, when all the others had fallen, was smitten by the Silver Death; and its peace descended upon him where he lay in his robes of blood-brightened purple, with features shining palely to the unclouded sun. And oblivion claimed the Isle of Uccastrog; and the Torturers were one with the tortured.

Decimate

Kristal Stittle

DECIMATE. The current definition is to kill, destroy, or remove a large percentage of. It's pretty accurate. I rather like the historical definition, however. It meant to kill one in every ten as punishment for the whole group. It's not totally accurate for what's happened, but it feels more fitting. What's the word for killing nine in every ten as punishment for the whole group?

When I first learned the word decimate, it was part of a story. I can't recall which one now. All I remember is people being put into groups of ten, then having to pick one among them whom they would stone to death. I think they were soldiers? I can't be certain. I'm sure someone could look it up if they really wanted to know. Anyway, we were less brutal than that. I mean, a lot more people died, but it was necessary. Our methods, however, were kinder. No one had to choose and the deaths were quicker than stones.

I'd like to take a minute to point out how amazing it is that this happened. Is happening. I mean, every government of every country eventually agreed on this plan. Every single one! Never in history has the entire world agreed to do something, especially not something so drastic and devastating. People always imagined that we'd come together over something good, to unify as a peaceful collective. Well, I guess we all have something to share now.

Do you remember where you were when you were first told about 'the plan'? I was graduating university at the time. A bunch of us had gathered around a TV in a hallway, all dressed up in our caps and gowns, the ceremony put on hold. There was horror, and outrage, and shock. I felt nothing, of course. No one who ended up being given the job I was felt anything. Okay, maybe that's not entirely true. I'm sure there were a bunch of us who were happy. We saw the problem for what it was and were excited that something was finally being done about it. It's why we were picked.

We started with the poor. I think that's how they made it work. First the homeless and the deadbeats were brought in, the meth heads and the wastrels. These were the people society had stopped caring about. After them, we worked our way through the prison system. That was an interesting time. We'd get murderers and rapists, but we'd also get drunk drivers, some kid who'd been caught selling heroin, and even people I truly believed were innocent. Innocence didn't matter though.

It got rough for a lot of people as we moved up the ladder. Next came the poor who were trying: those who were desperately holding onto their homes, working multiple jobs in order to support their families. Families. Kids. I've had newborns in my chair. You don't feel anything for the geriatrics – they've lived a full life – but it's the little ones that even I felt something for. I mean, we're doing what we're doing to save the world for them, right? But no one was safe from the process. Everyone has to take their turn in the chair.

It was once we had climbed up into middle class that the paranoia truly set in. Who had been tested already? Who had already passed? A lot of people came in here and told me that there had been a mistake, that they had taken the test already. That they got to live. But of course, they wouldn't have ended up here if that were the case. We screen everyone for the tattoo. Those who actually passed, learned really early on not to tell anyone about it. Everyone's now branded like money, with invisible ink only the governments have access to. And only the machines can make the design for the tattoo: human hands aren't that precise. I'm sure there are plenty of people who tried to trick the system and just as many who failed. For once, we had built something perfect.

I'm sure a couple of people who had passed the test got rounded up a second time by accident, but after being kept in a room for a little while, they were released without ever having to see the chair again. I hear that some people came in a second time on purpose. That they had lied to a loved one about having already taken and passed the test, and then accompany them when that person has to come in. If the loved one passes, great, you both leave together, talking about how lucky you are. If not, well, then they never know you kept something from them.

It's when we started to go through the rich that we really hit problems. They had somehow convinced themselves that they were exempt. That they were the elite and couldn't be touched. I had one guy in here who said that he had just come in as a formality. That enough people had died already, that everyone left would be allowed to live. His corpse was thrown down the chute with the others. You know, that's one of the most ingenious things about the chairs? That the burning corpses of the dead help power them.

The rich were also a problem because they used their money as a shield. I mean that almost literally. They would build compounds and bunkers and hire small armies to defend themselves. The poor and the middle class would go into hiding. They would be clever. We know where the rich holdouts are, we just haven't dug them all out yet. But we will.

The military was done within a couple of days. The whole world did them all at once, as agreed upon. It was for the best that way. There was this whole air of secrecy about it too. Only the heads really knew what was going on when the troops were packed on buses. Some countries took advantage that day, getting their own armies done quickly so that the survivors could rush the emptied bases of foreign powers. Or maybe they had just secretly recruited a bunch of people who had already survived to do that. I didn't see the point, really. Once the heads were to be chopped off, any plans they had would go up in smoke with the corpses.

Most of the government employees, both the elected and the hired, that sat in my chair handled it quite well. They were pretty dignified about it, although I think that's because they assumed they would pass like the rich had thought. Or they had already lost so many loved ones that they didn't care. No one who masterminded the plan came through here though. I didn't get to meet any of them, so I don't know what they were like. This room has seen so many different emotions. All ranges and combinations. Body fluids too. The fact that the chair is self-cleaning is probably my personal favourite bit about it. I mean, it's neat that it's impossible to dismantle the pneumatic piston without also destroying the tattoo mechanism – all its defensive measures are actually rather impressive – but the self-cleaning.... Whoever decided on that was a genius.

Although I suppose from a psychological standpoint, creating my position was the most genius aspect. We, the liars. People come in thinking that they can do something to pass. They see me, calmly asking them questions about their lives while they sit strapped in the chair, a camera recording beside me while I take notes. It's all just to give them hope. I don't decide anything, and neither does anyone else. The computer makes all the calls, and the computer knows nothing about these people. It doesn't see age, race, gender, sexual orientation, job, health, bank account, none of it. Every person is just a number to the computer, and the computer doesn't prefer any numbers over any other numbers. The chair is simply Russian roulette with really bad odds. Everyone has only a one in ten chance of surviving, of receiving the tattoo instead of the rod to the brain. Even me.

The chair is more comfortable than I thought it would be. Unlike everyone else, I don't get to have hope. I don't get to be asked questions by a calm, indifferent face. There's just me and the camera. My last moments put to tape. Well, maybe my last moments. There's still that one, right? We the liars, the last people to sit in the chair. Besides the holdouts that is. Besides the runaways, and the entrenched. But most of the chairs aren't needed anymore. They'll be destroyed, and those of us in the facilities who survived will go on to run the last of them, until everyone in the world is either tattooed or dead.

You know, pregnant women were always the ones I found the most unfair. Even more than the newborns. At least they had gotten to breathe the air, right? Even if it's so polluted that it's barely breathable in most places. But of course, when a pregnant woman passes, their baby passes too. I don't know how that works. I don't know how they tattoo the infants. Maybe they don't. Maybe there's something injected into the mother's blood stream that somehow tags the baby, like an isotope or something. I've always been curious about it, but of course, questions outside your area of responsibility are deeply frowned upon.

I wonder what the world is like out there? A lot of jobs opened up, that's for certain. Whole families will have been wiped out. Orphanages must be packed, but then again, a lot of parents might be looking to replace their lost kids. I don't actually know. I haven't left this building since we started. That was part of the deal. I could watch some limited news, and of course I heard many stories from those brought to my chair, but I haven't seen any of it for myself. Are we succeeding? Once we adjust, will the world be a better place? I think about the future of history. We can either be written as monsters or as heroes. Maybe, once enough time has passed, we'll have been both. I wonder if—

Whose Waters Never Fail

Rebecca E. Treasure

I STOOD in the dim light of swinging propane lamps while the 'fugees beat Susanna to death.

I swayed with the light when a rock split her lips, and tried to forget how soft they'd been. If I let the memory show on my lips, the Elders would suspect I knew Susanna, too.

Biblically.

Of course, they'd say it was more Leviticus and the abomination of lying with a woman than the one flesh of Genesis. Then it would be me pelted by hate-propelled rocks.

Heather had been Cleansed the day before. Now it was Susanna's turn.

Sinners, they called them. *Deviants.* Wasting their precious uteruses on perverted sex. They were dirty, and they must be Cleansed.

Susanna didn't even cry. The dust on her face mixed with the seeping blood and turned to mush on her cheeks. The wounds drove her to her knees, but still, she just looked at the ground. She didn't seem to see the blood pool in her lap, or the bone exposed on her forearm where someone had scored a lucky hit with a chunk of concrete.

Then she wilted sideways and I lost sight of her as the 'fugees moved in.

I wouldn't be missed now, so I headed down to the shore to throw a few rocks of my own.

Sounds morbid, but when you hit water with a rock, the result is predictable. Cohesive circles ripple out from impact, each ridge a little lower until it disappears into the glass surface. Even waves have rhythm.

Hit a person with a rock, and you never know what they'll do.

My brother Shem was already there, skipping stones across the waves. When we were kids we had a pond, round and full of fish. Now the pond was gone, and the black and brown dog, and our parents. Yellowstone and the Ring of Fire took care of the rest of the world. Everything was gone except the dying planet and the barely living camps, the ash-clogged water and the ice, the Elders and the 'fugees.

Shem nodded at me when I sank onto the rocky shore next to him. He waited while I threw up. When I'd finished, he patted me on the shoulder.

"Looking forward to your Service?" He skipped a rock. "Seems like I just got back and you're leaving."

He'd been home a month, back from the long trip to Alaska to wrangle icebergs. Just long enough to drag the 'bergs onto shore where'd they'd melt into water fit for drinking. I should have asked about the ice, snow, and storms. About being away from camp and the Elders.

Anything but Susanna. So I said, "Susanna wanted to stay on the trawler, do permanent service."

The slapping of waves on the rocks filled my ears, sucking a bit of the shore and my puke out to the bay. Finally, Shem sighed. "She and Heather shouldn't have gotten caught." He reached out and tried to squeeze my hand.

I slid away. "She was doing her marital duty by Ted. You heard them, night after night." Couldn't avoid hearing, with their tent right next to ours. "She'd have had a baby soon enough."

"You know that doesn't matter to the Elders." He intoned like a sermon. "She sinned and must therefore be Cleansed."

I picked up a flat rock and heaved it into black water. A satisfying splash peaked over the other sounds, reminding me of the last time I had met Susanna at the shoreline for a little sinning. "They weren't hurting anyone."

Shem grabbed at my hand. I couldn't jerk away this time. His voice dropped, too soft to carry. "Don't think about it, Bethy. You've got the whole year ahead on your Service to do whatever you want. Nobody cares, on the boat."

"Why should I listen to you?" I snorted. "Just 'cause you finished your service? You couldn't even get a wife."

Shem let go of my hand. "I'll get one from your batch, next year."

I shuddered, thinking of the leftover boys from Shem's Service. They'd have first pick for wives in the Choosing next year. I wasn't pretty, but my teeth were straight and I had a good figure. I'd get picked early. Made me want to puke again. "Got anyone in mind?"

I knew he didn't, but I really didn't want to think about Susanna, about her blonde hair over her face, downturned toward the dirt, and how by the end it dripped red.

Shem shifted on the rocks and picked through them, looking for a good skipper. When he found one, he cocked his arm back and sent it sliding over the waves, skimming the top without getting dragged under. "Nah," he replied. "I'm not picky."

"Yeah," I said. "Me neither." I sent a rock chasing the path his had taken, but in the moonlight mine sank after a few feet. "Me neither."

* * *

Next morning, I pulled my Service jumpsuit over my regular clothes. It was warmer once I zipped the front up, even if the bright orange stood out a mile.

Shem, curled under threadbare grey blankets, spoke around slurps of watery porridge. "They'll have good coats on the ship," he said, almost jealous. "Thick gloves. Boots and hats, too."

"You told me."

"I've never been so cold, and I've been cold since Yellowstone."

It wasn't like Shem to repeat himself. "I'll be okay." I sat on the foot of his cot. "I'll volunteer for the latrines, like you said, and I'll keep my head down."

Shem nodded. "Captain Lamech likes volunteers. She gets sick of forcing servicers to do the hard jobs. Ice wrangling is deadly, freezing work. Latrines are—"

"I know, Shem."

He frowned. "Let me get dressed and I'll walk you down."

Crossing over the main path to get to the dock, I stumbled over the wide stream of red in the dirt and fought my heaving stomach. The Elders were watching. I didn't want them to send me to the infirmary. There was no coming back from there, not since the epidemics wiped out most of the doctors and medicines. So I stood, staring at Susanna's blood, and swallowed the rancid fear trying to escape.

"Got what she deserved, eh?" The raw voice shocked me into movement. I glanced behind me, to the Elder sitting on a camp stool rubbing her arthritic knuckles.

I nodded, not daring to open my mouth for fear of what might come out. Shem pulled on my orange sleeve.

"Thank you for your service," the old lady said. She smirked, showing a mouth devoid of teeth. "Enjoy your trip."

Shem led me through the mess in the path. I trudged along, too scared and sick to pick my feet up. I didn't want to end up like Susanna, but I couldn't see a way to avoid it any more than I could avoid memories of Susanna or her blood in the path.

Unless...

Unless I got myself attached to a boy right away on the ship and stayed with him the whole time. When we got back, the Captain would tell the Elders – it was true love – and they'd excuse us from the Choosing. It had happened before. I'd have some choice, some control. And they couldn't Cleanse me, not if I behaved even on Service.

So when we got to the docks, I scanned the boys.

I didn't know what I was looking for. Someone like Shem, maybe. Shem wouldn't beat his wife, when he got one, or force himself on her. He'd take care of her.

I met sharp eyes peering up from under a mop of curly black hair, eyes that reminded me of the way Shem was always watching. I smiled into them. The boy blinked, then smiled back.

I forced my way into line next to him. "Hi," I said, forcing my voice into higher registers. "I'm Bethany."

He glanced, looking me over. Not much to see. Couldn't even see my so-so figure under the thick layers. Just dirty blond hair and a too-red complexion.

He seemed to like what he saw because he straightened and said, "My name's Jordan. Been here long?" He jerked his head at the camp.

I kept my eyes on his. They sparkled like lamplight on dark water. "Sure. Since about a year after."

He pursed his lips. I tried to like the way they rounded into a perfect circle, but black stubble made it hard. "Long time. I just got here. You've been here the whole time?"

I nodded. "When they set up a camp here, my brother and I got bussed in. There was still gasoline, then."

He glanced down the pier. "Your parents?"

I shook my head and Jordan heaved a great sigh. He didn't say anything, though. I decided he'd do. Most people said something stupid about God or fate, or worse, asked questions. I had a collection of lies I told when they asked.

"Oh," I'd say to their pitying, pitiful, faces, "a group of cannibals caught us just outside a camp. The Elders just watched while they ate my parents."

Or my favorite, "We were camping in Yellowstone when it happened. Shem and I made it out, but lava got mom and dad." Their faces paled, thinking about being anywhere near the start.

The truth was so much worse, and so much more tedious. Starvation and sacrifice. Noble, but boring. So I lied.

Jordan shook himself. "Yeah, mine too. You looking forward to this?" He jerked his head at the ship.

I looked at the ice trawler. It was long, low in the water, with a tower in the middle that had once been painted green. Now it looked like a stout bronze lizard in the middle of a particularly itchy molt. The gray water slapped and churned against it. The ship crawled with railings and round windows; steam and wood smoke rose from the stack at the top.

"Sure," I said. "My brother Shem went last year. Said the food was good." I tried for a girlish grin. "And no Elders."

Jordan smiled. "All the way to Alaska and back. They say the whole ocean is frozen over once you get past Cali, and the polar bears can climb right into the boat."

I nodded. "I think that's just supposed to scare us." Jordan looked scared, so I continued. "Shem said, volunteer for latrine duty. It's gross, but it keeps you inside."

Jordan nodded, blinking. "Bethany, right?"

I started to answer but saw *her* and trailed off. She was short, close-cut hair so dark it glistened in the frosty air. And chubby. Only gruel and potatoes to eat, and the occasional military meal or canned fruit or vegetable from the aid boxes. She worked hard at that body. She met my eyes and arched a sparkle-black eyebrow. A hot pulse spread into my hips from deep in my abdomen. How had I missed her in the camp?

Jordan cleared his throat and I remembered I was trying to stay alive. I pulled my eyes from the girl. "Yeah, Bethany. My brother calls me Bethy."

Jordan smiled. "Bethy. I like that." He gave me a lingering kind of look. I forced myself to hold his gaze. *This is good. Safe.* So, instead of glancing at the girl with dark hair, at her body straining at the seams of the orange jumpsuit, I returned his look.

I stuck with Jordan as we filed into the ship, got a tour of the tower section. His hand shot up moments after mine when Captain Lamech asked for latrine volunteers, and it looked like I'd done it. A match made in a metal privy, done up with a toilet paper bow.

Then my eyes found her, drawn like water down a drain, at the end of the row.

Her hand was up.

So instead of my safe romance, I found myself playing eyeball tug-of-war between what I needed to save my stupid skin and what I wanted, knowing full well that what I wanted would get me killed.

And what I wanted was Martha. The name suited her, a chewy mouthful. Martha didn't say much. I liked that, too. She slept in the bunk over mine and smelled like sweat and salt. I leaned into her when she spoke to catch a taste. She was a pool of deep crystal water I longed to dive into.

Jordan liked her, too, and we fell into a routine, with me in the middle like a magnet in a manic spin. After the camps with their blue boxes of vile slop and the Elders who seemed to take on the smell of not-quite sterilized feces like an odorous perfume, we got used to the smell. In between scrubbings, I worked hard at seducing Jordan. I sat next to him at meals, asked him about his before and after, lingered with him in the passageways.

But I thought about Martha. She ate with focused energy, tearing into the rich food with her wide, uneven teeth. Her before had been a lot like mine, a suburb and a family. After Yellowstone, she'd gotten to an army base. She'd missed out on a lot of the worst stuff, when the Pacific volcanoes all went at once and the sun went out. Her parents were still around, even. They moved from camp to camp, drifting south, trying to find someplace warm, a place they could call home.

"I don't believe in home," she said one night. The wind hissed outside the windows, pushing us north. We were at dinner, reveling in the sinful meatloaf and tomatoes with actual breading, and pudding for dessert. Freezer-burned and shared, it still beat out boiled potatoes.

"Why not?" I spilled some chocolate pudding on my chin watching her mouth move.

She smiled, watching me try to lick it off. "Home is what was. Home is safe. Predictable." She looked out to the white sky and black sea. "We'll never have that again."

I nodded, entranced.

Jordan sniffed. "You missed some, Bethy." He handed me a napkin. "Things will get better. They're trying to negotiate with Mexico, other nations with land that survived the Ring of Fire, to let us come south."

I shook my head. "We didn't want them – why would they want us?"

He shrugged and took a bite of pudding. Around it, he said, "Who wouldn't want me?"

Martha and I laughed, her giggle sounding as forced as mine felt.

That night Jordan and I had our first kiss. It was scratchy and made my stomach twist. I leaned into it, my hands gripping bony shoulders.

After a few moist moments, he pulled back. "What's wrong?"

A flash of panic chilled my face. "Nothing." I leaned in, but he shook his head.

"You're like a robot."

I tried to play it off. "I've never kissed anyone before."

He shook his head. "No, that's not it." He tilted his head. "It's Martha, isn't it?"

I froze like the ice we'd been sent to collect. "No."

He looked me over, sadness splashing into his eyes. "I understand why, but I can't pretend like that. Even with the world," he half-smiled, "I want the real thing."

So do I. But they'll kill me. "Don't—"

"I won't." He patted me on the shoulder. "Promise." He walked away.

I leaned against the bulkhead, hands clasped over my head, fighting waves of nausea. Instead of the cold hallway, I saw Susanna – in the dark in my tent, laughing on the beach in the moonlight, bleeding at the Cleansing. What would I do now?

I shuffled back to my bunk, shivering. Martha propped her head up.

"What's wrong, Bethy?"

I shook my head. "Doesn't matter."

"You and Jordan have a fight?"

A fight. So normal. Safe. Predictable. "Yes."

"He likes you, it'll be okay." She sounded sad, in the dark. All I could see was her head, rocking back and forth with the steady progress of the ship, and the black outline of the bunk against the distant passageway light.

"I don't think so." I pulled my jumpsuit off. "It's cold tonight."

"Do you want to climb in with me? It'll be warmer." I could barely hear her.

The back of my mind buzzed in warning, but I flipped my blankets back into place and nodded in the dark.

She was as soft as she looked, and the waves of heat coming from her washed away my fears and doubts, and before I knew it, we were kissing, but it wasn't like with Jordan, it was fast and smooth and when I fell asleep I wasn't worried about anything except not disturbing her perfect head on my arm.

The next day I went to Captain Lamech to volunteer for ice wrangling.

Martha would get me killed if I stayed on latrines. Worse, I'd get her killed. I'd never be able to stay away from her if I didn't start now.

The captain offered me a cup of coffee before settling behind her desk. Her eyes seemed warm, which was weird considering she spent most of her life in Arctic waters chasing icebergs. "You want to volunteer?" She peered at me over her enormous oak desk, bolted to the floor and scattered with maps.

I held her gaze. "I am tired of toilets. And ice wrangling is important. Fresh water."

She nodded, but her gaze didn't waver and little lines appeared over her eyebrows. "Sure. But why volunteer?"

I looked into the coffee, watching it slosh up and down the side of the blue and white metal cup. *Be predictable.* "Like I said, I'm sick of cleaning latrines."

She frowned and the lines on her forehead deepened. "I'm not sure you're up to it, frankly."

I couldn't shake the feeling that she knew, somehow, and wanted me to admit it. Well, I wouldn't. "I can handle it."

She raised an eyebrow, disrupting the level lines. "Wrangling is dangerous work. No guarantee. You fall in the water, you're dead."

"I know. My brother Shem told me."

"You're Shem's sister?" Somehow, that convinced her. She nodded. "Alright. Gretchen has been wailing about the weather nonstop. You can take her place."

I drained my coffee in one gulp and thanked the Captain.

She shook her head, not quite laughing. "You'll regret it soon enough."

I did. I lost feeling in my face and hands, and probably my feet, but I couldn't tell inside the three pairs of socks and huge steel-toed boots with nails on the bottom. The numbness crept up my arms and legs, reaching my hips and shoulders, stabbing at my body with icy fingertips. I thought of Susanna, of Shem losing me on top of everything else, and of Martha, and bent to the work.

Hammering pylons into the ice, fighting slushy water to get the heavy tarp around the 'berg, wrenching the ropes against the waves and the ice and the other boat. It took about four hours to harness one of the boulder-sized chunks of ice. When we'd get it into line with the others, we earned two hours downtime before going out and doing it all over again. Twice a day, every day.

The downtime was worse. Martha gave up trying to talk to me after the first day. I just walked away as fast as I could. Didn't she understand I was saving our lives? Instead, she just hovered nearby, staring at me. Jordan and my replacement, Gretchen, had no problems kissing. I was glad. Gretchen would make lots of red-blooded babies.

Then one day Martha showed up on my crew.

"What are you doing here?"

She shrugged and shivered. "Volunteered. If you could, I figured I could talk Captain Lamech into it." Martha glared at me. "You can't avoid me out here, Bethy."

I turned away, collecting pylons. The helmsman steered parallel with the other boat toward a little 'berg bobbing in the grey water. Martha slid next to me on the bench and picked up a coiled rope. I tried to ignore her. Might as well have tried to ignore the wind cutting into my exposed eyelids or the daggers of salt spray hitting my jacket.

"I just want to be with you. Before it's impossible."

"You should have stayed on latrines."

I think she nodded, but it might have been the boat rocking. Then we went to work with our mallets and pylons, the ropes and the tarps. Martha couldn't grip the pylons through the gloves, and kept dropping them when the waves shifted. The tarps flapped in the wind, the crinkling blue material slapping her in the face. Watching Martha struggling with the knots and the folds in the tarps I had the unfamiliar thought that wrangling was something I was good at.

Then Martha held onto a pylon for too long, determined to drive it into the 'berg. The ice rolled and dragged her into the water.

I dove before her legs left the boat, reaching out. My fingers met the nails on the bottoms of her boots instead of her ankles. The steel tips sliced through my gloves. I ignored the pain, plunging my hands into the water.

One of the other servicers pushed in beside me, shouting.

I couldn't understand where she'd gone, how she could have sunk so fast. The helmsman yanked me back, hollering something and shaking me. It took a few moments for his voice to cut through my panic and the wind. I fought him, trying to get to Martha.

"She's dead! Let her go."

Her hand appeared, clutching at the pylon as the ice bobbed back up out of the water. I shoved him so hard he almost fell in and threw myself toward Martha's hand. I grasped it, clamping down. The other servicer helped me drag her into the boat. She shook like an earthquake when the caldera blew, and her breath came in stuttering jumps.

The helmsman scowled but signalled the ship. After we got Martha up in a sling, the helmsman insisted I go up to the infirmary because of my hand. It didn't hurt, but it meant I could go with Martha, so I went.

I hesitated at the infirmary door. The white lights and smell of bleach reminded me of stiff bodies and empty cries. The doctor stripped Martha out of her coat and boots with precise hands. It looked like he might actually know how to save her.

I helped him cover her with cool towels, then warm ones. He rested her swollen hands and feet in heated water – only servicers warranted such luxury. When she fell asleep, I let him look at my hand. The cuts weren't deep and the ice water had stopped the bleeding.

"You can go."

"Can I stay with her? Our shift is done. We're friends."

He shrugged and turned away.

Some time later, she stirred and whimpered. She wasn't really awake, so I snuggled closer, smoothing her hair. I told her about way back, about how I'd wanted to be a DJ because my mom listened to pop music while she cleaned. I told her about Shem, how he'd been good at soccer. I even told her about after, when the dog had to be killed because he wouldn't stop barking, and how mom and dad just got thinner and thinner but Shem and I had food to eat, and then mom and dad…

I woke up the next day and Martha was alive. Color tinted her cheeks and a faint waft of sweat surrounded her.

That's as good as love gets, sometimes.

I pulled on my boots and gloves, and went back to wrangling. Between shifts I'd sit with Martha, all through the long winter and the slow crawl back down the coast. Our icebergs trailed behind us in the water like tarp-covered ducklings.

When we were a day or so out from camp, I went to see Captain Lamech again.

"I'd like to do permanent service," I said.

She steepled her fingers. "Tell me why."

This time, she wouldn't accept any dancing around the 'bergs. "There's nothing for me in the camps. I'd get Cleansed before your next service batch got on board anyway. I did the work."

Captain Lamech nodded. "You did. Move your things to the permanent crew bunks when we dock." She pointed at me. "Leave Martha out of it, though. That's over."

Martha was sitting up when I stepped into the infirmary. Her gauze bandages had come off a few days before. She'd lost good control of her hands, and her face bore angry scars, but she could walk and she would live. She smiled when I came in. I forced the deep pulse aside.

I spilled my guts before I could talk myself out of it. "I'm staying on the ship, doing permanent service."

Martha smiled, but her eyes were sad. "I'm glad for you, Bethy."

I settled on the bed next to her and squeezed her hand. We sat like that for a long time, just holding hands. The Choosing would happen the night we got back. Martha would be lost forever to the future the Elders imagined. Rebuilding the great dream, trying to regain a sense of predictability and safety in a chaotic, dangerous world.

* * *

Shem stood at the foot of the gangplank, waving with a wide overhead sweep like a flag of truce.

Or maybe, "Charge!" Other families pressed up to the edge of the dock over the black acid water. They formed a wave of their own, surging against one another in human unpredictability.

Martha walked past him. So did Jordan and Gretchen, clinging to one another in a way that left no doubt in anyone's mind as to their intentions. Shem peered at each orange-clad servicer as they passed, and from the sheltered place on deck I watched fear rise in his face.

When all the servicers were off, his shoulders slammed down with the weight of loss and familiar, new, grief. Another family stood behind him. A girl named Sara had gotten sick in Alaska and never recovered. They turned away but Shem stayed, watching the water.

He was still there when the permanent crew disembarked. I stopped next to him, wearing my grey jumpsuit and fur-lined coat. I counted three surges of waves slapping against the dock before his eyes met mine.

"Oh," Shem gasped. His face rebuilt itself from the chin up. "I should have known."

"I didn't mind the cold so much." I grinned. "And like you said, the food is good."

We fell against each other, hugging and slapping to share feelings we had no words for.

When we pulled apart, I patted his shoulder. "Follow me."

Martha had paused at the end of the dock, facing the assembled Elders and 'fugees cheering the return of life-giving water and servicers. She didn't want to take that last step from the unsteady dock to the still ground beyond. I stopped Shem and stepped around her, turning to look at her soft, scarred face.

Tears blossomed and dripped down her cheeks. I swallowed the lump in my throat. After all, if I couldn't have her, knowing she would marry the best man I knew would be better than nothing. Good, even. He'd understand. They'd have each other, and I'd have the water.

I looked into her eyes, smiling. "I'd like you to meet my brother."

Two Worlds

Francesco Verso

Translation by Sally McCorry

FROM THE repaired chronicles of Kilimanjaro.

Aruna turned to say good-bye to her parents, opened her arms and lifted them to free the plumage. She stretched out her neck and breathed in deeply. Her torso was ample, well suited to supporting her for a long time.

She was about to take-off from the shelter of the Solar Tree, three metres outside the Shining Corolla. In a line behind her were the faces of many friends, tense, nervous and distressingly thin. The song of the Aeromancers, arranged in a semicircle for the Ceremony of the Flight, could be so hypnotic as to make you believe anything.

The horizon that called her to maturity flattened into an opaque strip, infested with clouds of ammonia. Below her a 15,000 metre drop plunged down to the mass of the Global Ocean. Old Canderum of the Purple Feathers finished explaining the goal of the Flight for the thousandth time, then solemn and haggard approached Aruna. He bowed his beak in a gesture of good luck, and stopped singing. With a gentle push to the back of her neck, he cast Aruna into the emptiness.

"Fly, Aruna! Fly towards hope!"

Canderum's shout announced Aruna's eighteenth birthday, when for the first time she would leave without having a precise destination. The young woman dropped, together with another fifteen companions from the Solar Tree Major and perhaps none of them would ever return. Like everyone else who, year after year, had participated in the Ceremony.

Aruna closed her eyes, folded back her wings to gain speed and let the ascending currents take her westward. Going back empty handed would be a terrible dishonour.

Mnemonic relic 1.34.67 (source uncertain).

Not even the supercomputers had been able to predict that the hybrid genes would react so quickly and fill so many ecological niches. A number of sequences were defeated in a competition rendered ruthless by human alteration and an evolutional process millions of years long. Other sequences, a tough minority, took advantage of this situation to adapt, and incidentally, evolve into forms of life that from then onwards, populated the Modified Earth.

The "human race" in the form it presented before the Second Ecopoiesis, no longer existed. In their place, there were two races whose DNA shared 99.96% of their genes with the human race, but no longer walked the Earth. Because they had not discovered intergalactic flight in time to populate new worlds, human beings had discovered a way to bend the barrier of time and conserve their lives for centuries.

When the human genome was decoded in the Second Millennium, scientists were surprised to find that it consisted of a mere thirty-five thousand genes. So they enriched that sequence with a number of additional codes providing highly desirable qualities: qualities useful for adaptation and survival, values commonly found in species other than the human one.

Chimeric experimentation was the beginning of the end, when everything was mixed up together. The cancellation of the 2005 "Human Chimera Prohibition Act" was approved in accordance with the principle that human dignity should be applied exclusively to the individual and not generally to the whole species.

Even before Chimerism, it was common practice to exchange human cells with animal cells: cows secreted human proteins in their milk and sheep were the recipients of human liver and heart transplants. Vice-versa, many human beings possessed cardiac valves derived from pig and bovine hearts. Still, the phenomenon that followed chromosomic liberation – known as Genetic Confusion – was also the basis of *our* salvation.

It was demonstrated that there were no true genetic barriers between the different species, and the proof was that the human genome code clearly showed the presence of a genetic continuity between all the *animate beings.*

The high containment walls that had kept species separate for millennia crumbled within a few decades.

The Aeromancers learned to fly and oxygenate their blood better, enabling them to settle on the arid mountain tops. The Aquamancers became glabrous, acquired from fish the techniques of obtaining oxygen from water, and populated the seas.

This reconstruction is the result of a research study into how to ensure the survival of *animate beings.*

From the repaired chronicles of Saxayé.

On the twelfth day of nonstop flying over the Global Ocean, Aruna let herself fall, skimming over the surface of the sea. Exhausted, she succumbed to weariness.

Her worn out body, dehydrated and close to death, was intercepted a few hours later by a reconnaissance patrol who had never seen an Aeromancer before, except in films at school.

Drawn to the surface by a shadow, Karia, Coorny and Tsai Chin, moved closer to the creature with feathered arms and a beak instead of a mouth: the shape was of an *animate* like they were, even though there were differences, like the nails on her hands and feet, more like talons than their webbed fingers and toes.

The wings, folded behind her arms like drapes, were a rainbow of green, yellow and red stripes, dirtied with dust and dulled by marine contamination.

Karia sniffed the stranger, and turned to Tsai Chin, the patrol's leader.

"Should we take her down?"

"It could be risky."

The youth's narwhal like face looked worried. Although quick to act, Tsai Chin thought carefully about every decision.

"But she's dying!"

The girl's beak was withered and blackened. In some points, it shone like mercury.

Little Coorny looked towards the horizon and grimaced. Not only was there a storm coming that would generate fire twisters, but his nose could detect the stink of an enemy approaching.

"Quick.... That *orcark* knows exactly what to do with her."

Hearing their conversation, the girl regained consciousness and opened her beak.

"The Tower.... Do you know where...? I have to..."

Then she was quiet, overcome by exhaustion.

A big bubble of hydrogen from below reached the group and took them a few metres higher. Karia grabbed hold of the girl.

"She's raving, maybe she's ill."

Tsai Chin's prudence had made him head of the team even though he was so young.

Karia, on the other hand, was naturally curious. Her webbed fingers were expert in investigating coralline encrustations and fields of kelp. She loved the spores, microbes, and even the viruses. Life under water was prolific, and she had fun riding rays, flying on the back of mantas, and drawing with the cuttlefish and octopuses.

Tsai Chin blinked his nictitating membranes uncertainly. Then the air valve in his neck vented vigorously; Karia smiled.

"All right.... Your father will decide her fate."

Coorny took a breathing kit out of his pouch. After uncurling the tube, he placed the mouthpiece on the girl's beak and the oxygenating bands behind her shoulders. The bands' tiny fissures, acting as artificial gills, would allow the outsider to breathe underwater.

The orcark approached with its comic movements: its head rocking drunkenly. It was its hunger that made it look so ridiculous.

The patrol formed a diamond: Tsai Chin in front, Karia and Coorny on each side, and the outsider last, towed by her arms. They dived quickly, heading towards Saxayé: their underwater bubble.

The orcark, its mouth hanging open expecting to feed, missed its prey and resigned itself to going hungry yet again.

Mnemonic relic 2.98.36 (source Underwater Architecture Project).

The entrances to Saxayé were dug in the sand and its tunnels stretched across the seabed for several kilometres. Air was pumped into the corridors and the domes through porous walls made of osmotic membranes that absorbed oxygen from the sea water, releasing bubbles of carbon dioxide in the process.

Saxayé was situated close to two hydrothermal vents surrounded by prolific colonies tube worms, bivalves, and an abundance of prawns and mussels.

It was a complete ecosystem based not on photosynthesis, but chemosynthesis. The hydrothermal vents were the ocean's alternative to the old power stations. The springs also served to purify the salt water. As the water penetrated the Earth's crust, it lost minerals, was cleaned, and released back into circulation by thousands of steaming vents. It was an incredibly slow process, but the Aquamancers were in no hurry, they preferred efficiency to imbalance.

References were found in distributed memories of supercomputers to a few populations on the east coast, who mindful of time spent underground during the war, had installed these structures as dormitories for immigrant labour.

What for the Aquamancers turned out simple to get up and running again, having access to technology they had found surviving in watertight depots and laboratories, turned out to be disastrous for the Aeromancers. They had had to find shelter in the few Solar Trees left standing, surviving on inaccessible semi-desert terrain which had resisted the rising levels of the Global Ocean. Forced to live on land as hard as rock, their population had remained stable for centuries. This meant though that any chance or unforeseen event could easily compromise their survival.

Growing food crops was only possible at a certain altitude to make the most of the weak solar heat: cassava, sweet corn, beans, squash, and potatoes could be harvested up to an altitude of 3,600 metres. Between 3,600 and 5,000 metres, only potatoes would grow. Beyond that, every plant, even though modified by ancient biotechnology, stopped yielding any fruit.

According to local myths, the Little Ice Age had lasted for about 500 years, an exceptional phenomenon that had occurred at least another twice. Yet, according to the same legends, when the climate stabilised again, the tundra would recede, the parting waters would uncover fertile lands, and the Aeromancers would be able to come down from their heights; the heaths would flower again and their Solar Trees would prosper once more.

They had been waiting for this moment for centuries.

From the repaired chronicles of Saxayé.

Karia entered the med-lab pushing the gurney.

"Dad, we found this girl floating in the Ocean."

The stout shape of Iguain Celcantoss turned towards his daughter, then towards Aruna. She had regained consciousness, but she still couldn't make her talons clasp.

"An Aeromancer? And the rest of the flight? What was she doing in the sea?"

Iguain picked up a device and ran it over the girl's body. He stopped at her shoulders, where the inflammation was visible.

"There wasn't anybody else. She mentioned a Tower … She said she had to find it."

He turned to the Aeromancer. For centuries the inhabitants of Modified Earth had been using the oceanic language which had become the repository of idioms from before the Second Ecopoiesis.

"What's your name?"

She tried to grab his arm. At the sight of her talons, Iguain dodged out of the way and the young woman's hand dropped. The bone structure of her arms was elongated, especially near the hands where the metacarpals and phalanges were twice as long as those of an Aquamancer.

"Aruna Dalkey, of the Aeromancers of Kilimanjaro."

Iguains's cutaneous crests suggested he was smiling.

"You are not in danger.… You're just very tired. How did you manage to get this far? We're eleven days travel from the nearest coast."

"Eight days…flying."

He opened his eye membranes wide, exposing aquamarine irises. He was honestly surprised, as if Aruna had said something nonsensical. His surprise though owed as much to seeing an Aeromancer after such a long time; the floating bodies they sighted always ended up as food for the orcarks if the fire twisters didn't reduce them to shreds first.

"Where am I? And who are you?"

"Welcome to Saxayé, the capital of the Aquamancers. My name is Iguain Celcantoss and this is my daughter Karia."

"Saxayé? Never heard of it… But thank you for all you have done. Now I must continue with my journey."

"In your condition, you wouldn't beat your arms for a minute. It's better if you build up your strength before taking off again."

As soon as he turned away, Aruna burst into tears.

"You don't understand.… My people are dying. Only the Tower can save us."

"Calm down. Tell me about this Tower. Why are you looking for it? And why is it so important?"

The Aquamancers, as far as airborne reconnaissance had shown, were peaceful people. Aruna needed to trust someone and Karia had saved her life. That had to be a good sign.

The Aeromancer told them everything about the threat hanging over all of them, and hoped she wouldn't live to regret it.

Mnemonic relic 3.11.67 (source uncertain).

At the beginning of the third Millennium, on Spitsbergen, an island in the Svalbard archipelago, a building was erected, known to the future generations as the Tower of Seeds. Inside, thousands of samples of different varieties of seeds were stored in the hope that one day they would be able to survive an accident or natural catastrophe.

Following the Second Ecopoiesis, the island sank beneath the Global Ocean and from then on no-one heard about it. Despite this, the vault's construction and the care taken over its security led many Aeromancers to believe that if they could find the Tower, they would still be able to use the seeds.

According to various mnemonic fragments, the Tower, powered by a thermopile, consisted of three rooms located at the top of a 125 metre long tunnel. The seeds were kept at -20 degrees Celsius and sealed in specially designed containers of aluminium.

The low temperature and humidity levels in the Tower would limit the metabolic activity of the seeds and keep them integral. Preserved correctly, they could last for millennia.

From the repaired chronicles of Saxayé.

Aruna and Iguain meeting had unhoped-for consequences, the most important of which was their audience with the Council of Saxayé.

President Yecené Urus, in his uniform, a fluorescent overall with an opening on the back for his dorsal fin, had listened in silence to the words of the outsider.

"If I have understood correctly, you are saying that the existence of the Global Ocean is under threat?"

Aruna was standing in front of the assembly. Her plumage had regained the vigour of her genetic line, and shone with a myriad of colours. She found Iguain's presence by her side reassuring. The medic, for some reason, had believed her and seemed happy to help her.

Together, they had spent hours sifting through the mnemonic relics, hunting for information about the location of the Tower. The Aquamancers' network was not extensive, and lots of scouts explored the submerged ruins to hook up to old databases.

The fact that she might be the only survivor of that year's mission kept a flame of optimism alight in Aruna. She and her companions had left the Nest without knowing what to do, nor how to proceed if they had succeeded in finding the Tower.

Their flight was more a test of faith than of hope.

"Yes, the disappearance of humanity caused the evaporation of the coolant reservoirs of about 870 nuclear power stations and the meltdown of their reactors. The clouds that continued to form for decades afterwards turned out to be more of a problem than the radioactive material. 500 billion tons of methane deposits were released as the layers of ice they were trapped in melted. All that gas accelerated global warming to levels that had been unheard of since the end of the Permian period."

"This data is known to us. There are no boundaries between the ecosystems. The Global Ocean was the origin of everything that breathes and reproduces, and it seems that it is also their future. We see no threats on the horizon."

The round head of president Urus nodded up and down. The members of the assembly approved.

"Permit me to disagree."

If the Tower existed, and the Aquamancers could be convinced of the danger, maybe they would be able to help her.

"Have you ever left the sea? Have you ever analysed the situation of the Risen Lands?"

Some members of the assembly gasped, others vented their air valves, whispering to each other. Who did this outsider think she was to throw around accusations; how dare she seed amongst them doubt and fear about what the future might bring.

"Are you referring to the lands where *you* have made your nests?"

"Yes, before the Second Ecopoiesis, the lakes and the river deltas were suffocated by weeds and fertilisers. Our ancestors witnessed everything from above. When the algae collapsed from the lack of oxygen, their decomposition intensified the process. The lagoons, once crystal clear, became great expanses of sulphureous sludge; the river estuaries spread for hundreds of kilometres in unending dead zones. The plants and animals survived according to their tolerance to UV rays, or mutated beneath a bombardment of electromagnetic radiation."

Aruna's beak beat the words out with force. The Aquamancers kept listening.

"When the worst happened, life went on. It went on regardless, even though the parameters had changed. We, the *animate* races, are the result. Now though, the threat still hangs over us because there are no trees left to defend us."

"What have the trees got to do with the disappearance of the Ocean?"

"Like I said, our ancestors, on their first flights, saw everything from above. Their genetic memory preserved the memories of those events in the chemical composition of our plumage. If you don't believe my words, check the analyses against the fossils of the birds from the First Ecopoiesis."

Aruna turned to Iguain who lifted a translucent plate. They had come prepared, knowing that the Council would insist that they look at the matter in a rational manner.

"All right, continue.... We want to know about the trees."

"The disappearance of the trees together with heavy use of engineered seaweed to produce fuel hydrogen, once the fossil fuels ran out, caused the Earth's temperature to increase, and in consequence the level of the Ocean to rise. There is a limit beyond which the biosphere ceases to provide protection from the effects of these processes, and starts to magnify them instead. The only way we can save the Earth is by replanting trees. The clouds will give us water once more, and the Sun will heat and produce vapour from the watery mass of the ocean. In this way, the Global Ocean can be made to recede and the Risen Lands become fertile again. With the seeds, we'll have seasons again. Do you know what seasons are?"

The Aquamancers remained unmoved, like when the explanation about the mysteries of the universe, and the sheer size of the phenomena exceeds the mental capacity.

Aruna hoped she had managed to get the message across.

From the repaired chronicles of Saxayé.

At dawn of the following day, a squad left Saxayé heading northeast, towards the banks of Bioluminescent Plankton. Iguain had taken the place of young Coorny, while Tsai Chin had been moved down the squad's formation to Karia's side.

Aruna, unsuited to swimming, was transported in a capsule.

Their destination was a point near the North Pole. According to the mnemonic relics, this was a plausible position for the location of the Tower.

Iguain had managed to convince the Council to grant him permission to accompany the outsider, verify the entity of the threat, and "take possession" of the seeds. The risk that the legend might be true, must be taken seriously. Still, Iguain was not sure what meaning to attribute to the expression "take possession". He had a plan too, but of a completely different kind.

In the past, he had heard rumours about the Tower, but that information had been forgotten, until Aruna's story had brought it back and reactivated it.

Near Miami, the squad came across thousands of eels like silver ribbons, up to five metres long, swarming thanks to rudimentary fins and pointed snouts.

When they dived into the deeps, they saw the trail of pilings that had once held up a human civilisation's motorway. Following these, they reached a merchant ship resting on the seabed. Its corroded iron hulk fed a prolific mass of multicoloured seaweed. All around the wrecked ship, amidst statues covered with anemones, spores and starfish, spread a ten centimetre thick carpet of red seaweed. They decided to set-up their bubble and stop to rest.

Mnemonic relic 4 – (source: Wikipedia fragment).

Whoever wants to access the Tower must get passed four doors: the entrance, a second door in the tunnel, and a further two airtight doors.

Movement sensors are present all around the site. A work of art makes the vault visible from many kilometres away. The roof and entrance are covered with highly reflective mirrors and prisms designed by the artist Dyveke Sanne. This installation acts as a signal by reflecting the polar light in the summer months, whereas in the winter a network of 200 fibre optic cables illuminate the site with a colour changing light, varying from turquoise-green to white.

From the repaired chronicles of Saxayé.

On the seventh day of journey, beyond the Krill Fields, Aruna saw what must have been the beginnings of the fjords. Half hidden by teeming underwater life, she saw an encouraging sight. The images in the mnemonic relics that Iguain had shown her matched those from her childhood. Drawings and paintings that portrayed the Tower decorated the walls of the Aeromancer Academy and the Solar Tree Major.

Her people's dilemma consisted of having to make the terrible choice between sending its children out in search of the Tower, or hoping that it was all a lie, in other words the choice was between weakening the Nest or else seeing it destroyed within a few generations.

As old Canderum had explained, the decision to continue with the Ceremony of Flight was linked to the fact that legends needed to be valued according to their capacity to generate "morale" in those who stayed behind, rather than on the basis of their truth.

Because of the Flight, the life expectancy of the Aeromancers was shorter than that of their ancestors, though they had overcome this disadvantage by becoming sexually mature at an earlier age. They generally reproduced during puberty so the population had not shrunk as much as the elders had foreseen. The strongest individuals were excused from procreation, because of the risk they were to run. Candrum was known for saying "Better to raise heroes than orphans."

However, it was also plausible that the Second Ecopoiesis was hurrying along their natural selection, increasing the probability that new generations would be born with a greater tolerance of radiation. The Aeromancers knew that they were a transgenic form of life, which had evolved to face an extreme and continually mutating environment. A mutation that was guarded inside the Tower now before Aruna.

The squad was moving forward holding its formation when Tsai Chin realised that below them an intertwined mass of plants was rising rapidly. It was an enormous macrocyst of kelp.

Iguain motioned the group to move swiftly.

"Swim up!" was the sign he made to Tsai Chin, who vented his air valve as hard as possibile.

"No, we'll waste time."

Tsai Chin pushed the capsule with Aruna in to the head of the group to help the three Aquamancers push their way through the columns of seaweed.

"It's not common kelp. It's carnivorous and will rip us to shreds." Iguain's mouth was clamped shut.

Tsai Chin shook his head, he couldn't believe that the seabed could rouse itself and grow before his very eyes. As Iguain knew, courage didn't always make up for inexperience.

Less than twenty metres from the Tower, a compact wall of lianas forced them to slow down.

"It's been crossbred and I don't want to know what with…"

The lack of oxygen around them, so quickly sucked out by the kelp, would cause them to suffocate within a few minutes. Iguain distributed the breathing kits to gain time, but as soon as he did, a spongy tangle enveloped Tsai Chin and dragged him down with it.

Karia pushed Aruna ahead of her, while Iguain stopped and watched Tsai Chin armed with a dagger fighting those roots. If he went to help Tsai Chin, he would put the lives of the others at even greater risk.

Tsai Chin took out a bar of sodium, which on contact with the water, burned incandescently amidst a cloud of bubbles. The kelp, alarmed by his resistance, called up even more tentacles. At the sight of this, Iguain kicked his legs, beat his dorsal fins and resisted the tenacity with which the kelp was trying desperately to survive.

When he could no longer see Tsai Chin, Iguain filled his lungs, pushed with his pectorals, and swam away, helping his daughter and Aruna to safety in the narrow entrance of the Tower.

Mnemonic relic 5 (source: paper fragment).

The most alarming thing is that we have no idea about the mechanisms which enable a natural phenomenon to disrupt the Earth's temperature with such speed. As Elizabeth Kolbert observed in a mnemonic relic from the *New Yorker* "No known external force, or even any that has been hypothesised, seems capable of yanking the temperature back and forth as violently, and as often, as these cores have shown to be the case. [It seems] like some kind of vast and terrible feedback loop." We are a long way from understanding all of this.

From the repaired chronicles of Saxayé.

Shaken by the loss of Tsai Chin, Iguain pounded his fists on the Tower's door to the disbelief of Karia and Aruna. It was madness to think someone would come and open the door, nonetheless a display lit up by its side.

"Welcome to Spitsbergen island, I am the Custodian of the Vault, its security AI, how can I be of service?"

The girls came closer, intrigued. The supercomputer was still working, though it was not up-to-date with the situation on Modified Earth. The island no longer existed, covered by the Ocean.

"We have brought some seeds we'd like to deposit."

Aruna shook her feathers, a gesture typical of her race. She opened her beak angrily and pounded her hands against the capsule.

"You've got seeds?! And you didn't tell me?"

As soon as the doors opened, the three were pushed in by the pressure of the water. When they stood up again, after the doors had closed, they found themselves in a corridor sloping 20 degrees upwards. Emergency lighting indicated which way to go.

"I'm sorry, the Council forbade me from talking about it. It was the best way of getting us in."

"You lied to me..."

"No, I do have some seeds, but they are as old as fossils."

Iguain opened a bag and showed Aruna the contents. A strong smell of rotting hit her. A slightly sweeter version of the stench was also present in the corridor.

The interior of the Tower was covered by a film of dust, and as the AI led them to the top of the vault, the smell became the stink of mould.

When they reached the Seed Room, they could not hold back their disgust and horror: their hopes lay there rotting in an unending series of carefully labelled containers.

"They're all rotten! The seeds are useless... We got here too late."

Karia put her arm around the visibly upset Aeromancer. To return to the Nest only to tell her people that the seeds had turned to dust would throw everyone into deep despair.

"That is not exact. Some have survived."

The AI opened a door and inside a few cases, some names lit up: Himalayan Cedar, Caucasian Elm, Whitebeam, and then Rhododendrons, Azaleas, and Magnolias.

"The Barley seeds decomposed after 2,000 years, the Wheat seeds after 1,700, but the Whitebeam will last for another 10,000. You can leave your seeds here, I will take care to preserve them until the time is right for a new planting."

Aruna ran to see close to, drying her tears as she did so. Iguain, laid down his package and was about to move away when she grabbed him by the arm.

"Where are you going? We haven't come all this way to leave empty handed."

Iguain's eyelids dropped from the tops of his eyes until they were completely covered. The absence of eyelashes made him look strange to the Aeromancer.

"The aim of the mission was to verify the existence of the Tower and identify its position. Someone else will decide what to do with the seeds. We will report back to the Council and tell them what we have discovered."

"But my people need these seeds. We must take them back with us!"

"The Council will use its judgement to decide what to do. If it were not for them, we would not even be here."

"I know... but the seeds don't belong to anyone. The seeds belong to the Earth, and they must be returned to the Earth. The seeds are like the force of gravity and sunlight, they existed before the human race came along, and continued after its disappearance. No-one can *own* them."

"This is a decision the Council must make."

Aruna let her beak hang open, then tilted it to one side and unfolded her wings threateningly.

"No Iguain, this decision belongs to *you* too! We are alone here, and I don't think that you came all this way, at your age, only to satisfy your curiosity and to put a cross on a nautical map."

The Aquamancer vented his air valve. It was difficult to carry on doing his duty, now that he *knew.* The existence of the Seeds was a truth that could put his dream of repopulating the Risen Lands into motion.

When he was a boy, Iguain had loved to swim to the surface and gaze at the sky. The star fish were nothing compared to the stars that floated high above. During the night, under the spinning constellations, hypnotised by their mysterious movement, he would ask himself what was up there. On the edge of the outside world, he had never plucked up the courage to take the last step, the step that would have taken him out of the Ocean.

In the years that followed, his mind was often filled with thoughts of the Risen Lands. It was as if his memories held, in the folds of genetic memory, the panoramas and terrestrial landscapes that persisted with a certain melancholy within him.

This convinced him that his race should leave the Ocean, and that sooner or later the Aquamancers would return to dry land. It was a circle that would be closed.

He had taught Karia that the Risen Lands had been the cradle of civilisation, from where all the animate races had originated, and that that civilisation had *walked*, with its feet firmly on the ground.

Iguain couldn't get the mosaic of his thoughts in order.

As an Aquamancer he knew that the Risen Land Cultures had all ended badly, and that every land based civilisation was but a fragment in a distributed memory. They, vice-versa, were alive and would remain so until the Sun imploded.

For the Council, the Risen Lands were a fearsome environment, dry, exposed to intense radiation, and above all they offered none of that support provided by water that made moving in the sea so pleasant and less tiring than on land.

It was bizarre that a planet almost completely covered by the Ocean should be called Earth. Sooner or later it would have to be renamed "Aqua".

"I'm going to take the seeds anyway Iguain, with or without your permission. Even though you saved my life, you cannot expect me to sacrifice my people for a question of politics."

Aruna addressed the display with a pleading tone.

"Custodian, I beg you. The seeds must leave this place... I came here to take some samples. Allow my people to be able to plant them again."

"I have awaited a Planter for centuries. Preservation is a means unto planting. You may take two seeds of each type left in the vault."

Aruna was overjoyed, but did not know exactly what to do, nor did she have any idea how to transport the seeds. She was scared of ruining them, of accidentally destroying in an instant her own future.

Then Iguain had a change of heart, turning back with shuffling steps.

"Aruna, I have not told you everything. I did come here for another reason. I want to take us all back to a point when nothing had yet been compromised. I want to put evolution back on the right track."

"What do you mean?"

"I mean that any child born today inherits genes and learns from experience, but she also has the use of words, thoughts, and tools that were invented by others in other places and other eras. The animate beings exist because, on the contrary to other species, they know how to accumulate culture and pass on this information, not only across the Ocean, but also across time, from generation to generation. I think though, that this progress is cyclic, not linear. The human civilisation was a disaster for the biosphere. The next will be able to value the environment and read its signs.

"So, have you changed your mind?"

"Partially. Karia will return to the Council, whereas I will come with you, if you have nothing against the idea."

Iguain's daughter accepted the decision, perhaps she had already known in her heart that her father would not forgo this opportunity to finally leave the Ocean.

"I'll tell them that I got separated from you. And you dad, you can come back to Saxayé when you have finished."

As she said it, Karia feared that that day would not come any time soon.

From the repaired chronicles of Kilimanjaro.

The altitude caused Iguain some days of nausea and spells of dizziness. Born to resist the pressure of the water, his body was vulnerable to the rarefied air. However, when he saw the great size of the Giant Sequoias he forgot any suffering; these beings were the most incredible thing he had ever seen.

Aruna introduced him to her family and old Canderum of the Purple Feathers.

In the days that followed, the young woman was frequently away from the Nest, intent on coordinating the teams of planters that had started to work along the slopes of Kilimanjaro.

Returning in the evenings, tired but happy, Aruna told Iguain how in time every Aeromancer would inherit a mixture of seeds, a precious legacy to manage and make "yield". She imagined flights of Aeromancers flying around to pollinate plants and flowers. She imagined spreading the seeds to the other tribes. She imagined descending from the peaks, as the legend foretold.

Iguain, for his part, never went too far from the Nest, where the Aeromancers had prepared him a pool for his ablutions. He learned the local customs, he sat on the edge of the Solar Corolla contemplating the marine horizon, which, in his mind, would pull back and give way to a new unexplored Land, where people could return to walking.

He was not anxious to return to Saxayé, it did not worry him: he had initiated a process of transformation, and even though the consequences of his decision would take a very long time to reach their conclusion, he was at peace with himself.

Canderum glided down next to him. Standing on thin legs, he relied on the support of a stick.

"Look over there.... On the left."

The Aeromancer pointed with a finger, and Iguain, focussing, saw what the other was looking at: whole swarms of spores floating in the air.

"Our races will meet again, this time on the shores of the Ocean, Canderum."

"And from there we will go on together."

"As has already happened, but differently."

The two elderly men did not have much else to ask of life, except to observe it continue and recreate itself.

A Martian Odyssey

Stanley G. Weinbaum

JARVIS STRETCHED himself as luxuriously as he could in the cramped general quarters of the *Ares*.

"Air you can breathe!" he exulted. "It feels as thick as soup after the thin stuff out there!" He nodded at the Martian landscape stretching flat and desolate in the light of the nearer moon, beyond the glass of the port.

The other three stared at him sympathetically – Putz, the engineer, Leroy, the biologist, and Harrison, the astronomer and captain of the expedition. Dick Jarvis was chemist of the famous crew, the *Ares* expedition, first human beings to set foot on the mysterious neighbor of the earth, the planet Mars. This, of course, was in the old days, less than twenty years after the mad American Doheny perfected the atomic blast at the cost of his life, and only a decade after the equally mad Cardoza rode on it to the moon. They were true pioneers, these four of the *Ares*. Except for a half-dozen moon expeditions and the ill-fated de Lancey flight aimed at the seductive orb of Venus, they were the first men to feel other gravity than earth's, and certainly the first successful crew to leave the earth-moon system. And they deserved that success when one considers the difficulties and discomforts – the months spent in acclimatization chambers back on earth, learning to breathe the air as tenuous as that of Mars, the challenging of the void in the tiny rocket driven by the cranky reaction motors of the twenty-first century, and mostly the facing of an absolutely unknown world.

Jarvis stretched and fingered the raw and peeling tip of his frost-bitten nose. He sighed again contentedly.

"Well," exploded Harrison abruptly, "are we going to hear what happened? You set out all shipshape in an auxiliary rocket, we don't get a peep for ten days, and finally Putz here picks you out of a lunatic ant-heap with a freak ostrich as your pal! Spill it, man!"

"Speel?" queried Leroy perplexedly. "Speel what?"

"He means '*spiel*'," explained Putz soberly. "It iss to tell."

Jarvis met Harrison's amused glance without the shadow of a smile. "That's right, Karl," he said in grave agreement with Putz. "*Ich spiel es!*" He grunted comfortably and began.

"According to orders," he said, "I watched Karl here take off toward the North, and then I got into my flying sweat-box and headed South. You'll remember, Cap – we had orders not to land, but just scout about for points of interest. I set the two cameras clicking and buzzed along, riding pretty high – about two thousand feet – for a couple of reasons. First, it gave the cameras a greater field, and second, the under-jets travel so far in this half-vacuum they call air here that they stir up dust if you move low."

"We know all that from Putz," grunted Harrison. "I wish you'd saved the films, though. They'd have paid the cost of this junket; remember how the public mobbed the first moon pictures?"

"The films are safe," retorted Jarvis. "Well," he resumed, "as I said, I buzzed along at a pretty good clip; just as we figured, the wings haven't much lift in this air at less than a hundred miles per hour, and even then I had to use the under-jets.

"So, with the speed and the altitude and the blurring caused by the under-jets, the seeing wasn't any too good. I could see enough, though, to distinguish that what I sailed over was just more of this grey plain that we'd been examining the whole week since our landing – same blobby growths and the same eternal carpet of crawling little plant-animals, or biopods, as Leroy calls them. So I sailed along, calling back my position every hour as instructed, and not knowing whether you heard me."

"I did!" snapped Harrison.

"A hundred and fifty miles south," continued Jarvis imperturbably, "the surface changed to a sort of low plateau, nothing but desert and orange-tinted sand. I figured that we were right in our guess, then, and this grey plain we dropped on was really the Mare Cimmerium which would make my orange desert the region called Xanthus. If I were right, I ought to hit another grey plain, the Mare Chronium in another couple of hundred miles, and then another orange desert, Thyle I or II. And so I did."

"Putz verified our position a week and a half ago!" grumbled the captain. "Let's get to the point."

"Coming!" remarked Jarvis. "Twenty miles into Thyle – believe it or not – I crossed a canal!"

"Putz photographed a hundred! Let's hear something new!"

"And did he also see a city?"

"Twenty of 'em, if you call those heaps of mud cities!"

"Well," observed Jarvis, "from here on I'll be telling a few things Putz didn't see!" He rubbed his tingling nose, and continued. "I knew that I had sixteen hours of daylight at this season, so eight hours – eight hundred miles – from here, I decided to turn back. I was still over Thyle, whether I or II I'm not sure, not more than twenty-five miles into it. And right there, Putz's pet motor quit!"

"Quit? How?" Putz was solicitous.

"The atomic blast got weak. I started losing altitude right away, and suddenly there I was with a thump right in the middle of Thyle! Smashed my nose on the window, too!" He rubbed the injured member ruefully.

"Did you maybe try vashing der combustion chamber mit acid sulphuric?" inquired Putz. "Sometimes der lead giffs a secondary radiation—"

"Naw!" said Jarvis disgustedly. "I wouldn't try that, of course – not more than ten times! Besides, the bump flattened the landing gear and busted off the under-jets. Suppose I got the thing working – what then? Ten miles with the blast coming right out of the bottom and I'd have melted the floor from under me!" He rubbed his nose again. "Lucky for me a pound only weighs seven ounces here, or I'd have been mashed flat!"

"I could have fixed!" ejaculated the engineer. "I bet it vas not serious."

"Probably not," agreed Jarvis sarcastically. "Only it wouldn't fly. Nothing serious, but I had my choice of waiting to be picked up or trying to walk back – eight hundred miles, and perhaps twenty days before we had to leave! Forty miles a day! Well," he concluded, "I chose to walk. Just as much chance of being picked up, and it kept me busy."

"We'd have found you," said Harrison.

"No doubt. Anyway, I rigged up a harness from some seat straps, and put the water tank on my back, took a cartridge belt and revolver, and some iron rations, and started out."

"Water tank!" exclaimed the little biologist, Leroy. "She weigh one-quarter ton!"

"Wasn't full. Weighed about two hundred and fifty pounds earth-weight, which is eighty-five here. Then, besides, my own personal two hundred and ten pounds is only seventy on Mars, so, tank and all, I grossed a hundred and fifty-five, or fifty-five pounds less than my everyday earth-weight. I figured on that when I undertook the forty-mile daily stroll. Oh – of course I took a thermo-skin sleeping bag for these wintry Martian nights.

"Off I went, bouncing along pretty quickly. Eight hours of daylight meant twenty miles or more. It got tiresome, of course – plugging along over a soft sand desert with nothing to see, not even Leroy's crawling biopods. But an hour or so brought me to the canal – just a dry ditch about four hundred feet wide, and straight as a railroad on its own company map.

"There'd been water in it sometime, though. The ditch was covered with what looked like a nice green lawn. Only, as I approached, the lawn moved out of my way!"

"Eh?" said Leroy.

"Yeah, it was a relative of your biopods. I caught one – a little grass-like blade about as long as my finger, with two thin, stemmy legs."

"He is where?" Leroy was eager.

"He is let go! I had to move, so I plowed along with the walking grass opening in front and closing behind. And then I was out on the orange desert of Thyle again.

"I plugged steadily along, cussing the sand that made going so tiresome, and, incidentally, cussing that cranky motor of yours, Karl. It was just before twilight that I reached the edge of Thyle, and looked down over the gray Mare Chronium. And I knew there was seventy-five miles of *that* to be walked over, and then a couple of hundred miles of that Xanthus desert, and about as much more Mare Cimmerium. Was I pleased? I started cussing you fellows for not picking me up!"

"We were trying, you sap!" said Harrison.

"That didn't help. Well, I figured I might as well use what was left of daylight in getting down the cliff that bounded Thyle. I found an easy place, and down I went. Mare Chronium was just the same sort of place as this – crazy leafless plants and a bunch of crawlers; I gave it a glance and hauled out my sleeping bag. Up to that time, you know, I hadn't seen anything worth worrying about on this half-dead world – nothing dangerous, that is."

"Did you?" queried Harrison.

"*Did I!* You'll hear about it when I come to it. Well, I was just about to turn in when suddenly I heard the wildest sort of shenanigans!"

"Vot iss shenanigans?" inquired Putz.

"He says, 'Je ne sais quoi,'" explained Leroy. "It is to say, 'I don't know what.'"

"That's right," agreed Jarvis. "I didn't know what, so I sneaked over to find out. There was a racket like a flock of crows eating a bunch of canaries – whistles, cackles, caws, trills, and what have you. I rounded a clump of stumps, and there was Tweel!"

"Tweel?" said Harrison, and "Tveel?" said Leroy and Putz.

"That freak ostrich," explained the narrator. "At least, Tweel is as near as I can pronounce it without sputtering. He called it something like 'Trrrweerrlll.'"

"What was he doing?" asked the Captain.

"He was being eaten! And squealing, of course, as any one would."

"Eaten! By what?"

"I found out later. All I could see then was a bunch of black ropy arms tangled around what looked like, as Putz described it to you, an ostrich. I wasn't going to interfere, naturally; if both creatures were dangerous, I'd have one less to worry about.

"But the bird-like thing was putting up a good battle, dealing vicious blows with an eighteen-inch beak, between screeches. And besides, I caught a glimpse or two of what was on the end of those arms!" Jarvis shuddered. "But the clincher was when I noticed a little black bag or case hung about the neck of the bird-thing! It was intelligent! That or tame, I assumed. Anyway, it clinched my decision. I pulled out my automatic and fired into what I could see of its antagonist.

"There was a flurry of tentacles and a spurt of black corruption, and then the thing, with a disgusting sucking noise, pulled itself and its arms into a hole in the ground. The other let out a series of clacks, staggered around on legs about as thick as golf sticks, and turned suddenly to face me. I held my weapon ready, and the two of us stared at each other.

"The Martian wasn't a bird, really. It wasn't even bird-like, except just at first glance. It had a beak all right, and a few feathery appendages, but the beak wasn't really a beak. It was somewhat flexible; I could see the tip bend slowly from side to side; it was almost like a cross between a beak and a trunk. It had four-toed feet, and four fingered things – hands, you'd have to call them, and a little roundish body, and a long neck ending in a tiny head – and that beak. It stood an inch or so taller than I, and – well, Putz saw it!"

The engineer nodded. "*Ja!* I saw!"

Jarvis continued. "So – we stared at each other. Finally the creature went into a series of clackings and twitterings and held out its hands toward me, empty. I took that as a gesture of friendship."

"Perhaps," suggested Harrison, "it looked at that nose of yours and thought you were its brother!"

"Huh! You can be funny without talking! Anyway, I put up my gun and said 'Aw, don't mention it,' or something of the sort, and the thing came over and we were pals.

"By that time, the sun was pretty low and I knew that I'd better build a fire or get into my thermo-skin. I decided on the fire. I picked a spot at the base of the Thyle cliff, where the rock could reflect a little heat on my back. I started breaking off chunks of this desiccated Martian vegetation, and my companion caught the idea and brought in an armful. I reached for a match, but the Martian fished into his pouch and brought out something that looked like a glowing coal; one touch of it, and the fire was blazing – and you all know what a job we have starting a fire in this atmosphere!

"And that bag of his!" continued the narrator. "That was a manufactured article, my friends; press an end and she popped open – press the middle and she sealed so perfectly you couldn't see the line. Better than zippers.

"Well, we stared at the fire a while and I decided to attempt some sort of communication with the Martian. I pointed at myself and said 'Dick'; he caught the drift immediately, stretched a bony claw at me and repeated 'Tick.' Then I pointed at him, and he gave that whistle I called Tweel; I can't imitate his accent. Things were going smoothly; to emphasize the names, I repeated 'Dick,' and then, pointing at him, 'Tweel.'

"There we stuck! He gave some clacks that sounded negative, and said something like 'P-p-p-proot.' And that was just the beginning; I was always 'Tick,' but as for him – part of the time he was 'Tweel,' and part of the time he was 'P-p-p-proot,' and part of the time he was sixteen other noises!

"We just couldn't connect. I tried 'rock,' and I tried 'star,' and 'tree,' and 'fire,' and Lord knows what else, and try as I would, I couldn't get a single word! Nothing was the same for two successive minutes, and if that's a language, I'm an alchemist! Finally I gave it up and called him Tweel, and that seemed to do.

"But Tweel hung on to some of my words. He remembered a couple of them, which I suppose is a great achievement if you're used to a language you have to make up as you go along. But I couldn't get the hang of his talk; either I missed some subtle point or we just didn't *think* alike – and I rather believe the latter view.

"I've other reasons for believing that. After a while I gave up the language business, and tried mathematics. I scratched two plus two equals four on the ground, and demonstrated it with pebbles. Again Tweel caught the idea, and informed me that three plus three equals six. Once more we seemed to be getting somewhere.

"So, knowing that Tweel had at least a grammar school education, I drew a circle for the sun, pointing first at it, and then at the last glow of the sun. Then I sketched in Mercury, and Venus, and Mother Earth, and Mars, and finally, pointing to Mars, I swept my hand around in a sort of inclusive gesture to indicate that Mars was our current environment. I was working up to putting over the idea that my home was on the earth.

"Tweel understood my diagram all right. He poked his beak at it, and with a great deal of trilling and clucking, he added Deimos and Phobos to Mars, and then sketched in the earth's moon!

"Do you see what that proves? It proves that Tweel's race uses telescopes – that they're civilized!"

"Does not!" snapped Harrison. "The moon is visible from here as a fifth magnitude star. They could see its revolution with the naked eye."

"The moon, yes!" said Jarvis. "You've missed my point. Mercury isn't visible! And Tweel knew of Mercury because he placed the Moon at the *third* planet, not the second. If he didn't know Mercury, he'd put the earth second, and Mars third, instead of fourth! See?"

"Humph!" said Harrison.

"Anyway," proceeded Jarvis, "I went on with my lesson. Things were going smoothly, and it looked as if I could put the idea over. I pointed at the earth on my diagram, and then at myself, and then, to clinch it, I pointed to myself and then to the earth itself shining bright green almost at the zenith.

"Tweel set up such an excited clacking that I was certain he understood. He jumped up and down, and suddenly he pointed at himself and then at the sky, and then at himself and at the sky again. He pointed at his middle and then at Arcturus, at his head and then at Spica, at his feet and then at half a dozen stars, while I just gaped at him. Then, all of a sudden, he gave a tremendous leap. Man, what a hop! He shot straight up into the starlight, seventy-five feet if an inch! I saw him silhouetted against the sky, saw him turn and come down at me head first, and land smack on his beak like a javelin! There he stuck square in the center of my sun-circle in the sand – a bull's eye!"

"Nuts!" observed the captain. "Plain nuts!"

"That's what I thought, too! I just stared at him open-mouthed while he pulled his head out of the sand and stood up. Then I figured he'd missed my point, and I went through the whole blamed rigamarole again, and it ended the same way, with Tweel on his nose in the middle of my picture!"

"Maybe it's a religious rite," suggested Harrison.

"Maybe," said Jarvis dubiously. "Well, there we were. We could exchange ideas up to a certain point, and then – blooey! Something in us was different, unrelated; I don't doubt that Tweel thought me just as screwy as I thought him. Our minds simply looked at the world from different viewpoints, and perhaps his viewpoint is as true as ours. But – we couldn't get together, that's all. Yet, in spite of all difficulties, I *liked* Tweel, and I have a queer certainty that he liked me."

"Nuts!" repeated the captain. "Just daffy!"

"Yeah? Wait and see. A couple of times I've thought that perhaps we—" He paused, and then resumed his narrative. "Anyway, I finally gave it up, and got into my thermo-skin to sleep. The fire hadn't kept me any too warm, but that damned sleeping bag did. Got stuffy five minutes after I closed myself in. I opened it a little and bingo! Some eighty-below-zero air hit my nose, and that's when I got this pleasant little frostbite to add to the bump I acquired during the crash of my rocket.

"I don't know what Tweel made of my sleeping. He sat around, but when I woke up, he was gone. I'd just crawled out of my bag, though, when I heard some twittering, and there he came, sailing down from that three-story Thyle cliff to alight on his beak beside me. I pointed to myself and toward the north, and he pointed at himself and toward the south, but when I loaded up and started away, he came along.

"Man, how he traveled! A hundred and fifty feet at a jump, sailing through the air stretched out like a spear, and landing on his beak. He seemed surprised at my plodding, but after a few moments he fell in beside me, only every few minutes he'd go into one of his leaps, and stick his nose into the sand a block ahead of me. Then he'd come shooting back at me; it made me nervous at first to see that beak of his coming at me like a spear, but he always ended in the sand at my side.

"So the two of us plugged along across the Mare Chronium. Same sort of place as this – same crazy plants and same little green biopods growing in the sand, or crawling out of your way. We talked – not that we understood each other, you know, but just for company. I sang songs, and I suspect Tweel did too; at least, some of his trillings and twitterings had a subtle sort of rhythm.

"Then, for variety, Tweel would display his smattering of English words. He'd point to an outcropping and say 'rock,' and point to a pebble and say it again; or he'd touch my arm and say 'Tick,' and then repeat it. He seemed terrifically amused that the same word meant the same thing twice in succession, or that the same word could apply to two different objects. It set me wondering if perhaps his language wasn't like the primitive speech of some earth people – you know, Captain, like the Negritoes, for instance, who haven't any generic words. No word for food or water or man – words for good food and bad food, or rain water and sea water, or strong man and weak man – but no names for general classes. They're too primitive to understand that rain water and sea water are just different aspects of the same thing. But that wasn't the case with Tweel; it was just that we were somehow mysteriously different – our minds were alien to each other. And yet – we *liked* each other!"

"Looney, that's all," remarked Harrison. "That's why you two were so fond of each other."

"Well, I like *you*!" countered Jarvis wickedly. "Anyway," he resumed, "don't get the idea that there was anything screwy about Tweel. In fact, I'm not so sure but that he couldn't teach our highly praised human intelligence a trick or two. Oh, he wasn't an intellectual superman, I guess; but don't overlook the point that he managed to understand a little of my mental workings, and I never even got a glimmering of his."

"Because he didn't have any!" suggested the captain, while Putz and Leroy blinked attentively.

"You can judge of that when I'm through," said Jarvis. "Well, we plugged along across the Mare Chronium all that day, and all the next. Mare Chronium – Sea of Time! Say, I was willing to agree with Schiaparelli's name by the end of that march! Just that grey, endless plain of weird plants, and never a sign of any other life. It was so monotonous that I was even glad to see the desert of Xanthus toward the evening of the second day.

"I was fair worn out, but Tweel seemed as fresh as ever, for all I never saw him drink or eat. I think he could have crossed the Mare Chronium in a couple of hours with those block-long nose dives of his, but he stuck along with me. I offered him some water once or twice; he took the cup from me and sucked the liquid into his beak, and then carefully squirted it all back into the cup and gravely returned it.

"Just as we sighted Xanthus, or the cliffs that bounded it, one of those nasty sand clouds blew along, not as bad as the one we had here, but mean to travel against. I pulled the transparent flap of my thermo-skin bag across my face and managed pretty well, and I noticed that Tweel used some feathery appendages growing like a mustache at the base of his beak to cover his nostrils, and some similar fuzz to shield his eyes."

"He is a desert creature!" ejaculated the little biologist, Leroy.

"Huh? Why?"

"He drink no water – he is adapt' for sand storm—"

"Proves nothing! There's not enough water to waste any where on this desiccated pill called Mars. We'd call all of it desert on earth, you know." He paused. "Anyway, after the sand storm blew over, a little wind kept blowing in our faces, not strong enough to stir the sand. But suddenly things came drifting along from the Xanthus cliffs – small, transparent spheres, for all the world like glass tennis balls! But light – they were almost light enough to float even in this thin air – empty, too; at least, I cracked open a couple and nothing came out but a bad smell. I asked Tweel about them, but all he said was 'No, no, no,' which I took to mean that he knew nothing about them. So they went bouncing by like tumbleweeds, or like soap bubbles, and we plugged on toward Xanthus. Tweel pointed at one of the crystal balls once and said 'rock,' but I was too tired to argue with him. Later I discovered what he meant.

"We came to the bottom of the Xanthus cliffs finally, when there wasn't much daylight left. I decided to sleep on the plateau if possible; anything dangerous, I reasoned, would be more likely to prowl through the vegetation of the Mare Chronium than the sand of Xanthus. Not that I'd seen a single sign of menace, except the rope-armed black thing that had trapped Tweel, and apparently that didn't prowl at all, but lured its victims within reach. It couldn't lure me while I slept, especially as Tweel didn't seem to sleep at all, but simply sat patiently around all night. I wondered how the creature had managed to trap Tweel, but there wasn't any way of asking him. I found that out too, later; it's devilish!

"However, we were ambling around the base of the Xanthus barrier looking for an easy spot to climb. At least, I was. Tweel could have leaped it easily, for the cliffs were lower than Thyle – perhaps sixty feet. I found a place and started up, swearing at the water tank strapped to my back – it didn't bother me except when climbing – and suddenly I heard a sound that I thought I recognized!

"You know how deceptive sounds are in this thin air. A shot sounds like the pop of a cork. But this sound was the drone of a rocket, and sure enough, there went our second auxiliary about ten miles to westward, between me and the sunset!"

"Vas me!" said Putz. "I hunt for you."

"Yeah; I knew that, but what good did it do me? I hung on to the cliff and yelled and waved with one hand. Tweel saw it too, and set up a trilling and twittering, leaping to the top of the barrier and then high into the air. And while I watched, the machine droned on into the shadows to the south.

"I scrambled to the top of the cliff. Tweel was still pointing and trilling excitedly, shooting up toward the sky and coming down head-on to stick upside down on his beak in the sand. I pointed toward the south and at myself, and he said, 'Yes – Yes – Yes'; but somehow I gathered that he thought the flying thing was a relative of mine, probably a parent. Perhaps I did his intellect an injustice; I think now that I did.

"I was bitterly disappointed by the failure to attract attention. I pulled out my thermo-skin bag and crawled into it, as the night chill was already apparent. Tweel stuck his beak into the sand and drew up his legs and arms and looked for all the world like one of those leafless shrubs out there. I think he stayed that way all night."

"Protective mimicry!" ejaculated Leroy. "See? He is desert creature!"

"In the morning," resumed Jarvis, "we started off again. We hadn't gone a hundred yards into Xanthus when I saw something queer! This is one thing Putz didn't photograph, I'll wager!

"There was a line of little pyramids – tiny ones, not more than six inches high, stretching across Xanthus as far as I could see! Little buildings made of pygmy bricks, they were, hollow inside and truncated, or at least broken at the top and empty. I pointed at them and said 'What?' to Tweel, but he gave some negative twitters to indicate, I suppose, that he didn't know. So off we went, following the row of pyramids because they ran north, and I was going north.

"Man, we trailed that line for hours! After a while, I noticed another queer thing: they were getting larger. Same number of bricks in each one, but the bricks were larger.

"By noon they were shoulder high. I looked into a couple – all just the same, broken at the top and empty. I examined a brick or two as well; they were silica, and old as creation itself!"

"How you know?" asked Leroy.

"They were weathered – edges rounded. Silica doesn't weather easily even on earth, and in this climate—!"

"How old you think?"

"Fifty thousand – a hundred thousand years. How can I tell? The little ones we saw in the morning were older – perhaps ten times as old. Crumbling. How old would that make *them*? Half a million years? Who knows?" Jarvis paused a moment. "Well," he resumed, "we followed the line. Tweel pointed at them and said 'rock' once or twice, but he'd done that many times before. Besides, he was more or less right about these.

"I tried questioning him. I pointed at a pyramid and asked 'People?' and indicated the two of us. He set up a negative sort of clucking and said, 'No, no, no. No one-one-two. No two-two-four,' meanwhile rubbing his stomach. I just stared at him and he went through the business again. 'No one-one-two. No two-two-four.' I just gaped at him."

"That proves it!" exclaimed Harrison. "Nuts!"

"You think so?" queried Jarvis sardonically. "Well, I figured it out different! 'No one-one-two!' You don't get it, of course, do you?"

"Nope – nor do you!"

"I think I do! Tweel was using the few English words he knew to put over a very complex idea. What, let me ask, does mathematics make you think of?"

"Why – of astronomy. Or – or logic!"

"That's it! 'No one-one-two!' Tweel was telling me that the builders of the pyramids weren't people – or that they weren't intelligent, that they weren't reasoning creatures! Get it?"

"Huh! I'll be damned!"

"You probably will."

"Why," put in Leroy, "he rub his belly?"

"Why? Because, my dear biologist, that's where his brains are! Not in his tiny head – in his middle!"

"*C'est* impossible!"

"Not on Mars, it isn't! This flora and fauna aren't earthly; your biopods prove that!" Jarvis grinned and took up his narrative. "Anyway, we plugged along across Xanthus and in about the middle of the afternoon, something else queer happened. The pyramids ended."

"Ended!"

"Yeah; the queer part was that the last one – and now they were ten-footers – was capped! See? Whatever built it was still inside; we'd trailed 'em from their half-million-year-old origin to the present.

"Tweel and I noticed it about the same time. I yanked out my automatic (I had a clip of Boland explosive bullets in it) and Tweel, quick as a sleight-of-hand trick, snapped a queer little glass revolver out of his bag. It was much like our weapons, except that the grip was larger to accommodate his four-taloned hand. And we held our weapons ready while we sneaked up along the lines of empty pyramids.

"Tweel saw the movement first. The top tiers of bricks were heaving, shaking, and suddenly slid down the sides with a thin crash. And then – something – something was coming out!

"A long, silvery-grey arm appeared, dragging after it an armored body. Armored, I mean, with scales, silver-grey and dull-shining. The arm heaved the body out of the hole; the beast crashed to the sand.

"It was a nondescript creature – body like a big grey cask, arm and a sort of mouth-hole at one end; stiff, pointed tail at the other – and that's all. No other limbs, no eyes, ears, nose – nothing! The thing dragged itself a few yards, inserted its pointed tail in the sand, pushed itself upright, and just sat.

"Tweel and I watched it for ten minutes before it moved. Then, with a creaking and rustling like – oh, like crumpling stiff paper – its arm moved to the mouth-hole and out came a brick! The arm placed the brick carefully on the ground, and the thing was still again.

"Another ten minutes – another brick. Just one of Nature's bricklayers. I was about to slip away and move on when Tweel pointed at the thing and said 'rock'! I went 'huh?' and he said it again. Then, to the accompaniment of some of his trilling, he said, 'No – no – ,' and gave two or three whistling breaths.

"Well, I got his meaning, for a wonder! I said, 'No breath?' and demonstrated the word. Tweel was ecstatic; he said, 'Yes, yes, yes! No, no, no breet!' Then he gave a leap and sailed out to land on his nose about one pace from the monster!

"I was startled, you can imagine! The arm was going up for a brick, and I expected to see Tweel caught and mangled, but – nothing happened! Tweel pounded on the creature, and the arm took the brick and placed it neatly beside the first. Tweel rapped on its body again, and said 'rock,' and I got up nerve enough to take a look myself.

"Tweel was right again. The creature was rock, and it didn't breathe!"

"How you know?" snapped Leroy, his black eyes blazing interest.

"Because I'm a chemist. The beast was made of silica! There must have been pure silicon in the sand, and it lived on that. Get it? We, and Tweel, and those plants out there, and even the biopods are *carbon* life; this thing lived by a different set of chemical reactions. It was silicon life!"

"*La vie silicieuse!*" shouted Leroy. "I have suspect, and now it is proof! I must go see! *Il faut que je—*"

"All right! All right!" said Jarvis. "You can go see. Anyhow, there the thing was, alive and yet not alive, moving every ten minutes, and then only to remove a brick. Those bricks were its waste matter. See, Frenchy? We're carbon, and our waste is carbon dioxide, and this thing is silicon, and *its* waste is silicon dioxide – silica. But silica is a solid, hence the bricks. And it builds itself in, and when it is covered, it moves over to a fresh place to start over. No wonder it creaked! A living creature half a million years old!"

"How you know how old?" Leroy was frantic.

"We trailed its pyramids from the beginning, didn't we? If this weren't the original pyramid builder, the series would have ended somewhere before we found him, wouldn't it? – ended and started over with the small ones. That's simple enough, isn't it?

"But he reproduces, or tries to. Before the third brick came out, there was a little rustle and out popped a whole stream of those little crystal balls. They're his spores, or eggs, or seeds – call 'em what you want. They went bouncing by across Xanthus just as they'd bounced by us back in the Mare Chronium. I've a hunch how they work, too – this is for your information, Leroy. I think the crystal shell of silica is no more than a protective covering, like an eggshell, and that the active principle is the smell inside. It's some sort of gas that attacks silicon, and if the shell is broken near a supply of that element, some reaction starts that ultimately develops into a beast like that one."

"You should try!" exclaimed the little Frenchman. "We must break one to see!"

"Yeah? Well, I did. I smashed a couple against the sand. Would you like to come back in about ten thousand years to see if I planted some pyramid monsters? You'd most likely be able to tell by that time!" Jarvis paused and drew a deep breath. "Lord! That queer creature! Do you picture it? Blind, deaf, nerveless, brainless – just a mechanism, and yet – immortal! Bound to go on making bricks, building pyramids, as long as silicon and oxygen exist, and even afterwards it'll just stop. It won't be dead. If the accidents of a million years bring it its food again, there it'll be, ready to run again, while brains and civilizations are part of the past. A queer beast – yet I met a stranger one!"

"If you did, it must have been in your dreams!" growled Harrison.

"You're right!" said Jarvis soberly. "In a way, you're right. The dream-beast! That's the best name for it – and it's the most fiendish, terrifying creation one could imagine! More dangerous than a lion, more insidious than a snake!"

"Tell me!" begged Leroy. "I must go see!"

"Not *this* devil!" He paused again. "Well," he resumed, "Tweel and I left the pyramid creature and plowed along through Xanthus. I was tired and a little disheartened by Putz's failure to pick me up, and Tweel's trilling got on my nerves, as did his flying nosedives. So I just strode along without a word, hour after hour across that monotonous desert.

"Toward mid-afternoon we came in sight of a low dark line on the horizon. I knew what it was. It was a canal; I'd crossed it in the rocket and it meant that we were just one-third of the way across Xanthus. Pleasant thought, wasn't it? And still, I was keeping up to schedule.

"We approached the canal slowly; I remembered that this one was bordered by a wide fringe of vegetation and that Mud-heap City was on it.

"I was tired, as I said. I kept thinking of a good hot meal, and then from that I jumped to reflections of how nice and home-like even Borneo would seem after this crazy planet, and from that, to thoughts of little old New York, and then to thinking about a girl I know there – Fancy Long. Know her?"

"Vision entertainer," said Harrison. "I've tuned her in. Nice blonde – dances and sings on the *Yerba Mate* hour."

"That's her," said Jarvis ungrammatically. "I know her pretty well – just friends, get me? – though she came down to see us off in the *Ares*. Well, I was thinking about her, feeling pretty lonesome, and all the time we were approaching that line of rubbery plants.

"And then – I said, 'What 'n Hell!' and stared. And there she was – Fancy Long, standing plain as day under one of those crack-brained trees, and smiling and waving just the way I remembered her when we left!"

"Now you're nuts, too!" observed the captain.

"Boy, I almost agreed with you! I stared and pinched myself and closed my eyes and then stared again – and every time, there was Fancy Long smiling and waving! Tweel saw something, too; he was trilling and clucking away, but I scarcely heard him. I was bounding toward her over the sand, too amazed even to ask myself questions.

"I wasn't twenty feet from her when Tweel caught me with one of his flying leaps. He grabbed my arm, yelling, 'No – no – no!' in his squeaky voice. I tried to shake him off – he was as light as if he were built of bamboo – but he dug his claws in and yelled. And finally some sort of sanity returned to me and I stopped less than ten feet from her. There she stood, looking as solid as Putz's head!"

"Vot?" said the engineer.

"She smiled and waved, and waved and smiled, and I stood there dumb as Leroy, while Tweel squeaked and chattered. I *knew* it couldn't be real, yet – there she was!

"Finally I said, 'Fancy! Fancy Long!' She just kept on smiling and waving, but looking as real as if I hadn't left her thirty-seven million miles away.

"Tweel had his glass pistol out, pointing it at her. I grabbed his arm, but he tried to push me away. He pointed at her and said, 'No breet! No breet!' and I understood that he meant that the Fancy Long thing wasn't alive. Man, my head was whirling!

"Still, it gave me the jitters to see him pointing his weapon at her. I don't know why I stood there watching him take careful aim, but I did. Then he squeezed the handle of his weapon; there was a little puff of steam, and Fancy Long was gone! And in her place was one of those writhing, black, rope-armed horrors like the one I'd saved Tweel from!

"The dream-beast! I stood there dizzy, watching it die while Tweel trilled and whistled. Finally he touched my arm, pointed at the twisting thing, and said, 'You one-one-two, he one-one-two.' After he'd repeated it eight or ten times, I got it. Do any of you?"

"*Oui!*" shrilled Leroy. "*Moi – je le comprends!* He mean you think of something, the beast he know, and you see it! *Un chien* – a hungry dog, he would see the big bone with meat! Or smell it – not?"

"Right!" said Jarvis. "The dream-beast uses its victim's longings and desires to trap its prey. The bird at nesting season would see its mate, the fox, prowling for its own prey, would see a helpless rabbit!"

"How he do?" queried Leroy.

"How do I know? How does a snake back on earth charm a bird into its very jaws? And aren't there deep-sea fish that lure their victims into their mouths? Lord!" Jarvis shuddered. "Do you see how insidious the monster is? We're warned now – but henceforth we can't trust even our eyes. You might see me – I might see one of you – and back of it may be nothing but another of those black horrors!"

"How'd your friend know?" asked the captain abruptly.

"Tweel? I wonder! Perhaps he was thinking of something that couldn't possibly have interested me, and when I started to run, he realized that I saw something different and was warned. Or perhaps the dream-beast can only project a single vision, and Tweel saw what I saw – or nothing. I couldn't ask him. But it's just another proof that his intelligence is equal to ours or greater."

"He's daffy, I tell you!" said Harrison. "What makes you think his intellect ranks with the human?"

"Plenty of things! First, the pyramid-beast. He hadn't seen one before; he said as much. Yet he recognized it as a dead-alive automaton of silicon."

"He could have heard of it," objected Harrison. "He lives around here, you know."

"Well how about the language? I couldn't pick up a single idea of his and he learned six or seven words of mine. And do you realize what complex ideas he put over with no more than those six or seven words? The pyramid-monster – the dream-beast! In a single phrase he told me that one was a harmless automaton and the other a deadly hypnotist. What about that?"

"Huh!" said the captain.

"*Huh* if you wish! Could you have done it knowing only six words of English? Could you go even further, as Tweel did, and tell me that another creature was of a sort of intelligence so different from ours that understanding was impossible – even more impossible than that between Tweel and me?"

"Eh? What was that?"

"Later. The point I'm making is that Tweel and his race are worthy of our friendship. Somewhere on Mars – and you'll find I'm right – is a civilization and culture equal to ours, and maybe more than equal. And communication is possible between them and us; Tweel proves that. It may take years of patient trial, for their minds are alien, but less alien than the next minds we encountered – if they *are* minds."

"The next ones? What next ones?"

"The people of the mud cities along the canals." Jarvis frowned, then resumed his narrative. "I thought the dream-beast and the silicon-monster were the strangest beings conceivable, but I was wrong. These creatures are still more alien, less understandable than either and far less comprehensible than Tweel, with whom friendship is possible, and even, by patience and concentration, the exchange of ideas.

"Well," he continued, "we left the dream-beast dying, dragging itself back into its hole, and we moved toward the canal. There was a carpet of that queer walking-grass scampering out of our way, and when we reached the bank, there was a yellow trickle of water flowing. The mound city I'd noticed from the rocket was a mile or so to the right and I was curious enough to want to take a look at it.

"It had seemed deserted from my previous glimpse of it, and if any creatures were lurking in it – well, Tweel and I were both armed. And by the way, that crystal weapon of Tweel's was an interesting device; I took a look at it after the dream-beast episode. It fired a little glass splinter, poisoned, I suppose, and I guess it held at least a hundred of 'em to a load. The propellent was steam – just plain steam!"

"Shteam!" echoed Putz. "From vot come, shteam?"

"From water, of course! You could see the water through the transparent handle and about a gill of another liquid, thick and yellowish. When Tweel squeezed the handle – there was no trigger – a drop of water and a drop of the yellow stuff squirted into the firing chamber, and the water vaporized – pop! – like that. It's not so difficult; I think we could develop the same principle. Concentrated sulphuric acid will heat water almost to boiling, and so will quicklime, and there's potassium and sodium—

"Of course, his weapon hadn't the range of mine, but it wasn't so bad in this thin air, and it *did* hold as many shots as a cowboy's gun in a Western movie. It was effective, too, at least against Martian life; I tried it out, aiming at one of the crazy plants, and darned if the plant didn't wither up and fall apart! That's why I think the glass splinters were poisoned.

"Anyway, we trudged along toward the mud-heap city and I began to wonder whether the city builders dug the canals. I pointed to the city and then at the canal, and Tweel said 'No – no – no!' and gestured toward the south. I took it to mean that some other race had created the canal system, perhaps Tweel's people. I don't know; maybe there's still another intelligent race on the planet, or a dozen others. Mars is a queer little world.

"A hundred yards from the city we crossed a sort of road – just a hard-packed mud trail, and then, all of a sudden, along came one of the mound builders!

"Man, talk about fantastic beings! It looked rather like a barrel trotting along on four legs with four other arms or tentacles. It had no head, just body and members and a row of eyes completely around it. The top end of the barrel-body was a diaphragm stretched as tight as a drum head, and that was all. It was pushing a little coppery cart and tore right past us like the proverbial bat out of Hell. It didn't even notice us, although I thought the eyes on my side shifted a little as it passed.

"A moment later another came along, pushing another empty cart. Same thing – it just scooted past us. Well, I wasn't going to be ignored by a bunch of barrels playing train, so when the third one approached, I planted myself in the way – ready to jump, of course, if the thing didn't stop.

"But it did. It stopped and set up a sort of drumming from the diaphragm on top. And I held out both hands and said, 'We are friends!' And what do you suppose the thing did?"

"Said, 'Pleased to meet you,' I'll bet!" suggested Harrison.

"I couldn't have been more surprised if it had! It drummed on its diaphragm, and then suddenly boomed out, 'We are v-r-r-riends!' and gave its pushcart a vicious poke at me! I jumped aside, and away it went while I stared dumbly after it.

"A minute later another one came hurrying along. This one didn't pause, but simply drummed out, 'We are v-r-r-riends!' and scurried by. How did it learn the phrase? Were all of the creatures in some sort of communication with each other? Were they all parts of some central organism? I don't know, though I think Tweel does.

"Anyway, the creatures went sailing past us, every one greeting us with the same statement. It got to be funny; I never thought to find so many friends on this God-forsaken ball! Finally I made a puzzled gesture to Tweel; I guess he understood, for he said, 'One-one-two – yes! – two-two-four – no!' Get it?"

"Sure," said Harrison, "It's a Martian nursery rhyme."

"Yeah! Well, I was getting used to Tweel's symbolism, and I figured it out this way. 'One-one-two – yes!' The creatures were intelligent. 'Two-two-four – no!' Their intelligence was not of our order, but something different and beyond the logic of two and two is four. Maybe I missed his meaning. Perhaps he meant that their minds were of low degree, able to figure out the simple things – 'One-one-two – yes!' – but not more difficult things – 'Two-two-four – no!' But I think from what we saw later that he meant the other.

"After a few moments, the creatures came rushing back – first one, then another. Their pushcarts were full of stones, sand, chunks of rubbery plants, and such rubbish as that. They droned out their friendly greeting, which didn't really sound so friendly, and dashed on. The third one I assumed to be my first acquaintance and I decided to have another chat with him. I stepped into his path again and waited.

"Up he came, booming out his 'We are v-r-r-riends' and stopped. I looked at him; four or five of his eyes looked at me. He tried his password again and gave a shove on his cart, but I stood firm. And then the – the dashed creature reached out one of his arms, and two finger-like nippers tweaked my nose!"

"Haw!" roared Harrison. "Maybe the things have a sense of beauty!"

"Laugh!" grumbled Jarvis. "I'd already had a nasty bump and a mean frostbite on that nose. Anyway, I yelled 'Ouch!' and jumped aside and the creature dashed away; but from then on, their greeting was 'We are v-r-r-riends! Ouch!' Queer beasts!

"Tweel and I followed the road squarely up to the nearest mound. The creatures were coming and going, paying us not the slightest attention, fetching their loads of rubbish. The road simply dived into an opening, and slanted down like an old mine, and in and out darted the barrel-people, greeting us with their eternal phrase.

"I looked in; there was a light somewhere below, and I was curious to see it. It didn't look like a flame or torch, you understand, but more like a civilized light, and I thought that I might get some clue as to the creatures' development. So in I went and Tweel tagged along, not without a few trills and twitters, however.

"The light was curious; it sputtered and flared like an old arc light, but came from a single black rod set in the wall of the corridor. It was electric, beyond doubt. The creatures were fairly civilized, apparently.

"Then I saw another light shining on something that glittered and I went on to look at that, but it was only a heap of shiny sand. I turned toward the entrance to leave, and the Devil take me if it wasn't gone!

"I suppose the corridor had curved, or I'd stepped into a side passage. Anyway, I walked back in that direction I thought we'd come, and all I saw was more dimlit corridor. The place was a labyrinth! There was nothing but twisting passages running every way, lit by occasional lights, and now and then a creature running by, sometimes with a pushcart, sometimes without.

"Well, I wasn't much worried at first. Tweel and I had only come a few steps from the entrance. But every move we made after that seemed to get us in deeper. Finally I tried following one of the creatures with an empty cart, thinking that he'd be going out for his rubbish, but he ran around aimlessly, into one passage and out another. When he started dashing around a pillar like one of these Japanese waltzing mice, I gave up, dumped my water tank on the floor, and sat down.

"Tweel was as lost as I. I pointed up and he said 'No – no – no!' in a sort of helpless trill. And we couldn't get any help from the natives. They paid no attention at all, except to assure us they were friends – ouch!

"Lord! I don't know how many hours or days we wandered around there! I slept twice from sheer exhaustion; Tweel never seemed to need sleep. We tried following only the upward corridors, but they'd run uphill a ways and then curve downwards. The temperature in that damned ant hill was constant; you couldn't tell night from day and after my first sleep I didn't know whether I'd slept one hour or thirteen, so I couldn't tell from my watch whether it was midnight or noon.

"We saw plenty of strange things. There were machines running in some of the corridors, but they didn't seem to be doing anything – just wheels turning. And several times I saw two barrel-beasts with a little one growing between them, joined to both."

"Parthenogenesis!" exulted Leroy. "Parthenogenesis by budding like *les tulipes*!"

"If you say so, Frenchy," agreed Jarvis. "The things never noticed us at all, except, as I say, to greet us with 'We are v-r-r-riends! Ouch!' They seemed to have no home-life of any sort, but just scurried around with their pushcarts, bringing in rubbish. And finally I discovered what they did with it.

"We'd had a little luck with a corridor, one that slanted upwards for a great distance. I was feeling that we ought to be close to the surface when suddenly the passage debouched into a domed chamber, the only one we'd seen. And man! – I felt like dancing when I saw what looked like daylight through a crevice in the roof.

"There was a – a sort of machine in the chamber, just an enormous wheel that turned slowly, and one of the creatures was in the act of dumping his rubbish below it. The wheel ground it with a crunch – sand, stones, plants, all into powder that sifted away somewhere. While we watched, others filed in, repeating the process, and that seemed to be all. No rhyme nor reason to the whole thing – but that's characteristic of this crazy planet. And there was another fact that's almost too bizarre to believe.

"One of the creatures, having dumped his load, pushed his cart aside with a crash and calmly shoved himself under the wheel! I watched him being crushed, too stupefied to make a sound, and a moment later, another followed him! They were perfectly methodical about it, too; one of the cartless creatures took the abandoned pushcart.

"Tweel didn't seem surprised; I pointed out the next suicide to him, and he just gave the most human-like shrug imaginable, as much as to say, 'What can I do about it?' He must have known more or less about these creatures.

"Then I saw something else. There was something beyond the wheel, something shining on a sort of low pedestal. I walked over; there was a little crystal about the size of an egg, fluorescing to beat Tophet. The light from it stung my hands and face, almost like a static discharge, and then I noticed another funny thing. Remember that wart I had on my left thumb? Look!" Jarvis extended his hand. "It dried up and fell off – just like that! And my abused nose – say, the pain went out of it like magic! The thing had the property of hard x-rays or gamma radiations, only more so; it destroyed diseased tissue and left healthy tissue unharmed!

"I was thinking what a present *that'd* be to take back to Mother Earth when a lot of racket interrupted. We dashed back to the other side of the wheel in time to see one of the pushcarts ground up. Some suicide had been careless, it seems.

"Then suddenly the creatures were booming and drumming all around us and their noise was decidedly menacing. A crowd of them advanced toward us; we backed out of what I thought was the passage we'd entered by, and they came rumbling after us, some pushing carts and some not. Crazy brutes! There was a whole chorus of 'We are v-r-r-riends! Ouch!' I didn't like the 'ouch'; it was rather suggestive.

"Tweel had his glass gun out and I dumped my water tank for greater freedom and got mine. We backed up the corridor with the barrel-beasts following – about twenty of them. Queer thing – the ones coming in with loaded carts moved past us inches away without a sign.

"Tweel must have noticed that. Suddenly, he snatched out that glowing coal cigar-lighter of his and touched a cart-load of plant limbs. Puff! The whole load was burning – and the crazy beast pushing it went right along without a change of pace! It created some disturbance among our 'V-r-r-riends,' however – and then I noticed the smoke eddying and swirling past us, and sure enough, there was the entrance!

"I grabbed Tweel and out we dashed and after us our twenty pursuers. The daylight felt like Heaven, though I saw at first glance that the sun was all but set, and that was bad, since I couldn't live outside my thermo-skin bag in a Martian night – at least, without a fire.

"And things got worse in a hurry. They cornered us in an angle between two mounds, and there we stood. I hadn't fired nor had Tweel; there wasn't any use in irritating the brutes. They stopped a little distance away and began their booming about friendship and ouches.

"Then things got still worse! A barrel-brute came out with a pushcart and they all grabbed into it and came out with handfuls of foot-long copper darts – sharp-looking ones – and all of a sudden one sailed past my ear – zing! And it was shoot or die then.

"We were doing pretty well for a while. We picked off the ones next to the pushcart and managed to keep the darts at a minimum, but suddenly there was a thunderous booming of 'v-r-r-riends' and 'ouches,' and a whole army of 'em came out of their hole.

"Man! We were through and I knew it! Then I realized that Tweel wasn't. He could have leaped the mound behind us as easily as not. He was staying for me!

"Say, I could have cried if there'd been time! I'd liked Tweel from the first, but whether I'd have had gratitude to do what he was doing – suppose I *had* saved him from the first dream-beast – he'd done as much for me, hadn't he? I grabbed his arm, and said 'Tweel,' and pointed up, and he understood. He said, 'No – no – no, Tick!' and popped away with his glass pistol.

"What could I do? I'd be a goner anyway when the sun set, but I couldn't explain that to him. I said, 'Thanks, Tweel. You're a man!' and felt that I wasn't paying him any compliment at all. A man! There are mighty few men who'd do that.

"So I went 'bang' with my gun and Tweel went 'puff' with his, and the barrels were throwing darts and getting ready to rush us, and booming about being friends. I had given up hope. Then suddenly an angel dropped right down from Heaven in the shape of Putz, with his under-jets blasting the barrels into very small pieces!

"Wow! I let out a yell and dashed for the rocket; Putz opened the door and in I went, laughing and crying and shouting! It was a moment or so before I remembered Tweel; I looked around in time to see him rising in one of his nosedives over the mound and away.

"I had a devil of a job arguing Putz into following! By the time we got the rocket aloft, darkness was down; you know how it comes here – like turning off a light. We sailed out over the desert and put down once or twice. I yelled 'Tweel!' and yelled it a hundred times, I guess. We couldn't find him; he could travel like the wind and all I got – or else I imagined it – was a faint trilling and twittering drifting out of the south. He'd gone, and damn it! I wish – I wish he hadn't!"

The four men of the *Ares* were silent – even the sardonic Harrison. At last little Leroy broke the stillness.

"I should like to see," he murmured.

"Yeah," said Harrison. "And the wart-cure. Too bad you missed that; it might be the cancer cure they've been hunting for a century and a half."

"Oh, that!" muttered Jarvis gloomily. "That's what started the fight!" He drew a glistening object from his pocket.

"Here it is."

The Time Machine

H.G. Wells

Chapter I

THE TIME TRAVELLER (for so it will be convenient to speak of him) was expounding a recondite matter to us. His grey eyes shone and twinkled, and his usually pale face was flushed and animated. The fire burned brightly, and the soft radiance of the incandescent lights in the lilies of silver caught the bubbles that flashed and passed in our glasses. Our chairs, being his patents, embraced and caressed us rather than submitted to be sat upon, and there was that luxurious after-dinner atmosphere when thought roams gracefully free of the trammels of precision. And he put it to us in this way – marking the points with a lean forefinger – as we sat and lazily admired his earnestness over this new paradox (as we thought it) and his fecundity.

"You must follow me carefully. I shall have to controvert one or two ideas that are almost universally accepted. The geometry, for instance, they taught you at school is founded on a misconception.'

"Is not that rather a large thing to expect us to begin upon?" said Filby, an argumentative person with red hair.

"I do not mean to ask you to accept anything without reasonable ground for it. You will soon admit as much as I need from you. You know of course that a mathematical line, a line of thickness nil, has no real existence. They taught you that? Neither has a mathematical plane. These things are mere abstractions.'

"That is all right," said the Psychologist.

"Nor, having only length, breadth, and thickness, can a cube have a real existence.'

"There I object," said Filby. "Of course a solid body may exist. All real things –"

"So most people think. But wait a moment. Can an instantaneous cube exist?'

"Don't follow you," said Filby.

"Can a cube that does not last for any time at all, have a real existence?'

Filby became pensive. "Clearly," the Time Traveller proceeded, "any real body must have extension in four directions: it must have Length, Breadth, Thickness, and – Duration. But through a natural infirmity of the flesh, which I will explain to you in a moment, we incline to overlook this fact. There are really four dimensions, three which we call the three planes of Space, and a fourth, Time. There is, however, a tendency to draw an unreal distinction between the former three dimensions and the latter, because it happens that our consciousness moves intermittently in one direction along the latter from the beginning to the end of our lives.'

"That," said a very young man, making spasmodic efforts to relight his cigar over the lamp; "that...very clear indeed.'

"Now, it is very remarkable that this is so extensively overlooked," continued the Time Traveller, with a slight accession of cheerfulness. "Really this is what is meant by the Fourth Dimension, though some people who talk about the Fourth Dimension do not know they mean it. It is only another way of looking at Time. There is no difference between Time and any of the three dimensions of Space except that our consciousness moves along it. But some foolish people have got hold of the wrong side of that idea. You have all heard what they have to say about this Fourth Dimension?'

"I have not," said the Provincial Mayor.

"It is simply this. That Space, as our mathematicians have it, is spoken of as having three dimensions, which one may call Length, Breadth, and Thickness, and is always definable by reference to three planes, each at right angles to the others. But some philosophical people have been asking why three dimensions particularly – why not another direction at right angles to the other three? – and have even tried to construct a Four-Dimension geometry. Professor Simon Newcomb was expounding this to the New York Mathematical Society only a month or so ago. You know how on a flat surface, which has only two dimensions, we can represent a figure of a three-dimensional solid, and similarly they think that by models of three dimensions they could represent one of four – if they could master the perspective of the thing. See?'

"I think so," murmured the Provincial Mayor; and, knitting his brows, he lapsed into an introspective state, his lips moving as one who repeats mystic words. "Yes, I think I see it now," he said after some time, brightening in a quite transitory manner.

"Well, I do not mind telling you I have been at work upon this geometry of Four Dimensions for some time. Some of my results are curious. For instance, here is a portrait of a man at eight years old, another at fifteen, another at seventeen, another at twenty-three, and so on. All these are evidently sections, as it were, Three-Dimensional representations of his Four-Dimensioned being, which is a fixed and unalterable thing.

"Scientific people," proceeded the Time Traveller, after the pause required for the proper assimilation of this, "know very well that Time is only a kind of Space. Here is a popular scientific diagram, a weather record. This line I trace with my finger shows the movement of the barometer. Yesterday it was so high, yesterday night it fell, then this morning it rose again, and so gently upward to here. Surely the mercury did not trace this line in any of the dimensions of Space generally recognized? But certainly it traced such a line, and that line, therefore, we must conclude was along the Time-Dimension.'

"But," said the Medical Man, staring hard at a coal in the fire, "if Time is really only a fourth dimension of Space, why is it, and why has it always been, regarded as something different? And why cannot we move in Time as we move about in the other dimensions of Space?'

The Time Traveller smiled. "Are you sure we can move freely in Space? Right and left we can go, backward and forward freely enough, and men always have done so. I admit we move freely in two dimensions. But how about up and down? Gravitation limits us there.'

"Not exactly," said the Medical Man. "There are balloons.'

"But before the balloons, save for spasmodic jumping and the inequalities of the surface, man had no freedom of vertical movement.'

"Still they could move a little up and down," said the Medical Man.

"Easier, far easier down than up.'

"And you cannot move at all in Time, you cannot get away from the present moment.'

"My dear sir, that is just where you are wrong. That is just where the whole world has gone wrong. We are always getting away from the present moment. Our mental existences, which are immaterial and have no dimensions, are passing along the Time-Dimension with a uniform velocity from the cradle to the grave. Just as we should travel down if we began our existence fifty miles above the earth's surface.'

"But the great difficulty is this," interrupted the Psychologist. "You can move about in all directions of Space, but you cannot move about in Time.'

"That is the germ of my great discovery. But you are wrong to say that we cannot move about in Time. For instance, if I am recalling an incident very vividly I go back to the instant of its occurrence: I become absent-minded, as you say. I jump back for a moment. Of course we have no means of staying back for any length of Time, any more than a savage or an animal has of staying six feet above the ground. But a civilized man is better off than the savage in this respect. He can go up against gravitation in a balloon, and why should he not hope that ultimately he may be able to stop or accelerate his drift along the Time-Dimension, or even turn about and travel the other way?'

"Oh, this," began Filby, "is all –"

"Why not?" said the Time Traveller.

"It's against reason," said Filby.

"What reason?" said the Time Traveller.

"You can show black is white by argument," said Filby, "but you will never convince me.'

"Possibly not," said the Time Traveller. "But now you begin to see the object of my investigations into the geometry of Four Dimensions. Long ago I had a vague inkling of a machine –"

"To travel through Time!" exclaimed the Very Young Man.

"That shall travel indifferently in any direction of Space and Time, as the driver determines.'

Filby contented himself with laughter.

"But I have experimental verification," said the Time Traveller.

"It would be remarkably convenient for the historian," the Psychologist suggested. "One might travel back and verify the accepted account of the Battle of Hastings, for instance!'

"Don't you think you would attract attention?" said the Medical Man. "Our ancestors had no great tolerance for anachronisms.'

"One might get one's Greek from the very lips of Homer and Plato," the Very Young Man thought.

"In which case they would certainly plough you for the Little-go. The German scholars have improved Greek so much.'

"Then there is the future," said the Very Young Man. "Just think! One might invest all one's money, leave it to accumulate at interest, and hurry on ahead!'

"To discover a society," said I, "erected on a strictly communistic basis.'

"Of all the wild extravagant theories!" began the Psychologist.

"Yes, so it seemed to me, and so I never talked of it until –"

"Experimental verification!" cried I. "You are going to verify that?'

"The experiment!" cried Filby, who was getting brain-weary.

"Let's see your experiment anyhow," said the Psychologist, "though it's all humbug, you know.'

The Time Traveller smiled round at us. Then, still smiling faintly, and with his hands deep in his trousers pockets, he walked slowly out of the room, and we heard his slippers shuffling down the long passage to his laboratory.

The Psychologist looked at us. "I wonder what he's got?'

"Some sleight-of-hand trick or other," said the Medical Man, and Filby tried to tell us about a conjurer he had seen at Burslem; but before he had finished his preface the Time Traveller came back, and Filby's anecdote collapsed.

The thing the Time Traveller held in his hand was a glittering metallic framework, scarcely larger than a small clock, and very delicately made. There was ivory in it, and some transparent crystalline substance. And now I must be explicit, for this that follows – unless his explanation is to be accepted – is an absolutely unaccountable thing. He took one of the small octagonal tables that were scattered about the room, and set it in front of the fire, with two legs on the hearthrug. On this table he placed the mechanism. Then he drew up a chair, and sat down. The only other object on the table was a small shaded lamp, the bright light of which fell upon the model. There were also perhaps a dozen candles about, two in brass candlesticks upon the mantel and several in sconces, so that the room was brilliantly illuminated. I sat in a low arm-chair nearest the fire, and I drew this forward so as to be almost between the Time Traveller and the fireplace. Filby sat behind him, looking over his shoulder. The Medical Man and the Provincial Mayor watched him in profile from the right, the Psychologist from the left. The Very Young Man stood behind the Psychologist. We were all on the alert. It appears incredible to me that any kind of trick, however subtly conceived and however adroitly done, could have been played upon us under these conditions.

The Time Traveller looked at us, and then at the mechanism. "Well?" said the Psychologist.

"This little affair," said the Time Traveller, resting his elbows upon the table and pressing his hands together above the apparatus, "is only a model. It is my plan for a machine to travel through time. You will notice that it looks singularly askew, and that there is an odd twinkling appearance about this bar, as though it was in some way unreal." He pointed to the part with his finger. "Also, here is one little white lever, and here is another.'

The Medical Man got up out of his chair and peered into the thing. "It's beautifully made," he said.

"It took two years to make," retorted the Time Traveller. Then, when we had all imitated the action of the Medical Man, he said: "Now I want you clearly to understand that this lever, being pressed over, sends the machine gliding into the future, and this other reverses the motion. This saddle represents the seat of a time traveller. Presently I am going to press the lever, and off the machine will go. It will vanish, pass into future Time, and disappear. Have a good look at the thing. Look at the table too, and satisfy yourselves there is no trickery. I don't want to waste this model, and then be told I'm a quack.'

There was a minute's pause perhaps. The Psychologist seemed about to speak to me, but changed his mind. Then the Time Traveller put forth his finger towards the lever. "No," he said suddenly. "Lend me your hand." And turning to the Psychologist, he took that individual's hand in his own and told him to put out his forefinger. So that it was the Psychologist himself who sent forth the model Time Machine on its interminable voyage. We all saw the lever turn. I am absolutely certain there was no trickery. There was a breath of wind, and the lamp flame jumped. One of the candles on the mantel was blown out, and the little machine suddenly swung round, became indistinct, was seen as a ghost for a second perhaps, as an eddy of faintly glittering brass and ivory; and it was gone – vanished! Save for the lamp the table was bare.

Everyone was silent for a minute. Then Filby said he was damned.

The Psychologist recovered from his stupor, and suddenly looked under the table. At that the Time Traveller laughed cheerfully. "Well?" he said, with a reminiscence of the Psychologist. Then, getting up, he went to the tobacco jar on the mantel, and with his back to us began to fill his pipe.

We stared at each other. "Look here," said the Medical Man, "are you in earnest about this? Do you seriously believe that that machine has travelled into time?'

"Certainly," said the Time Traveller, stooping to light a spill at the fire. Then he turned, lighting his pipe, to look at the Psychologist's face. (The Psychologist, to show that he was not unhinged, helped himself to a cigar and tried to light it uncut.) "What is more, I have a big machine nearly finished in there" – he indicated the laboratory – "and when that is put together I mean to have a journey on my own account.'

"You mean to say that that machine has travelled into the future?" said Filby.

"Into the future or the past – I don't, for certain, know which.'

After an interval the Psychologist had an inspiration. "It must have gone into the past if it has gone anywhere," he said.

"Why?" said the Time Traveller.

"Because I presume that it has not moved in space, and if it travelled into the future it would still be here all this time, since it must have travelled through this time.'

"But," I said, "If it travelled into the past it would have been visible when we came first into this room; and last Thursday when we were here; and the Thursday before that; and so forth!'

"Serious objections," remarked the Provincial Mayor, with an air of impartiality, turning towards the Time Traveller.

"Not a bit," said the Time Traveller, and, to the Psychologist: "You think. You can explain that. It's presentation below the threshold, you know, diluted presentation.'

"Of course," said the Psychologist, and reassured us. "That's a simple point of psychology. I should have thought of it. It's plain enough, and helps the paradox delightfully. We cannot see it, nor can we appreciate this machine, any more than we can the spoke of a wheel spinning, or a bullet flying through the air. If it is travelling through time fifty times or a hundred times faster than we are, if it gets through a minute while we get through a second, the impression it creates will of course be only one-fiftieth or one-hundredth of what it would make if it were not travelling in time. That's plain enough." He passed his hand through the space in which the machine had been. "You see?" he said, laughing.

We sat and stared at the vacant table for a minute or so. Then the Time Traveller asked us what we thought of it all.

"It sounds plausible enough tonight," said the Medical Man; "but wait until tomorrow. Wait for the common sense of the morning.'

"Would you like to see the Time Machine itself?" asked the Time Traveller. And therewith, taking the lamp in his hand, he led the way down the long, draughty corridor to his laboratory. I remember vividly the flickering light, his queer, broad head in silhouette, the dance of the shadows, how we all followed him, puzzled but incredulous, and how there in the laboratory we beheld a larger edition of the little mechanism which we had seen vanish from before our eyes. Parts were of nickel, parts of ivory, parts had certainly been filed or sawn out of rock crystal. The thing was generally complete, but the twisted crystalline bars lay unfinished upon the bench beside some sheets of drawings, and I took one up for a better look at it. Quartz it seemed to be.

"Look here," said the Medical Man, "are you perfectly serious? Or is this a trick – like that ghost you showed us last Christmas?'

"Upon that machine," said the Time Traveller, holding the lamp aloft, "I intend to explore time. Is that plain? I was never more serious in my life.'

None of us quite knew how to take it.

I caught Filby's eye over the shoulder of the Medical Man, and he winked at me solemnly.

Chapter II

I THINK that at that time none of us quite believed in the Time Machine. The fact is, the Time Traveller was one of those men who are too clever to be believed: you never felt that you saw all round him; you always suspected some subtle reserve, some ingenuity in ambush, behind his lucid frankness. Had Filby shown the model and explained the matter in the Time Traveller's words, we should have shown him far less scepticism. For we should have perceived his motives; a pork butcher could understand Filby. But the Time Traveller had more than a touch of whim among his elements, and we distrusted him. Things that would have made the fame of a less clever man seemed tricks in his hands. It is a mistake to do things too easily. The serious people who took him seriously never felt quite sure of his deportment; they were somehow aware that trusting their reputations for judgment with him was like furnishing a nursery with egg-shell china. So I don't think any of us said very much about time travelling in the interval between that Thursday and the next, though its odd potentialities ran, no doubt, in most of our minds: its plausibility, that is, its practical incredibleness, the curious possibilities of anachronism and of utter confusion it suggested. For my own part, I was particularly preoccupied with the trick of the model. That I remember discussing with the Medical Man, whom I met on Friday at the Linnaean. He said he had seen a similar thing at Tubingen, and laid considerable stress on the blowing out of the candle. But how the trick was done he could not explain.

The next Thursday I went again to Richmond – I suppose I was one of the Time Traveller's most constant guests – and, arriving late, found four or five men already assembled in his drawing-room. The Medical Man was standing before the fire with a sheet of paper in one hand and his watch in the other. I looked round for the Time Traveller, and – "It's half-past seven now," said the Medical Man. "I suppose we'd better have dinner?'

"Where's –?" said I, naming our host.

"You've just come? It's rather odd. He's unavoidably detained. He asks me in this note to lead off with dinner at seven if he's not back. Says he'll explain when he comes.'

"It seems a pity to let the dinner spoil," said the Editor of a well-known daily paper; and thereupon the Doctor rang the bell.

The Psychologist was the only person besides the Doctor and myself who had attended the previous dinner. The other men were Blank, the Editor aforementioned, a certain journalist, and another – a quiet, shy man with a beard – whom I didn't know, and who, as far as my observation went, never opened his mouth all the evening. There was some speculation at the dinner-table about the Time Traveller's absence, and I suggested time travelling, in a half-jocular spirit. The Editor wanted that explained to him, and the Psychologist volunteered a wooden account of the "ingenious paradox and trick" we had witnessed that day week. He was in the midst of his exposition when the door from the corridor opened slowly and without noise. I was facing the door, and saw it first. "Hallo!" I said. "At last!" And the door opened wider, and the Time Traveller stood before us. I gave a cry of surprise. "Good heavens! man, what's the matter?" cried the Medical Man, who saw him next. And the whole tableful turned towards the door.

He was in an amazing plight. His coat was dusty and dirty, and smeared with green down the sleeves; his hair disordered, and as it seemed to me greyer – either with dust and dirt or because its colour had actually faded. His face was ghastly pale; his chin had a brown cut on it – a cut half healed; his expression was haggard and drawn, as by intense suffering. For a moment he hesitated in the doorway, as if he had been dazzled by the light. Then he came into the room. He walked with just such a limp as I have seen in footsore tramps. We stared at him in silence, expecting him to speak.

He said not a word, but came painfully to the table, and made a motion towards the wine. The Editor filled a glass of champagne, and pushed it towards him. He drained it, and it seemed to do him good: for he looked round the table, and the ghost of his old smile flickered across his face. "What on earth have you been up to, man?" said the Doctor. The Time Traveller did not seem to hear. "Don't let me disturb you," he said, with a certain faltering articulation. "I'm all right." He stopped, held out his glass for more, and took it off at a draught. "That's good," he said. His eyes grew brighter, and a faint colour came into his cheeks. His glance flickered over our faces with a certain dull approval, and then went round the warm and comfortable room. Then he spoke again, still as it were feeling his way among his words. "I'm going to wash and dress, and then I'll come down and explain things.... Save me some of that mutton. I'm starving for a bit of meat.'

He looked across at the Editor, who was a rare visitor, and hoped he was all right. The Editor began a question. "Tell you presently," said the Time Traveller. "I'm – funny! Be all right in a minute.'

He put down his glass, and walked towards the staircase door. Again I remarked his lameness and the soft padding sound of his footfall, and standing up in my place, I saw his feet as he went out. He had nothing on them but a pair of tattered, blood-stained socks. Then the door closed upon him. I had half a mind to follow, till I remembered how he detested any fuss about himself. For a minute, perhaps, my mind was wool-gathering. Then, "Remarkable Behaviour of an Eminent Scientist," I heard the Editor say, thinking (after his wont) in headlines. And this brought my attention back to the bright dinner-table.

"What's the game?" said the Journalist. "Has he been doing the Amateur Cadger? I don't follow." I met the eye of the Psychologist, and read my own interpretation in his face. I thought of the Time Traveller limping painfully upstairs. I don't think any one else had noticed his lameness.

The first to recover completely from this surprise was the Medical Man, who rang the bell – the Time Traveller hated to have servants waiting at dinner – for a hot plate. At that the Editor turned to his knife and fork with a grunt, and the Silent Man followed suit. The dinner was resumed. Conversation was exclamatory for a little while, with gaps of wonderment; and then the Editor got fervent in his curiosity. "Does our friend eke out his modest income with a crossing? or has he his Nebuchadnezzar phases?" he inquired. "I feel assured it's this business of the Time Machine," I said, and took up the Psychologist's account of our previous meeting. The new guests were frankly incredulous. The Editor raised objections. "What was this time travelling? A man couldn't cover himself with dust by rolling in a paradox, could he?" And then, as the idea came home to him, he resorted to caricature. Hadn't they any clothes-brushes in the Future? The Journalist too, would not believe at any price, and joined the Editor in the easy work of heaping ridicule on the whole thing. They were both the new kind of journalist – very joyous, irreverent young men. "Our Special Correspondent in the Day after Tomorrow reports," the Journalist was saying – or rather shouting – when the Time Traveller came back. He was dressed in ordinary evening clothes, and nothing save his haggard look remained of the change that had startled me.

"I say," said the Editor hilariously, "these chaps here say you have been travelling into the middle of next week! Tell us all about little Rosebery, will you? What will you take for the lot?'

The Time Traveller came to the place reserved for him without a word. He smiled quietly, in his old way. "Where's my mutton?" he said. "What a treat it is to stick a fork into meat again!'

"Story!" cried the Editor.

"Story be damned!" said the Time Traveller. "I want something to eat. I won't say a word until I get some peptone into my arteries. Thanks. And the salt.'

"One word," said I. "Have you been time travelling?'

"Yes," said the Time Traveller, with his mouth full, nodding his head.

"I'd give a shilling a line for a verbatim note," said the Editor. The Time Traveller pushed his glass towards the Silent Man and rang it with his fingernail; at which the Silent Man, who had been staring at his face, started convulsively, and poured him wine. The rest of the dinner was uncomfortable. For my own part, sudden questions kept on rising to my lips, and I dare say it was the same with the others. The Journalist tried to relieve the tension by telling anecdotes of Hettie Potter. The Time Traveller devoted his attention to his dinner, and displayed the appetite of a tramp. The Medical Man smoked a cigarette, and watched the Time Traveller through his eyelashes. The Silent Man seemed even more clumsy than usual, and drank champagne with regularity and determination out of sheer nervousness. At last the Time Traveller pushed his plate away, and looked round us. "I suppose I must apologize," he said. "I was simply starving. I've had a most amazing time." He reached out his hand for a cigar, and cut the end. "But come into the smoking-room. It's too long a story to tell over greasy plates." And ringing the bell in passing, he led the way into the adjoining room.

"You have told Blank, and Dash, and Chose about the machine?" he said to me, leaning back in his easy-chair and naming the three new guests.

"But the thing's a mere paradox," said the Editor.

"I can't argue tonight. I don't mind telling you the story, but I can't argue. I will," he went on, "tell you the story of what has happened to me, if you like, but you must refrain from interruptions. I want to tell it. Badly. Most of it will sound like lying. So be it! It's true – every word of it, all the same. I was in my laboratory at four o'clock, and since then...I've lived eight days...such days as no human being ever lived before! I'm nearly worn out, but I shan't sleep till I've told this thing over to you. Then I shall go to bed. But no interruptions! Is it agreed?'

"Agreed," said the Editor, and the rest of us echoed "Agreed." And with that the Time Traveller began his story as I have set it forth. He sat back in his chair at first, and spoke like a weary man. Afterwards he got more animated. In writing it down I feel with only too much keenness the inadequacy of pen and ink – and, above all, my own inadequacy – to express its quality. You read, I will suppose, attentively enough; but you cannot see the speaker's white, sincere face in the bright circle of the little lamp, nor hear the intonation of his voice. You cannot know how his expression followed the turns of his story! Most of us hearers were in shadow, for the candles in the smoking-room had not been lighted, and only the face of the Journalist and the legs of the Silent Man from the knees downward were illuminated. At first we glanced now and again at each other. After a time we ceased to do that, and looked only at the Time Traveller's face.

Chapter III

"**I TOLD** some of you last Thursday of the principles of the Time Machine, and showed you the actual thing itself, incomplete in the workshop. There it is now, a little travel-worn, truly; and one of the ivory bars is cracked, and a brass rail bent; but the rest of it's sound enough. I expected to finish it on Friday, but on Friday, when the putting together was nearly done, I found that one of the nickel bars was exactly one inch too short, and this I had to get remade; so that the thing was not complete until this morning. It was at ten o'clock today that the first of all Time Machines began its career. I gave it a last tap, tried all the screws again, put one more drop of oil on the quartz rod, and sat myself in the saddle. I suppose a suicide who holds a pistol to his skull feels much the same wonder at what will come next as I felt then. I took the starting lever in one hand and the stopping one in the other, pressed the first, and almost immediately the second. I seemed to reel; I felt a nightmare sensation of falling; and, looking round, I saw the laboratory exactly as before. Had anything happened? For a moment I suspected that my intellect had tricked me. Then I noted the clock. A moment before, as it seemed, it had stood at a minute or so past ten; now it was nearly half-past three!

"I drew a breath, set my teeth, gripped the starting lever with both hands, and went off with a thud. The laboratory got hazy and went dark. Mrs. Watchett came in and walked, apparently without seeing me, towards the garden door. I suppose it took her a minute or so to traverse the place, but to me she seemed to shoot across the room like a rocket. I pressed the lever over to its extreme position. The night came like the turning out of a lamp, and in another moment came tomorrow. The laboratory grew faint and hazy, then fainter and ever fainter. Tomorrow night came black, then day again, night again, day again, faster and faster still. An eddying murmur filled my ears, and a strange, dumb confusedness descended on my mind.

"I am afraid I cannot convey the peculiar sensations of time travelling. They are excessively unpleasant. There is a feeling exactly like that one has upon a switchback – of a helpless headlong motion! I felt the same horrible anticipation, too, of an imminent smash. As I put on pace, night followed day like the flapping of a black wing. The dim suggestion of the laboratory seemed presently to fall away from me, and I saw the sun hopping swiftly across the sky, leaping it every minute, and every minute marking a day. I supposed the laboratory had been destroyed and I had come into the open air. I had a dim impression of scaffolding, but I was already going too fast to be conscious of any moving things. The slowest snail that ever crawled dashed by too fast for me. The twinkling succession of darkness and light was excessively painful to the eye. Then, in the intermittent darknesses, I saw the moon spinning swiftly through her quarters from new to full, and had a faint glimpse of the circling stars. Presently, as I went on, still gaining velocity, the palpitation of night and day merged into one continuous greyness; the sky took on a wonderful deepness of blue, a splendid luminous color like that of early twilight; the jerking sun became a streak of fire, a brilliant arch, in space; the moon a fainter fluctuating band; and I could see nothing of the stars, save now and then a brighter circle flickering in the blue.

"The landscape was misty and vague. I was still on the hill-side upon which this house now stands, and the shoulder rose above me grey and dim. I saw trees growing and changing like puffs of vapour, now brown, now green; they grew, spread, shivered, and passed away. I saw huge buildings rise up faint and fair, and pass like dreams. The whole surface of the earth seemed changed – melting and flowing under my eyes. The little hands upon the dials that registered my speed raced round faster and faster. Presently I noted that the sun belt swayed up and down, from solstice to solstice, in a minute or less, and that consequently my pace was over a year a minute; and minute by minute the white snow flashed across the world, and vanished, and was followed by the bright, brief green of spring.

"The unpleasant sensations of the start were less poignant now. They merged at last into a kind of hysterical exhilaration. I remarked indeed a clumsy swaying of the machine, for which I was unable to account. But my mind was too confused to attend to it, so with a kind of madness growing upon me, I flung myself into futurity. At first I scarce thought of stopping, scarce thought of anything but these new sensations. But presently a fresh series of impressions grew up in my mind – a certain curiosity and therewith a certain dread – until at last they took complete possession of me. What strange developments of humanity, what wonderful advances upon our rudimentary civilization, I thought, might not appear when I came to look nearly into the dim elusive world that raced and fluctuated before my eyes! I saw great and splendid architecture rising about me, more massive than any buildings of our own time, and yet, as it seemed, built of glimmer and mist. I saw a richer green flow up the hill-side, and remain there, without any wintry intermission. Even through the veil of my confusion the earth seemed very fair. And so my mind came round to the business of stopping.

"The peculiar risk lay in the possibility of my finding some substance in the space which I, or the machine, occupied. So long as I travelled at a high velocity through time, this scarcely mattered; I was, so to speak, attenuated – was slipping like a vapour through the interstices of intervening substances! But to come to a stop involved the jamming of myself, molecule by molecule, into whatever lay in my way; meant bringing my atoms into such intimate contact with those of the obstacle that a profound chemical reaction – possibly a far-reaching explosion – would result, and blow myself and my apparatus out of all possible dimensions – into the Unknown. This possibility had occurred to me again and again while I was making the machine; but then I had cheerfully accepted it as an unavoidable risk – one of the risks a man has got to take! Now the risk was inevitable, I no longer saw it in the same cheerful light. The fact is that, insensibly, the absolute strangeness of everything, the sickly jarring and swaying of the machine, above all, the feeling of prolonged falling, had absolutely upset my nerve. I told myself that I could never stop, and with a gust of petulance I resolved to stop forthwith. Like an impatient fool, I lugged over the lever, and incontinently the thing went reeling over, and I was flung headlong through the air.

"There was the sound of a clap of thunder in my ears. I may have been stunned for a moment. A pitiless hail was hissing round me, and I was sitting on soft turf in front of the overset machine. Everything still seemed grey, but presently I remarked that the confusion in my ears was gone. I looked round me. I was on what seemed to be a little lawn in a garden, surrounded by rhododendron bushes, and I noticed that their mauve and purple blossoms were dropping in a shower under the beating of the hail-stones. The rebounding, dancing hail hung in a cloud over the machine, and drove along the ground like smoke. In a moment I was wet to the skin. 'Fine hospitality,' said I, 'to a man who has travelled innumerable years to see you.'

"Presently I thought what a fool I was to get wet. I stood up and looked round me. A colossal figure, carved apparently in some white stone, loomed indistinctly beyond the rhododendrons through the hazy downpour. But all else of the world was invisible.

"My sensations would be hard to describe. As the columns of hail grew thinner, I saw the white figure more distinctly. It was very large, for a silver birch-tree touched its shoulder. It was of white marble, in shape something like a winged sphinx, but the wings, instead of being carried vertically at the sides, were spread so that it seemed to hover. The pedestal, it appeared to me, was of bronze, and was thick with verdigris. It chanced that the face was towards me; the sightless eyes seemed to watch me; there was the faint shadow of a smile on the lips. It was greatly weather-worn, and that imparted an unpleasant suggestion of disease. I stood looking at it for a little space – half a minute, perhaps, or half an hour. It seemed to advance and to recede as the hail drove before it denser or thinner. At last I tore my eyes from it for a moment and saw that the hail curtain had worn threadbare, and that the sky was lightening with the promise of the sun.

"I looked up again at the crouching white shape, and the full temerity of my voyage came suddenly upon me. What might appear when that hazy curtain was altogether withdrawn? What might not have happened to men? What if cruelty had grown into a common passion? What if in this interval the race had lost its manliness and had developed into something inhuman, unsympathetic, and overwhelmingly powerful? I might seem some old-world savage animal, only the more dreadful and disgusting for our common likeness – a foul creature to be incontinently slain.

"Already I saw other vast shapes – huge buildings with intricate parapets and tall columns, with a wooded hill-side dimly creeping in upon me through the lessening storm. I was seized with a panic fear. I turned frantically to the Time Machine, and strove hard to readjust it. As I did so the shafts of the sun smote through the thunderstorm. The grey downpour was swept aside and vanished like the trailing garments of a ghost. Above me, in the intense blue of the summer sky, some faint brown shreds of cloud whirled into nothingness. The great buildings about me stood out clear and distinct, shining with the wet of the thunderstorm, and picked out in white by the unmelted hailstones piled along their courses. I felt naked in a strange world. I felt as perhaps a bird may feel in the clear air, knowing the hawk wings above and will swoop. My fear grew to frenzy. I took a breathing space, set my teeth, and again grappled fiercely, wrist and knee, with the machine. It gave under my desperate onset and turned over. It struck my chin violently. One hand on the saddle, the other on the lever, I stood panting heavily in attitude to mount again.

"But with this recovery of a prompt retreat my courage recovered. I looked more curiously and less fearfully at this world of the remote future. In a circular opening, high up in the wall of the nearer house, I saw a group of figures clad in rich soft robes. They had seen me, and their faces were directed towards me.

"Then I heard voices approaching me. Coming through the bushes by the White Sphinx were the heads and shoulders of men running. One of these emerged in a pathway leading straight to the little lawn upon which I stood with my machine. He was a slight creature – perhaps four feet high – clad in a purple tunic, girdled at the waist with a leather belt. Sandals or buskins – I could not clearly distinguish which – were on his feet; his legs were bare to the knees, and his head was bare. Noticing that, I noticed for the first time how warm the air was.

"He struck me as being a very beautiful and graceful creature, but indescribably frail. His flushed face reminded me of the more beautiful kind of consumptive – that hectic beauty of which we used to hear so much. At the sight of him I suddenly regained confidence. I took my hands from the machine.

Chapter IV

"**IN ANOTHER MOMENT** we were standing face to face, I and this fragile thing out of futurity. He came straight up to me and laughed into my eyes. The absence from his bearing of any sign of fear struck me at once. Then he turned to the two others who were following him and spoke to them in a strange and very sweet and liquid tongue.

"There were others coming, and presently a little group of perhaps eight or ten of these exquisite creatures were about me. One of them addressed me. It came into my head, oddly enough, that my voice was too harsh and deep for them. So I shook my head, and, pointing to my ears, shook it again. He came a step forward, hesitated, and then touched my hand. Then I felt other soft little tentacles upon my back and shoulders. They wanted to make sure I was real. There was nothing in this at all alarming. Indeed, there was something in these pretty little people that inspired confidence – a graceful gentleness, a certain childlike ease. And besides, they looked so frail that I could fancy myself flinging the whole dozen of them about like nine-pins. But I made a sudden motion to warn them when I saw their little pink hands feeling at the Time Machine. Happily then, when it was not too late, I thought of a danger I had hitherto forgotten, and reaching over the bars of the machine I unscrewed the little levers that would set it in motion, and put these in my pocket. Then I turned again to see what I could do in the way of communication.

"And then, looking more nearly into their features, I saw some further peculiarities in their Dresden-china type of prettiness. Their hair, which was uniformly curly, came to a sharp end at the neck and cheek; there was not the faintest suggestion of it on the face, and their ears were singularly minute. The mouths were small, with bright red, rather thin lips, and the little chins ran to a point. The eyes were large and mild; and – this may seem egotism on my part – I fancied even that there was a certain lack of the interest I might have expected in them.

"As they made no effort to communicate with me, but simply stood round me smiling and speaking in soft cooing notes to each other, I began the conversation. I pointed to the Time Machine and to myself. Then hesitating for a moment how to express time, I pointed to the sun. At once a quaintly pretty little figure in chequered purple and white followed my gesture, and then astonished me by imitating the sound of thunder.

"For a moment I was staggered, though the import of his gesture was plain enough. The question had come into my mind abruptly: were these creatures fools? You may hardly understand how it took me. You see I had always anticipated that the people of the year Eight Hundred and Two Thousand odd would be incredibly in front of us in knowledge, art, everything. Then one of them suddenly asked me a question that showed him to be on the intellectual level of one of our five-year-old children – asked me, in fact, if I had come from the sun in a thunderstorm! It let loose the judgment I had suspended upon their clothes, their frail light limbs, and fragile features. A flow of disappointment rushed across my mind. For a moment I felt that I had built the Time Machine in vain.

"I nodded, pointed to the sun, and gave them such a vivid rendering of a thunderclap as startled them. They all withdrew a pace or so and bowed. Then came one laughing towards me, carrying a chain of beautiful flowers altogether new to me, and put it about my neck. The idea was received with melodious applause; and presently they were all running to and fro for flowers, and laughingly flinging them upon me until I was almost smothered with blossom. You who have never seen the like can scarcely imagine what delicate and wonderful flowers countless years of culture had created. Then someone suggested that their plaything should be exhibited in the nearest building, and so I was led past the sphinx of white marble, which had seemed to watch me all the while with a smile at my astonishment, towards a vast grey edifice of fretted stone. As I went with them the memory of my confident anticipations of a profoundly grave and intellectual posterity came, with irresistible merriment, to my mind.

"The building had a huge entry, and was altogether of colossal dimensions. I was naturally most occupied with the growing crowd of little people, and with the big open portals that yawned before me shadowy and mysterious. My general impression of the world I saw over their heads was a tangled waste of beautiful bushes and flowers, a long neglected and yet weedless garden. I saw a number of tall spikes of strange white flowers, measuring a foot perhaps across the spread of the waxen petals. They grew scattered, as if wild, among the variegated shrubs, but, as I say, I did not examine them closely at this time. The Time Machine was left deserted on the turf among the rhododendrons.

"The arch of the doorway was richly carved, but naturally I did not observe the carving very narrowly, though I fancied I saw suggestions of old Phoenician decorations as I passed through, and it struck me that they were very badly broken and weather-worn. Several more brightly clad people met me in the doorway, and so we entered, I, dressed in dingy nineteenth-century garments, looking grotesque enough, garlanded with flowers, and surrounded by an eddying mass of bright, soft-colored robes and shining white limbs, in a melodious whirl of laughter and laughing speech.

"The big doorway opened into a proportionately great hall hung with brown. The roof was in shadow, and the windows, partially glazed with coloured glass and partially unglazed, admitted a tempered light. The floor was made up of huge blocks of some very hard white metal, not plates nor slabs – blocks, and it was so much worn, as I judged by the going to and fro of past generations, as to be deeply channelled along the more frequented ways. Transverse to the length were innumerable tables made of slabs of polished stone, raised perhaps a foot from the floor, and upon these were heaps of fruits. Some I recognized as a kind of hypertrophied raspberry and orange, but for the most part they were strange.

"Between the tables was scattered a great number of cushions. Upon these my conductors seated themselves, signing for me to do likewise. With a pretty absence of ceremony they began to eat the fruit with their hands, flinging peel and stalks, and so forth, into the round openings in the sides of the tables. I was not loath to follow their example, for I felt thirsty and hungry. As I did so I surveyed the hall at my leisure.

"And perhaps the thing that struck me most was its dilapidated look. The stained-glass windows, which displayed only a geometrical pattern, were broken in many places, and the curtains that hung across the lower end were thick with dust. And it caught my eye that the corner of the marble table near me was fractured. Nevertheless, the general effect was extremely rich and picturesque. There were, perhaps, a couple of hundred people dining in the hall, and most of them, seated as near to me as they could come, were watching me with interest, their little eyes shining over the fruit they were eating. All were clad in the same soft and yet strong, silky material.

"Fruit, by the by, was all their diet. These people of the remote future were strict vegetarians, and while I was with them, in spite of some carnal cravings, I had to be frugivorous also. Indeed, I found afterwards that horses, cattle, sheep, dogs, had followed the Ichthyosaurus into extinction. But the fruits were very delightful; one, in particular, that seemed to be in season all the time I was there – a floury thing in a three-sided husk – was especially good, and I made it my staple. At first I was puzzled by all these strange fruits, and by the strange flowers I saw, but later I began to perceive their import.

"However, I am telling you of my fruit dinner in the distant future now. So soon as my appetite was a little checked, I determined to make a resolute attempt to learn the speech of these new men of mine. Clearly that was the next thing to do. The fruits seemed a convenient thing to begin upon, and holding one of these up I began a series of interrogative sounds and gestures. I had some considerable difficulty in conveying my meaning. At first my efforts met with a stare of surprise or inextinguishable laughter, but presently a fair-haired little creature seemed to grasp my intention and repeated a name. They had to chatter and explain the business at great length to each other, and my first attempts to make the exquisite little sounds of their language caused an immense amount of amusement. However, I felt like a schoolmaster amidst children, and persisted, and presently I had a score of noun substantives at least at my command; and then I got to demonstrative pronouns, and even the verb 'to eat.' But it was slow work, and the little people soon tired and wanted to get away from my interrogations, so I determined, rather of necessity, to let them give their lessons in little doses when they felt inclined. And very little doses I found they were before long, for I never met people more indolent or more easily fatigued.

"A queer thing I soon discovered about my little hosts, and that was their lack of interest. They would come to me with eager cries of astonishment, like children, but like children they would soon stop examining me and wander away after some other toy. The dinner and my conversational beginnings ended, I noted for the first time that almost all those who had surrounded me at first were gone. It is odd, too, how speedily I came to disregard these little people. I went out through the portal into the sunlit world again as soon as my hunger was satisfied. I was continually meeting more of these men of the future, who would follow me a little distance, chatter and laugh about me, and, having smiled and gesticulated in a friendly way, leave me again to my own devices.

"The calm of evening was upon the world as I emerged from the great hall, and the scene was lit by the warm glow of the setting sun. At first things were very confusing. Everything was so entirely different from the world I had known – even the flowers. The big building I had left was situated on the slope of a broad river valley, but the Thames had shifted perhaps a mile from its present position. I resolved to mount to the summit of a crest, perhaps a mile and a half away, from which I could get a wider view of this our planet in the year Eight Hundred and Two Thousand Seven Hundred and One A.D. For that, I should explain, was the date the little dials of my machine recorded.

"As I walked I was watching for every impression that could possibly help to explain the condition of ruinous splendour in which I found the world – for ruinous it was. A little way up the hill, for instance, was a great heap of granite, bound together by masses of aluminium, a vast labyrinth of precipitous walls and crumpled heaps, amidst which were thick heaps of very beautiful pagoda-like plants – nettles possibly – but wonderfully tinted with brown about the leaves, and incapable of stinging. It was evidently the derelict remains of some vast structure, to what end built I could not determine. It was here that I was destined, at a later date, to have a very strange experience – the first intimation of a still stranger discovery – but of that I will speak in its proper place.

"Looking round with a sudden thought, from a terrace on which I rested for a while, I realized that there were no small houses to be seen. Apparently the single house, and possibly even the household, had vanished. Here and there among the greenery were palace-like buildings, but the house and the cottage, which form such characteristic features of our own English landscape, had disappeared.

"'Communism,' said I to myself.

"And on the heels of that came another thought. I looked at the half-dozen little figures that were following me. Then, in a flash, I perceived that all had the same form of costume, the same soft hairless visage, and the same girlish rotundity of limb. It may seem strange, perhaps, that I had not noticed this before. But everything was so strange. Now, I saw the fact plainly enough. In costume, and in all the differences of texture and bearing that now mark off the sexes from each other, these people of the future were alike. And the children seemed to my eyes to be but the miniatures of their parents. I judged, then, that the children of that time were extremely precocious, physically at least, and I found afterwards abundant verification of my opinion.

"Seeing the ease and security in which these people were living, I felt that this close resemblance of the sexes was after all what one would expect; for the strength of a man and the softness of a woman, the institution of the family, and the differentiation of occupations are mere militant necessities of an age of physical force; where population is balanced and abundant, much childbearing becomes an evil rather than a blessing to the State; where violence comes but rarely and off-spring are secure, there is less necessity – indeed there is no necessity – for an efficient family, and the specialization of the sexes with reference to their children's needs disappears. We see some beginnings of this even in our own time, and in this future age it was complete. This, I must remind you, was my speculation at the time. Later, I was to appreciate how far it fell short of the reality.

"While I was musing upon these things, my attention was attracted by a pretty little structure, like a well under a cupola. I thought in a transitory way of the oddness of wells still existing, and then resumed the thread of my speculations. There were no large buildings towards the top of the hill, and as my walking powers were evidently miraculous, I was presently left alone for the first time. With a strange sense of freedom and adventure I pushed on up to the crest.

"There I found a seat of some yellow metal that I did not recognize, corroded in places with a kind of pinkish rust and half smothered in soft moss, the arm-rests cast and filed into the resemblance of griffins" heads. I sat down on it, and I surveyed the broad view of our old world under the sunset of that long day. It was as sweet and fair a view as I have ever seen. The sun had already gone below the horizon and the west was flaming gold, touched with some horizontal bars of purple and crimson. Below was the valley of the Thames, in which the river lay like a band of burnished steel. I have already spoken of the great palaces dotted about among the variegated greenery, some in ruins and some still occupied. Here and there rose a white or silvery figure in the waste garden of the earth, here and there came the sharp vertical line of some cupola or obelisk. There were no hedges, no signs of proprietary rights, no evidences of agriculture; the whole earth had become a garden.

"So watching, I began to put my interpretation upon the things I had seen, and as it shaped itself to me that evening, my interpretation was something in this way. (Afterwards I found I had got only a half-truth – or only a glimpse of one facet of the truth.)

"It seemed to me that I had happened upon humanity upon the wane. The ruddy sunset set me thinking of the sunset of mankind. For the first time I began to realize an odd consequence of the social effort in which we are at present engaged. And yet, come to think, it is a logical consequence enough. Strength is the outcome of need; security sets a premium on feebleness. The work of ameliorating the conditions of life – the true civilizing process that makes life more and more secure – had gone steadily on to a climax. One triumph of a united humanity over Nature had followed another. Things that are now mere dreams had become projects deliberately put in hand and carried forward. And the harvest was what I saw!

"After all, the sanitation and the agriculture of today are still in the rudimentary stage. The science of our time has attacked but a little department of the field of human disease, but even so, it spreads its operations very steadily and persistently. Our agriculture and horticulture destroy a weed just here and there and cultivate perhaps a score or so of wholesome plants, leaving the greater number to fight out a balance as they can. We improve our favourite plants and animals – and how few they are – gradually by selective breeding; now a new and better peach, now a seedless grape, now a sweeter and larger flower, now a more convenient breed of cattle. We improve them gradually, because our ideals are vague and tentative, and our knowledge is very limited; because Nature, too, is shy and slow in our clumsy hands. Some day all this will be better organized, and still better. That is the drift of the current in spite of the eddies. The whole world will be intelligent, educated, and co-operating; things will move faster and faster towards the subjugation of Nature. In the end, wisely and carefully we shall readjust the balance of animal and vegetable life to suit our human needs.

"This adjustment, I say, must have been done, and done well; done indeed for all Time, in the space of Time across which my machine had leaped. The air was free from gnats, the earth from weeds or fungi; everywhere were fruits and sweet and delightful flowers; brilliant butterflies flew hither and thither. The ideal of preventive medicine was attained. Diseases had been stamped out. I saw no evidence of any contagious diseases during all my stay. And I shall have to tell you later that even the processes of putrefaction and decay had been profoundly affected by these changes.

"Social triumphs, too, had been effected. I saw mankind housed in splendid shelters, gloriously clothed, and as yet I had found them engaged in no toil. There were no signs of struggle, neither social nor economical struggle. The shop, the advertisement, traffic, all that commerce which constitutes the body of our world, was gone. It was natural on that golden evening that I should jump at the idea of a social paradise. The difficulty of increasing population had been met, I guessed, and population had ceased to increase.

"But with this change in condition comes inevitably adaptations to the change. What, unless biological science is a mass of errors, is the cause of human intelligence and vigour? Hardship and freedom: conditions under which the active, strong, and subtle survive and the weaker go to the wall; conditions that put a premium upon the loyal alliance of capable men, upon self-restraint, patience, and decision. And the institution of the family, and the emotions that arise therein, the fierce jealousy, the tenderness for offspring, parental self-devotion, all found their justification and support in the imminent dangers of the young. Now, where are these imminent dangers? There is a sentiment arising, and it will grow, against connubial jealousy, against fierce maternity, against passion of all sorts; unnecessary things now, and things that make us uncomfortable, savage survivals, discords in a refined and pleasant life.

"I thought of the physical slightness of the people, their lack of intelligence, and those big abundant ruins, and it strengthened my belief in a perfect conquest of Nature. For after the battle comes Quiet. Humanity had been strong, energetic, and intelligent, and had used all its abundant vitality to alter the conditions under which it lived. And now came the reaction of the altered conditions.

"Under the new conditions of perfect comfort and security, that restless energy, that with us is strength, would become weakness. Even in our own time certain tendencies and desires, once necessary to survival, are a constant source of failure. Physical courage and the love of battle, for instance, are no great help – may even be hindrances – to a civilized man. And in a state of physical balance and security, power, intellectual as well as physical, would be out of place. For countless years I judged there had been no danger of war or solitary violence, no danger from wild beasts, no wasting disease to require strength of constitution, no need of toil. For such a life, what we should call the weak are as well equipped as the strong, are indeed no longer weak. Better equipped indeed they are, for the strong would be fretted by an energy for which there was no outlet. No doubt the exquisite beauty of the buildings I saw was the outcome of the last surgings of the now purposeless energy of mankind before it settled down into perfect harmony with the conditions under which it lived – the flourish of that triumph which began the last great peace. This has ever been the fate of energy in security; it takes to art and to eroticism, and then come languor and decay.

"Even this artistic impetus would at last die away – had almost died in the Time I saw. To adorn themselves with flowers, to dance, to sing in the sunlight: so much was left of the artistic spirit, and no more. Even that would fade in the end into a contented inactivity. We are kept keen on the grindstone of pain and necessity, and, it seemed to me, that here was that hateful grindstone broken at last!

"As I stood there in the gathering dark I thought that in this simple explanation I had mastered the problem of the world – mastered the whole secret of these delicious people. Possibly the checks they had devised for the increase of population had succeeded too well, and their numbers had rather diminished than kept stationary. That would account for the abandoned ruins. Very simple was my explanation, and plausible enough – as most wrong theories are!

Chapter V

"**AS I STOOD** there musing over this too perfect triumph of man, the full moon, yellow and gibbous, came up out of an overflow of silver light in the north-east. The bright little figures ceased to move about below, a noiseless owl flitted by, and I shivered with the chill of the night. I determined to descend and find where I could sleep.

"I looked for the building I knew. Then my eye travelled along to the figure of the White Sphinx upon the pedestal of bronze, growing distinct as the light of the rising moon grew brighter. I could see the silver birch against it. There was the tangle of rhododendron bushes, black in the pale light, and there was the little lawn. I looked at the lawn again. A queer doubt chilled my complacency. 'No,' said I stoutly to myself, 'that was not the lawn.'

"But it was the lawn. For the white leprous face of the sphinx was towards it. Can you imagine what I felt as this conviction came home to me? But you cannot. The Time Machine was gone!

"At once, like a lash across the face, came the possibility of losing my own age, of being left helpless in this strange new world. The bare thought of it was an actual physical sensation. I could feel it grip me at the throat and stop my breathing. In another moment I was in a passion of fear and running with great leaping strides down the slope. Once I fell headlong and cut my face; I lost no time in stanching the blood, but jumped up and ran on, with a warm trickle down my cheek and chin. All the time I ran I was saying to myself: 'They have moved it a little, pushed it under the bushes out of the way.' Nevertheless, I ran with all my might. All the time, with the certainty that sometimes comes with excessive dread, I knew that such assurance was folly, knew instinctively that the machine was removed out of my reach. My breath came with pain. I suppose I covered the whole distance from the hill crest to the little lawn, two miles perhaps, in ten minutes. And I am not a young man. I cursed aloud, as I ran, at my confident folly in leaving the machine, wasting good breath thereby. I cried aloud, and none answered. Not a creature seemed to be stirring in that moonlit world.

"When I reached the lawn my worst fears were realized. Not a trace of the thing was to be seen. I felt faint and cold when I faced the empty space among the black tangle of bushes. I ran round it furiously, as if the thing might be hidden in a corner, and then stopped abruptly, with my hands clutching my hair. Above me towered the sphinx, upon the bronze pedestal, white, shining, leprous, in the light of the rising moon. It seemed to smile in mockery of my dismay.

"I might have consoled myself by imagining the little people had put the mechanism in some shelter for me, had I not felt assured of their physical and intellectual inadequacy. That is what dismayed me: the sense of some hitherto unsuspected power, through whose intervention my invention had vanished. Yet, for one thing I felt assured: unless some other age had produced its exact duplicate, the machine could not have moved in time. The attachment of the levers – I will show you the method later – prevented any one from tampering with it in that way when they were removed. It had moved, and was hid, only in space. But then, where could it be?

"I think I must have had a kind of frenzy. I remember running violently in and out among the moonlit bushes all round the sphinx, and startling some white animal that, in the dim light, I took for a small deer. I remember, too, late that night, beating the bushes with my clenched fist until my knuckles were gashed and bleeding from the broken twigs. Then, sobbing and raving in my anguish of mind, I went down to the great building of stone. The big hall was dark, silent, and deserted. I slipped on the uneven floor, and fell over one of the malachite tables, almost breaking my shin. I lit a match and went on past the dusty curtains, of which I have told you.

"There I found a second great hall covered with cushions, upon which, perhaps, a score or so of the little people were sleeping. I have no doubt they found my second appearance strange enough, coming suddenly out of the quiet darkness with inarticulate noises and the splutter and flare of a match. For they had forgotten about matches. 'Where is my Time Machine?' I began, bawling like an angry child, laying hands upon them and shaking them up together. It must have been very queer to them. Some laughed, most of them looked sorely frightened. When I saw them standing round me, it came into my head that I was doing as foolish a thing as it was possible for me to do under the circumstances, in trying to revive the sensation of fear. For, reasoning from their daylight behaviour, I thought that fear must be forgotten.

"Abruptly, I dashed down the match, and, knocking one of the people over in my course, went blundering across the big dining-hall again, out under the moonlight. I heard cries of terror and their little feet running and stumbling this way and that. I do not remember all I did as the moon crept up the sky. I suppose it was the unexpected nature of my loss that maddened me. I felt hopelessly cut off from my own kind – a strange animal in an unknown world. I must have raved to and fro, screaming and crying upon God and Fate. I have a memory of horrible fatigue, as the long night of despair wore away; of looking in this impossible place and that; of groping among moon-lit ruins and touching strange creatures in the black shadows; at last, of lying on the ground near the sphinx and weeping with absolute wretchedness. I had nothing left but misery. Then I slept, and when I woke again it was full day, and a couple of sparrows were hopping round me on the turf within reach of my arm.

"I sat up in the freshness of the morning, trying to remember how I had got there, and why I had such a profound sense of desertion and despair. Then things came clear in my mind. With the plain, reasonable daylight, I could look my circumstances fairly in the face. I saw the wild folly of my frenzy overnight, and I could reason with myself. 'Suppose the worst?' I said. 'Suppose the machine altogether lost – perhaps destroyed? It behoves me to be calm and patient, to learn the way of the people, to get a clear idea of the method of my loss, and the means of getting materials and tools; so that in the end, perhaps, I may make another.' That would be my only hope, perhaps, but better than despair. And, after all, it was a beautiful and curious world.

"But probably, the machine had only been taken away. Still, I must be calm and patient, find its hiding-place, and recover it by force or cunning. And with that I scrambled to my feet and looked about me, wondering where I could bathe. I felt weary, stiff, and travel-soiled. The freshness of the morning made me desire an equal freshness. I had exhausted my emotion. Indeed, as I went about my business, I found myself wondering at my intense excitement overnight. I made a careful examination of the ground about the little lawn. I wasted some time in futile questionings, conveyed, as well as I was able, to such of the little people as came by. They all failed to understand my gestures; some were simply stolid, some thought it was a jest and laughed at me. I had the hardest task in the world to keep my hands off their pretty laughing faces. It was a foolish impulse, but the devil begotten of fear and blind anger was ill curbed and still eager to take advantage of my perplexity. The turf gave better counsel. I found a groove ripped in it, about midway between the pedestal of the sphinx and the marks of my feet where, on arrival, I had struggled with the overturned machine. There were other signs of removal about, with queer narrow footprints like those I could imagine made by a sloth. This directed my closer attention to the pedestal. It was, as I think I have said, of bronze. It was not a mere block, but highly decorated with deep framed panels on either side. I went and rapped at these. The pedestal was hollow. Examining the panels with care I found them discontinuous with the frames. There were no handles or keyholes, but possibly the panels, if they were doors, as I supposed, opened from within. One thing was clear enough to my mind. It took no very great mental effort to infer that my Time Machine was inside that pedestal. But how it got there was a different problem.

"I saw the heads of two orange-clad people coming through the bushes and under some blossom-covered apple-trees towards me. I turned smiling to them and beckoned them to me. They came, and then, pointing to the bronze pedestal, I tried to intimate my wish to open it. But at my first gesture towards this they behaved very oddly. I don't know how to convey their expression to you. Suppose you were to use a grossly improper gesture to a delicate-minded woman – it is how she would look. They went off as if they had received the last possible insult. I tried a sweet-looking little chap in white next, with exactly the same result. Somehow, his manner made me feel ashamed of myself. But, as you know, I wanted the Time Machine, and I tried him once more. As he turned off, like the others, my temper got the better of me. In three strides I was after him, had him by the loose part of his robe round the neck, and began dragging him towards the sphinx. Then I saw the horror and repugnance of his face, and all of a sudden I let him go.

"But I was not beaten yet. I banged with my fist at the bronze panels. I thought I heard something stir inside – to be explicit, I thought I heard a sound like a chuckle – but I must have been mistaken. Then I got a big pebble from the river, and came and hammered till I had flattened a coil in the decorations, and the verdigris came off in powdery flakes. The delicate little people must have heard me hammering in gusty outbreaks a mile away on either hand, but nothing came of it. I saw a crowd of them upon the slopes, looking furtively at me. At last, hot and tired, I sat down to watch the place. But I was too restless to watch long; I am too Occidental for a long vigil. I could work at a problem for years, but to wait inactive for twenty-four hours – that is another matter.

"I got up after a time, and began walking aimlessly through the bushes towards the hill again. 'Patience,' said I to myself. 'If you want your machine again you must leave that sphinx alone. If they mean to take your machine away, it's little good your wrecking their bronze panels, and if they don't, you will get it back as soon as you can ask for it. To sit among all those unknown things before a puzzle like that is hopeless. That way lies monomania. Face this world. Learn its ways, watch it, be careful of too hasty guesses at its meaning. In the end you will find clues to it all.' Then suddenly the humour of the situation came into my mind: the thought of the years I had spent in study and toil to get into the future age, and now my passion of anxiety to get out of it. I had made myself the most complicated and the most hopeless trap that ever a man devised. Although it was at my own expense, I could not help myself. I laughed aloud.

"Going through the big palace, it seemed to me that the little people avoided me. It may have been my fancy, or it may have had something to do with my hammering at the gates of bronze. Yet I felt tolerably sure of the avoidance. I was careful, however, to show no concern and to abstain from any pursuit of them, and in the course of a day or two things got back to the old footing. I made what progress I could in the language, and in addition I pushed my explorations here and there. Either I missed some subtle point or their language was excessively simple – almost exclusively composed of concrete substantives and verbs. There seemed to be few, if any, abstract terms, or little use of figurative language. Their sentences were usually simple and of two words, and I failed to convey or understand any but the simplest propositions. I determined to put the thought of my Time Machine and the mystery of the bronze doors under the sphinx as much as possible in a corner of memory, until my growing knowledge would lead me back to them in a natural way. Yet a certain feeling, you may understand, tethered me in a circle of a few miles round the point of my arrival.

"So far as I could see, all the world displayed the same exuberant richness as the Thames valley. From every hill I climbed I saw the same abundance of splendid buildings, endlessly varied in material and style, the same clustering thickets of evergreens, the same blossom-laden trees and tree-ferns. Here and there water shone like silver, and beyond, the land rose into blue undulating hills, and so faded into the serenity of the sky. A peculiar feature, which presently attracted my attention, was the presence of certain circular wells, several, as it seemed to me, of a very great depth. One lay by the path up the hill, which I had followed during my first walk. Like the others, it was rimmed with bronze, curiously wrought, and protected by a little cupola from the rain. Sitting by the side of these wells, and peering down into the shafted darkness, I could see no gleam of water, nor could I start any reflection with a lighted match. But in all of them I heard a certain sound: a thud – thud – thud, like the beating of some big engine; and I discovered, from the flaring of my matches, that a steady current of air set down the shafts. Further, I threw a scrap of paper into the throat of one, and, instead of fluttering slowly down, it was at once sucked swiftly out of sight.

"After a time, too, I came to connect these wells with tall towers standing here and there upon the slopes; for above them there was often just such a flicker in the air as one sees on a hot day above a sun-scorched beach. Putting things together, I reached a strong suggestion of an extensive system of subterranean ventilation, whose true import it was difficult to imagine. I was at first inclined to associate it with the sanitary apparatus of these people. It was an obvious conclusion, but it was absolutely wrong.

"And here I must admit that I learned very little of drains and bells and modes of conveyance, and the like conveniences, during my time in this real future. In some of these visions of Utopias and coming times which I have read, there is a vast amount of detail about building, and social arrangements, and so forth. But while such details are easy enough to obtain when the whole world is contained in one's imagination, they are altogether inaccessible to a real traveller amid such realities as I found here. Conceive the tale of London which a negro, fresh from Central Africa, would take back to his tribe! What would he know of railway companies, of social movements, of telephone and telegraph wires, of the Parcels Delivery Company, and postal orders and the like? Yet we, at least, should be willing enough to explain these things to him! And even of what he knew, how much could he make his untravelled friend either apprehend or believe? Then, think how narrow the gap between a negro and a white man of our own times, and how wide the interval between myself and these of the Golden Age! I was sensible of much which was unseen, and which contributed to my comfort; but save for a general impression of automatic organization, I fear I can convey very little of the difference to your mind.

"In the matter of sepulture, for instance, I could see no signs of crematoria nor anything suggestive of tombs. But it occurred to me that, possibly, there might be cemeteries (or crematoria) somewhere beyond the range of my explorings. This, again, was a question I deliberately put to myself, and my curiosity was at first entirely defeated upon the point. The thing puzzled me, and I was led to make a further remark, which puzzled me still more: that aged and infirm among this people there were none.

"I must confess that my satisfaction with my first theories of an automatic civilization and a decadent humanity did not long endure. Yet I could think of no other. Let me put my difficulties. The several big palaces I had explored were mere living places, great dining-halls and sleeping apartments. I could find no machinery, no appliances of any kind. Yet these people were clothed in pleasant fabrics that must at times need renewal, and their sandals, though undecorated, were fairly complex specimens of metalwork. Somehow such things must be made. And the little people displayed no vestige of a creative tendency. There were no shops, no workshops, no sign of importations among them. They spent all their time in playing gently, in bathing in the river, in making love in a half-playful fashion, in eating fruit and sleeping. I could not see how things were kept going.

"Then, again, about the Time Machine: something, I knew not what, had taken it into the hollow pedestal of the White Sphinx. Why? For the life of me I could not imagine. Those waterless wells, too, those flickering pillars. I felt I lacked a clue. I felt – how shall I put it? Suppose you found an inscription, with sentences here and there in excellent plain English, and interpolated therewith, others made up of words, of letters even, absolutely unknown to you? Well, on the third day of my visit, that was how the world of Eight Hundred and Two Thousand Seven Hundred and One presented itself to me!

"That day, too, I made a friend – of a sort. It happened that, as I was watching some of the little people bathing in a shallow, one of them was seized with cramp and began drifting downstream. The main current ran rather swiftly, but not too strongly for even a moderate swimmer. It will give you an idea, therefore, of the strange deficiency in these creatures, when I tell you that none made the slightest attempt to rescue the weakly crying little thing which was drowning before their eyes. When I realized this, I hurriedly slipped off my clothes, and, wading in at a point lower down, I caught the poor mite and drew her safe to land. A little rubbing of the limbs soon brought her round, and I had the satisfaction of seeing she was all right before I left her. I had got to such a low estimate of her kind that I did not expect any gratitude from her. In that, however, I was wrong.

"This happened in the morning. In the afternoon I met my little woman, as I believe it was, as I was returning towards my centre from an exploration, and she received me with cries of delight and presented me with a big garland of flowers – evidently made for me and me alone. The thing took my imagination. Very possibly I had been feeling desolate. At any rate I did my best to display my appreciation of the gift. We were soon seated together in a little stone arbour, engaged in conversation, chiefly of smiles. The creature's friendliness affected me exactly as a child's might have done. We passed each other flowers, and she kissed my hands. I did the same to hers. Then I tried talk, and found that her name was Weena, which, though I don't know what it meant, somehow seemed appropriate enough. That was the beginning of a queer friendship which lasted a week, and ended – as I will tell you!

"She was exactly like a child. She wanted to be with me always. She tried to follow me everywhere, and on my next journey out and about it went to my heart to tire her down, and leave her at last, exhausted and calling after me rather plaintively. But the problems of the world had to be mastered. I had not, I said to myself, come into the future to carry on a miniature flirtation. Yet her distress when I left her was very great, her expostulations at the parting were sometimes frantic, and I think, altogether, I had as much trouble as comfort from her devotion. Nevertheless she was, somehow, a very great comfort. I thought it was mere childish affection that made her cling to me. Until it was too late, I did not clearly know what I had inflicted upon her when I left her. Nor until it was too late did I clearly understand what she was to me. For, by merely seeming fond of me, and showing in her weak, futile way that she cared for me, the little doll of a creature presently gave my return to the neighbourhood of the White Sphinx almost the feeling of coming home; and I would watch for her tiny figure of white and gold so soon as I came over the hill.

"It was from her, too, that I learned that fear had not yet left the world. She was fearless enough in the daylight, and she had the oddest confidence in me; for once, in a foolish moment, I made threatening grimaces at her, and she simply laughed at them. But she dreaded the dark, dreaded shadows, dreaded black things. Darkness to her was the one thing dreadful. It was a singularly passionate emotion, and it set me thinking and observing. I discovered then, among other things, that these little people gathered into the great houses after dark, and slept in droves. To enter upon them without a light was to put them into a tumult of apprehension. I never found one out of doors, or one sleeping alone within doors, after dark. Yet I was still such a blockhead that I missed the lesson of that fear, and in spite of Weena's distress I insisted upon sleeping away from these slumbering multitudes.

"It troubled her greatly, but in the end her odd affection for me triumphed, and for five of the nights of our acquaintance, including the last night of all, she slept with her head pillowed on my arm. But my story slips away from me as I speak of her. It must have been the night before her rescue that I was awakened about dawn. I had been restless, dreaming most disagreeably that I was drowned, and that sea anemones were feeling over my face with their soft palps. I woke with a start, and with an odd fancy that some greyish animal had just rushed out of the chamber. I tried to get to sleep again, but I felt restless and uncomfortable. It was that dim grey hour when things are just creeping out of darkness, when everything is colourless and clear cut, and yet unreal. I got up, and went down into the great hall, and so out upon the flagstones in front of the palace. I thought I would make a virtue of necessity, and see the sunrise.

"The moon was setting, and the dying moonlight and the first pallor of dawn were mingled in a ghastly half-light. The bushes were inky black, the ground a sombre grey, the sky colourless and cheerless. And up the hill I thought I could see ghosts. There several times, as I scanned the slope, I saw white figures. Twice I fancied I saw a solitary white, ape-like creature running rather quickly up the hill, and once near the ruins I saw a leash of them carrying some dark body. They moved hastily. I did not see what became of them. It seemed that they vanished among the bushes. The dawn was still indistinct, you must understand. I was feeling that chill, uncertain, early-morning feeling you may have known. I doubted my eyes.

"As the eastern sky grew brighter, and the light of the day came on and its vivid colouring returned upon the world once more, I scanned the view keenly. But I saw no vestige of my white figures. They were mere creatures of the half light. 'They must have been ghosts,' I said; 'I wonder whence they dated.' For a queer notion of Grant Allen's came into my head, and amused me. If each generation die and leave ghosts, he argued, the world at last will get overcrowded with them. On that theory they would have grown innumerable some Eight Hundred Thousand Years hence, and it was no great wonder to see four at once. But the jest was unsatisfying, and I was thinking of these figures all the morning, until Weena's rescue drove them out of my head. I associated them in some indefinite way with the white animal I had startled in my first passionate search for the Time Machine. But Weena was a pleasant substitute. Yet all the same, they were soon destined to take far deadlier possession of my mind.

"I think I have said how much hotter than our own was the weather of this Golden Age. I cannot account for it. It may be that the sun was hotter, or the earth nearer the sun. It is usual to assume that the sun will go on cooling steadily in the future. But people, unfamiliar with such speculations as those of the younger Darwin, forget that the planets must ultimately fall back one by one into the parent body. As these catastrophes occur, the sun will blaze with renewed energy; and it may be that some inner planet had suffered this fate. Whatever the reason, the fact remains that the sun was very much hotter than we know it.

"Well, one very hot morning – my fourth, I think – as I was seeking shelter from the heat and glare in a colossal ruin near the great house where I slept and fed, there happened this strange thing: Clambering among these heaps of masonry, I found a narrow gallery, whose end and side windows were blocked by fallen masses of stone. By contrast with the brilliancy outside, it seemed at first impenetrably dark to me. I entered it groping, for the change from light to blackness made spots of colour swim before me. Suddenly I halted spellbound. A pair of eyes, luminous by reflection against the daylight without, was watching me out of the darkness.

"The old instinctive dread of wild beasts came upon me. I clenched my hands and steadfastly looked into the glaring eyeballs. I was afraid to turn. Then the thought of the absolute security in which humanity appeared to be living came to my mind. And then I remembered that strange terror of the dark. Overcoming my fear to some extent, I advanced a step and spoke. I will admit that my voice was harsh and ill-controlled. I put out my hand and touched something soft. At once the eyes darted sideways, and something white ran past me. I turned with my heart in my mouth, and saw a queer little ape-like figure, its head held down in a peculiar manner, running across the sunlit space behind me. It blundered against a block of granite, staggered aside, and in a moment was hidden in a black shadow beneath another pile of ruined masonry.

"My impression of it is, of course, imperfect; but I know it was a dull white, and had strange large greyish-red eyes; also that there was flaxen hair on its head and down its back. But, as I say, it went too fast for me to see distinctly. I cannot even say whether it ran on all-fours, or only with its forearms held very low. After an instant's pause I followed it into the second heap of ruins. I could not find it at first; but, after a time in the profound obscurity, I came upon one of those round well-like openings of which I have told you, half closed by a fallen pillar. A sudden thought came to me. Could this Thing have vanished down the shaft? I lit a match, and, looking down, I saw a small, white, moving creature, with large bright eyes which regarded me steadfastly as it retreated. It made me shudder. It was so like a human spider! It was clambering down the wall, and now I saw for the first time a number of metal foot and hand rests forming a kind of ladder down the shaft. Then the light burned my fingers and fell out of my hand, going out as it dropped, and when I had lit another the little monster had disappeared.

"I do not know how long I sat peering down that well. It was not for some time that I could succeed in persuading myself that the thing I had seen was human. But, gradually, the truth dawned on me: that Man had not remained one species, but had differentiated into two distinct animals: that my graceful children of the Upper-world were not the sole descendants of our generation, but that this bleached, obscene, nocturnal Thing, which had flashed before me, was also heir to all the ages.

"I thought of the flickering pillars and of my theory of an underground ventilation. I began to suspect their true import. And what, I wondered, was this Lemur doing in my scheme of a perfectly balanced organization? How was it related to the indolent serenity of the beautiful Upper-worlders? And what was hidden down there, at the foot of that shaft? I sat upon the edge of the well telling myself that, at any rate, there was nothing to fear, and that there I must descend for the solution of my difficulties. And withal I was absolutely afraid to go! As I hesitated, two of the beautiful Upper-world people came running in their amorous sport across the daylight in the shadow. The male pursued the female, flinging flowers at her as he ran.

"They seemed distressed to find me, my arm against the overturned pillar, peering down the well. Apparently it was considered bad form to remark these apertures; for when I pointed to this one, and tried to frame a question about it in their tongue, they were still more visibly distressed and turned away. But they were interested by my matches, and I struck some to amuse them. I tried them again about the well, and again I failed. So presently I left them, meaning to go back to Weena, and see what I could get from her. But my mind was already in revolution; my guesses and impressions were slipping and sliding to a new adjustment. I had now a clue to the import of these wells, to the ventilating towers, to the mystery of the ghosts; to say nothing of a hint at the meaning of the bronze gates and the fate of the Time Machine!

And very vaguely there came a suggestion towards the solution of the economic problem that had puzzled me.

"Here was the new view. Plainly, this second species of Man was subterranean. There were three circumstances in particular which made me think that its rare emergence above ground was the outcome of a long-continued underground habit. In the first place, there was the bleached look common in most animals that live largely in the dark – the white fish of the Kentucky caves, for instance. Then, those large eyes, with that capacity for reflecting light, are common features of nocturnal things – witness the owl and the cat. And last of all, that evident confusion in the sunshine, that hasty yet fumbling awkward flight towards dark shadow, and that peculiar carriage of the head while in the light – all reinforced the theory of an extreme sensitiveness of the retina.

"Beneath my feet, then, the earth must be tunnelled enormously, and these tunnellings were the habitat of the new race. The presence of ventilating shafts and wells along the hill slopes – everywhere, in fact, except along the river valley – showed how universal were its ramifications. What so natural, then, as to assume that it was in this artificial Underworld that such work as was necessary to the comfort of the daylight race was done? The notion was so plausible that I at once accepted it, and went on to assume the how of this splitting of the human species. I dare say you will anticipate the shape of my theory; though, for myself, I very soon felt that it fell far short of the truth.

"At first, proceeding from the problems of our own age, it seemed clear as daylight to me that the gradual widening of the present merely temporary and social difference between the Capitalist and the Labourer, was the key to the whole position. No doubt it will seem grotesque enough to you – and wildly incredible! – and yet even now there are existing circumstances to point that way. There is a tendency to utilize underground space for the less ornamental purposes of civilization; there is the Metropolitan Railway in London, for instance, there are new electric railways, there are subways, there are underground workrooms and restaurants, and they increase and multiply. Evidently, I thought, this tendency had increased till Industry had gradually lost its birthright in the sky. I mean that it had gone deeper and deeper into larger and ever larger underground factories, spending a still-increasing amount of its time therein, till, in the end –! Even now, does not an East-end worker live in such artificial conditions as practically to be cut off from the natural surface of the earth?

"Again, the exclusive tendency of richer people – due, no doubt, to the increasing refinement of their education, and the widening gulf between them and the rude violence of the poor – is already leading to the closing, in their interest, of considerable portions of the surface of the land. About London, for instance, perhaps half the prettier country is shut in against intrusion. And this same widening gulf – which is due to the length and expense of the higher educational process and the increased facilities for and temptations towards refined habits on the part of the rich – will make that exchange between class and class, that promotion by intermarriage which at present retards the splitting of our species along lines of social stratification, less and less frequent. So, in the end, above ground you must have the Haves, pursuing pleasure and comfort and beauty, and below ground the Have-nots, the Workers getting continually adapted to the conditions of their labour. Once they were there, they would no doubt have to pay rent, and not a little of it, for the ventilation of their caverns; and if they refused, they would starve or be suffocated for arrears. Such of them as were so constituted as to be miserable and rebellious would die; and, in the end, the balance being permanent, the survivors would become as well adapted to the conditions of underground life, and as happy in their way, as the Upper-world people were to theirs. As it seemed to me, the refined beauty and the etiolated pallor followed naturally enough.

"The great triumph of Humanity I had dreamed of took a different shape in my mind. It had been no such triumph of moral education and general co-operation as I had imagined. Instead, I saw a real aristocracy, armed with a perfected science and working to a logical conclusion the industrial system of today. Its triumph had not been simply a triumph over Nature, but a triumph over Nature and the fellow-man. This, I must warn you, was my theory at the time. I had no convenient cicerone in the pattern of the Utopian books. My explanation may be absolutely wrong. I still think it is the most plausible one. But even on this supposition the balanced civilization that was at last attained must have long since passed its zenith, and was now far fallen into decay. The too-perfect security of the Upper-worlders had led them to a slow movement of degeneration, to a general dwindling in size, strength, and intelligence. That I could see clearly enough already. What had happened to the Under-grounders I did not yet suspect; but from what I had seen of the Morlocks – that, by the by, was the name by which these creatures were called – I could imagine that the modification of the human type was even far more profound than among the 'Eloi,' the beautiful race that I already knew.

"Then came troublesome doubts. Why had the Morlocks taken my Time Machine? For I felt sure it was they who had taken it. Why, too, if the Eloi were masters, could they not restore the machine to me? And why were they so terribly afraid of the dark? I proceeded, as I have said, to question Weena about this Under-world, but here again I was disappointed. At first she would not understand my questions, and presently she refused to answer them. She shivered as though the topic was unendurable. And when I pressed her, perhaps a little harshly, she burst into tears. They were the only tears, except my own, I ever saw in that Golden Age. When I saw them I ceased abruptly to trouble about the Morlocks, and was only concerned in banishing these signs of the human inheritance from Weena's eyes. And very soon she was smiling and clapping her hands, while I solemnly burned a match.

Chapter VI

"**IT MAY** seem odd to you, but it was two days before I could follow up the new-found clue in what was manifestly the proper way. I felt a peculiar shrinking from those pallid bodies. They were just the half-bleached colour of the worms and things one sees preserved in spirit in a zoological museum. And they were filthily cold to the touch. Probably my shrinking was largely due to the sympathetic influence of the Eloi, whose disgust of the Morlocks I now began to appreciate.

"The next night I did not sleep well. Probably my health was a little disordered. I was oppressed with perplexity and doubt. Once or twice I had a feeling of intense fear for which I could perceive no definite reason. I remember creeping noiselessly into the great hall where the little people were sleeping in the moonlight – that night Weena was among them – and feeling reassured by their presence. It occurred to me even then, that in the course of a few days the moon must pass through its last quarter, and the nights grow dark, when the appearances of these unpleasant creatures from below, these whitened Lemurs, this new vermin that had replaced the old, might be more abundant. And on both these days I had the restless feeling of one who shirks an inevitable duty. I felt assured that the Time Machine was only to be recovered by boldly penetrating these underground mysteries. Yet I could not face the mystery. If only I had had a companion it would have been different. But I was so horribly alone, and even to clamber down into the darkness of the well appalled me. I don't know if you will understand my feeling, but I never felt quite safe at my back.

"It was this restlessness, this insecurity, perhaps, that drove me further and further afield in my exploring expeditions. Going to the south-westward towards the rising country that is now called Combe Wood, I observed far off, in the direction of nineteenth-century Banstead, a vast green structure, different in character from any I had hitherto seen. It was larger than the largest of the palaces or ruins I knew, and the facade had an Oriental look: the face of it having the lustre, as well as the pale-green tint, a kind of bluish-green, of a certain type of Chinese porcelain. This difference in aspect suggested a difference in use, and I was minded to push on and explore. But the day was growing late, and I had come upon the sight of the place after a long and tiring circuit; so I resolved to hold over the adventure for the following day, and I returned to the welcome and the caresses of little Weena. But next morning I perceived clearly enough that my curiosity regarding the Palace of Green Porcelain was a piece of self-deception, to enable me to shirk, by another day, an experience I dreaded. I resolved I would make the descent without further waste of time, and started out in the early morning towards a well near the ruins of granite and aluminium.

"Little Weena ran with me. She danced beside me to the well, but when she saw me lean over the mouth and look downward, she seemed strangely disconcerted. 'Good-bye, little Weena,' I said, kissing her; and then putting her down, I began to feel over the parapet for the climbing hooks. Rather hastily, I may as well confess, for I feared my courage might leak away! At first she watched me in amazement. Then she gave a most piteous cry, and running to me, she began to pull at me with her little hands. I think her opposition nerved me rather to proceed. I shook her off, perhaps a little roughly, and in another moment I was in the throat of the well. I saw her agonized face over the parapet, and smiled to reassure her. Then I had to look down at the unstable hooks to which I clung.

"I had to clamber down a shaft of perhaps two hundred yards. The descent was effected by means of metallic bars projecting from the sides of the well, and these being adapted to the needs of a creature much smaller and lighter than myself, I was speedily cramped and fatigued by the descent. And not simply fatigued! One of the bars bent suddenly under my weight, and almost swung me off into the blackness beneath. For a moment I hung by one hand, and after that experience I did not dare to rest again. Though my arms and back were presently acutely painful, I went on clambering down the sheer descent with as quick a motion as possible. Glancing upward, I saw the aperture, a small blue disk, in which a star was visible, while little Weena's head showed as a round black projection. The thudding sound of a machine below grew louder and more oppressive. Everything save that little disk above was profoundly dark, and when I looked up again Weena had disappeared.

"I was in an agony of discomfort. I had some thought of trying to go up the shaft again, and leave the Under-world alone. But even while I turned this over in my mind I continued to descend. At last, with intense relief, I saw dimly coming up, a foot to the right of me, a slender loophole in the wall. Swinging myself in, I found it was the aperture of a narrow horizontal tunnel in which I could lie down and rest. It was not too soon. My arms ached, my back was cramped, and I was trembling with the prolonged terror of a fall. Besides this, the unbroken darkness had had a distressing effect upon my eyes. The air was full of the throb and hum of machinery pumping air down the shaft.

"I do not know how long I lay. I was roused by a soft hand touching my face. Starting up in the darkness I snatched at my matches and, hastily striking one, I saw three stooping white creatures similar to the one I had seen above ground in the ruin, hastily retreating before the light. Living, as they did, in what appeared to me impenetrable darkness, their eyes were abnormally large and sensitive, just as are the pupils of the abysmal fishes, and they reflected the light in the same way. I have no doubt they could see me in that rayless obscurity, and they did not seem to have any fear of me apart from the light. But, so soon as I struck a match in order to see them, they fled incontinently, vanishing into dark gutters and tunnels, from which their eyes glared at me in the strangest fashion.

"I tried to call to them, but the language they had was apparently different from that of the Over-world people; so that I was needs left to my own unaided efforts, and the thought of flight before exploration was even then in my mind. But I said to myself, 'You are in for it now,' and, feeling my way along the tunnel, I found the noise of machinery grow louder. Presently the walls fell away from me, and I came to a large open space, and striking another match, saw that I had entered a vast arched cavern, which stretched into utter darkness beyond the range of my light. The view I had of it was as much as one could see in the burning of a match.

"Necessarily my memory is vague. Great shapes like big machines rose out of the dimness, and cast grotesque black shadows, in which dim spectral Morlocks sheltered from the glare. The place, by the by, was very stuffy and oppressive, and the faint halitus of freshly shed blood was in the air. Some way down the central vista was a little table of white metal, laid with what seemed a meal. The Morlocks at any rate were carnivorous! Even at the time, I remember wondering what large animal could have survived to furnish the red joint I saw. It was all very indistinct: the heavy smell, the big unmeaning shapes, the obscene figures lurking in the shadows, and only waiting for the darkness to come at me again! Then the match burned down, and stung my fingers, and fell, a wriggling red spot in the blackness.

"I have thought since how particularly ill-equipped I was for such an experience. When I had started with the Time Machine, I had started with the absurd assumption that the men of the Future would certainly be infinitely ahead of ourselves in all their appliances. I had come without arms, without medicine, without anything to smoke – at times I missed tobacco frightfully – even without enough matches. If only I had thought of a Kodak! I could have flashed that glimpse of the Underworld in a second, and examined it at leisure. But, as it was, I stood there with only the weapons and the powers that Nature had endowed me with – hands, feet, and teeth; these, and four safety-matches that still remained to me.

"I was afraid to push my way in among all this machinery in the dark, and it was only with my last glimpse of light I discovered that my store of matches had run low. It had never occurred to me until that moment that there was any need to economize them, and I had wasted almost half the box in astonishing the Upper-worlders, to whom fire was a novelty. Now, as I say, I had four left, and while I stood in the dark, a hand touched mine, lank fingers came feeling over my face, and I was sensible of a peculiar unpleasant odour. I fancied I heard the breathing of a crowd of those dreadful little beings about me. I felt the box of matches in my hand being gently disengaged, and other hands behind me plucking at my clothing. The sense of these unseen creatures examining me was indescribably unpleasant. The sudden realization of my ignorance of their ways of thinking and doing came home to me very vividly in the darkness. I shouted at them as loudly as I could. They started away, and then I could feel them approaching me again. They clutched at me more boldly, whispering odd sounds to each other. I shivered violently, and shouted again – rather discordantly. This time they were not so seriously alarmed, and they made a queer laughing noise as they came back at me. I will confess I was horribly frightened. I determined to strike another match and escape under the protection of its glare. I did so, and eking out the flicker with a scrap of paper from my pocket, I made good my retreat to the narrow tunnel. But I had scarce entered this when my light was blown out and in the blackness

I could hear the Morlocks rustling like wind among leaves, and pattering like the rain, as they hurried after me.

"In a moment I was clutched by several hands, and there was no mistaking that they were trying to haul me back. I struck another light, and waved it in their dazzled faces. You can scarce imagine how nauseatingly inhuman they looked – those pale, chinless faces and great, lidless, pinkish-grey eyes! – as they stared in their blindness and bewilderment. But I did not stay to look, I promise you: I retreated again, and when my second match had ended, I struck my third. It had almost burned through when I reached the opening into the shaft. I lay down on the edge, for the throb of the great pump below made me giddy. Then I felt sideways for the projecting hooks, and, as I did so, my feet were grasped from behind, and I was violently tugged backward. I lit my last match…and it incontinently went out. But I had my hand on the climbing bars now, and, kicking violently, I disengaged myself from the clutches of the Morlocks and was speedily clambering up the shaft, while they stayed peering and blinking up at me: all but one little wretch who followed me for some way, and well-nigh secured my boot as a trophy.

"That climb seemed interminable to me. With the last twenty or thirty feet of it a deadly nausea came upon me. I had the greatest difficulty in keeping my hold. The last few yards was a frightful struggle against this faintness. Several times my head swam, and I felt all the sensations of falling. At last, however, I got over the well-mouth somehow, and staggered out of the ruin into the blinding sunlight. I fell upon my face. Even the soil smelt sweet and clean. Then I remember Weena kissing my hands and ears, and the voices of others among the Eloi. Then, for a time, I was insensible.

Chapter VII

"**NOW, INDEED**, I seemed in a worse case than before. Hitherto, except during my night's anguish at the loss of the Time Machine, I had felt a sustaining hope of ultimate escape, but that hope was staggered by these new discoveries. Hitherto I had merely thought myself impeded by the childish simplicity of the little people, and by some unknown forces which I had only to understand to overcome; but there was an altogether new element in the sickening quality of the Morlocks – a something inhuman and malign. Instinctively I loathed them. Before, I had felt as a man might feel who had fallen into a pit: my concern was with the pit and how to get out of it. Now I felt like a beast in a trap, whose enemy would come upon him soon.

"The enemy I dreaded may surprise you. It was the darkness of the new moon. Weena had put this into my head by some at first incomprehensible remarks about the Dark Nights. It was not now such a very difficult problem to guess what the coming Dark Nights might mean. The moon was on the wane: each night there was a longer interval of darkness. And I now understood to some slight degree at least the reason of the fear of the little Upper-world people for the dark. I wondered vaguely what foul villainy it might be that the Morlocks did under the new moon. I felt pretty sure now that my second hypothesis was all wrong. The Upper-world people might once have been the favoured aristocracy, and the Morlocks their mechanical servants: but that had long since passed away. The two species that had resulted from the evolution of man were sliding down towards, or had already arrived at, an altogether new relationship. The Eloi, like the Carolingian kings, had decayed to a mere beautiful futility. They still possessed the earth on sufferance: since the Morlocks, subterranean for innumerable generations, had come at last to find the daylit surface intolerable. And the Morlocks made their garments, I inferred, and maintained them in their habitual needs, perhaps through the survival of an old habit of service. They did it as a standing horse paws with his foot, or as a man enjoys killing animals in sport: because ancient and departed necessities had impressed it on the organism. But, clearly, the old order was already in part reversed. The Nemesis of the delicate ones was creeping on apace. Ages ago, thousands of generations ago, man had thrust his brother man out of the ease and the sunshine. And now that brother was coming back changed! Already the Eloi had begun to learn one old lesson anew. They were becoming reacquainted with Fear. And suddenly there came into my head the memory of the meat I had seen in the Under-world. It seemed odd how it floated into my mind: not stirred up as it were by the current of my meditations, but coming in almost like a question from outside. I tried to recall the form of it. I had a vague sense of something familiar, but I could not tell what it was at the time.

"Still, however helpless the little people in the presence of their mysterious Fear, I was differently constituted. I came out of this age of ours, this ripe prime of the human race, when Fear does not paralyse and mystery has lost its terrors. I at least would defend myself. Without further delay I determined to make myself arms and a fastness where I might sleep. With that refuge as a base, I could face this strange world with some of that confidence I had lost in realizing to what creatures night by night I lay exposed. I felt I could never sleep again until my bed was secure from them. I shuddered with horror to think how they must already have examined me.

"I wandered during the afternoon along the valley of the Thames, but found nothing that commended itself to my mind as inaccessible. All the buildings and trees seemed easily practicable to such dexterous climbers as the Morlocks, to judge by their wells, must be. Then the tall pinnacles of the Palace of Green Porcelain and the polished gleam of its walls came back to my memory; and in the evening, taking Weena like a child upon my shoulder, I went up the hills towards the south-west. The distance, I had reckoned, was seven or eight miles, but it must have been nearer eighteen. I had first seen the place on a moist afternoon when distances are deceptively diminished. In addition, the heel of one of my shoes was loose, and a nail was working through the sole – they were comfortable old shoes I wore about indoors – so that I was lame. And it was already long past sunset when I came in sight of the palace, silhouetted black against the pale yellow of the sky.

"Weena had been hugely delighted when I began to carry her, but after a while she desired me to let her down, and ran along by the side of me, occasionally darting off on either hand to pick flowers to stick in my pockets. My pockets had always puzzled Weena, but at the last she had concluded that they were an eccentric kind of vase for floral decoration. At least she utilized them for that purpose. And that reminds me! In changing my jacket I found...'

The Time Traveller paused, put his hand into his pocket, and silently placed two withered flowers, not unlike very large white mallows, upon the little table. Then he resumed his narrative.

"As the hush of evening crept over the world and we proceeded over the hill crest towards Wimbledon, Weena grew tired and wanted to return to the house of grey stone. But I pointed out the distant pinnacles of the Palace of Green Porcelain to her, and contrived to make her understand that we were seeking a refuge there from her Fear. You know that great pause that comes upon things before the dusk? Even the breeze stops in the trees. To me there is always an air of expectation about that evening stillness. The sky was clear, remote, and empty save for a few horizontal bars far down in the sunset. Well, that night the expectation took the colour of my fears. In that darkling calm my senses seemed preternaturally sharpened. I fancied I could even feel the hollowness of the ground beneath my feet: could, indeed, almost see through it the Morlocks on their ant-hill going hither and thither and waiting for the dark. In my excitement I fancied that they would receive my invasion of their burrows as a declaration of war. And why had they taken my Time Machine?

"So we went on in the quiet, and the twilight deepened into night. The clear blue of the distance faded, and one star after another came out. The ground grew dim and the trees black. Weena's fears and her fatigue grew upon her. I took her in my arms and talked to her and caressed her. Then, as the darkness grew deeper, she put her arms round my neck, and, closing her eyes, tightly pressed her face against my shoulder. So we went down a long slope into a valley, and there in the dimness I almost walked into a little river. This I waded, and went up the opposite side of the valley, past a number of sleeping houses, and by a statue – a Faun, or some such figure, minus the head. Here too were acacias. So far I had seen nothing of the Morlocks, but it was yet early in the night, and the darker hours before the old moon rose were still to come.

"From the brow of the next hill I saw a thick wood spreading wide and black before me. I hesitated at this. I could see no end to it, either to the right or the left. Feeling tired – my feet, in particular, were very sore – I carefully lowered Weena from my shoulder as I halted, and sat down upon the turf. I could no longer see the Palace of Green Porcelain, and I was in doubt of my direction. I looked into the thickness of the wood and thought of what it might hide. Under that dense tangle of branches one would be out of sight of the stars. Even were there no other lurking danger – a danger I did not care to let my imagination loose upon – there would still be all the roots to stumble over and the tree-boles to strike against.

"I was very tired, too, after the excitements of the day; so I decided that I would not face it, but would pass the night upon the open hill.

"Weena, I was glad to find, was fast asleep. I carefully wrapped her in my jacket, and sat down beside her to wait for the moonrise. The hill-side was quiet and deserted, but from the black of the wood there came now and then a stir of living things. Above me shone the stars, for the night was very clear. I felt a certain sense of friendly comfort in their twinkling. All the old constellations had gone from the sky, however: that slow movement which is imperceptible in a hundred human lifetimes, had long since rearranged them in unfamiliar groupings. But the Milky Way, it seemed to me, was still the same tattered streamer of star-dust as of yore. Southward (as I judged it) was a very bright red star that was new to me; it was even more splendid than our own green Sirius. And amid all these scintillating points of light one bright planet shone kindly and steadily like the face of an old friend.

"Looking at these stars suddenly dwarfed my own troubles and all the gravities of terrestrial life. I thought of their unfathomable distance, and the slow inevitable drift of their movements out of the unknown past into the unknown future. I thought of the great precessional cycle that the pole of the earth describes. Only forty times had that silent revolution occurred during all the years that I had traversed. And during these few revolutions all the activity, all the traditions, the complex organizations, the nations, languages, literatures, aspirations, even the mere memory of Man as I knew him, had been swept out of existence. Instead were these frail creatures who had forgotten their high ancestry, and the white Things of which I went in terror. Then I thought of the Great Fear that was between the two species, and for the first time, with a sudden shiver, came the clear knowledge of what the meat I had seen might be. Yet it was too horrible! I looked at little Weena sleeping beside me, her face white and starlike under the stars, and forthwith dismissed the thought.

"Through that long night I held my mind off the Morlocks as well as I could, and whiled away the time by trying to fancy I could find signs of the old constellations in the new confusion. The sky kept very clear, except for a hazy cloud or so. No doubt I dozed at times. Then, as my vigil wore on, came a faintness in the eastward sky, like the reflection of some colourless fire, and the old moon rose, thin and peaked and white. And close behind, and overtaking it, and overflowing it, the dawn came, pale at first, and then growing pink and warm. No Morlocks had approached us. Indeed, I had seen none upon the hill that night. And in the confidence of renewed day it almost seemed to me that my fear had been unreasonable. I stood up and found my foot with the loose heel swollen at the ankle and painful under the heel; so I sat down again, took off my shoes, and flung them away.

"I awakened Weena, and we went down into the wood, now green and pleasant instead of black and forbidding. We found some fruit wherewith to break our fast. We soon met others of the dainty ones, laughing and dancing in the sunlight as though there was no such thing in nature as the night. And then I thought once more of the meat that I had seen. I felt assured now of what it was, and from the bottom of my heart I pitied this last feeble rill from the great flood of humanity. Clearly, at some time in the Long-Ago of human decay the Morlocks" food had run short. Possibly they had lived on rats and such-like vermin. Even now man is far less discriminating and exclusive in his food than he was – far less than any monkey. His prejudice against human flesh is no deep-seated instinct. And so these inhuman sons of men –! I tried to look at the thing in a scientific spirit. After all, they were less human and more remote than our cannibal ancestors of three or four thousand years ago. And the intelligence that would have made this state of things a torment had gone. Why should I trouble myself? These Eloi were mere fatted cattle, which the ant-like Morlocks preserved and preyed upon – probably saw to the breeding of. And there was Weena dancing at my side!

"Then I tried to preserve myself from the horror that was coming upon me, by regarding it as a rigorous punishment of human selfishness. Man had been content to live in ease and delight upon the labours of his fellow-man, had taken Necessity as his watchword and excuse, and in the fullness of time Necessity had come home to him. I even tried a Carlyle-like scorn of this wretched aristocracy in decay. But this attitude of mind was impossible. However great their intellectual degradation, the Eloi had kept too much of the human form not to claim my sympathy, and to make me perforce a sharer in their degradation and their Fear.

"I had at that time very vague ideas as to the course I should pursue. My first was to secure some safe place of refuge, and to make myself such arms of metal or stone as I could contrive. That necessity was immediate. In the next place, I hoped to procure some means of fire, so that I should have the weapon of a torch at hand, for nothing, I knew, would be more efficient against these Morlocks. Then I wanted to arrange some contrivance to break open the doors of bronze under the White Sphinx. I had in mind a battering ram. I had a persuasion that if I could enter those doors and carry a blaze of light before me I should discover the Time Machine and escape. I could not imagine the Morlocks were strong enough to move it far away. Weena I had resolved to bring with me to our own time. And turning such schemes over in my mind I pursued our way towards the building which my fancy had chosen as our dwelling.

Chapter VIII

"**I FOUND** the Palace of Green Porcelain, when we approached it about noon, deserted and falling into ruin. Only ragged vestiges of glass remained in its windows, and great sheets of the green facing had fallen away from the corroded metallic framework. It lay very high upon a turfy down, and looking north-eastward before I entered it, I was surprised to see a large estuary, or even creek, where I judged Wandsworth and Battersea must once have been. I thought then – though I never followed up the thought – of what might have happened, or might be happening, to the living things in the sea.

"The material of the Palace proved on examination to be indeed porcelain, and along the face of it I saw an inscription in some unknown character. I thought, rather foolishly, that Weena might help me to interpret this, but I only learned that the bare idea of writing had never entered her head. She always seemed to me, I fancy, more human than she was, perhaps because her affection was so human.

"Within the big valves of the door – which were open and broken – we found, instead of the customary hall, a long gallery lit by many side windows. At the first glance I was reminded of a museum. The tiled floor was thick with dust, and a remarkable array of miscellaneous objects was shrouded in the same grey covering. Then I perceived, standing strange and gaunt in the centre of the hall, what was clearly the lower part of a huge skeleton. I recognized by the oblique feet that it was some extinct creature after the fashion of the Megatherium. The skull and the upper bones lay beside it in the thick dust, and in one place, where rain-water had dropped through a leak in the roof, the thing itself had been worn away. Further in the gallery was the huge skeleton barrel of a Brontosaurus. My museum hypothesis was confirmed. Going towards the side I found what appeared to be sloping shelves, and clearing away the thick dust, I found the old familiar glass cases of our own time. But they must have been air-tight to judge from the fair preservation of some of their contents.

"Clearly we stood among the ruins of some latter-day South Kensington! Here, apparently, was the Palaeontological Section, and a very splendid array of fossils it must have been, though the inevitable process of decay that had been staved off for a time, and had, through the extinction of bacteria and fungi, lost ninety-nine hundredths of its force, was nevertheless, with extreme sureness if with extreme slowness at work again upon all its treasures. Here and there I found traces of the little people in the shape of rare fossils broken to pieces or threaded in strings upon reeds. And the cases had in some instances been bodily removed – by the Morlocks as I judged. The place was very silent. The thick dust deadened our footsteps. Weena, who had been rolling a sea urchin down the sloping glass of a case, presently came, as I stared about me, and very quietly took my hand and stood beside me.

"And at first I was so much surprised by this ancient monument of an intellectual age, that I gave no thought to the possibilities it presented. Even my preoccupation about the Time Machine receded a little from my mind.

"To judge from the size of the place, this Palace of Green Porcelain had a great deal more in it than a Gallery of Palaeontology; possibly historical galleries; it might be, even a library! To me, at least in my present circumstances, these would be vastly more interesting than this spectacle of oldtime geology in decay. Exploring, I found another short gallery running transversely to the first. This appeared to be devoted to minerals, and the sight of a block of sulphur set my mind running on gunpowder. But I could find no saltpeter; indeed, no nitrates of any kind. Doubtless they had deliquesced ages ago. Yet the sulphur hung in my mind, and set up a train of thinking. As for the rest of the contents of that gallery, though on the whole they were the best preserved of all I saw, I had little interest. I am no specialist in mineralogy, and I went on down a very ruinous aisle running parallel to the first hall I had entered. Apparently this section had been devoted to natural history, but everything had long since passed out of recognition. A few shrivelled and blackened vestiges of what had once been stuffed animals, desiccated mummies in jars that had once held spirit, a brown dust of departed plants: that was all! I was sorry for that, because I should have been glad to trace the patent readjustments by which the conquest of animated nature had been attained. Then we came to a gallery of simply colossal proportions, but singularly ill-lit, the floor of it running downward at a slight angle from the end at which I entered. At intervals white globes hung from the ceiling – many of them cracked and smashed – which suggested that originally the place had been artificially lit. Here I was more in my element, for rising on either side of me were the huge bulks of big machines, all greatly corroded and many broken down, but some still fairly complete. You know I have a certain weakness for mechanism, and I was inclined to linger among these; the more so as for the most part they had the interest of puzzles, and I could make only the vaguest guesses at what they were for. I fancied that if I could solve their puzzles I should find myself in possession of powers that might be of use against the Morlocks.

"Suddenly Weena came very close to my side. So suddenly that she startled me. Had it not been for her I do not think I should have noticed that the floor of the gallery sloped at all. (*Note bene:* It may be, of course, that the floor did not slope, but that the museum was built into the side of a hill. – ED.) The end I had come in at was quite above ground, and was lit by rare slit-like windows. As you went down the length, the ground came up against these windows, until at last there was a pit like the 'area'" of a London house before each, and only a narrow line of daylight at the top. I went slowly along, puzzling about the machines, and had been too intent upon them to notice the gradual diminution of the light, until Weena's increasing apprehensions drew my attention. Then I saw that the gallery ran down at last into a thick darkness. I hesitated, and then, as I looked round me, I saw that the dust was less abundant and its surface less even. Further away towards the dimness, it appeared to be broken by a number of small narrow footprints. My sense of the immediate presence of the Morlocks revived at that. I felt that I was wasting my time in the academic examination of machinery. I called to mind that it was already far advanced in the afternoon, and that I had still no weapon, no refuge, and no means of making a fire. And then down in the remote blackness of the gallery I heard a peculiar pattering, and the same odd noises I had heard down the well.

"I took Weena's hand. Then, struck with a sudden idea, I left her and turned to a machine from which projected a lever not unlike those in a signal-box. Clambering upon the stand, and grasping this lever in my hands, I put all my weight upon it sideways. Suddenly Weena, deserted in the central aisle, began to whimper. I had judged the strength of the lever pretty correctly, for it snapped after a minute's strain, and I rejoined her with a mace in my hand more than sufficient, I judged, for any Morlock skull I might encounter. And I longed very much to kill a Morlock or so. Very inhuman, you may think, to want to go killing one's own descendants! But it was impossible, somehow, to feel any humanity in the things. Only my disinclination to leave Weena, and a persuasion that if I began to slake my thirst for murder my Time Machine might suffer, restrained me from going straight down the gallery and killing the brutes I heard.

"Well, mace in one hand and Weena in the other, I went out of that gallery and into another and still larger one, which at the first glance reminded me of a military chapel hung with tattered flags. The brown and charred rags that hung from the sides of it, I presently recognized as the decaying vestiges of books. They had long since dropped to pieces, and every semblance of print had left them. But here and there were warped boards and cracked metallic clasps that told the tale well enough. Had I been a literary man I might, perhaps, have moralized upon the futility of all ambition. But as it was, the thing that struck me with keenest force was the enormous waste of labour to which this sombre wilderness of rotting paper testified. At the time I will confess that I thought chiefly of the *Philosophical Transactions* and my own seventeen papers upon physical optics.

"Then, going up a broad staircase, we came to what may once have been a gallery of technical chemistry. And here I had not a little hope of useful discoveries. Except at one end where the roof had collapsed, this gallery was well preserved. I went eagerly to every unbroken case. And at last, in one of the really air-tight cases, I found a box of matches. Very eagerly I tried them.

They were perfectly good. They were not even damp. I turned to Weena. 'Dance,' I cried to her in her own tongue. For now I had a weapon indeed against the horrible creatures we feared. And so, in that derelict museum, upon the thick soft carpeting of dust, to Weena's huge delight, I solemnly performed a kind of composite dance, whistling The Land of the Leal as cheerfully as I could. In part it was a modest cancan, in part a step dance, in part a skirt-dance (so far as my tail-coat permitted), and in part original. For I am naturally inventive, as you know.

"Now, I still think that for this box of matches to have escaped the wear of time for immemorial years was a most strange, as for me it was a most fortunate thing. Yet, oddly enough, I found a far unlikelier substance, and that was camphor. I found it in a sealed jar, that by chance, I suppose, had been really hermetically sealed. I fancied at first that it was paraffin wax, and smashed the glass accordingly. But the odour of camphor was unmistakable. In the universal decay this volatile substance had chanced to survive, perhaps through many thousands of centuries. It reminded me of a sepia painting I had once seen done from the ink of a fossil Belemnite that must have perished and become fossilized millions of years ago. I was about to throw it away, but I remembered that it was inflammable and burned with a good bright flame – was, in fact, an excellent candle – and I put it in my pocket. I found no explosives, however, nor any means of breaking down the bronze doors. As yet my iron crowbar was the most helpful thing I had chanced upon. Nevertheless I left that gallery greatly elated.

"I cannot tell you all the story of that long afternoon. It would require a great effort of memory to recall my explorations in at all the proper order. I remember a long gallery of rusting stands of arms, and how I hesitated between my crowbar and a hatchet or a sword. I could not carry both, however, and my bar of iron promised best against the bronze gates. There were numbers of guns, pistols, and rifles. The most were masses of rust, but many were of some new metal, and still fairly sound. But any cartridges or powder there may once have been had rotted into dust. One corner I saw was charred and shattered; perhaps, I thought, by an explosion among the specimens. In another place was a vast array of idols – Polynesian, Mexican, Grecian, Phoenician, every country on earth I should think. And here, yielding to an irresistible impulse, I wrote my name upon the nose of a steatite monster from South America that particularly took my fancy.

"As the evening drew on, my interest waned. I went through gallery after gallery, dusty, silent, often ruinous, the exhibits sometimes mere heaps of rust and lignite, sometimes fresher. In one place I suddenly found myself near the model of a tin-mine, and then by the merest accident I discovered, in an air-tight case, two dynamite cartridges! I shouted 'Eureka!' and smashed the case with joy. Then came a doubt. I hesitated. Then, selecting a little side gallery, I made my essay. I never felt such a disappointment as I did in waiting five, ten, fifteen minutes for an explosion that never came. Of course the things were dummies, as I might have guessed from their presence. I really believe that had they not been so, I should have rushed off incontinently and blown Sphinx, bronze doors, and (as it proved) my chances of finding the Time Machine, all together into non-existence.

"It was after that, I think, that we came to a little open court within the palace. It was turfed, and had three fruit-trees. So we rested and refreshed ourselves. Towards sunset I began to consider our position. Night was creeping upon us, and my inaccessible hiding-place had still to be found. But that troubled me very little now. I had in my possession a thing that was, perhaps, the best of all defences against the Morlocks – I had matches! I had the camphor in my pocket, too, if a blaze were needed. It seemed to me that the best thing we could do would be to pass the night in the open, protected by a fire. In the morning there was the getting of the Time Machine. Towards that, as yet, I had only my iron mace. But now, with my growing knowledge,

I felt very differently towards those bronze doors. Up to this, I had refrained from forcing them, largely because of the mystery on the other side. They had never impressed me as being very strong, and I hoped to find my bar of iron not altogether inadequate for the work.

Chapter IX

"**WE EMERGED** from the palace while the sun was still in part above the horizon. I was determined to reach the White Sphinx early the next morning, and ere the dusk I purposed pushing through the woods that had stopped me on the previous journey. My plan was to go as far as possible that night, and then, building a fire, to sleep in the protection of its glare. Accordingly, as we went along I gathered any sticks or dried grass I saw, and presently had my arms full of such litter. Thus loaded, our progress was slower than I had anticipated, and besides Weena was tired. And I began to suffer from sleepiness too; so that it was full night before we reached the wood. Upon the shrubby hill of its edge Weena would have stopped, fearing the darkness before us; but a singular sense of impending calamity, that should indeed have served me as a warning, drove me onward. I had been without sleep for a night and two days, and I was feverish and irritable. I felt sleep coming upon me, and the Morlocks with it.

"While we hesitated, among the black bushes behind us, and dim against their blackness, I saw three crouching figures. There was scrub and long grass all about us, and I did not feel safe from their insidious approach. The forest, I calculated, was rather less than a mile across. If we could get through it to the bare hill-side, there, as it seemed to me, was an altogether safer resting-place; I thought that with my matches and my camphor I could contrive to keep my path illuminated through the woods. Yet it was evident that if I was to flourish matches with my hands I should have to abandon my firewood; so, rather reluctantly, I put it down. And then it came into my head that I would amaze our friends behind by lighting it. I was to discover the atrocious folly of this proceeding, but it came to my mind as an ingenious move for covering our retreat.

"I don't know if you have ever thought what a rare thing flame must be in the absence of man and in a temperate climate. The sun's heat is rarely strong enough to burn, even when it is focused by dewdrops, as is sometimes the case in more tropical districts. Lightning may blast and blacken, but it rarely gives rise to widespread fire. Decaying vegetation may occasionally smoulder with the heat of its fermentation, but this rarely results in flame. In this decadence, too, the art of fire-making had been forgotten on the earth. The red tongues that went licking up my heap of wood were an altogether new and strange thing to Weena.

"She wanted to run to it and play with it. I believe she would have cast herself into it had I not restrained her. But I caught her up, and in spite of her struggles, plunged boldly before me into the wood. For a little way the glare of my fire lit the path. Looking back presently, I could see, through the crowded stems, that from my heap of sticks the blaze had spread to some bushes adjacent, and a curved line of fire was creeping up the grass of the hill. I laughed at that, and turned again to the dark trees before me. It was very black, and Weena clung to me convulsively, but there was still, as my eyes grew accustomed to the darkness, sufficient light for me to avoid the stems. Overhead it was simply black, except where a gap of remote blue sky shone down upon us here and there. I struck none of my matches because I had no hand free. Upon my left arm I carried my little one, in my right hand I had my iron bar.

"For some way I heard nothing but the crackling twigs under my feet, the faint rustle of the breeze above, and my own breathing and the throb of the blood-vessels in my ears. Then I seemed to know of a pattering about me. I pushed on grimly. The pattering grew more distinct, and then I caught the same queer sound and voices I had heard in the Under-world. There were evidently several of the Morlocks, and they were closing in upon me. Indeed, in another minute I felt a tug at my coat, then something at my arm. And Weena shivered violently, and became quite still.

"It was time for a match. But to get one I must put her down. I did so, and, as I fumbled with my pocket, a struggle began in the darkness about my knees, perfectly silent on her part and with the same peculiar cooing sounds from the Morlocks. Soft little hands, too, were creeping over my coat and back, touching even my neck. Then the match scratched and fizzed. I held it flaring, and saw the white backs of the Morlocks in flight amid the trees. I hastily took a lump of camphor from my pocket, and prepared to light it as soon as the match should wane. Then I looked at Weena. She was lying clutching my feet and quite motionless, with her face to the ground. With a sudden fright I stooped to her. She seemed scarcely to breathe. I lit the block of camphor and flung it to the ground, and as it split and flared up and drove back the Morlocks and the shadows, I knelt down and lifted her. The wood behind seemed full of the stir and murmur of a great company!

"She seemed to have fainted. I put her carefully upon my shoulder and rose to push on, and then there came a horrible realization. In manoeuvring with my matches and Weena, I had turned myself about several times, and now I had not the faintest idea in what direction lay my path. For all I knew, I might be facing back towards the Palace of Green Porcelain. I found myself in a cold sweat. I had to think rapidly what to do. I determined to build a fire and encamp where we were. I put Weena, still motionless, down upon a turfy bole, and very hastily, as my first lump of camphor waned, I began collecting sticks and leaves. Here and there out of the darkness round me the Morlocks" eyes shone like carbuncles.

"The camphor flickered and went out. I lit a match, and as I did so, two white forms that had been approaching Weena dashed hastily away. One was so blinded by the light that he came straight for me, and I felt his bones grind under the blow of my fist. He gave a whoop of dismay, staggered a little way, and fell down. I lit another piece of camphor, and went on gathering my bonfire. Presently I noticed how dry was some of the foliage above me, for since my arrival on the Time Machine, a matter of a week, no rain had fallen. So, instead of casting about among the trees for fallen twigs, I began leaping up and dragging down branches. Very soon I had a choking smoky fire of green wood and dry sticks, and could economize my camphor. Then I turned to where Weena lay beside my iron mace. I tried what I could to revive her, but she lay like one dead. I could not even satisfy myself whether or not she breathed.

"Now, the smoke of the fire beat over towards me, and it must have made me heavy of a sudden. Moreover, the vapour of camphor was in the air. My fire would not need replenishing for an hour or so. I felt very weary after my exertion, and sat down. The wood, too, was full of a slumbrous murmur that I did not understand. I seemed just to nod and open my eyes. But all was dark, and the Morlocks had their hands upon me. Flinging off their clinging fingers I hastily felt in my pocket for the match-box, and – it had gone! Then they gripped and closed with me again. In a moment I knew what had happened. I had slept, and my fire had gone out, and the bitterness of death came over my soul. The forest seemed full of the smell of burning wood. I was caught by the neck, by the hair, by the arms, and pulled down. It was indescribably horrible in the darkness to feel all these soft creatures heaped upon me. I felt as if I was in a monstrous spider's web. I was overpowered, and went down. I felt little teeth nipping at my neck. I rolled over, and as I did so my hand came against my iron lever. It gave me strength. I struggled up, shaking the human rats from me, and, holding the bar short, I thrust where I judged their faces might be. I could feel the succulent giving of flesh and bone under my blows, and for a moment I was free.

"The strange exultation that so often seems to accompany hard fighting came upon me. I knew that both I and Weena were lost, but I determined to make the Morlocks pay for their meat. I stood with my back to a tree, swinging the iron bar before me. The whole wood was full of the stir and cries of them. A minute passed. Their voices seemed to rise to a higher pitch of excitement, and their movements grew faster. Yet none came within reach. I stood glaring at the blackness. Then suddenly came hope. What if the Morlocks were afraid? And close on the heels of that came a strange thing. The darkness seemed to grow luminous. Very dimly I began to see the Morlocks about me – three battered at my feet – and then I recognized, with incredulous surprise, that the others were running, in an incessant stream, as it seemed, from behind me, and away through the wood in front. And their backs seemed no longer white, but reddish. As I stood agape, I saw a little red spark go drifting across a gap of starlight between the branches, and vanish. And at that I understood the smell of burning wood, the slumbrous murmur that was growing now into a gusty roar, the red glow, and the Morlocks" flight.

"Stepping out from behind my tree and looking back, I saw, through the black pillars of the nearer trees, the flames of the burning forest. It was my first fire coming after me. With that I looked for Weena, but she was gone. The hissing and crackling behind me, the explosive thud as each fresh tree burst into flame, left little time for reflection. My iron bar still gripped, I followed in the Morlocks" path. It was a close race. Once the flames crept forward so swiftly on my right as I ran that I was outflanked and had to strike off to the left. But at last I emerged upon a small open space, and as I did so, a Morlock came blundering towards me, and past me, and went on straight into the fire!

"And now I was to see the most weird and horrible thing, I think, of all that I beheld in that future age. This whole space was as bright as day with the reflection of the fire. In the centre was a hillock or tumulus, surmounted by a scorched hawthorn. Beyond this was another arm of the burning forest, with yellow tongues already writhing from it, completely encircling the space with a fence of fire. Upon the hill-side were some thirty or forty Morlocks, dazzled by the light and heat, and blundering hither and thither against each other in their bewilderment. At first I did not realize their blindness, and struck furiously at them with my bar, in a frenzy of fear, as they approached me, killing one and crippling several more. But when I had watched the gestures of one of them groping under the hawthorn against the red sky, and heard their moans, I was assured of their absolute helplessness and misery in the glare, and I struck no more of them.

"Yet every now and then one would come straight towards me, setting loose a quivering horror that made me quick to elude him. At one time the flames died down somewhat, and I feared the foul creatures would presently be able to see me. I was thinking of beginning the fight by killing some of them before this should happen; but the fire burst out again brightly, and I stayed my hand. I walked about the hill among them and avoided them, looking for some trace of Weena. But Weena was gone.

"At last I sat down on the summit of the hillock, and watched this strange incredible company of blind things groping to and fro, and making uncanny noises to each other, as the glare of the fire beat on them. The coiling uprush of smoke streamed across the sky, and through the rare tatters of that red canopy, remote as though they belonged to another universe, shone the little stars. Two or three Morlocks came blundering into me, and I drove them off with blows of my fists, trembling as I did so.

"For the most part of that night I was persuaded it was a nightmare. I bit myself and screamed in a passionate desire to awake. I beat the ground with my hands, and got up and sat down again, and wandered here and there, and again sat down. Then I would fall to rubbing my eyes and calling upon God to let me awake. Thrice I saw Morlocks put their heads down in a kind of agony and rush into the flames. But, at last, above the subsiding red of the fire, above the streaming masses of black smoke and the whitening and blackening tree stumps, and the diminishing numbers of these dim creatures, came the white light of the day.

"I searched again for traces of Weena, but there were none. It was plain that they had left her poor little body in the forest. I cannot describe how it relieved me to think that it had escaped the awful fate to which it seemed destined. As I thought of that, I was almost moved to begin a massacre of the helpless abominations about me, but I contained myself. The hillock, as I have said, was a kind of island in the forest. From its summit I could now make out through a haze of smoke the Palace of Green Porcelain, and from that I could get my bearings for the White Sphinx. And so, leaving the remnant of these damned souls still going hither and thither and moaning, as the day grew clearer, I tied some grass about my feet and limped on across smoking ashes and among black stems, that still pulsated internally with fire, towards the hiding-place of the Time Machine. I walked slowly, for I was almost exhausted, as well as lame, and I felt the intensest wretchedness for the horrible death of little Weena. It seemed an overwhelming calamity. Now, in this old familiar room, it is more like the sorrow of a dream than an actual loss. But that morning it left me absolutely lonely again – terribly alone. I began to think of this house of mine, of this fireside, of some of you, and with such thoughts came a longing that was pain.

"But as I walked over the smoking ashes under the bright morning sky, I made a discovery. In my trouser pocket were still some loose matches. The box must have leaked before it was lost.

Chapter X

"**ABOUT EIGHT** or nine in the morning I came to the same seat of yellow metal from which I had viewed the world upon the evening of my arrival. I thought of my hasty conclusions upon that evening and could not refrain from laughing bitterly at my confidence. Here was the same beautiful scene, the same abundant foliage, the same splendid palaces and magnificent ruins, the same silver river running between its fertile banks. The gay robes of the beautiful people moved hither and thither among the trees. Some were bathing in exactly the place where I had saved Weena, and that suddenly gave me a keen stab of pain. And like blots upon the landscape rose the cupolas above the ways to the Under-world. I understood now what all the beauty of the Over-world people covered. Very pleasant was their day, as pleasant as the day of the cattle in the field. Like the cattle, they knew of no enemies and provided against no needs. And their end was the same.

"I grieved to think how brief the dream of the human intellect had been. It had committed suicide. It had set itself steadfastly towards comfort and ease, a balanced society with security and permanency as its watchword, it had attained its hopes – to come to this at last. Once, life and property must have reached almost absolute safety. The rich had been assured of his wealth and comfort, the toiler assured of his life and work. No doubt in that perfect world there had been no unemployed problem, no social question left unsolved. And a great quiet had followed.

"It is a law of nature we overlook, that intellectual versatility is the compensation for change, danger, and trouble. An animal perfectly in harmony with its environment is a perfect mechanism. Nature never appeals to intelligence until habit and instinct are useless. There is no intelligence where there is no change and no need of change. Only those animals partake of intelligence that have to meet a huge variety of needs and dangers.

"So, as I see it, the Upper-world man had drifted towards his feeble prettiness, and the Under-world to mere mechanical industry. But that perfect state had lacked one thing even for mechanical perfection – absolute permanency. Apparently as time went on, the feeding of the Under-world, however it was effected, had become disjointed. Mother Necessity, who had been staved off for a few thousand years, came back again, and she began below. The Under-world being in contact with machinery, which, however perfect, still needs some little thought outside habit, had probably retained perforce rather more initiative, if less of every other human character, than the Upper. And when other meat failed them, they turned to what old habit had hitherto forbidden. So I say I saw it in my last view of the world of Eight Hundred and Two Thousand Seven Hundred and One. It may be as wrong an explanation as mortal wit could invent. It is how the thing shaped itself to me, and as that I give it to you.

"After the fatigues, excitements, and terrors of the past days, and in spite of my grief, this seat and the tranquil view and the warm sunlight were very pleasant. I was very tired and sleepy, and soon my theorizing passed into dozing. Catching myself at that, I took my own hint, and spreading myself out upon the turf I had a long and refreshing sleep.

"I awoke a little before sunsetting. I now felt safe against being caught napping by the Morlocks, and, stretching myself, I came on down the hill towards the White Sphinx. I had my crowbar in one hand, and the other hand played with the matches in my pocket.

"And now came a most unexpected thing. As I approached the pedestal of the sphinx I found the bronze valves were open. They had slid down into grooves.

"At that I stopped short before them, hesitating to enter.

"Within was a small apartment, and on a raised place in the corner of this was the Time Machine. I had the small levers in my pocket. So here, after all my elaborate preparations for the siege of the White Sphinx, was a meek surrender. I threw my iron bar away, almost sorry not to use it.

"A sudden thought came into my head as I stooped towards the portal. For once, at least, I grasped the mental operations of the Morlocks. Suppressing a strong inclination to laugh, I stepped through the bronze frame and up to the Time Machine. I was surprised to find it had been carefully oiled and cleaned. I have suspected since that the Morlocks had even partially taken it to pieces while trying in their dim way to grasp its purpose.

"Now as I stood and examined it, finding a pleasure in the mere touch of the contrivance, the thing I had expected happened. The bronze panels suddenly slid up and struck the frame with a clang. I was in the dark – trapped. So the Morlocks thought. At that I chuckled gleefully.

"I could already hear their murmuring laughter as they came towards me. Very calmly I tried to strike the match. I had only to fix on the levers and depart then like a ghost. But I had overlooked one little thing. The matches were of that abominable kind that light only on the box.

"You may imagine how all my calm vanished. The little brutes were close upon me. One touched me. I made a sweeping blow in the dark at them with the levers, and began to scramble into the saddle of the machine. Then came one hand upon me and then another. Then I had simply to fight against their persistent fingers for my levers, and at the same time feel for the studs over which these fitted. One, indeed, they almost got away from me. As it slipped from my hand, I had to butt in the dark with my head – I could hear the Morlock's skull ring – to recover it. It was a nearer thing than the fight in the forest, I think, this last scramble.

"But at last the lever was fitted and pulled over. The clinging hands slipped from me. The darkness presently fell from my eyes. I found myself in the same grey light and tumult I have already described.

Chapter XI

"**I HAVE ALREADY** told you of the sickness and confusion that comes with time travelling. And this time I was not seated properly in the saddle, but sideways and in an unstable fashion. For an indefinite time I clung to the machine as it swayed and vibrated, quite unheeding how I went, and when I brought myself to look at the dials again I was amazed to find where I had arrived. One dial records days, and another thousands of days, another millions of days, and another thousands of millions. Now, instead of reversing the levers, I had pulled them over so as to go forward with them, and when I came to look at these indicators I found that the thousands hand was sweeping round as fast as the seconds hand of a watch – into futurity.

"As I drove on, a peculiar change crept over the appearance of things. The palpitating greyness grew darker; then – though I was still travelling with prodigious velocity – the blinking succession of day and night, which was usually indicative of a slower pace, returned, and grew more and more marked. This puzzled me very much at first. The alternations of night and day grew slower and slower, and so did the passage of the sun across the sky, until they seemed to stretch through centuries. At last a steady twilight brooded over the earth, a twilight only broken now and then when a comet glared across the darkling sky. The band of light that had indicated the sun had long since disappeared; for the sun had ceased to set – it simply rose and fell in the west, and grew ever broader and more red. All trace of the moon had vanished. The circling of the stars, growing slower and slower, had given place to creeping points of light. At last, some time before I stopped, the sun, red and very large, halted motionless upon the horizon, a vast dome glowing with a dull heat, and now and then suffering a momentary extinction. At one time it had for a little while glowed more brilliantly again, but it speedily reverted to its sullen red heat. I perceived by this slowing down of its rising and setting that the work of the tidal drag was done. The earth had come to rest with one face to the sun, even as in our own time the moon faces the earth. Very cautiously, for I remembered my former headlong fall, I began to reverse my motion. Slower and slower went the circling hands until the thousands one seemed motionless and the daily one was no longer a mere mist upon its scale. Still slower, until the dim outlines of a desolate beach grew visible.

"I stopped very gently and sat upon the Time Machine, looking round. The sky was no longer blue. North-eastward it was inky black, and out of the blackness shone brightly and steadily the pale white stars. Overhead it was a deep Indian red and starless, and south-eastward it grew brighter to a glowing scarlet where, cut by the horizon, lay the huge hull of the sun, red and motionless. The rocks about me were of a harsh reddish colour, and all the trace of life that I could see at first was the intensely green vegetation that covered every projecting point on their south-eastern face. It was the same rich green that one sees on forest moss or on the lichen in caves: plants which like these grow in a perpetual twilight.

"The machine was standing on a sloping beach. The sea stretched away to the south-west, to rise into a sharp bright horizon against the wan sky. There were no breakers and no waves, for not a breath of wind was stirring. Only a slight oily swell rose and fell like a gentle breathing, and showed that the eternal sea was still moving and living. And along the margin where the water sometimes broke was a thick incrustation of salt – pink under the lurid sky. There was a sense of oppression in my head, and I noticed that I was breathing very fast. The sensation reminded me of my only experience of mountaineering, and from that I judged the air to be more rarefied than it is now.

"Far away up the desolate slope I heard a harsh scream, and saw a thing like a huge white butterfly go slanting and fluttering up into the sky and, circling, disappear over some low hillocks beyond. The sound of its voice was so dismal that I shivered and seated myself more firmly upon the machine. Looking round me again, I saw that, quite near, what I had taken to be a reddish mass of rock was moving slowly towards me. Then I saw the thing was really a monstrous crab-like creature. Can you imagine a crab as large as yonder table, with its many legs moving slowly and uncertainly, its big claws swaying, its long antennae, like carters" whips, waving and feeling, and its stalked eyes gleaming at you on either side of its metallic front? Its back was corrugated and ornamented with ungainly bosses, and a greenish incrustation blotched it here and there. I could see the many palps of its complicated mouth flickering and feeling as it moved.

"As I stared at this sinister apparition crawling towards me, I felt a tickling on my cheek as though a fly had lighted there. I tried to brush it away with my hand, but in a moment it returned, and almost immediately came another by my ear. I struck at this, and caught something threadlike. It was drawn swiftly out of my hand. With a frightful qualm, I turned, and I saw that I had grasped the antenna of another monster crab that stood just behind me. Its evil eyes were wriggling on their stalks, its mouth was all alive with appetite, and its vast ungainly claws, smeared with an algal slime, were descending upon me. In a moment my hand was on the lever, and I had placed a month between myself and these monsters. But I was still on the same beach, and I saw them distinctly now as soon as I stopped. Dozens of them seemed to be crawling here and there, in the sombre light, among the foliated sheets of intense green.

"I cannot convey the sense of abominable desolation that hung over the world. The red eastern sky, the northward blackness, the salt Dead Sea, the stony beach crawling with these foul, slow-stirring monsters, the uniform poisonous-looking green of the lichenous plants, the thin air that hurts one's lungs: all contributed to an appalling effect. I moved on a hundred years, and there was the same red sun – a little larger, a little duller – the same dying sea, the same chill air, and the same crowd of earthy crustacea creeping in and out among the green weed and the red rocks. And in the westward sky, I saw a curved pale line like a vast new moon.

"So I travelled, stopping ever and again, in great strides of a thousand years or more, drawn on by the mystery of the earth's fate, watching with a strange fascination the sun grow larger and duller in the westward sky, and the life of the old earth ebb away. At last, more than thirty million years hence, the huge red-hot dome of the sun had come to obscure nearly a tenth part of the darkling heavens. Then I stopped once more, for the crawling multitude of crabs had disappeared, and the red beach, save for its livid green liverworts and lichens, seemed lifeless. And now it was flecked with white. A bitter cold assailed me. Rare white flakes ever and again came eddying down. To the north-eastward, the glare of snow lay under the starlight of the sable sky and I could see an undulating crest of hillocks pinkish white. There were fringes of ice along the sea margin, with drifting masses further out; but the main expanse of that salt ocean, all bloody under the eternal sunset, was still unfrozen.

"I looked about me to see if any traces of animal life remained. A certain indefinable apprehension still kept me in the saddle of the machine. But I saw nothing moving, in earth or sky or sea. The green slime on the rocks alone testified that life was not extinct. A shallow sandbank had appeared in the sea and the water had receded from the beach. I fancied I saw some black object flopping about upon this bank, but it became motionless as I looked at it, and

I judged that my eye had been deceived, and that the black object was merely a rock. The stars in the sky were intensely bright and seemed to me to twinkle very little.

"Suddenly I noticed that the circular westward outline of the sun had changed; that a concavity, a bay, had appeared in the curve. I saw this grow larger. For a minute perhaps I stared aghast at this blackness that was creeping over the day, and then I realized that an eclipse was beginning. Either the moon or the planet Mercury was passing across the sun's disk. Naturally, at first I took it to be the moon, but there is much to incline me to believe that what I really saw was the transit of an inner planet passing very near to the earth.

"The darkness grew apace; a cold wind began to blow in freshening gusts from the east, and the showering white flakes in the air increased in number. From the edge of the sea came a ripple and whisper. Beyond these lifeless sounds the world was silent. Silent? It would be hard to convey the stillness of it. All the sounds of man, the bleating of sheep, the cries of birds, the hum of insects, the stir that makes the background of our lives – all that was over. As the darkness thickened, the eddying flakes grew more abundant, dancing before my eyes; and the cold of the air more intense. At last, one by one, swiftly, one after the other, the white peaks of the distant hills vanished into blackness. The breeze rose to a moaning wind. I saw the black central shadow of the eclipse sweeping towards me. In another moment the pale stars alone were visible. All else was rayless obscurity. The sky was absolutely black.

"A horror of this great darkness came on me. The cold, that smote to my marrow, and the pain I felt in breathing, overcame me. I shivered, and a deadly nausea seized me. Then like a red-hot bow in the sky appeared the edge of the sun. I got off the machine to recover myself. I felt giddy and incapable of facing the return journey. As I stood sick and confused I saw again the moving thing upon the shoal – there was no mistake now that it was a moving thing – against the red water of the sea. It was a round thing, the size of a football perhaps, or, it may be, bigger, and tentacles trailed down from it; it seemed black against the weltering blood-red water, and it was hopping fitfully about. Then I felt I was fainting. But a terrible dread of lying helpless in that remote and awful twilight sustained me while I clambered upon the saddle.

"So I came back. For a long time I must have been insensible upon the machine. The blinking succession of the days and nights was resumed, the sun got golden again, the sky blue. I breathed with greater freedom. The fluctuating contours of the land ebbed and flowed. The hands spun backward upon the dials. At last I saw again the dim shadows of houses, the evidences of decadent humanity. These, too, changed and passed, and others came. Presently, when the million dial was at zero, I slackened speed. I began to recognize our own petty and familiar architecture, the thousands hand ran back to the starting-point, the night and day flapped slower and slower. Then the old walls of the laboratory came round me. Very gently, now, I slowed the mechanism down.

"I saw one little thing that seemed odd to me. I think I have told you that when I set out, before my velocity became very high, Mrs. Watchett had walked across the room, travelling, as it seemed to me, like a rocket. As I returned, I passed again across that minute when she traversed the laboratory. But now her every motion appeared to be the exact inversion of her previous ones. The door at the lower end opened, and she glided quietly up the laboratory, back foremost, and disappeared behind the door by which she had previously entered. Just before that I seemed to see Hillyer for a moment; but he passed like a flash.

"Then I stopped the machine, and saw about me again the old familiar laboratory, my tools, my appliances just as I had left them. I got off the thing very shakily, and sat down upon my bench. For several minutes I trembled violently. Then I became calmer. Around me was my old workshop again, exactly as it had been. I might have slept there, and the whole thing have been a dream.

"And yet, not exactly! The thing had started from the south-east corner of the laboratory. It had come to rest again in the north-west, against the wall where you saw it. That gives you the exact distance from my little lawn to the pedestal of the White Sphinx, into which the Morlocks had carried my machine.

"For a time my brain went stagnant. Presently I got up and came through the passage here, limping, because my heel was still painful, and feeling sorely begrimed. I saw the Pall Mall Gazette on the table by the door. I found the date was indeed today, and looking at the timepiece, saw the hour was almost eight o'clock. I heard your voices and the clatter of plates. I hesitated – I felt so sick and weak. Then I sniffed good wholesome meat, and opened the door on you. You know the rest. I washed, and dined, and now I am telling you the story.

"I know," he said, after a pause, "that all this will be absolutely incredible to you. To me the one incredible thing is that I am here tonight in this old familiar room looking into your friendly faces and telling you these strange adventures.'

He looked at the Medical Man. "No. I cannot expect you to believe it. Take it as a lie – or a prophecy. Say I dreamed it in the workshop. Consider I have been speculating upon the destinies of our race until I have hatched this fiction. Treat my assertion of its truth as a mere stroke of art to enhance its interest. And taking it as a story, what do you think of it?'

He took up his pipe, and began, in his old accustomed manner, to tap with it nervously upon the bars of the grate. There was a momentary stillness. Then chairs began to creak and shoes to scrape upon the carpet. I took my eyes off the Time Traveller's face, and looked round at his audience. They were in the dark, and little spots of colour swam before them. The Medical Man seemed absorbed in the contemplation of our host. The Editor was looking hard at the end of his cigar – the sixth. The Journalist fumbled for his watch. The others, as far as I remember, were motionless.

The Editor stood up with a sigh. "What a pity it is you're not a writer of stories!" he said, putting his hand on the Time Traveller's shoulder.

"You don't believe it?'

"Well –"

"I thought not.'

The Time Traveller turned to us. "Where are the matches?" he said. He lit one and spoke over his pipe, puffing. "To tell you the truth…I hardly believe it myself…. And yet…'

His eye fell with a mute inquiry upon the withered white flowers upon the little table. Then he turned over the hand holding his pipe, and I saw he was looking at some half-healed scars on his knuckles.

The Medical Man rose, came to the lamp, and examined the flowers. "The gynaeceum's odd," he said. The Psychologist leant forward to see, holding out his hand for a specimen.

"I'm hanged if it isn't a quarter to one," said the Journalist. "How shall we get home?'

"Plenty of cabs at the station," said the Psychologist.

"It's a curious thing," said the Medical Man; "but I certainly don't know the natural order of these flowers. May I have them?'

The Time Traveller hesitated. Then suddenly: "Certainly not.'

"Where did you really get them?" said the Medical Man.

The Time Traveller put his hand to his head. He spoke like one who was trying to keep hold of an idea that eluded him. "They were put into my pocket by Weena, when I travelled into Time." He stared round the room. "I'm damned if it isn't all going. This room and you and the atmosphere of every day is too much for my memory. Did I ever make a Time Machine, or a model of a Time Machine? Or is it all only a dream? They say life is a dream, a precious poor dream at times – but I can't stand another that won't fit. It's madness. And where did the dream come from? …I must look at that machine. If there is one!'

He caught up the lamp swiftly, and carried it, flaring red, through the door into the corridor. We followed him. There in the flickering light of the lamp was the machine sure enough, squat, ugly, and askew; a thing of brass, ebony, ivory, and translucent glimmering quartz. Solid to the touch – for I put out my hand and felt the rail of it – and with brown spots and smears upon the ivory, and bits of grass and moss upon the lower parts, and one rail bent awry.

The Time Traveller put the lamp down on the bench, and ran his hand along the damaged rail. "It's all right now," he said. "The story I told you was true. I'm sorry to have brought you out here in the cold." He took up the lamp, and, in an absolute silence, we returned to the smoking-room.

He came into the hall with us and helped the Editor on with his coat. The Medical Man looked into his face and, with a certain hesitation, told him he was suffering from overwork, at which he laughed hugely. I remember him standing in the open doorway, bawling good night.

I shared a cab with the Editor. He thought the tale a "gaudy lie." For my own part I was unable to come to a conclusion. The story was so fantastic and incredible, the telling so credible and sober. I lay awake most of the night thinking about it. I determined to go next day and see the Time Traveller again. I was told he was in the laboratory, and being on easy terms in the house, I went up to him. The laboratory, however, was empty. I stared for a minute at the Time Machine and put out my hand and touched the lever. At that the squat substantial-looking mass swayed like a bough shaken by the wind. Its instability startled me extremely, and I had a queer reminiscence of the childish days when I used to be forbidden to meddle. I came back through the corridor. The Time Traveller met me in the smoking-room. He was coming from the house. He had a small camera under one arm and a knapsack under the other. He laughed when he saw me, and gave me an elbow to shake. "I'm frightfully busy," said he, "with that thing in there.'

"But is it not some hoax?" I said. "Do you really travel through time?'

"Really and truly I do." And he looked frankly into my eyes. He hesitated. His eye wandered about the room. "I only want half an hour," he said. "I know why you came, and it's awfully good of you. There's some magazines here. If you'll stop to lunch I'll prove you this time travelling up to the hilt, specimen and all. If you'll forgive my leaving you now?'

I consented, hardly comprehending then the full import of his words, and he nodded and went on down the corridor. I heard the door of the laboratory slam, seated myself in a chair, and took up a daily paper. What was he going to do before lunch-time? Then suddenly I was reminded by an advertisement that I had promised to meet Richardson, the publisher, at two. I looked at my watch, and saw that I could barely save that engagement. I got up and went down the passage to tell the Time Traveller.

As I took hold of the handle of the door I heard an exclamation, oddly truncated at the end, and a click and a thud. A gust of air whirled round me as I opened the door, and from within came the sound of broken glass falling on the floor. The Time Traveller was not there. I seemed to see a ghostly, indistinct figure sitting in a whirling mass of black and brass for a moment – a figure so transparent that the bench behind with its sheets of drawings was absolutely distinct; but this phantasm vanished as I rubbed my eyes. The Time Machine had gone. Save for a subsiding stir of dust, the further end of the laboratory was empty. A pane of the skylight had, apparently, just been blown in.

I felt an unreasonable amazement. I knew that something strange had happened, and for the moment could not distinguish what the strange thing might be. As I stood staring, the door into the garden opened, and the man-servant appeared.

We looked at each other. Then ideas began to come. "Has Mr. – gone out that way?" said I.

"No, sir. No one has come out this way. I was expecting to find him here.'

At that I understood. At the risk of disappointing Richardson I stayed on, waiting for the Time Traveller; waiting for the second, perhaps still stranger story, and the specimens and photographs he would bring with him. But I am beginning now to fear that I must wait a lifetime. The Time Traveller vanished three years ago. And, as everybody knows now, he has never returned.

Epilogue

ONE CANNOT choose but wonder. Will he ever return? It may be that he swept back into the past, and fell among the blood-drinking, hairy savages of the Age of Unpolished Stone; into the abysses of the Cretaceous Sea; or among the grotesque saurians, the huge reptilian brutes of the Jurassic times. He may even now – if I may use the phrase – be wandering on some plesiosaurus-haunted Oolitic coral reef, or beside the lonely saline lakes of the Triassic Age. Or did he go forward, into one of the nearer ages, in which men are still men, but with the riddles of our own time answered and its wearisome problems solved? Into the manhood of the race: for I, for my own part, cannot think that these latter days of weak experiment, fragmentary theory, and mutual discord are indeed man's culminating time! I say, for my own part. He, I know – for the question had been discussed among us long before the Time Machine was made – thought but cheerlessly of the Advancement of Mankind, and saw in the growing pile of civilization only a foolish heaping that must inevitably fall back upon and destroy its makers in the end. If that is so, it remains for us to live as though it were not so. But to me the future is still black and blank – is a vast ignorance, lit at a few casual places by the memory of his story. And I have by me, for my comfort, two strange white flowers – shrivelled now, and brown and flat and brittle – to witness that even when mind and strength had gone, gratitude and a mutual tenderness still lived on in the heart of man.

Black Isle

Marian Womack

0001

THE OSPREYS' deaths – by the dozens – are inexplicable, as is the bluish taint on their beaks, heads and chests. It simply should not be there. I should know, for I designed the birds.

Every morning, day breaks over the mudflats, covered in osprey corpses and unexpected bluish reflections, as if a hundred will-o-the-wisps of the wrong colour were advancing over the watery surface. The smooth flat mirror of the mudflats shines indigo: fluorescent, freakish, *wrong*. From their beaks, and from sores on their chests and bellies, there pours a tainted viscous liquid that resembles watery gelatine, odourless and sticky to the touch.

This is, of course, not what our star product for the Scottish ecosystem should do. Our fabricated birds, to start with, should not die this soon, a mere fifteen years after their release into nature. They are engineered: to sustain longer life, eternal in some cases, to maintain fish and insect numbers – a delicate dance of environmental equilibrium.

"Dr Hay, your presence is required, code A-001."

A summons from God himself. I cannot recall being asked to Philip's office since our last disagreement, and that was months ago. But I do what I'm told. Things are changing, and I am now treated by everyone as a newcomer, an embarrassing uncle. No one seems to remember that at the beginning it was me, and Philip, and Barbara, fighting against the elements. Fighting against those who believed our work unethical. I risked as much as he did, more in fact. Barbara risked it all.

"Thank you, Dolores."

I close the intercom, walk towards the cabinet, and slide open its glass doors with a light wave of my hand. I find the bottle of vodka behind a row of gold-tooled volumes, and take it gently to my lips with a furtive movement: the light is flashing red by a corner of the ceiling, little rubies of a warning. I'm being observed.

0002

THE GREEN rocks and hills of the Highlands reflect the yellow glow of the bio-engineered grass, and the landscape shines on the other side of the glass and white-aluminium dome. The colossal hall, built to the proportions of our greatest achievement to date, the de-extinct monolithic squid, is a vast oblong chamber of pure whiteness into which the landscape pours its new colours. On sunnier days the yellow and orange reflections are almost unbearable, and the glass octahedrons taint themselves a shade or two darker to keep us sheltered. This part of Scotland can be particularly hot during the winter months.

The dome resembles a hive made of the glass panels supported by white aluminium, a triumph of de-modernized architecture imitating late twenty-first century design. The vast column of the aquarium occupies its centre, placed there to greet the visitors with our impressive bio-engineered reproductions: sharks, whales, dolphins, coral, moonfish. The squid moves gracefully among its fellow inmates as I walk round the watery cylinder. It takes me seventeen minutes to complete the circle. I notice new species locked in there. Apparently we have starfish now. Only the natural-correct colours, in accordance with the Scottish Law on Bio-Ethics and the International Consensus on De-Extinction. We pride ourselves on reproducing environments; no one is interested here in the new fashions for violet sheep or pink cows. We leave these frivolities as the pets of rich Russians.

Philip's office has its own private elevator, as well as another entry-escape route: a helipad on its balcony. I press the only button in the white capsule. The answer comes back in flashing red; it has been a while since I have been granted direct access to him.

Two members of the security staff push the doors open to find me there.

"Sorry, sir," one of them says, their attitude relaxing a bit. They have obviously been briefed. They put down their white machine-guns, one of them presses the button again, and the system reacts, positively this time, to his DNA.

The doors close and the elevator moves upwards.

0003

PHILIP IS STANDING behind his desk when I enter. His office is immaculately white, as is everything else in XenoLab.

The genetically-engineered Siberian tiger, re-imagined by Neo-Bio to be as tame as a gigantic cat, is stretching in the middle of the chamber, causing echoes as he plays with a worn-out red plastic sphere. I cross the vast space, cavernous with the sounds of the beast, and those of my own shoes over the white marble.

"Andrew, dear friend," Philip's voice resonates. His hair and his trimmed beard are also white now, I notice, in communion with our corporate surroundings.

"Philip. You wanted to see me." I hope I don't sound like an obedient child.

He looks down, turns awkwardly and advances towards the glass wall on the south side of the chamber. He looks diminutive with his hands behind his back, looking through the glass in the direction of the distant aviary, an external structure of gigantic proportions, shaped like a huge pine cone.

"How have you been?"

I would like to imagine that there is some genuine interest in his tone of voice. But I know my ex-business partner well enough not to hold false illusions. Nonetheless, his question brings Barbara's face back to my mind. It was probably designed to do exactly that, throw salt into the old wound, and I hate him for it.

"Marvellous." There's no point hiding the lie. "What's up, Philip?"

He cannot see the birds from where he stands. It is obvious he's looking in the direction of the cone to avoid turning to face me.

"The ospreys were one of our first, were they not?" he says laconically. I notice he still speaks the same way, ending sentences with a negative answer. Manipulation 101.

"That is correct."

"I am sorry to say this requires swift action. We cannot allow the reputation of our company to be affected."

Our company.

"What do you propose to do?"

"Go there, back to Black Isle, and take a small team of your choosing. Find out what is wrong with the birds."

"Why me?"

"I need someone I can trust." I believe him, God knows why. Perhaps because I want to believe him, even after everything that has happened.

"Why are a bunch of birds so important, Philip? What aren't you telling me?"

He turns and smiles briefly, more with his squinting eyes than with his mouth.

"Nothing, old friend, nothing." Now he is the one who doesn't bother to hide the lie. "But they were some of our first, were they not?" he repeats.

His meaning dawns on me at last. I never had his powers of memory, and it's been fifteen years. Fifteen years in which I have had reason enough to forget.

I reply that I'll do all in my power, turning in the direction of the elevator. Before leaving I specify that I will go on my own. He does not refuse me this small request, the only victory I contemplate gaining anytime soon. I savour it in silence.

"Andrew," he calls as the elevator doors are closing. I push them open, and wait for him to speak. "Mendez has already been there." This surprises me. I thought I had kept myself informed of the company's recent goings-on. It had obviously been a secret outing. "He went and returned with no conclusive results. You should seek him out, talk to him."

"Of course, I will do so first thing." I let the doors go.

"Andrew!" I put my foot just in time once more between the doors before they close.

"Yes, Philip?" My tone is ironic, disdainful. Each one of us is back in his proper place, and mine is obviously that of the delivery boy.

He looks in my direction again, advancing towards the elevator. I did not expect this; I tense unexpectedly. Even at a distance he looks haggard, strangely old. I wonder if my ex-friend has stopped following his rejuvenating bio-treatments. "Mendez is in Hospital Zero Zero Sixteen. Committed. Mental ward." The matter-of-fact manner with which he delivers this piece of significant information freezes me out. I leave at last.

The elevator takes me back down into the hall. This time I fancy that I see a bluish foam coming out of the whale's mouth as she exhales. There is nothing there. It is only a reflection of a rare passing cloud over the cylindrical structure, staining the glass with its dark shadow.

0004

I AM alone in bed. Dolores has just left me and gone back to her own compound. I get up, go to the bathroom and splash my face with cold water.

I open my computer and connect myself to the company hive. "Black Isle," I say to the screen that waits flat like the surface of calm stagnant water. The requested information starts popping up fast over the screen, reports and charts and scientific articles, and I am startled by the number of species that we have introduced into that particular environment. Not only birds, but fish and mammals as well. Insects, some species genetically engineered to help decimate the rapidly multiplying ones. Genetically modified grass, the kind that won't miss the disappearing clouds. Flowers. I wonder how much of the landscape is fake in the place, how much of it remains original, if any.

Close to us, Black Isle was one of our first proving-grounds. A small peninsula twenty minutes to the west of Inverness, it is placed right in front of the vast watery expanse of the Bauly Firth in the North Sea. On the opposite shore, the hills and the glens of The Aird are visible in the distance, with its farmland and its pretty copses, a soft mist dancing over the small summits.

The Bauly Firth is an unusual spot. The place is subjected to dramatic changes in its ecosystem every few hours following the tides. For half a day, twice a day, the water recedes, and an expanse of mudflats extends itself further into the distance, crossing the whole bay and reaching the Aird, a strange black mirror filled with the inevitable quicksands, a deceptive landscape that looks barren but that is full of life. I notice this landscape of an entire bay without water has been referred to in the company reports somehow unflatteringly as "a long view of a lot of mud."

The mud houses a particular type of animal life. Afterwards, in a mere few hours, the water reconquers it all with its undulating dark glimmer. It is then when the birds reappear, together with certain types of fish, seals, dolphins, crossing the bay in direction to Inverness. Enormous hen harriers and cormorants, diving gracefully into the water to hunt their prey, small martens running around, birds coming and going, ever-changing, as subtly as the rhythms of the water. The place is utterly fascinating for a biologist. The bay becomes a completely different biological environment in each of its distinctive phases.

Black Isle is also one of many self-contained late twenty-first century environments, protected by its own glass and aluminium dome. The company will organise the necessary paperwork to grant me access.

The ospreys were not simply one of our first; they were our first one hundred per cent success story. After the ospreys, everything else came swiftly, easily, and Neo-Bio took a massive leap forward. Everything changed. We weren't ready, when the birds first disappeared, for our ecosystem's metamorphosis: but we could see the danger it posed to our species. Hundreds of birds suffered a sudden decline in numbers, vanishing at the same time as their main food, small insects, multiplied in dangerous proportions. The swarms destroyed lives, destroyed property. The latter was determinant in making the powers that be act.

Maintaining the insect eaters constant became XenoLab's first mission. After the success with the ospreys, that was our next job, to re-imagine the insects-eaters with a supra-hunger. Success after success, our reputation grew without equal. We were like God himself, reestablishing the balance in His creation.

I remember the day we freed the ospreys. They all had a white tag embedded in their legs, shiny, easy to spot with binoculars.

0005

I GLIDE OVER the avenues and the open squares, marvelling as always at the daring of some of our competitors. I ascertain, even from manoeuvring-height, that the new fashion for taking polar bears as pets has reached our city, as has the one that prizes giant lizards, tigers, and other unusual animals for human company. My opinion about this hasn't changed: it does not matter how tame these beasts have been re-imagined by Neo-Bio, it is obvious that this new fashion for modifying the instincts of species not suited for human company has to pose some kind of danger.

At least the Scottish Republic's law spares us from the blue bears, the orange lizards. I will not be able to stand seeing them around when they are legally available, which will surely happen eventually.

I negotiate the narrow entry into the parking dock at the block where the hospital is located. I do not know this area of the city well, but my vehicle has brought me in with the autopilot. It is a new model provided by the company, a convertible which will also run over ground once I am granted access to the domed zone of Black Isle.

I show my credentials and am ushered quickly to the exact place by a young assistant doctor. I am impressed by the effectiveness and power that a card from XenoLab still commands.

The hospital is as white as every other building in the city – Scotland still misses, all these decades later, its snowy winter landscapes – but I am led through one white corridor after another until we reach a back area outside of the main wards, and here the paint is peeling, the plumbing is exposed over the walls and the lights flick, covering each turn in increasing darkness.

We stop in front of a metal door with a hatch for food. The door is unlocked. I am pushed in, the door locked again quickly after me.

The place is hardly illuminated by an orange bulb. Mendez is a formless bundle in one corner.

"Mendez?" There's no answer. "Mendez?"

He turns and finally sees me. He tries to focus his eyes on me, tries to recognise me.

"I am waiting for him."

"Who?"

"My master."

"Do you mean Philip?"

He looks up, and crawls closer. He has aged beyond recognition. His rejuvenation program had stopped him at age twenty-four. He looks nearly forty now, or perhaps fifty. It is difficult to know.

"God," he says simply. Just before I ask again if he is talking about Philip, he utters a few words that I don't quite catch, and takes something into his mouth.

He is eating flies. I don't even know where from. There are no flies – not officially at least – under the city's dome.

"What have you said?" I ask.

"Pan. I am waiting for him."

I do not have a clue what he is talking about, but understand I will get no useful information. His mind seems to be gone completely.

As I'm turning round, I hear the loud thump, wettish and sudden, of meat hitting the wall. It is followed by a distant whining, some lonely animal conjured up into this narrow chamber to devour us. I do not want to turn back, but I do. The blood has already formed a miniature lake, darker than redder, and Mendez is convulsing on the floor. There is no animal there, unless he is the animal. But I know that animals do not harm themselves. I am pushed to one side unceremoniously as the attendants get in. I do not desire to see the outcome to my visit, and escape quickly through the open door. I can't feel pity, not now; I'm sorry for Mendez, but I've seen enough to pity him.

0006

I STAY with Peter and Anita, the allocated occupants of Pier Cottage, exactly like I did fifteen years ago. The house enjoys a privileged situation, a mere five minutes walk from the Gothic ruins of Red Castle, a small turreted structure abandoned to rot at the end of the twentieth century when its owner decided he could not pay more taxes on the property and removed the roof to stop is mounting debt to the government.

On the right side of the cottage there is a path that leads into the old quarry, with its oddly flat and reddish walls cut into the hill. The house and the Castle are both built out of this local stone, as it is the abandoned Victorian pier that gives its name to the cottage, put there in order to transport the stone from the quarry into Inverness over the bay. The pier's abandonment means it is no more than an overgrown greenish and rocky structure that advances into the water, hard to walk over, and which gets dangerously covered by the regular tides.

Apart from the striking landscape, and the Gothic ruin of Red Castle, Black Isle is particularly rich in Megalithic chambered cairns. It was inhabited in 3000 BC by prehistoric men, and New Stone Age folk constructed these tomb-buildings. There seems to be two main types on the isle, the Orkney and the Clava, one rectangular and one a stone ring, with a circular burial chamber underground. I promise myself to visit some before my field trip is over, something I did not manage to do during the release-trip all those years ago.

0007

EVERYTHING IS PRETTY much unchanged over the past fifteen years. Anita's cat startles me as much as it did back then, its red eyes marking him out as one of the first, discarded models of genetic manufacture of the old days, re-imagined not to attack the birds but unsuccessful in every other aspect. Everything is pretty much the same, including Anita. Her smile still awakens something in me. The way she looks at me makes me think that she hasn't entirely forgotten our brief affair.

The place is quite magical, utterly unspoiled. That is, unspoiled but at present subtly different from what it was, due to the interaction of companies such as ours with the landscape, *precisely* so as to keep it unspoiled. It is strangely unreal, this truthful version of a late twenty-first century Scottish ecosystem. The irony does not escape me. It has been my major point of conflict with Philip in recent times.

The green expanses reflect the yellow glow of the genetically engineered grass. Once the motorway crosses the bridge over the water, you find yourself negotiating narrow winding country roads framed by little stone walls, trees and thickets. Some of the moss over the fake walls is also fabricated. I can see it plainly even from the moving vehicle.

From the window of the kitchen one can observe even without binoculars the birds that come to the feeders, mostly chaffinch, greenfinch, blue tits, bullfinch and a rare young woodpecker. Several of these birds are of our own manufacture, as an inspection with the binoculars reveals the white tags in their legs, shining with their unusual plastic glimmer. Not the woodpecker, however. He seems the genuine article.

0008

WE WALK over to the pier. To reach its end a short walk is necessary, no more than three hundred metres, but I am soon reminded how hard is to advance over the abandoned structure. The overgrown reeds and the muddy grass have covered it all. The seaweed climbs onto it from its deceptive little shores. But the worst is that the remaining rocks of the man-built pier are now out of place and out of shape, as if a giant had scattered the original square stones from the sky without looking to see where they would fall. Time and abandonment have covered them in the green of the reeds and the grass, so much so that it is impossible to find steady ground, or even to avoid holes and uneven spots where it would be easy to twist one's ankle.

We need nearly half an hour to get to its rounded end.

Halfway onto the pier, the grass is spotted here and there with the corpses of crabs of different sizes. They are all the same kind of local specimen, and they are all tainted with the irregular bluish-green. I collect several of them, and some of the bluish-tainted grass around their emptied bodies. The cottage is provided with a small working lab, well enough equipped to carry out small tasks. Anita is carrying plastic sample bags. Peter is taking digital photographs for my initial report, for which these notes are intended. They both have been most helpful.

I see a figure over the mud, and I put my binoculars to my eyes: a man is dragging a net-fishing bag full of what I can make out as the huge cadavers of birds, bleeding their cobalt liquid into the darkened mirror of the mud as he walks.

"Who is that?" I ask.

"Oh no. Good gracious!"

Peter advances to the uneven border of the pier and starts shouting at the man.

"McKenzie! You're going to drown, you stupid son of a bitch!"

I am startled by his reaction. I remember Peter as an educated, mild-mannered, retired science teacher. He turns in my direction and explains.

"Tomorrow morning those birds will be laid at our door."

"What?"

I am not offered an explanation as to how the man McKenzie, who is braving the quicksand in such reckless fashion, knows of Peter and Anita's connection to XenoLab, or why he directs the birds' death towards the inhabitants of Pier Cottage. Or how much he knows about our de-extinction work in the area. But that he is angry at us is clear.

Later in the day we observe the tide covering the mud, rapidly filling the Bay, splashing around the pier. The remains of the structure get completely covered except for its round tip. I make a mental note to find out the tide times as soon as possible; it is more than likely that venturing onto the pier again will be needed, and I do not desire to get stranded there with the vicious winds and the vicious seagulls.

I see the man McKenzie is walking along the shore, dragging behind him his trophy of dead fabricated birds.

0009

I AM THINKING of how quiet this new nature has turned out to be. There are hardly any bird sounds, an unexpected silence. I know by memory the osprey's call, as described in my field guide: *A short, cheeping whistle, sometimes slightly declining.* I guess I can remember it; I certainly can imagine a sound described like that. But I haven't heard it once here, and it has been a while since I've heard it anywhere else.

What I have seen is their clear white bellies, the black wing patches, when the birds glide overhead. I have seen them, alive and flying; and I have also by now collected their cadavers and dissected them by the dozens. The man McKenzie has not graced us so far with his grim reaping, despite Peter's assurances that he would.

Evening approaches, and my hosts must be preparing dinner. I am out for an evening walk after one of the dissecting sessions, trying to regain my appetite with some much-needed fresh air. Almost by impulse I turn at the last moment in a two-way path and venture into Red Castle's abandoned grounds. I reach the structure, inspect the plaque on the wall, inscribed with the date 1641, and look over the Bauly Firth, the bay in front of me in its formidable vastness. I admire the Castle's defensive position. I decide to push into the extensive woods and come out on the other side of my hosts' home. I trust my instinct not to get lost, and cross eventually into the area of the old farmlands, now covered in decorative crops.

Barbara would have liked this contrasting landscape. I bury the thought as deep as possible.

Something is shinning blue on the Castle's grounds. It's a hare, or a rat. It is difficult to ascertain, as all there remains is a furry wet pulp of flesh, and something that looks like a strange bluish-green gelatine.

I pack the remains of the animal into a sample bag and carry it back home with me.

0010

I AM in bed when I hear a dry bump against the main door. I look out of my window but see nothing. The next morning Anita shows me a robin, dead from the collision with the door of Pier Cottage. Inside his breast a bluish heart is shining. The right leg displays its whitish plastic tag.

0011

MY NOTES from the previous trip to Black Isle are little more than useless. Apart from the observations of the releasing day proper, they contain nothing helpful. The acquired wisdom of observations relating to the weather. Indications for sowing the seed, for when to begin harvesting. Customs outmoded now, since we have completely eradicated hunger with our genetically engineered crops, destroyed death and illness with the widely available rejuvenating processes.

I remember those nights in which Anita explained these wonders to me: that tomorrow's weather starts to be foretold the previous evening, that if swallows fly high in their search for insects there will be good weather. If the cattle bunch together in a corner of the field, rain may be expected.

There is only nice weather now; it was one the first things man learned to interact with. Our satellites, strategically placed around the globe, provide a never-ending provision of cloudless skies, mild temperatures, constant and bright sunshine.

If the lights of the Aurora Borealis, or *Merry Dancers*, sweep across the sky, and Scottish countryfolk can see them from their homes, disturbed weather is on the way. I do not know very well what the Aurora Borealis is. Must find records on the company hive; I remember clearly making the same promise to Anita fifteen years ago, while I noted down all these. I obviously wasn't interested enough, and only took notes on these useless bits of local information as a means to flirt with her.

Fifteen years ago, Barbara waited for me back home. There had not yet been any renal failure, no transplant from the genetically-engineered pigs, performed strictly against her religious wishes, and no final rejection of the animal's harvested organ by her body. Fifteen years ago we had not managed to crack that side of our business, I'm afraid, and Barbara was little more than an experiment for Philip, a stoat, small but vicious, a little guinea pig.

Red rowan berries protect against witches. Some flowers (broom, hawthorn, foxglove) should never be taken into the houses. Robins have a drop of God's blood in its veins. It is unlucky to hurt one of them for that reason.

Barbara would have said that God himself was angry with us, producing the blue viscous liquid. Was Jesus's blood meant to be bluish? Or was that what was said about kings and queens in the tales of the old days? I wish I had kept the meaning of these things buried in some field notebook. I wish I had my own archive, my own private hive, my personal stack of useless knowledge from past days.

0012

WHEN I SEE him is too late to hide. The stone circle, in the middle of a round, dark meadow, half covered by the treetops falling on it from its side, offers no other hiding place than the actual cairn that I have come to visit, which turns out to be a mound with a little excavation entrance. I glance over it; it seems blocked, or rather leading nowhere. It is too late anyhow to escape. Are the Neolithic tombs also a decoration, perhaps? No time to muse about it.

"Morning," I say.

"Morning," he answers. He stops in front of me, and says nothing else. He has his hands in his pockets.

Attack is as good a defence as any and, since I've got the notion that he considers me the enemy, I waste no time.

"I guess you know who I am, and what I am doing here."

He smiles crookedly but says nothing, taken aback by my forwardness no doubt.

"Oh yes, I know who you are," he says at last.

"And how can I help you?"

"Oh, no, you cannot help me… You cannot help us."

This is leading nowhere. I start again:

"Look, man… McKenzie, isn't it?"

"I just want to show you something."

I am not surprised by his offer. I had expected something similar to these: proofs of the company's mismanagement of the environment, threats of dismal intensity, perhaps just expecting some kind of compensation, maybe in the form of rejuvenating credit.

"Very well," I say at last. "I'll come."

We head deep into the woods, leaving the quarry behind. Very soon there is no sight of the sea, although it can clearly be heard from practically everywhere in Black Isle due to the lack of animal noise I have already noted. The sound of the water makes me feel strangely at ease.

His cabin is quite well kept, a fresh lick of whitewash on the walls, recently fixed wooden fences.

He takes me towards the back, into a small working hut. I wonder who this man is, why he is allowed inside the dome, what role he performs, if any, on Black Isle. I gather that he has what are called "historical rights" – that is to say, his family has always belonged to the area and therefore he can stay. A controversial idea. But I cannot imagine any other way in which he would be allowed to be here, in the middle of our delicately engineered dance.

He opens the door and then I see it.

There is absolutely no smell, but the animals, of all sizes and shapes, are the bluish mash I have half expected. Shockingly, not only birds. A bucket is filled with what looks like different kinds of insects and rodents. The birds are hanging upside down. At the back of the hut there is a dead blue-sheep lying on a worktable. I have no idea such large species have also been affected. I turn round in disbelief.

"Where did you find her?" I asked.

"She was mine, my sheep." That is all the information he offers.

When I leave I am asking myself two questions. What have we done here, and what should we do next?

0013

I FINISH and send my report. The experiments I have conducted with Anita's help have formulated no final theory, although I am still waiting on the samples I have sent Philip's way. But I really see no way to stop this extravagant virus, which is not a virus, but which seems nonetheless to be spreading all over the area at a level I could not have anticipated. The animals themselves seem to be carrying this possibility of de-continuation. I offer no possible solution. There is none until we look in more detail into the issue. I recommend the creation of a research team back in XenoLab to start working with immediate effect. Secretly, of course. I understand the sensitivity of the issue. My final prediction is to expect more cases outside of this particular dome, quite soon.

The cat is staring at me with his "evil" fake red eyes. He comes and rubs himself against my leg and I shudder. I go to sleep and my mind is uneasy, heavy images of what I have been shown hanging on me. I dream of Barbara, of the days prior to her operation.

I was privately offered another option before that fatal day: a experimental dose of proto-phomaldeion to keep her in animated suspension, living eternally, until the xeno was not experimental anymore and we had better results with the harvesting of organs from animals. I never got to see the huge capsule where the substance would be provided, but in my dream a blue syrup is injected into her small arm, and Barbara cries blue tears as the liquid fills her up.

Philip is also crying blue tears while his face, no longer treated with the rejuvenation process, collapses into old age all of a sudden, in front of my very eyes, while he communicates to me her passing.

I wake up covered in cold sweat, and wet with tears, thinking about xeno-suspension, xeno-cloning and other rapidly progressing issues I simply cannot cope with, but which nonetheless are under way, even in the minutes of the Scottish parliament's Bio-Regulation Commission's latest meetings. I lie in bed thinking that, perhaps, Philip has been right to cast me away from the front line of things. I am an old-fashioned man, typing these notes with my fingers on my computer instead of talking into it, collecting field notebooks written with ink, or rather a succedaneum of ink manufacture by myself, since it is impossible to buy it. A man unable, as it were, to accept the realities that surround me. Perhaps I should commission a shiny red goat as a pet and snap out of it once and for all.

0014

PHILIP HAS READ my report and demands to talk with me through HiveCam. I do not have my profile active anymore, although that goes strictly against company regulations. I then receive a strange message through an encoded email provider, contracted during the early days of the company, and which we used to communicate delicate matters. We have not used it to talk in years. I am confused when I see the red flag on my screen, until I suddenly remember what it means.

I command the computer to open the message. I am even more confused after reading it: "Code Z-666". Get out. Leave. Abort. I've always prided myself on knowing the company's code-protocols by heart. I helped write them, after all.

0015

I TRUST I'll find the cabin of the man McKenzie. I trust that I will not get lost. I reach without problem the stone circle with its Neolithic tomb, and from there I try to reorient myself. I do reach the cabin, and the hut, eventually. I hardly notice the twilight, which is nothing more than a pale-grey sky miles higher, beyond the distant dome.

"You're back."

It's a statement, and affirmation. I walk in the direction of the strange man.

"What do you want?"

"Talk, just to talk."

I am not sure what kind of help I expect to get from him, but if nothing else I want his assistance to conduct a larger survey of Black Isle. I'm also carrying the digital camera, and want to ask permission to photograph the animals in his hut. For now, I let myself be led into the cabin, where the man flicks on the electric kettle.

The man rinses a few herbs and puts them inside a teapot. He pours the water.

"Do you take sugar?"

I say no. He puts some in my cup anyway. The infusion is still acidic in my tongue.

"Do you want any of this?" he says holding a small bottle of whisky. I say no, wishing it was vodka instead.

"What do you think is happening here?" I ask.

He shrugs for an answer, but says:

"Nature will reconquer, will she not?"

I am startled for a second. Something unexpected has happened: the way he has spoken has reminded me of Philip.

"She will battle back," he continues, in his dark Scottish drawl.

I look into his eyes, and then I see it. Philip's eyes, his nose. In a body twenty years his senior. What the hell is going on here?

I get up and go towards an old-fashioned static-photograph on the wall, where two children are showing the animals they've hunted to the camera, each of them holding a huge bird by the legs. The Bauly Firth's mudflats shine behind them.

I turn to say something more, but I feel unexpectedly dizzy. My vision blurs, and I try to find something to grab.

The herbs. I am a biologist. I suddenly recognise the herbs he has made me drink. I think I've seen a hedge of it outside, with its horny stems and foxglove-like flowers. *Datura stramonium.*

Thorn apple, devil's apple, devil's trumpet, feuille du diable, herb du diable, green thorn apple.

I fall to the floor at last. I look up, and a blurry image walks in my direction. McKenzie. Or rather a re-imagined version of the man McKenzie, completed with hooves and horns and the face of a sheep.

I close my eyes to the hallucination, and doze happily into oblivion.

Z-666

Thorn apple, devil's apple, devil's trumpet, feuille du diable, herb du diable, green thorn apple. Datura stramonium. Get out. Leave. Abort. She is running in my direction. Behind her, the red ruin of the Castle is shedding blue tears. I'm crying, but my hands get cover in the same indigo slime when I touch my face. She is running, but is not her; or rather, it is an older version of my wife, as if she had declined our rejuvenating credit. Barbara gets to where I am and slaps my face with the full force of her rage. She is shouting now. Zero Zero Sixteen. Zero Zero Sixteen. Wake up. Wake up!

0016

I WAKE UP cold, uncomfortable, wet. It takes me a few seconds to understand where I am, lying at the very end of the pier. The tide is coming in, in full spate. I notice that there is water all around me. Only the rounded end where I have been dropped is not covered by it. There is no escape now until the tide goes down.

I see them then: hundreds and thousands of dead fish, floating over the grey-bluish surface. Then the birds start falling from the sky.

Behind me, a huge roar announces that the trees in the Castle's grounds are collapsing as well.

Everything is dying, at the exact same moment. As if someone had orchestrated it all, or pushed the required button from a safe and distant location.

I notice the sea is exploding: here, where it has always been an unmoving mirror of greyness.

From the sea, an enormous whale is coming in my direction. Where from? How did she get into the domed space? Only it doesn't look like a whale, exactly. It looks like a shapeless monster, bleeding its blue foam as it advances into the pier.

I try to remember a prayer, but I can't.

I close my eyes and think of Barbara, her image slapping my face, through a rare moment of clarity. Not in the domed Black Isle, not in my compound. Am I still here? Zero Zero Sixteen. The reality is too harsh to contemplate. I close my eyes once more, and I'm back there, alone in the pier. The whale opens her mouth, and prepares to swallow me up.

Biographies & Sources

Barton Aikman
How to Reclaim Water
(First Publication)
Barton Aikman is a graduate of the Clarion Writers' Workshop and holds an MFA in Creative Writing from California Institute of the Arts. Born and raised in Southern California, he continues to live and write in Los Angeles. Barton is a fan of many genres and is interested in how they might be combined and subverted to create startling and memorable stories. You can find him on Twitter @BartonAikman.

V.K. Blackwell
The Hollow Journal
(First Publication)
V.K. Blackwell is a biochemical scientist and student from Dallas, Texas. Virginia has been writing science fiction/fantasy short stories and novels for nearly a decade. The eldest of four children, she began storytelling to share her fascination with the natural and magical. When not in the laboratory conducting research, she can be found volunteering for science communication events in her community, rolling dice as a Dungeon Master, or playing video games. Visit her on Twitter (@vk_blackwell).

Steve Carr
Power Grid
(Originally Published in *Kingdoms in the Wild*, 2018)
Steve Carr, who lives in Richmond, Virginia, has had over 340 short stories published internationally in print and online magazines, literary journals and anthologies since June, 2016. Five collections of his short stories, *Sand*, *Rain*, *Heat*, *The Tales of Talker Knock* and *50 Short Stories: The Very Best of Steve Carr*, have been published. His plays have been produced in several states in the U.S. He has been nominated for a Pushcart Prize twice. Find him on Twitter @carrsteven960 or visit his website: stevecarr960.com.

Brandon Crilly
Rainclouds
(Originally Published in *Electric Athenaeum*, 2018)
An Ottawa teacher by day, Brandon Crilly has been previously published by *Daily Science Fiction*, *Abyss & Apex*, *PULP Literature*, *On Spec*, *Electric Athenaeum* and other markets. He received an Honorable Mention in the 2016 Writer's Digest Popular Fiction Awards, reviews fiction for BlackGate.com and serves as a Programming Lead for Can*Con in Ottawa. Brandon is the co-host of the podcast *Broadcasts from the Wasteland*, described as 'eavesdropping on a bunch of writers at the hotel bar.' You can find him at brandoncrilly.wordpress.com or on Twitter, @B_Crilly.

AnaMaria Curtis
A Quiet, Lonely Planet
(First Publication)
AnaMaria Curtis is from the part of Illinois that is very much not Chicago, where she spent her childhood reading, correcting people who mispronounced her name, and trying to avoid people her own age. She's the winner of the 2019 Dell Magazines Award and a graduate of the Alpha Workshop. AnaMaria likes starting debates about 19th century British Literature and getting distracted by other people's dogs. Please look for her on Twitter (@AnaMCurtis) and remind her to water her plants.

Kate Dollarhyde
The Arrow of Time
(Originally Published in *Gamut Magazine*, 2017)
Kate Dollarhyde is a writer of speculative fiction, the former Editor-in-Chief of SFF magazine *Strange Horizons*, and a Writers Guild of America-nominated Narrative Designer at video game developer Obsidian Entertainment. Her short fiction has been published in Flame Tree anthologies, *Fireside Fiction*, *Lackington's*, *Beneath Ceaseless Skies*, *Gamut*, and *Lamplight*. Her game writing appears in *The Outer Worlds* and *Pillars of Eternity 2: Deadfire* – as well as its three expansions, *Beast of Winter*, *Seeker Slayer Survivor*, and *Forgotten Sanctum*. She lives in California.

Megan Dorei
Acrylics for a Wasteland
(First Publication)
Megan Dorei lives in Lawrence, KS with her fiancée and several friendly ghosts. She has been published in such works as Sirens Call Publications' *Bellows of the Bone Box*, *Dark Moon Digest #14*, Flame Tree Publishing's *Dystopia Utopia Short Stories*, and Transmundane Press' *On Fire* anthology. She is fuelled by a love of strange horror and survival stories, both new and classic, and will never tire of fictional apocalypses.

Stephanie Ellis
Milking Time
(First Publication)
Stephanie Ellis is a horror writer residing in Southampton, UK. Her most recent short stories can be found in Snowbooks' industrial horror anthology, *Thread of the Infinite* and Things in the Well Publications charity anthology, *Trickster's Treats 3*. Her novella, *Bottled*, will be published by Silver Shamrock Publishing in early 2020 and her ebook novelette, *Asylum of Shadows* from Demain Publishing is due to come out in print before the end of the year. She is co-editor of *Trembling With Fear*, HorrorTree.com's online magazine. She is an affiliate member of the HWA.

George Allan England
The Air Trust (chapters I–XV)
(Originally Published by Phil Wagner, 1915)
George Allan England (1877–1936) was an American writer and explorer, best known for his speculative science fiction inspired by authors such as H.G. Wells and Jack London. After a period of translating fiction he published his first story in 1905,

leading to over 330 pieces now accounted for. England attended Harvard University and later in life ran for Governor of Maine. Though unsuccessful in that endeavour, he transferred his interest in politics into his writing, where themes of socialist utopia often appear.

Gini Koch writing as Anita Ensal
The Last Day on Earth
(Originally Published in *The Book of Exodi*, 2009)
Anita Ensal has always been intrigued by possibilities inherent in myths and legends. She likes to find both the fantastical element in the mundane and the ordinary component within the incredible. She writes in all areas of speculative fiction and has stories in several fine anthologies including *Love and Rockets* and *Boondocks Fantasy* from DAW Books, *Guilds & Glaives* and *Portals* from Zombies Need Brains, *The Book of Exodi* from Eposic, and the novella, *A Cup of Joe*. She will be re-releasing *The Neighborhood* series in 2020. You can reach Anita (aka Gini Koch) at her website, Fantastical Fiction. (www.ginikoch.com/aebookstore.htm)

Camille Flammarion
Omega: The Last Days of the World (Part I)
(Originally Published by The Cosmopolitan Publishing Company, 1894)
Camille Flammarion (1842–1925) was a French astronomer and author. He wrote many books, including popular science and astronomy non-fiction works as well as science fiction novels and was interested in paranormal research. His books include *Distances of the Stars* (1874), *Popular Astronomy* (1894), *Urania* (1890) and the *Death and its Mystery* series. *Omega: The Last Days of the World* was originally published in French as *La Fin du Monde* in 1893 and was received well.

Dave Golder
Foreword Writer
Dave Golder is a former editor of *SFX* magazine (which he helped to launch), SFX.co.uk and *Comic Heroes* magazine, but he first began writing professionally about science fiction with a regular feature in *Your Sinclair* called The Killer Kolumn From Outer Space. He has also written for various gaming magazines despite only ever having finished two games completely. And one of those was *Kung Fu Panda*. He now works freelance and is pretending to write a novel.

William Hope Hodgson
The House on Borderland
(Originally Published by Chapman and Hall, 1908)
William Hope Hodgson (1877–1918) was born in Essex, England but moved several times with his family, including living for some time in County Galway, Ireland – a setting that would later inspire *The House on the Borderland*. Hodgson made several unsuccessful attempts to run away to sea, until his uncle secured him some work in the Merchant Marine. This association with the ocean would unfold later in his many sea stories. After some initial rejections of his writing, Hodgson managed to become a full-time writer of both novels and short stories, which form a fantastic legacy of adventure, mystery and horror fiction.

E.E. King
The Rediscovery of Plants
(First Publication)
E.E. King is a painter, performer, writer, and biologist – she'll do anything that won't pay the bills, especially if it involves animals. Ray Bradbury called her stories, 'marvelously inventive, wildly funny and deeply thought-provoking. I cannot recommend them highly enough.' King has won numerous various awards and fellowships for art, writing, and environmental research. She's worked with children in Bosnia, crocodiles in Mexico, frogs in Puerto Rico, egrets in Bali, mushrooms in Montana, archaeologists in Spain, and butterflies in South Central Los Angeles. Check out paintings, writing, musings and books at www.elizabetheveking.com.

Michael Kortes
The Sun Takers
(First Publication)
Michael Kortes lives in Mississauga, Canada but commutes daily to Toronto on a rickety train. It's his favourite time to write. He knows that if the rider sitting next to him stops reading over his shoulder then his story hasn't made the grade. Michael has been a janitor, a river rafting guide, a YouTuber and a barrister. He currently spends copious amounts of time studying and thinking about pandemics and extinction events. Probably more than is healthy. 'Sun Takers' is Michael's first foray into short story writing.

Raymond Little
Scream and I'll Come to You
(Originally Published in *DOA II*, 2013)
Raymond Little was born and brought up in South London and now lives in Kent, though he returns regularly to Brixton to head the creative writing group he set up in 2017. He has had short stories published in anthologies in both the UK and USA, and his debut novel, *Eyes of Doom*, was published by Blood Bound Books in 2017. *Dark Matter*, a collection of the best of Ray's short stories, was published in 2019. Discover more about the author on his website: www.raymondlittle.co.uk.

Ken Liu
Mono no aware
('Mono no aware' copyright © 2012 Ken Liu. First published in *The Future is Japanese*, 2012)
Ken Liu (http://kenliu.name) is an American author of speculative fiction. A winner of the Nebula, Hugo, and World Fantasy awards, he wrote The Dandelion Dynasty, a silkpunk epic fantasy series (starting with The Grace of Kings), as well as The Paper Menagerie and Other Stories and The Hidden Girl and Other Stories, short story collections. He also authored the Star Wars novel, The Legends of Luke Skywalker. Prior to becoming a full-time writer, Liu worked as a software engineer, corporate lawyer, and litigation consultant. Liu frequently speaks at conferences and universities on a variety of topics, including futurism, cryptocurrency, history of technology, bookmaking, the mathematics of origami, and other subjects of his expertise.

Jack London
The Dream of Debs
(Originally Published in *International Socialist Review*, January 1909)
Jack London (1876–1916) was born as John Griffith Chaney in San Francisco, California. As a young man he went to work in the Klondike during the Gold Rush, which became the setting for two of his best-known novels, *White Fang* and *The Call of the Wild*. Coming from a working-class background, London was a keen social activist and wrote several stories and articles from a socialist standpoint. His dystopian novel *The Iron Heel* is one of the clearest displays of this, in which he focuses on the political and social changes that have taken place in his fictional future.

Thana Niveau
And Fade Out Again
(Originally Published in *Great British Horror Vol. 2: For Those in Peril*, 2018)
Thana Niveau is a horror and science fiction writer. Originally from the States, she now lives in the UK, in a Victorian seaside town between Bristol and Wales. She is the author of the short story collections *Octoberland*, *Unquiet Waters*, and *From Hell to Eternity*, as well as the novel *House of Frozen Screams*. Her work has been reprinted in *Best New Horror* and *Best British Horror*. She has been shortlisted three times for the British Fantasy award – for *Octoberland* and *From Hell to Eternity*, and for her story 'Death Walks En Pointe'.

John B. Rosenman
Free Air
(Originally Published in an earlier version in *The Leading Edge Magazine of Science Fiction and Fantasy #11*, 1986)
John B. Rosenman is a retired English professor who lives in Virginia Beach VA. He and his wife Jane recently celebrated their 52nd wedding anniversary. He has published fiction in *Galaxy*, *Weird Tales*, *Whitley Strieber's Aliens* and elsewhere. He is the author of *The Merry-Go-Round Man* (young adult) and science-fiction adventure novels such as *Beyond Those Distant Stars*, *A Senseless Act of Beauty*, and the *Inspector of the Cross* series, published by MuseItUp Publishing. John was inspired by EC Comics, Ray Bradbury, and terrifying SF movies of the fifties. He is also a tennis addict.

Sydney Rossman-Reich
A Line Cutting Canvas
(First Publication)
Sydney Rossman-Reich lives in Orlando, Florida where she works in her family's small real estate business. Prior to moving home, Sydney spent most of her working life building software at big and small tech companies in Silicon Valley. She draws on this experience extensively in her fiction. Sydney is a proud alumnus of Viable Paradise Writers Workshop, and you can find more of her stories in *Reckoning 4* and forthcoming with *Stupefying Stories*. Outside of writing, Sydney is passionate about reading, baking ambitious cakes, and besting her husband at video games. You can find her on Twitter at @Sydkick.

Elizabeth Rubio
What Treasures We Store on Earth
(First Publication)
Elizabeth Rubio writes science fiction, fantasy, and nonfiction in Austin, Texas, where people take pride in being weird. Once a professional biochemist, Elizabeth believes that every person is a scientist, and hopes optimistic scientists of all kinds can work together to avert climate disaster and build a green and living future. You can find her stories in *Analog*, *Mythic*, and *Little Blue Marble*, or look for her nonfiction series of children's books from Enslow Publishing.

Zach Shephard
The Final Chapter of Marathon Mandy
(Originally Published in *The Binge-Watching Cure*, 2018)
Zach Shephard lives in Enumclaw, Washington, where he's written stories that have appeared in places like *Fantasy & Science Fiction*, *Galaxy's Edge*, and his computer's Recycle Bin. He loves kickboxing and Brazilian jiu-jitsu, but rather dislikes the back pain that comes with being a thirty-seven-year-old exercise junkie. Like the protagonist of 'The Final Chapter of Marathon Mandy', Zach occasionally does his writing out in nature, away from modern distractions. He's now appeared in Flame Tree's Gothic Fantasy series five times – his other contributions can be found in the *Science Fiction*, *Swords & Steam*, *Endless Apocalypse*, and *Haunted House* volumes.

Shikhandin
Communal
(First Publication)
Shikhandin is the *nom de plume* of an Indian writer, whose recent published books include a story collection *Immoderate Men* (Speaking Tiger Books, India), and a children's book *Vibhuti Cat* (Duckbill Books, India). Shikhandin has won several awards and accolades for her poetry and fiction in India and abroad. Her work has been published in journals and anthologies worldwide. You can find out more about Shikhandin on her Facebook page: facebook.com/AuthorShikhandin.

Alex Shvartsman
Ambassador to the Meek
(Originally Published in *The Sum of Us*, 2017)
Alex Shvartsman is a writer, translator, and anthologist from Brooklyn, NY. Over 120 of his short stories have appeared in *Nature*, *Analog*, *Strange Horizons*, and many other magazines and anthologies. He won the 2014 WSFA Small Press Award for Short Fiction and was a two-time finalist for the Canopus Award for Excellence in Interstellar Fiction (2015 and 2017). He is the editor of the Unidentified Funny Objects annual anthology series of humorous SF/F, and of *Future Science Fiction Digest*. His epic fantasy novel, *Eridani's Crown*, was published in 2019. His website is www.alexshvartsman.com.

Clark Ashton Smith
The Empire of the Necromancers
(Originally Published in *Weird Tales*, September 1932)
The Isle of the Torturers

(Originally Published in *Keep on the Light*, Selwyn & Blount, 1933)
Clark Ashton Smith (1893–1961) was born in Long Valley, California. He is well regarded as both a poet and a writer of horror, fantasy and science fiction stories. Along with H.P. Lovecraft and Robert E. Howard, he was a prolific contributor to the magazine *Weird Tales*. His stories are full of dark and imaginative creations, and glimpses into the worlds beyond. His unique writing style and incredible vision have led to many of his stories influencing later fantasy writers.

Kristal Stittle
Decimate
(First Publication)
Kristal Stittle was born and raised in Toronto, Canada, where she still lives with her cat, although she's known to frequently flee to the lakes and forests of Muskoka. Trained in 3D animation, she continues to paint and illustrate regularly while dabbling in photography whenever she's not writing. She's the author of the zombie *Survival Instinct* series, and the thriller *Merciless*, as well as many short stories. You can find her on Twitter @KristalStittle, where she's probably lurking in the comments of her favourite horror authors' posts.

Rebecca E. Treasure
Whose Waters Never Fail
(First Publication)
Rebecca E. Treasure grew up reading science fiction in the foothills of the Rocky Mountains. She received a degree in history from the University of Arkansas and a Masters degree from the University of Denver. After graduate school, she began writing fiction. Rebecca has lived many places, including the Gulf Coast of Mississippi and Tokyo, Japan. She currently resides in Texas Hill Country with her husband, where she juggles two children, a corgi, a violin studio, and writing. She only drops the children occasionally.

Francesco Verso
Two Worlds
(Originally Published in *in English on Future Fiction, Mincione Edizioni,* April 2014)
Francesco Verso is one of the most interesting author of contemporary Italian Science Fiction. Over the last ten years he has won many SF awards and since 5 years he's the editor of Future Fiction multicultural project. His books include: Antidoti umani, e-Doll (Urania Award 2009), Livido (Odissea and Italia Award 2013), Bloodbusters (Urania Award 2015) and I camminatori book 1 The Pulldogs and book 2 No/Mad/Land (Future Fiction, 2018.) His novel Livido – translated by Sally McCorry – has been published in the USA by Apex Books in 2018. Livido and Bloodbusters will be published in China for Bofeng Culture in 2020. His short stories appeared in many genre magazines like 'Robot', 'Fantasy Magazine', 'Futuri', 'MAMUT', 'International Speculative Fiction #5', 'Chicago Quarterly Review #20', 'Words Without Borders' and 'Future Affairs Administration'.

Stanley G. Weinbaum
A Martian Odyssey
(Originally Published in *Wonder Stories*, July 1934)

Stanley Grauman Weinbaum (1902–35) was a science fiction writer born in Louisville, Kentucky. He is best known for the groundbreaking short story 'A Martian Odyssey', which was the first of its kind to present an alien life form that was complex in nature. Many of Weinbaum's short stories were published in *Astounding Science Fiction and Fact* or *Wonder Stories*. His premature death cut short his very promising career as a writer.

H.G. Wells
The Time Machine
(Originally Published by William Heinemann, 1895)
Herbert George Wells (1866–1946) was born in Kent, England. Novelist, journalist, social reformer and historian, Wells is one of the greatest ever science fiction writers and along with Jules Verne is sometimes referred to as a 'founding father' of the genre. With Aldous Huxley and, later, George Orwell he defined the adventurous, social concern of early speculative fiction where the human condition was played out on a greater stage. Wells created over fifty novels, including his famous works *The Time Machine*, *The Invisible Man*, *The Island of Dr. Moreau* and *The War of the Worlds*, as well as a fantastic array of short stories.

Marian Womack
Black Isle
(First Publication)
Marian Womack is a bilingual writer (English and Spanish), and co-founder of Calque Press. She is a graduate of the Clarion Writer's Workshop, and her debut English-language eco-storytelling collection, Lost Objects, was published in 2018 by Luna Press . Her fiction has been part of an installation in Somerset House about activism and ecology, translated into Italian, and nominated for both BSFA and British Fantasy Awards. She teaches creative writing at Oxford University, and works for Cambridge University Libraries in a teaching and engagement role. Her doctoral research looks at the communication of climate change through fiction, and the intersections of eco-storytelling, independent publishing, and activism. Find out more on her website: marianwomack.com.

FLAME TREE PUBLISHING
Short Story Series

New & Classic Writing

Flame Tree's Gothic Fantasy books offer a carefully curated series of new titles, each with combinations of original and classic writing:

Chilling Horror • Chilling Ghost • Science Fiction
Murder Mayhem • Crime & Mystery • Swords & Steam
Dystopia Utopia • Supernatural Horror • Lost Worlds
Time Travel • Heroic Fantasy • Pirates & Ghosts
Agents & Spies • Endless Apocalypse • Alien Invasion
Robots & AI • Lost Souls • Haunted House • Cosy Crime
Urban Crime • American Gothic • Epic Fantasy
Detective Mysteries • Detective Thrillers

Also, new companion titles offer rich collections of classic fiction, myths and tales in the gothic fantasy tradition:

H.G. Wells • Lovecraft • Sherlock Holmes
Edgar Allan Poe • Bram Stoker • Mary Shelley
African Myths & Tales • Celtic Myths & Tales
Chinese Myths & Tales • Norse Myths & Tales
Greek Myths & Tales • Japanese Myths & Tales • Irish Fairy Tales
King Arthur & The Knights of the Round Table
Alice's Adventures in Wonderland • The Divine Comedy
The Wonderful Wizard of Oz • The Age of Queen Victoria • Brothers Grimm

Available from all good bookstores, worldwide, and online at
flametreepublishing.com

See our new fiction imprint
FLAME TREE PRESS | FICTION WITHOUT FRONTIERS
New and original writing in Horror, Crime, SF and Fantasy

And join our monthly newsletter with offers and more stories:
FLAME TREE FICTION NEWSLETTER
flametreepress.com

GOTHIC FANTASY

Paris
ATIONALE
AGE MERCREDI
LOTER
PROCHAI
HOTEL

OULANGERIE
RUE PIAT

TRANSVAAL HOTEL
21
LA CORDONNERIE 21
21 AU PETIT CARREFOUR BOIS et CHARBONS

UH
UH
AH
BOIS CHA

au Repos de la Montagne' VINS

NICOL
21

Paris

ANDI WATSON
story
SIMON GANE
art

IMAGECOMICS.COM

ISBN: 978-1-5343-2120-5.

CHÉRI
BONJOUR.

POUR LA JOLIE FILLE.

MERCI, MONSIEUR.

BEEP!
an image publication

BAC
BRASSERI

HOTEL
ANGLAIS
ONALE

written by

andi watson

DEBORAH, CLOSE THAT WINDOW AND GET DRESSED AT ONCE, CHILD.

YES, AUNT CHAPMAN.
WE'RE DUE AT THE CRICKET CLUB FOR ELEVENSES, FOLLOWED BY TEA WITH MRS. HEREFORD-SOAMES, OR HAD YOU FORGOTTEN?

COME, COME, WE SHALL FINALLY HAVE A PROPER CUP OF TEA.

SSSsiiiiip
HOTE
ANGLA

DUBONNET

drawn by

VENEZ À TRAVERS!
?

simon
gane

42 Rue de Seine

AC
de
2en

ADÉMIE
STAËL
ne etage

Paris
ACADÉMIE de STAËL

chapter
one

HERE AT ACADÉMIE DE STAËL YOU WILL CAST YOUR EYES UP FROM THE GUTTER, AWAY FROM THE NEON LIGHTS AND VULGAR DISTRACTIONS OF MODERN LIFE.

I WILL DIRECT YOU TO A HIGHER CALLING, SHARING WITH YOU A VISION OF THE HEAVENS AND OF THE ETERNAL VIRTUES.
YOU ARE STUDYING NOT ONLY ART BUT HISTORY, TRAINING YOUR EYES AND YOUR MINDS, LEARNING FROM ANTIQUITY, FROM THE POEMS OF HOMER AND THE PAINTING OF RAPHAEL.

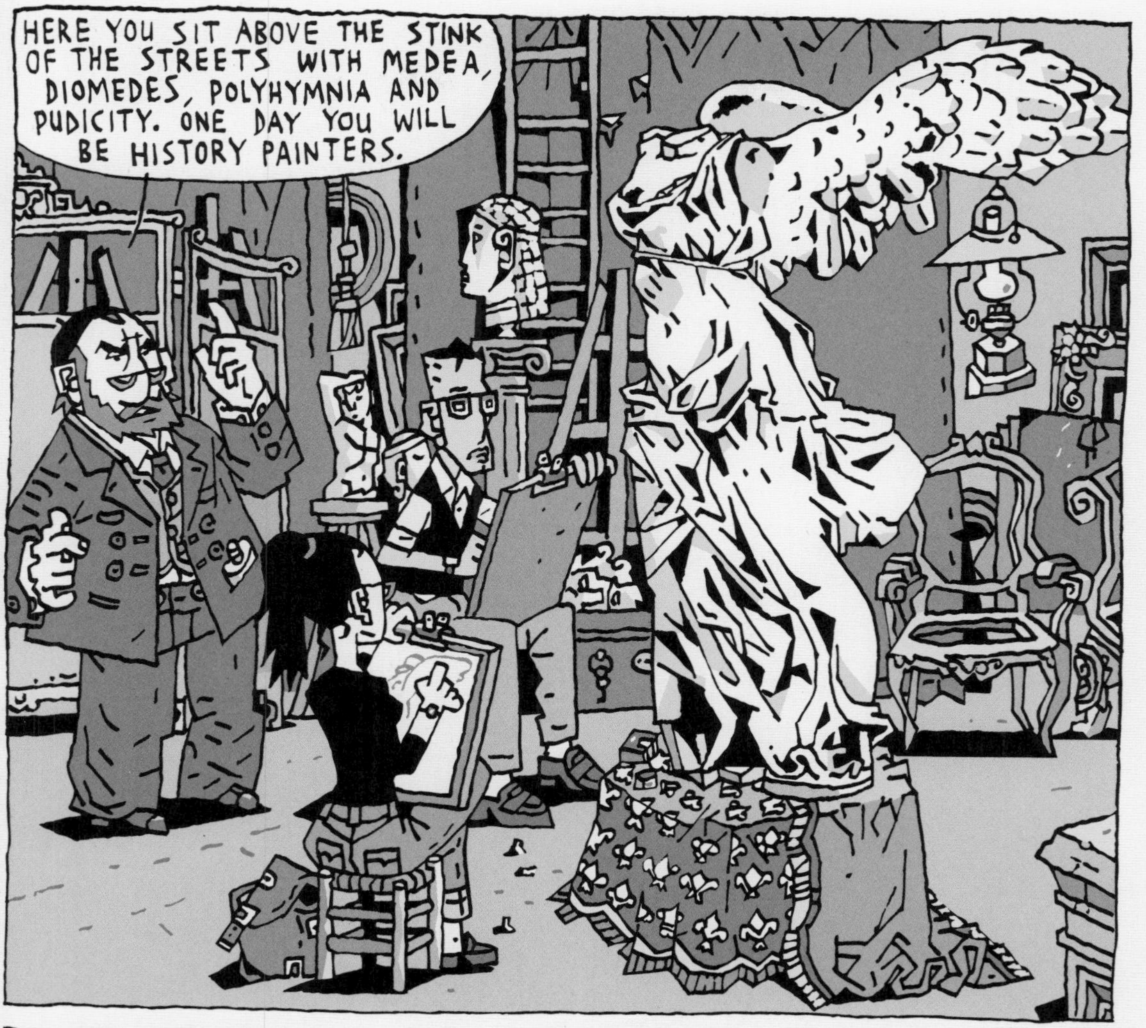

HERE YOU SIT ABOVE THE STINK OF THE STREETS WITH MEDEA, DIOMEDES, POLYHYMNIA AND PUDICITY. ONE DAY YOU WILL BE HISTORY PAINTERS.

GIBERT JEUNE
Cafe St.M
GD COMPTOIR Telephone
Salon Blonde
HOTEL
TABAC
RANT Bar
CAF
HEBDO LATIN
JAZZ
HIS BREATH IS LIKE DÉCAPANT, NON? HOW DO YOU LIKE IT?

I DON'T, GERARD. WHA' D'YA WANT ME TO DO, SLINK BACK TO NEW YORK WITH MY TAIL BETWEEN MY LEGS?
RICAR
BYRRH

M. ANCIEN RÉGIME, THAT IS WHERE HE WOULD PUT HIS TAIL.

I'LL MAKE LIKE I DIDN'T HEAR THAT.
NOIR

SO, HE MAKES GIFT OF PAINTS TO YOU?

NO. I HAVE TO GIVE THEM BACK. LIKE YOU I'M SANS LE SOU. I HAVE TO BE FEMME D'AFFAIRES.
NOIR

YOU COME SEE ME CETTE NUIT, LIKE YOU PROMISE?

YOU BOP SANS JULIET.

TING TING TING TING
ABROAD IS BLOODY, ISN'T IT? THANK YOU SO MUCH FOR HAVING US OVER. SUCH A RELIEF TO BE AMONG ONE'S OWN WHO STICK TO THE OLD WAYS.

SHALL I POUR?

I WAS ALWAYS LED TO BELIEVE PARISIANS WERE TERRIBLY SOPHISTICATED, BUT WHAT DO I FIND?

THEY PRINT, NOT ENGRAVE THEIR VISITING CARDS.

AND THE FOOD.
FORTUNATELY FOR DEBORAH, HER MOTHER ...YOU REMEMBER ROSEMARY DON'T YOU?

WELL ROSEMARY SENDS OVER HER HOMEMADE WHEAT-GERM LOAVES AND WE PRACTICALLY LIVE ON THE STUFF.

FRIGHTFULLY GOOD FOR MY FIGURE. I'LL NEED A WHOLE NEW WARDROBE WHEN WE'RE HOME FOR THE SHOOTING SEASON.

HAH HAR!

WON'T I DEAR?
NICOLAS

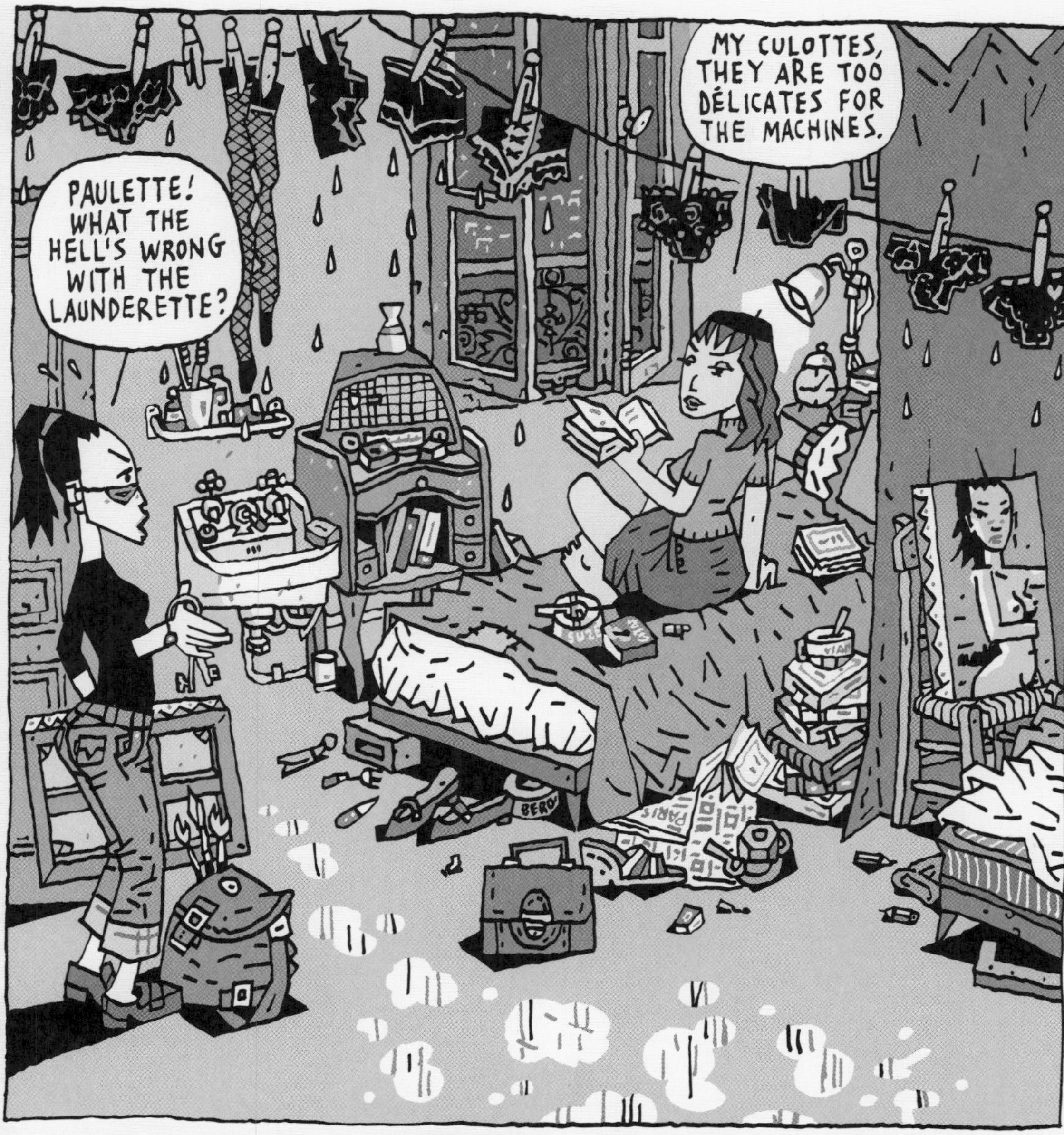

PAULETTE! WHAT THE HELL'S WRONG WITH THE LAUNDERETTE?

MY CULOTTES, THEY ARE TOO DÉLICATES FOR THE MACHINES.

WHAT IS SO TERRIBLE NOW?
I HAVE ANOTHER HORSESHIT PORTRAIT TO PAINT.

SOON THERE WILL BE NO MONEY. YOUR PROFESSEUR WILL BURN IN HIS ATELIER.

I HAVE TO PAINT PRECIOUS LITTLE DADDY'S GIRLS. BECAUSE THEY WON'T ALLOW A MAN TO STARE AT THEIR PRETTY LITTLE BODIES.

WOOF.
THEY GO UP IN THEIR DRESSES.

WITH THEIR EXPENSIVE DRESSES AND THEIR DAMNED EMPTY HEADS.

WOOOF!
CLINK

IVRY

HOTEL ANGLAIS
WHY AREN'T YOU PAINTING?
PREPARATORY SKETCHES, MA'AM.
HOW LONG IS IT LIKELY TO TAKE?

I WON'T KNOW UNTIL I START.

DO LET US GET ON WITH IT, CHAP.

TING TING TING

CHAP.

I SEE MIDDY FINALLY DRAGGED POOR CLIVE LEISCESTER-ROWLANDS TO THE ALTAR.
"Glamorous Princess"
NYLON
Dress overall
5/.
The Lady

CHAP! PLEASE, GO FOR A WALK.
OH, ALL RIGHT. I THINK I CAN TRUST YOU.

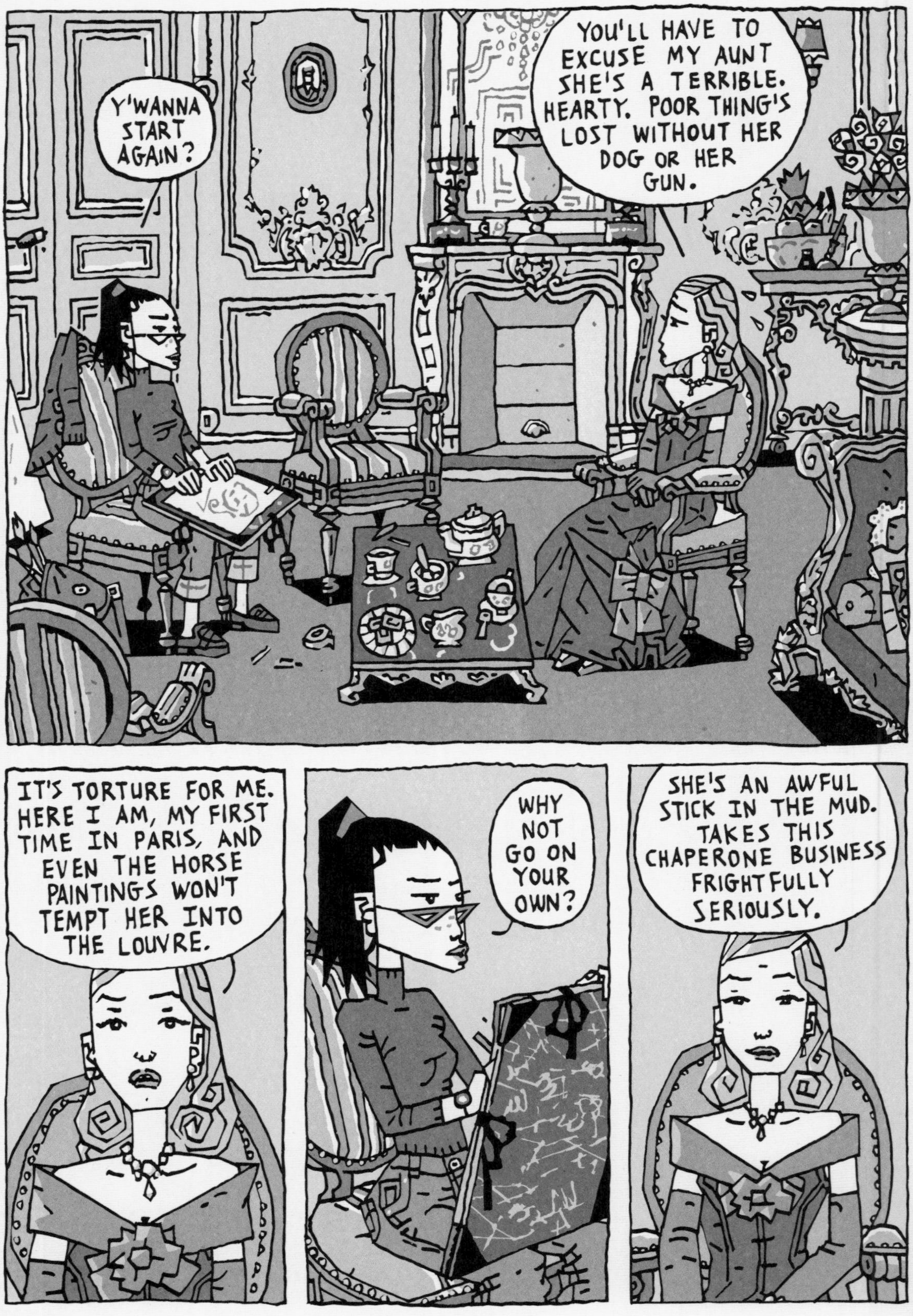

Y'WANNA START AGAIN?

YOU'LL HAVE TO EXCUSE MY AUNT SHE'S A TERRIBLE. HEARTY. POOR THING'S LOST WITHOUT HER DOG OR HER GUN.

THANK GOD BILLY'S COMING. I'LL SHAKE OFF THE OLD CHAP AND HE'LL SHOW ME PARIS.

THAT'S GREAT.

MAY I SEE?
ALL THREE LINES, SURE.

THEN YOU WOULDN'T MIND AWFULLY IF I HAD AN IDEA?
HAVE AS MANY AS YOU LIKE.

I COULDN'T SHOW YOU THIS BEFORE BECAUSE CHAP THINKS HE'S AN ABSOLUTE SINK.
INGRES. YOU DIG HIM?

CHAP CALLS THEM IMMORAL PICTURES. WHAT DO YOU THINK?

THE VICOMTESSE?

OH. I'M BEING SILLY?
INGRES

NO. THAT'S COOL.

AND WITH THE LOOKING GLASS? BILLY WILL ADORE IT.

l'ascenseur
A TELEGRAM FOR MADAME CHAPMAN.
Daily Mail
FRENCH

JUST LEAVING? I EXPECTED YOU'D BE FINISHED BY NOW.

I'VE BARELY STARTED ON THE FACE. AS FOR THE DRESS AND...
NONSENSE. NEVER MIND THE GOWN.

I CAN HARDLY ...
TAKE A PHOTOGRAPH. I STEADFASTLY REFUSE TO PAY ANOTHER TWO HUNDRED FOR A SITTING.

FRANKLY I DON'T SEE WHERE THE MONEY GOES. PERHAPS YOU DRIVE ONE OF THOSE MONSTROUS CARS YOU HAVE IN YOUR COUNTRY.

WAIT A MINUTE, LADY. I DON'T SEE A CENT OF THAT MONEY. IT GOES STRAIGHT TO M. DE STAËL TO COVER MY TUITION. I CAN'T EVEN AFFORD MY OWN PAINTS.

HOW UNFORTUNATE. HOWEVER, DEBORAH'S PORTRAIT WILL BE DELIVERED HERE TO ME IN A FORTNIGHT'S TIME.

HUH
?

TWO WEEKS, FOURTEEN DAYS. UNDERSTAND? REALLY, AT LEAST WITH THE FRENCH THEY UNDER-STAND WHEN I TALK LOUDLY AND SLOWLY.

C'MON. CUT ME SOME SLACK WILLYA
?

THIS TELEGRAM MEANS I NEED THAT PICTURE IN TWO WEEKS. IT'S AN IMPORTANT GIFT AND IF IT'S NOT FINISHED ON TIME YOU WON'T GET PAID.

EVEN IF I GET IT FINISHED ON TIME, YOU REALISE IT WON'T BE DRY FOR MONTHS?

PUT IT OUT IN THE SUN THEN.

YOU THINK DEBS WILL APPRECIATE A BIG, FAT FLY STUCK IN HER PIGMENT?

HER NAME IS DEBORAH, MISS MORROW.

GOOD EVENING.

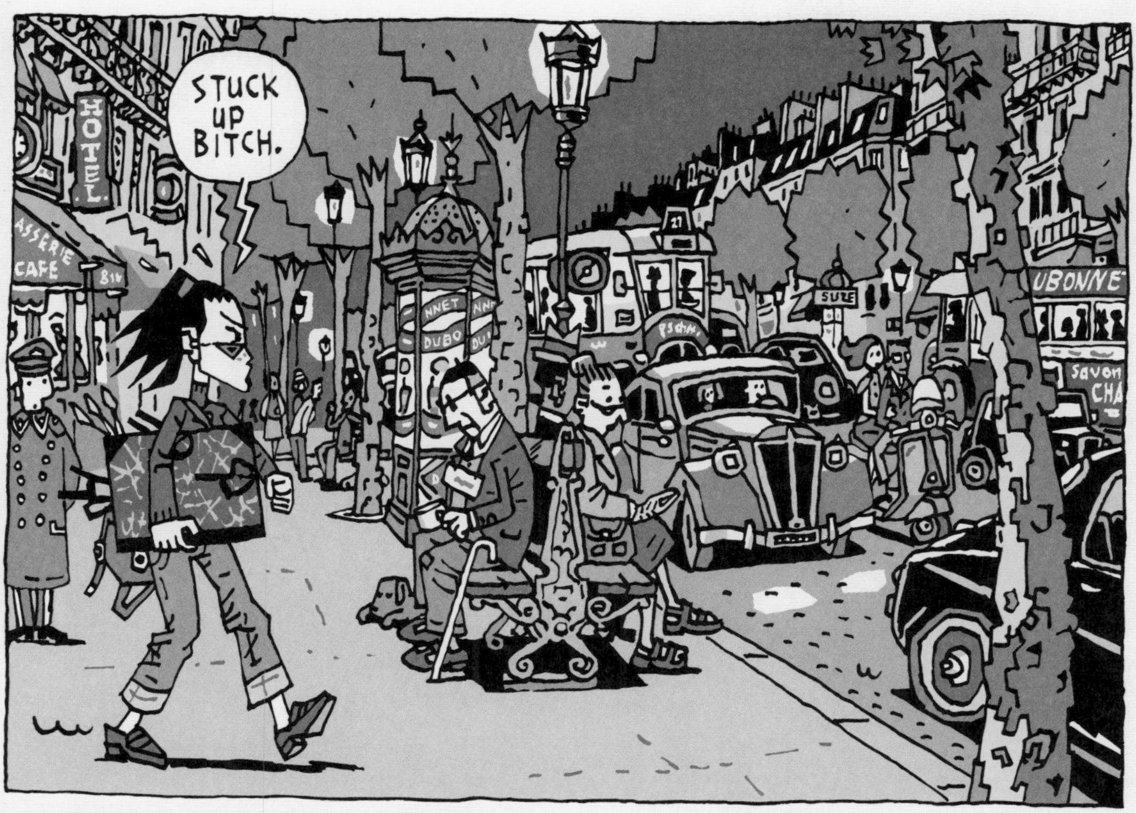

STUCK UP BITCH.

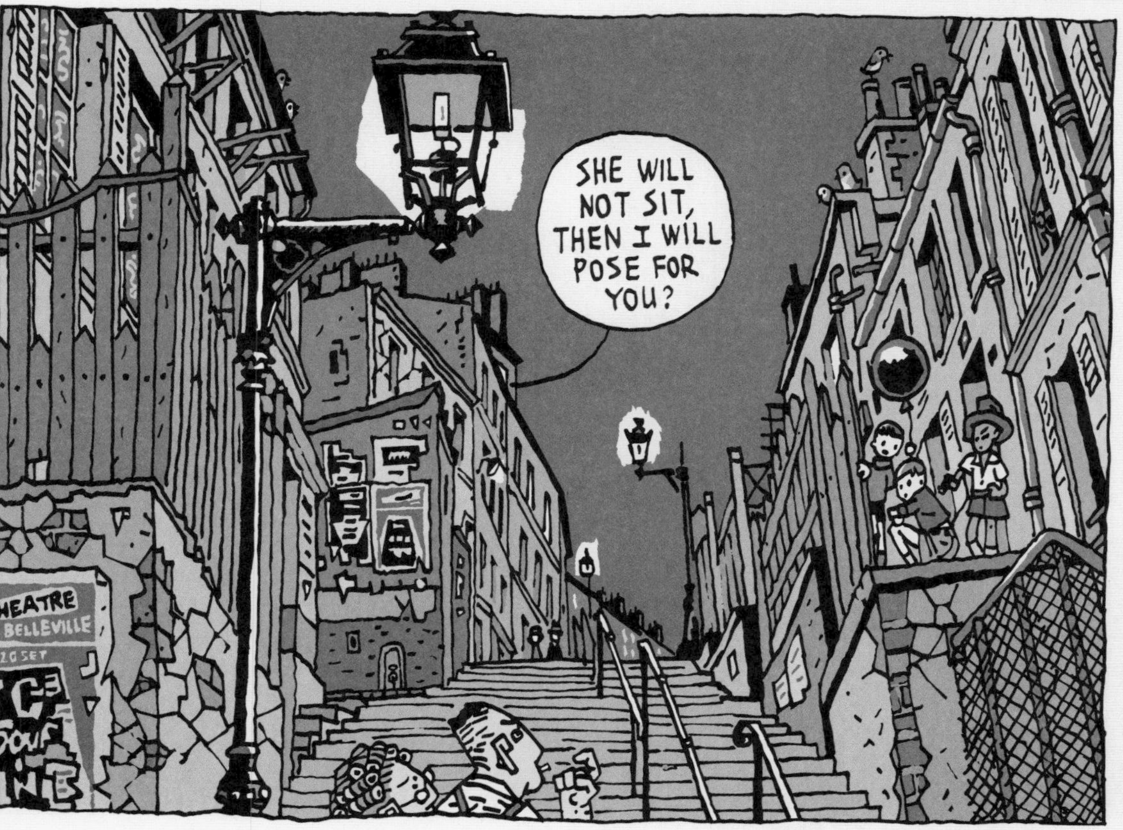

SHE WILL NOT SIT, THEN I WILL POSE FOR YOU?

BIG TABOO. DE STAËL FORBIDS LIFE DRAWING UNTIL WE REACH THE NEXT CLASS.
BERGE

YOU THINK, MAYBE, WHY YOU DRAW PLASTER IT IS CHEAPER THAN MODÈLE, NON?

EITHER YOU DO THINGS RIGHT OR YOU DON'T.
BER

YOU ARE DOING THINGS RIGHT? WHEN WILL YOU CAST OFF YOUR PETIT BOURGEOIS...

PAULETTE, PAULETTE!

YOU WILL NOT COME ?

I'M UP TO MY EARS.

BONSOIR !

BERGER

HAUT
ESCAFE

chapter
two

...EVERY PERSON SAUTILLÈRENT, IT WAS CRAZY. AND YOU SEE, YOU MISS BON TEMPS AND...

...AND I SEE YOU ONLY HEAR WITH YOUR EYES.

SHE IS GIRL YOU PAINT, WHAT IS HER NAME?

DEBORAH.

SHE IS, BELLE, TRÈS BELLE, NOT LIKE YOU.
GEE THANKS, GERARD, THAT'S VERY SWEET OF YOU.

NON, NON, I MEAN SO YOU ARE VÉRITABLE, THAT IS GOOD.
IT'S COOL, I KNOW WHAT YOU MEANT.

SO YOU SEE ME, WE HAVE BON TEMPS, NON?

YEAH, SURE, NEXT TIME. LIKE I PROMISED.

UH
UH
UH.

AH
AH
AH.

AHH
AHH

AH ...

...AHHH HHHHhh.
SLAP

Hee hee.
BON-SOIR.

MY PETITE GIROFLÉE, YOU NOT FINIS YET?
I CAN'T CAPTURE HER FACE, NOT FROM SNAP-SHOTS.
SUZE

WHY YOU CARE? IS PAPIER PEINT FOR HAUTE BOURGEOISIE!

SHE'S DIFFERENT, SHE APPRECIATES ART.

AHHHH.

JE COMPRENDS.

PLÂTRE IS NOT ENOUGH, OR PHOTOGRAPH. YOU WISH TO SEE HER ROUGEUR, FEEL HER BREATH ON YOUR SKIN, SMELL AND HEAR HER TO SAVOIR TOUT À FAIT.

THAT OLD CRONE OF AN AUNT WON'T LET ME NEAR HER.

OH, YOU GIVE UP YOUR DEBORAH TO VIEILLE SORCIÈRE SANS BATAILLE? NON, YOU CUT LES RONCES TO CLAIM PRINCESSE PRÉCIEUSE.

SPLENDIDES NICHONS!

COCHON!

HOTEL ANGLAI
ANGLAIS
FRENCH PHRASE BOOK

MADAME CHAPMAN? AH, BONSOIR, JE M'APPELLE HUGHINA. ÇA SENT MAUVAIS, IL Y A UNE ERREUR DANS L'ADDITION. VOUS AVEZ UNE INTOXICATION ALIMENTAIRE.
FRENCH PHRASE BOOK

DEBORAH, DEAR, IT'S NO GOOD. YOU'LL HAVE TO ANSWER IT. THE WRETCHED FROG CAN'T SPEAK A WORD OF THE QUEEN'S ENGLISH.

POURRIEZ-VOUS RÉPETER, S'IL VOUS PLAIT?
YOU'D THINK, WILLIAM, WHEN ONE STAYS IN AN ENGLISH HOTEL THE HELP WOULD SPEAK PROPERLY.

DEBS? IT'S ME, JULIET. LISTEN, I NEED TO SEE YOU.
JULIET? ONE MOMENT, PLEASE.

THEY'RE HOLDING A PARCEL FOR US AT THE DESK. I'LL POP DOWN AND FETCH IT.
SPLENDID, ANOTHER RATION OF WHEAT-GERM LOAF. I DO HOPE ROSEMARY TREATED US TO A POT OF GENTLEMAN'S RELISH.
DO HURRY, DEBORAH DARLING, OR WE'LL NEVER FINISH THIS WRETCHED HAND.

I'VE BEEN HAVING A HELL OF A TIME WITH THIS DAMNED PAINTING. I CAN'T FINISH IT WITHOUT SEEING YOUR FACE AGAIN.
I WAS SO LOOKING FORWARD TO MY SITTING, BUT CHAP HAS BEEN EXTRAORDINARILY VICTORIAN.

SHE DOESN'T LIKE AMERICANS?
SHE SEES ALL FOREIGNERS AS SEDUCERS, BUT NOW BILLY'S HERE I'LL BE FREE.

BILLY?

YES, YOU'LL SIMPLY ADORE HIM. EVERYONE DOES. WE'RE GOING TO THE LOUVRE TOMORROW. WHY DON'T YOU MEET US THERE?
UH, I DUNNO, THREE OF US?

BE UNDER "ROGER DELIVERING ANGELICA" AT NOON. AND DO BRING THE PAINTING.

PAVILLION TURGOT

AWFULLY SORRY WE'RE LATE. JULIET, THIS IS BILLY.
MWAH
MWAH
ERR, HI.

MY SISTER HAS BEEN QUITE SICK-MAKING ABOUT HOW FRIGHTFULLY TALENTED YOU ARE. SHE WILL NOT SHUT UP ABOUT YOU.

DON'T BE BEASTLY, BILLY.

YOU TWO ARE BROTHER AND SISTER?

WE BOTH HAVE AN EYE FOR A PRETTY THING.
DADDY WANTED HEARTY OFFSPRING. WE'RE A FRIGHTFUL DISAPPOINT-MENT.

MUST DASH, I HAVE BUSINESS TO PUT IN ORDER. PROMISE ME YOU'LL MISBEHAVE AND NOT LET ON TO CHAPPERS, OR SHE'LL HAVE MY GUTS FOR GARTERS.

DID YOU BRING THE PORTRAIT? I'M ACHING TO SEE IT.
'FRAID IT'S STILL WET. EITHER YOU COME OVER TO THE STUDIO OR YOU WAIT 'TIL IT'S DONE.

I'LL DIE OF ANTICIP-ATION.

I ONLY WISH I HAD YOUR TALENT.
WHAT MAKES YOU THINK YOU DON'T?

I'VE TAKEN CLASSES. MY TUTOR PAINTED TANKS IN THE WAR.

THEN I TOOK A COURSE ON THE ROMANTIC POETS, PIANO LESSONS, TENNIS. THE MORTIFYING TRUTH IS THAT I EXCEL AT NOTHING.

YOU COULD BE A MUSE, A MODEL?

WHAT KIND OF LIFE IS THAT FOR A YOUNG LADY? NO, UNLESS I MARRY SOMEONE BEASTLY RICH I'LL BE CONSIDERED A TERRIBLE LOST CAUSE. ONE MUST KEEP THE SIDE UP.

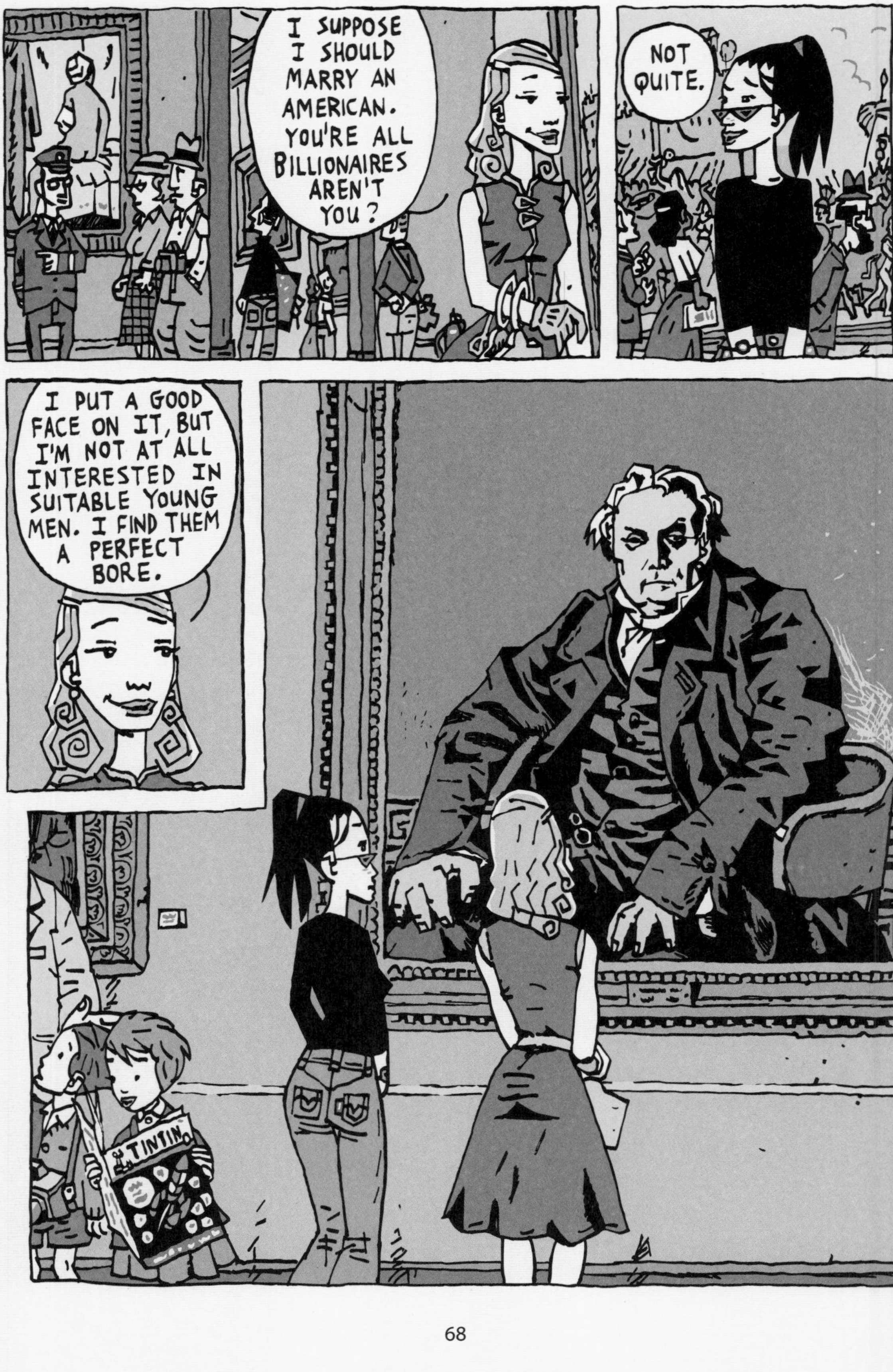

I PUT A GOOD FACE ON IT, BUT I'M NOT AT ALL INTERESTED IN SUITABLE YOUNG MEN. I FIND THEM A PERFECT BORE.

TINTIN

NOW, JULIET, YOU MUST NOT LET ME RUN ON SO. TELL ME, HOW DID YOU COME TO BE HERE, IN THIS HEAVENLY PLACE?

I'M AN ARTIST AND SO THIS IS IT, Y'KNOW? THE PLACE TO LEARN. SO I LEARN THE OLD WAY, THE ACADEMY WAY. I FIGURE I LEARN THE RULES BEFORE I BREAK THEM, RIGHT?

ONLY, I HATE THE OLD WAY, SO MAYBE I'M NOT CUT OUT TO BE AN ARTIST.

I THINK ABOUT TAKING THAT TICKET HOME. BACK TO MOM AND DAD WHO THINK EVERY PAINTING I MAKE IS AN UNMADE BED OR AN UNCOOKED MEAL.

ONLY I DON'T WANT TO STAY AND I DON'T WANT TO GO.

OH, I WANT TO STAY. TO LIVE IN PARIS WOULD BE DIVINE.

UPONT
BOULEVARD
Jazz
HUMERIE MARTINIQ
DUBO

YOU'RE SURE YOU'RE SAFE?
YES, I CALLED BILLY AT THE CRICKET CLUB AND HE'S TOLD CHAP HE AND I ARE ATTENDING A BACH STRING QUARTET. CHAP REVILES EVERYTHING GERMAN.

THIS AIN'T NO BACH! IT'LL PUT YOU OUT OF YOUR SHOES!
DELIGHTFUL!

GRACIOUS, I'M QUITE DIZZY. YOU DON'T SUPPOSE I'M DRUNK DO YOU?

LIPPY'S SO EXPENSIVE. I'LL SHOW YOU HOW I MAKE IT LAST.

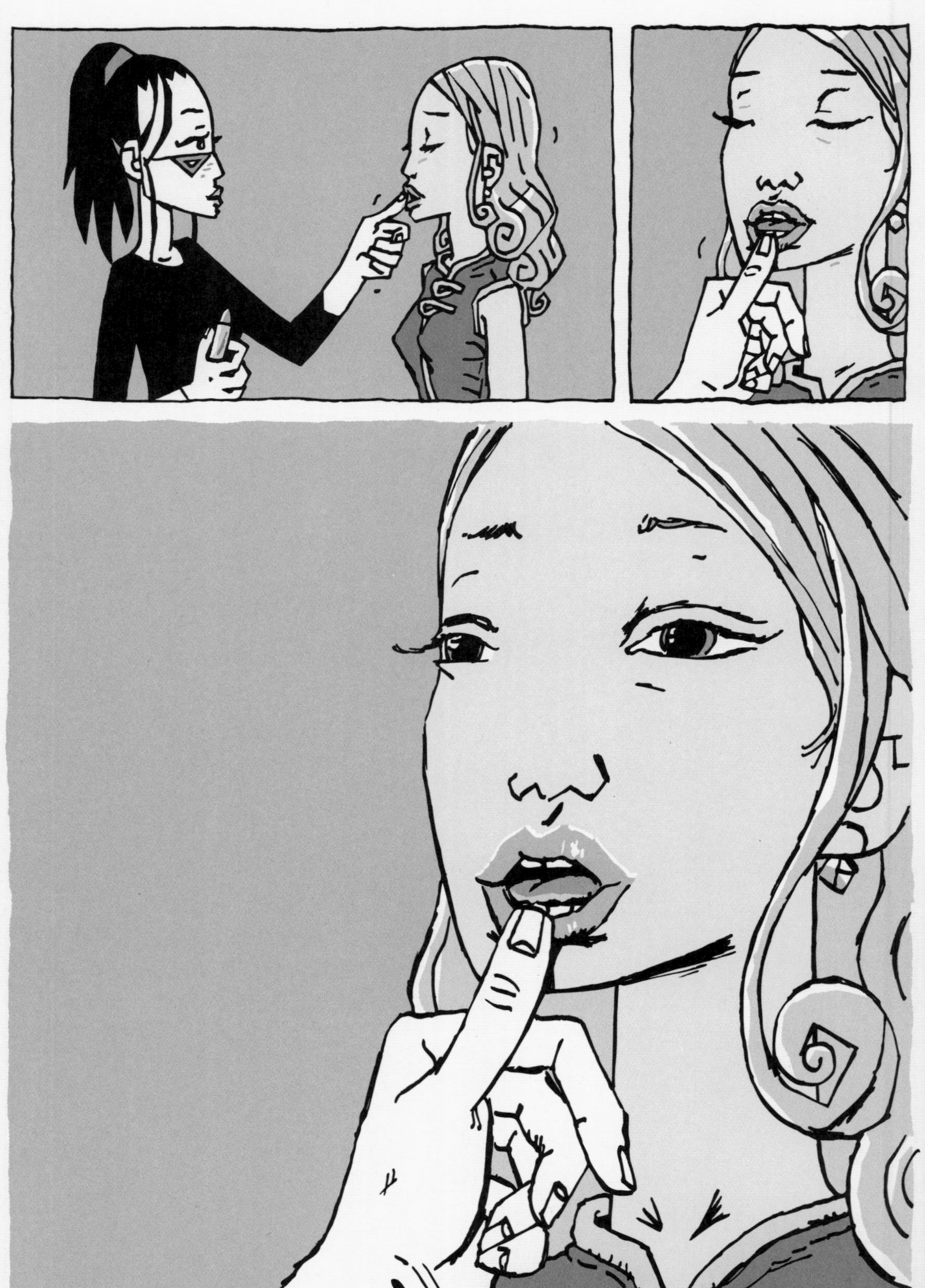

AU PETIT CARREFOUR CA
GHM
A75
chapter three

YOU AN INSOMNIAQUE, JULIET?

THE DAMN PORTRAIT HAS TO BE FINISHED TODAY AND I STILL CAN'T GET IT RIGHT.
TU VAS DÉPÊCHER ET L'HABILLER, NO?

LETTRE D'AMOUR?
RIIIP!

THE CRICKET CLUB
It will be frightfully dull, but Billy has organised a ball in my honour. Formal dress, and do bring the painting.
Yours longingly,
Debs

A BALL! PAULETTE, DO YOU HAVE ANYTHING I CAN WEAR TO A BALL?
BALLON?
de BEAUVOIR

Y'KNOW, A BIG PARTY WITH PUNCH BOWLS, GOWNS AND DANCING.
LES PARASITES DE LA CLASSE OUVIÈRE!

SIGH.

KNOCK
KNOCK

PARDON, I HAVE WOKEN YOU?
GERARD, COME IN.

SORRY, I'VE BEEN AT IT ALL NIGHT. COFFEE?
YOU ARE ABSENCE IRRÉGULIÈRE FROM L'ACADÉMIE. I WORRY OVER YOU.

WE'RE OUT OF COFFEE. WINE?

I'M UP TO MY EARS WRESTLING WITH THIS DAMN PAINTING.
M. ANCIEN RÉGIME DEMANDE YOU, HE WANT HIS FRANCS.

YOU CAN TELL THE PROFESSEUR HE'LL HAVE HIS DOUGH TONIGHT.

YOU AIMÉS LE JAZZ?

YEAH, IT WAS CRAZY. THE PLACE FLIPPED.

I WORRY OVER YOU, JULIET.

DON'T.

I CANNOT RÉPRIMER MES SENTIMENTS.

RED WINE GIVES ME A HEAD-ACHE.

MORE BECAUSE YOU ARE PERPLEXE, HMMM?

GERARD, I HAVE SO MUCH WORK TO DO BEFORE THIS EVENING.
YOU SEE ALL FRENCH MEN AS PIGS, NON?

I LOVE YOU TOO, GERARD.

BUT NOT LIKE THAT.

NOT LIKE THIS?

LE PROFESSEUR SERA INTÉRESSÉ COMMENT VOUS FAITES VOTRE ARGENT DE POCHE FROM YOUR PRETTY GIRLS!

THE CRICKET CLUB

SIR WORFIELD-LAMB AND LADY ROUGHLY.
CHIN UP, OLD GIRL. IT'S NOT EATON SQUARE, BUT IT BEATS CROCHETING ANTIMACASSARS OR ANOTHER TEDIOUS HAND OF BRIDGE.

IT'S TOO, TOO DREARY, BILLY. I SUPPOSE FOR YOU IT'S A JOLLY OLD LARK, HAVING A BALL IN MY HONOUR AND PARADING ME BEFORE EVERY DECAYING COLONEL AND SOUR-FACED AMBASSADOR'S WIFE IN PARIS?

IF YOU'RE GOING TO BE A DISMAL BITCH ABOUT IT, DEBS, I'LL FETCH CHAP AND YOU CAN BOTH GO HOME AND NIBBLE MUMMY'S WHEAT-GERM BREAD LIKE A PAIR OF OLD SPINSTERS.
OH, DON'T BE SUCH A HEAD GIRL, BILLY.

DO ADMIT IT'S SIMPLY KILLING TO SEE CHAP HOBBLE AROUND IN THOSE SHOES. WALKING ON COALS WOULD BE LESS AGONY FOR THE OLD GIRL.
THE POOR THING IS CRIPPLED BY A HEEL HIGHER THAN A RIDING BOOT.

HERE, SIP A GLASS OF THIS SWILL. I EXPECT SOME FAMILIAR FACES WILL ARRIVE SOONER OR LATER.

I DO HOPE SO.

FINISHED.

JULIET! DO YOU HAVE ROBE DESOIRÉE?
I'M NOT GOING. I'LL SEND THE PAINTING OVER IN A CAB.

BUT YOU MUST. DÉPÊCHE-TOI! COME, COME.
I DON'T WANNA RUB SHOULDERS WITH A ROOM FULL OF STUFFED SHIRTS AND OLD DAMES.

PFF, YOU BAIGNÉ DANS L'HUILE DE LIN?
PAULETTE!

HERE, JULIET. YOU LIKE?
MONE EAVOIR

I... I... WHERE DID YOU GET IT?
WE LIBERATION. NO MORE INTERROGATION. YOU DÉSHABILLER.

COCHON!

SPLENDIDES NICHONS.

DÉPÊCHE-
TOI !

Almasy
Almasy
33
!

PECK

MISS JULIET MORROW.

OH JULIET, YOU LOOK UTTERLY DIVINE. I FEEL LIKE QUITE THE SCARECROW IN MY ENGLISH RAGS. IT HAS BEEN AN ABSOLUTE SINK WITHOUT YOU.
AND I SEE YOU HAVE THE PAINTING, I MUST SEE IT AT ONCE.

MISS CHAPMAN, YOU MOVE LIKE A GAZELLE.
WHERE THE BLOODY HELL IS DEBS?
HAVE YOU BEEN ABUSING THE PUNCH BOWL AGAIN, WILLIAM?

WE'RE ABOUT TO MAKE THE ANNOUNCEMENT. WE HAVE TO GET HER OUT HERE OR IT WILL LOOK DAMNED PECULIAR, DON'T YOU THINK?
COMPOSE YOURSELF, MY BOY. I'LL HAVE HER IN A JIFFY.

I WAS PAINTING LIKE A BENNY ADDICT TO MAKE THE DAMNED DEADLINE. THE PAINT'S STILL WET IF YOU WANT ME TO CHANGE ANYTHING.

IT'S... IT'S QUITE SICK-MAKINGLY BEAUTIFUL.

I SIMPLY ADORE YOU.

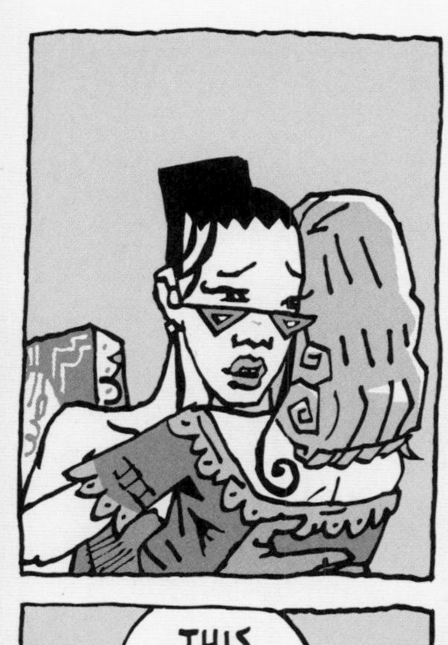

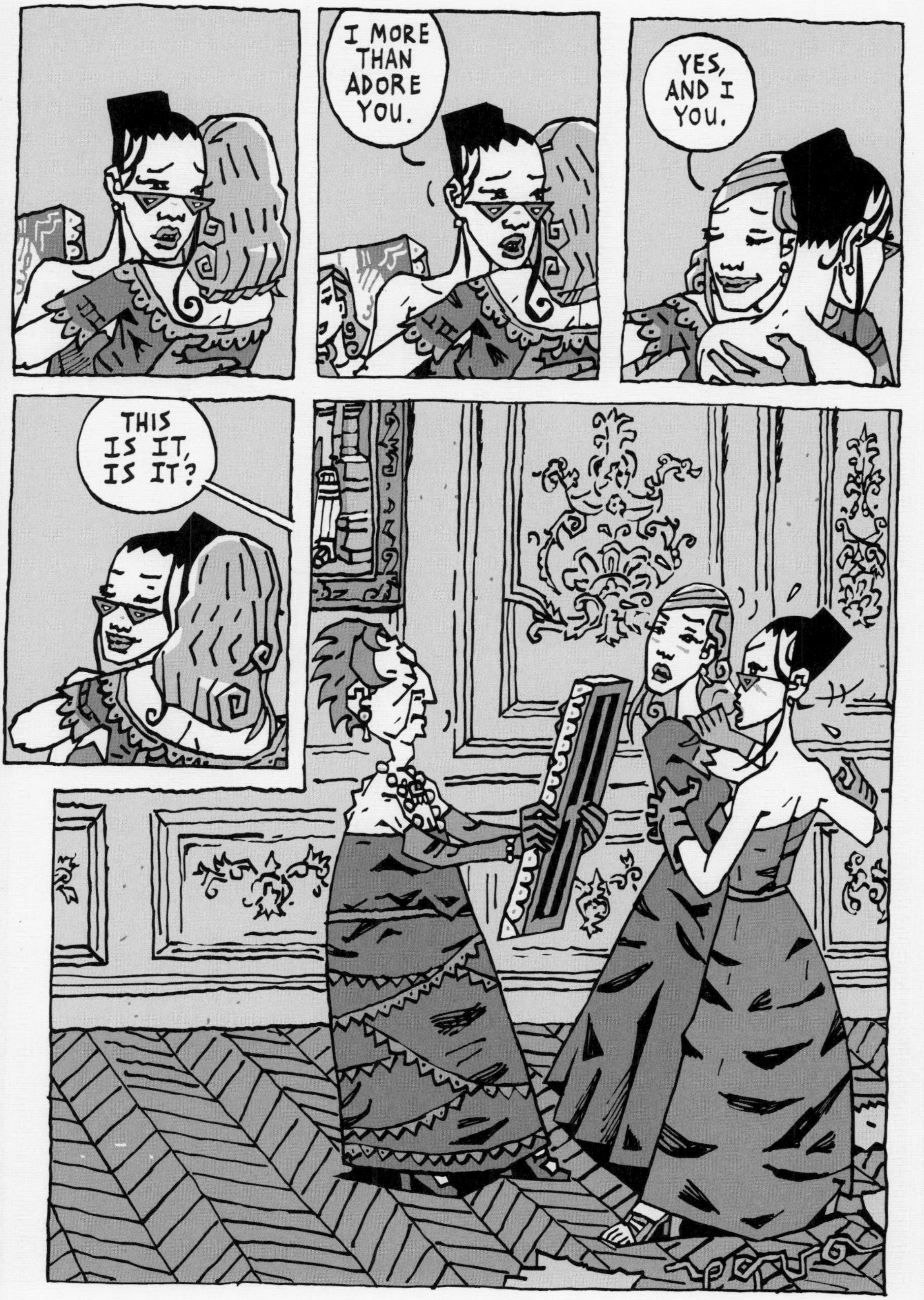

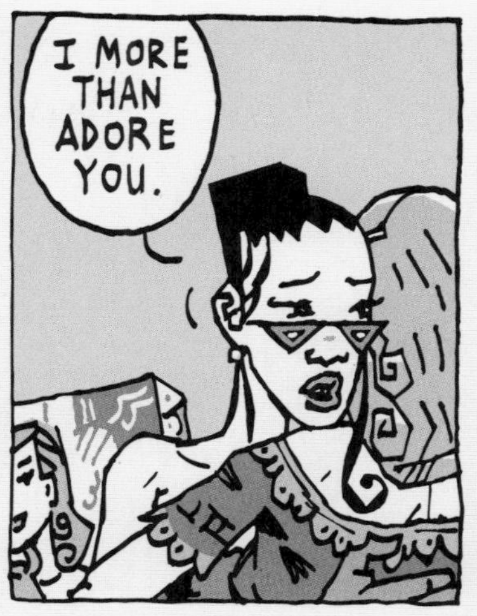

I MORE THAN ADORE YOU.

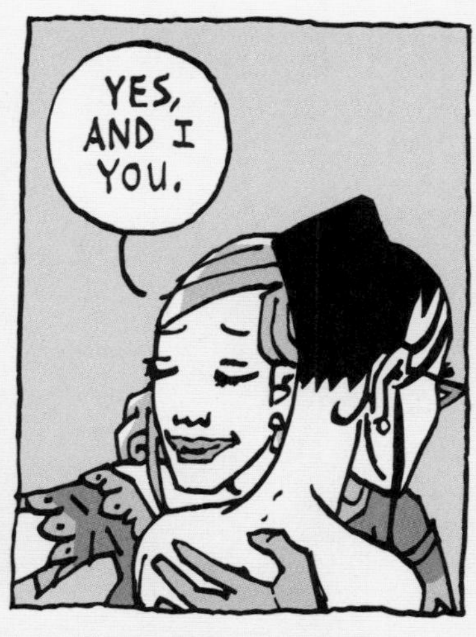

YES, AND I YOU.

THIS IS IT, IS IT?

COME NOW, DEBORAH, I REQUIRE YOUR PRESENCE ELSEWHERE.
CHAP, I'M RATHER PREOCCUPIED WITH...

NO TIME FOR BACK-CHAT, YOUNG LADY. OFF YOU TROT.

I KNOW YOUR GAME, MISSY. DON'T THINK YOU HAVE ME FOOLED.
WHAT-EVER CAN YOU MEAN, MA'AM?

TAKE THIS MUCK BACK TO YOUR FILTHY SWEATSHOP AND INFORM MR. STALE THAT HE HAS MORE CHANCE OF SQUEEZING BLOOD FROM A STONE THAN PRYING A PENNY OUT OF MY FINGERS.

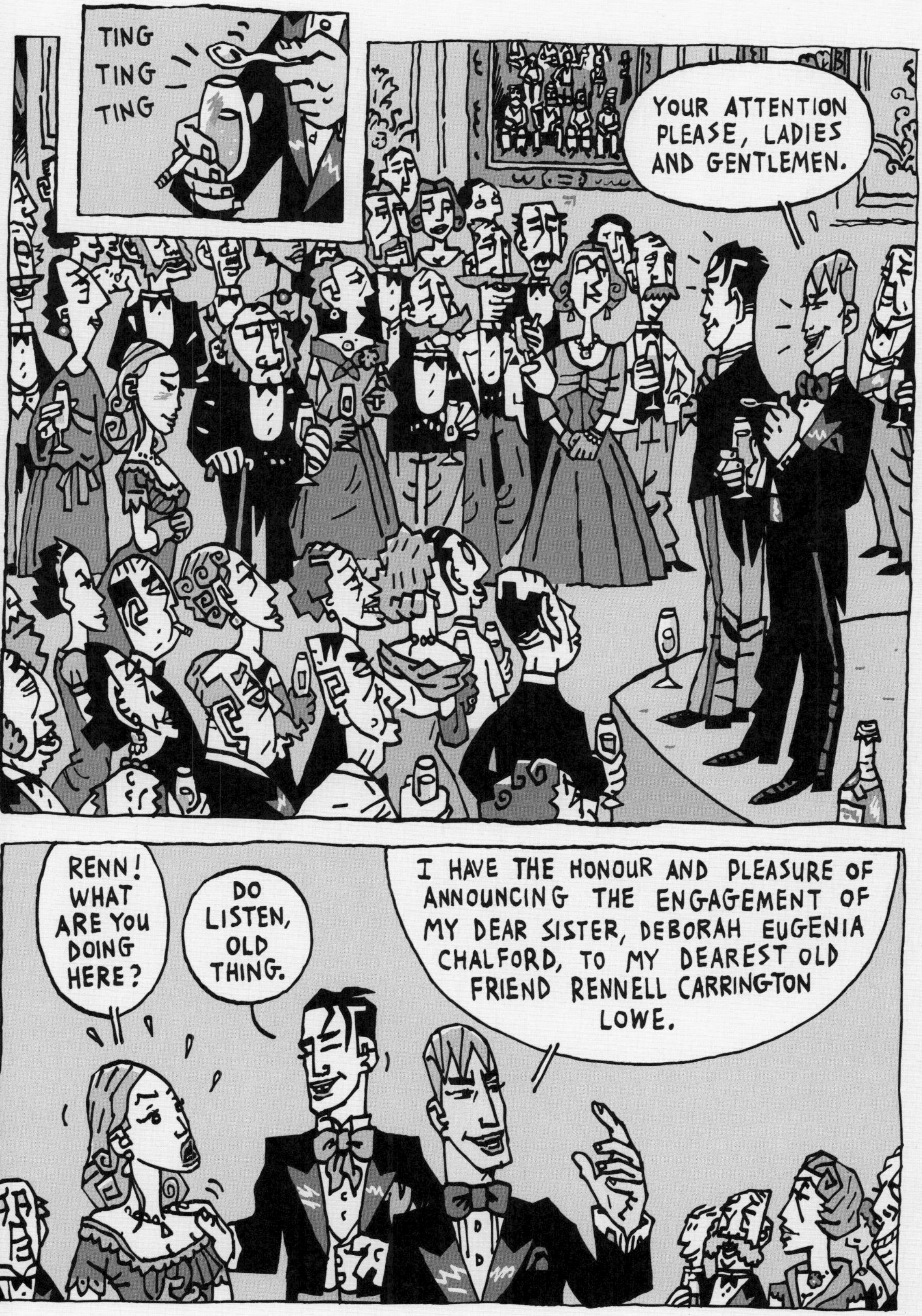

TING
TING
TING

YOUR ATTENTION PLEASE, LADIES AND GENTLEMEN.

NOW RAISE YOUR GLASSES IN A TOAST TO THE HAPPIEST COUPLE IN PARIS.

TINK

YOU CLEVER THING, DEBORAH. AT LAST YOU'VE MANAGED TO DRAG RENNELL TO THE ALTAR.

YOUR PORTRAIT WAS TO HAVE BEEN AN ENGAGEMENT GIFT FOR HIM. NEVER FEAR, WE'LL FIND SOMETHING MUCH SUPERIOR WHEN WE RETURN TO ENGLAND TOMORROW AND BEGIN THE WEDDING PREPARATIONS.

FIVE MORE MAGNUMS, GARÇON.

SUZE SUZ
SUZE

chapter
four

OVER THERE. IT'S IN THE GORSE, YOU STUPID ANIMAL!

YOU SICK IT, TINKS. LORD STRATHCLAIR'S BLASTED LAB HAS TROUBLE FINDING ITS OWN TAIL.

AS I TOLD YOU, RENN, FOLLOW THE SOUND OF CHAP BLASTING THEIR LORDSHIP'S DOGS AND WE'LL FIND THEM IN NO TIME.

YOU LOOK QUITE FROZEN, DEAR THING.
YES, I AM RATHER.

NANNY RENN TO THE RESCUE.

WE'RE HEADING HOME FOR A HOT TODDY, CHAP.
YES, DO. DEBORAH IS QUITE USELESS OUT OF DOORS.

HOTEL
UPER
MARKET
FRUIT
Delicatessen
Drugs
BUS
STOP
Mobilgas
US MAI
Mobilgas
Mobilgas

SHELLACS
VARNISHES
OILS
ENAMELS
MORROW'S
HARDWARE
METAL
SHADES
POLISHES
KEROSENE
HOUSEWARES
PAINTS
MORROW'S HARDWARE
SALE ON TOOL
CUT KEYS
MORROW'S
HARDWARE
TOMORROW'S HARDWARE
AT YESTERDAY'S PRICES

JULIET! STOP DAY-DREAMING AND GET TO WORK.

DOING WHAT, PA?
Sunbeam
new
Comet

YOU COULD GET TO KNOW THE STOCK. YESTERDAY YOU TRIED TO SELL MR. MATHIESSON PICTURE HOOKS WHEN HE WANTED TACKS.
PAINT
BLAC FLAG
ROACH SPRAY
SOS
SOS

YES, SIR.

SIGH

HOW LONG IS THIS GOING TO DRAG ON FOR?

WHAT?

THIS, THIS HALF-DEAD POSSUM ACT. WHERE'S MY JULIET? THE ONE WITH THE PEP IN HER STEP AND FIRE IN HER BELLY, NOT THIS HANG-DOG GIRL SHUFFLING AROUND IN A DAZE.

I MUST HAVE LOST THAT ONE SOMEWHERE IN PARIS.

IT'S TIME TO WAKE UP, HON', TIME TO WAKE UP.

LISTEN, LET'S DO A DEAL. IF I LEAVE YOU TO DO SOME PAINTING FOR ME...

PAINTING ?

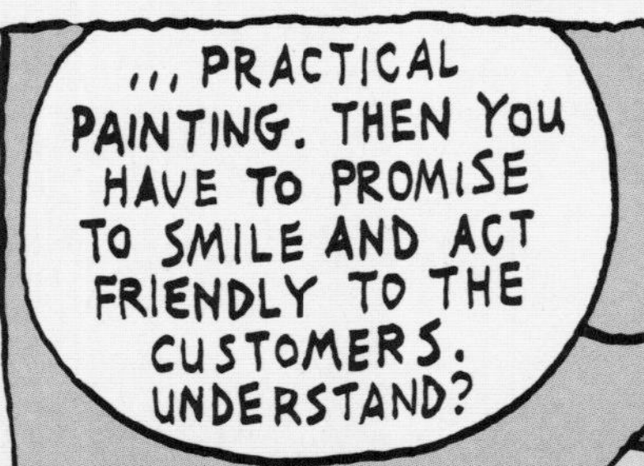
... PRACTICAL PAINTING. THEN YOU HAVE TO PROMISE TO SMILE AND ACT FRIENDLY TO THE CUSTOMERS. UNDERSTAND?

WHAT AM I S'POSED TO PAINT WITH?

WE HAVE PAINT, WE HAVE BRUSHES.
YOU WANT ME TO DECORATE ?

PAINT SIGNS. HELP THE CUSTOMERS FIND WHAT THEY WANT, QUICK AS THEY WANT.
DUPONT

THE ORCHIDS ARE SIMPLY TOO, TOO DIVINE, RENN.
THEY ARE BEAUTIFUL, AREN'T THEY?

RENN?
YES, DARLING?

DO YOU REALLY LOVE ME? I MEAN REALLY AND TRULY?

DEBORAH ...

I HAVE BEEN OFF AND ON FOR A WICKEDLY LONG TIME AND I DO FEEL TERRIBLY ABOUT IT, REALLY I DO.
AND WILLIAM THINKS SO TOO. SO AFTER BEING SENT DOWN IT SEEMED QUITE THE TIME TO DO THE RIGHT THING BY YOU, DEAR GIRL, AFTER STRINGING YOU ALONG SO DREADFULLY IN THE PAST.

SENT DOWN? BUT WHY, HOW?
IT'S TERRIBLY DREARY AND NOTHING AT ALL FOR YOU TO WORRY ABOUT, DARLING.

WHY DIDN'T BILLY TELL ME?

IT'S NOTHING AT ALL, MY SWEET. QUITE SORDID TO TALK OF ONE'S GAMBLING DEBTS TO ONE'S FIANCÉE, DON'T YOU THINK?
YES, I SUPPOSE IT IS.

DON'T WORRY, MY DARLING. AS A MARRIED MAN I WILL PUT SUCH TEMPTATIONS BEHIND ME.

YES. OF COURSE YOU WILL.

YOU'RE THE ONLY GIRL I COULD MARRY, DEBBY. WHO ELSE COULD I TALK TO ABOUT BOOKS AND PAINTINGS AND SUCH THINGS?

YOU ALWAYS SAID SELINA PRESTON-STUART HAD THE MOST DIVINE TASTE OF ANYONE YOU KNEW.

HA HA HA!
YOU CHALFORDS ARE SUCH FOUL, JEALOUS CREATURES.

A TEASE, DARLING. SELLY IS A DREADFUL HOG.

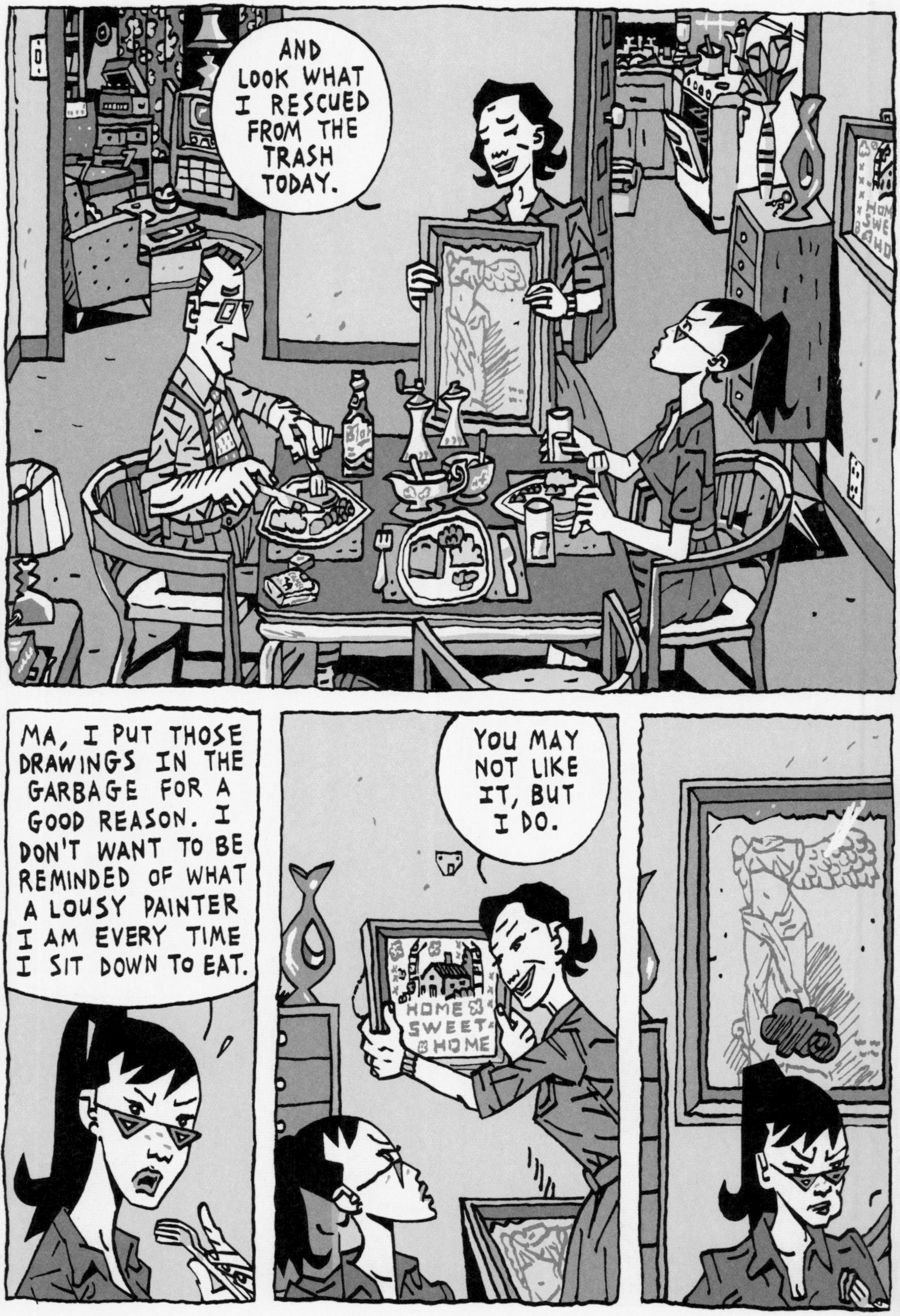

AND LOOK WHAT I RESCUED FROM THE TRASH TODAY.

MA, I PUT THOSE DRAWINGS IN THE GARBAGE FOR A GOOD REASON. I DON'T WANT TO BE REMINDED OF WHAT A LOUSY PAINTER I AM EVERY TIME I SIT DOWN TO EAT.

TAKE A LOOK AT THESE. NEAT, HUH?
JULIET, DID YOU PAINT THEM?

AIN'T THEY SOMETHIN'? THEY'RE FOR THE STORE, BUT I'VE HALF A MIND TO FRAME THEM AND HANG 'EM RIGHT HERE AT HOME.

YOU KNOW HONEY, WHEN YOU PUT YOUR MIND TO IT YOU CAN REALLY PUT YOUR GIFT TO A PRACTICAL USE.

THAT'S EXACTLY WHAT I SAID, YOU HAVE TO KEEP YOUR FEET ON THE GROUND, BE REALISTIC.

I WISH I'D HAD A HOBBY ONCE YOU'D GROWN OUT OF DIAPERS AND STARTED SCHOOL.

OPEN
YOUR MOTHER AND FATHER HAVE GIVEN YOU THIS.

GOOD GRACIOUS!

BUT WHAT IS IT FOR?
IT'S FOR SPENDING ON ADDITIONAL, UM, INTIMATE ITEMS FOR YOUR FUTURE LIFE.

I'M SORRY CHAP, BUT I CAN'T FOR THE LIFE OF ME UNDERSTAND WHAT YOU MEAN.

DON'T BE SO ODIOUS, CHILD.

SHE MEANS FOR UNDERWEAR AND THE LIKE, DEBBY DARLING.

WILLIAM, DO KEEP YOUR VOICE DOWN.

I DON'T SUPPOSE YOU COULD LEND ME FIVE GUINEAS DO YOU DEBS? I'M AWFULLY SHORT.
SHIR, YOUR SHIGARETTE.

TERRIBLY SORRY.
ABSOLUTELY UNDER NO CIRCUMSTANCES. IF YOU WANT A PURSE OF YOUR OWN YOU'LL HAVE TO GET MARRIED, WILLIAM.

NO FEAR OF THAT CHAPS, OLD THING.

"A CANVAS SCARCELY DRY, SHUT UP FOR A LONG TIME, AWAY FROM LIGHT AND AIR. YOU KNOW VERY WELL THAT THAT WOULD CHANGE IT TO CHROME-YELLOW NO. 3."

RENN,
DO YOU
RECOGNISE
THIS QUOTE
ABOUT DRY
...

UCO

DUPONT
Wall Paint

ATEX-B

Gold Bond
FLOW

YOU, YOU WON'T TELL, WILL YOU? IF MOTHER AND FATHER EVER ...
DON'T BE A DREADFUL PRIG, THERE'S A GOOD GIRL.

OF COURSE, SHE KNEW? SHE DID KNOW, DIDN'T SHE BILLY?
DON'T BE RIDICULOUS.

I'M TERRIBLY SORRY FOR INTERRUPTING.

WELL, THE CAT'S OUT OF THE BAG, ISN'T IT RATHER?

I'D LIKE TO SPEAK TO RENNELL ALONE, BILLY.

FOR PITY'S SAKE DEBORAH, DON'T START SOBBING LIKE SOME TART FROM A CHEAP MELODRAMA.

GET OUT, WILLIAM!

YOU CAN'T BLAME ME, DEBBY DARLING, YOU'VE ALWAYS SAID WE BOTH HAVE AN EYE FOR A PRETTY THING.

I DON'T QUITE UNDERSTAND. YOU WANTED US TO BE MARRIED.
I STILL DO, DARLING, TERRIBLY MUCH SO. IS IT REALLY SUCH A SHOCK?

VERY MUCH SO.

BECAUSE WE'VE ALWAYS UNDERSTOOD EACH OTHER, HAVEN'T WE? PERFECTLY I MEAN? WE'VE NEVER BEEN INTIMATE. YOU'VE NEVER BEEN THE PASSIONATE SORT.
I'VE PUSHED YOU TO IT, BEING SUCH A COLD FISH?

WE'VE ALWAYS BEEN TERRIBLY GOOD FRIENDS DARLING, EXACTLY BECAUSE THE BED-ROOM HAS NEVER COME INTO IT.

IT WAS DIFFERENT WITH SELINA, THAT WAS WHY I COULDN'T BEAR TO BE IN COMPANY WITH HER WHEN SHE MADE HER INTENTIONS CLEAR.

WITH YOU IT'S DIFFERENT, WITH YOU I'VE NEVER FELT SO MUCH AS A LUSTFUL GLANCE.

MY DESIRES HAVE NEVER REALLY COME INTO IT, HAVE THEY? IT'S ALWAYS BEEN AN IDEA OF OUR FAMILIES IN GENERAL.

I'VE BEEN SUCH A DREADFUL DISAPPOINTMENT TO MY CLAN THAT I CAN'T AFFORD ANOTHER.
IT'S THIS OR A POSITION IN A BANK IN HONG KONG.

BILLY WOULD RATHER YOU WERE HERE. HE'S ARRANGED THINGS WONDERFULLY.

THERE'S NO GOING BACK NOW, DARLING.

NEW AMERICAN PAINTIN
TARD
GALLERY

ELSEA WATCH
RY CO.

WHAT KIND OF PAINT IS THAT?
WHATEVER I CAN GET FROM THE HARDWARE STORE.

IT'S RAW, I CAN MAYBE FIND SPACE FOR ONE.
ONE?

YOU WALK OFF THE STREET AND GET A SPOT IN MY NEXT SHOW? I'D SAY THAT'S PRETTY DAMN LUCKY.

LET'S TAKE THAT ONE. IF IT'S NOT ON CANVAS IT WON'T SELL. WHAT'S IT CALLED?
THAT ONE, ERR, THAT ONE'S CALLED ...

WHAT?
"CHROME YELLOW No. 3"?
IT'S YOUR PAINTING, HONEY.
I'LL GIVE YOU A CALL IF IT SELLS.

SHELLACS
VARNISHES
OILS
ENAMELS
HAVE A NICE DAY!

WHO IS IT?
I DON'T KNOW.

YOURS WAS THE FIRST TO SELL. WHY DON'T YOU COME DOWN FOR YOUR MONEY, AND BRING YOUR PAINTINGS WITH YOU?

SOLD?

BUT I DON'T HAVE ...
THINK OF SOME MORE TITLES LIKE THE LAST ONE.

TITLES AREN'T THE PROBLEM, IT'S THE PAINT...
I'LL SEE YOU THIS AFTERNOON.

GODDAMN!

THE BANK FOR SAVINGS
PARK AV SO on 22 ST

N PAINTING
NEW AMERIC

"Chrome Yellow No.3"
$ SOLD

IT TOOK ME AN AWFULLY LONG TIME TO FIND YOU.

I TRAWLED THROUGH PRACTICALLY EVERY GALLERY IN THE CITY.

I DIDN'T RECOGNISE THE PAINTING, BUT I KNEW THE TITLE INSTANTLY.

IT'S DEGAS, TALKING ABOUT ONE OF HIS PAINTINGS.

AH, DEGAS. HE WAS A GREAT ADMIRER OF INGRES.

WELL, I WON'T DETAIN YOU ANY LONGER. HERE, FOR THE PAINTING.

I DON'T WANT YOUR MONEY.

NEW

SHOULD WE?
HERE, I MEAN.
YES.

The End

Notes

The French and English terms translated and featured artworks credited...

Page 13
Panel 2 *Women Ironing* by Edgar Degas, c. 1884.
Page 14
Bonjour, Chérie Hello, my dear
Page 15
Panel 2
Pour la jolie fille For the pretty girl
Panel 3
Merci, monsieur Thank you, sir

Page 27
The Apotheosis of Homer by Jean Auguste Dominique Ingres, 1827.
Page 29
Panel 1 *The Winged Victory of Samothrace,* c.190BC.
Page 30
Panel 2 *Dècapant* Paint stripper
Page 31
Panel 2 *M. Ancien Régime* Mr. Old Fashioned
Panel 5 *sans le sou* penniless
femme d'affaires business woman
Panel 6 *cette nuit* tonight
Panel 7 *sans* without
Page 33
Panel 6 *shooting season* hunting game animals in the Fall and Winter months.
Page 35
Panel 1 *culottes* panties

délicat delicate
Panel 2 *rouge* red wine
Page 36
Panel 2 *atelier* studio
Page 40
Panel 1 *hearty* outdoorsy
Page 42
Panel 1 *sink* corrupting
Panel 2 *The Turkish Bath* by Ingres, 1862.
Page 43
Panel 2 *The Countess d'Haussonville* by Ingres, 1845.
Page 48
Panel 4 *petit bourgeois* the middle class/upholders of the status-quo
Page 49
Panel 3 *bonsoir* good night
Page 54
Panel 2 *sautillèrent* jumping/dancing
bon temps good times
Page 55
Panel 1 *très belle* very beautiful
Panel 2 *véritable* real/not fake
Page 57
Panel 4 *Bonsoir* Good evening
Panel 5 *petite giroflée* little wallflower
finis finish
Page 58
Panel 1 *papier peint for haute bourgeoisie* wallpaper for the middle classes
Panel 4 *Je comprende* I understand
Panel 5 *plâtre* plaster
rougeur blush
savoir tout à fait know completely
Page 59
Panel 2 *vieille sorcière* old witch
sans bataille without a fight
ronces brambles
princesse précieuse precious princess
Panel 3 *Splendides nichons!* Splendid boobs!
Panel 4 *Cochon!* Pig!
Page 60
Panel 2 *Conversation In A Park* by Thomas Gainsborough, c. 1740.
Page 61
Panel 1 *je m'appelle* my name is
Ça sent mauvais, il y a une erreur dans l'addition. Vous avez une intoxication alimentaire. It smells bad, there's a problem with the bill. You have food poisoning.
Panel 3 *Pourriez-vous répeter, s'il vous plait?* Could you repeat that, please?
Page 64
Panel 1 *Roger Delivering Angelica* by Ingres, 1819.
Page 66
Panel 1 *Liberty Guiding the People* by Eugene Delacroix, 1830.
Page 67
Panel 5 *The Intervention of the Sabine Women* by Jacques Louis David, 1799.
Page 68
Panel 1 *The Bather of Valpinçon* by Ingres, 1808.
Panel 4 *Louis-François Bertin* by Ingres, 1832.
Page 69
Panel 1 *The Grande Odalisque* by Ingres, 1814.
Page 79
Panel 1 *Insomniaque* insomniac
Panel 3 *Tu vas dépêcher et l'habiller, no?* You will hurry and dress her, no?
Page 80
Panel 2 *lettre d'amour* love letter
Panel 4 *ballon* balloon
Panel 5 *Les parasites de la classe ouvière!* parasites of the working class!
Page 81
Panel 4 *absense irrégulière from l'académie* A.W.O.L from art school
Page 82
Panel 1 *demande* ask
Panel 3 *aimé* enjoy
Page 83
Panel 3 *réprimer mes sentiments* repress my feelings
Panel 5 *perplexe* lost/confused
Page 84
Panel 1 *Je ne rêve que de toi.* I only dream of you.
Panel 2 *Je ne veux que toi.* I only want you.
Page 85
Panel 4 *Le professeur sera intéressé comment vous faites votre argent de poche* The professeur will be interested what you do to earn your pocket money
Page 89
Panel 2 *robe de soirée* evening gown
Panel 3 *Dépêche-toi!* Hurry!
Panel 4 *baigné dans l'huile de lin?* bathed in linseed oil?
Page 90
Panel 2 *déshabiller* undress
Page 136 *The Cock* and *Bird in Space*, sculpted by Constantin Brancusi in 1924 and 1925 respectively.

Extras

PAIN
BISCOTTES
Jacquet
BOULANGER
PATISSER

RICARD

GAZ
15

The original book cover published by SLG in 2007.

The cover illustration for Paris No.1 (2005), after a photograph of Picasso by David Douglas Duncan.

HOTEL
HOTEL
OSTES
HONK